Maxim Jakubowski is a London-based novelist and editor. He was born in the UK and educated in France. Following a career in book publishing, he opened the world-famous Murder One bookshop in London in 1988 and has since combined running it, now online (www.murderone.co.uk), with his writing and editing career. He compiles two acclaimed annual series for the Mammoth list: *Best New Erotica* and *Best British Crime*. He is a winner of the Anthony and the Karel Awards, a frequent TV and radio broadcaster, crime columnist for the *Guardian* newspaper and Literary Director of London's Crime Scene Festival.

THE MAMMOTH BOOK OF BEST BRITISH MYSTERIES

Volume 8

EDITED AND INTRODUCTION BY MAXIM JAKUBOWSKI

ROBINSON

RUNNING PRESS
PHILADELPHIA · LONDON

Constable & Robinson Ltd
3 The Lanchesters
162 Fulham Palace Road
London W6 9ER
www.constablerobinson.com

First published in the UK by Robinson,
an imprint of Constable & Robinson, 2011

A copy of the British Library Cataloguing in Publication
Data is available from the British Library

UK ISBN 978-1-84901-567-7

1 3 5 7 9 10 8 6 4 2

First published in the United States in 2011 by Running Press Book Publishers

9 8 7 6 5 4 3 2 1
Digit on the right indicates the number of this printing

US Library of Congress Control number: 2010925954
US ISBN 978-0-7624-4096-2

Running Press Book Publishers
2300 Chestnut Street
Philadelphia, PA 19103-4371

Visit us on the web!
www.runningpress.com

Printed and bound in the UK

CONTENTS

INTRODUCTION

Maxim Jakubowski

INTRODUCING LAST YEAR'S volume of our annual anthology collecting the best crime and mystery stories penned by British authors during the course of the preceding calendar year, I mentioned the fact that Ian Rankin had called a halt to the perennially popular series featuring Edinburgh cop Inspector Rebus. Well, mourn not, our much-loved character returns briefly to open this year's volume with a short but intriguing story which Ian initially agreed to write for charity! And to please our readers even further, there is a double helping of Ian Rankin, as we close the book with another great tale set in Edinburgh. Two for the price of one can't be bad. And a heartfelt vote of thanks to Ian and his agent Peter Robinson for allowing us to feature him twice this year.

Crime writing in the UK continues to thrive ever vigorously and in addition to several handfuls of stalwart regulars, it's also a great pleasure to welcome to our series many new names who have not previously appeared herein, including such luminaries as Kate Atkinson, Louise Welsh, Stephen Booth, Christopher Brookmyre, Colin Bateman, literary star A. L. Kennedy, Sheila Quigley, Lin Anderson, Simon Kernick and David Hewson.

In addition, it's a decided pleasure to be able to introduce many new talents who've mostly hitherto only appeared in the proliferating web magazines devoted to the genre: Nick Quantrill, Jay Stringer, Paul D. Brazill and Nigel Bird. Also comforting is the ability to feature stories by father and son, with Peter Lovesey and Phil Lovesey sharing our pages, together with a wide assortment of other talented writers whose imagination somehow never fails them when it comes to creating stories which blend thrills, puzzles, emotions, shock and great writing.

Long may all these fictional criminals thrive and keep on entertaining us with a dash or more of blood, a zest of death and a galaxy of grey cells involved in solving the dastardly crimes that pepper our pages and delight us in myriad ways.

Another good year for crime!

Maxim Jakubowski

THE VERY LAST DROP

AN INSPECTOR REBUS STORY

Ian Rankin

" **A**ND THIS IS where the ghost's usually seen," the guide said. "So I hope nobody's of a nervous disposition." His eyes were fixed on Rebus, though there were four other people on the tour. They had wandered through the brewery in their luminous health-and-safety vests and white hard-hats, climbing up flights of steps, ducking for low doorways, and were now huddled together on what seemed to be the building's attic level. The tour itself had been a retirement present. Rebus had almost let the voucher lapse, until reminded by Siobhan Clarke, whose gift it had been.

"Ghost?" she asked now. The guide nodded slowly. His name was Albert Simms, and he'd told them to call him "Albie" – "not alibi, though I've provided a few in my time." This had been said at the very start of the tour, as they'd been trying the protective helmets for size. Siobhan had made a joke of it, warning him that he was in the presence of police officers. "Officer singular," Rebus had almost interrupted.

Almost.

Simms was currently looking uncomfortable, eyes darting around him. "He's usually only seen at night, our resident ghost. More often, it's the creaking of the floorboards the workers hear. He paces up and down...up and down..." He made a sweeping gesture with his arm. The narrow walkway was flanked by rectangular stainless-steel fermentation tanks. This was where the yeast did its work. Some vats were three-quarters full, each topped with a thick layer of brown foam. Others were empty, either clean or else waiting to be sluiced and scrubbed.

"His name was Johnny Watt," Simms went on. "Sixty years ago he died – almost to the day." Simms's eyes were rheumy, his face blotchy and pockmarked. He'd retired a decade back, but liked leading the tours. They kept him fit. "Johnny was up here on his own. His job was to do the cleaning. But the fumes got him." Simms pointed towards one of the busier vats. "Take too deep a breath and you can turn dizzy."

"He fell in?" Siobhan Clarke guessed.

"Aye," Simms appeared to agree. "That's the story. Banged his head and wasn't found for a while." He slapped the rim of the nearest vat. "They were made of stone back then, and metal-lined." His eyes were on Rebus again. "A fall like that can do some damage."

There were murmurs of agreement from the other visitors.

"Two more stops," Simms told them, clapping his hands together. "Then it's the sample room … "

The sample room was laid out like a rural pub, its brickwork exposed. Simms himself manned the pumps while the others removed their safety-ware. Rebus offered a brief toast to the guide before taking his first gulp.

"That was interesting," Siobhan offered. Simms gave a nod of thanks. "Is it really sixty years ago? Almost exactly, I mean – or do you tell all the tours that?"

"Sixty years next week," Simms confirmed.

"Ever seen the ghost yourself, Albie?"

Simms's face tightened. "Once or twice," he admitted, handing her a glass and taking Rebus's empty one. "Just out the corner of my eye."

"And maybe after a couple of these," Rebus added, accepting the refill. Simms gave him a stern look.

"Johnny Watt was real enough, and he doesn't seem to want to go away. Quite a character he was, too. The beer was free to employees back then, and no limits to how much you had. Legend has it, Johnny Watt could sink a pint in three seconds flat and not be much slower by the tenth." Simms paused. "None of which seemed to stop him being a hit with the ladies."

Clarke wrinkled her nose. "Wouldn't have been a hit with me."

"Different times," Simms reminded her. "Story goes, even the boss's daughter took a bit of a shine to him…"

Rebus looked up from his glass, but Simms was busy handing a fresh pint to one of the other visitors. He fixed his eyes on Siobhan Clarke instead, but she was being asked something by a woman who had come on the tour with her husband of twenty years. It had been his birthday present.

"Is it the same with you and your dad?" the woman was asking Clarke. "Did you buy him this for his birthday?"

Clarke replied with a shake of the head, then tried to hide the fact that she was smiling by taking a long sip from her glass.

"You might say she's my 'companion'," Rebus explained to the woman. "Charges by the hour."

He was still quick on his toes; managed to dodge the beer as it splashed from Siobhan Clarke's glass…

The next day, Rebus was back at the brewery, but this time in the boardroom. Photos lined the walls. They showed the brewery in its heyday. At that time, almost a century ago, there had been twenty other breweries in the city, and even this was half what there had been at one time. Rebus studied a posed shot of delivery men with their dray-horse. It was hitched to its cart, wooden barrels stacked on their sides in a careful pyramid. The men stood with arms folded over their three-quarter-length aprons. There was no date on the photograph. The one next to it, however, was identified as "Workers and Managers, 1947". The faces were blurry. Rebus wondered if one of them belonged to Johnny Watt, unaware that he had less than a year left to live.

On the wall opposite, past the large, polished oval table, were portraits of twenty or so men, the brewery managers. Rebus looked at each of them in turn. The one at the end was a colour photograph. When the door opened and Rebus turned towards the sound, he saw the man from the portrait walk in.

"Douglas Cropper," the man said, shaking Rebus's hand. He was dressed identically to his photo – dark blue suit, white shirt, burgundy tie. He was around forty and looked the type who liked sports. The tan was probably put there by nature. The hair showed only a few flecks of grey at the temples. "My secretary tells me you're a policeman..."

"Was a policeman," Rebus corrected him. "Recently retired. I might not have mentioned that to your secretary."

"So there's no trouble then?" Cropper had pulled out a chair and was gesturing for Rebus to sit down, too.

"Cropper's a popular name," Rebus said, nodding towards the line of photographs.

"My grandfather and my great-grandfather," Cropper agreed, crossing one leg over the other. "My father was the black sheep – he became a doctor."

"In one picture," Rebus said, "the inscription says 'workers and managers'..."

Cropper gave a short laugh. "I know. Makes it sound as if the managers don't do any work. I can assure you that's not the case these days..."

"Your grandfather must have been in charge of the brewery when that accident happened," Rebus stated.

"Accident?"

"Johnny Watt."

Cropper's eyes widened a little. "You're interested in ghosts?"

Rebus offered a shrug, but didn't say anything. The silence lengthened until Cropper broke it.

"Businesses weren't so hot on health and safety back then, I'm afraid to say. Lack of ventilation... and nobody partnering Mr Watt." Cropper leaned forward. "But I've been here the best part of twenty years, on and off, and I've never seen anything out of the ordinary."

"You mean the ghost? But other people have?"

It was Cropper's turn to shrug. "It's a story, that's all. A bit of shadow... a squeaky floorboard... Some people can't help seeing things." Cropper sat back again and placed his hands behind his head.

"Did your grandfather ever talk to you about it?"

"Not that I remember."

"Was he still in charge when you started here?"

"He was."

Rebus thought for a moment. "What would have happened after the accident?" he asked.

"I dare say the family would have been compensated – my grandfather was always very fair. Plenty of evidence of it in the annals."

"Annals?"

"The brewery's records are extensive."

"Would they have anything to say about Johnny Watt?"

"No idea."

"Could you maybe look?"

Cropper's bright blue eyes drilled into Rebus's. "Mind explaining to me why?"

Rebus thought of Albie Simms's words: Johnny Watt was real ... and he doesn't seem to want to go away ... But he didn't say anything, just bided his time until Douglas Cropper sighed and began getting to his feet.

"I'll see what I can do," Cropper conceded.

"Thank you, sir," Rebus said.

"You're supposed to be retired," Dr Curt said.

In the past, the two men would normally have met in the city mortuary, but Rebus had arrived at the pathologist's office at the university, where Curt maintained a full teaching load between autopsies. The desk between them was old, ornate and wooden. The wall behind Curt was lined with bookshelves, though Rebus doubted the books themselves got much use. A laptop sat on the desk, its cover closed. There was no paperwork anywhere.

"I am retired," Rebus stated.

"Funny way of showing it ... " Curt opened a drawer and lifted out a leather-bound ledger-book. A page had been marked. He opened the book and turned it to face Rebus.

"Report of the post-mortem examination," Curt explained. "Written in the finest copper-plate lettering by Professor William Shiels."

"Were you ever taught by him?" Rebus asked.

"Do I really look that old?"

"Sorry." Rebus peered at the handwritten notes. "You've had a read?"

"Professor Shiels was a great man, John."

"I'm not saying he wasn't."

"Contusions...fractured skull...internal bleeding to the brain... We see those injuries most days even now."

"Drunks on a Saturday night?" Rebus guessed. Curt nodded his agreement.

"Drink and drugs, John. Our friend Mr Watt fell eleven feet on to an inch-thick steel floor. Unconscious from the fumes, no way to defend himself..."

"The major damage was to the base of the skull," Rebus commented, running a finger along the words on the page.

"We don't always fall forehead first," Curt cautioned. Something in his tone made Rebus look up.

"What is it?" he asked.

Curt gave a twitch of the mouth. "I did a bit of digging. Those vats give off carbon dioxide. Ventilation's an issue, same now as it was back then. There are plenty of recorded cases of brewery employees falling into the vats. It's worse if someone tries to help. They dive into the beer to rescue their friend, and come up for air... take a deep breath and suddenly they're in as much trouble as the other fellow."

"What a way to go..."

"I believe one or two had to climb out and go to the toilet a couple of times prior to drowning," Curt offered. Rebus smiled, as was expected.

"Okay," he said. "Carbon dioxide poisoning...but what is it you're not saying?"

"The vat our friend fell into was empty, John. Hence the injuries. He didn't drown in beer – there was no beer."

Finally, Rebus got it.

"No beer," he said quietly, "meaning no fermenting. No carbon dioxide." His eyes met the pathologist's. Curt was nodding slowly.

"So what was it caused him to pass out?" Curt asked. "Of course, he could have just tripped and fallen, but then I'd expect to see signs that he'd tried to stop his fall."

Rebus rubbed a hand over the ledger-book. "No injuries to the hands," he stated.

"None whatsoever," Professor Curt agreed.

Rebus's next stop was the National Library of Scotland, where a one-day reader's pass allowed him access to a microfiche machine. A member of staff threaded the spool of film home and showed Rebus how to wind it to the relevant pages and adjust the focus. It was a slow process – Rebus kept stopping to read various stories and sports reports, and to smile at some of the advertisements. The film contained a year's worth of *Scotsman* newspapers, the year in question being 1948. I was one year old, Rebus thought to himself. Eventually he came to news of Johnny Watt's demise. It must have been a quiet day in the office: they'd sent a journalist and a photographer. Workers had gathered in the brewery yard. They looked numbed. The manager, Mr Joseph Cropper, had been interviewed. Rebus read the piece through twice, remembering the portrait of Douglas Cropper's grandfather – stern of face and long of sideburn. Then he spooled forwards through the following seven days. There was coverage of the funeral, along with another photograph. Rebus wondered if the horse pulling the carriage had been borrowed from the brewery. Warriston Cemetery was the destination. Watt and his family had lived in the Stockbridge area for umpteen generations. He had no wife, but three brothers and a sister. Watt had died at the age of twenty, and had served a year in the army towards the end of World War Two. Rebus paused for a moment, pondering that: you survived a war, only to die in your home town three years later. Watt had only been working at the brewery for eleven months. Joseph Cropper told the reporter that the young man had been "full of energy, a hard worker with excellent prospects". In the photo showing the procession into the cemetery, Cropper was central. There was a woman next to him, identified as his wife. She wore black, her eyes to the ground, her husband gripping her arm. She was skinny and slight, in contrast to the man she'd married. Rebus leaned in a little further towards the screen, then wound the film back to the previous photo. Twenty minutes later, he was still looking.

Albert Simms seemed surprised to see him.

Simms had just finished one of his brewery tours. Rebus was sitting at a table in the sample room, nursing the best part of a pint of IPA. It had been a busy tour: eight guests in all. They offered Rebus half-smiles and glances but kept their distance. Simms poured them their drinks but then seemed in a hurry for them to finish, ushering them from the room. It was five minutes before he returned. Rebus was behind the pumps, topping up his glass.

"No mention of Johnny Watt's ghost," Rebus commented.

"No." Simms was tidying the vests and hard-hats into a plastic storage container.

"Do you want a drink? My shout."

Simms thought about it, then nodded. He approached the bar and eased himself on to one of the stools. There was a blue folder lying nearby, but he tried his best to ignore it.

"Always amazes me," Rebus said, "the way we humans hang on to things – records, I mean. Chitties and receipts and old photographs. Brewery's got quite a collection. Same goes for the libraries and the medical college." Rebus handed over Simms's drink. The man made no attempt to pick it up.

"Joseph Cropper's wife never had a daughter," Rebus began to explain. "I got that from Joseph's grandson, your current boss. He showed me the archives. So much stuff there … " He paused. "When Johnny Watt died, how long had you been working here, Albie?"

"Not long."

Rebus nodded and opened the folder, showing Simms the photo from the *Scotsman*, the one of the brewery workers in the yard. He tapped a particular face. A young man, seated on a corner of the wagon, legs dangling, shoulders hunched. "You've not really changed, you know. How old were you? Fifteen?"

"You sound as if you know." Simms had taken the photocopy from Rebus and was studying it.

"The police keep records, too, Albie. We never throw anything away. Bit of trouble in your youth – nicking stuff; fights. Brandishing a razor on one particular occasion – you did a bit of juvenile time for that. Is that when Joseph Cropper met you? He was the charitable type, according to his grandson. Liked to visit prisons, talk to the men and the juveniles. You were about to be released, he offered you a job. But there were strings attached, weren't there?"

"Were there?" Simms tossed the sheet of paper on to the bar, picked up the glass and drank from it.

"I think so," Rebus said. "In fact, I'd go so far as to say I know so." He rubbed a hand down his cheek. "Be a bugger to prove, mind, but I don't think I need to do that."

"Why not?"

"Because you want to be caught. You're an old man now, maybe only a short while left, but it's been plaguing you. How many years is it, Albie? How long have you been seeing Johnny Watt's ghost?"

Albert Simms wiped foam from his top lip with his knuckles, but didn't say anything.

"I've been to take a look at your house," Rebus continued. "Nice place. Semi-detached; quiet street off Colinton Road. Didn't take much searching to come up with the transaction. You bought it from new a couple of months after Johnny Watt died. No mortgage. I mean, houses were maybe more affordable back then, but on wages like yours? I've seen your pay slips, Albie – they're in the company files, too. So where did the money come from?"

"Go on then – tell me."

"Joseph Cropper didn't have a daughter. You told me he did because you knew fine well it would jar, if I ever did any digging. I'd start to wonder why you told that particular lie. He had a wife though, younger than him." Rebus showed Simms a copy of the photo from the cemetery. "See how her husband's keeping a grip on her? She's either about to faint or he's just letting everyone know who the boss is. To be honest, my money would be on both. You can't see her face but there's a photo she sat for in a studio … " Rebus slid it from the folder.

"Very pretty, I think you'll agree. This came from Douglas Cropper, by the way. Families keep a lot of stuff, too, don't they? She'd been at school with Johnny Watt. Johnny, with his eye for the ladies. Joseph Cropper couldn't have his wife causing a scandal, could he? Her in her late teens, him in his early thirties … " Rebus leaned across the bar a little, so that his face was close to that of the man with the sagging shoulders and face.

"Could he?" he repeated.

"You can't prove anything, you said as much yourself."

"But you wanted someone to find out. When you found out I was a cop, you zeroed in on me. You wanted to whet my appetite, because you needed to be found out, Albie. That's at the heart of this, always has been. Guilt gnawing away at you down the decades."

"Not down the decades – just these past few years." Simms took a deep breath. "It was only meant to be the frighteners. I was a tough kid but I wasn't big. Johnny was big and fast, and that bit older. I just wanted him on the ground while I gave him the warning." Simms's eyes were growing glassy.

"You hit him too hard," Rebus commented. "Did you push him in or did he fall?"

"He fell. Even then I didn't know he was dead. The boss... when he heard... " Simms sniffed and swallowed hard. "That was the both of us, locked together... we couldn't tell. They were still hanging people back then."

"They hanged a man at Perth jail in 1948," Rebus acknowledged. "I read it in the *Scotsman*."

Simms managed a weak smile. "I knew you were the man, soon as I saw you. The kind who likes a mystery. Do you do crosswords?"

"Can't abide them." Rebus paused for a mouthful of IPA. "The money was to hush you up?"

"I told him he didn't need to – working for him, that was what I wanted. He said the money would get me a clean start anywhere in the world." Simms shook his head slowly. "I bought the house instead. He didn't like that, but he was stuck with it – what was he going to do?"

"The two of you never talked about it again?"

"What was there to talk about?"

"Did Cropper's wife ever suspect?"

"Why should she? Post-mortem was what we had to fear. Once they'd declared it an accident, that was that."

Rebus sat in silence, waiting until Albert Simms made eye contact, then asked a question of his own. "So what are we going to do, Albie?"

Albert Simms exhaled noisily. "I suppose you'll be taking me in."

"Can't do that," Rebus said. "I'm retired. It's up to you. Next natural step. I think you've already done the hard part."

Simms thought for a moment, then nodded slowly. "No more ghosts," he said quietly, almost to himself, as he stared up at the ceiling of the sample room.

"Maybe, maybe not," Rebus said.

"Been here long?" Siobhan Clarke asked as she entered the Oxford Bar.

"What else am I going to do?" Rebus replied. "Now I'm on the scrap-heap. What about you – hard day at the office?"

"Do you really want to hear about it?"

"Why not?"

"Because I know what you're like. Soon as you get a whiff of a case – mine or anyone else's – you'll want to have a go at it yourself."

"Maybe I'm a changed man, Siobhan."

"Aye, right." She rolled her eyes and told the landlord she'd have a gin and tonic.

"Double?" he asked.

"Why not?" She looked at Rebus. "Same again? Then you can make me jealous by telling me stories of your life of leisure."

"Maybe I'll do that," said Rebus, raising his pint-glass and draining it to the very last drop.

DOLPHIN JUNCTION

Mick Herron

I

"DON'T TRY TO find me," the note began. It was written on the back of a postcard. "Believe me, it's best this way. Things aren't working, David, and they haven't been for a long time. I'm sorry, but we both know it's true. I love you. But it's over. Shell."

On the kitchen wall, the clock still ticked, and outside the window, one of the slats in the fence still hung loose, and the fence remained discoloured where ivy had been peeled from it during the garden makeover two weeks previously. The marks where it had clung still resembled railway lines as seen on a map. If you could take a snapshot of that moment, nothing would have changed. But she was gone.

"And this card was on the kitchen table."

"As I've already told you, yes."

"And there's no sign of a break-in, no disturbance, no—"

"I've told you that too. There's no sign of anything. She's just disappeared. Everything else is the same as always."

"Well. You say disappeared. But she's fairly clearly left of her own accord, wouldn't you say?"

"No. I wouldn't say that at all."

"Be that as it may, sir, that's what the situation suggests. Now, if there were no note I'd be suggesting you call her friends, check with colleagues, maybe even try the hospitals just in case. But where there's a note explaining that she's gone of her own free will, all I can advise is that you wait and see."

"Wait and see? That's what you're telling me? I should wait and *see*?"

"I've no doubt your wife will be in touch shortly, sir. These things always look different in the plain light of day."

"Is there someone else I can talk to? A detective? Somebody?"

"They'd tell you exactly what I'm telling you, sir. That ninety-nine point nine per cent of these cases are exactly what they appear to be. And if your wife decides to leave you, there's not a lot the police can do about it."

"But what if she's the point one per cent? What happens then?"

"The chances of that are a billion to one, sir. Now, what I suggest you do is go home and get some rest. Maybe call into the pub. Shame not to take advantage, eh?"

He was on the other side of a counter, in no position to deliver a nudge in the ribs. But that's what his expression suggested. Old lady drops out of the picture? Have yourself a little time out.

"You haven't listened to a word, have you? My wife has been abducted. Is that so difficult to understand?"

He bristled. "She left a note, sir. That seems clear enough to me. Wrote and signed it."

"But that's exactly the problem," I explained for the fourth time. "My wife's name isn't Shell. My wife – Michelle – she'd never sign herself Shell. She hated the name. She hated it."

* * *

In the end I left the station empty-handed. If I wanted to speak to a detective, I'd have to make an appointment. And it would be best to leave this for forty-eight hours, the desk sergeant said. That seemed to be the window through which missing persons peered. Forty-eight hours. Not that my wife could be classed a missing person. She had left of her own accord, and nothing could convince him otherwise.

There'd be a phone call, he said. Possibly a letter. He managed to refrain from asserting that he'd put good money on it, but it was a close-run thing.

His unspoken suggestion that I spend the evening in the pub I ignored, just as he'd ignored the evidence of the false signature. Back home, I wandered from room to room, looking for signs of disturbance that might have escaped me earlier – anything I could carry back to the station to cast in his smug stupid face. But there was nothing. In fact, everything I found, he'd doubtless cite as proof of his view of events.

The suitcase, for example. The black suitcase was in the hall where I'd left it on getting home. I'd been away at a conference. But the other suitcase, the red one, was missing from its berth in the stair-cupboard, and in the wardrobe and the chests of drawers were unaccustomed gaps. I have never been the world's most observant husband. Some of my wife's dresses I have confidently claimed never to have seen before, only to be told that that's what she'd been wearing when I proposed, or that I'd bought it for her last Christmas. But even I recognized a space when I saw one, and these gaps spoke of recent disinterment. Someone had been through Michelle's private places, harvesting articles I couldn't picture but knew were there no longer. There were underlinings everywhere. The bathroom cabinet contained absences, and there was no novel on the floor on Michelle's side of the bed. Some of her jewellery was gone. The locket, though, was where it ought to be. She had far from taken everything – that would have entailed removal lorries and lawyerly negotiation – but it seemed as if a particular version of events were establishing itself.

But I didn't believe Michelle had been responsible for any of this. There are things we simply know; non-demonstrable things; events or facts at a tangent from the available evidence. Not everything is susceptible to interrogation. This wasn't about appearances. It was about knowledge. Experience.

Let me tell you something about Michelle: she knows words. She makes puns the way other people pass remarks upon the weather. I remember once we were talking about retirement fantasies: where we'd go, what we'd do, places we'd see. Before long I was conjuring Technicolor futures, painting the most elaborate visions in the air, and she chided me for going over the top. I still remember the excuse I offered. "Once you start daydreaming," I told her, "it's hard to stop."

"That's the thing about castles in Spain," she said. "They're very moreish."

Moreish. Moorish. You see? She was always playing with words. She accorded them due deference. She recognized their weight.

And she'd no more sign herself Shell than she'd misplace an apostrophe.

When I eventually went to bed, I lay the whole night on my side of the mattress, as if rolling on to Michelle's side would be to take up room she'd soon need; space which, if unavailable on her return, would cause her to disappear again.

II

The mattress is no more than three inches thick, laid flat on the concrete floor. There is a chemical toilet in the opposite corner. The only light spills in from a barred window nine foot or so above her head. This window is about the size of eight bricks laid side by side, and contains no glass: air must come through it, sound drift out. But here on floor level she feels no draught, and outside there is no one to hear any noise she might make.

But he will find her.

She is confident he will find her.

Eventually.

III

Forty-eight hours later, I was back in the police station.

Much of the intervening period had been spent on the telephone, speaking to an increasingly wide circle of friends, which at its outer reaches included people I'd never met. Colleagues of Michelle's; old university accomplices; even schoolmates – the responses I culled varied from sympathy to amusement, but in each I heard that chasm that lies between horror and delight; the German feeling you get when bad things happen to other people.

At its narrower reach, the circle included family. Michelle had one parent living, her mother, currently residing in a care home. I'm not sure why I say "currently". There's little chance of her future involving alternative accommodation. But she's beyond the reach of polite conversation, let alone urgency, and it was Michelle's sister – her only sibling – that I spoke to instead.

"And she hasn't been in touch?"

"No, David."

"But you'd tell me if she had?"

Her pause told its own story.

"Elizabeth?"

"I would reassure you that nothing bad had happened to her," she said. "As I'm sure it hasn't."

"Can I speak to her?"

"She's not here, David."

"No, it certainly sounds like it. Just put her on, Elizabeth."

She hung up at that point. I called back. Her husband answered. We exchanged words.

Shortly after that, I began drinking in earnest.

Thursday evening was the forty-eight-hour mark. I was not at my best. I was, though, back at the police station, talking to a detective.

"So your wife hasn't been in touch, Mr Wallace?"

I bit back various answers. No sarcasm; no fury. Just answer the question. Answer the question.

"Not a word. Not since this."

At some point I had found a polythene envelope in a desk drawer; one of those plastic flippancies for keeping documents pristine. Michelle's card tucked inside, it lay on the table between us. Face down, which is to say, message-side up.

"And there's been no word from anyone else?"

"I've called everyone I can think of," I said.

This wasn't quite true.

"You have my sympathy, Mr Wallace. I know how difficult this must be."

She – the detective – was young, blonde, jacketless, with a crisp white shirt, and hair bunched into the shortest of tails. She wore no make-up. I have no idea whether this is a service regulation. And I couldn't remember her name, though she'd introduced herself at the start of our conversation. Interview, I should probably call it. I'm good with names, but this woman's had swum out of my head as soon as it was spoken. Then again, I had distractions. My wife was missing.

"Can we talk about background details?"

"Whatever will help."

"What about your finances? Do you and your wife keep a joint account?"

"We have a joint savings account, yes."

"And has that been touched at all?"

"We keep our current accounts separate." It was important to spell out the details. One might prove crucial. "I pay a standing order into her account on the fifteenth, and she deals with the bills from that. Most of them. The mortgage and council tax are mine. She pays the phone and the gas and electricity." I came to a halt. For some reason, I couldn't remember which of us paid the water rates.

"And your savings account, Mr Wallace," she reminded me, quite gently. "Has that been touched at all?"

I said, "Well, yes. Yes, it probably has."

"Emptied?" she asked.

"No," I told her. "Quite the opposite. Well, not the opposite. That would be doubling it, wouldn't it? Or something." Rambling, I knew. I took a breath. "Half of our savings have been withdrawn," I told her.

"Half?"

"Precisely half," I said. "To the penny."

She made a note on the pad in front of her.

"But don't you see?" I told her. "If they'd taken it all, that would have alerted me, alerted *you*, to the fact that there's funny business going on."

"They?" she asked.

"Whoever's taken her," I said. "She hasn't just left. She can't have."

"People do leave, Mr Wallace. I'm sorry, but they do. What is it your wife does? She works, is that right?"

"She's a librarian."

"Whereabouts? Here in town?"

"Just down the road, yes."

"And you've spoken to her colleagues? Have they… shed any light on your wife's departure?"

"Disappearance."

She nodded: not agreeing. But allowing my alternative term the way you might allow a child to have his way on an unimportant matter, on which he was nevertheless mistaken.

I said: "She handed in her notice."

"I see."

You had to hand it to her. There was no inflection on this.

"And when did she do that, do you know?"

"A few days ago," I said. Suddenly I felt very tired. "On Monday."

"While you were away."

"That's right."

"Didn't she have notice to serve? Under the terms of her contract?"

"Yes. But she told them that she had personal reasons for needing to leave right away. But… " I could hear my voice trailing away. There was another *but*; there'd always be a *but*, but I couldn't for the life of me work out what this particular one might be.

"Mr Wallace."

I nodded, tiredly.

"I'm not sure we can take this matter further." She corrected herself. "We the police, I mean. It doesn't seem like a matter for us. I'm very sorry."

"What about the handwriting?" I asked.

She looked down at exhibit one, which just now seemed all that remained of my wife.

"It's a postcard," I explained. I was half sure I'd told her this already, but so many facts were drifting loose from their moorings that it was important to nail some down. "It didn't come through the post. It's just a card we both liked. It's been on our fridge a long time. Years, even. Stuck there with a magnet."

In a few moments more, I might have begun to describe the magnet it was stuck with.

"And you recognize it?"

"The card?"

"The handwriting, Mr Wallace."

"Well, it looks like hers. But then it would, wouldn't it? If someone was trying to make it look like Michelle's?"

"I'm not sure that impersonating handwriting is as easy as all that. If it looks like your wife's, well..." She glanced down at whatever note she'd been making, and didn't finish.

"But the name! I keep telling you, Michelle wouldn't call herself Shell. It's—" I had to stop at this point. *It's the last thing she would do* was what I didn't say.

"Mr Wallace. Sometimes, when people want a new life for themselves, they find a new name to go with it. Do you see? By calling herself Shell, she's making a break with the past."

"That's an interesting point – I've forgotten your name. Whatever. It's an interesting point. But not as important as handwriting analysis. Maybe, once that's been done, we can discuss your psychological insight."

She sighed. "Handwriting analysis is an expensive business, sir. We're not in the habit of diverting police resources to non-criminal matters."

"But this is a criminal matter. That's precisely what I'm trying to get across. My wife has been abducted."

I might have saved my breath.

"When your wife's worked out her new place in the world, I'm sure she'll be in touch. Meanwhile, do you have a friend you can stay with? Someone to talk things over with?"

"You won't have the card analysed," I informed her. We both already knew this. That's why I didn't make it a question.

"There's nothing to stop you having it done privately," she said.

"And if I'm right? *When* I'm right? Will you listen to me then?"

"If you can provide credible evidence that the note's a forgery, then we'd certainly want to hear about it," she said.

It was as if we'd sat next to each other at a dinner party, and I'd described a trip I was planning.

Well, if you have a good time, I'd certainly like to hear about it.

The kind of thing you say when you're certain you'll never meet again.

IV

I've read books where they say things like *I took an indefinite leave of absence*. Do you have a job like that? Does anyone you know

have a job like that? By Friday, my phone was ringing off the hook.
Was I sick? Had I forgotten the appropriate channels for alerting
HR to health issues? I spat, fumed and mentally consigned HR to
hell, but once I'd raged my hour I bit the bullet and saw my GP, who
listened sympathetically while my story squirmed out, then signed
me off work for the month. I returned home and delivered the news
to the fools in HR. Then I fished out *Yellow Pages* and looked for
handwriting experts.

Here's another. Have you ever tried looking for a handwriting
expert in *Yellow Pages*?

Nothing under *handwriting*. *Calligraphy* offers sign-writers and
commercial artists. And—

And that's all I came up with.

I sat next to the phone for a while, useless directory in my hands.
What other guise might a handwriting expert adopt? I couldn't
imagine. I failed to deduce.

In the end, I looked up Detective Agencies instead.

You're probably thinking that was the thing to do. That once the
professional arrived on the scene I'd fade into the background where
I belonged, while some hard-bitten but soft-centred ex-cop with an
alcohol problem and an interestingly named cat reravelled my life
for £250 a day plus expenses. But it was just another trip to Dolphin
Junction. I gave my story twice, once over the phone and once in
person to an acne-scratched twentysomething who couldn't get his
digital recorder to work and forgot – thank God – to take the
postcard when he left. I didn't hear from him again. He probably
lost my address. And if he couldn't find me, missing persons were
definitely out of his league.

Anyway. I went back to the police.

V

This time, it was a man. A thin, dark-featured man whose tie
featured small dancing elephants, a detail which stuck with me a
long time afterwards. He was a detective sergeant, so at least I was

being shuffled upwards, rather than down. His name was Martin Dampner, and I wasn't a stranger to him.

"We've met before, Mr Wallace. You probably don't remember."

"I do," I told him. "I think I do. When Jane was killed."

It would have had to be then. When else had I been in a police station?

"That's right. I sat in on the interview. Don't think I said anything. I was a DC then. A Detective Constable."

"It was a long time ago," I said.

He digested that, perhaps examining it for hidden barbs. But I hadn't meant anything special. It had been twelve years ago. If that was a long time to rise from DC to DS, that was his problem.

He said, "It was a bad business."

"So is this."

"Of course," he said.

We were in an office which might have been his or just one he was using for our conversation. I've no idea whether Detective Sergeants get their own office. My impression was that life was open-plan at that rank.

"How are you?" he now asked.

This stumped me.

"What do you mean?"

He settled into the chair his side of the desk. "How are you feeling? Are you eating properly? Drinking too much? Getting to work okay?"

I said, "My GP signed me off."

"Sensible. Good move."

"Can we talk about my missing wife?"

"We can. We can." He put his hands behind his neck, and stared at me for what felt a long while. I was starting to quite seriously wonder if he were mad. Then he said, "I've looked at the notes DC Peterson made. She seems convinced your wife left of her own accord."

"Well it's nice to know she's formed an opinion. That didn't take much effort on her part, did it?"

"You're underestimating my colleague. She followed some matters up after speaking to you. Did you know that?"

I didn't. And had more important subjects to raise: "Did she explain about the name? The name the note was signed with?"

"Shell, yes?"

"That's right."

"For Michelle."

"My wife never called herself that. Never would. She hated it."

"I got that much. But if you don't mind my saying so, Mr Wallace, that's a pretty flimsy base on which to assume – what is it you're assuming? Abduction?"

"Abduction. Kidnapping. Whatever you call it when someone is taken against their will and the police won't do *a bloody thing about it!*"

I was shaking suddenly. How did that happen? For days I'd been calm and reasonably controlled, and now this supercilious cop was undoing all that work. Did he have any idea what I was going through? These days of *not knowing*; these endless nights of staring at the ceiling? And then, just when it felt the dark would never end, light pulling its second-storey job; bringing definition to the furniture, and returning all the spooky shapes to their everyday functional presences. With this came not fresh hope. Just an awareness that things weren't over yet.

Days of this. More than a week now. How much longer?

"Let's calm down," he suggested.

"Why," I asked, pulling myself together, "did you agree to see me? If you've made up your mind nothing's wrong?"

"We serve the public," he said.

I didn't have an answer to that.

"My colleague, DC Peterson. She did some follow-up after you spoke." Martin Dampner pushed his chair back, to allow himself room to uncross his legs, then cross them the other way. "She went to the library where Mrs Wallace worked. Spoke to the librarian."

"And?"

Though I knew what was coming.

"When your wife handed her resignation in, she was perfectly in control. She handed her letter over, discussed its ramifications. Refused to be swayed. There was no coercion. Nobody waiting outside. No whispered messages for help."

"And I'm sure you've drawn all the conclusions you need from that."

He steamrollered on. "She also went, DC Peterson, to your building society. Where she didn't just ask questions. She saw the tape."

I closed my eyes.

"They record everything on CCTV. You probably know that already. DC Peterson watched footage of Mrs Wallace withdrawing money, having a brief chat with the cashier – who has no memory of their conversation, other than that it probably involved the weather or holidays – and leaving. On her own. Uncoerced."

It was like pursuing an argument with a filing cabinet. I stood.

"Mr Wallace, I am sorry. But you need to hear this."

"Which is why you agreed to see me. Right?"

"Also, I was wondering if you'd had a handwriting test done."

I stared.

"Have you?"

"No. No, I haven't."

"And does that mean you're now convinced it is her writing? Or so convinced it isn't that mere proof isn't likely to sway you?"

"It means, Sergeant, that I haven't yet found anywhere that'll do the job for me." I didn't want to tell him about the spotty private eye. I already knew that was a road heading nowhere. "And I don't suppose you're about to tell me you've had a change of heart? And will do it yourselves?"

He was shaking his head before I'd finished. "Mr Wallace. Believe me, I'm sorry for what you're going through. I've been there myself, and there aren't many I'd wish it on. But the facts as we understand them leave little room for doubt. Your wife quit her job, withdrew half your savings, and left a note saying she was leaving. All of which suggests that wherever Mrs Wallace is, she's there of her own accord."

"My wife's name is not Shell," I said.

He handed me a piece of paper with a phone number on it. "They're pretty good. They won't rip you off. Take another sample of Mrs Wallace's writing with you. Well, you'd probably worked that out for yourself."

I should have thanked him, I suppose. But what I really felt like was a specimen; as if his whole purpose in seeing me had been to study what my life looked like. So I just shovelled the paper into a pocket, and stood.

"You've aged well," he said. "If you don't mind my saying."

"I'm surprised you've not made Inspector yet," was the best I could manage in reply.

Back home, I sat at the kitchen table and rang the number Martin Dampner had given me. The woman who answered explained what I could expect from her firm's services: a definitive statement as to whether the handwriting matched a sample I knew was the subject's. There was no chance of error. She might have been talking of DNA. She might have been talking of a lot of things, actually, because I stopped listening for a bit. When I tuned back in, she was telling me that they could also produce a psychometric evaluation of the subject. I wasn't thinking of offering the subject a job, I almost said, but didn't. If they couldn't work that out from the postcard, they weren't much use to anyone.

There was a notepad on the window ledge, as ever. I scribbled down the address she gave me. And then, before anything could prevent my doing so, I transferred my scribble to an envelope, found a stamp, and went out and popped my wife's last words in the post.

VI

She does not have much spatial awareness – few women do, many men say – but sees no reason to doubt the information she has been given: that this room measures 24 foot by 18, with a ceiling some 20 foot high. It is a cellar, or part of a cellar. The handkerchief of light way over her head is the only part of the room set above ground level. Built into a hillside, see? *he'd told her. Yes. She saw.*

Apart from herself and the mattress and a thick rough blanket, and the chemical toilet in the corner, this room holds three articles: a plastic beaker three inches deep; a plastic fork five inches long; and a stainless steel tin-opener.

And then there is the second room, and all that it contains.

VII

Had I been asked, during the days following, what I imagined had happened to Michelle, I would have been unable to give an answer. It wasn't that there was any great dearth of fates to choose from. Open any newspaper. Turn to any channel. But it was as if my imagination – so reliably lurid in other matters – had discreetly changed the locks on this particular chamber, deeming it better, or safer, if I not only did not know what had occurred, but was barred from inventing a version of my own. I can see Michelle in our kitchen last week – of course I can. Just as I can see no trace of her here today, or in any other of her domestic haunts. But what happened to merge the former state into the latter remains white noise. Who stood by while she wrote that note and packed a case? What thrill of inspiration moved her to sign herself Shell? And in quitting her job, in withdrawing half our savings, what threat kept her obedient; made her perform these tasks unassisted?

And underneath all this a treacherous riptide that tugged with subtly increasing force. What if all this was as it seemed? What if she'd left of her own free will?

Things aren't working, David, and they haven't been for a long time. I'm sorry, but we both know it's true.

That's what her note had said. But that's true of any marriage. All have their highs and lows, and some years fray just as others swell.

These past few years, you could describe as frayed. We'd had fraught times before – the seven-year itch, of course. A phrase doesn't get to be cliché just by being a classic movie title. If ever the wheels were to come off, that would have been the time. But we survived, and it bonded us more securely. I truly believe that. And if these past few years had been less than joyful, that was just another dip in a long journey – we've been married nineteen years, for goodness' sake. You could look on this period as one of adjustment; a changing of gear as the view ahead narrows to one of quieter, calmer waters; of a long road dipping into a valley, with fewer turnings available on either side.

But maybe Michelle had other views. Maybe she thought this her last chance to get out.

Once, years ago, a train we were on came to a halt somewhere between Slough and Reading, for one of those unexplained reasons that are the motivating force behind the English railway network. Nearby was a scatter of gravel, a telephone pole, a wire fence and a battleship-grey junction box. Beyond this, a desultory field offered itself for inspection. On the near side of the fence, a wooden sign declared this to be Dolphin Junction.

"Dolphin Junction," Michelle said. "If you heard the name, you'd summon up a picture easily enough, wouldn't you? But it wouldn't look like this."

Afterwards, it became part of our private language. *A trip to Dolphin Junction* meant something had turned out disappointing, or less than expected. It meant things had not been as advertised. That anytime soon would be a good moment to turn back, or peel away.

And maybe that was it, when all was said and done. Maybe Michelle, during one of these dips in our journey, caught a glimpse of uninspiring fields ahead, and realized we were headed for Dolphin Junction. Would it have taken more than that? I didn't know any more. I didn't know what had happened. All I knew, deep in the gut, was that all wasn't, in fact, said and done.

Because she had signed her name Shell. Michelle had done that? She'd have been as likely to roll herself in feathers and go dancing down the street.

She just wouldn't.

*   *   *

A few days later the card came back. Until I heard the thump on the doormat I hadn't been aware of how keenly I'd been awaiting it, but in that instant everything else vanished like yesterday's weather. And then, as I went to collect it, a second thing happened. The doorbell rang.

She's back, was my first thought. Swiftly followed by my second, which was – what, she's lost her *keys*?

Padded envelope in hand, I opened the door.

Standing there was Dennis Farlowe.

There are languages, I know, that thrive on compound construction; that from the building blocks of everyday vocabulary cobble together one-time-only adjectives, or bespoke nouns for special circumstances. Legolanguages, Michelle would say. Perhaps one of them includes a word that captures my relationship with Dennis Farlowe: a former close friend who long ago accused me of the rape and murder of his wife; who could manage only the most tortured of apologies on being found wrong; who subsequently moved abroad for a decade, remarried, divorced; and who ultimately returned here a year or so ago, upon which we achieved a tenuous rapprochement, like that of a long-separated couple who remember the good times, without being desperate to relive them.

"David," he said.

"Dennis."

"I'm sorry about—" He grimaced and made a hand gesture. Male semaphore. For those moments when speech proves embarrassing.

We went into the kitchen. It's odd how swiftly an absence can make itself felt in a room. Even had Dennis not already heard the news, it wouldn't have cost him more than a moment's intuition to discern a problem.

"Good of you to come," I said.

Which it probably was, I thought – or he probably thought it was. Truth was, he was the last man I wanted to see. Apart from anything else, the envelope was burning my fingers.

But he had his own agenda. "You should have called."

"Yes. Well. I would have done." Leaving open the circumstances this action would have required, I put the kettle on instead. "Coffee?"

"Tea, if you've got it."

"I think we run to tea."

That pronoun slipped out.

It was history, obviously, that had prevented me from phoning Dennis Farlowe; had kept him the missing degree in the circle I'd rung round. Some of this history was the old kind, and some of it newer. I poured him a cup of tea, wondering as I did so how many gallons of the stuff – and of coffee, beer, wine, spirits; even water – we'd drunk in each other's company. Not an immeasurable amount,

I suppose. Few things, in truth, are. But decanted into plastic containers, it might have looked like a lifetime's supply.

"Milk?" he asked.

I pointed at the fridge.

He fixed his tea to his liking, and sat.

Twelve years ago, Jane Farlowe was found raped and murdered in a small untidy wood on the far side of the allotments bordering our local park. The year before, Jane, Dennis, Michelle and I had holidayed together in Corfu. There are photographs: the four of us around a café table or on a clifftop bench. It doesn't matter where you are, there's always someone will work your camera for you. Jane and Michelle wear dark glasses in the photos. Dennis and I don't. I've no idea why.

After Jane's death, I was interviewed by the police, of course. Along with around eighty-four other people, in that first wave. I've no idea whether this is a lot, in the context. Jane had, I'd guess, the usual number of friends, and she certainly had the usual number of strangers. I would have been interviewed even if Dennis hadn't made his feelings known.

Long time ago. Now, he said: "Has she been in touch?"

"No," I said.

"It's just a matter of time, David."

"So I've been told."

"Everyone wishes you well, David. Nobody's … gloating."

"Why on earth would anyone do that?"

"No reason. Stupid word. I just meant – you know how it is. There's always a thrill when bad things happen to people you like. But there's none of that going on."

I was about as convinced of this as I was that Dennis Farlowe was the community's spokesperson.

But I was no doubt doing him a disservice. We had a complicated past. We've probably grown used to shielding our motives from each other. And more than once in the past year, I've come home to find him seated where he is now; Michelle where I am. And I've had the impression, on those occasions, that there was nothing unusual about them. That there'd been other times when I didn't come home to find them there, but still: that's where they'd been. In my absence.

That's what I meant by *newer history*.

He said, "David. Do you mind if I make an observation?"

"Have you ever noticed," I said, "that when people say that, it would take a crowbar and a gag to prevent them?"

"You're a mess."

"Thank you. Fashion advice. It's what I need right now."

"I'm talking hygiene. You want to grow a beard, it's your funeral. But you should change your clothes, and you should – you really should – take a shower."

"Right."

"Or possibly two."

"Am I offending you?" I asked him. "Should I leave?"

"I'm trying to help. That's all."

"Did you know this was going to happen?"

"Michelle leaving?"

"Well yes, I – Christ, what did you think I meant? That we'd have *tea* this morning?"

He said, "I didn't know, no."

"Would you have told me if you did?"

"No," he said. "Probably not."

"Great. Thanks for the vote of confidence."

"I'm her friend too, David."

"Don't think I'm not aware of that."

He let that hang unanswered.

We drank tea. There were questions I wanted to ask him, but answers I didn't want to hear.

At length he said, "Did she leave a note?"

"Did the grapevine not supply that detail?"

"David—"

"Yes. Yes, she left a note."

Which was in a padded envelope, on the counter next to the kettle. And I couldn't wait a moment longer. It didn't matter that Dennis was here; nor that I already knew in my bones what the experts would have decreed. I stood, collected the envelope, and tore its mouth open. Dennis watched without apparent surprise as I poured on to the table the postcard, still in its transparent wrapper; the letter I'd supplied as a sample of Michelle's hand, and another letter, this one typed, formal, beyond contradiction.

Confirm that this is … no room for doubt … invoice under separate cover.

I crumpled it, and dropped it on the floor.

"Bad news?" Dennis asked after a while.

"No more than expected."

He waited, but I was in no mood to enlighten him. I could see him looking at the postcard – which had fallen picture-side up – but he made no move for it. I wondered what I'd have done if he had. What I'd have said if he asked to read it.

At length, he told me: "I'm going away for a while."

I nodded, as if it mattered.

"I've a new mobile. I'll leave you the number." He reached for the writing tablet on the sill, and scrawled something on it. "If she calls, if you hear anything – you'll let me know, David?"

He tore the uppermost leaf from the pad, and pushed it towards me. "David?"

"Sure," I said. "I'll let you know."

He let himself out. I remained where I was. Something had shifted, and I knew precisely what. It was like the turning of the tide. With an almanac and a watch, I've always assumed, you can time the event to the second. But you can't see it happen. You can only wait until it becomes beyond dispute; until that whole vast sprawl of water, covering most of the globe, has flexed its will, and you know that what you've been looking at has indisputably changed direction.

With a notepad available on the windowsill, Michelle had chosen to unclip a postcard from the door of the fridge, and leave her message on its yellowing back.

Flipping it over, I looked at its long-familiar picture for what felt like the first time.

VIII

The doorway into the second room is precisely that: a doorway. There is no door. Nor even the hint of a door, in fact; no hinges on the jamb; no screwholes where hinges might have swung. It's just an oblong space in the wall. The ghost of stone. She steps through it.

This is a smaller room. As wide, but half as long as the other. In a previous life of this building – before it succumbed to the fate all buildings secretly ache for, and became a ruin, scribbled on by weeds and tangled brambles – this would have been a secondary storeroom; only accessible via its larger twin, which itself can only be entered by use of a ladder dropped through the trap in its roof. Hard to say what might have been stored here. Wine? Grain? Maybe cheese and butter. There's no knowing. The room's history has been wiped clean.

And in its place, new boundaries:

To her left, a wall of tin. To her right, a screen of plastic.

IX

The Yard of Ale was one of those theme pubs whose theme is itself: a 400-year-old wooden-beamed structure on a crossroads outside Church Stretton, it was plaqued and horse-brassed within an inch of Disneyland. There wasn't a corner that didn't boast an elderly piece of blacksmith's equipment with the sharp bits removed, or something somebody found in a derelict dairy, and thought would look nice scrubbed up and put next to a window. The whole place reeked of an ersatz authenticity; of a past replicated only in its most appealing particulars, and these then polished until you could see the present's reflection in it, looking much the same as it always did, but wearing a Jane Austen bonnet.

Michelle and I had stayed there four years ago. It was spring, and we'd wanted a break involving long fresh days on high empty ground, and slow quiet evenings eating twice as much as necessary. An internet search produced the Yard of Ale, and for all my dismissive comments, it fitted the bill. Post-breakfast, we hiked for miles on the Long Mynd; counted off the Stiperstones and scaled the Devil's Chair. In hidden valleys we found the remnants of abandoned mines, and sheep turned up everywhere, constantly surprised. And in the evenings we ate three-course meals, and drank supermarket wine at restaurant prices. The bed was the right degree of firm, and the shower's water-pressure splendid. Everyone was polite. As we checked out Michelle picked up one of the hotel's self-promoting postcards, and when we got home she clipped it to the fridge door, where it had remained ever since.

I set off about thirty minutes after Dennis had left.

The rain began before I'd been on the road an hour. It had been raining for days in the south-west; there'd been weather warnings on the news, and a number of rivers had broken banks. I had not paid attention: weather was a background babble. But when I was stopped by a policeman on a minor road on the Shropshire border, and advised to take a detour which would cost a couple of hours – and offered no guarantee of a passable road at the end of it – it became clear that my plan, if you could call it that, wanted rethinking.

"You're sure I can't get through this way?"

"If your vehicle's maybe amphibious. I wouldn't try it myself. Sir."

Sir was an afterthought. He'd drawn back as I'd wound down the window to answer him, as if rain were preferable to the fug of unwashed body in my car.

I said, "I need somewhere to stay."

He gave me directions to a couple of places, a few miles down the road.

The first, a B&B, had a room. There'd been cancellations, the man who checked me in said. Rain was sheeting down, and the phone had been ringing all morning. He'd gone from fully booked to empty without lifting a finger. But there'd be more in my situation; folk who couldn't get where they were headed, and needed a bed for the night. It was still early, but he seemed confident there'd be little travelling on the local roads today.

"I was headed for Church Stretton," I said.

"You'll maybe have better luck tomorrow."

He seemed less worried than the policeman by my unwashed state. On the other hand, the smell of dog possibly masked my odour. The room was clean though. I could look down from its window on to a rain-washed street, and on light puddling the pavements outside the off-licence opposite. When I turned on the TV, I found footage of people sitting on rooftops while water swirled round their houses. I switched it off again. I had my own troubles.

I lay on the bed, fully clothed. If it weren't for the rain, where would I be now? Arriving at the Yard of Ale, armed with enquiries. I had a photograph – that was about it, as far as packing had gone – and I'd be waving it at somebody. It wasn't the best picture of Michelle ever taken (she'd be the first to point out that it made her nose look big) but it was accurate. In some lights, her nose does look big. If Michelle had been there, the photo would be recognized. Unless she'd gone out of her way to change her appearance – but what sense would that make? She'd left me a clue. If she hadn't wanted me to follow, why would she have done that?

Always supposing it really was a clue.

Perhaps the rain was a blessing. It held off the moment of truth; the last ounce of meaning I could dredge from the note she'd left. The note there was *no room for doubt* that she'd written.

But had signed *Shell*. An abbreviation she'd detested. And what was that if not a coded message? It was a cry for help.

And no one was listening but me.

* * *

At length, I turned the TV on again. I got lucky with a showing of *Bringing Up Baby*, and when that was finished I swam across the road to the shiny off-licence, and collected a bottle of Scotch. Back indoors, before broaching it, I belatedly took Dennis Farlowe's advice and stood under the shower for twenty minutes, using up both small bottles of complimentary gel. There were no razors. But the mirror suggested I'd crossed the line between being unshaven and having a beard.

And then I lay back on the bed, and drank the scotch.

Alcohol never helps. Well, alcohol always helps, but when there are things you need to keep at bay, alcohol never helps. Dennis Farlowe's appearance had disturbed me. Dennis's appearances inevitably did, though on most occasions I could mask the visible symptoms: could smile, give a cheery hello; ask him how things were going while I manoeuvred my way into my own kitchen; stood behind my own wife; put my hand on her shoulder, still smiling. All that newer history I mentioned. The history in which Michelle and Dennis had re-established the relationship we'd once all enjoyed, before the older history had smashed it all to pieces.

That history didn't end with Dennis's wife's murder. Ten days after Jane Farlowe's body was found a second victim came to light, in a town some distance from ours. I was at a conference at the time – that phase of business life was already in full swing – so didn't see the local press reports until they were old news. Wounds on the body indicated that the same man was responsible for both murders. You could sense our local tabloid's frustration at the vagueness of this detail, as if it had hot gossip up its sleeve it was bound not to share. Gossip relating to the nature of those wounds.

"Have you spoken to Dennis?" were my first words to Michelle on reading this.

"I tried calling him."

"But he wouldn't talk?"

"He wouldn't answer."

He would have been in shock, of course. Just a week and a half since his own wife's body had been found: did this make it worse for him? To understand that his wife's end was sealed by random encounter, not precise obsession? Because there was surely – can I say this? – something of a compliment buried in the murder of one's wife, if it was intended. If it didn't turn out that the murder was just *one of those things*; a passing accident that might have happened to anyone's wife, had they been in the wrong place at the right time.

The random nature of the murders was confirmed with the discovery of a third body: a little later, a little further away.

I poured more scotch. Switched the TV on. Switched it off. It was suppertime, but I didn't want to eat. Nothing was happening outside. The rain had eased off, and I could see the puddles dancing under the streetlights' glare.

In the gap between the discovery of the first two bodies – Jane and the second woman, whose name I've forgotten – Dennis

Farlowe had suggested that I was the man responsible. That I was a rapist and murderer. We had been friends for years, but in his grief he found it possible to say this: *You wanted her. You always wanted her.* The police would have interviewed me anyway – as they did all Jane's male friends – but Dennis's words no doubt interested them. Though they subsequently had to spread their net wider, with the second death; and wider still with the third... A local murder became a two-county hunt, but the man responsible was never caught, though he stopped after the third death. Not long after that, Dennis moved abroad.

He returned to England years later, a quieter, more intense man. Our friendship could never be what it was, but Michelle had done all she could. Jane was gone, she told me (I didn't need reminding). Dennis's life had been shattered; his attempt to rebuild it with a second marriage had failed too. With Michelle, he seemed to rediscover something of his old self, but between the two of us were barriers which could never fall, for all our apparent resolve to leave the past behind.

And it occurred to me that Dennis's old accusation – *You always wanted her* – could as justly be levelled at him. Wasn't his relationship with Michelle a little *too* close? How often had he dropped round in my absence; little visits I never heard about? Some evenings I'd find small evidences littered about: too many coffee cups draining on the board; a dab of aftershave in the air. But it's easy to paint pictures like that when the canvas has been destroyed. And doesn't this sort of tension often arise, when couples are close friends?

Not that Dennis was part of a pair any more, of course. And who could tell what effect a violent uncoupling like his might have had?

These thoughts chased me into sleep.

Where dreams were whisky-coloured, and stale as prison air.

X

She puts her hand to the wall of plastic. It gives, slightly; she has touched it at a gap between two of the objects it shields. An image startles her, of an alien egg-sac pulsing beneath her palm, about to spawn. But this is not an egg-sac; nor a wall; it is, rather, dozens upon dozens of two-litre bottles of mineral water, plastic-wrapped in batches of six, the wrapper stretched tight across the gaps between the bottles. That's what her palm lit on: a plastic-shrouded gap between bottles.

And opposite, the wall of tin; hundreds upon hundreds of cans of food. If they reach seven foot deep – which they might, if this room's as wide as the one adjoining – and reach ten foot in height, which they seem to, then…

But the number outreaches her ability to compute. Thousands, for sure. Possibly tens of thousands.

Put another way, a lifetime's supply.

XI

Next morning the rain had ceased, and though roads remained down all over Shropshire – and in neighbouring counties, marooned villagers waved at helicopters from the roofs of submerged cottages – it was possible to be on the move. But there were no shortcuts. Nor even reliable long cuts: twice I had to turn back at dips in B-roads, where the off-run from waterlogged fields had conjured lagoons. In one sat an abandoned van, rust-red water as high as its door handle. I reversed to the nearest junction, and consulted my map. I should have brought a thick fat marker pen. Instead of marking possible routes, I could have deleted impossible ones.

But if progress was slow, it was at least progress. At last I reached the car park of the Yard of Ale, not much more than some poorly tarmacked waste ground opposite the pub. Three other cars were there. I'm not good on cars. I've been known to walk past my own while trying to remember where it was. But for some reason, one of those vehicles struck a chord, and instead of heading over the road, I sat for a while, trying to work out why.

There was nobody around. A stiff breeze ruffled the nearby hedge. The more I looked at the car, the more it troubled me. It was the configuration of the windscreen, I decided. But how? One windscreen was much the same as another…At last I got out and approached the offending vehicle, and halfway there, the penny dropped. A parking permit on the driver's side was almost identical to one on my own windscreen. Same town, different area. This was Dennis Farlowe's car.

The breeze continued to ruffle the hedge. After another moment or two, I got back into my car and drove away.

XII

It was dark when I returned. The intervening hours, I'd spent in Church Stretton; partly sitting in a coffee bar, trying to make sense of events; the rest in one of the town's several camping shops. I'd intended to buy binoculars, but ended up with a small fortune's worth of equipment: the 'nocs, but also a torch, a waterproof jacket, a baseball cap, a new rucksack – with no real idea of what I was doing, I had a clear sense of needing to be prepared. I bought a knife, too. The instructions (knives come with instructions: can you believe it?) indicated the efficient angle for sawing through rope.

I believe in coincidence – if they didn't happen, we wouldn't need a word for them. But there's a limit to everything, and coincidence's limit fell far short of Dennis Farlowe's presence. He'd looked at Michelle's postcard, hadn't he? At the picture side, with the pub's name on. How long would it take to Google it?

Another possibility was that he already knew where it was; had already intended to come here. Which opened up various avenues, all reaching into the dark.

Whatever the truth of it, if not for the weather, I'd have been here first.

This time I drove straight past the pub and parked in a layby half a mile down the road, then walked back to the Yard, weaving a path with my new finger-sized torch. There was little traffic. When I reached the car park, my watch read 6.15. Dennis's car was still there.

For four-and-a-half hours I waited in the cold. *Lurked* is probably the word. Behind its thick velvety curtains the Yard was lit like a spacecraft, yellow spears of light piercing the darkness at odd angles.

I could picture Dennis in the restaurant, enjoying a bowl of thick soup, or pork medallions with caramelized vegetables. Memories of my own last meal were too distant to summon. When I could stand it no longer – and was certain he was holed up for the night – I trudged back to my car and drove to a petrol station, where I ate a microwaved pasty. Then I returned to my layby, crawled into the back seat, and tried to get some sleep.

But first I rang the Yard of Ale, and asked to speak to Mrs Farlowe. There was a puzzled moment while it was established that there was a *Mr* Farlowe in residence, but no *Mrs*. It must have been the inverse of a familiar sort of conversation, if you worked at a hotel desk. I hung up.

Sleep was a long time coming.

***

It was light by seven, but looked set to be a grey day. I drove back to the pub and a little beyond, hoping to find a vantage point from which I could keep an eye on Dennis's car. But nowhere answered, the best I could manage being another layby. If Dennis passed, I'd see him. But if he headed another way, he'd be history before I knew it.

I sat. I watched. I'd have listened to the radio, but didn't want to drain the battery. All I had to occupy me was the road, and the cars that used it. My biggest worry was the possibility that he'd drive past without my recognizing the car, and my next biggest that he'd see me first. There was a third, a godless mixture of the two, in which Dennis saw me without my seeing him: this further confusing a situation which already threatened to leave me at a waterlogged junction, rust-red water lapping at my throat. Is it any wonder I fell asleep? Or at least into that half-waking state where nightmares march in without bothering to knock, and set up their stalls in your hallway. There were more prison visions. Stone walls and tiny barred windows. I came back with a start, the taste of corned beef in my mouth, and a car heading past, Dennis at its wheel. In the same alarmed movement that had brought me out of sleep I turned the ignition, and drove after him.

I'd never tailed anyone before. When you get down to it, hardly anyone's ever tailed anyone before, and few of us have been tailed. It sounds more difficult than it is. If you're not expecting it, you're not likely to notice. I followed Dennis from as far behind as I could manage without losing track, once or twice allowing another car to come between us. This led to anxious minutes – he might turn off; I could end up following a stranger – but at the same time had a relieving effect, as if the intermission wiped the slate clean, leaving my own car fresh and new in his rearview mirror when I took up position again.

But it turned out I couldn't follow and pay attention to roadsigns at the same time. I've no idea where we were when he pulled in at one of those gravelled parking spots below the Long Mynd, leaving me to drive past then stop on the verge a hundred yards on. I grabbed my equipment – the new rucksack holding the waterproof, the torch, the binoculars, the knife – and hurried back.

It was midweek, and there was little evidence of other hikers. Besides Dennis's, two other cars sat sulking; the rest was empty space, evenly distributed round a large puddle. The surrounding hills looked heavy with rain, and the clouds promised more.

On the far side was a footpath, which would wind up on to the Mynd. That was clearly where he'd gone.

Stopping by the puddle, I pulled the black waterproof from the rucksack; tugged the cap over my eyes. From the puddle's wavery surface, a bearded stranger peered back. Far behind him, grey skies rolled over themselves.

The footpath dipped through a patch of woodland before setting its sights on the skyline. Just rounding a bend way ahead was Dennis. He wore a waterproof too: a bright red thumbprint on the hillside. If he'd wanted me to be following, he couldn't have made it easier.

XIII

Twenty minutes later, I'd revised that. He could have made it easier. He could have slowed down a little.

To any other watcher, it might have seemed odd. Here was a man on a hike, on a midweek morning – what was his hurry? Dennis moved like a man trying to set a record. But I wasn't any other watcher, and his speed only confirmed what I already knew: that this was no hike. Dennis wasn't interested in exercise or views. He had a specific destination in mind. He'd always known where he was going.

I couldn't tell whether his thighs ached, or his lungs burnt like mine, but I hoped so.

The red jacket bobbed in and out of view. I knew every disappearance was temporary; no way could a red jacket weave itself out of sight forever. But it also seemed that Dennis wasn't heading for the top. Every time the footpath threatened to broach the summit, he found another that dipped again, and some of them couldn't entirely be called footpaths. We broached hollows where newly formed ponds had to be jumped, and gaps where I couldn't trust my feet. I needed both hands on the nearest surface: rock, tree limb, clump of weed. More than once, a fallen tree blocked the way. At the second I was forced to crawl under its trunk, and an absent-minded branch scratched me as I passed, leaving blood on my cheek.

From the heavy grey clouds, which seemed closer with every minute, I felt the first fat splatter of rain at three o'clock.

I'm not sure why I'd chosen that moment to check my watch. Nor whether I was surprised or not. It can't have been later than ten when we started, though even that was a guess – what I really felt was that I'd never been anywhere else, doing anything else; that all the existence I could remember had been spent in just this manner: following a man in a bright red jacket through an alien landscape. But I do know that two things followed immediately upon my establishing what time it was.

The first was that I realized I was overpoweringly, ravenously hungry.

The second was that I looked up, and Dennis was nowhere in sight.

For some moments I stood still. I was possessed by the same understanding that can fall on a sudden awakening: that if I remain acutely still, refusing to accept the abrupt banishment from sleep, I can slip back, and be welcomed open-armed by the same waiting dream. It never works. It never works. It didn't work then. When I allowed myself to breathe again, I was exactly where I'd been. The only living thing in sight, nature apart, was a worm at my foot.

I took two steps forward, emerging from a canopy of trees. The ground sucked at my feet, and the rain picked up a steadier rhythm.

In the past hundred yards, the terrain had changed. Not four steps ahead, the path widened: I was near the bottom of one of the many troughs Dennis had led me through. Against the hillside rising steeply up to meet the falling rain was sketched the brick outline of what I assumed was a worked-out mine – Michelle and I had seen others like it on our holiday. On the opposite side, the incline was less steep, though you'd have needed hands and feet to scale it. Had Dennis gone that way, he'd have been pinned like a butterfly on a board. And as for directly ahead—

Directly ahead, the valley came to a dead end. The incline to my right became steeper on its passage round this horseshoe shape, and the cliffside in front of me was obscured by a rustic tangle of misshapen trees and unruly bushes. With no sign of Dennis, unless – and there it was: a ribbon of red flapped behind a bush, then merged again with the brown grey and green. A strap from a jacket, nipped by a gust of wind. The rain was coming down harder, as loud as it was wet, and Dennis must have thought this the right place to take shelter … Had Dennis really thought that, though? Or had Dennis just had enough of playing cat-and-mouse?

Hard to say when the game began. When I set off after him on the footpath? When his car passed mine in the layby near the Yard of Ale? Or further back, even; back in my kitchen, with Michelle's postcard in front of him, and an unused notepad next to the phone? He might have picked up on that clue. Dennis wasn't a fool. No one could call him a fool.

In fact, now I thought about it, you could almost say he'd drawn it to my attention.

Which might have been the moment to pause. I could have stood in the rain a little longer, my cap soaking to a cardboard mess as memory made itself heard: *He reached behind him for the writing*

*tablet on the sill, and scrawled something on it ... tore the uppermost
leaf from the pad, and pushed it towards me.* Was there more to it
than that? If Dennis wanted me here, that was a point in favour of
being anywhere else. I could have turned and retraced that long
long ramble. Reached my car, eventually, and got in it, and driven
away.

But I didn't. Momentum carried me forward. Only my cap stayed
behind; plucked from my head by a delinquent branch just as I
reached the bush I was after: surprise! Dennis's jacket hung like a
scarecrow, flapping in the wind. What a foolish thing. The man
must be getting wet.

Something stung my neck, and if it had been a mosquito, it would
have been the biggest bastard this side of the equator. But it wasn't
a mosquito.

Brown grey and green. Green grey and brown. Grey brown and

I'd forgotten what the third colour was even as it rushed up to
meet me.

XIV

"Do you remember?" he asks.

Well of course I do. Of course I do.

"Do you remember we used to be friends?"

It was long ago. But I remember that too.

I'll never know what Dennis Farlowe injected me with. Something
they use to pacify cows with, probably: it acted instantly, despite not
being scientifically applied. He must have stepped from behind and
just shoved the damn thing into my neck. I lie now on a three-inch
mattress on a concrete floor. The only light spills from a barred
window nine foot or so above Dennis's head. There is a strange
object behind him. It reaches into the dark. My rucksack, with all it
contains – the knife, especially – is nowhere.

Vision swims in and out of focus. I feel heavy all over, and everything aches.

I say, "Where is she?"

"She's dead."

And with that, something falls away, as if a circle I never wanted completed has just swum into existence, conjured from the ripples of a long-ago splash.

"But then, you already know that. You killed her."

I try to speak. It doesn't come out right. I swallow. Try again. "That's your plan?"

He cocks his head to one side.

"To make out I did it? To kill her, and make out—"

But that same head shakes in denial.

"I think," he says, "we need to clarify some issues."

It is only now that I realize what that strange object behind Dennis is. It is a ladder. There is no door into this room; there is only a ladder out of it. This reaches up to a trap in the ceiling.

And at almost the same time I realize that the room is part of a pair; that the shadow against one wall is actually a space leading somewhere else. And that somebody is hovering on that threshold.

"I don't mean your wife," Dennis goes on. "I mean mine."

The somebody walks forward.

Michelle says, "I found the locket."

XV

At last she nods. All this is fine. Barring one small detail.

"We need to unwrap these bottles," she says to Dennis Farlowe.

"Because?"

"So he can't stack them. Build himself a staircase."

She looks up at the barred window, about the size of eight bricks laid side by side, containing no glass.

"You think he can squeeze through that?"

"We're leaving him a tin-opener. He might hack a bigger hole."

"He wants to treat that thing with care. If he doesn't want to starve to death." But he concedes that she has a point. "You're right, though. We'll unwrap them."

In fact, she does this after he leaves. Leaves to return home; to find out what David's up to. To give him a nudge in the direction of the postcard.

Some things are best not left to chance.

XVI

"I believed you," she says. "For so long, I believed you. I mean, I always knew you had a thing for Jane – I'd have had to be blind not to – but I honestly, truly didn't think you'd killed her. Raped and killed her."

I so much want to reply to this, to deliver a devastating refutation, but what can I say? What can I say? That I never wanted it to happen? That would sound lame, in the circumstances. Of course I never wanted it to happen. Look where it's left me.

"But then I found her locket, where you'd kept it all these years. Behind that tile in the bathroom. Dear god, I thought. What's this? What's this?"

Jane and I had grown close, and that's the truth of it. But there are missteps in any relationship, and it's possible that I misread certain signs. But I never wanted any of it to happen. Or have I already said that?

"But Dennis recognized it."

And there you go. What precisely is going on with you and Dennis, I want to ask. Am I supposed to lie here while she reveals how close *they've* become? But lie here is all I can do. My limbs are like tree trunks. There is an itch at my neck, where Dennis stuck me with his needle.

"And those other women," she continues. "The way you made it look random – the way you killed them to make it look random. How can you live with yourself, David? How could I have lived with you? You know what everyone thinks when this happens. They always think the same thing – that *she must have known*. They'll think *I* must have known."

So it's all about you, I want to tell her. But don't.

"You told me you were at a conference."

Well, I could hardly tell you where I really was, I want to explain. I was doing it for *us*, can't you see that? To take Jane's story and put it at a remove, so we could continue with our lives. Besides, I *was* at a conference. Or registered at one, anyway; was there enough to make my presence felt. It passed muster, didn't it? Or it did until Dennis came back, and poured poison in your ear.

Did you really just find the locket, Michelle? Or did you go looking for it? It was the one keepsake I allowed myself. Everything else, all those events of twelve years ago – my seven-year itch – they happened to somebody else. Or might as well have done.

And I thought things were okay again. That's why I came looking for you. I didn't think your disappearance had anything to do with all *that*. All that was over long ago. And you said you loved me – in your note, you said *I love you*. Or was that just part of your trap?

And now Dennis says, "She's right, you know. All this will reflect on her. It always does. And that's not right. You destroyed my life, you ended Jane's. You killed those other poor women. You can't destroy Michelle's, too. We won't let you."

At last I find my voice again. "You're going to kill me."

"No," Dennis says. "We're going to leave you alone."

And very soon afterwards, that's exactly what they do.

I sometimes wonder whether anyone is looking for me, but not for very long. They'll have parked my car far away, near an unpredictable body of water; the kind which rarely returns its victims. Besides, everyone I spoke to thought Michelle had disappeared of her own accord – only I believed otherwise; only I attached weight to the clue so carefully left me. I remember the conversation with her sister, and it occurs to me that of course Michelle had spoken to her – of course Elizabeth knew Michelle was fine. She had promised not to breathe a word to me, that was all. Just one more thing to be produced in evidence when Michelle returns, and I do not.

She hadn't known I'd take it so hard, she'll say.

I never imagined he'd take his own life—

Meanwhile, I have drunk one hundred and three two-litre bottles of water; eaten eighty-nine tins of tuna fish, forty-seven of baked beans, ninety-four of corned beef. There are many hundreds left. Possibly thousands. I do not have the will to count them.

I already know there's a lifetime's supply.

CHRIS TAKES THE BUS

Denise Mina

THEY STOOD OUTSIDE the plate glass window at the bus station, because inside was so bright and cheerful, so full of happy milling people, that neither could bear it.

The cold was channelled here, into a snaking stream that lapped at their ankles, a bitter snapping cold that chilled them both. His eyes were fixed on the ground and she could feel him shrinking, sinking into the concrete.

"Jees-ho!" She shivered theatrically, trying to bring his attention back to her.

Chris looked at her and pulled the zip up at his neck, making a defiant face that said, see? I can look after myself, I know to do my coat up against the cold. They were huddled in their coats, shoulders up at their ears, each alone.

He tried to smile at her but she glanced down at the bag on the floor because his eyes were so hard to look into. The backlit adverts tinged the ground an icy pink and she saw that Chris had put the heel of his bag in a puddle.

"Bag's getting soggy," she smiled nervously, keeping her eyes averted.

He looked at it, dismayed at yet another fuck-up, and then shrugged, shaking his head a little, as if trying to shake off the concern she must be feeling. "Dry out on the bus."

She nodded, "Yeah, it'll get hot in there."

"Phew," he looked away down the concrete fairway. "Last time I only had a T-shirt and jeans on and I was sweating like a menopausal woman."

His turn of phrase made her mouth twitch.

"When I got off I had salt rings under my arms."

She tutted disbelievingly.

"True," he insisted. "I stood still at King's Cross and a couple of deer came up and licked me."

She smirked away from him, felt her eyes brimming up at the same time and frowned to cover it up.

"One of them offered me a tenner for a gobble, actually."

She was crying and laughing at the same time, spluttering ridiculously, the pink glow from the adverts glinting off her wet cheeks. His whole fucking venture depended on a lie and she wasn't a good liar.

"So," she wiped her face and turned back to him, "so when you get there you're off to—"

"My Auntie Margie's, yeah." He had done her the courtesy of looking away, giving her the chance to get it together before he looked back. "Yeah, she'll be waiting in for me, got my room ready."

"D'you get on with her?"

Chris shrugged, "She's my auntie … "

He tipped gently forward on his heels, leaning out into the brutal wind beyond the shelter. A coach pulled past the mouth of the bus station, slowly, dim yellow lights behind the shaded windows. They both saw the rabbit-ear side mirrors. It was a luxury coach, luxury in as much as coaches ever could be. Full of fat tourists coming to see the Castle and the Mile, the pantomime of the city. Not the London Bus, not Chris's bus.

He stepped back and they watched the bus pass, heads swinging around in unison like a pair of kittens watching a ball swing in front of them.

"I'll not get that one," he said, joking that he had a choice. "I'll just wait for the shit bus and get that one."

"Yeah," she said cheerfully, and looking up saw him flinch, arcing his head back as his neck stiffened. He was still bleeding, she knew, had asked her if it was showing through the seat of his jeans, made her look. It wasn't showing. She'd given him a fanny pad to put down there and he joked about having a period. She didn't know who'd raped him, but it was someone they both knew, or else he wouldn't be leaving. He confided in her because she was mousey, would give him the money for the ticket without asking too much detail, wouldn't make him go to the police.

It came suddenly, a hot molten gush of dread from the base of her gut, rolling up her chest until it bubbled and burst out of her mouth: "Don't go." Her voice was flat and loud, ridiculous, a voice from the middle of a heated argument.

Chris looked at her, eyebrows tented pitifully. "I have tae … "

She nodded, looked away.

"I have," he whispered. "Have to. You'll come and visit me."

"Of course. Of course, and we'll phone all the time."

"Yeah, phone. We'll phone."

As a coach slowly eased its way around the sharp turn into the St Andrew Bus Station, the destination lit up brightly above the windscreen.

The passengers who had waited inside, in the warm, filtered out behind them, talking excitedly, swinging bags, forming a messy queue.

Conscious of the company, Chris shifted his weight, brushing her shoulder lightly, shifting away. She felt the loss quite suddenly, a wrench, another cherished friend swallowed by the promise of London, loading the coach boot with bags stuffed with the offal of their own history.

THE MADWOMAN OF USK

Edward Marston

1188

OF ALL THE gifts with which I've been blessed by the Almighty, none is perhaps as striking as my ability to sense the presence of evil. It's uncanny. I can detect venom behind a benign smile, lust in the loins of a virgin and blackness in the heart of the outwardly virtuous. The first time I was acquainted with this strange power was when I was still a youth, studying in Paris. One of the many churches I visited harboured such a wondrous collection of holy relics that it had become a place of pilgrimage. Local people and visitors to the city flocked to view the sacred bones, leaving coins beside them as a mark of respect. One old woman, to whom my attention was drawn, came to the church every day to pay homage.

"She's an example to us all," I was told in a respectful whisper. "Though she's seen seventy summers or more, she never misses her daily visit to the shrine. Behold her, Gerald."

I did as I was bidden and watched her with care. After trudging down the aisle with the help of a stick, she lowered herself painfully to her ancient knees, dropped a coin on to the pile before her then bent her head in prayer. There she stayed until the discomfort grew too great. Hauling herself to her feet, she genuflected before the altar then struggled back down the aisle. It was a touching sight and I was duly moved – until, that is, she passed within a foot of me.

"Isn't she remarkable?" said my companion.

"In some ways, she is," I conceded.

"Such dedication is inspiring. Truly, she is a species of saint."

I was blunt. "I don't feel that she's ready for canonization yet."

My comment was felt to be unkind but I held my ground with characteristic tenacity. I knew something was amiss. Witnessed from a distance, the old woman's commitment was stimulating. She herself had become an object of veneration. When she brushed past me, however, I caught a scent that was less than saintly. Keeping my thoughts to myself, I returned to my studies and lost myself in the beauty of the Scriptures.

On the following day, I made sure that I was in the same church at exactly the same time. The woman was punctual. Through the door she came as the bell of the nearby abbey was signalling tierce. I let her shuffle past me and make her way to the side chapel where the relics were housed. She was so preoccupied with the effort of lowering herself to her knees that she didn't see me sink down a yard away from her. Like me, she deposited a small coin on the altar rail then lowered her head in prayer. The difference between us was that I kept my eyes open so that I could watch her.

What I saw outraged me. Down went her head and up it came again in a movement so slight as to be invisible to anyone not right beside her. As it went down once more, her lips fastened upon a coin and lifted it up before dropping it into a fold in her gown. Instead of praying to her Maker, she was instead plundering the church. In place of the one coin she had deposited, I counted over a dozen that she took. She was nothing but a common thief. I reported what I'd seen and, though nobody believed me, it was agreed that the old woman would be kept under surveillance the next day. Almost twenty coins were filched by her greedy lips on that occasion. Arrest and retribution soon followed.

I was thanked and congratulated. "How on earth did you spy her out?" I was asked.

"It's a gift from God," I replied.

"What's your name, young man?"

"Gerald de Barri – though some call me Gerald of Wales."

By the time I accompanied Archbishop Baldwin on his journey around my native country to find recruits for the Third Crusade, I

was in my early forties and held, among other positions, that of
archdeacon of Brecon in the diocese of St David's. Instances of my
remarkable skill in unmasking wrongdoers wherever I went are far
too numerous to recount so I'll merely offer one case that's
emblematic of them all. It occurred near Usk and tested my powers
to the limit.

Thanks to a sermon by Archbishop Baldwin, an address by that
good man, William, Bishop of Llandaff, and some stirring words in
both Latin and French from myself – my contribution was much
admired – a large group of men was signed for the Cross. To the
astonishment of all but me, many of those converted were notorious
robbers, highwaymen and horse thieves from the area, evil men
who sought to cleanse themselves by taking part in a holy crusade.
Their strong arms could now be put to a useful purpose. Before we
could make our way to Caerleon, we were diverted by a commotion
in Usk itself. I was sent to investigate.

Murder was afoot. Idwal the Harpist, a man renowned for his
glorious voice and nimble musicianship, had been a guest at the
home of Owain ap Meurig where he'd entertained the family for
three nights. The harpist was due to visit Monmouth Castle but he
never arrived and nobody who lived along the road that would
have taken him there had seen him pass by. Idwal had vanished
into thin air. Foul play was suspected. It fell to Roger de Brionne to
accuse Owain of the crime to his face. Tempers flared up into a
veritable inferno.

Nobody is better placed than I to understand the deep hatred and
mutual fear that exists between the Welsh and the Norman aristocracy. Born at Manorbier Castle in Dyfed, I'm a man of mixed
blood, having kinsfolk from both nations. I share in the privileges of
conquest while sympathizing, to a lesser extent, with the conquered.
When it came to mediating in a dispute between two sworn enemies,
Owain and Roger, who could doubt my credentials or match my
wide experience? I felt obliged to offer my services.

After prising accused and accuser apart, I first talked to Owain ap
Meurig at his house. A local chieftain whose family had held estates
in the region for generations, he was a proud, fierce, white-haired

man in his sixties with the build and attitudes of a warrior. It took me some time to calm him down and to assure him that – unlike Roger de Brionne – I had no prejudice against the Welsh. He was impressed by the fact that I'd heard Idwal the Harpist and was able to talk knowledgeably about him. The Welsh consider the playing of the harp to be the greatest of all accomplishments. Idwal was without peer.

"I hear that he stayed with you for three nights," I said.

"That's true," answered Owain. "He bewitched us all with the magic of his art. My late wife and my niece learned to master the instrument but they could not compare with Idwal."

"Did you see him off at your door?"

"I waved until he was out of sight. He'd delighted us so much that I rewarded him handsomely and pressed him to come again."

"Who else saw him leave?" I asked.

Owain bristled. "Is my word not good enough for you?"

"Of course, my friend – but corroboration is always useful."

"You sound as if you don't believe me."

"I accept your word without question, Owain."

That seemed to reassure him. "Well, then," he said. "There *was* someone else who bade him farewell – my niece, Gwenllian. She had cause to be grateful to Idwal. He found time to listen to her playing the harp and favoured her with advice. Gwenllian was thrilled."

"May I speak with her?"

"Is that necessary?"

"I would like to hear what she thought of Idwal's playing."

A defensive look had come into his eye. It was clear that he didn't want me to talk to his niece yet, at the same time, he calculated that his refusal might count against him, leading to the suspicion that he was trying to hide something. Owain eventually capitulated. He despatched a servant to fetch his niece. Gwenllian soon appeared.

Entering the room out of obedience to her uncle rather than enthusiasm to meet me, she was both wary and slightly fearful, as if fearing a rebuke. She glanced at Owain, at me, then back again at him. When she spoke, her voice was sweet and melodic.

"You wanted me, Uncle?" she enquired, politely.

While he explained who I was and why I was there, I took the opportunity to subject the girl to scrutiny. Gwenllian was beautiful. Natural modesty and my vow of celibacy prevent me from going into anatomical detail about a member of the fairer sex. Suffice it to say that I had seen few fairer and none so graceful. Gwenllian could have been no more than seventeen, combining the bloom of youth with a rare maturity. After telling her that she'd nothing to fear, Owain eased her gently towards me.

"I understand that you're a harpist," I began.

Her laugh was deprecating. "After hearing Idwal play," she said, "I realize that I'm a mere beginner on the harp. He makes it produce the most enchanting music."

"Which of his songs did you enjoy most?"

It was a clever question, allowing her to lose some of her anxiety as she talked about Idwal's visit. The longer she went on, the more she relaxed and – I duly noted – the more relaxed Owain became. I wasn't there to subject the girl to a rigorous interrogation and he was relieved by that. What I was simply trying to do was to assess her character and disposition. The information I sought was volunteered before I even asked for it.

"Uncle and I waved him off until our arms ached," she said, smiling at the memory. "Our loss is Monmouth's gain."

I had the feeling that she was repeating a phrase that Owain had first used but I didn't hold it against her. Gwenllian had been honest and unguarded. There'd been no dissemblance. I turned back to her uncle with my searching gaze.

"Is there any truth in Roger de Brionne's accusation?" I said.

"None at all!" was the defiant reply.

I believed him and thanked them both for their help. As I took my leave of them, I warned them that I'd probably call on them again before the matter was cleared up. Spreading his arms wide, Owain told me that I was always welcome. As he led me to the front door, I passed close to Gwenllian and had a curious sensation. It was similar to the unease I'd felt in that Parisian church all those years ago. Though I concealed my feelings, I was quite upset. Could this innocent girl have been involved in an evil act?

* * *

Roger de Brionne owned extensive land to the south of Owain's estates and they'd been arguing about the border between them for years. Each claimed to have had territory stolen by the other. Both swore that his neighbour had rustled livestock from them. It was not my business to sit in judgement on their respective claims. All that concerned me was to decide whether or not a murder had been committed and, if it had, to solve the crime.

Roger was confident he already knew the name of the culprit.

"Owain is a killer!" he yelled at me. "Place him under arrest."

"I've neither the right nor the inclination to do so," I replied, stoutly. "All I've heard so far is wild accusation. I need evidence."

"Then you must search for it."

"Where?"

"Where else but on Owain's land?" he said. "That's where the harpist is buried and where his instrument remains."

"You seem very certain of that."

"I can even tell you where the harp has been hidden."

"Oh?"

"It is somewhere in the stables."

"How do you know that, my lord?"

"I was told by an informant."

"And did this informant give any motive for the murder," I wondered, "because I'm at a loss to find one. I've questioned both Owain and his niece. The two of them worshipped Idwal. Why should Owain want to kill a man who gave him so much pleasure?"

"I can see that you don't know the villain."

"I know enough about him. I took him for a testy old Welshman with all the faults of his nation – that's to say, he's quarrelsome, inconstant and wedded to memories of a heroic past that no longer exists. I've lived among the Welsh, my lord."

"Then you'll appreciate their legendary skill at lying. Never a true word passes their lips. They break promises, say anything that suits their purpose and let you down as if it's their duty to do so."

"It's their way of resisting the invader," I observed.

"We've been here for over a hundred years," he affirmed, waving a fist. "We're no longer invaders."

"You are in Welsh eyes and will be so for another thousand years. However," I went on, stifling his impatience, "let's return to the question of motive. According to Owain, the harpist stayed with them for three days and was well-paid before he left."

Roger snorted. "Well-paid!" he exclaimed. "He's certainly pulled the wool over *your* eyes, archdeacon. Owain is a born miser. Ask anyone in the county and they will say as much. It was exactly what Idwal told me when he played for Owain last year. On his way south, the harpist spent the night here and earned generous recompense for the entertainment he provided. Idwal said that, as usual, he'd been given a pittance by Owain."

I weighed this information in the balance, trying to decide if it was the truth or arose out of Roger's malice. He was a tall, slim man in his fifties with a gaunt face and a glinting eye. There was an air of nobility about him that impressed me, albeit tempered by a combative nature. He and Owain would never be happy bedfellows. They were so accustomed to trade insults that they would sooner die than agree. Something about Roger's argument nevertheless did ring true. Though he was a wealthy man, Owain's house showed all the signs of deliberate parsimony. In Roger de Brionne's manor, by contrast, riches were openly on display. It was likely that Idwal the Harpist would earn more from one night with Roger than from three with Owain.

"As to the question of motive," said Roger, pursuing his argument, "you've already met the young lady."

"Are you referring to Owain's niece?"

"Gwenllian would tempt a pope."

"She didn't tempt *me*," I was at pains to assure him, "but I did observe how well-favoured the girl was. And now I think about it, Idwal was always a man with an interest in feminine company."

"It wasn't interest, archdeacon," said Roger, bitterly, "it was an obsession. When you listed the faults of the Welsh, you forget to mention their rampant carnality. Anyone with Welsh blood in him is as lecherous as a goat."

"I deny that!" I retorted. "I have the honour to have Welsh blood in my veins and it hasn't inclined me to anything that can remotely be considered goatish."

"Did you ever *hear* Idwal play?"

"Yes, my lord – many times."

"Then you'll know the seductive power of his music. It can enthral adults and work upon their emotions. Think how much greater its effect might be on an impressionable young woman."

It was an apt comment. Idwal had been a handsome man in his late thirties with magic in his fingers and persuasion in his smile. I remembered that he'd given Gwenllian instruction in how to play the harp, sitting behind her no doubt, guiding her hands, making the most of his licensed touch. Though such intimacies between man and woman are outside my ken, I can well imagine what might have taken place. Owain ap Meurig had been affectionate and protective towards his niece. If he'd seen something untoward occurring between the girl and the harpist – something that Gwenllian herself was too young to recognize as improper – it might well have aroused his jealousy.

Yet he and the girl had waved off Idwal together. Was it possible that Owain had later overtaken the harpist and murdered him? Was I investigating revenge? Roger was so convinced about the chain of events that I had to take him seriously.

"This informant of yours was a witness, was he?" I asked.

"In a manner of speaking," he explained. "Except that it was not a man but a woman." He took a deep breath before blurting out the truth. "She saw it all in a dream."

I couldn't hide my surprise. "A *dream*, my lord?" I said with utter disbelief. "You expect me to denounce Owain as a murderer because a woman has a troubled night? This is absurd."

"That's what *I* thought at first, archdeacon."

"Who is this creature?"

"Angharad FitzMartin."

I was astounded. It was the Madwoman of Usk.

While I'd never set eyes on her, I knew her well by repute. Angharad FitzMartin was the offspring of a Welsh mother and a Norman father, both of whom had been killed in a tragic accident. The event had had a profound effect on her, changing her from a young woman with the normal expectations of her class into a wild, haunted, hortatory being who preached her own eccentric version of the gospel of Christ and who, it was rumoured, could quote the Bible in three languages. Some feared her, others reviled her, others again simply mocked her but most people showed Christian compassion towards a woman who had clearly lost her mind at the cruel death of her parents.

It was market day in the village and I soon found her. The Madwoman of Usk was living up to her name, standing on a cask as she proclaimed her message to a small crowd. Peppered with snatches of Holy Writ, it was a rambling homily but delivered with such fervour that it held some onlookers spellbound. When she'd finished her blistering attack on the wickedness of human existence, I helped her down from her pulpit and took her aside. As soon as I introduced myself, Angharad became truculent.

"You'll not stop me, archdeacon," she warned. "The Lord has called me and I answer only to Him."

"Then we've something in common," I said, tolerantly. "Having heard you speak, I'd argue with your theology but I don't call your sincerity into question. You are brave, Angharad."

"It's not bravery – it's a blessed duty."

I could've taken issue over that remark but I chose to ignore it. I also pretended not to notice the unpleasant odour that came from the woman. Her hair was straggly and unwashed, her apparel mean. She wore sandals on her bare feet. Still in her twenties, her once appealing face was now blotched and haggard. I might have been looking at a beggar but one with an intelligence that shone out of her like a flaming beacon. For a moment, I wasn't sure if I was in the presence of madness or of divine inspiration.

"I want to ask you about Idwal the Harpist," I said.

"He was killed by Owain ap Meurig," she responded.

"Do you have any proof of that?"

"I saw it happen in a dream."

"We need more positive evidence than that, Angharad."

"My dreams never deceive," she insisted. "On the night that my parents died, I woke up screaming because I'd foreseen it in a nightmare. Every detail of my dream turned out to be correct. I was able to take people to the very spot where the rocks had tumbled down the mountain and buried them. I can give you other examples, if you wish."

"No, no," I said, staving off a long litany of her disturbed sleep. "I want to know what you saw – or *thought* you saw – with regard to Idwal the Harpist."

"Then first, you must know that I live on Owain's land. My cottage lies due south of here near the road that leads to Monmouth."

"Go on."

"The dream was short but vivid. I saw Owain and his niece bidding the harpist farewell. Idwal set off on his horse. It picked up a stone along the way and he dismounted to remove it from the animal's hoof. He walked beside it for a while, his harp in a bag that hung from the saddle. When he came to a stand of trees, he was set upon and stabbed to death. His body was buried nearby."

"What about the harp?"

"It was taken back to Owain's house and hidden in the stables. That's how I know Owain was the murderer."

"Yet you saw him and Gwenllian wave off the harpist."

"Idwal rode slowly. It would have been easy to catch him up and overtake him. He was in no hurry. He was on foot when he was attacked. Owain took him by surprise."

"And are you *certain* that it was Owain?"

"It looked vaguely like him, archdeacon."

Angharad went on to add more detail. My first impulse was to dismiss the whole thing as nonsense but I came to feel that her story was at least worth investigation.

"To whom have you told this tale?" I asked.

"It's not a tale, archdeacon – it's the truth."

"Did you confront Owain with it?"

"I tried," she said, "but he sent me away with harsh words and threatened to throw me off his land if I repeated what I'd seen in my dream." She drew herself up to her full height. "Nobody can threaten me, archdeacon. When my way of life was chosen for me, I put on the whole armour of God and it's protected me well. If I lose my little home, I'll sleep in barns or byres or wherever my feet are directed. Owain ap Meurig doesn't frighten me."

"You also spoke to Roger of Brionne."

"He, at least, had the courtesy to listen to me."

"So I was told."

"He believes me." She fixed me with a shrewd look. "What about you, archdeacon?"

"The only thing that will convince me is ocular proof," I told her. "If your dream was a true reflection of what happened – and we know from the Bible that dreams *can* act as warnings – then there's an easy way to establish it. I'll institute a search of the stables at Owain ap Meurig's house."

"Shall I come with you, archdeacon?"

"That might not be wise."

"But you'll tell me what you find, I hope."

"It's the least I can do, Angharad. Thank you for your help."

"It's I who must thank you," she said with a wan smile. "Most of those in holy orders think I'm a madwoman who perverts the word of God. You heard me preach yet raised no objection. I cannot tell you how grateful I am for that. You are a good man, archdeacon."

"I've striven hard to achieve goodness," I admitted.

"Then let good triumph over evil. Bring a killer to justice."

Anticipating resistance, I took the precaution of detaching two men-at-arms from our retinue and travelled with them to the house of Owain ap Meurig. The sight of Norman soldiers in helm and hauberk enraged the old Welshman and he rid himself of a few choice curses. He was even more vociferous when I explained the purpose of my second visit, his anger spilling over into uncontrollable rage.

"You'd listen to the word of that madwoman?" he demanded.

"I have a duty to test its veracity," I said, calmly.

"Her brain is addled, man! You only have to look at her to see that she's descended into babbling idiocy. Angharad is always making stupid accusations about people. Her dreams are like a plague on the rest of us. Out of misguided kindness, I gave her the use of a hovel on my land but she really belongs in a madhouse."

I let him rant on until his fury was spent then I pointed out it was in his interests to let us search the stables. If no harp were found there, he'd be exonerated. Under protest, he accepted my advice and we walked away from the house. As we did so, I caught sight of Gwenllian, peering from a window in consternation. Was she indirectly the cause of a heinous crime? Only time would tell.

It took longer than I expected. When we got to the stables, my two companions searched it thoroughly, using their swords to poke about in the straw. In an effort to show that he was innocent of the charge, Owain joined in the search, going into stall after stall in pursuit of the harp. We were on the point of abandoning the exercise when I received what I can only describe as guidance from above. I heard a noise that didn't reach the ears of the others, the soft, coaxing, resonant sound of harp strings being plucked.

"What's up there?" I asked, pointing to the rafters.

"That's where I store the hay," replied Owain, "as these two Norman ruffians have already discovered."

"Let me take a second look."

Moving the ladder into position, I clambered up it to the rafters. Boarding had been laid across part of the timbers so that sheaves of hay could be kept there. I wasn't worried about the fodder. My eye went upwards to a piece of dark cloth that hung from the apex of the roof. It had been so artfully arranged that it blended with the rafters and was difficult to pick out in the gloom. Going to the very top of the ladder, I reached up and felt something solid beneath the cloth. When I drew the object out, there was a gasp of horror from Owain ap Meurig. It was a harp.

Roger de Brionne was overjoyed to hear the news. He clapped me on the back in congratulation then offered me wine. As we drank together in his solar, I supplied him with full details.

"The praise should go to Angharad," I pointed out. "The harp was exactly where she said it would be and we found the body of

Idwal the Harpist in a shallow grave among some trees. That dream of hers was providential. The Madwoman of Usk deserves our thanks."

"Where is Owain being held?"

"In a dungeon at the castle – he protests his innocence and calls me such foul names that I blush to hear them. His niece could not believe he was guilty yet she provided some of the evidence that helped to secure his arrest."

Roger's interest sharpened. "Indeed?"

"Yes, my lord. Gwenllian confessed that, as soon as she and her uncle had waved off the harpist, Owain mounted his horse and rode off in the same direction. He was wearing his dagger."

"Did the girl say anything about Idwal's behaviour to her?"

"It was as you suggested," I said. "In the presence of her uncle, Idwal was polite and restrained. When she and the harpist were alone together, however, he did take certain liberties. One night, he even tapped upon her chamber door but she kept it firmly locked."

"Was this reported to her uncle?"

"Of course – she keeps nothing from him."

Roger drained his cup. "This is not the first crime that Owain has committed," he said, licking his lips, "but it's the one that will finally bring him down. You've done well, archdeacon. Without your intercession, the case would never have been resolved and Idwal would have lain undiscovered in his grave."

"I was glad to be of assistance, my lord."

"As for Angharad, she'll be rewarded."

"In what way?"

"That hovel she inhabits is on land that's rightly mine. Now that Owain is no longer here to contest ownership, it will revert to me and I'll grant her free use of the dwelling in perpetuity."

"Your generosity does you credit, my lord," I said, taking another sip of wine, "but we mustn't forget that Owain allowed her to live on his estate without any payment. He even gave her food from time to time. An evil man was capable of some goodness."

Roger of Brionne smiled grimly. "That thought may comfort him at his execution."

On my ride back, I took the trouble to seek out the hovel where the so-called Madwoman of Usk spent her nights when she was not roaming the county in search of random congregations. Having left her with severe reservations about the significance of her dream, I could now return with all my doubts answered. Angharad had a gift that was almost as extraordinary as some that I possess. I needed to bestow my gratitude and to acquaint her with the consequences of what she'd told me.

The dwelling was no more than a ramshackle hut and I couldn't understand how a woman who'd once lived in a fine house and slept on a soft bed now chose to endure such privations. It was a self-imposed martyrdom. Angharad was not at home but, since the door was unlocked, I ventured inside the building. The single room was hardly fit for human habitation. There were gaps in the roof, holes in the wall and inches of space around the door to let in wind and rain. Apart from a few sticks of furniture and a mattress, the place was bare. It was as cheerless as a monastic cell.

The only items of value were the crucifix on the table and the books wrapped up in sealskin to save them from being soaked. When I glanced through the little collection, I was diverted by the sight of a religious pamphlet that I'd once written in the elegant Latin for which I'm justifiably famous. The Madwoman of Usk had sanity in her library. I was about to leave when my eye fell on something I didn't expect to find there, something concealed behind the mattress with a sense of shame. Its protruding top caught the sunlight that slanted in through the only window.

When I stopped to pick it up, I was shocked to find myself holding a flagon of wine. It was half-empty. Instinct urged me to taste the wine and I did so. It was a revelation.

Gwenllian was in despair. Calling at the house, I found her still weeping over the dramatic turn of events. Once again, she swore to me that her uncle was not capable of murder and that some grotesque mistake had been made. I silenced her with a raised palm.

"If you wish to help your uncle," I advised, "answer a question. Did you see the horse on which Idwal the Harpist rode?"

"Yes, I did, archdeacon."

"And would you recognize the animal again?"

"I'm certain of it," she said.

"Why is that, Gwenllian?"

"It was so distinctive – and so was the saddle. I'd know it anywhere." She drew back from me. "It's not in our stables, if that's what you mean. I've been there to look."

"I'd like you to look again – in another place altogether."

As a sign of the importance of my embassy, I took four armed men with me this time. On the journey there, none of them could take his eyes off Gwenllian, who rode beside me with the breeze plucking at her hair. Roger of Brionne came out of his house to greet us with a frown. Hands on hips, he was smouldering with anger.

"What's the meaning of this, archdeacon?" he demanded.

"We'd like to inspect your stables," I said. "A horse has gone astray and I wondered if it might have ended up here."

His eyes darted and I caught the slight tremble of his lip. Though he tried to deny us access, I deprived him of the power to resist us in one sentence. I thanked him for the wine he gave me. He was rocked. While two of the soldiers flanked Roger, the others took Gwenllian to the stables to begin their search. It was short-lived. They soon emerged with a bay mare in tow. One of the men carried a saddle. He held it up to show me.

"This horse belonged to Idwal the Harpist," Gwenllian attested. "And so did that saddle. How did they end up here?"

"That's something that the lord Roger will have to explain," I said, glancing at his ashen countenance. "Meanwhile, he can replace your uncle in the castle dungeon. He'll be charged with murder, theft and the wilful manipulation of a vulnerable woman."

"It's not I who manipulated a woman," howled Roger, "but that devil of a harpist. When he stayed with us last year, he left more than the sound of his music in the air. As a result of his visit, my daughter was with child. I had to send her to Normandy to give birth in order to avoid disgrace. Idwal deserved to die!"

"And you sought to take full advantage of his death," I noted. "In killing him, you not only wreaked your revenge – you saw the chance to ensnare Owain ap Meurig by hiding that harp in his stables."

***

Gwenllian was mystified. As we rode back to Usk, I made sure that she and I stayed at the rear so that the soldiers couldn't ogle her and so that I could give her an account of what had happened.

"I first began to suspect the lord Roger," I said, solemnly, "when he told me how much he admired Idwal's playing. Yet he didn't invite the harpist back to his house even though Idwal would pass his door on the way to Monmouth. That struck me as odd. There had to be a reason why he didn't offer hospitality to Idwal. He's now told us what it was. Knowing exactly when the man would depart from your house, the lord Roger lay in wait for Idwal and struck him down."

"Then he blamed it on Uncle Owain."

"I fear that he did, Gwenllian."

She was dismayed. "Are you telling me that Angharad was his confederate?" she asked, querulously. "I know that the poor woman has lost her wits but I didn't think she'd forgotten the difference between right and wrong."

"Angharad is free from any blame. A dream she had and much of it foreshadowed the heinous crime. When she recalled it to me, however," I went on, "she admitted that she only saw the figures in dim outline. Angharad knew that Idwal was the victim because she saw the harp. She *assumed* that your uncle was the killer because the man in her dream resembled him. When she took her story to Roger of Brionne, he couldn't believe his good fortune. He plied her with wine and put flesh on the bare bones of her dream."

"How did she know that the harp was hidden in our stables?"

"Because that's where the lord Roger had it placed," I explained, "and where he convinced Angharad that it would be. Her dream was real but it was peopled by the lord Roger, whispering in the ear of a woman affected by strong drink. I can vouch for its strength," I added, "for he offered some to me. When I found a flask of it at Angharad's hovel, I knew who her benefactor was."

"Poor woman!" she cried. "He practised upon her."

"The full truth will emerge at the trial – the full truth about the murder, that is." When I turned to look at her, she dropped her head guiltily to her chest. "There's something you held back from me, isn't there?" I probed. "It's to do with the night when Idwal tapped on your chamber door in search of your favour."

"I'd rather not speak about it."

"It's a shame that must be acknowledged, Gwenllian. It may be habitual among the Welsh but it's wrong and I've preached against it many times. Tell me the truth, child."

"No, no," she whispered. "I dare not."

"Then let me put the words into your mouth," I said, recalling that moment when I passed by her and felt that peculiar sensation. "You didn't open the door to Idwal that night for one simple reason. Someone was already sharing your bed."

Her face turned white and she brought a hand up to her mouth to smother a cry. Owain ap Meurig would be released from custody but, in truth, he was no innocent man. Roger of Brionne had exploited the weakness of the Madwoman of Usk and implicated her in a murder plot. Owain had seduced his niece and turned her into his mistress. Both men would answer for their sins before God. I was once again honoured to be chosen as the instrument of His divine purpose.

DEAD AND BREAKFAST

Marilyn Todd

"GEORGES, HAVE YOU put those pillows in number twenty-two yet?"

Pillows. Pillows. Georges dragged his eyes away from the grebes out on the lake as he remembered the pile of goosedown in his arms.

"Doing it now, Mother."

But it was so comical, the way they dived for fish. You watch them go down, follow the ripples on the surface, then pick a spot where you think they'll come up. Except you're wrong. Every time, it's that much further from where you expect them to, and this time one of the grebes had caught a fish. A big one. Georges watched, fascinated by the contest between predator and prey. One false move and the fish was gone forever. Both sides fighting for survival.

"And don't forget to unblock that drain in the second-floor bathroom while you're up there, love."

Drain? He looked at the spanner in his hand. Oh. Drain. "No, no," he called down. "I won't forget."

Georges loved this lake. He loved the way the boats bobbed on smooth days as well as in rough weather, their yards clanking gentle lullabies, their hulls gleaming in the sun. He loved the way that spring dawns glimmered hazy and yellow on the surface, like melted Camembert. How fiery sunsets multiplied out and flickered on the water. How autumn mists swirled round the islands and then disappeared, as if by magic, and how the moon reflected double on the lake. And none of this would be possible, were it not for the pines that surrounded it, repelling the winds that drove in from the west, fending off the snows that swept up from the Pyrénées, thwarting the desiccating frosts that gripped the rest of France. In fact, he thought, if it wasn't for the gulls, flapping round the perimeter in search of tiddlers in the shallows, you'd think the coast was a lot further than eight kilometres away.

Except not everyone enjoyed neat promenades that served up ice creams and carousels, or took pleasure in roasting themselves on broad, white sandy beaches that stretched to infinity in both directions. The people who holidayed at Georges's lake were more discriminating. Not for them long treks through woods, laden with parasols and picnic hampers, just to then do battle with the highest dunes in Europe. Let others wrestle with deck chairs and drink lukewarm lemonade—

"Oh, Georgie!" His mother jerked the pillows from his arms with a good-natured, but nonetheless exasperated sigh. "Will you ever stop your silly daydreaming?" She gave his cheek an affectionate squeeze, before setting off down the corridor to give 22 their extra pillows. "But if you don't mind, love. The drain?"

The what? Oh, that. Second floor. Blocked. At last, the grebe managed to turn the wriggling fish and gulp it down. Almost at once, it was diving back down for more.

"Now, if you wouldn't mind." She didn't seem entirely surprised to find her son still staring out of the window when she returned. "Breakfast'll be over any minute, and the guests are bound to need the bathroom."

"Right-oh."

He mightn't have won any prizes for spelling, maths, or grammar, but Georges was handy with his hands. In no time at all, he'd unscrewed the waste and was flushing out the pipe, though he didn't see what all the fuss was for. A few hairs, a bit of gunge, and *bien sûr*, it would reduce the drainage to a trickle, but that was no reason to go grumbling to his mother. She went to a lot of trouble to make the guests feel welcome. She set vases of flowers in their rooms, left them boiled sweets on the dressing table, and placed mothballs in the drawers. The sheets always smelled crisp and clean and fresh.

But then, some folk were never satisfied, he thought, his big, strong hands spannering the pipes back into place. If they weren't griping about lumpy mattresses, they were moaning because there wasn't an ashtray, or could someone change their bedside lamp, it wasn't bright enough to read by. Still. He mopped up the puddle of dirty water with a towel. Surrounded by such stunning scenery, people probably expected the same level of perfection from Les Pins. Most of the time, they blooming got it, too.

"I don't believe it!" An hour must have passed before his mother came storming into the dining room, where he was cramming the last of the unwanted croissants in his mouth. "Look what you've done to Madame Fouquet's towels!"

Eh?

She held up the filthy, sopping linen. "She's absolutely livid, and quite frankly, so am I."

Oh. *Those* towels. "Then she should have taken them back to her room," he said, spraying crumbs over the table. "Instead of leaving them in the bathroom for anyone to use."

"That's still no excuse for you to use them as rags. And to just leave them lying there, as well, you lazy toad!"

"Sorry."

It wasn't often that he saw his mother angry, and it wasn't simply because she had endless patience with him. She simply could not afford to lose control. Georges's father, Marcel, was the chef, and since food was his passion as well as the foundation for his business, he was either shopping for it at the market or else creating magnificent works of art with it in the kitchen. The hotel management was Irène's responsibility, something she accomplished with a combination of politeness, style, and military crispness, being just strict enough to keep the chambermaids on their toes, but not so tough that they looked for work elsewhere. Welcoming enough towards the guests, but not so sociable that they might be tempted to take advantage.

"Oh, Georgie, it's not you," she said, instantly calm again. "It's that wretched bloody bathroom that's got me so worked up." She swiped her hair out of her eyes with the back of her hand. "I'm going to have to call a plumber out, and God knows how long that'll take in August."

"Why?" He might be big and slow and clumsy, but Georges took great pride in his work.

"Why?" Her voice rose. "Because that stupid, bloody wash-basin's blocked up again already—"

Wash…basin… "I'll take another look."

"Not sure there's any point, you've only just been up there."

"Yes, but I'll check further down the pipes." He turned away, so she wouldn't see how red his cheeks had gone.

"Will you? Oh, you are an angel. And while you're up there, would you put clean towels in thirty-four for Madame Fouquet? I can hardly leave the poor woman with just a hand towel for her bath."

"Right-oh."

Washbasin. He wrote it on the back of his hand with a Biro, so as not to forget. Second floor, he scribbled underneath. And towels.

Which was just as well, because by the time he'd brushed Minou the cat, topped up the birdbath, and then fed the ducks out on the lake, it was fast approaching midday. Four o'clock before he actually got round to fixing it.

Madame Fouquet never saw her towels.

For all its pine-scented air and picture-postcard views, it wasn't always easy here for Georges. Life was comfortable enough. Marcel and Irène were the first to think of shipping in sand, to create a private lakefront beach. They revamped the gardens with Mediterranean palms and oleanders, tacked on a veranda, then a terrace, and built moorings for the hotel clients' boats. This was good. With every improvement, the hotel grew and prospered.

The trouble was, in order to capitalize on a silence broken only by the croaking of frogs and the splash of fish – the very qualities their middle-aged, middle-class guests looked for in a holiday – his parents also banned transistor radios and banished TV to the public lounge. Their intention was that busy Parisians should come down, plug into two weeks of time-warp bliss, then go home refreshed and free of stress. But for Georges, this was his home. And, rather like the resort itself, which had grown up to create its own identity but in doing so had paradoxically isolated itself from the outside world, so he, too, became disconnected.

While other teenagers were rebelling, flower power passed him by, and whatever the Summer of Love might be, it never came his way. But not being "groovy" didn't trouble him. To be honest, he didn't know what groovy was, so it didn't matter that Jesus might be loving Mrs Robinson more than she would ever know, much less that Mick Jagger was having his mind and other things blown by honky-tonk girls. But then he turned sixteen and things began to change. Not being clever enough to stay on at school, he quickly lost touch with the few friends that he'd had, and though he took over as the hotel handyman from doddery old René, the staff were invariably too busy to stop for idle chit-chat. Naturally, Georges picked up the broad outline of events from the national news, but what he wasn't getting was life's rich tapestry of trivia, and this became a problem. All he wanted was to do what the Parisians did, only in reverse. Plug into normal life. But how?

The more time passed, the more his desire – his need – to tap into normality intensified. It wasn't that he was lonely, exactly. He'd always enjoyed his own company, but there was a hole somewhere, a big black hole that needed to be filled, and whoever said it was the little things that mattered was absolutely right. And it was the little things that were missing from his life.

At least, that was the case until one warm and sunny April morning when his mother asked him to oil the sticky lock on Number 17. And would you believe it, there was the answer. Staring him right in the face. He oiled, he turned, he oiled, he turned. No sticking. No rubbing. No catching.

No noise …

At long last, Georges had found a way to connect to the world beyond Les Pins.

The idea of being called a Peeping Tom would have cut him to the quick. There was nothing mucky about what he was doing. Nothing sinister about his motives. He was simply using his master key to slip into rooms, and there, just being among the guests while they slept, he was able to note other people's eccentricities and foibles. The big, black void was filled.

While Irène was just delighted that her son had at last showed some initiative by oiling all the bedroom locks, not just the one.

"Madame Garnier's eldest daughter's getting married," Georges told Parmesan, the heavy horse who used to pull a plough but had long since been put out to pasture. "I saw the telegram on her dressing table."

MAMAN PAPA GUESS WHAT STOP HENRI PROPOSED AT LAST STOP ISN'T THIS JUST WONDERFUL STOP

"Both Monsieur *and* Madame Garnier were smiling in their sleep," he added. "So they must be pleased about it."

Although he still spent the same amount of time fishing, bird-watching, and watching squirrels in the woods, Georges and Parmesan tended to see a lot more of each other these days. Blissfully unaware, of course, that Marcel was having to drop his *bœuf bordelaix* and drive at breakneck speed so the Gérards – the LeBlancs – the St Brices or whoever – didn't miss their trains. Or that the Duponts, the Brossards, and the new people in 38 had to lug their cases up several flights of stairs, because the handyman had forgotten to reconnect the lift after regreasing the cogs and chains.

"Mother doesn't like that Madame Dupont, with the blue-rinse hair, who rustles when she walks. She thinks she's hard and crusty, but she's not." Georges passed the horse an apple. "She's soft as dough inside."

He knew this because of the soppy romances Madame Dupont read, and more than once he'd had to pick up a paperback that had fallen from her hand, replacing the bookmark and laying it gently on the cover next to her.

"You wouldn't think it, but twenty-seven wears a toupee." It gave Georges quite a fright, seeing it draped over the footstool. He thought it was a rat. "Someone should tell him he looks a lot younger without it, though." Unlike Madame 27, whose teeth snarled at him from the glass beside the bed. "She snores, as well," he said.

In fact, it was quite a revelation, seeing what the guests were really like, as opposed to what they wanted you to think. For instance, Georges could tell who was putting on a front, pretending to read highbrow literature when they were sneaking tabloid news inside their daily papers. He knew who was sloppy and who was not from the way they folded their clothes or tossed them on a chair, and, even more importantly, by squeezing the towels, he knew who took a bath every day and who only took one once a week and disguised their lack of personal hygiene with cologne.

Darker secrets came out, too. Major Chabou, for instance, swapped dirty pictures with the banker in the room upstairs. Suzette the chambermaid was having an affair with Number 14, even sleeping in his bed after his poor wife had had to rush back home to see to her sick mother. Mind you, Suzette didn't sleep in curlers, like the other female guests. Or wear a hairnet, either, for that matter.

So summers came and summers went, and even though Georges assumed the Year of the Cat was just one more Chinese holiday, who cared? The same people booked the same rooms for the same two weeks in the season, and simply by taking stock of their toothbrushes, their writing pads, their cosmetics, and their clothes, he was able to follow the changes in their lives and circumstances.

Some guests never changed, of course. Monsieur Prince still put his dirty shoes on Irène's clean white linen sheets. The Bernards still stashed the hotel's face flannels at the bottom of their suitcase. Madame Morreau still treated Georges the same way she did when he was seven, only now instead of ruffling his hair and giving him a bag of aniseed, she had to reach up on tippy-toes to pat his shoulder. But she still brought him aniseed, which Georges had never liked but which he could at least feed to Parmesan, even though it made him kick and swish his tail. And Georges still very much looked forward to her visits.

Which made it doubly hard when Madame Morreau died.

"Take a look at these architect's plans, love, and tell me what you think."

From the outset, his parents had involved him in their projects, but to be honest, the squares and boxes on the page confused him. What did it mean, "drawn to scale", he wondered? Fish had scales. Kitchens had scales. But gardens? And this 250:1 stuff. Georges didn't understand where bookmakers fitted into plans for new extensions, and whenever he saw things like this, he was glad he hadn't been forced to stay on at school.

"Ten new bedrooms to be built during the winter shut-down, and what about this?" The excitement in his mother's voice was catching. "No more trotting down the corridor in the middle of the night for *our* guests. As of next spring, they'll all have their own individual, private bathroom!"

"And now the world's opening up to foreign travel, son, what do you think about including couscous on the menu?" Marcel said.

Would that be meat, or some exotic vegetable, he wondered?

"Every room'll have its own mini shampoo and soap."

"Osso buco, perhaps?"

"Hair dryers in the bathrooms."

"Definitely paella – are you all right, son?"

"Yeah."

But there was no fooling his mother. "Oh, Georges." She laid down her fountain pen. "You're not still upset about Madame Morreau, are you?"

Marcel had brought him up that it was wrong to tell a lie, but for some reason he felt ashamed of saying yes out loud. Madame Morreau had been different from the other guests, somehow. Special. For a start, she was one of the few who weren't wary of this big, shambling young man, who was constantly wandering round the hotel with a distant expression on his face and a toolbox in his hand. And she didn't talk down to him, either. In fact, quite often she had to rebuke that weasel-faced nephew of hers for poking fun at him.

Georges is a wee bit slow, Jean-Paul. You need to make allowances.

Jean-Paul. That was Weasel's name. Jean-Paul. And it was a funny thing, but until Madame Morreau said that, Georges had never thought of himself as slow. And yet, now he came to think of it, he *had* always been in the tail of any school race. How she knew all that was a mystery to him, but even so, Georges always made a point of quickening his pace when he saw her coming. Especially once Jean-Paul began to mouth *Slowpoke* at him behind her back.

"A bit," Georges admitted.

"Don't be, love." His mother squeezed his hand. "The old dear had a long and happy life, and you should be pleased she died peacefully, snuggled in her pillows." She turned to Marcel and pulled a face. "Even if it was in our hotel."

"The undertakers were very discreet, I thought."

"Only because you slipped them lorry loads of francs, but it's the chambermaids I'm proudest of. None of them so much as screamed."

"They wouldn't bloody dare," Marcel muttered under his breath, but Irène wasn't listening.

"The guests had no idea that anything was amiss, and even Madame Morreau's nephew carried himself well, I thought. Considering."

When Georges closed his eyes, he could see Jean-Paul in conversation with the doctor that the hotel had been obliged to call. Saw him showing him the pills Madame Morreau took for her bad heart. Heard him telling how she'd had two seizures this year already.

"Nice boy," Irène added, with a sigh. "Always so conscientious when he stayed here with his aunt."

"No, he wasn't."

If anyone was an expert on the subject of being chivvied up, it was Georges. But never on account of being lazy.

It's very good of you to do this for me, Georges.

I like doing it, Madame Morreau. Honest.

Unlike some, who wouldn't be seen dead supporting an old lady's arm while she took a walk along the lake.

I don't know where Jean-Paul's got to, I really don't.

Georges did. As soon as she said she wouldn't mind a stroll, Weasel had been off. Greyhounds on a track don't run that fast.

It's so nice to be able to take a walk, while I'm still able. He remembered the sad little smile she'd shot him, as she patted his arm. *I'll be in a wheelchair next year, Georges.*

That'll be good, though, won't it? I'll be able to push you round the lake. In fact, I'll run.

Will you? Will you, Georges? Her laugh suddenly became happy and girlish, and for a moment he saw how she must have looked sixty years ago. *You've no idea how exciting it'd be for an old woman to feel the wind in her hair again.*

You bet, he'd promised, and he meant it.

"Jean-Paul thought fetching things and looking after her beneath him," he told Marcel and Irène.

It wasn't because he sneered at him, or called him names behind her back, that Georges despised the nephew. More the way he scowled at having to trek upstairs to fetch her cardigan because her legs weren't up to it, or screwed up his face when she forgot things. Georges scuffed his foot. He knew all about forgetting things, and saw how much it embarrassed Madame Morreau, being dependent on someone else to put it right. Especially someone who resented doing it...

"I don't think he was even sorry that she died."

Georges had never encountered sudden death before, so he couldn't be certain. But that look on Weasel's face when the doctor signed that piece of paper—

"I wish I could put a name to that expression," he said, but his parents were back poring over their plans, discussing colour charts and debating whether the floor tiles in the bathrooms would be better white or cream. To them, the incident was closed. But for Georges, the misgivings wouldn't go away, and though the winter gales came lashing in from the Atlantic, bending the pines around the lake and causing them to hiss like angry snakes, his mind remained on aniseed and ruffled hair. On cardigans that smelled of lavender, and happy, girlish giggles.

People imagined Madame Morreau was as well-heeled as the other guests, but Georges knew otherwise. Her suits were quality, but seconds, he'd seen the crossed-out labels. Also, her petticoats had worn thin, her stockings were darned, and her shoes, although good quality and polished to a shine, were almost through to holes. And even he, who didn't understand figures very much, knew that red ink on a bank statement was bad news. Which is why he thanked her so politely for the candy every year, and refused a tip for carrying her bags. She'd had to really scrimp and save for her fortnight at Les

Pins, and go without a lot of things to pay for her nephew to come with her. He knew all this, because he'd read it in her diary.

And her diary said nothing about heart attacks and seizures—

"Oh, Georgie. You've let the paste go hard."

Paste? Then he remembered why he was up this blooming ladder. Sticking fresh wallpaper on Number 21. "It's not right, Mum."

"Not now it isn't, love. It's set like concrete in this wretched bucket."

"I don't mean the glue. Madame Morreau."

But by the time he'd trundled down the ladder, both his mother and the tub of paste were gone, and he'd painted the whole of the first-floor corridor and was halfway through emulsioning the ceiling in Reception before it dawned on him.

"You said pillows," he said, laying down his brush.

"No, I didn't, love. I said windows. Can you wash the windows when you're done? Only Suzette's gone and got herself pregnant, and God only knows who the father is. But the point is, I don't want her up a stepladder, not in her condition."

"You said she died snuggled into her pillows," Georges said, except she couldn't have. Madame Morreau never used a pillow, stacking all four neatly in a pile beside the bed, and that's where she used to rest her diary when she'd finished writing up her day. On the pile of pillows, with her specs. "She liked to sleep flat," he added. For her neck.

"Suzette?" Irène looked confused. "Anyway, the thing is, the hotel inspector's coming down to view the new extension, and I would really like to have the whole place looking its best for when he comes. Sparkling from roof down to the cellar!"

Georges tried to imagine the roof sparkling, but couldn't. "Madame Morreau had a good heart."

"Indeed she did, love. She was kind and patient, just like you, and I know you were fond of her, Georgie, but you have to accept that her poor old heart was simply worn out with age."

Was it? All night he couldn't sleep for worrying, because who could he tell? Who'd listen to the ramblings of a daydreaming handyman who couldn't spell and couldn't add up, either?

Who would believe a man who crept in people's rooms at night?

***

"Hey, Carrot Top!"

The season was in full swing again.

"Fetch me a cold beer, will you? I'm absolutely gasping."

Georges paused from emptying the hedge clippings on the compost. That voice— He peered round the corner and could hardly believe his eyes. Madame Morreau's nephew!

"Yes, you. Gingernut." Jean-Paul was addressing a girl, whose bare feet were half buried in the sand. "You wouldn't allow a man to die of thirst, would you?"

"She's not staff," Georges said. "She's—" For the first time he took a good, hard look at her. "She's—"

"Recently moved in across the lake." Her little snub nose wrinkled in apology. "Sorry. Am I trespassing? Only I was curious to see what our village looked like from this side."

"No. I mean, yes, but—"

He could see how Jean-Paul mistook her for a waitress. Black skirt, white blouse. Red hair tied back from her face.

"What he means is, can't you read?" Weasel pointed to the big, bold sign that proclaimed *Private Property*. "It specifically says 'No Carrot Tops Allowed'."

"Don't call her that." Georges felt something stir inside. "It's mean."

"True." The nephew winked, then turned and walked off whistling. "I'll stick with Gingernut instead."

Over in the car park, Georges saw Madame Morreau's ancient Peugeot straddling two bays. The mirror shine had gone, the number plate was black with flies, and rust had begun to creep along the sills. A pair of fluffy dice, one pink, one blue, dangled above the grimy walnut console.

"Thanks for sticking up for me," the girl said, scuffing her toe deeper into the sand. "But I'm used to being ribbed about my hair."

The teasing still hurt, though. He could tell by the way her skin had turned bright pink, right down to her neck. "Is that why you tie it back? To hide it?"

"Wouldn't you?" The greenest eyes he'd ever seen misted over. "I tried dyeing it, but that made it ten times worse." This time the nose wrinkled in disgust. "It's horrible hair. I hate it."

"You shouldn't." For some reason, he had an urge to reach out and feel how its curls would spring about between his fingers. "It's beautiful."

"It's bright red!"

"Like maple leaves in autumn," Georges said, nodding. "The colour of a robin's breast and squirrels' fur and sunsets on the lake, and you know what else? Your face. It reminds me of a wren's egg."

"Because of the mass of brown freckles on a very white background?"

"Because it's small and smooth and fragile," he corrected.

Across the lake? He glanced at the dots that were the village in the distance. She did. She definitely said, across the lake.

"Is it true you know where every swan and heron has its nest?"

Her name was Sandrine and she worked in the boat-hire office that her father had just opened and which, according to her, was doing exceptionally well. Despite her leaving customers lined up outside because she forgot to open up, or else stranded on the open water, having not filled up their gas tanks.

"Are there otters in the lake?" she asked, peering through her binoculars.

"No, but there's a family in the river that feeds into it." Her legs were long and slim, and covered in the same pretty freckles that covered her face and arms. "I built a hide to watch them."

He could have talked for hours, and the odd thing was, he had the feeling Sandrine would have listened, too. But round the door of Reception, he could see a finger being crooked, beckoning him. An arrogant, bony finger, with a weaselly sneer on the end of it.

"Going to carry my cases for me, Slowpoke?"

Through the office, Georges could see Irène had had to take an urgent phone call, and remembered that although he'd serviced the lift earlier this morning, this was yet another occasion when he'd gone off to cut the hedge without reconnecting the blasted electricity.

"Number forty-five," Jean-Paul said, grinning. "Top floor."

In many ways, Georges had inherited his mother's temperament. In many ways, he had not. He chewed his lips. Almost smelled the aniseed.

"Certainly, sir." A phrase he'd never used before, but one which he'd heard Irène trot out a thousand times each season. "This way, please."

He glanced at the *Out of Order* sign. Would that have made things worse, or better? Four flights of stairs made for a long, slow climb, but at least they went up separately. In the lift, they'd have been locked in, face-to-face.

"Here we are, sir. Your aunt's old room."

"Nice view." Jean-Paul let his breath out in an admiring whistle as he stepped out on to the balcony. "Better than that crummy cupboard she used to put me in. I mean, who wants to overlook a bloody car park?"

Georges wanted to tell him that the single rooms weren't crummy, and they weren't much smaller, either. It was because they had ordinary windows, rather than French doors, that they appeared darker.

"The view will be better once the new swimming pool's installed."

"I can't swim, so who cares, and in any case," Jean-Paul sniffed, "wild horses wouldn't bring me back to this dump."

Georges had the same urge he'd had when he was eight years old and Jacques Dubois kicked down the matchstick train that Georges had spent all winter building. He wanted to punch him on the nose.

"This is the best room in the house," he said instead.

Madame Morreau used to stay here with her husband before he died, he'd read that in her diary, too. The reason why she scrimped and saved to come back again each year. To relive the happy memories they'd shared.

"Two weeks of R and R in the best room in the house, all paid for in advance? Not bad, eh?" Weasel threw himself down on the bed. "Not quite the Côte d'Azur I'd had in mind, of course. But since the old girl coughed without a penny, it's better than bloody nothing, I suppose."

No money, poor health, and a nephew who couldn't give a damn.

"Y'know, Slowpoke, I'm betting the beds in this place could tell a tale or two." He chuckled as he bounced up and down on the mattress.

Georges swore his heart stood still. "That one could."

The bouncing stopped. "Oh?" Jean-Paul's eyes narrowed as he advanced across the room. "And just what might you mean by that?"

Never tell a lie if you can help it, son. Marcel's voice echoed in his head. *It'll only come back to trip you up.*

"Honeymooners," he said. "The last guests were honeymooners."

Weasel's shoulders went slack again, but for a second Georges saw the same expression cross his face as when the doctor signed the death certificate. At last, he could put a name to it. Relief.

"Will there be anything else?" he asked in the same neutral tone he'd heard the chambermaids use.

"Just that beer – and Slowpoke?" Jean-Paul dipped his hand in his pocket. "A tip for carrying my cases."

His generosity took Georges by surprise. "Thank you," he said warmly.

"Look both ways before you cross the road."

Weasel seemed to think this was the funniest joke he'd ever heard, while Georges was so ashamed that he'd actually held his hand out to this man that he forgot to switch the lift back on, and once again Marcel had to abandon his *canard à l'orange* and dash the Brandons to the station, while Irène couldn't understand what a cold beer should be doing on her desk, but was so glad to see it that she downed it in one go.

"He killed her," Georges told Parmesan, feeding him the carrots that Marcel had earmarked for his julienne vegetables in garlic. "Jean-Paul murdered Madame Morreau, and it isn't right."

It wasn't right that she should die, simply so he could get his hands on her money. It wasn't right that he should run around in her beloved Peugeot, letting it go rusty and not even washing it, or that he should profit from a holiday she'd had to make huge sacrifices for.

"Then to come back to the hotel where he killed her, throwing his weight around, bouncing on the bed where she died, and making tasteless jokes. It's not right, Parmesan. It's not right at all."

And so another night passed in which Georges didn't get a wink of sleep, but this time it was different. Lying on his back, with his hands folded behind his head, he watched the Milky Way swirling across a cloudless sky with only one thought in his head.

She knows what wren's eggs look like …

The following week Georges took Sandrine to watch the otters from the seclusion of his hide, showed her all the secret places where rare warblers could be found, pointed out the heronry and the favourite perches of the kingfishers, and introduced her to Parmesan at her request.

"I used to slip him aniseed balls."

Sandrine dug around in her handbag and eventually came out with half a roll of extra-strong mints. "Do you think he'd like these?"

Like was a moot point. With the aniseed, he used to kick and swish his tail. The effect of the extra-strong mints made him snicker, buck, and, considering his age and size, practically gallop round the field, his nostrils snorting out peppermint strong enough to fell an oak. But since he kept coming back for more, they made a point of packing them with the carrots, oats, and apples every time they paid a visit.

"I think he's addicted," she giggled.

"Guess that makes us pushers," Georges quipped back, because her laugh was as magical as rainbows, hoarfrost, and snow-melt waterfalls, and he was as hooked on its sound as this old plough horse on mints. Sometimes he feared he would drown in those freckles.

And in return for otters, squirrel drays, and badgers setts, Sandrine introduced Georges to the Bee Gees, *Star Wars*, and the thrill of racing powerboats, courtesy of her father's hire business.

"Night fever, night fever," they'd sing together, Sandrine clicking her fingers, while Georges sped the sleek blue-and-white "Hire Me for 30F an Hour" advertisement past the new resorts that were springing up around the lake.

He'd never known anything like it.

Music that stirred his feet and his blood.

Tragedy.

A girl with hair the colour of the rich, red, Gascony soil and eyes greener than pastures in spring.

And now this. Scenery whizzing past in a blur, shirt billowing wide, and the wind in his hair – Georges cut the motor.

The powerboat went dead.

"What's wrong?"

"Madame Morreau," he said sombrely. "All she wanted was to feel the wind in her hair."

Instead, Jean-Paul was feeling it in his for thirty francs an hour. Using Madame Morreau's money.

"That's the first I've heard of any fishing competition." Irène looked up from her accounts. "Funny time of year, isn't it?"

Never tell a lie if you can help it.

"This is something new they're trying out for tourists." Georges crossed his fingers behind his back. "You're not allowed to keep the fish, you have to throw them back, but there's a prize of—" He'd been going to say a hundred francs. "Three hundred francs."

"Goodness me, I think I'll dash out and buy a fishing rod myself," Irène laughed. "Who's putting up the money, do you know?"

Georges was prepared for this. "The man who runs that new boat-hire company." He sneaked a peek at the notes scribbled in the palm of his hand. "He says the prize money is nothing compared to what he'll fetch, renting out his boats to the competitors."

"Sharp," Irène said admiringly. "Maybe I should try to find something that'll attract more visitors to Les Pins. Afternoon tea? Apéritifs on the terrace?"

"You will tell Jean-Paul Morreau, won't you, Mother?"

This was how the conversation had started. With him asking her to pass the message on.

"I don't really see him as the fishing type," she said doubtfully.

"None of the other guests is interested, I've asked," he cut in quickly, because the last thing he wanted was for her to broadcast it round the hotel, only to discover it was a better work of fiction than the Harold Robbins he was reading. Also … "It would be good publicity for us, too, if he won."

"Good heavens, Georges, you do surprise me sometimes!" Every mother is proud of her children, but at that moment Irène thought her heart would burst out of her chest. "But you're right, and what young man could possibly resist the lure of such a competition, given the right motivation by his hotelier!" Irène cocked her head. "Pity you're not a tourist. I'll bet you know exactly where the big fish live."

Bingo! The moment he'd been waiting for.

"Oh yes," he said, unable to hide the big, broad beam that cut his face in half. "I know where to find the winner."

As the door closed behind him, Irène became aware of hot tears coursing down her cheeks. She couldn't pinpoint the precise moment when her son had grown into a man. But she was fiercely proud of what he had become.

Fishing is as much about patience as anything else. Having baited his hook, Georges sat back, ready to reel in Jean-Paul, but even he was surprised at the speed with which he bit.

"Got a proposition for you," he said, less than one hour later. "You help me catch the winner and I'll go fifty-fifty with you."

Georges swallowed. "The best time's dusk. That's when they rise to the surface."

Weasel looked suspicious. "I thought they sank to the bottom."

Never tell a lie if you can help it. Suddenly, they were trotting out like ants. "Not the big ones."

"Dusk it is, then." Jean-Paul rubbed his hands together. "Tonight?"

Georges studied the sky, confident the weather would hold. "Perfect." The only thing that could have spoiled his plans was a storm that whipped up the water. But on a moonless night there'd be no tourists on the lake, and with his parents busy serving dinner, there'd be no one around to notice that two men went out but only one came back.

"What was that about?" Sandrine asked Jean-Paul, seeing him swagger out of Georges's shed. She was about to get on her scooter to ride home. He was off to the coast for livelier entertainment than what was on offer at Les Pins.

"That, my little Gingernut, is about winning a competition, and you know the best thing?" He chuckled as he unlocked the car. "We're going fifty-fifty."

"What's fifty-fifty?" Sandrine wasn't good with maths.

Jean-Paul slung his jacket on the passenger seat and winked. "It means he catches me a fish and I give him a hundred and fifty francs."

"I wish someone would give me a hundred and fifty francs," she sighed. "I'd buy myself a haircut just like Farrah Fawcett's."

* * *

"Bloody dark out there. Sure you can see to row?"

"I've fished loads of times at night," Georges said truthfully, but all the same his hands were clammy. "I know this lake like the back of my hand."

"Not surprised, considering they're the same size," Jean-Paul sniggered. "Where'd you say the big boy lives?"

Georges couldn't meet his eyes. "Far side of the island."

Jean-Paul squinted towards a dark lump in the distance. "Wake me up when we get there." He leaned back and pulled his cap down over his eyes.

Georges listened to the slapping of the oars and the pounding of his heart. It wasn't too late. He could turn round. Tell Jean-Paul he had a headache or stomach pains, even admit he'd made the whole thing up...

It's so nice to be able to take a walk, while I'm still able.

Madame Morreau's sad smile hung in the air like the Cheshire cat's. *Will you run? Will you, Georges?*

And that was the problem, wasn't it? Madame Morreau was never going to feel the wind in her hair. He looked at the shoreline, growing thinner with each stroke. Glanced over his shoulder, at the island looming closer. She'd never see the sunset from the room where she'd shared so many good times with her husband. Never smell the leather of the seats of her old Peugeot, or run her hands across its walnut dash. She wouldn't even have the chance to chide her nephew, or wonder where he'd got to when she needed him.

"We're here." He nudged Jean-Paul with his foot.

"It's the middle of bloody nowhere!" Lights from villages twinkled like miniature fireflies around the lake as black as soot. "Still, for three hundred smackers, it's worth getting spooked, eh, Slowpoke?"

"Stop calling me that, my name's Georges."

His tone made Jean-Paul look up. "Right." Both smile and voice were unusually tight. "Georges." He shifted in his seat. "So how long do you reckon it'll take to track down our little winner?"

"Depends." Georges pulled out a flashlight and leaned over the water. "Could be minutes, could be hours – whoa! Look! It's—"

"Give me that." Jean-Paul's unease vanished as he grabbed the torch from George's hand. "Where? I can't see any—"

The rest was drowned by the splash of two giant hands tipping him over the side.

"Hey! Hey, I can't swim!"

"I know," Georges said, rowing out of range with a speed that would have surprised Madame Morreau's nephew, had he not been gulping so much water. "You told me."

"All right, all right, you've had your fun. You've humiliated me, shown me who's boss, and fair dos. I called you names, bullied you a bit, and now you've got your revenge – but for Chrissakes, man, I'm drowning."

"No, you're not. Not if you kick your feet about a bit."

Jean-Paul had nothing to lose. He kicked his feet about a bit, but the fear of being sucked in wouldn't leave. "Enough's enough, you stupid bloody halfwit."

"You killed her," Georges said, pulling out a piece of paper and reading it by flashlight.

"What?" Jean-Paul's arms flailed and flapped in the water. "Is that what this is about? My stupid bloody aunt, you stupid moron?"

"My mother thinks she had a long and happy life, but Mother's wrong."

For one thing, Madame Morreau was only sixty-eight. Georges saw her identity papers lying on the table once, and sixty-eight was no age at all these days. Also, reading her diary, he saw that she'd never got over the devastation of not having children, sinking all her love in her husband instead.

"When he fell ill with cancer, she had no qualms about spending every last *centime* on finding him a cure." He didn't know what a qualm was, but it sounded so good that he'd quoted it anyway. "She even mortgaged her house."

"I know that, you stupid idiot."

"Not when you killed her, you didn't."

"I don't know what you're talking about. Now listen to me, Georges. You've had your laugh, you've made a fool of me, so come back and pull me out before I drown, you bloody retard."

"She was too proud to let people know she hadn't got two francs to rub together—" Or, more accurately, too ashamed to admit she'd blown their entire fortune on charlatans and quack cures. "—and like everybody else, you assumed she was well off. You were her only heir, and so you killed her. For her money."

"Yeah, well, prove it, dumb-ass." But the fight had gone out of Jean-Paul as the struggle of trying to keep afloat began to tell.

"You smothered her with her own pillows, then tried to make it look like natural causes, and because she was old and because you convinced the doctor that she had a bad heart, you thought you'd got away with it."

"All right, all right, I killed the old bitch, so what? She was like a bloody succubus, *Can you fetch this, I forgot that, Would you mind giving me a hand to the table.* I lost my temper that night and rammed the pillow over her face, all right? She was sick and old. I was doing her a favour – oh God, help—"

The water glugged and gurgled as it covered his head. Georges felt his stomach turning somersaults.

"Please," Jean-Paul said, bobbing up at last, and Georges could tell that he was crying. "Help me—"

"You didn't lose your temper. You planned to kill her long before you left Paris."

"I swear to God, it was the heat of the moment. For God's sake, don't let me die! I'll give you anything. The car. Take the car … "

"You brought the medication with you. That's premeditated murder."

"Whatever you want, name it, it's yours."

"A confession," Georges said. "I just want to hear you admit it."

"All right, all right." Jean-Paul was spluttering words and water in equal amounts now. "I thought she was rolling, I bought heart pills from a chemist's in Paris, I held the pillow over her face and—"

"Did she struggle?"

"Yes, of course she bloody struggled! I had to wake her up to get her to unlock the door, spinning some cock-and-bull story about needing to talk, put her back to bed, and guess what? No pillows."

"She used to pile them on the floor."

"I know that now, but at the time I had to search for them, so yes, the old bitch put up a fight – oh, Christ."

His head went underwater, and once more, it took forever before it surfaced. Even Jean-Paul, who couldn't swim, knew the third time was his last.

"You don't know what it's like," he screamed. "Do this, do that—"

"You wanted her money, you just didn't want to earn it."

"I'm young! I'm not cut out for fishing false teeth out of glasses, just because the stupid bitch forgot to put them in before going down to dinner! I killed her, and the only thing I'm sorry about is that she didn't have the money. Satisfied?"

"We certainly are," boomed a voice from nowhere, and suddenly the night was filled with blinding sunshine. It took Jean-Paul a few seconds to realize they were searchlights from other boats.

"Help," he spluttered, and it didn't matter the water was swarming with police uniforms. He was saved. "Help me, I'm drowning!"

"No, you're not," Georges said. "If you put your feet down, you could walk to the island."

Autumn came, and the leaves on the trees turned the colour of her hair, fluttering across the ground like the freckles on her skin. Out on the lake, grebes dived, the last of the swallows fattened up on flies, and in a rowboat a young couple talked of wedding rings and babies.

Irène was already converting the old barn into a cottage.

"I'm so proud of you," Sandrine said, dabbling her fingers in the water. "The way you went to the police, told them the only way to prove Madame Morreau had been murdered was by a confession by her killer, and then offering them a way they could get it."

She hadn't cut her hair like Farrah Fawcett, why would she? Not when a big man with a broad smile loved to run his fingers through it, telling her it shone like fire and smelled of lollipops and roses.

"I may have thought up the competition, but you gave it substance by saying your father was sponsoring it." He'd had to lie, telling Sandrine that Madame Morreau confided in him on their walks. But this would be the last lie he ever told, he promised himself. "Without you to hold my hand, I'd never have plucked up the courage to walk into the commissariat."

"In that case, come over here and show your appreciation properly," she giggled.

"I'd rather do it improperly," he grinned back, "but first."

He prised the master key from his ring and, with great solemnity, consigned it to the lake. As it sank, a breeze sprang up, rippling across the open water and ruffling his hair. Georges swore it smelled of aniseed.

AFFAIRS
OF THE HEART

Kate Atkinson

FRANKLIN MET CONNIE one evening outside the Queen's Hall. It was raining and when Connie slipped on the wet pavement Franklin helped her up and offered the shelter of his umbrella. "It was incredibly romantic," she said afterwards. "Like something out of Forster." Franklin happened to have been walking past when Connie was coming out of the Beethoven recital, but in her uncharacteristically flustered state she received the impression that he had also been at the concert.

"It was wonderful, wasn't it?" she said to him fifteen minutes later in the Café Royal. "How challenging Beethoven's late string quartets are," she added, decorously sipping a glass of Merlot.

"Yet how rewarding," Franklin said. He had never been to a classical concert in his life and certainly hadn't listened to a Beethoven string quartet, late or otherwise.

Connie seemed eager to share the details of her life with him. She was twenty-eight years old, educated at St George's and then at Aberdeen University and now worked as an account handler in an advertising agency in Leith. She was the second in a clutch of three girls, Patience, Constance and Faith. ("Mummy", apparently, was a stalwart churchwoman who believed in virtue.) "No Charity?" Franklin said and Connie said, "No, and don't mention Hope to Mummy if you meet her.

"My sister, Patience, is a cellist with the RSNO," Connie continued blithely. "And Faith is a senior registrar at the Royal Infirmary. Daddy's a heart surgeon and Mummy does—" at this point Connie made rabbit ears, something Franklin particularly disliked "—'good works'. She's a very keen gardener too. Her roses are legendary."

Franklin in a nutshell. *Ab ovo*. English. Thirty-four years old, five foot ten, one hundred and fifty pounds. Eyes of blue, hair of brown. Born in a Swiss clinic beneath the benign and sunny sign of the Lion three weeks after his father was immolated in the Austrian Grand Prix. His much-married mother, the slovenly scion of a minor, ruined aristocratic family, was notorious for having been involved in a sleazy sex-scandal (*Top Totty Brings Down Government*, according to one tabloid headline at the time).

Franklin left London for Scotland, managing to scrape into Stirling University on a media studies course, and after graduation he joined a local radio station from which starting point he climbed, like a salmon up a ladder, to the dizzy heights of being a script editor on a Scottish TV soap, *Green Acres* – a violent yet couthy mix, as if *The Sopranos* had relocated to *Brigadoon* and all the script editors had media studies degrees from Stirling.

Franklin felt that one day he would be tested, that a challenge would appear out of the blue – a war, a quest, a disaster – and that he would rise to this challenge and not be found wanting. It would be the making of him, he would come into his own. But what if this never happened, what if nothing was asked of him? Would he have to ask it of himself? And how did you do that?

Franklin was also unbelievably unlucky, descended from a long line of bad luck, only child of an only child of an only child and so on, and had become reconciled to the fact that no matter how many times the wheel of fortune turned he would always find himself stuck on the underside like gum on a shoe. Connie seemed like the very person who might change his luck.

"What does *your* family do, Franklin?" Connie asked.

Franklin, unfortunately, had only his lone, infamous parent to offer.

"There's just my mother, I'm afraid," he said. "She's" (he made rabbit ears) "a widow."

* * *

Franklin was surprised when less than an hour after leaving the pub he found himself naked on the beech laminate flooring of Connie's basement flat in Cumberland Street, kissing her grazed knees in an odd combination of first aid and foreplay. Their modest intake of wine, the Beethoven and her generally demure demeanour had led him to think that Connie wasn't the kind of girl who kissed on a first date, let alone shed her clothes before she'd hardly got the key in her front door. He said something to this effect to her afterwards when they were lying in a tangled, sweaty knot on her "Beware of the Cat" doormat and she laughed and said, "Of *course* I'm not that kind of girl, but it's not every day you fall – literally – head over heels in love." Franklin felt both alarmed and flattered in equal measure by this statement.

It turned out that Connie had the easygoing nature of a girl who had never had a worry in her life greater than whether or not flat shoes made her calves look fat. She was "almost a vegetarian", did Pilates twice a week and played for the Edinburgh Netball Club. She was thrillingly well-organized with no self-doubt whatsoever. For Franklin, a person continually in the throes of an apprehensive nihilism, this last was a compelling quality. Furthermore, Connie's hair was straight and brown and never seemed to tangle, her breath was always slightly minty no matter the time of day and she was possessed of the kind of flawless complexion that you only got from a clear conscience.

Conversations with Connie tended to be based on an endless series of ethical dilemmas. Franklin knew it was a test he was bound to fail eventually. "If I was trapped in a burning building with a cat, which of us would you rescue?" Connie asked as they came out of the Cameo cinema.

"You, of course," Franklin said without hesitation.

"What about the cat?"

"What *about* the cat?"

"You would just leave it to burn to death, Franklin?"

They pursued a hectic month of courtship. It was an exhausting and somehow very public chase – theatres, cinemas, museums, cafés, endless meals out in restaurants. On top of that there were race meetings in Musselburgh, walks in the Botanics and Holyrood Park, athletic ascents of Arthur's Seat. Connie seemed particularly fond of the outdoors. Franklin would have preferred to have stayed home and had sex, although, thankfully, Connie's diary managed to make room for a lot of that too.

Franklin found it difficult to keep up with Connie – literally – when they were out together, rather than being intimately coupled up, arm in arm, Connie was always shooting ahead (he'd never met anyone who walked so fast), leaving him trailing behind. He hoped the pace would slow down soon.

Barely a month after meeting Connie, Franklin found himself meeting "Mummy and Daddy" for the first time, invited for the weekend to their house in Cramond.

"Sherry?" Mr Kingshott asked, hefting a heavy crystal decanter. ("Daddy can be a wee bit gruff," Connie had murmured, to Franklin's alarm, as they made their way up the Kingshott's impressive drive.)

"Thank you," Franklin said. He felt acutely conscious of his manners in this delicate environment. It seemed inevitable that something would be broken. Drinking sherry before lunch – lunch itself – was just one of the many attractive things that Connie would bring to his life if he married her. He would swim in the Kingshott gene pool like a happy sun-kissed otter.

Mr Kingshott was smaller than Franklin had expected, a little gamecock of a man, strutting around his lovely Cramond drawing room, pecking at his brood. Franklin felt that if he were going to have his heart operated on he would prefer it to be done by a bigger man, a man whose hand was large enough to hold his heart firmly without any danger of it slipping from his overly petite fingers. He also felt that he would not like his heart to be tended by a man who continually grunted and sighed with irritation and impatience, Mrs Kingshott apparently being the usual beneficiary of this malcontent. ("Daddy's a bit of a tyrant," Connie said cheerfully.) Franklin thought that he would like the man operating on his heart to be singing, light opera, nothing too dramatic, Gilbert and Sullivan perhaps.

"Mummy!" Connie exclaimed as a rather large, soft woman entered the drawing room, holding a wooden spoon in her hand as if it were a wand. She had the distracted air of someone who had wandered into a room without having the slightest idea why she was there.

Mummy smiled sadly at Franklin as if she knew some terrible thing that was to befall him and then wandered out of the room again, spoon aloft.

All of Mummy's brood had pitched up at the Cramond house. ("The nest full again," Connie said.) "So we can meet the beau," Patience said. Patience was both the eldest and the largest of the three sisters. (No Chekhovian gloom in the Kingshott household, no longing for a golden somewhere else, Franklin was relieved to note. Except possibly from Mummy.) Patience, in Birkenstocks and a paisley blouse, had a suggestion of heaviness about her, as if one day she would be in possession of the stout figure and bovine slowness of her mother. Faith, the youngest, on the other hand, had her father's height and his bird-boned frame. Franklin was struck by the sight of the three sisters together, Patience was too big and serious, Faith too small and flighty, but Connie was, in the wise words of Goldilocks, just right. If he could love anyone, surely it would be her.

"Have a seat," Connie said, indicating a sofa that wouldn't have looked out of place in a royal palace. It was more a mansion than a house. There was a library and a tennis court, endless well-kept lawns.

"Mind the cat," Connie said hastily as Franklin narrowly missed sitting on what he had taken to be some kind of strange cushion but which turned out to be a dish-faced, long-haired white cat that glared malevolently at him. "Pedigree," Patience muttered, as if that explained everything.

Patience, who clearly lacked Connie's sunny nature, downed a schooner of sherry in one and said to Franklin, "If you were a musical instrument what musical instrument would you be, Franklin?" She seemed to regard the question as one of real interest. She had a kind of Germanic earnestness about her that made Franklin feel shallow.

All three sisters stared at him, waiting for an answer. "Violin," he hazarded. To say "Cello" would have seemed sycophantic, given that it was Patience's own instrument. A violin seemed a safe bet, like the cello it had strings, and it wasn't quirky like a bassoon or a tuba or grandstanding like a piano, but Patience raised her eyebrows at his answer as if he'd just fulfilled her expectations by saying something banal.

Franklin was relieved when they moved into the dining room and settled at the (enormous) table. Mrs Kingshott carried in a platter and ceremoniously presented a poached salmon (one dull eye glared out at them) to Mr Kingshott. The salmon, apparently, fitted happily into Connie's "almost vegetarian" philosophy. Mr Kingshott dissected the fish as if he were conducting a post-mortem. Franklin found himself wondering what Connie would taste like if he bit through her smooth skin and into the firm yet tender flesh beneath. The breast of an Aylesbury duck or a particularly good pork sausage perhaps. Franklin realized that the very fact that he had thoughts like this made him incredibly unsuitable to be in possession of the Kingshott's middle child. He suspected that in her parent's eyes (and in his own too if he was honest) he must seem feckless and totally unworthy of the gift of their daughter.

"What is it you actually *do*, Franklin?" Mr Kingshott asked suddenly, as if he'd been struggling with this quandary since the sherry. For a moment Franklin thought this might also be some kind of game (*If you were a job what job would you be?*). "For a living," Mr Kingshott clarified when Franklin looked blank.

"Oh," Franklin said. "I work in television."

"Television?" Mr Kingshott repeated, his face contorted as if he was in some kind of exquisite pain. Previously Franklin had always felt a certain amount of pride when announcing this fact, it had taken him a long time to squirm his way up to where he was now. "On *Green Acres*," he added.

"A farming programme?" Mr Kingshott looked incredulous, as well as he might. "You?"

"Oh, Daddy," Mummy laughed. "It's a soap opera, everyone knows that. Daddy likes Wagner," she said to Franklin, as if that explained everything.

"Mummy's an addict, Frankie," Faith said.

"God," Franklin said to Mrs Kingshott, "how awful for you."

"Of *Green Acres*," Connie said.

"Of course," Franklin said.

He suddenly realized that Faith was studying his face across the centrepiece of yellow roses ("St Alban," Mummy said) as if he were a fascinating new life form. He felt something rubbing against his calf and wondered if it was the cat again. He glanced down and was shocked to see a naked foot, the scarlet nails like drops of blood, arching and contracting as it stroked the denim of his jeans. The foot could only belong to Faith unless Patience, sitting at the other end of the table, possessed freakishly long legs. Perhaps he wouldn't be such a happy otter if Connie's sisters were in the pool with him, circling like sharks.

"So, Frankie," Faith purred, "If you were a disease what disease would you be?"

* * *

There was a mutually declared break before the appearance of a raspberry mille-feuille that was waiting rather anxiously in the wings. "I really wasn't in the mood for pastry-making," Mummy said, frowning at the yellow roses as if they were about to do something unpredictable.

"Still on the Prozac, Mummy?" Patience said. ("Daddy fills all Mummy's prescriptions," Connie said.)

Connie leaned closer to Franklin. She smelt fresh and flowery. "Let's go outside," she said.

"Mummy's pride and joy," Connie said, rather brutally snapping off a delicate rose the colour of peaches and cream and holding it beneath Franklin's nose. It was a lovely perfume, the inside of old wardrobes, China tea on a summer lawn, Connie's skin. "Pretty Lady," she said.

"You are," Franklin affirmed.

"No, it's the name of the rose," Connie said. "I think we should get married."

For some reason, Franklin's dumbfounded silence was taken as an affirmative and the next thing he knew he was lost in a shrieking

scrum of Kingshott women, only Mr Kingshott, more interested in
the raspberry mille-feuille, remained aloof from the hysteria.
Franklin wasn't sure why they were shrieking. He wondered if it
was horror. "Just like Jane Austen," Connie said, fanning her
flushed face with her hand.

Seeing that a romantic gesture was expected of him, Franklin drove
back into town, put a thousand pounds on a handy little bay running
in the last race at Beverley that came in at 10/1, strolled down the
street with a winner's easy gait and bought a diamond engagement
ring from Alastair Tait, the jeweller. ("Any vices, Franklin?" Mr
Kingshott had asked with mock amiability after the celebratory
champagne was opened and the raspberry mille-feuille was finally
consumed. "Oh, just the usual," Franklin laughed.)

On his return, Mr Kingshott coerced Franklin into a game of
tennis on the hard court at the back of the house. "Reach for it,
boy!" Mr Kingshott yelled at him, lobbing an impossible ball high
over Franklin's head towards the back of the court. Despite his
size, Mr Kingshott, it turned out later, was the doyen of the local
tennis club, whereas Franklin hadn't played since listlessly
knocking a ball about at university.

Mr Kingshott took great pleasure in reporting back, over an elaborate afternoon tea that Mummy had prepared, that he had "soundly
trounced" Franklin. "Well, Daddy wouldn't play anything he
couldn't win," Connie said later to Franklin as if that was the most
reasonable thing in the world.

By the time they had eaten a supper of chicken sandwiches and
drunk more champagne (they seemed to do nothing but eat and drink)
Franklin couldn't wait to retreat to the attic guest-room. Kingshott
daughters were not allowed to share a bed with their beaux beneath
the family roof. ("Daddy likes to pretend that we're all virgins.")

Franklin opened the door to the little room under the eaves and
nearly had a heart attack. A figure was standing quite still at the
open casement window, gazing out at the darkness. The figure
turned around and to Franklin's relief it was only Mrs Kingshott.

"Mrs Kingshott?" Franklin said softly. For an awful moment he wondered if she was thinking of jumping.

"Oh, Franklin," she said as if she was surprised to see him. "I was just … " she gestured vaguely at the narrow single bed. She was holding a carafe of water and a glass which she placed gently down on the bedside table. She moved carefully like someone made of something breakable. She sat on the bed and stroked the cover as if it were a sick animal. "Sometimes I wish … " she said.

"What do you wish for, Mrs Kingshott?"

"Oh, nothing. Silly me," she said. "It's just … " she sighed, a tremulous, sob-bearing sigh, and absentmindedly plumped up the pillows on the bed. "You know. The death of hope."

Franklin tried to think of something to say that would mollify this rather bleak existential statement but Mummy jumped up and said brightly, "Night, night, Franklin."

Soundly asleep, Franklin incorporated the opening of the squeaking bedroom door into a dream he was in the midst of. The monstrous but indeterminate predator that had been hunting him through an abandoned railway goods yard was closing in on him. He could hear its ragged breath, could feel the heat of it, the strange, soft texture of it. It was smaller than he had imagined but it wrapped itself around him and started to probe and pull at his body with its small hands. Perhaps not a monster but an alien? Without warning, it thrust its tongue into his mouth. He screamed the mute scream of the nightmare victim.

"It's all right, Frankie," a familiar female voice said quietly in his ear. "It's just the doctor here to examine you."

There was a festive air about the house the next morning. "Not every day we manage to get one of them off our hands," Mr Kingshott said, over an extensive cooked breakfast. "Although, of course, no man should marry, Balzac says, until he has studied anatomy and dissected at least one woman."

Franklin tried very hard not to catch faithless Faith's eye over the table. He needn't have worried, she hardly gave him a second glance and if it hadn't been for the scratches and the teeth-marks on his body (more wildcat than woman) he might have dismissed last night as the nightmare that it was.

"Sleep well?" Connie said, kissing him lightly on the cheek before sitting down at the table. Franklin almost choked on his guilt.

Mummy slid a fried egg on to his plate and patted him on the shoulder as if he was a dog.

Franklin felt compelled to accompany Connie and Mrs Kingshott to church.

"Then you can meet the minister who'll be marrying us."

She spent most of the service admiring her ring in the sunlight that cascaded through the church windows while Franklin weighed his soul and found it sadly wanting.

More sherry before lunch. Franklin hadn't realized what a potent drink it was.

"Fetch another bottle from the kitchen, would you?" Mr Kingshott said to Franklin in the same tone of voice he might have used with a waiter.

The big six-door Aga that Mrs Kingshott treated with a mixture of servitude and fear (much the same relationship as she had with Mr Kingshott) was pumping out heat on what was an already stifling day. Mrs Kingshott was putting the finishing touches to a peach pavlova.

"Can I do something to help?" Franklin asked. He felt strangely compelled to treat Mrs Kingshott like an invalid.

She shook her head in a tragic way as if to say no but then said, "That's very kind of you. Perhaps you could slice a lemon for me?"

"Of course," Franklin said. He felt strangely comfortable with Mrs Kingshott (or "Mummy" as he had begun to think of her). How much better off he would have been with a mother like Mrs Kingshott. She would have sent him to scout camps and concert performances of *A Young Person's Guide to the Orchestra* and given him sound advice, unlike his own mother. ("Remember the rule of the three Fs, Franklin – if it flies, floats or fucks, then, for God's sake, *rent it.*")

Mrs Kingshott handed him a knife to cut the lemon with, holding it delicately at the edges of the handle as if she was worried that she might suddenly turn it on herself.

They lunched al fresco on a roast chicken, a bird which was also nearly vegetarian, apparently. Mr Kingshott wielded the carving knife as if it were a particularly large scalpel.

"Breast or leg?" he asked Franklin. "Which do you prefer?" For a confusing moment Franklin thought that he was somehow referring to his daughters.

"Leg," Franklin said, incapable of saying the word "breast" to Mr Kingshott when surrounded by his flock of women. Mr Kingshott passed Franklin the delicately carved slices of dark meat and said, "No breast? Sure?"

"Sure," Franklin said.

The peach pavlova made its entrance before the chicken had exited. Faith ripped the wishbone from the remains of the bird (it was hard to believe that someone so savage had received the same upbringings as Connie) and held out the little bony arch and said, "Make a wish, Frankie," but before he could even begin to think of anything he wanted to wish for (where to start?) Faith had yanked aggressively on the fragile bone and claimed the greater part. Franklin could see a little shred of chicken flesh lodged between her front teeth. He hoped she was never in a position to perform a medical procedure on him.

"Then Aunt Jefferson and Mr Bray," Mummy said. "And all of the string section," Patience said. It took Franklin a while to realize it was his own wedding that was being discussed.

"Who's on your guest list, Franklin?" Connie asked. "There's your mother, of course," she reminded him before he could answer. The thought of his mother at the wedding filled Franklin with feverish horror. The only thing that was certain was that it all would go badly. If only Franklin had told Connie that he was an orphan. Perhaps he could put his mother in a coma, it was always a handy device in

Green Acres, when you wanted to shelve a cast member for a while.
And his mother was pretty much a soap opera character anyway.

"Patience and Faith will be the bridesmaids, of course," Connie was
saying to her mother. "It's just a shame they're different heights."

"You could cut Patience's feet off," Faith suggested.

"Or stretch Faith," Patience said.

Mrs Kingshott stood up from the table suddenly and said, "There
should be three bridesmaids." Connie reached out for her hand and
tried to get her to sit down again.

"Come on, Mummy," Faith said, surprisingly gentle. "Don't get
upset."

"Sit down," Mr Kingshott barked at his wife. "And don't start all
that nonsense again."

Mrs Kingshott stood rigid and wild-eyed, like some terrible figure
in a Greek tragedy. A dramatic clap of thunder exploded overhead
and the heavens opened. From the look of her, Mrs Kingshott
would still have been out there at bedtime and it took the persuasive
powers of all three girls to coax her indoors. The pavlova was left to
melt in the rain, the peach slices like beached fish in the surf.

"What was all that about?" Franklin asked later.

"Hope," Connie said.

"Hope?"

"Our sister, the youngest. She died of meningitis when she was
five. Mummy wanted to take her to the hospital but Daddy said she
was making a fuss about nothing and it was just a fever. Hope died
in Mummy's arms."

"That's *terrible*," Franklin said, fresh to the tragedy.

"Yes," Connie said. "It is, isn't it? Daddy's such a brute. You
have no idea," she added, staring at something out of sight.

"So let me get this right, the building's on fire and I have to choose
between rescuing a cat and rescuing the cure for cancer?"

"Yes," Connie said.

"And I definitely can't save both?"

"No."

"Is it the cure for all cancers? Or just some?"

"All."

"Is the cat old?"

"What difference does that make? Is its life worth less because it's old? Will it suffer less when it's burnt alive?"

Franklin wondered if Connie's hypothetical cat was a distant relative of Schrödinger's Cat. "And you're definitely not in the building? It's just a straight choice – cat or cancer? Cancer or cat?"

"Yes."

"Where are *you*? Just out of interest?"

"I'm standing on the pavement watching, Franklin."

Mr Kingshott retired to the gloom of the library while the women of the household embarked on a furiously paced game of Monopoly in the course of which even Mrs Kingshott became a cut-throat (*Park Lane! Mine!*).

Franklin excused himself and dozed on the sofa. He did feel extraordinarily tired and woozy and the Kingshott's sofa was as comfy as a fairy-tale feather bed.

When he woke, the drawing room was empty, no sign of any Kingshotts and the Monopoly board had been tidied away. It felt late and Franklin wondered how long he had slept. The clock on the mantelpiece said eight o'clock but surely someone would have woken him to partake in the endless round of eating and drinking that seemed to go on in the house.

There was no sign of life anywhere and Franklin wandered from room to room, occasionally shouting "Hello?" to the air until only the library remained unexplored. Franklin paused before the closed door. The idea of disturbing the bear in his lair was unnerving. He put his ear to the door. There was no sound from within. Perhaps Mr Kingshott had jumped ship with his women. Franklin knocked sharply twice and when there was no answer he turned the handle and opened the door cautiously, half expecting to find Bluebeard's wives hanging from butchers' hooks.

There was nothing, a faint tang in the air, iron and salt and something faintly raw.

And a foot. A smallish foot, poking out from behind the desk. A foot encased in a beige wool sock and a tan handmade brogue that looked very like one that Mr Kingshott was wearing the last time Franklin saw him.

Franklin approached the desk and discovered that the foot was (thankfully) still attached to the rest of Mr Kingshott. Unfortunately, there was a knife sticking out of his chest, exactly where his heart was. It seemed an ironic death for a man who spent his life sticking knives into other people's hearts.

Mr Kingshott's eyes were open, as fixed and dull as a dead salmon. It was just like Cluedo, Franklin thought – Mr Kingshott in the library with a dagger. Not a dagger exactly but a small sharp knife, very like the one Franklin had used earlier to slice a lemon for Mrs Kingshott, although, when he thought about it now, the lemon had never made an appearance at lunch.

Franklin's feet were sticking to the carpet and he realized he had walked in Mr Kingshott's blood. He felt sick. He knew he should phone the police but his brain was still fogged up. Had he been drugged? Faith must be pretty handy with narcotics.

He retreated to the hallway and was fumbling in his pocket for his mobile when the front door burst open and several policemen rushed in, followed by all the Kingshott women.

"That's him," Patience said, pointing dramatically at Franklin.

"Yes," Connie said, "that's definitely him. He's been stalking me for weeks, everywhere I go he follows." She was a stagy actress, Franklin noted.

"We have photographs," Patience said in her own histrionic style. It was like being in the middle of a poor amateur dramatic production. *An Inspector Calls*. From nowhere Patience produced a folder of black-and-white photographs. Franklin managed to catch a glimpse of them over the shoulder of one of the policemen. They all seemed to show Franklin loitering in Connie's wake in a variety of venues he recognized – Hollywood Park, George Street, coming out of the Lyceum. "I was trying to catch up with her, not follow her," he protested.

"Daddy tried to warn him off," Connie said.

"And so he killed him," Faith said. "Obviously."

The cat appeared suddenly, arching its back and spitting at Franklin.

"He's an awfully good judge of character," Connie said.

"Mrs Kingshott?" one of the policemen said, turning to her, as if she had some kind of casting vote on Franklin's fate.

Mrs Kingshott gazed into Franklin's face and gave a tremendous sigh. "I'm afraid so," she said. "He's been giving us all so much bother."

Franklin had an unnerving flashback to last night and the condom that Faith had produced and magicked away when she had finished ravishing him. He remembered the rabid biting and scratching – how many samples of DNA had she managed to steal off him? He had stood in Mr Kingshott's blood, his own bloody footprints tracking his journey all the way from the body. And what about the knife? He remembered the delicate way Mrs Kingshott had handed it to him, so that no prints were on that knife except his.

"I thought you loved me," Franklin said to Connie. Even to his own ears he sounded pathetic.

"He's so deluded," Patience said to the policemen.

"I believe the medical term is erotomania," Faith said. "It often leads to violence, I'm afraid."

"Don't listen to them!" Franklin said.

All four women stood on the doorstep and watched as Franklin was bundled into a police car. By now the place was swarming with more police, with forensics, with photographers, although it was a relatively subdued crime scene compared with anything in *Green Acres*. Franklin made a mental note for future use. If he had a future.

As the car drove away, Franklin caught sight of Mrs Kingshott. She gave him a regretful smile and waved goodbye to him.

Franklin waved back. Even now, he found himself not wanting to hurt Mummy's feelings.

THE BALLAD OF MANKY MILNE

Stuart MacBride

A ND THAT WAS why, on a cold night in February, Duncan Milne was up to his neck in shite. Literally. There was a small stunned pause, and then the swearing started. "FUCK, Jesus, fuck! Aaaaaaargh!" then some spitting, then more swearing.

A silhouette blocked out the handful of stars visible through the septic tank's inspection hatch. "You OK?"

"No I'm not fucking OK!" More spitting. "Argh! Jesus – that tastes horrible!"

"Aye, well … it is shite."

Duncan "Manky" Milne wiped his eyes and flicked the scummy liquid away. The smell was appalling. "Don't tell me it's shite, OK? I know it's fucking shite! I'm bloody swimming in it!" He screwed his face up and spat some more. Breaking into Neil McRitchie's septic tank had seemed like such a good idea at the time – smacked out of their tits and jacked up on shoplifted vodka – but treading "water" in a subterranean vat of raw sewage, Milne had to admit it was losing its appeal.

"Can you see it?"

He scowled up at the dark shape. "Help me out!"

A pause, then, "But—"

"Josie, I swear: if you don't help me out of here I'm gonnae stab you in the fucking eye!"

"But you're down there anyway …" Wheedling, putting on her "little girl" voice, because she thinks it makes men squirm.

"It's pitch black down here. I can't—"

"So feel about for it! It'll be easy enough to find. I'll bet it floats."

Milne spat again, trying to get rid of the aftertaste. "Why the hell would it float?"

Pause. "Well, it's powder, it should—"

"Oh for God's sake. If it was bloody powder it'd be dissolved in all this crap! It'll be wrapped in polythene. And parcel tape. Like in the movies." A kilo of heroin for their very own.

"OK, so it'll sink. You just have to feel about for it."

"You fucking 'feel about for it'! Jump down here and see how you like it!"

"Come on, Duncan, pwease?" She was bringing out the big guns now – the fake lisp. Silly cow. It hurt to admit it, but she was probably right – he might as well look while he was down here. Wasn't as if he was going to get any mankier than he already was.

Grumbling and swearing, he groped about in the lukewarm liquid. Trying not to think about what was bobbing about his throat. Thank God he was six foot tall – four inches shorter and his mouth and nose would be submerged. The scum layer was warm, steaming gently all around him, further down it got colder – between the putrid froth and the knee-deep sludge at the bottom of the tank. That was slightly warm too, saturating his nylon tracksuit and socks, filling his trainers.

Milne cursed again. A kilo of heroin would sink. And that meant he'd have to duck under the surface to get it. Not that he hadn't already been there, having fallen head-first through the inspection hatch. But still: fuck this shite.

Gritting his teeth he waded forward, feeling for the parcel in the sludge with his feet. Nothing. "It's not—" was as far as he got before Josie hissed, "Shut up! Someone's coming!"

He froze.

Thin light swept past the access hatch, caught in the steam rising from the rotting sewage, and then voices: "What the hell do you think you're doing?" A man. Angry. Very, very angry.

"I...I was looking for someone." Josie trying her "little girl" voice again. Only this time there were no takers.

"You think I don't know what you are? Eh? Think I'm stupid?"

"I don't think you're—"

"We've had ENOUGH! Whores and drug addicts coming round here all hours!"

"But—"

"ENOUGH!"

"You know what: *fuck you* granddad—" A muffled "thunk" and the sound of something hitting the ground: something undernourished and three months shy of her nineteenth birthday. "Thunk." "Thunk." "Thunk."

"Enough..." And then it went quiet for a bit. And then there was some crying. And then some grunting. And then scraping, like someone was being dragged – the stars were blotted out again. Milne backed away quietly until he was against the far wall of the septic tank.

"Click" and a beam of cold white light leapt through the access hatch, making the milky-brown liquid glow. More grunting and then an almighty splash as the something was unceremoniously dumped in, making a tidal wave of human waste. Milne closed his mouth and his eyes and prayed for the best.

When it was over he wiped his face, and stared at the thing floating face-up in front of him.

Some fumbling and a curse and then the torch was hurled in after her, bouncing off Josie's cheek and spinning away into the scum. It stayed lit, sinking through the layers of liquid, glowing like a firefly. Flickering. Then dying. Leaving the tank in darkness once more.

The sound of heavy lifting came from above and slowly the patch of stars disappeared. "Clunk!" And they were gone. Milne and Josie were entombed.

Two days was a long time to spend trapped in a septic tank. Especially when the shakes started to set in. Coming down from a heroin buzz to the depths of cold turkey – making him sweat and shiver, even though the liquid waste was just warm enough to steam. To start with he'd held Josie close, like a child would its teddy bear, but then she started to smell worse than the sewage and he'd been forced to push her to the far side of the tank. Wedging her under the inlet valve so she stayed beneath the surface.

Now it was just smells and darkness. He knew it was two days because the watch he'd taken from Josie's dead wrist glowed in the dark. Two days shivering and sweating. Feeling terrible. Scratching at the holes in his arms, unable to stop, even though he knew they'd get infected. Didn't matter now anyway. He was dead.

He'd spent hours trying to get the tank's thick concrete lid to move, but it was too heavy and too high above his head. He was well and truly trapped.

Two days without a hit and the hallucinations were in full swing, following him in and out of consciousness as he floated on the surface with the frothy scum. Where it was warmest. Trying to stay beneath the ventilation pipe, hoping enough air would be drawn down by the internal/external temperature difference to keep him from suffocation as he slowly died of dehydration.

Drifting on a sea of warm shite and cold turkey...

Within eighteen months of meeting Duncan "Manky" Milne, Josie has gone from a plump happy teenager to a straggly scarecrow with sunken eyes and track marks down both arms. Red and angry like hornet stings around the crook of her elbow.

And Duncan hasn't fared much better – his boyish good looks are gone, now he's just skin and bone with a drug habit. And it's *all* about where the next fix is coming from. Which is why they're standing at the bar of the Dunstane Arms on George Street, trying to scrape together enough change for two pints of cider. An apéritif before they head down the docks to see if anyone wants to rent Josie for a quick blowjob.

Of course, in the old days they both tried it, but no one wants to screw Manky Milne for cash any more. So these days he's her Pimp Daddy. Even if he can only come up with enough cash for a pint and a half. Being a gentleman, Milne lets her take the pint – after all, she'll be the one doing all the work tonight – and they settle back into a booth, out of sight of the barman who's been giving them the evil eye since they slouched in five minutes ago, looking like shite.

And that's when they hear about Neil McRitchie.

Two blokes standing by the bandit – poking the buttons, making the wheels spin, the light flash, and the music ding – laughing about how Neil McRitchie just got this big consignment in from Amsterdam: a kilo of uncut heroin. How Grampian Police decide to raid his house, but McRitchie flushes the whole parcel down the toilet before they break down the door. A kilo of smack, right down the drain. And then they drag him off to the station.

Milne sits back in his seat, face creased in thought, trying to get his drug-addled mind to work. Neil McRitchie ... A small-time dealer on the south side of the city – Kincorth, Nigg and Altens. Milne's bought from him before: blow, smack, and a bit of speed. Always from the guy's house.

A smile creeps on to Milne's dirty face. McRitchie's house is on the back road between Nigg and Charlestown, the end cottage in a row of four. Not so far off the beaten track that you can't walk there, but far enough to need private drainage. And private drainage means a septic tank.

The police won't have a bloody clue. They'll think it's gone for good, but McRitchie's kilo of heroin isn't wheeching its way out to the North Sea – it's bobbing about in a vat of shite, buried at the bottom of the garden. That's one good thing about being the son of a plumber: Milne knows his drainage. And that's when the plan—

He's hiding behind the Christmas tree, cowering down behind the sharp, dry needles, trying not to breathe, because he knows they'll fall and spatter against the bare floorboards. And then his father will find him. A scream from the corridor and a thump – his mother hitting the floor, then a thud – his father hitting her. Other kids want Giga Pets and Furbies for Christmas. He wants his father to die. Six years old and all he wants—

Milne spluttered, dragging his head back above the surface. Coughing. Shivering. He was burning up – cold, aching, feverish. It wasn't just the DTs: it was the sewage. Oozing in through the open sores on his arms and legs. Spreading tendrils of septicaemia through his already battered system.

And it was all for nothing. He'd searched the tank from top to bottom and there was no heroin. No kilo of smack wrapped up in a nice plastic package, sealed off with parcel tape. They'd been stupid to ever think there was: how was it going to get through the pipes? The package wouldn't have got round the toilet U-bend. They'd been stupid and now—

Half ten and Josie's on her knees, earning them enough cash for three wrappers of heroin and a Big Mac with fries. The guy's something in accounting from the look of him, dressed in a Barbour jacket and checked shirt with his chinos round his ankles. Leaning against the wall, grunting as Josie's mouth works its magic.

Hiding in the shadows, Milne gives the guy's car a once over. It's an anonymous Renault with all the panache of a bottle of brown sauce. Perfect. Milne fingers the half brick in his pocket and crosses the road. He doesn't even let the guy finish before smashing him over the back of the head.

Josie sits back on the doorstep, giggling as Milne pops the Renault's boot and tries to manhandle the guy inside. He's still breathing, but the bastard weighs a ton! A quick search of his pockets turns up car keys, house keys, credit cards, a wallet with a hundred quid in it – result – and half a packet of cigarettes. Milne strips him naked and ties him up with his own clothes. The man just lies there, pale, curled up like a foetus, bleeding into the dark blue carpet. Not moving. Milne slams the boot shut, then he and Josie smoke the guy's cigarettes. Telling jokes about—

It's cold, barely past dawn, but he's running for all he's worth, chasing down the blond kid from Robert Gordon's private school, diving at him, dragging him to the ground. The rugby ball flies off to one of the other wee boys on the opposite team, but Milne doesn't care, just starts punching and kicking the blond kid. Hammering away until the teacher acting as a referee drags him off. Shouting and swearing.

The wee blond kid lies on the frosty grass, curled up in a ball, bleeding and crying. And Milne has no idea why he did it. But he's crying too. And the teacher hauls him round and screams in his face—

* * *

It's after midnight, but they're nowhere near sleepy. A hundred quid goes a long way if you know what you're doing. A woman Josie knows sells them a couple of wrappers of heroin each and a litre bottle of Asda's own-label vodka – shoplifted fresh that afternoon by a gang of eight-year-old girls. And then Josie and Milne are driving off to McRitchie's house in the guy's stolen car, pausing to shoot-up in a lay-by off the A90. Taking the long way round.

Milne parks down the road a bit, where they've got a good view of the cottages, but far enough away not to draw any attention. This is the difficult bit, figuring out where the septic tank is. Sometimes it's right up close to the house, sometimes it's more than a field away. But it always—

He couldn't tell if the noise was coming from inside his head or not. A dull rasping, grinding sound, like two stones being dragged apart. And then the air burst into fiery light. He opened his mouth to cry for help, but nothing came out. Not even a dry croak.

"Bloody hell…" A man's voice. It took a minute for Milne's brain to catch up, but he knew it was the same one who'd shouted at Josie. Who'd battered her head in with the heavy, metal torch. Milne had found it when he was searching the tank – lying buried in the bottom layer of sludge – the casing all battered and dented round the bulb end. Like someone had used it as a club.

The sound of gagging from above and the light drifted away, then swung back in through the inspection hatch. Milne pulled back against the wall, screwing his eyes shut, unaccustomed to the change from perpetual darkness—

Standing at the side of the grave, looking down at the shiny brown coffin. Holding his mother's hand. Pretending not to see the woman in the dark blue uniform cuffed to her other wrist—

A long pole reached in through the hatch, bringing the sound of muttered swearing with it. Something about backed-up plumbing and blocked pipes and people starting to notice … The pole slipped into the layer of frothy scum, leaving a trail behind it as the man above swept it through the sewage. Looking for something.

Prod, prod, prod. And then Josie's bloated corpse floated to the surface, bringing with it a smell even worse than before. Her face appeared above the froth for a moment, then slipped sideways. Eyes open, looking at Milne one last time, before sliding over on to her front.

The pole clattered down into the tank as the sound of retching erupted from above. The light disappeared again. Then more retching. Spattering. Swearing. Coughing. And finally the light returned.

The Angry Man's voice: "Come on, you can do this … " The pole, poking away at Josie's shoulder, trying to hook on to the tatty lumberjack shirt. Failing. More swearing.

Milne shook his head, trying to make things settle down. Trying to think clearly for the first time in a year and a half.

A bright-yellow Marigold rubber glove appeared in the opening, and then another one, attached to a disgusted-looking man in his late forties with a plastic torch clenched between his teeth. His greying hair just visible in the torchlight as it bounced back from the layer of sewage-froth. He stretched out, reaching for Josie's body … And that was when Milne grabbed him—

Sitting cross-legged in Colin's bedroom, ignoring the blaring of the television next door, sinking the needle into his virgin arm. Biting his lip at the bee-sting pain. Pressing the plunger—

There was a high-pitched scream and the man toppled forward, dropping the torch as he pitched head-first into the tank. Arms flailing—

Standing down the docks, selling himself for the price of a hamburger. Enough to pay for a single wrapper. Feeling disgusted as he goes down on a man old enough to be his dead dad—

Milne curled a bony hand into a fist and slammed it into the
screaming man. Over and over again, splashing and hitting and
punching and biting in the dark. And all the time Josie's body bumps
against them. Like she's trying to intervene. Trying to break it up.
Make them—

Breaking into an old lady's house in the dead of night. Rifling
through her things as she sleeps in the next room. Stealing anything
he can sell down the pub for a couple of quid. Passing them out
through the window to Josie, who's standing watch. Punching the
old lady in the face when she wakes up to see what all the noise is
about. Watching as she lies there on the floor, not moving, too
scared to check if she's still alive—

The man gurgled, struggling as Milne grabbed him by the lapels and
forced his head under the surface. Holding him there. An arm swept
up from the stinking water, catching Milne on the side of the head,
but he didn't let go. Grunting, teeth gritted, feeling the man start to
go limp. Keeping him submerged. Drowning him in piss and shite—

There's no one in the cemetery at this time of night. No one to
watch him drop his trousers and squat over his father's grave—

The struggling stopped after a couple of minutes, but Milne didn't
let go. Just in case. A long, slow count to 500: that should be
enough. The bastard deserved what he got. Milne released his grip
and the body bobbed to the surface.

He rummaged through the guy's pockets, taking everything he
could find – keys, wallet, spare change, handkerchief – before
releasing the body to sink into the sludge. And then he reached up
and clambered out of the tank, back into the real world.

He lay on his back, staring up at the night sky. Shivering. Steaming
gently. According to Josie's glow-in-the-dark watch it was half past
eleven. Wednesday. Two days without food or water. He was lucky
to be alive at all. And that thought set off a fit of the giggles. And
then some coughing. And finally some sort of seizure. He was

pouring with sweat, juddering away, teeth clamped shut so he wouldn't bite his tongue in half. Not healthy. Not healthy at all.

Milne rolled over on to his front and levered himself up on to his knees. Trembling all the time. Knowing that without something to drink soon, he was going to die. The world tangoed round his head as he stood upright, the night sky swirling and pulsing. He took a deep breath and lurched towards the darkened row of cottages.

A security light blared into life, catching him halfway down the path, but he staggered on to the front door. Locked. Milne dragged out the keys he'd taken from the bastard who'd killed Josie and tried them in the lock, one by one. None of them worked.

He lurched across the garden and nearly fell over the waist-high fence, clambering into next door. The keys still didn't fit. But another dose of the tremors grabbed him, shaking him to his knees. Leaving him gasping and wracked with cramp on the top step. The third house was the same, only this time he had to crawl through the garden to get to the front door. The keys were useless.

Give up. Just curl up on the path and die: get it over with.

But there was one more house left – the one on the end. Where McRitchie lived. McRitchie would still be banged up in Craiginches, Milne could break in without having to worry about an irate house-holder coming after him with a shotgun.

It was pitch-dark round the back of the cottages. Milne felt his way along the wall, stumbling over a pile of something that rattled and clattered, before finding McRitchie's back door. It was one of the part-glazed kind beloved of housebreakers everywhere. Smiling, Milne tried to smash one of the panes with his elbow. It bounced, sending shooting pains racing round his body, making his whole arm feel like it was on fire. Biting his tongue he sank to his knees and nearly passed out.

Deep breaths. Deeeeeeep breaths… Oh God, he was going to be sick. But there was nothing to be sick with, just a thin string of bile, spiralling bitterly down the front of his soaking, stained clothes. He grabbed a rock from the garden and did the window properly, sending shards of glass shattering into the kitchen. Fumble with the lock and doorknob. And he was in. Oh thank God.

He slumped against the worktop and tried not to pass out. And tried—

It's his birthday and he'll cry if he wants to. Nineteen years old and his present is getting the crap beaten out of him by Colin McLeod over a small matter of an unpaid debt. Fifteen pounds. That's all it takes for Colin McLeod to give him two weeks in hospital. Happy birthday.

The doctors come past and the councillors and the police too, but he doesn't say anything. Just lies there and tries to move his toes again. They give him methadone and group therapy, but as soon as he gets out he's back on heroin again. Borrowing money and—

BANG! And his head hit the linoleum floor. Milne lay flat on his back, staring up at McRitchie's kitchen ceiling, wondering how he got there. He was in hospital and the next thing…He closed his eyes and shivered. He needed a drink.

There was a bottle of whisky on the kitchen table – illuminated by the faint green light from the clock on the microwave. He picked it up with trembling hands and fumbled the lid off, swallowing mouthful after mouthful, not caring that it burnt all the way down. Until it hit his stomach and bounced, spewing out through his mouth and nose, making a slick of alcohol on the kitchen floor.

Water, he needed *water*, not whisky. Lurch to the sink, turn on the tap and stick his mouth against it. Sucking it down. This time he was bright enough to stop after a couple of mouthfuls, feeling his stomach rebel after two days on "nil by mouth". Two gulps, then a break, then another couple. Slowly building up until he wasn't thirsty any more. He was ravenous.

McRitchie's fridge wasn't exactly packed with tasty goodies, but Milne didn't care. He grabbed things at random, stuffing them in his mouth, barely chewing. Eating by the cold-white glow of the fridge light. Cheese, cold mince, raw bacon. For a moment he thought he was going to bring it all up again, but it stayed down. Now all he had to worry about was the—

"Click." Light blossomed in the kitchen and someone said, "What the FUCK?"

Milne span round, eyes wide, cold beans falling from his open mouth. It was McRitchie, looking very pissed off. The man was easily as tall as Milne, but a hell of a lot broader. Muscled, not junky stick-thin. Someone who didn't sample his own product.

Milne raised his hands, dropping the tin of beans. It bounced off the linoleum, exploding red sauce and pale beans everywhere, joining the whisky vomit. He tried to explain what he was doing there, but his throat wouldn't work.

McRitchie yanked a drawer open and dragged out a long-bladed kitchen knife. "Break into *my* house? You stupid smack-head bastard!" He charged forward. "I'll fucking—" and stepped right in the slick of spilled beans and whisky. His left leg shot out from underneath him and for a brief second everything went into slow motion: the knife sailing through the air, his head sweeping downward and catching the edge of the kitchen table. The loud "thunk!" as it hit. The knife skittering away across the working surface, clattering into the sink. Another thump as McRitchie hit the floor hard. Eyes shut, mouth open wide. Not moving.

Milne grabbed the knife from the sink and crept forward. Trembling. McRitchie was still breathing. But it didn't take long to fix that.

The guy's car was in exactly the same place he and Josie had left it two days ago. It even started first time. Milne sat behind the wheel, shivering and shaking, coughing until the world slipped into shades of black and yellow then disappeared.

He came to with his head resting against the wheel and the car's horn braying in his ear. Snatched himself back upright, felt everything whooooosh around him. And closed his eyes. Forcing it all back down. Turning the key in the ignition.

It had taken every last ounce of strength to drag McRitchie's heavy arse round to the septic tank, tumbling him in with Josie and her killer. Then a considerable breather before levering the inspection hatch cover back into place. Good job McRitchie had a HUGE stash of speed hidden in his bedroom or there was no way Milne would have managed it. In fact all of McRitchie's stash was now stuffed into the glove compartment, Milne's pockets, and under the driver's seat. He had enough to last a couple of months, if he was careful and didn't go mad in the first week.

All he had to do now was get back to the squat and he'd be fine. Sell the car, get some spare cash and live on drugs and delivery pizza until April. Every junkie's dream.

The A90 was quiet as he pulled on to it, face screwed up in concentration, keeping the car at a steady thirty, trying to stay between the white lines. And doing a pretty good job of it too. Three tablets of speed and he was back on form. No more shakes and shivers. No, he was feeling— Oh shite.

A flash of blue light in the rear-view mirror. SHITE!

Eyes front. Maybe it wasn't for him? Maybe the police wanted to pull someone else over and they were just ... No. It was him. And he was too wasted to make a run for it. He pulled over.

The traffic policeman was a woman. She rapped on the driver's window and Milne fumbled with the electric button thing until it slid down. She recoiled back, one hand covering her mouth, gagging. "Holy shit!" she said at last, spluttering. "What the hell is that *stink*?"

Milne shrugged. After two days in the tank he couldn't smell himself any more. "I fell in some shite," he said, trying not to twitch, or shiver, or sound like he was out of his face on stolen drugs.

"You OK, sir?" she asked, shining a torch into the car, spot-lighting him in all his manky glory. "You look ill."

Milne nodded, she had him there, he could see himself in the rear-view mirror: pale-grey, sweaty, dark purple bags under his eyes, threads of fiery red spreading through his skin. "I fell in some shite."

She turned and shouted back at the traffic car, "Norm, get an ambulance up here sharpish!" then knelt down, breathing through her mouth, like she didn't want to smell him any more. "You're going to be OK, we're going to get you to the hospital."

He opened his mouth to tell her he just wanted to go home, but couldn't. All that came out was, "I fell in some shite ... "

Sitting there, watching the policewoman fading away until there was nothing left but darkness and—

* * *

Headache. Killer, bastard headache. Like a chisel driven between the ears. Milne cracked open an eye to see a pretty nurse hovering over him with a syringe.

"Where am I?" was what he tried to say, but all that came out was a dry croaking sound. The nurse didn't smile at him, just held a squeezy bottle to his lips and let him take a small sip. "Thank you..." – weak, but almost sounding human again.

The nurse nodded, then said, "There's someone here to see you." Brisk, matter of fact, beckoning over a uniformed constable and a big, fat bald bloke with a tight suit and a constipated expression.

"Mr Milne," said the fat one, looming over the bed, "we'd like to talk to you about the car you were driving when you were brought here."

Milne frowned. "I..." Shite – they'd found the drugs. All of McRitchie's lovely drugs and he'd barely had a chance to sample any of them.

"Specifically, we'd like to talk to you about the car's original owner. And how his dead body wound up in the boot covered in your fingerprints."

And that was it: Duncan "Manky" Milne was up to his neck in shite again.

THE CIRCLE

David Hewson

THE TUBE LINE ran unseen beneath the bleak unfeeling city, round and round, day and night, year after year. Under the wealthy mansions of Kensington the snaking track rattled, through cuttings and tunnels, to the bustling mainline stations of Paddington, Euston and King's Cross where millions came and left London daily, invisible to those below the earth. Then the trains travelled on to the poorer parts in the east, Aldgate, with its tenements and teeming immigrant populations, until the rails turned abruptly, as if they could take the poverty no more, and longed to return to the prosperous west, to civilization and safety, before the perpetual loop began again. *The Circle*. Melanie Darma had travelled this way so often she sometimes imagined she was a part of it herself.

Today she felt tired. Her head hurt as she slumped on the worn, grubby seat in the noisy, rattling carriage, watching the station lights flash by, the faces of the travellers come and go. Tower Hill, Monument, Cannon Street, Mansion House... Somewhere to the south ran the thick, murky waters of the Thames. She remembered sitting next to her father as a child, bewildered in a shaking train from Charing Cross to Waterloo, a stretch that ran deep beneath the old, grey river. Joking, he'd persuaded her to press her nose to the grimy windows to look for passing fish, swimming in the blackness flashing by. On another occasion, when he was still as new to the city as she was, in thrall to its excitement and possibilities, they'd both got out at the station called Temple, hoping to see something magical and holy, finding nothing but surly commuters and tangles of angry traffic belching smoke.

This was the city, a thronging, anonymous world of broken promises. People, millions of them, whatever the time of day. Lately, with her new condition, they would watch on the train as she moved heavily, clutching the swelling bundle in her belly. Most would stand aside and give her a seat. A few would smile, mothers mostly, she thought. Some, men in business suits, people from the City, stared away as if the obvious extent of her state, and the apparent nearness of her release from it, amounted to some kind of embarrassment to be avoided. She could almost hear them praying... *if it's to happen please God let it not be this instant, when I've a meeting scheduled, a drink planned, an assignation with a lover. Any time but now.*

She sat the way she had learned over the previous months: both hands curved protectively around the bump in her fawn summer coat, which was a little heavy for the weather, bought cheaply at a street market to encompass her temporary bulk. Her fingers felt comfortable there nevertheless. It was as if this was what they were made for.

So much of her life seemed to have been passed in these tunnels, going to and fro. She felt she could fix her position on the Circle's endless loop by the smell of the passengers as they entered the carriage: sweet, cloying perfume in the affluent west, the sweat of workmen around King's Cross, the fragrant, sometimes acrid odour of the Indians and Pakistanis from the sprawling, struggling ethnic communities of the east. Once she'd visited the museum in Covent Garden to try to understand this hidden jugular which kept the city alive, uncertainly at times, as its age and frailty began to show. Melanie Darma had gazed at the pictures of imperious Victorian men in top hats and women in crinoline dresses, all waiting patiently in neat lines for miniature trains with squat smoke stacks and smiling crew. It was the first underground railway ever built, part of a lost and entirely dissimilar age.

When the London bombers struck in 2005 they chose the Circle Line as one of their principal targets, through accident, she thought, not from any conscious attempt to strike at history. The first bomb exploded on an eastbound train between Liverpool Street and Aldgate. The second in a westbound train that had just left Edgeware Road. Fifty-two unsuspecting men and women died in all that day, thirteen of them on the Circle. The entire system was closed for almost a month, forcing her to take buses, watching those around her nervously, glancing at anyone with a dark skin and a backpack, wondering.

She might have been on one of those two carriages had it not been for her father's terminal sickness, a cruel cancerous death eked out on a hard, cheap bed in some cold public ward, one more body to be rudely nursed towards its end by a society that no longer seemed to care. Birth, death, illness, accident ... Sudden, fleeting joy, insidious, lasting tragedy ... All these things lay in wait on the journey that was life, ambushes, large and small, hidden in the wings.

Sometimes, as she sat on the train rattling through the black snaking hole in the dank London earth, she imagined herself falling forwards in some precipitous, headlong descent towards an unknown, endless abyss. Did the women in billowing crinoline dresses ever imagine themselves the same way? She doubted it. This was a modern affliction. It had a modern cure too. Work, necessity, the daily need to earn sufficient money to pay the rent for another month, praying the agency would find her some other temporary berth once the present ran out.

There were two more stops before Westminster, the station she had come to know so well, set in the shadow of Big Ben and the grandiose, imposing silhouette of the Houses of Parliament. The train crashed into the darkness of the tunnel ahead. The carriage shook so wildly the lights flickered and then disappeared altogether. The movement and the sudden black gloom conspired to make the weight of her stomach seem so noticeable, such a part of her, she believed she felt a slow, sluggish movement inside, as if something were waking. The fear that idea prompted despatched a swift, guilty shock of apprehension through her mind. The thought: *this is real and will happen, however much you may wish to avoid it.*

Finally the rolling, careering carriage reconnected with whatever source of energy gave it light. The carriage stabilized, the bulbs flickered back to life.

On the opposite seat sat a young foreign-looking man who wore a dark polyester jacket and cheap jeans, the kind of clothes the people from Aldgate and beyond seemed to like. He had a grubby, red, webbed rucksack next to him, his hand on the top, a possessive gesture, though there was no one there who could possibly covet the thing.

He stared at her, openly, frankly, with a familiarity she didn't appreciate. His eyes were dark and deep, his face clean shaven, smiling, attractive.

The train lurched again, the lights flashed off and on as they dashed downwards once more.

The young man spoke softly as he gazed at her, and it was difficult to hear over the crash of iron against iron.

Still, she thought she knew what he said, and that was, "They will remember my name."

* * *

She tried to focus on the book in her hands. It came from the staff library. The Palace of Westminster didn't pay its workers well, but at least they had access to decent reading.

"Are you scared?" the young traveller opposite asked pleasantly, nodding at the bump beneath her hands.

It was a book on philosophy. She chose it for the image on the cover: *Ouroboros*, the serpent that devoured itself. If she squinted hard she could imagine the familiar London Transport poster, with its yellow rounded rectangle for the Circle Line, transposed in its place.

"Not at all," she answered immediately without taking her attention off the page.

There was a paragraph from Plato, a description of Ouroboros as the very first creature in the universe, the beast from which everything sprang, and to which everything returned.

She felt a little giddy when she realized the words of some ancient Greek, who had been dust when Christ was born, made some sense to her. It was almost as if she could hear his ancient, cracked voice.

The living being had no need of eyes when there was nothing remaining outside him to be seen; nor of ears when there was nothing to be heard; and there was no surrounding atmosphere to be breathed; nor would there have been any use of organs by the help of which he might receive his food or get rid of what he had already digested, since there was nothing which went from him or came into him: for there was nothing beside him.

It was impossible to concentrate. Melanie Darma didn't want to ask, not really. But she had to.

"Who will remember?"

Before he could answer they clattered into Temple. The bright station lights made her blink. The doors opened. A burly, scarlet-faced man in a creased, grubby dark suit entered the carriage, looked at their half, then the other, and sat down in the seats opposite her, as far away from the young man with the rucksack as he could. She could still smell the rank stink of beer though.

"And why?" she wondered.

The newcomer grunted, pulled out a copy of the *Standard*, thrust his coarse face into it. Then he raised his head and stared hard at both of them, as if they'd broken some kind of rule by speaking to each other across the chasm of a Tube train carriage, strangers conversing beneath the streets of London on a breathless July day.

"I don't know what you mean ... " the young man answered quietly.

Perhaps she'd misheard. The train was noisy. She didn't feel well. But now he had his hands curled round the rucksack the way hers fell in place about her stomach, and his eyes wouldn't leave her document bag from work, the green canvas carry-all bearing the insignia of the Palace of Westminster, a golden portcullis, crowned, with two chains. It sat in the seat next to her looking important, though in truth it contained nothing of moment.

The train lurched into darkness once more, for several seconds this time. She wondered whether someone had moved during that time. But when the lights returned they were both in the same seats, the older man face deep in his paper, the younger, smiling a little vacantly, glancing in her direction.

She thought of the offices and who would be there, waiting. It was temporary work, six months, no more, until her ... "confinement" as one of the older women put it. Temps didn't get maternity pay, even when they were forced to go through interminable interviews and vetting processes, just so they could answer irate emails to MPs she never met. The men and women there were, for the most part, kind, in an officious, offhand way. Each day she would nod and smile to the policemen on the door, place her bag on the security machine to be scanned, her ID card against the entry system reader to be checked. Nothing ever changed, nothing ever happened. Behind the imposing, ornate doors of the Palace of Westminster, beyond the gaze of the tourists who snapped and gawped at the great building that sat beneath the tower of Big Ben, lay nothing more than the world writ small: little people doing little jobs, leading insignificant lives, just looking, like her, to pay the bills.

No one ever asked who the father was. She was a temp. There was, of course, no point.

She leaned forward, needing to ask him something.

"I was wondering…?" she began.

The man in the creased dark suit glared at her, swore, screwed up his paper, and got to his feet.

Her heart leapt in her chest, her hands gripped the shape beneath her fingers more firmly. It was the middle of the day. Violence on the Tube at that hour was rare, but not unknown.

"Don't do anything…" she heard herself murmur.

There was an exchange of intemperate words, and the thick-set man stomped off to sit in the far end of the carriage. The train burst into Embankment with a deafening clatter. One more stop to go. In her early days working at the Houses of Parliament she had sometimes abandoned the Tube here and walked the rest of the way, along the Embankment. She enjoyed the view, her left side to the river and the London Eye on the opposite bank, ahead the familiar outline of Westminster Bridge and the great iconic symbol of Big Ben beneath which – and this had long ceased to astonish her – she worked, humbly tapping away at a computer.

There was no possibility that she could walk such a distance any more. She kept her eyes on the grimy carriage floor and said nothing else. At Westminster station she got up and left the train without looking at anyone.

The day seemed brighter than when she first went underground. She glimpsed up at the impossibly tall clock tower to her right, blinking at the now fierce sky.

Then, patiently, as she always did, because that was how she was brought up, she waited at the first pedestrian crossing, until the figure of the green man came and it was safe to walk. It was only a few hundred yards from the mouth of the Tube station to the heavily guarded gate of the Palace of Westminster, close to the foot of the tower, the entrance she had to use. As always, there were police officers everywhere, many carrying unsightly black automatic weapons in their arms, cradling them as if they were precious toys.

No one looked at a pregnant young woman out on the street in London. They were all too busy to notice such a mundane sight. She walked over the final stretch of road when the last pelican crossing allowed, wondering who would be on duty at the security post that day. There was one nice police officer, a friendly sergeant, tall, with close-cropped grey hair, perhaps forty, or a fit fifty, it was difficult to tell. She knew his name: Kelly. Everyone else among the staff who scrutinized her bag and her ID card from time to time, asking pointless questions, picking curiously at her belongings, was still a stranger.

Twenty yards from the high iron gates of the security entrance she turned and saw him.

The young man from the train had his rucksack high over his head. He was running and screaming something in a language she didn't understand. He looked both elated and scared. There were policemen beginning to circle him, fumbling at their weapons.

Melanie Darma watched all this as if it were a dream, quite unreal, a spectacle from some TV show that had, perhaps, been granted permission to film in the shadow of Big Ben, though this was, she felt sure, improbable.

She walked on and found herself facing the tower of Big Ben again. Kelly – *Sergeant* Kelly, she corrected herself – was there, yelling at her. He didn't have a weapon. He never carried one. He was too nice for that, she thought, and wondered why at that moment she chose, quite consciously, not to listen to his hoarse, anxious voice.

"Melanie ...!"

The bright, angry sky shook, the horizon began to fall sideways. She found herself thrust forcefully to one side, and felt her hands grip the shoulder bag with the golden portcullis close to her, out of habit, not fear, since all it contained was the book on Ouroboros, a few bills, a purse with £20 and a few coins.

Falling, she clutched the canvas to herself, defending the tender swell at her stomach as she tumbled towards the hard London stone.

Two strong arms were attempting to knock her down to the ground. She broke the fall with one knee and his chin jabbed hard against her skull. Her stockinged skin grazed against the paving. She felt a familiar, stabbing pain from childhood, loose flesh damaged by grit. Tears pricked at her eyes. She was in someone's arms and she knew, immediately, whose.

She couldn't see him, but he was still on her, tight arm around her throat.

When she looked up three men in black uniforms circled them, weapons to their shoulders, eyes fixed on a target that was, she understood, as much her as it was him.

* * *

Half crouched, gasping for breath she could see the iron security gates were just a few short steps away: security, a safe, private world, guarded so carefully against violent young men carrying mysterious rucksacks. Someone came into view, face in darkness initially since she was now in the shadow cast by the gigantic clock tower and the day seemed suddenly almost as dark as the mouth of the Tube from which she had so recently emerged.

"Don't shoot me," she said quietly, and realized there were tears in her eyes. "Don't ... "

Her hands stayed where they were, on her stomach. Somehow she couldn't say the words she wanted them to hear. *Don't shoot us ...*

The grip on her neck relaxed, just a little. She caught the eyes of the man in front of her. Sergeant Kelly – she had never known his second name, and feared now she never would – had his hands out in front, showing they were empty. His face was calm and kind, unflustered, that of a gentle man, she thought, one for whom violence was distasteful.

"It doesn't need to end this way…" he pleaded quietly.

"What way?" the voice behind her demanded.

"Badly," the policeman said, and moved forward so that they could see his eyes. "Let the young lady get to her feet. Can't you see she's hurt?"

Laughter from an unseen mouth, his breath hot against her scalp. She found the courage to look. The old red rucksack was high in the air. From its dirt-stained base ran a slender black cord, dangling down towards the arm that gripped her. Tight in his fingers lay some small object, like a television remote control.

She couldn't count the black shapes gathering behind Sergeant Kelly. They wore heavy bullet-proof vests and soft caps. Black, ugly weapons stood in their arms tight to the shoulder, the barrels nodding up and down, like the snouts of beasts sniffing for prey.

"She's pregnant," the sergeant went on. "You see that? *Can't you?*"

The unseen man sighed softly, a note, perhaps, of hesitation. She felt there was some flicker of hope reflected in Sergeant Kelly's eyes.

"Get up…" the foreign voice ordered.

She stumbled to her feet. Her knee hurt. Her entire body seemed racked by some strange, unfamiliar, yet not unwanted pain.

Her captor's young face was now just visible. He was looking towards the tower of Big Ben.

"We're going in there," he insisted, nodding towards the black iron security gates. "If you try to stop me…she's dead." He nodded at the armed officers circling them. "Them or me. What's the difference?"

She wondered how long the men with guns would wait, whether they were already gauging how wide to make the arc of their circle so that they might shoot safely in order to guarantee a kill, yet not be subject to their own deadly fire when the moment came.

It will be soon… she thought, and found her hands returning to her belly, as if her fingers might protect what was there against the hot rain of gunfire.

Someone thrust aside the barrel of the closest weapon. It was the sergeant again, swearing furiously, not at her assailant, but at the officers with guns. Harsh words. Harsher than she'd ever heard him speak before.

"There are choices," Sergeant Kelly insisted as he pushed them back.

Hands high, empty, face still calm, determined, he wheeled round to confront the man who held her.

"Choices…" the policeman repeated quietly. "She's pregnant. Isn't there," he shook his head, struggling to locate the right words, "…some rule that says it's wrong to kill an unborn child?" Sergeant Kelly shrugged. "For me there is, and I don't believe in anything much, except what I can see and touch. If you believe," his right hand swept briefly towards the sky, "…something, isn't it the same?"

"You are not my preacher, policeman," the voice behind her spat at him.

"No." Sergeant Kelly was so close that she could feel the warmth of his breath on her face and it smelled of peppermints and stale tobacco. "I'm no one's priest. But tell me this. What will your god say of a man who knowingly takes the life of an unborn child?" The man gripping her leaned forward, bending his head to one side, as if listening, curiously. "Will he be pleased? Or…"

A stream of angry, foreign words filled the air. The London policeman stood there, his hand out, beckoning.

"She doesn't belong here," he said. "Let her go with me. After that…"

He shrugged.

"You…and *they*…" The way he nodded at the others, the men with the guns, shocked her. It was as if there was no difference between them and the one who had snatched her, out in the bright, stifling day in Parliament Square. "You can do what the hell you like."

Silence, followed by the distant caterwauling of sirens. This was, she knew, the moment.

"I beg you…" Melanie Darma murmured, not knowing to whom she spoke.

The grip on her neck relaxed. A choking sob rose in her throat. She stumbled forward, out of the young man's grip, still clutching the bag with the portcullis logo close to her stomach.

"Quickly ... " the policeman ordered, beckoning.

She lurched forwards, slipped. Her knee went to the ground once more. The pain made her shriek, made her eyes turn blurry with tears.

One set of arms released her. Another took their place. She was in the grip of Sergeant Kelly, and the smells of peppermint and tobacco were now secondary to the stink of nervous sweat, hers or his, she didn't know and didn't care.

She fell against him. His arms slipped beneath hers, pulling, dragging, demanding.

They were close to the gate. She found herself falling again, turning her head around. She had to. It was impossible to stop.

The young man from the Tube had his hands in the air. He was shouting, words she couldn't understand, foreign, incomprehensible words, a lilting chant that seemed to veer between anger and fear, imprecation and beseechment.

"Melanie ... " the police sergeant muttered, as he pulled her away. "Don't look ... Don't ... "

It was futile. No one could not watch a scene like this. It was a kind of theatre, a staging, a play in real life, performed on a dirty stone stage in the heart of London, for all to see.

Not far away there were men with cameras, people holding cell phones, recording everything. Not running the way they should have been.

That puzzled her.

She fell to one knee again, and felt glad the pain made her wake, made her pay more attention.

The dark shapes with the rifles were around him again, more close this time, screaming obscenities and orders in equal measures. Yet his eyes were on the sky, on something unseen and unseeable.

The rucksack flew from his hand. The ugly black metal creatures burst into life in the arms of their owners and began to leap and squeal. She watched the young man she had spoken to on the Tube twitch and shriek at the impact, dancing to their rhythm as if performing some deadly tarantella.

His bag tumbled through the air, falling to the ground, the wire that linked device to owner flailing powerlessly like a snapped and useless tendon.

That part of the performance was over. It was the dance now, nothing but the dance.

Sergeant Kelly didn't drag her at that moment. Like Melanie Darma he realized the bomb, or whatever it was, had refused to play its part. Like her, he could only watch in shock and terrified wonder.

She closed her eyes, gripping her stomach firmly, intent on ensuring everything there was normal, as it ought to be. As she half-knelt there, feeling the policeman's strong arms on her shoulder, she was aware of two thin lines of tears trickling slowly down her face. And something else...

"Melanie," Sergeant Kelly murmured, looking scared.

She looked at him. There was worry, concern in his face, and it was more personal now, more direct than such a vague and ephemeral threat as explosives in a young man's bag.

Following the line of his gaze she saw what he did. Blood on the pavement. Not that of the man from the Tube. Hers. A line of dark, thick liquid gathering around her grazed knee, pooling as it trickled down her leg.

The wailing of sirens grew louder. Vans and police cars seemed to be descending upon them from every direction. Men were shouting, screaming at one another. A couple were bent down over the broken body leaking on to the ground a few yards away.

Before she could say another thing he bent down, looked in her face, breathed deeply, then scooped her up in his strong, certain arms.

"There's a nurse inside," Sergeant Kelly muttered, a little short of breath, as he carried her through the security gate, past the door, and the gawping, wide-eyed officers next to their untended machines, and on into the cool, dusty darkness of the Houses of Parliament.

* * *

She knew the medical room, could picture it as he half-stumbled, half-ran along the narrow corridors. In the very foot of the tower, a clean and windowless cubicle with a single medic in attendance, always. Twice, she'd stopped by, for advice, for support, only to be told to see her own doctor instead of troubling the private resources of the Palace of Westminster.

Except in emergencies.

Sergeant Kelly turned down the final passageway, one that led into the very core of the building. The stonework was so massive here it scared her. Trapped beneath several hundred feet and untold tons of grimy London stone, an insignificant creature, like some tiny insect in the bowels of a towering anthill, she felt herself carried into the brightly lit room, lifted on to a bed there, placed like a specimen to be examined.

It was the same nurse. Thickset, ugly, fierce. The place smelled of drugs and chemicals. The lights were too bright, the walls so thick she couldn't hear a note of the chaos that must have ensued outside.

The nurse took one look at the drying stain on her ankle and asked, "When are you due?"

"Four weeks."

Her flabby face contorted in a scowl.

"And you're coming to work? Good God…Let's take a look."

She was reaching for a pair of scissors, casually, with no panic, no rush. It was as if life and death cohabited happily in this place, one passing responsibility to the other the way day faded into night.

He was still there as the woman came towards the hem of her dress with the sharp, shiny instrument, staring at the Palace of Westminster bag which she continued to clutch tight against the bump, as if it still needed protection.

"You don't need that any more," Sergeant Kelly said, half amused, reaching down for the carry-all in her hands.

She let go and released it into his grip. The nurse advanced again with the scissors, aiming at her dress.

"Sergeant…?" Melanie Darma objected, suddenly anxious.

"I'm a London copper, love," he answered, laughing a little. "There's nothing I haven't seen."

"I don't want you to see me," she told him firmly.

The nurse gave him a fierce stare.

Sergeant Kelly sighed, held the bag up for her to see, and said, "I'll look after your things outside."

As he opened the door, the faint wail of sirens scuttled through then died as he closed it again.

It wasn't like an anthill, she thought. More akin to being in the foundations of a cathedral, feeling the weight of ages, the massive load of centuries of tradition, of a civilization that had, at one time, dominated the known world and now had the power to do nothing more than bear down on her remorselessly.

"The doctor might be a man, love," the nurse said as she cut the fabric of the cheap dress in two, all the way up to the waist.

Then she stepped back, eyes wide with surprise, unable to speak.

It was all there. The plastic bag with the fake blood, and the tell-tale path it had left down the side of her leg after she burst it with her fingers. And the bulge. The hump. The being she had brought to life, day-by-day, out of stockings and underclothes, napkins and tea towels, until that very morning. *The* morning. When something else took its place.

She knew the wires, every one, because he'd told her about each as he placed them there, around the soft, fat wad of material they'd given him, the night before. There was, she wanted to tell the nurse, no other way to penetrate this old and well-protected inner sanctum of a world she had come to hate. No other means to escape the attention of the electric devices, the sniffers, the security people prying into everything that came and went in this great palace, a monument that meant so much to so many.

"I'm sorry," she murmured, reaching for the band of yellow cable, taking the tail to the mouth, as she'd learned and practised so many times in the small, fusty bedroom of the apartment she could barely afford.

The foreign phrase he taught her wouldn't come. They were, in any case, his words, not hers, codes from a set of beliefs she did not share.

What she did know was the Circle. It seemed to have been with her forever, since the moment she first set foot in the dark world beneath the ground, hand in hand with her father, as he took the first step on the journey to his bleak, cruel end. Ahmed – this was not his real name, she understood and accepted that – had woken the slumbering beast one cold morning that spring when he talked his way into her life after she left the Palace of Westminster. But he was its creature too, not that he recognized the fact.

Her mind could not dismiss the image of Ouroboros at that moment, the picture of the serpent devouring itself. Or the words of the book that was now in the hands of Sergeant Kelly who was, perhaps, a little way away, outside even, eyeing the shattered body in the street.

The living being had no need of eyes when there was nothing remaining outside him to be seen; nor of ears when there was nothing to be heard; and there was no surrounding atmosphere to be breathed. And all that he did or suffered took place in and by himself.

From nothing to nothing, round and round.

With unwavering hands Melanie Darma held the wires above her belly like a halo, bringing together the ends with a firm and deliberate motion, filled with the deepest elation that this particular journey was at an end.

A GOOSE
FOR CHRISTMAS

Alexander McCall Smith

1

OLD FARMER HONDERCOOTER had a place near a hill that everybody called Birds' Hill. He had 250 acres, which was a reasonable size for a dairy farm in that part of the country. Sheep people had far more – thousands of acres, whole plains, it seemed, whole mountainsides, but dairy people had no need of such wide horizons. "I can walk across my land," he sometimes said. "I know every inch of it. The good bits, the bad bits – I know the lot."

As well as keeping cows, Hondercooter usually had at least six geese about the farmyard, a flock of laying hens, and a dog of indeterminate breed, Old Dog Tray. This dog was named after a dog in the German children's book, *Struwelpeter*, in which the faithful dog Tray is tormented by a cruel boy. Eventually Tray turns on the boy and defends himself. Hondercooter had that book read to him when he was a child and found it frightening. But the name *Tray* struck him as being a good name for a dog, and so he chose it when the dog first came to him as a puppy.

"Old Tray is a good dog," he said to visitors. "Looks after the place. Follows me round. Barks. Does everything you need a dog to do."

2

Hondercooter was of Dutch extraction. His father had gone to New Zealand as a young man and taken up farming near the Abel Tasman in the South Island. In those days it was not a particularly fashionable part of the country. Later, it became popular with people of an alternative outlook – hippies, in particular, liked the atmosphere, and settled there to grow their own vegetables and run small pottery and batik workshops. The farmers were bemused by these people, but by and large got on well with them.

Hondercooter was a New Zealander through and through, although he was proud of his Dutch ancestry. "Dairy farming is what we do," he said. "You can't find a better dairy farmer than a Dutchman. It's in the blood."

He had never married. "Wives are expensive," he joked. "Look at what it costs to keep a wife. Just look!"

The fact that he was unmarried meant that there were no obvious heirs. "He may have cousins somewhere," people speculated. "You never know."

3

Hondercooter's nearest neighbour was a farmer called Ted Norris. Ted was a bit younger than Hondercooter, and, unlike him, was married. His wife was called Betty, and she had a substantial reputation as a cheese-maker. She had won prizes for her cheeses in Auckland and Wellington, and had even been chosen for a New Zealand Cheese exhibition in Melbourne. That trip to Australia was her first trip abroad. "It opened my eyes," she said when she returned.

After that experience, Betty hankered for another foreign trip.

"Waste of money," said Ted Norris. "Airports. Rush. All that stuff. Why don't we drive down to Dunedin instead? Or Christchurch, maybe."

Betty got her way, though, and a few years later they went on a trip to Rome and Paris. Rome was chosen because Ted was a devout Catholic. Paris was for Betty. She had never converted to Catholicism, although she was on good terms with the local priest, who regularly dropped in on the farm to play a game of chess with Ted.

Another regular social engagement for Ted and Betty was the visit of Hondercooter, who came for Sunday dinner once a month.

After the meal the three of them would sit in the living room and drink a cup of coffee while Ted erected a screen to show his slides of the trip to Rome. Hondercooter knew these slides well, but did not mind looking at views of St Peter's while Ted explained the finer points of its architecture. It reassured him to hear these facts – in a changing world, it was helped to be reminded that there were people who took the long view, who thought in terms of eternity.

4

Hondercooter reciprocated this hospitality, even though he was not much of a cook. Ted and Betty came for dinner every other month, and they then played canasta for the rest of the evening. Betty took the opportunity, too, to tidy up Hondercooter's house a bit. This became something of a private joke with them, and Hondercooter would issue his invitation by saying that he would be pleased if Betty came round to tidy things up a bit. She could bring Ted, of course, and there would be a bite to eat afterwards. This never failed to amuse them.

5

Hondercooter was quite well-off. His father had done well for himself and had made good investments. By the time he died and they came to Hondercooter, they were worth a considerable sum. Hondercooter never touched them. They were looked after by a lawyer in Nelson, a cadaverous-looking man called Bollingworth, who sent a report every six months of the state of the investments. He usually used the same words to describe the portfolio of shares. "Very good, on the whole."

Hondercooter also had one or two personal items of some value. One of these was a small painting in an ornate gilded frame. This had belonged to his maternal grandmother's family, and had been brought out to New Zealand by Hondercooter's father. It was typical of Dutch painting of the late sixteenth century, and depicted a group of peasants working on the harvest. In the background, the sails of a windmill could be made out, half hidden by a stand of trees.

This painting was by Pieter Brueghel, although the small gilt lozenge glued on to the bottom of the frame claimed the artist as Jan Brueghel the Younger. This attribution, which would have considerably reduced the painting's value, was false.

"Nice painting, that," commented Ted Norris. "By a Dutchman?"

"I think so," said Hondercooter. "It was my grandmother's. There are an awful lot of Dutch paintings, you know. Lots of old ones."

Ted was more interested in the agricultural detail. "What are they harvesting?" he asked.

"Hard to tell," said Hondercooter. "Probably wheat. You like that painting, Ted?"

"Yes," said Ted Norris. "I saw a lot of paintings like that in Rome. Only they were bigger and they were by Italians. No, I like it a lot."

"I'll leave it to you in my will," said Hondercooter.

Ted Norris thought he was joking, but Hondercooter assured him he was not.

"Well, that's decent of you," said Ted Norris.

6

Hondercooter was fattening one of the geese for Christmas. He had chosen the goose, which was the largest of the flock, and also the most bad tempered. He remembered something that he had learned about geese in school. The Romans kept geese as watchdogs, did they not? And hadn't the geese hissed to alert the Romans that somebody was about to attack Rome? He would have to ask Ted Norris whether he knew that story; he had been to Rome, of course.

This bad-tempered goose seemed to sense that something was up. As Christmas approached, he became increasingly aggressive, going so far as to hiss at Hondercooter himself as he walked past him in the yard. Hondercooter even had to aim a kick at the goose on one occasion and almost tripped up as a result.

"You don't know it, but you're ending up on the table," he warned. "Ted, Betty, me – we're going to eat you, my hissy friend!"

The goose looked at him. There was venom in his gaze.

7

Old Dog Tray particularly disliked the geese and barked at them
ferociously whenever they came near him. The geese ignored this
barking, emboldened by the senior goose, who seemed as unafraid
of dogs as he was of humans. Tray lay on the grass and watched the
geese from the corner of his eye. He would deal with them in due
course. They would overstep the mark one day, and he would show
them that a dog can only be pushed so far. There were some sheep
down the road who also needed to be dealt with. Stupid creatures.
Irritating beyond belief to a dog.

8

Ted Norris came to tell Hondercooter about what happened.

"Your dog, Tray," he said. "You seen him today?"

"This morning," said Hondercooter. "He's about the place."

"Sorry about this, Hondy, but he's killed two of my sheep. At
least I think it's him. Betty saw something and couldn't quite make
out what it was, but we think it's your Tray. Really sorry to have to
tell you this, you know."

Hondercooter was silent. He knew how serious this was. In a
farming community, if a dog is a sheep-killer there was only one
solution.

"Let's go and look for him," suggested Ted Norris. "If he's
clean, then it won't have been him. But if he's covered in blood ... "
He shrugged.

"All right," said Hondercooter. "We can try the barn. Sometimes
he goes there. He likes lying in the straw."

9

They found Old Dog Tray where Hondercooter had suggested he
might be – in the barn. And, as predicted, he was lying in the
straw. There was blood on his chin and all across the white patch
on his chest. There were feathers, too, and the body of a goose,
limp and ruffled.

Tray looked up at Hondercooter and Ted Norris. There was guilt in his eyes. Alone of animals, it seems that dogs experience feelings of guilt, although there is some argument as to whether it is real guilt or merely a dread of punishment. Whatever the source of the emotion, that was what Tray demonstrated.

Hondercooter shook his head. He knew what he had to do.

10

Walking back to the house, Ted Norris tried to cheer his neighbour up. He looked about him, at the contented herd of dairy cows, at the well-kept fences, at the neat fields. "You've got a really good place here, Hondy," he said.

Hondercooter nodded. "Yes, it's a good place. Left it to you and Betty in my will, you know."

Nothing was said. Ted was surprised, and pleased. It would make him a wealthy man. And every farmer, however much he has, convinces himself that he needs more.

11

The following day there was an accident. A parcel delivery man, bringing a package of veterinary remedies to the farm, spotted Hondercooter on the ground near the barn. He ran over, thinking that the farmer may have had a heart attack or something of that sort. It was not that: Hondercooter had been shot. His shotgun lay beside him, not far from his right hand. A few yards away, lying on the ground watching the delivery man, was Old Dog Tray. He growled faintly when the delivery man appeared, but then he wagged his tail and came up to him, ready to be patted.

12

The police spoke to everybody, including Ted and Betty. "Was Mr Hondercooter depressed, do you think? Was there any reason why he would take his life?"

The answer from everybody was the same. "No, he was a pretty level-headed sort of man. His farm was doing well – you can understand it when a farmer is up to his eyes in debt – people can get desperate then. But none of this applied to Hondercooter."

There was an inquest, the conclusion of which was that it had been accidental death. The police produced photographs of the ground near Hondercooter's feet. It looked as if he had slipped, as it was muddy there, and there were marks which looked as if they had been made by a stumbling man.

13

Ted Norris looked after the dairy herd. He went through Hondercooter's papers in the drawers of his large desk. He found a letter from Bollingworth, the lawyer in Nelson, and he telephoned him. "Mr Hondercooter's dead," he said. "I believe you're his lawyer."

"Who am I speaking to?" asked Bollingworth.

"Ted Norris. I'm his neighbour."

There was a silence, which might have been shock, or a moment for recollection. Then, "You're the principal executor, you know, Mr Norris. And under Mr Hondercooter's will you and your wife are the main beneficiaries."

Ted Norris was cool. "He said something about that. I didn't pay much attention, but he did say something."

14

Ted and Betty Norris decided that they would go ahead with their Christmas meal in spite of the sad circumstances. They took one of the geese – not the one that Hondercooter had been fattening – and they roasted that. They sat in their dining room, both wearing a paper hat from a Christmas cracker. On the wall behind Betty was the Brueghel. "I love that painting," she said to Ted. "Brueghel's very famous, I think. We'd better get it valued."

"We must find out what they're harvesting," said Ted. "Hondy thought it was wheat."

15

Underneath the table, replete after the dinner of goose scraps fed to him by his new owners, reprieved because Ted could not bring himself to shoot him – not after what had happened – lay Old Dog Tray. A dog's memory is strange: it is full of smells and random impressions; there is little sense of chronology to it. But he did remember having to defend himself; having deliberately to trip up his master – not something that a good dog liked to have to do. The memory came, and then faded; came back and faded again. And there had been a goose.

AN ARM AND A LEG

Nigel Bird

COLD AIR POURED in when they opened the doors. It would soon be over. All Carlo had to do was accept his punishment and they could wake up in the morning and start over.

The ride had been at high speed and in a straight line, so they'd either gone south down the A1 or round the Edinburgh bypass. It wasn't easy to tell in the dark, but he figured south was the more likely when he factored in the roundabouts.

Rolling round inside the back of the van, he'd been reminded of driving his wife and first-born home from the maternity ward at Little France in the restaurant's Berlingo. Maria had been bumped around as sleeping-policemen and pot-holes took turns to attack the suspension; even with her newly stitched episiotomy, she didn't utter a noise the whole way. Nor had Chris, the poor child, head bobbing in the seat they'd spent an age working out how to secure.

That was ten years earlier. Since then Maria had given birth to a second child and, when her patience finally wore through, filed for divorce and sent him packing from the family home and business.

If he'd kept away from the booze, he might still have been in line for taking over one of the most successful eateries in the city. He could have been sitting back counting cash and sipping orange juice while his shoulders were rubbed and he watched the Hoops put one past the Jambos or the 'Gers. Instead he was in some God-forsaken place wondering how they were going to take their revenge.

It wasn't long before they dropped him to the ground, his head hitting something hard and sharp.

The icy wind from the Forth cut through his jacket and the smell of the salt filled his nostrils. He guessed they were at the cement works – that's where he'd be doing it if the steel toe-caps were on the other foot.

The men standing over him took a moment to spark up cigarettes. Carlo rested his cheek upon the smooth metal rail, so chilled that his tongue might have stuck to it if he'd given it a lick. His fingers identified wooden sleepers with pebbles scattered in between and his legs found the parallel rail exactly where he knew it would be. The bleating of a goat was the last piece he needed to complete his picture. They weren't at the cement works but the East Lothian Family Park, built to entertain the kiddies.

Sure, what he'd done wouldn't be winning him an MBE, but using trains as weapons should have died out with silent movies.

These guys were animals. Perhaps the farm was the best place for this to end after all.

* * *

Tranent needed another chip shop like it needed another teenage pregnancy. When Carlo Salvino impregnated Kylie on the same night that he opened "The Golden Fry", he really managed to hit the bull's eye.

Belters they were called, the people from the town. Some said it was on account of the tanneries in the area way back when, others that it was because of the way the miners had worn their lamps. As far as Carlo could make out it made more sense that it was because they were likely to settle a disagreement with punches rather than words and that they could hit as hard as anyone he'd ever come across.

If he'd had the money he'd have set up in the city, moved over to Glasgow even, but at least he was within ten miles of his kids, the rates on the High Street were cheap as his chips and with four pubs on the doorstep success seemed a sure thing.

"The Golden Fry" opened on Valentine's Day. Carlo fixed up ribbons and fairy lights, ordered in cases of cheap sparkling wine and sprinkled heart-shaped chocolates along the window seat for the kids.

At six the place was buzzing. By half past, the cava and chocolates gone, the only person left was a girl who'd been giving him the eye since walking in.

They chatted about something, the weather or football or the price of fish. Whatever it was, Carlo couldn't remember. Nor could he fully recall sharing a quick one against the wall in the Wynd when he walked her home. He had a vague recollection of some fumblings, but they weren't enough for him to even daydream about while he stood around waiting for customers.

Kylie came in the next day for a poke of onion rings wearing her school sweatshirt. She may have looked at least eighteen and he knew nothing illegal had taken place, but if he could have run a mile without needing to stop for a rest, he might well have done.

Hers was the only sale that day and the next. The competition had put out word and the Belters were sticking together against the new blow-in on the block with his one-eighth Italian blood and fading good looks.

It was Kylie who gave him the idea. If he could lure in the kids from the High School, he'd be quids in.

He took on two extra staff, a couple of older ladies who'd never travelled further than Prestonpans, hand wrote signs and offered food at half the price of anyone else. "Credit Crunch Lunch" he called it and it took off like it was supersonic.

There were still queues of black sweatshirts at the bakeries and the other chippies, but he had the lion's share, the line of youngsters stretching back to where he and Kylie had had their fun. Hot plates full of fried pizza (Maria's father would have had a heart attack), burgers, puddings, pies and fish were emptied daily within half an hour, as if a plague of locusts had descended and licked them clean.

They were getting through two hundred polystyrene trays at a sitting, twice that on a Friday when the primary school kids piled in to kick-off their weekend with a healthy fry-up.

After a month of success, Carlo felt that he had finally earned the slice of the luck he'd always deserved.

Things started to change when two lads came in after the rush hour, all swagger and spiky hair with the familiar white line down the middle that always made him think of wobbly skunks.

When they spoke, he just listened until they'd finished and watched them leave without ordering a thing, their mullets bobbing against their designer gear.

Turning to Mrs Edgar, who was wiping grease from the wall tiles, he asked for an interpretation.

They wanted him to put the prices up, she told him, and they wouldn't be asking so nicely the next time. And, if he didn't mind her putting in her two shillings worth, the Ramsay boys were nasty pieces of work and it might be worth listening to what they'd said.

Listening? He'd tried that and hadn't understood a single word.

The wee shites. Who did they think they were telling him how to run his business? They'd have been plankton in Leith if they ever ventured from their tiny pond into those shark-infested waters.

That same afternoon, Kylie told him about the baby. She wasn't ready to tell her dad and her mum would beat her enough to make sure the kid never saw out the first trimester.

She wanted to keep it, leave school and live with Carlo. She could serve at the counter for six months and after that she'd be a stay at home mum, make a nest they could share, a cosy place that would be a cut above the council scheme she was used to.

Carlo didn't say anything. Instead, a hug of reassurance, a pat on the behind and a poke of chips "on the house" did their job and she left with a half smile on her lips.

Turning the open sign to closed, he hooked up his apron, left the ladies to get on with things and headed for the Cross Keys. Having a glass in his hand always made life easier to understand.

The landlord, Billy, knew all about the Ramsays. They'd graduated from the Tranent Young Team and had a brief spell with the Hibs Casuals.

Local folklore had it that they used the derelict farm up near the cemetery as their base. There were tales of broken bones, cuttings and even a crucifixion. He'd seen clips of them on YouTube working away on some bloke with a pair of pliers. Their faces were hidden, but everyone in town knew who they were watching.

They were involved in drugs, loan-sharking and a bit of dog-fighting every now and then.

Their mother was known to everyone as Nan. Nan was where Carlo and just about everyone else went to get cheap fags. She sold them singly to those that were really hard up or too young to know better, with special deals for the under nines. The Ramsays were likely to be allied to "The Happy Haddock" given that the older one of them was sleeping with Nan's half-sister, whose brother owned the joint.

As Billy pulled Carlo another pint, he started on about Kylie's dad. Bert was put away for tying a man to a car and dragging him around the Heugh for slapping his sister, that and for driving underage and without a licence. Family life had cooled the fire in his belly, though Billy saw him as a dormant volcano.

The stories that followed were hardly better news.

Opposite Carlo's place was the "Quick N Eazy", run by Ray and Jim McMerry. They worked like a tag team when it came to a scrap, the kind that would have had grannies screaming at their sets when wrestling was still taken seriously.

Then there was Kwok or Kwang or whatever his name was at "Peking Cuisine". He was bound to be Bruce Lee or a Triad or both.

No, it wasn't looking good for Carlo Salvino, not until his fifth whisky gave him inspiration. There was nothing to be scared of.

Who, he asked himself, who outside of the area had ever heard of the town? They didn't even have a football team. It was a blackhead on the face of a giant and it was about time someone gave it a squeeze.

First he went for the McMerrys. The "Quick N Eazy" had slashed its prices to keep up with him and the Ramsay boys were likely to have paid a visit to them too.

As far as he could see, outside of a good fight and making a few quid, there was only one thing that Ray and Jim cared about. Their cat was pure Russian Blue and worth a few bob. An elegant thing, Carlo imagined she was the sort of creature a pharaoh might have wanted to have with him in his tomb.

Beautiful she may have been, but loyal she was not. It took nothing more than chocolate drops and catnip to get her to go with him.

Making sure she was safely secured in his laundry basket, Carlo went on to complete the next part of the plan.

Sitting with Kylie's dad, he could see why she wanted to move. The furniture stank, the carpet was hardly worth the name and the swirls on the wallpaper were making him dizzy. Outside the dirty brown render on the houses made it look like God had puked over every single one of them and the line of satellite dishes made it look like everyone on the street was trying to contact alien beings to get them the hell out of there.

Bert hadn't switched off the TV as Carlo talked, but at least he turned the sound down. He listened carefully, his expression remaining unchanged from beginning to end, a cold stare fixed upon Carlo as he talked of love and babies, apologies and marriage.

Speech over, Bert stood and, for a moment, it appeared that he was weighing up the penalty for the dragging of another human being against the satisfaction it would give him to take the bastard outside and tie him to the bumper. Instead, he left the room momentarily and returned with two glasses of vodka.

Without exchanging words, they clinked glasses and downed their drinks simultaneously. There was no ice and it hadn't been kept in the fridge, but what could one expect at ten in the morning.

Carlo received a slap on the back that would have knocked anyone under twelve stone flying. They shared vodka after vodka until, by mid afternoon, they were practically old friends.

Job done. With Kylie's dad on side, the odds had tilted in his favour.

"The Golden Fry" didn't open that day as Carlo toured the bars. Staggering home, he was pleased to see the sign, a colour photo with "Lost, Minky. Reward. Ray and Jim @ Quick N Eazy" written above it.

He considered collecting the cash, but decided to stick to the plan instead.

Three days he waited, watching the McMerrys stew and savouring every moment of their anxiety.

On Tuesday night, Kylie stood with him frying fish, a small diamond ring telling of their engagement. It had only cost a few quid down at the pawnbrokers, but he promised her that they'd get a proper one when they got the chance.

At the end of the evening, Carlo sent Kylie home early then set about his work before the oil cooled. Flicking the fryer back on, he turned out the lights and headed upstairs.

They say that animals can sense when things aren't right, that they have a sixth sense about imminent danger. It was a load of tosh as far as Carlo could see, the way Minky burrowed cosily into his armpit as if he were the earth mother herself.

He carried her downstairs, put her on the floor and threw her a few fish scraps. She hadn't chosen it exactly, but as a last meal it seemed to be up to the job.

The batter was in a bucket he'd prepared that afternoon and, before she knew it, so was Minky. She couldn't get a grip on the smooth plastic walls, scratched at them to get a grip, bit at the hand that held her down, but all to no avail.

Carlo's rubber gloves protected him well. Grabbing her tail and her scruff he threw her into the fat in one smooth movement. Minky opened her eyes as she sank, the beautiful blue spheres peering out from the white paste that covered her. A few strokes of doggy paddle and it was all over.

To her credit, she went down without a word of complaint and Carlo thought again of Maria in the van.

He fished Minky out, shook off the excess oil and spooned her into a box looking like a cartoon character who'd been in a road accident.

It took hours for the streets to empty and when they did, Carlo crossed the road to deliver his package.

Returning to his shop, he picked up a sledgehammer and gave it a baseball slugger's swing. Thousands of lines appeared in the window and it bulged out over the pavement.

Something gave in his back as he swung, so he decided that breaking through completely wasn't necessary. When the McMerrys found their cat and saw "The Golden Fry", they'd put two and two together and the Ramsays wouldn't have any legs left to stand on.

Unfortunately for Carlo, Ray and Jim had never been much good at arithmetic. It was the way the window looked that gave it away, the fact that it bulged out instead of in. He'd avoided the CCTV cameras, but not fooled the McMerrys; they'd put enough folk through glass to know it was an inside job.

* * *

The diesel engine coughed into action.

Carlo had ridden behind it six times one summer's day when his dad was still alive. Chris and Jack had loved it, the circular tour of the farm, throwing badly aimed nuggets of food at sheep, donkeys and llamas. Nursery rhymes cheered the passengers, taking their minds off the fumes.

That visit was expensive. This one was going to cost him an arm and a leg. His left wrist and ankle had been cuffed to one of the rails. As he felt the train approach, the vibrations tickling his flesh and rattling his bones, he stretched out the rest of his body like a starfish and turned his face away.

He pictured the time they were there last, the four of them standing by the ostriches, his dad holding out a scoop full of seed. The things had stretched their necks out so far and with such zeal that they'd practically taken his hand off. How they'd laughed, him and the boys, at the way his dad had dropped the whole lot and jumped back three paces at a speed that might be expected of one thirty years younger.

The drivers of the train felt the bump under the wheels and gave a quick toot in celebration. The whistle and the scream were heard by the night staff at the brewery and the insomniacs of Dunbar alike.

Before leaving, Ray and Jim broke into the small animal shed and shone their torch from one enclosure to the next.

"We'll try one of these this time, eh?" Ray said, stepping over the board and getting in amongst the rabbits.

"Aye. Let's have the black and white yen," Jim said.

Ray picked it out by the ears, handed him over to his brother and the two men set off for home, talking gently to their new pet every step of the way.

THE LOVER AND LEVER SOCIETY

Robert Barnard

THE NEW (AND most unlikely) literary society finally came into existence in one of the buildings of Pisa University, hardly more than a hop, skip, and jump from the world-renowned *torre pendente*. The hall where the delegates to the "Lover and Lever Conference" gathered was more than large enough to accommodate those who were interested in the two Irish writers being honoured, but the specialness of their enthusiasm more than made up for the relative sparseness of their numbers. By 10.30 officers for the new society had been elected, and over coffee the delegates got to know each other. The Irish delegates had to apologize that interest in these two admittedly Anglo-Irish writers was not greater, but the Englishness of their take on Ireland was controversial. There was a strong undertow of Italian interest (this was the country in which Lever spent his last years), and the rest of Europe had provided most of the other delegates, mostly Ph.D. students, with one jet-lagged customer from Australia.

By lunchtime there had been the election (actually nomination and election by acclamation) of a secretary and a treasurer, and in addition, two lectures had been given. It was over lunch, in fact, that things began – not to go wrong, no no! – but to acquire an edge. When they reached the fifth and last course, the prime mover in the conference, a man called Terry Butterfield whose bloodhound good looks had over the years set hearts of all sexes aquiver, rose to give the speech of welcome.

"It is a great pleasure," he began, "to welcome to Pisa all those lovers of Irish literature who believe that much more needs to be done to celebrate the impressive body of work of two unjustly neglected literary figures, Samuel Lover and Charles Lever. Here I would pay particular tribute to Professor Mario Pollini, of the English Department here in Pisa, without whose sterling work this two-day conference – really almost a festival – could never have taken place. Also Professor Jim Northcote, newly retired from his august position at London University, and Brian Bracewell, the well-known writer of … the well-known writer."

He paused.

"We also owe a great debt to Declan Donnelly, my friendly rival in matters bibliographical, for his custodianship of the financial side of this wonderful coming-together of Lever-lover and Lover-lovers."

Smiles all round, rather self-satisfied. It was a joke they had seen coming since the day they registered. One or two in the audience thought that in the references to Declan Donnelly they had heard the sound of gritted teeth.

"Does it sound like friendly rivalry to you, mate?" asked the delegate from Australia, any trace of Irish in his accent being subsumed into the cockney tones which are the Australian language.

"No," said Brian Bracewell, on the other side of the table. "But why rivalry? Does Lever fetch astronomical prices? It seems unlikely. And Lover didn't write all that much fiction."

"I should say it's a question of numbers, mate. Lever went on writing long after anybody much wanted to read him. Scarcity value, that's what it'll be. There's not much logic in the secondhand trade, apart from that. Some subject is taken up, or some writer, often following a television series, and suddenly all the books on Vermeer, or Franz-Joseph of Austria, or Ned Kelly, are fetching sky-high prices. It's a mad world, and I've always kept well out of it."

Terry Butterfield was coming to the end of his speech, working up to a bit of eloquence.

"I leave it to others to talk about Samuel Lover. I am a Lever man. Charles Lever spent the later years of his life not in Ireland, not in England, but mainly on the continent of Europe, for most of the last twenty-two years in Italy. He was, in his thoughts and spirit, a European. It may seem that his years here have left little trace. We can see buildings that he knew, but we can see buildings that Attila the

Hun knew, and he was around fifteen hundred years before Lever."
(Some laughter.) "But if there are only one or two buildings that we
know that he lived in, places we know he went to regularly, like the
Casino in Bagni di Luca, we are perhaps looking in the wrong place.
We should be looking for Italy in his books. And there we find the sun,
the love of pleasure, of sheer fun, the realized life which Englishmen
find difficult to cope with but which suits Irishmen down to the ground.
Instead of looking for traces of Lever in Italy, which are few, we
should be looking for traces of Italy in Lever, and they are legion."

He sat down to warm applause.

Sitting opposite him at the table was the delegate from Helsinki, a
man who had made no impression hitherto except for an
unquenchable thirst. Now he leaned across the table and put his
mouth close to Terry Butterfield's ear.

"He left something in Italy. There's a descendant lives in Siena."

Terry Butterfield's eyebrows shot up.

"Surely not."

"Quite legit, at least I think so. Descendant of one of his daughters.
Name of Teresa Spagnoli. You should have asked her to be here."

"I would have if I'd known," said Butterfield. But he was lying. If
she really was a descendant of Charles Lever he would have kept her
very quiet from everyone, which meant in particular from his "friendly
rival" in matters bibliographical, Declan Donnelly. Their "friendly
rivalry" was particularly "friendly" when it came to first editions of
Malcolm Merrivale – that late Lever novel, published reluctantly by
Newby, and given the sort of print run usually only awarded to silly
girls from Yorkshire who thought they had written great novels.

Further down the table Declan Donnelly was taking in the little
scene that had taken place after the speech's end.

"What the hell's going on there?" he mused.

"Don't know," said Morag O'Connor, a close friend of Terry's.
"But he's interested, Terry is. I know the signs."

"What in the world could that Finn be telling him?"

"Search me. Does it matter? I could ask him."

"*No.* Don't do that. Things always emerge in conversation. I
always get to know things if I go about it in the right way."

"Aren't you a judge? I can't imagine many people gossiping with a judge."

"Oh, I'm not the sort of judge who used to enjoy putting on the black cap! People talk to me as if I'm an agony aunt. My current wife says I'm 'the judge next-door'."

This particular agony aunt, Morag noticed, went in search of agony. When the lunchtime was drawing to a close and groups were breaking up she saw Declan Donnelly, glass in hand, casually wandering up towards the talkative Finn. Or not *towards* him, but taking a path that, with the odd stop and detour, would land him next to the rather unsteady university lecturer.

"Declan Donnelly," he said, holding out his hand. "And you must be Jyrki Kaapola. Did I pronounce that right?"

"Not really. Nobody doesh. Why bother? Just call me Jerk."

"All right, Jerk, I will. I've been called worse things than that in my time, by people in the dock."

"Are you a pleeshman?"

"Judge, Jerk. Terry's just been telling me what you told him."

"Oh, yes? This woman – the descendant on the distaff side. Did I say that right?"

"No, but I get the idea. On the female side."

"Thash right. Daughters – more than one. I mean: daughter of a daughter of a daughter."

"Daughters of—?"

"Charles Lever, of course. Lives in Shiena. No distance. She should have been asked to come."

"How do you know about her?"

"Colleague in the English Department in Helsinki. Has a holiday home in Tuscany. Liquor's cheaper here. He'd met her."

"*Her* being…?"

Jerk swayed. He looked as if he had only seconds in which he would remain upright. But he put his hand on the table and with practised skill maintained a vertical stance.

"Name…It's gone…I had it, but Shpanish shounding…Like an ancestor from…di Spagna. That'sh it. Di Spagna."

"Christian name?"

"Oh … Matilda, Teresa, or … one of those."

"I don't see the connection between the two."

"End with 'a'. Trishyllabic."

Though Declan was about to say practically all Italian women's names ended with an "a", the Finn at last lost out in his battle with gravity and sank with a grunt to the floor. The delegates clustered around him, but not before Judge Donnelly had made a strategic retreat. He did not feel himself compromised in the least by talking to a drunk, but he didn't want Terry Butterfield to see him doing it.

He considered what to do next. He could, of course, take off for Siena at once. He was just one of many delegates, and he had no special duties during the weekend. On the other hand, he was the financial brain behind the weekend and the new society, and he had just been elected treasurer. It would not look good. And judges these days had to be very aware of what would and would not look good.

And the other token in the balance was that Terry Butterfield *was* occupied the whole weekend. He was in overall charge, and down to do this or that pretty much till midnight that night, and till lunchtime on Sunday, when the conference ended. He, Donnelly, could take off midmorning on Sunday without his absence attracting any comment. And he could be in Siena by around lunchtime, or mid-siesta, if they still had them in Siena. Meanwhile, he slipped back to his hotel, secured the Siena telephone directory, and established the existence of a *di Spagna, M* – living in Via Fontegiusta 41. He went to the nearest bookshop and bought himself a road map of Siena.

Meanwhile, Terry Butterfield pursued a similar course. His hotel was a more modest one than the judge's, but it was close to one of the entrances to the Campo Santo, and the famous tower was only a few yards away from its windows. Terry recognized the cheapness as his duty as conference organizer, and his view of the tower as one of the perks of office. The proprietor came up with a telephone directory of Siena and also a very grubby street guide to the town which had obviously been lent to generations of tourists. No one noticed during the Sunday lunch that he was itching to get away: Terry had the reputation of a solid bloke, unflappable, with a touch of gravitas. But he was, in fact, on tenterhooks, and the moment he could say his farewells and get away to the station without arousing any thoughts of a quick getaway he did so.

Judge Declan Donnelly stood on the step of Via Fontegiusta 41 and pulled an antique door handle, resulting in a cacophony inside and outside the dwelling. He heard footsteps in the house, and then he was conscious of being observed through the spy-hole in the door.

"*Che vuole?*"

"My name is Declan Donnelly. Do you speak English?"

"Yes. What you want?"

"I—" It sounded to his ear a bit absurd however he put it "—I want to talk to you about an ancestor of yours who wrote books."

There was a long pause. He was conscious of being observed closely, and was glad he had dressed with the utmost care, and had assumed the facial expression of one of the pillars of the community.

"You come in," said the voice. The door opened and closed behind him, and he followed an ample (but not fat, let alone obese) figure down the ill-lit hallway into a large room furnished with the usual bulky pieces that spoke of plush and respectability. Miss or Mrs di Spagna was an attractive and lively forty-something, and she spoke the language of the plush of her flat, but less so the language of respectability.

"Who this writer, then?"

Declan sat down where she gestured him to.

"The writer is an Irish novelist called Charles Lever. He wrote in the mid-nineteenth century and he lived the last years of his life in Italy. I was hoping—" the hope was fading though "—you had a collection of his novels."

The well-upholstered shoulders shrugged.

"I never 'eard of 'im. Maybe my 'usband."

"Your husband? I heard that the descendant of Charles Lever was a woman."

"Oh, maybe 'is first wife. She died last year. She was a great reader, 'e's a great reader, they 'ave a fine library. I lock it up. I don't give 'im time to *read*. I didn't marry 'im for *books*."

She gave him a meaningful glance, a slight smile, then looked away.

"And your husband – can I talk to him?"

"No. 'E is away. Three 'ole weeks. Can you imagine? It is so lonely."

"It must be. And you not long married."

"*Esattamente!* You are good-looking man. Well-dressed, smooth, a touch James Bond. Experienced, eh?"

"I have been married more often than was perhaps wise. People assume that you are fickle, like a bee flitting from flower to flower."

"What is that – a bee?"

"*Bzzzz,*" said Declan. "They think you want variety."

"And you?"

"I want variety."

"Then what say we 'ave a little bargain. A deal you call it, no? You come to bed with me for an hour or two. That is a pleasure for both of us. And I give you the key to my 'usband's library. 'Is and 'is first wife's, the book people."

Declan was sorely tempted. His devotion to his habitual parade of a respectable façade never applied once he was behind closed doors. None of his wives had been in any doubt as to what he did when exposed to sexual temptation. He did what Oscar Wilde recommended.

"Done," he said.

When he banged on the peeling door of the small, ancient house in Via Dante, Terry had no idea what to expect. The steps to the door were so faint that he could hardly hear them. Or the voice, either.

"*Si – chi è?*"

"Signora Spagnoli? I am English. Do you speak English?"

"Yes, a little. What do you want?"

"I want to speak to you on important business."

There was a pause. Then he was shocked to hear the chains on the door being taken down – just what he had always advised his mother never to do. It's a good job it's just me, he thought. The door was pulled open with difficulty.

"Well, come in," said the tiny lady, all skin and bone, wrapped up against the cold that did not exist. She closed the door as he came in, and led the way through the unlighted hall to a high-ceilinged room, once rather grand, but now dirty, peeling, without pictures, almost without furniture – nothing more than two chairs and a cupboard. She led him to one chair and sat down herself in the other.

"It's very good of you to see me," said Terry. "But you really shouldn't—"

"Open the door. So people tell me. But why not? If it was someone who wanted to batter me and rob me, wouldn't he see at once there was nothing to be gained? And if he did assault me and leave me to die, what would I be losing? A few months of a life that is no longer worth living. As I'm sure you can see, and guess, all is gone, little by little. To the man who gives little bits of money for nice things. Now there are no nice things, and no money. That is why I do not offer you even a cup of coffee."

Terry was struck by the precise, almost literary English she spoke.

"You have excellent English," he said.

"Oh, it was Miss Cavendish, who helped in the shop. A very precise and prim person. She came to live in Italy because of her admiration for Mussolini – one I did not understand or share. After the war she had nothing except her beautiful voice and her precise and grammatical English. Some of the English tourists thought she was funny, but luckily Siena does not attract many of that type."

"You had a shop. What was it? A bookshop?"

"Oh dear, no. Leather goods, just off the Piazza del Duomo. Lovely soft gloves, elegant handbags, evening shoes. All beautiful and expensive. But when my husband died—" She gestured with her hand, downwards. Terry nodded.

"Your name was given to me as a possible descendant of an English – well, Irish – novelist called Charles Lever." He saw no response in her eyes. "He was fairly well known in his time – the Victorian era."

"I have never heard of him. I have seen Charles Dickens on television and Jane Austen. Oh, I like Jane Austen *very* much. But the television broke down and could not be repaired, and of course I could not afford … The Bible says we take nothing out of this world. I shall soon have nothing even though I am still in it."

"So you have never heard of Lever?"

"Never in my life. I know my grandfathers and my great-grandfathers. I assure you there were no English novelists among them. One fought for a time in Garibaldi's red-shirted army, but that is as near to fame as we have ever got."

"And your husband? You never heard him talk of a writer in his family tree?"

She laughed, almost merrily.

"Never! Not a chance of it. My Aldo, he fought the Germans all the way up Italy, and was wounded in Pisa. Perhaps one day those brave Italians will be as famous as Garibaldi's men. But he and his family were shopkeepers, men of commerce. There was not a literary person among them."

"So you have no copy of *Malcolm Merrivale*, no first edition?"

"No, alas. I have never heard of it, yet it must be famous for you to come all this way in search of it."

"Not famous at all. Almost unknown, even to specialists in Irish literature. But we collectors – we must have our holding complete: a first of every title." He saw incomprehension in her gaze. "I am wasting your time."

"What else can I do with my time but waste it?"

Terry stood up and fumbled in the back pockets of his jeans.

"I must pay you for it nevertheless," he added hurriedly, in case she was insulted. "Please regard this like any other commercial transaction, like selling a pair of gloves."

But she was not insulted, and sat fingering and looking at the note.

"Oh, it's the new stuff. So shoddy-looking..."

"But much the best stuff for buying things: food, coffee, medicines."

"Oh, I know *that*. But the old stuff was so much more like real money, and the price looked so good on a pair of gloves in the window – so many lovely noughts in it, you felt like a millionaire if you sold anything."

Terry escaped from the room, feeling as if he had escaped from a very classy sort of madhouse.

Declan Donnelly got out of bed, after two eventful hours. Every part of him seemed exhausted, and his legs seemed to have gone off on a separate existence. He pulled on his trousers and then put on his shirt, buttoning down the front in the wrong buttonholes. He tried to tie his tie, failed, and threw it down on the floor in disgust. He grabbed his coat and pulled it on. He was aware of a movement from the bed.

"You want to see the library?"

"Delightful and exciting though the last few hours have been," he said in his suavest voice, "the library was part of our deal, as I'm sure you remember."

"It is very good. You like," said Signora di Spagna, jumping to the floor and leading him from the bedroom. They went back to the sitting room, the signora fetching a key from the mantelpiece and throwing open a door in the corner of the room and switching on a light.

Declan found himself looking into something between a large cupboard and a small room. It was packed with books, almost all paperbacks. The first title that met Declan's eye was *Kane and Abel*. Then he saw a whole shelf-ful of Wilbur Smith. Then *Riders*, Joanna Trollope, Andy McNab. Another shelf-ful, this time of Barbara Cartland. *Gaudy Night*, which Declan had often thought the dullest book he had ever read. *Goldfinger* and *Casino Royale*. Several James Hiltons and *The Blue Lagoon*.

Declan Donnelly turned to his hostess.

"I ought to recommend you to take up reading," he said. "There is a lifetime of experience awaiting you here. However, I am loath to direct you away from the activity which clearly you do best."

And he turned tail and fled the flat.

There were many small bars between the Via Dante and the railway station. Terry went into several of them, and began to lose sight of which direction the railway station lay in. It was as he was coming out of the bar in the Via Rossi that he saw a familiar face.

"*Scellerato! Ladro! Traditore!*"

"Nothing of the sort," said Declan, putting out a hand to steady Terry's wavering body (though the hand itself shook). "Perfectly normal behaviour between competing collectors."

"I saw you talking to that bloody Finn."

"Why shouldn't I talk to a Finn? Particularly one with information for a Leverite."

"Ha! Information! Well, I can save you a bit of time if you're on your way to talk to Signora Spagnoli."

"To who? Never heard of her. I've been talking to Signora di Spagna. I can save *you* a bit of time if you're on your way to talk to her."

"I'm not." They looked at each other. "That bloody Finn," said Terry. "He couldn't even remember her name, he was so drunk."

"Finns are always drunk," said Declan. "I wouldn't mind betting there's no descendant of Lever here, legit or illegit…Here's a bar. Have another drink. Then we'll get a taxi and take the last train home."

So they had a last drink, swore eternal friendship, swore the finding of a first edition of *Malcolm Merrivale* was a game not worth the candle, and they'd give it up pronto. Then they went back out into the street, hailed lots of taxis, none of whose drivers wanted to pick up two drunken Brits (for they were both, in their different ways, respectable and casual, very recognizable) then began to make their way on foot to the station.

By chance, as they made their way like silent-film drunks, they walked along Via d'Orti, where at number 46, in a neat little upstairs flat, Valentine della Spanna was eating from a large box of chocolates, drinking from a bottle of finer wine than she had drunk for years, and contemplating a small gap in the dusty books on a high shelf in a dim part of the room – books written by some old geezer who somehow or other was connected with her, and which the slightly tipsy man from a country she had barely heard of had bought from her for a price (for he was a fair-minded man, this Finn, drunk or sober) which was a bargain for him and a prodigious windfall for her. He was a nice man, she thought, as she took another soft centre. And he had a lovely sense of humour.

AUTHOR'S NOTE: It should be emphasized that there is no resemblance in the characters or events in this story to the characters or events at the International Conference on Charles Lever in Pisa in September 2006, which the author attended.

DEAD CLOSE

Lin Anderson

Doug Cameron stared wide-eyed into the darkness, his heart racing, fear prickling his skin. The dream. As fresh now as it had been seventeen years ago. For a few moments Rebecca was alive, the swell of her pregnancy as clear as her terrified expression, then she was running from him as though he was the source of her fear.

A police siren wailed past in tune with his thoughts, its blue light flickering his rain-splattered window. He rose and went to watch the squad car's progress, leaning against the window frame, reminding himself that in forty-eight hours that sound would belong to his past. Just like the view from the bedroom window. Just like Rebecca.

When he felt steadier, he went through to the kitchen and began the process of making coffee, glancing at the photograph on the fridge door as he fetched out the milk carton. He'd taken the picture from the garden of his future home. A view of the flat-topped slopes of Dun Caan on the Island of Raasay instead of Edinburgh Castle. Not a bad exchange, he decided.

Cameron settled at the kitchen table, pulled over his work box and began the intricate task of tying a new fishing fly. The only thing that helped him forget the dream, and the past.

Detective Sergeant James Boyd woke with a start. Immediately his body reacted to its cramped position on the sofa sending waves of pain through his knees and lower back. Boyd wasn't sure which noise had wakened him, the screaming baby or his mobile. Through the open bedroom door he could see Bev put their young son to the breast, silencing his cries. Boyd answered the duty officer in mono-syllables, pulling on his trousers and shirt as he did so. He turned, sensing Bev in the doorway. She looked pointedly at him.

"I have to go to work."

Bev said nothing, but her expression was the same as always. Tired, resentful, desperate.

"I'm sorry," he tried.

"Will Susan be there?" she said sharply.

Boyd covered guilt with irritation. "She's forensic. If there's a crime she's there."

Bev turned on her heel, Rory still attached to her breast. The last thing Boyd saw before the bedroom door banged shut was a small chubby hand clutching the air.

When his phone rang, Cameron contemplated ignoring it. The only call he would get at this time was one he didn't want.

"Glad you're up, sir," his Detective Sergeant's voice was suspiciously cheery. "We've had a call out."

"I've retired," Cameron tried.

"Not till Tuesday," Boyd reminded him.

Cameron listened in silence to the details. A serious incident had been reported at Greyfriars Churchyard, a stone's throw from his flat.

"I'll walk round," he offered.

"No need, sir. I'll be with you in five minutes."

Cameron wondered if Boyd suspected he wouldn't come otherwise.

Boyd's car stank of stale vinegar, the door pocket stuffed with fish and chip wrappers, a sure sign he wasn't eating at home. His DS looked rough, stubble-faced and bleary-eyed.

"How's the new arrival?" Cameron asked.

"Only happy when he's attached to Bev's tit."

"A typical male then."

Boyd attempted a smile. Cameron thought about adding something, like "Hang on in there. Things'll get better", but didn't know if that was true.

They were at the graveyard in minutes, sweeping past the statue of Greyfriars Bobby and through the gates of the ancient churchyard. Ahead, the pale edifice that was the church loomed out of an early morning mist.

A couple of uniforms stood aside to let the two men enter the mausoleum, one of many that lined the walls of the graveyard.

Inside, the air was musty and chill. The light-headed feeling Cameron had experienced earlier returned and he reached out to steady himself against the doorframe, bowing his head to relieve the sudden pressure between his eyes. The beam from Boyd's high-powered torch played over the interior, finally settling on a pool of fresh blood next to a stone casket.

"The caller reported seeing a figure run in through the gate. Then they heard a woman scream."

Cameron said nothing. He wanted to make it plain that if Boyd expected to take over as DI, this was the time to start.

"We've done an initial search of the graveyard. Nothing so far. And no blood except in here."

Cameron registered the oddity of this, but made no comment. He didn't want to be drawn in. He didn't want his brain to focus on anything other than his departure.

They emerged to find a parked forensic van and two SOCOs getting kitted up. Cameron watched as Boyd and the young woman exchanged looks. He walked out of hearing, not wanting to be party to something he couldn't prevent. Besides, what could he say? Don't piss on your wife or you could end up like me?

He had no idea what made him look up. The medieval stone tenement behind him merged with the back wall of the crypt. It was blank-faced except for one narrow window. The young woman who watched him was in shadow but Cameron briefly made out a pale face and long dark hair, before she stepped out of sight.

It took him five minutes to circumnavigate the building and gain entry. The internal stairwell spiralled swiftly from ground level, one door on each floor. He climbed to the second landing and knocked.

When the young woman opened the door, Cameron's voice froze in his throat.

Cameron had been a detective long enough to read body language pretty accurately. Susan was on her knees on the muddy grass, Boyd trying hard not to look at her upturned buttocks. He stood to attention when he spotted Cameron. Another sign.

"I spoke to a girl living up there," Cameron pointed at the window. "She says she was wakened by the siren. Didn't see or hear anything before that."

Boyd gave him an odd look. Cameron wasn't planning to say the girl looked so like Rebecca it'd almost given him a heart attack, but wondered if the shock still showed on his face.

"Well the police dog was right. It is a grave, but not a fresh one." Susan sat back to reveal a sunken area in the muddy trampled grass. "They buried plague victims here in medieval times. There were so many it raised the ground level by twenty feet. Heavy rain sometimes washes the top soil away, exposing the remains."

Cameron stepped closer, his eye caught by a glint of metal.

"What's that?"

Susan fished it out and wiped off the mud. "Looks like a brooch." She handed it over.

Cameron felt the prick as the pin caught his thumb. Blood oozed from the wound to form a red bubble. The sight of it made him nauseous.

"The plague bacteria are way out of date," Susan quipped, "but I'd renew your tetanus if I were you." She slipped the brooch into an evidence bag. "I should have something for you on the blood in the crypt in twenty-four hours."

"That's Boyd's department now," Cameron told her.

He left them to it, giving the excuse of packing to cover his early departure. The truth was, in his head he was no longer a policeman. Thirty-five years of detective work had come and gone and the city was no better or safer now than when he'd begun. Worse than that, the dream this morning and the young woman he'd spoken to in the flat above the graveyard had only served to remind Cameron that the one case he should have solved, he never had.

It wasn't much for a lifetime. Cameron surveyed the meagre group of boxes. Everything had been packed except the books. There wasn't much shelf space at the cottage. He would have to be ruthless.

He started well, splitting the books into two piles, one for Cancer Research, the other destined for Raasay. There were at least half a dozen on fly fishing, all of which went on the Raasay pile. The last book on the shelf was one about Edinburgh's past. Cameron recognized it as belonging to Rebecca. Not a native to the city, she'd taken an amused interest in its medieval history, both fact and fiction. The photograph fell out as he transferred the book to the Raasay pile.

Rebecca stood by a dark expanse of water, laughing as she tried to anchor her long dark hair against the wind. On the lapel of her jacket she wore a brooch. Cameron suddenly remembered buying her the brooch from a silversmith near Glendale as a birthday present – a swirling Celtic pattern not unlike the one they'd found in the ancient grave.

The flashback had all the power and detail of the original event. Rebecca standing next to the counter, her head bowed as she examined the selection. He could even smell her perfume as she turned to show him which one she'd chosen.

Cameron sat down heavily, his legs like water. This was how it had been when she'd first disappeared. The powerful, terrible dreams, the intensity of her presence. The fear that she was in danger and he couldn't save her.

He had no idea how long he sat there unmoving before he heard the buzzer.

Boyd stood awkwardly amidst the packing cases. Cameron thought again how much he liked his DS. He wanted to tell Boyd he would make a good inspector but he shouldn't let the job take over his life. Instead Cameron said nothing.

He'd laid the Edinburgh book on the Raasay pile. Boyd picked it up, checked out the cover and flicked through a few pages. Cameron was aware his DS was stalling for time. There was something he wanted to say, but didn't know how.

"You don't believe in all this stuff, sir?"

"What stuff?"

"Ghosts?"

Boyd's eyes were shadowed from lack of sleep. The pregnancy, Cameron gathered, had been unplanned. The timing wasn't good for him or Bev, Boyd had said. Cameron suddenly recalled his own reaction when Rebecca had told him she was pregnant. The worry and confusion mingled with his desire to say the right thing.

"We're all haunted, one way or another, Sergeant." Cameron handed Boyd the photograph. "This is Rebecca, my wife, taken just before she went missing. Look at the brooch she's wearing."

Boyd studied the picture. "That's what I came about, sir. We've found something I think you should see."

On the way, Cameron had this expectant feeling. It was something he'd experienced countless times on the job, the breakthrough moment, when the pieces of the jigsaw fell into place.

An incident tent had been raised over the plague pit. A foot below the surface they'd exposed a mummified body. Cameron could make out strands of long dark hair.

"There's a lot of sandy soil in this section," Susan was saying. "It leeched the fluids from the body. That's why it's preserved. The brooch must have been attached to the clothes."

Cameron's heart was in his mouth. "How long has it been there?"

"At a guess a couple of decades," Susan avoided his eye.

Cameron stared into the grave. Was it possible that this could be Rebecca? That all the time she'd been buried here, half a mile from her home?

He recalled with utmost clarity the morning he'd returned from work to find the flat empty, Rebecca gone. She'd been tearful when he'd been called out the previous night. The pregnancy had made her vulnerable – something he'd resented, because it made his life difficult. Cameron still felt guilty at the relief he'd experienced when the door had closed on the sound of her distress.

The months following her disappearance had been hell. He'd been in charge of missing person cases himself, interviewed husbands about their wives, known the statistics that pointed to the partner as the prime suspect. He'd had to endure the same accusations himself.

It had all ended nowhere. No Rebecca, no body. And all the time Cameron had hoped she'd simply left him. That they were both alive somewhere, Rebecca and the child. This morning when the girl opened the door, her extraordinary likeness to Rebecca, for a moment he'd hoped…

"The girl in the flat. Have you spoken to her?"

The look he'd seen earlier was back on Boyd's face.

"The flat's unoccupied, sir."

"Nonsense. I spoke to a young woman. She looked like…" Cameron stopped himself.

"According to the neighbours, the flat's been empty for months, sir."

Cameron took the stairs two at a time. He was already banging on the door when Boyd caught him up. Boyd let him go through the process three times, before he intervened.

"There's no one there, sir."

"I saw her, Sergeant." Cameron was pissed off by Boyd's expression. He might be about to retire, but he wasn't senile yet. Cameron put his shoulder to the door.

The room was empty – of everything. For a terrible moment Cameron thought the dream that haunted his nights had somehow spilled over into the day. The fantasy of Rebecca being alive, of the child surviving had fuelled his daytime imagination. But why here? Why now?

Boyd was standing silently in the doorway.

Cameron pushed past, suddenly desperate to be out of that room.

*　*　*

"I don't see how that's possible." Boyd looked again at the DNA results. Anyone working with the police had their DNA taken and stored on the database. It was routine. Susan's tests on the blood traces in the crypt had come up with two types. One matched the boss, the other was an unknown.

"There must have been contamination when the samples were taken," Boyd insisted.

Susan was adamant. "The only way for this to happen is for him to have bled in that room."

"He cut his finger on the brooch," he tried in desperation.

"That was afterwards."

Boyd was at a complete loss. He would have to bring Cameron in, ask him how the hell his blood got in that crypt. Boyd didn't relish the thought.

"What about the body?" he asked.

"Tests are ongoing. Superficially it's the same build as Rebecca, but what's left of the clothes suggest it may be older. We're checking the teeth against Rebecca's dental records. The brooch is the only real match and it's not unique."

Boyd had pulled the file on Rebecca's disappearance and spent most of the previous night reading it. Seventeen years ago he hadn't even joined the force so anything he'd heard about the boss's missing wife was hearsay. Boyd wished he'd read the story sooner. It would have explained a lot about the old man.

He thought about the last few weeks, the boss's odd behaviour. Boyd knew he hadn't been sleeping. The DI had made a joke of it, suggesting it was excitement at getting out at last, but Boyd suspected that wasn't the real reason.

He flicked through the well-thumbed documents in the file. There were transcripts of at least six interviews with Cameron.

"What if the boss did have something to do with his wife's disappearance?"

Susan looked unconvinced. "Why? There was nothing wrong between them. No evidence of an affair ... " She halted mid-sentence.

A sick feeling anchored itself in the pit of Boyd's stomach. He had a sudden image of life repeating itself. The same stupid people doing the same stupid things.

"Susan ... "

She held up her hand to stop him. "Don't."

The Royal Mile hummed with life in the late summer light. Cameron passed the usual mix of street artists and musicians circled by enthusiastic tourists. Near the Mercat Cross a young woman was regaling a group with stories of Edinburgh's past. Cameron checked the nearby advertising boards for city tours.

The poster he sought had been on the wall of the flat. He'd spotted it when the girl opened the door. An advert for a ghost tour, one of several that roamed the old city, above and below ground. Like many Edinburghers Cameron had left that sort of thing to the tourists. *Dead Close*. Had he imagined the poster in the same way he'd imagined the girl?

He spotted a board for a ghost tour of Greyfriars Churchyard with a cancelled notice stuck across it. There was nothing advertising *Dead Close*.

In the end he found it by chance. Later Cameron would recall the entrance, remember it as the one in his dream, yet knowing there were scores of such archways lining the Royal Mile.

A young man wearing a long black cloak was calling a group to order outside a heavy wooden door, asking who among them was willing to cross the threshold of *Dead Close*.

The passageway was narrow, low and rough underfoot, dropping steeply. Cameron knew of Underground Edinburgh, the bowels of the older city beneath its current counterpart, but had never visited it before. He was fascinated by the narrow stone passageway, the small cell-like rooms to either side. It was bare and clean now, but the squalor in medieval times must have been horrendous. No wonder plague had broken out here.

The tour guide had brought them to a halt, encouraging the group to view one of the rooms. Cameron took his place at the back. The guide was telling the story of a child, separated from its mother when plague broke out and the city authorities quarantined the Close.

Cameron wasn't shocked by the story, but by the room. Rough shelves housed a multitude of toys and sweets left by visitors who'd professed to sense the ghost-child's loneliness. Cameron turned away, irritated by the guide's tone, no longer willing to be part of this make-believe. It was then he saw the doll, wedged in the corner, three shelves up.

"We're not supposed to touch the presents."

Cameron showed him his ID card.

The guide lifted the doll down and handed it over. A ripple of excitement moved through the group. They were wondering if this was for real or just part of the tour. Cameron examined the doll. It looked just like the one he'd seen on the window seat in the flat, one eye dropped in its socket, the blue dress faded.

"I believe a young woman may have left this here. She was in her late teens, long dark hair?"

The guide looked blank. He must have taken scores of people round this place. "Wait a minute. There was a girl, a couple of nights ago. She joined just as we came in. I wasn't sure she'd paid, but I decided to let it go."

"Did she give a name?"

The guide shook his head.

This wasn't fucking real. Boyd shifted his feet, discomfort showing in every inch of his body. Across the table the old man looked calm. Boyd tried to work out what he was thinking and couldn't. Had it been anyone else, the interview would have been formal.

"You've never been in there before that night?"

Cameron shook his head.

"Then how did traces of your blood get on the scene, sir?"

"I have no idea."

Jesus, he didn't want this to end up as an investigation into an officer contaminating a scene of crime. Boyd contemplated keeping quiet about it, at least until the boss handed in his badge.

Cameron looked impatient as though he had no interest in the fact that his blood had been found in the crypt.

"What about the body? Is it Rebecca?"

Boyd hesitated. The tests weren't complete yet, but there was no point keeping the old man thinking they'd found his dead wife. He shook his head. "Forensic think it's much older."

Cameron gave a small nod as though he wasn't surprised.

"The girl I met in the flat looked like Rebecca. Our daughter would have been her age by now. Rebecca had an old-fashioned doll that was hers as a kid. It was the only thing missing from the house when she left."

Boyd's heart was sinking fast. He didn't want the old man to go on, but couldn't bring himself to stop him.

Cameron produced a china-faced doll in a faded blue dress. One eye hung low in its socket.

Something cold crawled up Boyd's spine.

Cameron's eyes were bright with excitement. "The girl I spoke to had this doll in the flat. There was a poster on the wall. It advertised a ghost tour called *Dead Close*. I took that tour. There's a room dedicated to a child ghost. This doll was on the shelf."

Cameron was staring at him, waiting for Boyd to respond.

What the hell was he supposed to say? That he'd had the flat searched again, even had Susan go over it forensically. That she'd been adamant no one had set foot in it for months. That this girl the DI kept going on about didn't exist, except in his imagination.

Pity engulfed Boyd. Thirty-five years of service, on the point of retirement and the old man had lost it.

Cameron wandered down the Royal Mile, silent and deserted in the dark hours before dawn. It was the time he liked best. The right time to say goodbye. Without people, cars and lights the city felt like his alone.

Boyd had humoured him. Organized a search for the mysterious girl, but apart from the tour guide no one had professed to seeing her. The other occupants of the tenement continued to insist the flat had lain empty for months.

So he'd imagined it all, conjured up a daughter who didn't exist? Cameron could have accepted that had it not been for the doll.

The rain had come on, beating heavily on his head and shoulders. Cameron was impervious to it, his gaze fastened on the arch leading to *Dead Close*. The Royal Mile had grown darker under the sudden downpour, the space around him airless, making it difficult to breathe. Cameron leaned against the stone wall, his legs suddenly weak.

He watched as a figure emerged from the archway opposite. The figure turned towards him, the swell of her pregnancy suddenly visible.

"Rebecca?"

The figure turned and for a moment Cameron believed she recognized him. A sob rose in his throat. Then she was off, hurrying up the steep cobbles of the Mile, turning left towards Greyfriars.

Cameron ran like he had never run before, yet always her fleeing figure was the same distance ahead. Fear drove him forward. He knew this time he must catch her up or else lose her forever.

He reached the Greyfriars gate, his breath rasping in his throat, his heart crashing. Ahead, the door of the mausoleum lay open. Cameron slithered across the rain-soaked grass and stood at the crypt door.

"Rebecca?" he called.

The moon broke through the cloud, dropping a faint line of light on the stone casket. Cameron could see nothing but that line of light yet every nerve and fibre of his body told him someone was in there and that they could hear him.

He poured out his heart to the darkness and shadows. He loved her. He should never have left her alone that night. He should never have stopped searching.

He fell silent as a figure stepped from behind the casket. Cameron called out Rebecca's name, but the woman wasn't looking at him but at someone else.

The shadow of a male loomed against the wall, then took form. Words were exchanged between them. Words that Cameron did not understand. His own voice was silenced, his body frozen in time.

The woman screamed and launched herself at the man. Cameron heard a grunt of surprise then saw him crumple and fall. Blood pooled at Cameron's feet. He looked round in vain for its source, for there was no longer anyone there but him.

Boyd steeled himself and went inside the flat. Packing cases were stacked neatly in the hallway, each one with its contents detailed on the side. Two fishing rods stood upright in the corner.

He hesitated before pushing open the sitting room door. The place was empty. Boyd chose the kitchen next. He had been in this room many times. It was where the DI liked to sit. From the window, the castle stood resolute against the sky. Cameron's tin box sat open on the table, a part-assembled fishing fly nearby.

Boyd listened outside the bedroom door. Maybe the old man was fast asleep? Praying wasn't something Boyd did, but he made an exception as he pushed open that door.

Cameron was lying fully clothed on top of the bed. For a moment Boyd thought he was sleeping. The Edinburgh book lay open on his chest. The doll he'd pestered Boyd about sat in the crook of his arm. Blood running from his nostrils, eyes and ears had caked on his face and neck.

The book was just one of many that told the story of Edinburgh's haunted places. Most of the stories were invented. This one was no different. Boyd read the passage the boss had circled.

The mausoleum is haunted by the ghost of the man responsible for quarantining Dead Close. He was killed by the mother of a child he'd walled in to die. The authorities executed the woman and she was buried in a mass grave with other plague victims. Visitors have reported seeing a pool of blood on the floor of the Mausoleum and hearing the woman scream.

Boyd closed the book and slipped it in a drawer of his filing cabinet. Whatever it said, he didn't believe in ghosts.

Blood, on the other hand, was real.

They'd had no luck trying to find the person who'd bled in the crypt. As for the boss's contribution – that was the warning they'd all missed.

Boyd wondered if the boss knew his life had sat on a knife edge. Maybe that was why he'd made up the story of the girl – the daughter he'd never had. Perhaps the old man just wanted one last chance to make things right.

The pathology report had stated that the brain aneurysm that killed Cameron had been developing for some time. He would have experienced all the symptoms; light-headedness, rapid heartbeat, nose bleeds and finally a massive drop in blood pressure as it burst.

Detective Inspector Boyd sat for a minute in the darkness of his office. Everyone else had gone. He picked up the phone and called home. After a few moments Bev answered.

"What's wrong?"

"Nothing," Boyd said, happy just to hear her voice.

Bev lay on her right side, her swollen breasts leaking through the T-shirt. She was sound asleep, her breath coming in small puffs. Boyd went to the cot and looked in at the other male in Bev's life,

the one who had stolen those breasts. The lips were puckered from
sucking, eyes moving behind blue lids.

"I know what you're dreaming about," Boyd whispered.

The eyes flickered open, a tiny fist thrust the air. Bev stirred in
response as though the two were still attached, umbilical cord
unbroken.

Boyd offered his finger. At his touch, the fist fastened round him.
Boyd was amazed at its strength.

He undressed and got into bed, gathering his wife in his arms. Bev
pressed against him, damp, smelling of milk. Boyd kissed her hair,
her eyes, her mouth.

THE TURNIP FARM

Allan Guthrie

L ESTER CLOSED THE gate, stepped into the field, wiped his brow with the back of his hand. Sweat glistened in the creases of his skin. He wiped his hands, front and back, on the legs of his dungarees.

It was only five o'clock but already Lester could tell it was going to be a hot one. Yep, by doodly, he'd better do it now rather than chance it later during the heat of the day.

Decision made, he felt his dangle stir. He gazed at the dozens of rows of turnips poking through the soil like a field of breasts, round and firm and ripe, and his dangle stirred some more.

He glanced around. Nothing moved apart from a couple of crows gliding in the thermals above the barn. Back in the cottage, everyone was still asleep.

Lester dropped to his knees, reached down, brushed surface dirt off a pair of fine wee beauties and placed them in the palms of his hands. He grasped them tightly, pressed against their fullness, and relaxed. Pressed and relaxed. As he kneaded the turnips, his breathing grew faster. He shifted, leaned forward, squeezed and stroked and tugged and nipped. He drew circles with his thumbs on the skin of the turnips, whispering, "Like this? Oh, yeah." He squeezed and stroked again until his fingers were tired and the muscles in his thighs burned.

"Use my mouth? Okay."

He lay on his stomach and wrapped his lips around the sweet, bare turnip flesh, and sucked and licked and nibbled, first one turnip and then the other, until the earth beneath him moaned.

"You want me to touch you there? In a minute." He liked to tease.

When his lips were numb and his tongue was raw, he gently placed his fingers between the turnips and traced a line in the soil towards his belly, stopping only when he felt the earth under his fingers part. He prodded and pushed until his fingers sank inside a delicious softness, the soil still moist from yesterday's spurts of rain. His fingers stiffened and he thrust them deep into the welcoming shaft that wrapped around his skin, clinging to him as he probed deeper and deeper, his fingers throbbing like over-excited hearts about to explode.

He was about to unzip himself when something caught his eye. He squinted. It was Sheena, his tractor, the shiny jealous ring of her exhaust pipe glinting in the sun. This is where his fumble with the turnips ended. Sheena wanted him inside her. She wanted him to ride her hard and fast, up and down the field, in and out of the turnips, harder and faster, engine roaring and screaming, until she shuddered, finally, to a furious climax, and came to rest by the gate, spent.

That's what he did most mornings and he'd have done it again today if his oldest brother, Anne, hadn't shouted at him from Mum's bedroom window, "Lester, come up here. We've got a problem."

* * *

It was still early, and Lester was surprised that Anne was up, but he saw right away when he stepped into Mum's bedroom that she hadn't budged from her usual position. Lester couldn't remember the last time he'd seen her out of bed. When their dad had got ill, she'd watched them move him into the barn, and then she'd sunk between the covers and stayed there.

Lester supposed she must have got up to go to the bathroom now and then, but he'd never seen her do it. And she didn't have to get up to eat cause Lester's youngest brother, Bamber, brought her food that he'd caught himself in his traps and prepared in the kitchen. He wasn't a bad cook, but all he'd cook was meat. Lester liked to prepare the vegetables, but the rest of the family were often reluctant to let him. They'd seen what he'd done with a carrot once, a long thick one. Walked in on him on his back on the table with his pants down and his legs in the air. Wasn't his fault. He was only human, with human desires.

Mum was in bed but she was awake. Sitting up, propped up against the pillows. Petey, one of Lester's other brothers, had his back to her, facing the wall, and his body shook under the covers. Made a change that the pair of them weren't curled up together. They were always giggling. Lester used to giggle too, but not for a while.

Dad would have been mad if he'd seen them, Mum and Petey. He was mad when he saw his friend, Alf, between the sheets with Mum. He'd shot Alf and then fed him to the pigs. Course, they didn't have the pigs any longer, not since animal welfare had visited. Lester missed the pigs. He liked how they snuffled and squealed and how sometimes they looked like they were smiling.

Anne stroked his beard and looked round the room.

"What's going on?" Lester said.

Petey snuffled.

"Waiting on Bamber," Anne said.

"Want me to fetch him?" Lester said.

Anne shook his head. "He knows we're meeting here. We'll wait."

They waited, fidgeting, listening to Petey's slavering sobbing noises.

When Bamber finally appeared an hour or so later, he was carrying a tray with steaming plates of food on it. "Sorry I'm late," he said. "But I thought you might be hungry."

They all tucked in, except for Petey, who ignored everybody and groaned now and then. Mum had Petey's, along with her own.

"Very good," Lester said to Bamber. Rabbit. Would have been better with potatoes, though. Potatoes in their skins. Lester enjoyed peeling the skin back and nuzzling the exposed potato underneath.

After Lester had finished licking his plate, he turned to Anne. "What did you want us all here for?" he asked.

Anne rose to his full height of six foot eight and bit his lip. "Mum," he said. "You better tell Lester and Bamber the news."

Mum looked a little worried. Her hair looked even wispier than usual and her bald patch seemed larger. She looked more worried when the bed began to shake with Petey's sobs. She slid down the bed and out of sight under the covers.

Anne sighed. "It's Dunlop." Dunlop was their nearest neighbour. He lived four miles away, called himself a farmer but he just rented out his land and lived off the proceeds. Didn't even own his own tractor. "He's asked her to marry him."

Lester felt the undigested meat in his stomach come alive. He looked at Bamber and Bamber shook his head sadly. "No," Lester said. "She can't, by doodly. Dunlop's not right in the head." He'd never been the same since Ruby, his daughter, got her tongue pierced. After the accident, Dunlop had started to talk to himself, not like normal folk, but whole conversations. And not just one side either as if he was talking to an imaginary friend. With Dunlop, you got both sides.

"Mum," Anne said. He walked over to the bed, prodded the figure huddled under the covers where her head might be. "Mum. Tell them."

"I'll tell them," Petey yelled, throwing off the bedclothes, and rolling out of bed with his fence post that hadn't left his side for nigh on four years now. "I'll tell them," he repeated, his dangle waggling as he shook the post. "She only went and said yes."

"But she can't," Lester said. "Mum, you can't. What about Dad?"

"Why don't we go ask him?" Bamber suggested.

* * *

Dad lived in the barn. Well, most of him did. When he'd taken ill a while back, he'd cut off one of his arms and a foot with a machete. Anne had said measles could do that to you, but Lester wasn't convinced it was measles.

Anne had patched him up pretty good, anyway, and you could hardly tell the arm had been sewn on again. Pup, the dog, had got to the foot, though, and eaten most of it. Bamber had given what was left to the girl who lived in the cupboard under the stairs to play with and Pup ran away soon afterwards and hadn't been seen since.

Dad hardly spoke these days. All a bit of a trauma for him. He just sat in his chair in the middle of the barn, head slumped to the side, jaw hanging open. They'd tied him to the chair for his own protection. Didn't want him trying to hurt himself again.

"I think he might be dead," Bamber said.

Anne smacked Bamber with the back of his hand.

"Ow," Bamber said. "I'm just saying."

"Well, don't," Anne said. "He's clearly not dead."

"He looks dead, that's all I'm saying."

"What happens to dead people, Bamber?"

"I don't know," Bamber said. "They stop moving?"

"And?"

"They stop breathing?"

"And?"

"I don't know."

"They go to Heaven," Lester said.

"Exactly," Anne said. "And where's Dad? Right here."

"So he can't be dead," Lester said. "Right?"

"But when we had the pigs," Bamber said, "they didn't go anywhere when they died."

"Cause they're pigs," Anne said. "Pigs don't go to Heaven, stupid."

Petey rubbed his eyes. "Mum can't marry Dunlop if Dad's not dead."

"That's right."

Petey smiled. "So that means everything's okay."

"Far from it," Anne said. "If Dunlop and Mum are planning on getting married, it can only mean one thing."

They all looked at him, waiting.

He coughed, stretched, coughed again. "They're planning on killing Dad."

"Wow," Lester said.

"Mum wouldn't do that," Petey said, clutching his fence post to his chest.

"No," Lester said. "But Dunlop would. Lightning strikes your daughter's tongue stud and kills her, it's sure to drive you batty. And batty people get up to all sorts of evil."

"So what are we going to do?" Anne said.

They were silent for a moment. Then Bamber spoke up. "I have an idea," he said. "How about we hire a hitman?"

"Brilliant," Anne said. "Anybody know any hitmen?"

* * *

Anne and Lester went into the village the next day and asked around. Bit of a wasted journey, since nobody at the post office or the shop was able to help. Lester suggested they try the pub.

There were six people inside, not including them or Domenic, the barman, who'd left home a few years ago when he was still called Susan. He asked how Mum and Dad were and Lester asked if he could see Domenic's Teflon rod again that he slipped inside his dangle to make it stiff, and Domenic showed him, and then they ran out of conversation. So Anne and Lester played some darts while they knocked back a few pints.

After an hour or so, one of the blokes at the table nearest them challenged Anne to a game.

Lester let them get on with it, went to empty his bladder.

There was a guy in the toilet with a monkey. "Hello," the guy said.

"Hello," Lester said.

"I hear you're looking for a hitman."

"Hang on," Lester said. "I'll go fetch my brother."

* * *

The hitman followed them back to the farm in his Mini.

"Nice guy," Lester said.

Anne grunted.

"Don't you think he looks like Mum with a moustache?" Lester said.

Anne grunted again.

"What's the matter?" Lester asked.

"That monkey," Anne said. "Don't trust it."

* * *

Lester grabbed Bamber out of the kitchen, dragged Petey out of Mum's bed, and led them to the barn where the hitman was pointing at the monkey who'd jumped on to Dad's lap.

"I've killed over a thousand people," the hitman was saying. "I should know when someone's dead."

"You would think so," Anne said. "Makes me doubt your thingumabobs."

"My what?"

"You know. Makes me doubt you can do what you say you can do."

"I've never been doubted," the hitman said. "I take great exception to that comment. Your father's definitely dead."

Anne smacked him with the back of his hand.

"Ow," he said.

"Watch your monkey," Lester said.

The monkey had been playing with Dad's flies. Pulling the zip down, and chattering, pulling it back up, chattering. He'd pulled it down again, grinned and stuck his little fist inside.

Lester said, "He's going too far."

The hitman rubbed his cheek, looked at the monkey and yelled at it. It yanked its hand out of Dad's pants and leapt on to the floor and scurried away into the corner, out of sight behind the large freezer that Dad used to climb inside when the weather was too warm.

"He's not dead," Anne said.

"Right," the hitman said, still rubbing his cheek. "I want ten grand. Half now, half later."

"I don't know," Anne said. "We're a bit strapped."

"Eight, then."

"Well..."

"Six."

"I don't know..."

"Five?"

"Okay," Anne said. "How about we give you a hundred and fifty quid now and the rest when it's done."

"What do you think?" the hitman said, looking over to the monkey.

The monkey jumped on top of the freezer, screeched, then chattered its way over to the hitman and whispered something in his ear.

"It's a deal," the hitman said.

They all shook hands with the hitman. And then they all shook hands with the monkey. And then they all shook hands with each other.

Then they stood around, looking at one another and shuffling their feet.

The hitman said, after a while, "So where's my down payment?"

"Go fetch the cheque book," Anne told Bamber.

"I want cash," the hitman said.

"Don't have any," Anne said. "Leave cash lying around this place, one of these fellas'd nick it soon as look at it."

That wasn't true. But what was true was that they didn't have much money. They had heavy loan repayments, and it was hard to make a living growing turnips, in any case.

Bamber left to fetch the cheque book.

"So you've done a thousand hits?" Lester said.

"Yep. At least."

"You and the monkey?"

"Yep. Well, he's probably done more than me."

"Yeah?" Anne said.

"I just go along to help, usually," the hitman said. "He's the one who pulls the trigger. In fact, I've never actually killed anyone. No need. He's happy to do the dirty work."

"Isn't he scared of the noise?" Petcy asked.

"Nah," the hitman said. "He uses a .22. Delicate little piece. Sounds no louder than a cap gun." He looked at his watch. "We have to go soon."

"Another job?"

"Nah. Got my dance class tonight."

"You dance?"

"Oh, yeah." He showed them. Nifty piece of footwork ending up with a 360-degree turn. The monkey applauded, so they joined in. "You want to see some more?"

* * *

An hour later and the hitman had well and truly missed his dance class. But he seemed happy enough that he'd had the chance to entertain them and he'd forgotten about (or forgiven) the slap on the cheek. And the truth was, he was extremely good at dancing. All that spinning around and never once getting dizzy. Apparently, so he told them, it was all in the way you twisted your head to the side, focused on a particular spot, and let your body turn.

Like Petey had said, if the hitman was as good at killing people as he was at dancing, Dunlop didn't stand a chance.

Anne wrote the hitman his cheque and handed it over.

"If you don't cough up the rest when I'm done," the hitman said, "I'll have that fine-looking tractor I saw out in the turnip field."

Lester stiffened. Nobody was getting their hands on his tractor. "You'll get the money," he said. "When are you going to do it?"

The hitman looked at his watch. "Well," he said. "I've no other plans for the rest of the night."

* * *

"What are we going to do?" Lester asked, after he'd gone. "He'll be back for his money later."

"What do you mean?" Anne asked.

"We don't have any. He'll take my tractor."

"It's not yours," Bamber said. "It belongs to all of us."

"He's not getting it," Lester said.

Anne stroked his beard. "I don't know that we have any choice."

* * *

Lester went back in the house and knocked on the door of the cupboard under the stairs.

The girl who lived in there opened it. She was about nine, wore clothes that were far too big for her, the sleeves of her jumper hanging over her wrists, trouser legs flapping over her feet.

"What?" she said.

"I want to borrow your shotgun," Lester said.

She tilted her head, licked her lips. "Why?"

"Doesn't matter."

"What're you going to do with it?"

"Please just let me borrow it."

She stood there, hands on her hips. "You know what happened the last time I leant it to someone."

That was the time Dad had found Alf in bed with Mum.

"So?" Lester said.

"You going to shoot someone too?"

"Maybe."

"I can't let you do that."

Lester stared at her. "But this guy, he's going to take my tractor," he said.

"Oh," the girl said. "Oh, dear." She pouted. "That's probably for the best, don't you think?" Then she swivelled on the balls of her feet and closed the door.

* * *

When the hitman returned, about eleven, he was covered in blood, and alone. They all went out to meet him. He climbed out of his Mini and they all wandered over to the barn together.

"Is it done?" Anne asked, once they were inside.

"Crazy coot, that Dunlop," the hitman said. "You people never told me. Just kept talking to himself."

"Is he dead?" Petey asked.

The hitman was out of breath. He held up a hand, then said, "Yeah."

"Where's the monkey?" Bamber asked.

Lester was glad Bamber had asked. He wanted to know too but was afraid of what the answer might be.

"Didn't make it," the hitman said, lowering his eyes. "Dunlop did something to him. He said, 'What are you doing here?' 'Oh, I've come to kill you.' 'That's nice. Why?' 'I don't know, it's what I do.' 'But you're a monkey.' 'And?' 'You shouldn't be shooting people. In fact, you shouldn't be talking like this.' 'I'll talk how I like,' the monkey said. And fired his first shot. Wide. The second got Dunlop in the leg. Dunlop said, 'You're a freak of nature.' 'I'm a monkey.' 'A monkey freak.' The third shot got Dunlop between the eyes and that was him.

But the monkey wasn't finished. He looked at me and I told him no, he wasn't a freak, but he didn't believe me. He put the gun in his mouth and squeezed the trigger. That's how I got covered in all this crap."

"Bit of a mess, right enough," Anne said.

"Sorry about your monkey," Bamber told him.

"Never mind that," the hitman said. "Where's my money?"

Anne ran a hand through his hair, looked at Lester. Then away. "Don't have it. You'll have to take the tractor."

"Fine," he said.

But it wasn't fine. It wasn't fine at all.

Lester lunged towards Petey. Grabbed the fence post from him and swung it down, two-handed, on the hitman's head. There was a thunk and the hitman reeled. Lester whacked him again. And again. The hitman dropped to his knees and groaned. Lester hit him again. Kept pounding his skull with the fence post.

Thunk.

Thunk.

Thunk.

When Lester's arms hurt too much, he stopped.

Nobody spoke for a while.

Then Petey said, "Can I have it back?"

Lester held out the fence post. It was covered in blood, and bits of hair and scalp were stuck to it.

Petey started to cry.

Lester said, "He's not getting my tractor."

"No," Anne said. "He's not."

Anne took the hitman's arms and Bamber took his legs and they carried him over to the freezer. Lester helped them lift him inside.

When they closed the lid, it was as if nothing had changed.

"You okay?" Anne asked.

* * *

Lester got up at 4.30 the next morning. He washed, brushed his teeth, dressed, and was outside by 4.45. The sky was cloudy and drops of rain fell on his face.

In the field, the turnips poked through the soil like rows of naked scalps. He didn't want to touch them. Didn't want to go anywhere near them.

He tiptoed through the field towards his tractor. He opened the door, climbed inside the cab.

He sat there, shaking.

Then he got out again and ran back into the house. He stopped outside the cupboard under the stairs and thought about asking the girl once again if he could borrow her shotgun. But he walked on, upstairs, into his mum's bedroom where he took his clothes off and climbed into bed beside her and Petey.

Mum woke up, stroked his hair.

Birds chirped, Petey snored, and his mum kept stroking his hair.

Lester thought he might stay here for a long, long time.

AS GOD MADE US

A. L. Kennedy

D AN NEVER EXPLAINED why he woke up so early, or what it was that made him leave the flat. Folk wouldn't get it if he told them, so he didn't tell. He'd just head off out there and be ready for the pre-light, the dayshine you could see at around 4 a.m. – something about 4 at this point in the year – he'd be under that, stood right inside it. Daily. Without fail. Put on the soft shoes, jersey, tracky bottoms and the baseball cap and then off down the stairs to his street. His territory. Best to think of it as his – this way it was welcoming and okay.

He'd lean on the railings by number 6 and listen and settle his head, control it, and watch the glow start up from the flowers someone had planted in these big round-bellied pots, ceramic pots with whole thick fists of blossom in them now: a purple kind and a crimson, and both shades luminous, really almost sore with brightness, especially when all else was still dim. They only needed a touch of dawn and they'd kick off, blazing. Dan liked them. Loved them. He would be sorry when they went away.

Since the birds would be more of a constant, he made sure he loved them as well: their first breaks of song across the stillness, the caution and beauty in signals that hid their location, became vague and then faded as you hunted them. He thought there was practically nothing so fine as feeling their secrets pass round him and do no harm and he'd let himself wish to hook out the notes with his fingers like smooth, hot stones: little pebbles with a glimmer he could easily hold, could picture putting in his pockets, saving them. He'd imagine they might rattle when he walked: his weight landing and swinging and landing in the way it did, the only way it could, providing enough clumsiness to jar them. Or maybe they'd call out again when they took a knock, maybe that would happen. In his head, anything could happen – it was freedom in there: big horizons and fine possibilities, that kind of balls – and chirping whenever he moved would be nice. So Dan would have it. He'd insist.

The other noises Dan could do without – there were too many of them and they were too much. They came in at him off the bare walls in his new digs, rebounded and propagated among the landlord's efforts at furniture. He'd to put up with clatters and small impacts – perhaps impacts – and vehicles – engines, metal sounds – and shouting and murmuring: voices that might be planning, that could have a bad intent, and footfalls: creeping, dashes, jogging. Fox screams were the worst – they sounded like bone pain and being lost, losing.

Caught in the house, you could not assess your situation, could neither prepare nor react – you were held in an impermissible state. Being caught at the railings wasn't as bad. Standing there you would realize that you were naked: no cover, no recourse: and so you would send a ghost of yourself running down to the basement door – send this lump from your thoughts that would chase and then lie out flat in the shadows you've seen at the foot of the steps. It could hide there, your mind between it and any harm. It could even curl up like a child, like a hiding boy, while you mother it, father it, let it be secure. The rest of you, which was the part that was real and existed and knew what's appropriate: that part could stay where it was and be firm – nothing going wrong – and could appreciate a mercy was taking place, a chance of survival all over again, and a measure to show your recovery's success.

This kind of trick in his thinking was needed because, as had been previously and very often discussed with professionals of several kinds, he was a brave bastard – the brave bastards being the ones who were shitting themselves and did what they had to, anyway.

He managed.

He'd begun to use earplugs when it was night. He'd be snug in his pit by ten and the covers up over his head – which made him hot, but then again he'd been hotter and covers up over would let him sleep – and the plugs would be in and packing his skull with the racket of being alive: swallowing and a background thrum – like he had engines and they were running – and his breath pacing back and forth and keeping as restless as you'd want it, keeping on.

Sometimes the press of the foam would make his ears hurt, or start to tickle, but that he could tolerate. Putting in the right one was very slightly awkward. Could be worse, though – could be having to sew on a button as part of his personal maintenance, or peeling potatoes, or that whole palaver of taking a crap – which, these days, he really noticed how often he did, even though he'd cut back on eating potatoes, obviously – except for chips from the chipper, from Frying Tonite, which were made by either Doris, or Steve, who was her other son, the one who wasn't dead. Those things were personally developmental and necessary tasks. They were interesting challenges in his reconstructed life. They were fucking pains in the arse.

When he's together with the lads he doesn't much mention such details because they are obvious and aren't important, not like they seem when he's alone.

"Oh, the many, many pains in young Daniel's delicate arse … But on the other hand … "

"On the other hand – Aaw … look, I dropped it."

"Well, fucking pick it up again, hands are expensive."

Once every month they swim together: six gentlemen sharing a leisurely day. They choose whoever's turn it is to be host, fire off the emails, travel however far, and then rendezvous at a swimming baths and christen the Gathering.

They call it that because of the movies with the Highlander in, the ones with everybody yelling at each other – there can be only one – and mad, immortal buggers slicing off each other's heads with these massive swords.

You have only got the one head and shouldn't lose it.

For this Gathering they'll do the usual: swimming in the morning and then a big lunch and then getting pissed and then going back to Gobbler's place, because this was his turn, and eating all his scran and some carry-out and then watching DVDs of their films and

getting more pissed and maybe some porn and maybe not. They'd
tried going to clubs in the early days – strip clubs, lap dancing – and
one night in Aberdeen they'd gone to a neat, wee semi full of prossies
– foreign prossies in fact, prossies from Moldova – but that never
worked out too well. Porn was better sometimes.

In the baths everything is standard, predictable, doesn't matter
what pool they come to. First there's the push or the pull on heavy
doors and that walk into a thump of hot air – stuns your breath – and
then chlorine smell and kiddie smell and there'll be that knowledge
of a space nearby, light and high with the huge tearing windows – the
windows will take out at least the one wall – and all of that water
trapped underneath the airiness, that pressure and weight.

Dan and the others, they'll start mucking about, getting wound
up by the anticipation of effort – flailing themselves from one place
to another, hither and yon – the idea of fitness, applicable force –
and more mucking about.

"Hey! Salt and vinegar!" Gobbler is shouting at Dan. Gobbler
with an accent that is east of Scotland and Dan who sounds west –
sounds, he supposes, like he's from Coatbridge, because he is.
Gobbler is from salt and sauce land and Dan is from salt and vinegar.
On occasion, they set out the subtleties of this to the others.

"Gobbler's from the heathen side – they put salt and sauce on
their chips."

"Jockanese bastards – everything's spuds with you. Like the
bloody Micks." Frank dodges in with this, yelling – sounds like he's
near to Gobbler, out of sight behind a row of changing cubicles.
"How long are you meant to live, anyway, on fried Mars bars and
fried pizza and fried fucking pies?"

"About till we're twenty." Dan remembers the trip they had to
Kettering – which is where Frank has settled. It's a wee, grey hoor
of a place. "Twenty years in Kettering, that'd feel like eighty. I'd
top myself."

The lot of them of them shouting back and forth at each other,
scattered in the room, while they change and are overexcited and
Dan thinks of being at school and how that was: swimming days
with rubbish pals – pals who weren't pals at all – and not wanting

to get undressed, being scared that he'd maybe sink this time, choke, scared of standing in nothing but trunks and somebody picking him out, starting something, having a go, and then the teachers coming in to the troublemakers and saying they had to behave and this being a relief to Dan, but also shaming – he knew it wasn't right, that he should sort his own problems, but couldn't. He'd been shy then and not aware of his potential and people could miss things in children – this happens constantly, he's certain – and even if an adult might try to be helpful, they might not do it a good way. Not enough care is taken. He worries for kids quite often. He wonders how they get through. He is extremely concerned that each possible kid should get through. He considers doing voluntary work with youngsters.

Dan as a youngster, he'd got his head down and tried to be correct, quiet and correct, tucked himself out of sight inside the rules. It was two years back, three, since he'd left that stuff – such a long while. He'd not forgotten, though – how he'd been useless.

Gobbler is hammering on the lockers between him and Dan and asking, bellowing, "You got your kit off yet?" Gobbler who had another name in other times and places, when he was with other Gobblers, but now he is by himself and not in a regiment, so he is the Gobbler – he is the representative of his type. "Oh, Danny Boy … You having trouble?"

No one will come in and tell them they have to do anything today. They will misbehave.

"Piss off."

"Your pants are removed over the feet, remember – not over the head. Poor bloody Paras, you do get confused."

"Fuck off." And they are none of them useless.

"Are you naked yet, though, Danny? Getting hard just thinking about it." Gobbler rattles something that sounds metallic and laughs. "And here's old Fez, living up to his name … a dapper and fragrant man. Your heady aroma, sir, reminds me of those lovely evenings back at the mess when I ran the naked bar."

A few strangers are in here too, but they are minding their own business. Mostly. Dan catches one of them giving him a walty look, in fact, the most perfectly walty look he's met: that civilian mix of need and disgust, someone who thinks he might like being scared, but wouldn't want the whole real deal, not a bit – wants to flirt, not end up being fucked. Dan stares at him while shouting back to Gobbler, shouting hard so that spittle leaves him, so that his heartbeat wakes.

"Bollocks!" "Exactly. And where there's boliocks..." "Don't start." "There's the mighty Gobbler javelin of Spam. You know when I get hard now—" Everyone joining in here, because they know the words, "It looks like I've got two dicks."

Gobbler's left leg gone from above the knee – which is called a transfemoral amputation – this allowing him to repeatedly assert a lie that keeps him merry, or relatively so. There are six of them today: Gobbler, Petey, Fezman, Jason, Frank and Dan. That's two transfemoral – one with a transtibial to match – an elbow disarticulation, a transradial, a double wrist disarticulation – Frank's been hopeless at knitting ever since – and then there's Dan: he's a right foot disarticulation and a right arm transhumeral – roughly halfway between the elbow and the shoulder – the elbow which is not there any more and the shoulder which is – the elbow which Dan still feels – the elbow which is frequently wet: warm and wet, like it was when he last saw it. This is another variety of repeatedly asserted lie.

"Here we go, then. Where'd you get the trunks from, Fezman?" This from Jason who's hidden by the lockers nearest the exit.

"Girlfriend."

"Got the DILAC trunks from his girlfriend, everyone."

When they move out for the main event, Jason will be on one side of Petey and Fezman will be on the other. They will cradle him, but won't talk about it. They will look mainly straight ahead. They will halt when they get to the footbath and threaten to dip in Petey's arse. This will make them laugh.

"He doesn't have a bloody girlfriend." Gobbler again – a man who's fond of the chat, who probably was the same before.

Jason answers him from the footbath, "Ah, but he's definitely got the trunks."

"Got it the wrong way round again, Fez, you minging big window-licker. You want to have the girlfriend and fuck the trunks."

"No. I want to fuck the girlfriend and have the trunks."

They're all giggling, Dan can hear from every side, pissing them-selves over nothing, letting themselves get daft, because that's what they want.

Gobbler's all set now for his own trip to the poolside. So, "Come and get it then, you big Marys."

Gobbler calls for him exactly as Dan drops his locker key, has to reach it back up, pin it to his trunks without stabbing anything precious. He removes his foot before swimming. In the thickness of the water he can feel he doesn't know it isn't there, but meanwhile he grabs on to the lockers to make his way, works himself round the houses in hops and sways like he does at home.

The other two are waiting by the time he reaches them.

Then Dan and Frank and Gobbler huddle up and start to stumble themselves along – four feet between them out of the possible six.

"Mind where you put your hand, ducky. None of that 3 Para Mortar Platoon stuff here." Gobbler sways them too close to a wall and then back.

Dan isn't much of a talker except out on the Gatherings. "Make your bloody mind up, Gobbler." The rest of the time he'll maybe ask for his stop on a bus, or say something mumbly and stupid to Doris at the chipper, because she wants him to be guilty and he agrees. Probably in her mind she has the truth that there's a set amount of death and what missed Dan found someone else. She misunderstands the working of that truth, but he won't help her to figure it out. It's none of her business. "Are you scared that we're gay, or are you just worried about yourself ?" And Dan maybe does eat more chips than he should. "Because we've always thought you were a fudge packer." He could give them a bye and not have to meet her again. "Didn't want to say so in case you got upset." Except she needs him to be there, he can feel that. "You'll just end up crying and then your mascara'll run." He needs it, too.

Frank listens and smiles down at a skinny coffin-dodger who's folding his kecks on the bench nearest to them and trying to act invisible. Frank enunciates very clearly past Gobbler's ear, "I can give you a special handjob, help you decide – clear all your pipework." He waggles his free stump and winks. "Just bend over and kiss Danny's ring."

They stagger on, holding tight, and under other circumstances it might simply be that they're drunk already and out somewhere late at night – it might be there's years not happened yet and they've some other reason for being mates.

Hospital – great place to meet folk, get new mates. Get proper pals. Once they're out at the pool, Dan breathes in warm and wet and is harmed by the sharp light and the din from the kids, hard noises.

A school party's here, maybe a couple – lots of primary-age heads and bodies – the water's splitting and heaving with them – all polystyrene floats and nervous piss.

Dan is aware they could prove to have an overwhelming nature, could defeat him, and he never does handle this bit too well. The panic is up and in him before he can jump and be ears full of water, wrapped by it and washed and free. He concentrates on being glad of Frank and Gobbler: the carrying, discomfort, distraction.

And he knows that once he's swimming he'll be fine. These days he goes on his back and is quite accomplished, purposeful, almost steers in the directions he intends.

"Nearly there, then."

"Well, I had actually guessed that, you mong – cos of the fucking pool being right fucking here." Gobbler shifts his weight and they stagger to the edge faster than intended.

Dan makes a point of exhaling and starting to grin. He is about to improve himself. He has grasped the theory, read the leaflets – people like him need a way to ignore their reminders, the signs of wounding which are their obvious and inconvenient new shape. His body is not an aid to mental rehabilitation. So he swims, makes everything glide and be jolly. This means he'll improve faster. But never as fast as he would without his injuries. That's a medical fact – if he still had his foot and the rest of his arm, he'd be finding life much better than he is.

He frowns, brings his thinking forward, peers ahead of his skin and his skull to the spot where Pete is already bobbing, hand at rest on the side and frowning up at a woman who is pacing and speaking to Fezman and Jason. They are both still dry and standing on the tiles, Fezman in these mad, knee-length trunks like he's going to play football in the 1920s but with Day-Glo palm trees and dolphins and surf on them. You can tell he fancies himself in them and they're new. They maybe are from a girlfriend.

The speaking woman is round-shouldered and wears a blouse and a long skirt so tight it almost stops her walking, only this isn't good because she has no arse, no pleasantness to see. When she angles herself and faces Dan, he ends up looking right at the curve of her little belly and her little mound and he doesn't want to. They make him sad. Everything about her is sad – browny grey and bloody depressing – hair, clothes, shoes that she clips and quarter-steps along in – and Dan can tell she's a teacher, because she's got that fake cheerful thing about her mouth and darty little eyes that are tired and want to find mistakes. Every now and then, her lips thin together and it gets obvious that her job has gone badly for her, and probably also her life. And here she is taking her class for swimming lessons on a Tuesday afternoon – for safety and fitness and possibly something else that she can't quite control. Dan is of the opinion that she should not have any kind of care over children.

"Excuse me." The teacher doesn't speak to Dan, although she has left the others and drawn really near to him. She's maybe only in her forties, but he notices she smells of old lady.

"Excuse me." She focuses on Gobbler. "I realize you've been here, that you come here quite often…" She swallows and angles her head away, starts seriously watching the children – you'd think they were going to catch on fire, or something – not that she'd be any use to save them. "And I've explained you to them, but now—"

"What d'you say, love?" Gobbler interrupts her and his arm around Dan flexes. "You've explained…?"

"Yes, I could explain you to them."

Gobbler's arm getting ready for something, thoughts roaring about inside it, Dan can hear them.

"Don't know what you mean though, love. How you'd explain me. What you'd be explaining." Gobbler is nearly giggling which the woman shouldn't think is him being friendly, because Dan knows he's not. "Is that like I need translating? Like I'm a foreign language, because that's not it – British me, British to the core."

Dan wanting to clear off out of it, avoid, and also wanting to do what he must, what he does – he goes along with the lads: Fezman, Frank, Jason, even Petey in the water, they close up alongside Gobbler, make a curvy sort of line, and they watch the woman regret herself, but still think she's in the right. "It's the children – I know you can't help it – but they get upset."

Dan's voice out of him before he realizes, "They don't look upset."

"One of the girls was crying."

"They look fine. Splashing away and happy. I mean, they do. I wouldn't say it, if they weren't."

She tries going at Gobbler again which is unwise and Dan wonders how she managed to qualify, even get to be a teacher, when she is this thick and this shit at understanding a situation. "I told them you were as God made you."

"What?"

"But with so many… it isn't your fault, but you must see that you're disturbing." Her hands waver in front of her, as if she can't quite bear to point at them. "You are disturbing. I'm sorry, but you are." She nods. "There must be places you can go to where you'd be more comfortable." Her fingers take hold of her wrists and cling.

And the lads don't speak. She stays standing there and hasn't got a fucking clue. And the lads don't speak. Dan can tell that she has no idea they're deciding to be still, to be the nicest they can be, working up to it by deciding they will mainly forget her and what she's said and who they are.

And the lads don't speak.

She gives them a disapproving face, touch of impatience.

And Fezman nods, thoughtful, and says – he's very even, gentle with every word – says to her, "These are new trunks. I like these trunks. They are DILAC trunks, which you don't understand." He presses his face in mildly, mildly towards her, "They are Do I Look

A Cunt in these trunks? trunks and I am going to swim in them this morning. And you look a cunt and you are a cunt, you are an utter cunt and I am sorry for this, but you should know and you should maybe go away and try being different and not a cunt, but right here, right now – a cunt – you're a cunt. You are a cunt." He nods again, slowly, and turns his face to the water and the girls and boys.

Dan watches while the woman stares and her head jumps, acts like they've spat at her, or grabbed her tits and his gone arm trembles the same way that Gobbler's does and he wants to run, can't run, wants to – wants to throw up.

The woman kind of freezes for a moment and then takes a little, hobbled step and then another, everything unsteady, leaves them.

The lads wait.

Dan sees when she reaches the opposite wall and starts yakking to a guy in a DILAC suit, guy who's standing with a Readers' Wives type of bint – they're colleagues, no doubt, fellow educators. He decides that he has no interest in what may transpire.

Dan and the lads take a breath, the requisite steps, and drop themselves into the water. They join Petey. They swim – show themselves thrashing, ugly, wild.

Dan watches the ceiling tiles pass above him and has his anger beneath him, has it pushing at the small of his back, bearing him up. It wouldn't be useful anywhere else.

And he makes sure that he watches – regularly watches out – twists and raises his head and strains to see, makes sure that the kids have cleared out of his way, out of everyone's. He wants no accidents.

In his heart, though, in his one remaining heart, there is a depth, a wish that some morning there will be an accident: a frightened kid, scared boy, choking and losing his way. When this happens Dan will be there and will save him.

He practises in his head and in the water – the paths that his good arm will take, the grip, the strength he's already developed in his legs.

Once that's over it will mean he has recovered himself again – become a man who would rescue a boy, who would always intend and wish to do that – would not be any other man than the man who would do that, who would be vigilant, be a brave bastard and take care.

He never would have done the thing that he couldn't have. He never would have been the man he couldn't be. He never would.

No tricks of the darkness, no sounds in the pre-light, no panic, no confusion, no walking downstairs to find it, to see how it lies like it's frightened and shouldn't be hurt. No mistake.

There should be no mistake. There should be no mistake. There should be no mistake.

ROBERT HAYER'S DEAD

Simon Kernick

"**I** USED TO have a boy like you," the man said quietly. "A son. His name was Robert."

The kid didn't say anything, just kept his position, sitting on an upturned plastic bucket in the corner of the cellar. He was staring down at the bare stone floor, staring hard like it mattered. His naturally blond hair was a mess – all bunched and greasy – and his clothes, which were the usual early teen uniform of baggy jeans, white trainers, white football shirt, had a crumpled, grimy look like he'd been sleeping in them, which he had.

"I'm going to tell you about my son," continued the man whose name was Charles Hayer. He was standing five feet away from the boy, watching him intently, his face tight and lined with the anguish he felt at recounting the story. "He was all I ever had. You know that? Everything. His mother and me, we were still together but things between us...well, y'know, it just wasn't right. Hadn't been for a long time. We'd been married getting on for twenty years, and the spark, the love, whatever you want to call it, it had just gone. You're too young to understand but that's sometimes the way it goes between a man and a wife. You'll find out one day."

"Will I?" asked the kid, still not looking up. No obvious fear in the voice. More resignation.

Charles Hayer gave the kid a paternal smile that the kid missed. "Sure you will," he said. "But you've got to listen to me first. The fact is, Robert was my life. He was a good kid, he never hurt anyone, and he was everything a father would ever want in a child.

"Then one day when he was thirteen years and two months old, they came and took him."

He paused. Waited. The kid said nothing. The kid *knew*.

Hayer continued. "There were three of them involved. The one driving the car was called Louis Belnay. He was forty-two and he had convictions going back to when he was in his mid teens. Bad convictions. The kind that get you segregated when they put you behind bars. He should have been locked up for life because everyone knew he was going to remain a constant danger to young boys, because he always had been, and even one of his psychiatrists said he was untreatable, but I suppose that's not enough for some people. And Belnay was no fool. He knew how to pull the wool over people's eyes. That's why he'd only ever done time twice, just a couple of years on each count, which isn't a lot considering he'd been a child molester for more than a quarter of a century.

"He didn't look like a child molester, though, that was the thing. They often say they don't. He just looked like a normal guy. One of his tricks if he didn't have a kid he knew to hand, and he needed to get hold of one, was to impersonate a police officer, a plainclothes guy. Flash the badge, call them over, and bingo, he was away. That's how he did it with my son. Robert was walking home from his friend's place – and we're talking about a walk of a hundred yards here – one night last summer. It was about a quarter past nine, and it wasn't even fully dark. Somewhere on that hundred yards, Louis Belnay pulled up beside him, flashed that false badge of his, and called Robert over. Robert was a trusting kid. He had no reason not to be. His mother and me had warned him about talking to strangers plenty of times but this guy was a cop, so of course it should have been no problem. He did as he was told and approached the vehicle, and while Belnay spoke to Robert, his accomplice came round the other side of the car, had a quick check round to see that the coast was clear, then bundled him in the back, putting a cloth soaked in chloroform over his face to make sure he stayed nice and quiet. The accomplice's name was Patrick Dean."

Hayer couldn't entirely suppress a shudder. Just repeating Dean's name aloud could do that to him. Always would now.

"Now some people say that child molesters can't help what they do, that they're diseased rather than wicked, and I don't know, maybe that's true for some of them. But not Dean. Dean was – is – just pure fucking evil. He just liked to hurt people, kids especially. It was a power trip to him, a way of showing how strong he was to the world, that nothing was sacred to him. If he was here with you now, he'd hurt you bad. Do things to you that you cannot even begin to imagine. Sexual things, painful ones. And he'd enjoy every minute of it too, right up to the moment he put his hands round your neck and squeezed, or put the knife across your throat."

The kid flinched. Hayer saw it. Like someone had threatened him with a slap. He still didn't look up. Hayer felt bad. He didn't like putting the kid through it, didn't like putting himself through it. But there was no other way. He had to *explain*.

"Dean was strong. Big too. Six-three and fifteen stone. That's why they used him for the physical stuff. That, and the fact that he didn't scare easily. Ten years ago, while he was in Brixton prison, serving time for some assault and molestation charges, he made a formal complaint to the governor about the way he was being treated. The guards doing the mistreatment warned him if he didn't drop the complaint, they'd stick him in with the general jail population and let him take his chances. He told them to go fuck themselves. They carried out their threat, he got the shit kicked out of him, but he still went through with the complaint. The guards ended up suspended, several of them lost their jobs, and he got released early even though he was what one detective called 'a walking timebomb'.

"And on that night, the walking timebomb met my son and Robert never stood a chance. He must have seen Dean coming round the car but because he thought he was a cop he didn't run. Maybe if he'd been a couple of years older he would have done, and I guess they counted on that. It was all over in seconds. One minute he was walking down the street minding his own business, looking forward to the holiday the three of us were going to be going to have in Spain the following week, the next he was unconscious in the back of a car, being driven away by two dangerous paedophiles who should never have been out on the streets in the first place. And no one saw a thing.

"I don't know how long he lived after that. I don't like to think about it, to tell you the truth. It's too much. Either way, they took him back to the home of the third guy, Thomas Barnes, and that's where they raped and killed him. Barnes said that the other two made him film it ... everything ... but the police never found the tape, so I don't know if he was telling the truth or not. But then, why would you lie about something like that?"

Hayer sighed. His throat was dry. He felt awkward standing there, looking down at a silent boy who was only a few months older than Robert had been on the night they'd taken him. Hayer wanted to cry again, to let his emotions do their work, if only because it would show the kid that he wasn't such a bad man – that he too felt pain – but no tears came out in the way they'd done on so many occasions before. It seemed like the well of sorrow and self-pity had finally run dry.

"After they'd finished with him, they cut up the body. Took off his legs, his arms, his head, and tried to burn the pieces separately. It didn't work properly – apparently the body fat melts and it acts to stifle the flames – so they ended up having to put everything in separate bin bags and dumping them at different sites. The bag containing one of his partially burned legs and a section of his torso was found washed up on a riverbank a couple of months later by a man walking his dog. Other parts turned up after that beside a railway line, and at a landfill site. But they never found his head. We had to bury him in pieces."

This time the kid did look up. His face was streaked with tears. "Listen, please. Why are you telling me all this? I don't want to hear it." His eyes were wide, imploring. Innocent.

Hayer's inner voice told him to be strong. "You have to hear it," he said firmly.

"But I don't ... "

"Just listen," snapped Hayer.

The kid stopped speaking. His lower lip began to quiver and his face crinkled and sagged with emotion. Robert had pulled an expression like that once. It had been after he'd broken an expensive vase while he'd been fooling about in the family kitchen. The vase had been a birthday present from Hayer to his wife, and on discovering what Robert had done, Hayer had blown his top on the boy, shouting so loudly that he could have sworn his son's hair was standing on end by the time he'd finished. But when Robert had pulled that powerless, defeated face, all the anger had fallen away to be replaced by guilt at his own unnecessary outburst. God knows, he hadn't wanted to hurt him. His only child. His dead and gone son.

"They found DNA on some of the bodyparts," he continued, his voice as dispassionate as he could manage under the circumstances. "The DNA belonged to Barnes, who was also a convicted child sex offender. Barnes was arrested, admitted his part in the death of my son, and expressed terrible regret. He also named Belnay and Dean as being involved.

"Belnay and Dean both went on the run but were caught quickly enough and charged with murder, as was Barnes. We buried what was left of our son and waited for some sort of closure with the trial. But of course we never got it. Because a man called Gabriel Mortish denied us that."

"Oh God," said the kid.

Hayer nodded. "Oh God, indeed. Gabriel Mortish QC, one of *the* best defence barristers in the country, well known for taking on the cases that no one else wants to touch. He's defended all sorts. Terrorists, serial killers, rapists. If you're one of the bad guys, he'll be there supporting your right to maim, torture and murder with everything he's got. If you've never done a thing wrong in your life, tried to treat others like you'd want to be treated yourself, then he's not interested in you. So, of course, it went without saying that Mortish took on the defence of Belnay and Dean. Not Barnes, because Barnes had shown some remorse for what he'd done, admitted that he'd played a part in it. That made him part-human and Mortish is only interested in helping out sub-humans.

"Belnay and Dean denied everything. Said it was nothing to do with them, but it came out that a neighbour remembered seeing the two of them leaving Barnes's house the day after Robert had disappeared, and when the police found the car used to abduct him, they found Belnay's DNA in that. But the two of them stuck to their story. Said that they knew Barnes, and had been round his house, but that that was the extent of their involvement. Instead, they blamed him, claiming that he'd been acting very erratically when they were round there, and came close to admitting that he'd been the one responsible for the abduction. But Barnes said it was the other way round. According to him, it was Dean doing the killing with Belnay encouraging him, and it was Dean who did the chopping up of the body afterwards."

Hayer sighed. "Your dad did a good job, son. I had to give him that. I watched him every day in that courtroom. He sowed doubt like it was a breeding rabbit, put it everywhere. Sure, he said, Belnay and Dean were not nice guys, no question of that, but were they guilty of this heinous crime? He said the evidence suggested strongly that they weren't. He made the neighbour, the witness who'd seen them leave Barnes's place, sound all confused about whether it was actually them she'd seen. Then Barnes got put on the witness stand and your dad wound him up in knots. Did he see Dean or Belnay kill Robert? If so, why didn't he try to stop it? Wasn't he just blaming them to take the heat off himself?"

Hayer sighed, addressing the kid directly now. "You know what happened? Course you do. Barnes ended up admitting that he hadn't seen either of them actually kill him, that he'd been out of the room at the time, but he came across like a shifty witness – someone you weren't going to believe. Your dad made him look like that. Your dad discredited the evidence to such an extent that Barnes, who didn't have him as a lawyer, got life for murder, but Belnay got away with seven years as an accessory. And Dean…" He spat the name this time. "The judge directed the jury to acquit him. Said the evidence against him just wasn't reliable. That was your dad's doing. He got one of them seven years, meaning the bastard'll be out in four, and the other – the one who was pure fucking evil, who cut my son into little pieces – he got him off. He walked free, and now he's living on the outside with police fucking protection, just to make sure that no one tries to take the law into their own hands and trample on his precious human rights, even though no one gave a shit about my son's human rights. He's even strode past this house a couple of times, just to fucking torment me. THAT IS NOT JUSTICE!" He shouted these last four words, shouted them at the non-existent heavens, his voice reverberating round the dull confines of the cellar.

The kid opened his mouth, started to say something, but Hayer was not to be interrupted. "That man ... your father destroyed me. He took away the last thing I had left: closure. A week after the trial, two months ago, Robert's mother and I split up. Neither of us could take any more. She's contacted a lawyer and the divorce'll be going through sometime soon. All I've got left is my job. Adding up numbers on one side of a page, taking them away on another."

"Please, I ... "

"Shut up. Just shut up. Listen to me." He paused for a moment, tried to calm himself down, knew it wouldn't happen. Not until he'd said his piece. "I can't stand my job, I can't stand what my life has become. I can't ... I can't stand fucking any of it, and that's why you're here. You've got to understand that. What those men did to Robert, what they stole from me, that half put me in the grave. What your dad did, what he did on behalf of bastards who do not deserve to even be alive let alone walking free, well that pushed me the rest of the way. I've got nothing left to lose now. That's why I snatched you. That's why you're here. Because I've got to make him suffer like I've suffered. It's the only way. Some people say two wrongs don't make a right, some people say that you can't stoop down to a bad man's level, but it's bullshit. It's all fucking bullshit propagated by people who haven't been torn apart by suffering, by injustice."

"But you don't understand."

"Don't understand what?" he yelled. "Don't understand what? I understand fucking everything, that's the problem!"

The kid shook his head. Fast. "No you don't. Honestly. The man you're talking about ... " The voice quietened, almost to a whisper. "He's not my dad."

"What?"

"This man, Mortish, he's not my dad. My name's Blake. Daniel Blake. Lucas Mortish goes to my school. We've got the same colour hair, but my dad's an IT director. Please, I promise you."

The tension in Hayer collapsed, replaced by a thick black wave of despair. He looked closely at the boy. Was he wrong? What if he was?

"Oh shit. Oh no."

The cellar seemed to shrink until it was only inches square. A heavy silence squatted in the damp air. The kid snivelled. Hayer just stood there, defeat etched deep on a face that had seen far too much of it during the previous year.

Ten seconds passed. The kid snivelled again. Hayer didn't know what else to say.

It was the kid who finally broke the silence. "I'm sorry about your son," he said, trying to look like he understood, "but it was nothing to do with me."

This time it was Hayer who couldn't bear to look the kid in the eye. Instead the whole world finally fell apart for him and with a hand that was shaking with emotion, he reached into the pocket of his jacket and pulled out the .22 calibre handgun he'd bought illegally three weeks ago in a pub (for either a murder or a suicide, he hadn't known which), fumbled and released the safety, then placed the cold barrel hard against his temple, and pulled the trigger.

He died instantly.

* * *

Lucas Mortish sighed with relief, then stood up, staring down impassively at the body of the deranged lunatic who'd abducted him from the street the previous afternoon, chloroforming him in the process. He was hungry. And thirsty. The lunatic's head was pouring out blood on to the uneven concrete floor and already the corpse was beginning to smell. Lucas Mortish wrinkled his nose and stepped over it, making for the steps that would take him to freedom.

It had been an uncomfortable experience and one in which he'd had to use all his natural cunning to survive, but it had also been a very interesting one. He couldn't wait to tell his friends about it. And his father. His father especially would be proud of the way he'd thought on his feet, catching his kidnapper out so smartly.

His father had taught him so many good lessons. That words can tear an opponent to pieces far more effectively than even the strongest blade.

And of course, that in law, as in life, there is no place for sentiment.

So what if the lunatic's son had died? His death had had nothing to do with Lucas, nor with his father. His father had simply done his job. Why then should they be made to pay for this other man's misery?

He mounted the steps, opened the door and walked out into the Hayer's hallway. Ignoring the photographs on the wall, quite oblivious to them, he went over to the phone, even allowing himself a tiny triumphant smirk as he dialled the police.

Didn't hear the footsteps behind him. Only knew that something was wrong when the phone suddenly went dead before it was picked up at the other end. As if it had been unplugged.

He turned round slowly, the hairs prickling on the back of his neck. Saw the man.

Stocky, with close-cropped hair and narrow, interested eyes. Dressed in an ill-fitting blue boiler suit. Stained. An unpleasant familiarity about him.

Found his eyes moving almost magnetically towards the huge, gleaming blade of the carving knife in the man's huge paw-like hand.

The fear came in a quivering rush.

Now it was Patrick Dean's turn to smirk.

ANOTHER LIFE

Roz Southey

I'D ALWAYS KNOWN it was either me or Keeg. Mates then enemies. One of us was going to have to die.

It was never fucking well going to be me.

* * *

The flat is dark, full of shadows. As I walk naked across the room, moonlight stripes the floor. The polished-wood, paid for with my hard-earned. Floor to ceiling windows, velvet curtains. Chrome and glass furniture, plasma screen TV, pictures worth a fortune. We used to look up at blocks like this, me and Keeg, back when we were fourteen. Ponsy fuckers, we'd yell. Fucking fat-cats. And pudgy-faced wankers in posh suits would peer out at us in a mixture of fury and fear.

Now I'm the one looking out.

Down below, in the courtyard, there are four yobs, toting beer cans, shadowboxing. Keeg's there, doubling up in mock agony at a play kick to his guts. One of the yobs lumbers over to an ornamental tree, hikes down his zip and pisses. My mates. Twenty somethings who still think like fourteen-year-olds. Who spend their lives stoned out of their minds. Drink or drugs, who cares. We started with glue nicked from Woollies then bought E on street corners then moved on to the hard stuff. Okay, so I have that kind of stuff now, stashed at the bottom of the biscuit tin. But *I* earned the cash to buy it with; Keeg and his mates just pinched something.

Keeg's shouting up at me. He sees me. Our eyes meet. And hate. He hates me for going over to the other side. I hate him for reminding me what I once was.

I let the blind snap back into place. How the hell did they get through the security gate? You have to show the guard your ID, look into a camera, that sort of shit. And *why* are they here, anyway? To piss me off, that's why.

There were five of us, and me and Keeg were top dogs. Kev and Keegan – unbelievable – we thought it was meant. We bossed the gang, we said what fucking went and we fucking did it. Go to school? What the fuck do you learn at school? You've got to be out there, grabbing the world by the balls and letting it know what's what. Want some money? Take it. Want some drink? Steal it.

We lived it up like crazy. We had the entire neighbourhood shitting its pants when they saw us. Standing outside the super-market with our hoods up, kicking at the walls, leering at the kids in their prams, running straight at the oldies, swerving only at the last moment so they'd totter and shout.

Christ, it was good.

Except.

Except for those lousy evenings when it was pissing it down and no one would let us in the pubs, and even the students in Kentucky Fried Chicken chased us out. Bizzy cars cruised past, winding their windows down and the pigs taking a good long insolent look at us. Those were the nights we'd break windows, to hear the glass break and alarm bells howl. The nights we wondered what the fuck we were doing here, what the world was all about, and who cared anyway. Bored as hell.

I dress. Jeans, T-shirt, leather jacket, trainers. Only the best. The guy who stares back at me from the mirror looks good. Good face, good body. Not your average wanker. And all the clothes're top quality, none of your mass-produced shit. I've left all that behind. Way behind. Only the best.

Particularly when you're going out to kill.

***

First time we did it, we were scruffy. Worse than scruffy, we looked shite. Keeg's T had more holes than shirt, I'd spilt beer down my hoodie, hell, I'd been sick down it. And my jeans. Frayed to start with and I wore them right down on my hips so I could get the crotch real low. Keeg said they made me waddle and he could see my underpants and they weren't clean. Not pretty at all.

He was a kid, the one we found. Homeless. Huddled in a doorway, with big eyes full of tears and a nose dripping snot. Eighteen maybe. We were fourteen. And there were five of us – that made up for him being bigger than us.

"Hey, mate," Keeg said. "Want some beer?" He held out the half-full can, the kid grabbed for it. Keeg upended the can and poured it over his head.

The kid went mental. He screamed and shouted and kicked out with his feet and flailed around with his arms. One of his feet caught Keeg on the shin and he swore. "Fucking fucking fucking shit," he yelled. "What the fuck are you doing?" And he kicked back.

Then we were all doing it. Kicking and stamping and jumping up and down and hearing cloth tear and bone crack. And I stomped, and went on stomping, and on and on until there was only blood, and the shrieks subsided into groans. And all the anger went into my feet and came out again with every jump and in the end there was nothing left except the kind of relieved emptiness you get after wanking.

And you know why we didn't get caught? Some fucker had smashed the CCTV. We washed off the blood in puddles, then lit a bonfire under our clothes in one of the sheds on the allotments and burnt the whole place down. Vandalism, they called it. Fucking cops didn't have a clue.

The next one, me and Keeg did on our own. This time we went looking. Maybe three weeks later. Fucking truant officer had been round and my mum's boyfriend gave me a beating for skipping school. As if he'd never done it when he was a kid. Doesn't like me around all day, that's it, not since I walked in on him and mum fucking on the sofa. Christ, that was horrible.

So we were out in the frost and the hail, and it was a Monday night in November and we'd already been thrown out of three pubs for being too young. We'd tried nicking beer from the off-licence but they'd run us off. So we pissed around the city centre, getting stared at by bouncers and sniggered at by girls wearing damn all.

"Hey," Keeg said to one of them. "Fancy a bit of something, then?"

She was twice his height and six times his weight and I bet she'd never pulled a bloke in her life. But she just looked down her nose at Keeg and said, "I bet your willy's no bigger than my kid sister's pinkie."

Keeg went for her.

She screeched and kicked out and grabbed at his hair. His head smashed into her boobs and she bullied him back against the shop window, then kneed him in the groin. Then she marched off with a sneer and a swagger.

"Bitch," Keeg spluttered.

So we went looking for someone to kill. Keeg was raging. "I'll find a bitch somewhere and fuck her and fuck her and then I'll slice her tits off and fry them up for my supper!"

"Yeah, yeah," I said not believing him.

"I will. I fucking will!"

We found someone at last, an elderly bloke by a cashpoint, peering with rheumy eyes at the huge letters and trying to fit his card into the slot with a shaking hand. We leapt on him from behind and he threw up his hands and went down at once with a great gusting sigh that scared the shit out of us. And then he lay still and never moved again.

"What kind of fucking fun was that?" Keeg said. So we went and killed a dog as well. And that wasn't much fun either.

I reckon we killed four maybe five people all told. I don't remember exactly. We were stoned half the time, or pissed. No one ever got near us, not cops, not neighbours. I remember me mam saying once how dirty my jeans were – we'd had to roll around in the mud with this wino before we could finish him off. Accidental death, they said that one was – fell in the river and drowned. Anyway, it was only a tramp – who cares about them?

But somewhere along the line I stopped enjoying it. There wasn't any anger left to come out. Or maybe it got changed into fear and that was scary in itself. I kept thinking it couldn't last. The cops aren't stupid. They'd catch us. Maybe they were on to us already and we just didn't know it. And then we'd spend the rest of our lives in jail and everyone would forget about us. There'd be nothing to do except kick the shit out of the walls.

I got stressed out about it. I kept looking over my shoulder. Every time a bizzy car went past, I thought they were playing with us and would just drive round the corner and catch us. So when Keeg said, "Let's go get a wino," only a couple of weeks after the old guy, I puked in the gutter.

"You're scared," Keeg said.

"Don't talk crap."

"You're shitting your pants."

"It's that fucking burger," I said. "It's giving me the runs."

"Fuck the burger," Keeg said. "Let's go get some fun."

"I'm going home. I'm sick."

"Scaredy cat!" he said contemptuously.

"Fuck off."

I went home. Keeg went off by himself but didn't find anyone. Later, he said it hadn't seemed right without me.

Then he broke his leg. Running to get out of the way of his old man when he was beating up everyone in sight. Ended up in hospital for a month. Like he said, it wasn't fun on my own. So I got into the way of going to the library and mucking around on the internet. Then mam threw out the boyfriend cos he slapped her and we went off to live with her sister down south. And that was that – I didn't see Keeg for ten years.

It wasn't any better down south. No one in my new school wanted to know me – I had a stupid accent and didn't know anything. So I stopped going and went down the library to surf the internet and then mam won a bit on the lottery and gave me a games station.

And it took off from there really. All the games were stupid. Fantasy stuff, dragons, and aliens and other dull shit. I reckoned I ought to make up my own games, based on what me and Keeg had done.

You don't wanna hear all of this – the bits about how I got myself sorted. I found this guy who taught me how to do the computer stuff – he made me pay of course but it was worth it. Faggot. I went to school to keep everyone off my back, but I didn't do anything, I just kept scribbling away, planning the games. Okay, so the first game I made up was shite and anyone playing it would have known exactly what me and Keeg had done and we would have ended up behind bars for the rest of our natural, but the later stuff was better. Much better.

I got it made in the end. I got a job with this small firm, just three of us. Made a name for ourselves and pulled in a mint of money. And that's how I'm here, in this flat, with all this cash, and these clothes, and girls queuing up for fucks. And Keeg's out there, swigging beer and still wearing a hoodie and trainers he bought years ago. Sod all in his pockets and he's probably fucking the barmaid in the pub. That's why he hates me.

I saw him last week. First time in ten years. In the street outside Smiths. Still the same Keeg, the same tatty jeans and holey T-shirt. He looked me up and down and laughed.

"Wanker," he said.

"Yeah," I said. "Well, at least I'm not a loser."

We stood toe to toe, face to face.

"I know stuff about you," he said, softly. "I know about homeless kids and winos, and old gits whose hearts go pop the first time you say boo. Don't you piss *me* off!"

"I know things about you too," I said.

Maybe I've lost my accent a bit, being away. A huge grin cracked his face and he said in a prissy precious voice, "Know things too? Can't speak proper any more, right?"

That got to me somehow. Like saying I wasn't real. "Sod off," I said.

He muscled in on me, till we were nose to nose. I could feel his hard-on.

"This is my town," he said. "*You* sod off!" And he added, whispering, "You were the one that chickened out, remember. You were the one who sicked his guts up rather than tackle a pansy pervert."

"Sod off," I said again, and walked away.

And ever since, he and his mates – once my mates – have been prancing around outside my flat. Fuck knows how they found me.

First couple of nights they tossed stones into the courtyard and against the wall of the flats. The security guard went out and yelled at them; minutes later a bizzy car cruised by. By then Keeg and his mates had gone.

But tonight they're in the courtyard and the guard's nowhere to be seen. Course, I could call the law, but if I did that, Keeg could land me in the shit. That's what he's betting on, that I won't dare do anything. Shop him and I shop myself. Of course someone else in the flats is probably calling the cops. That's why I'm going to have to sort it. Now.

Keeg doesn't stand a chance.

I take the lift down. From the glass doors in the foyer, I can see the security booth at the gate, which I couldn't see from above. I can see feet in polished black shoes, toes up on the floor. That takes care of what happened to the security guard, I guess.

They come for me the minute I walk out the door but Keeg roars at them; they give him sour looks but stop.

"Me and you," I say, hands in the pockets of my leather jacket.

"Yeah," he says, and the others jump on the low walls of the ornamental flowerbeds and sit there, beer cans in hand, legs swinging like they were at the football.

"Make it fast," Keeg said. "Someone'll have called the cops."

"Sure," I say and swagger up to him. He stinks of beer and piss and vomit, and once I stank like that too. This is what I left behind, this is what I could have been. And what's he seeing? A smart guy, with looks and brains, the kid he once was, who made it out of here and who got everything life has to offer. And what do I feel?

Sick to the heart. It's all shit and show. Nothing but nothing.

Nothing like what Keeg and me had. Why am I here? Because I left him behind. I walked out on him, and left him to the shit and the crap and the boredom and the beer, and all the rest of the nothing we had when we were kids. I let him down. He was my mate and I walked out on him. He's shit but I'm shit too, just shit covered with a fine coat and we both know it.

We stand nose to nose, face to face, chest to chest and Keeg's not the only one with a hard-on. And I'm thinking: this is it, this is real.

All that other shit is just pretend. The only difference is that it pays, and means you can stand up and say *look at me. I'm an executive with my own internet business. I'm respectable.*

Yeah. Right. I let him down and that makes me worse than him. Ten times worse.

And that's the way it's going to stay. If I can't be better, I'll be worse. No way he's going to get the drop on me. No way he can take me down. And I slip the kitchen knife between his ribs and he stares wide-eyed and gives an odd little gurgle and slips down the length of me, like an old pair of jeans shucking off. And then he's lying on the ground and there's a smear of blood down my T-shirt.

Simple as that. No big deal. And you know – no fun at all. It's all shite. But at least I don't feel guilty any more. What's to feel guilty about? Keeg got left behind and I didn't. I look at the three yobos. They're still staring at Keeg's body with the knife in it.

"So he got in and killed the guard," I said. "Then he panicked and did for himself. Right?"

They hop down from the walls, pause, nod. Then they're sauntering away towards the gate as if nothing has happened. So long, Keeg. So long, mate. No offence, but you're just history.

I bend to wipe the knife clean of my fingerprints and close Keeg's hand around it.

And why didn't I get caught? Keeg took the cameras out of course, when he did for the guard. Just like I knew he would. So no one would see what happened. He knew tonight was the night we sorted it.

* * *

In the dark room, the moon stripes the polished floorboards. I look out of my window at the courtyard. Empty. Just a new guard in the security cabin, a cat prowling round the flowerbeds.

Empty.

I did what was necessary. It was always going to come down to me and Keeg facing off. And there could be only one winner.

But that's the point. He's dead, just a pile of ashes scattered for the dogs to crap on. And without him, I'm nothing. Just another fucking bag of shite with nowhere to go. We were two sides of one coin and I destroyed it.

In a way, *he* won.

I'm going to go get myself someone. A wino maybe or a *Big Issue* seller, or a foreign student who doesn't know where the hell he is. Someone to kill some time. Someone to kill.

Hey, Keeg, this one's for you.

THE WOMAN WHO LOVED ELIZABETH DAVID

Andrew Taylor

On the evening that Charles died I actually heard the ambulance, the one that Edith Thornhill called. I was putting out the milk bottles on the porch. I didn't take much notice. Our house was on Chepstow Road and so was the hospital; we often heard ambulances.

He died on the evening of the day the rat-catcher came – the last Thursday in October. Our house was modern, built just before the war, but in the garden was a crumbling stone stable. Charles planned to convert it into a garage if we ever bought a car, which was about as likely as his agreeing to install a telephone. In the meantime we used it as a sort of garden shed and apple store. Almost all the apples had been ruined by rats in the space of a week. Hence the rat-catcher.

Charles was late but I had not begun to get worried. After he closed the shop, he often dropped into the Bull Hotel for a drink. Then the doorbell rang and I found Dr Bayswater and Mrs Thornhill on the doorstep. I know Edith from church, and Dr Bayswater is our doctor.

"I'm sorry, Anne," Edith said. "It's bad news. May we come in?"

I took them into the lounge. Edith suggested I sit down.

"Charles? It's Charles, isn't it?"

"I'm afraid he's dead," Edith said.

I stared at her. I did not know what to say.

The doctor cleared his throat. "Coronary thrombosis."

"A coronary? Do you mean a heart attack? But he was only forty-eight."

"It does happen."

"But he doesn't have a weak heart. Surely there'd have been some—"

"I'd seen him three times in the last month." Bayswater examined his fingernails. "Didn't he tell you?"

"Of course he did. But that was indigestion."

"Angina. Some of the symptoms can be similar to indigestion."

The doctor and Edith went on talking to me. I didn't listen very much. All I could think of was the fact that Charles hadn't told me the truth. Instead of grieving that he was gone, I felt angry with him.

My memory of the next few weeks is patchy, as if a heavy fog lies over that part of my mind. Certain events rear out of it like icebergs from a cold ocean. The funeral was at St John's and the church was full of people wearing black clothes, like crows. Marina Harper was there, which surprised me because she wasn't a churchgoer. Charles had an obituary in the *Lydmouth Gazette*. It was not a very long one. It said that he came of a well-respected local family and referred in passing to Nigel.

It was unfortunate that Nigel, Charles's younger brother, was in Tanganyika, looking at some sawmills he was thinking of buying. I never really understood what Nigel did for a living. Whatever it was, it seemed to bring him a good deal of money. Once I asked him and he said, "I just buy things when they're cheap, and sell things when they're expensive. Nothing to it, really."

I sent a telegram to Dar es Salaam. Nigel cabled back, saying he would be home as soon as possible. He and Charles had always been very close, though Nigel was my age, a good ten years younger than his brother. He was also Charles's executor.

In the meantime, everything was in limbo. Until Nigel came home, I could have very little idea of what the future held for me. I did not even know whether I would be able to stay in the house. In the meantime, the shop – Butter's, the men's outfitters in the High Street – was left in the charge of the manager, a man who had worked for Charles and his father for many years.

What struck me most was the silence. In the evenings, when I sat by the fire in the lounge, there was a quietness that I could not drive away by turning on the wireless. After a while, I stopped trying. I would sit in my chair, with a book unopened on my lap, and stare at the familiar room which had grown suddenly un-familiar: at my mother-in-law's dark oak sideboard, which I had always loathed; at the collected editions of Kipling, which Charles and Nigel had laboriously assembled when they were boys; at the patch on the hearthrug where Charles had left a cigarette burning one Christmas-time.

I don't know when I realized something was wrong. I think the first thing that struck me was the key. When the hospital sent back Charles's belongings, the contents of his pockets had been put in a separate bag. There was nothing unexpected except for the key. Charles had other keys in a leather pouch with a buttoned flap – keys for the house, for the shop. This key, however, was loose – a Yale, made of brass and obviously quite new. I tried it unsuccess-fully in our only Yale lock, the one on the old stable. I took it down to the shop, but it didn't fit any of the locks there, either.

On the same morning, I went to the bank to draw some cash – something I had to do for myself now Charles wasn't here. The cashier said the manager would like a word. Our account was over-drawn. The manager suggested that I transfer some money from the deposit account.

As I was walking down the High Street on my way from the bank to the bus stop, Mr Quale was sweeping the doorstep of the Bull Hotel.

"Morning, ma'am. Sorry to hear about Mr Butter."

"Thank you."

"Very nice gentleman. I saw him just before it happened."

"How did he seem?"

"Right as rain. He'd been in for a quick drink – left a bit earlier than usual. Thought he must be in a hurry for his supper."

"Earlier?" Charles had collapsed on the pavement outside the Thornhills' house in Victoria Road a little after seven-thirty. "Surely you mean later?"

Quale shook his head. "It was about a quarter-past six."

"I expect he looked in at the shop on the way home."

I said goodbye and joined the queue at the bus stop. Charles had never worked in the evening. I was standing there, turning over in my mind what Quale had said, when there was a loud tooting from the other side of the road. It was Marina Harper in her little two-seater. She drove across the road and pulled up at the bus stop.

"Hop in, Anne. I'll give you a lift."

I was tired, and it was beginning to rain. Otherwise I might have tried to find an excuse. I never knew quite what to make of Marina. She had fair, coarse hair and a high-coloured face with small, pale eyes. She was comfortably off – her father used to own the local bus company. We had known each other since we were children but we weren't particular friends. And I was old-fashioned enough to feel that a wife should live with her husband.

Marina talked unceasingly as she drove me home. "I've just had a couple of days in town." Her husband worked in London. He and Marina had a semi-detached marriage: his job kept him in London while she preferred to live in Lydmouth. " ... And you'll never guess who we met at a party last night. Elizabeth David – yes, *really*. Absolutely wonderful. Such style. She looks how she writes, if you know what I mean."

"Elizabeth who?"

Marina raised plucked eyebrows. "Elizabeth David. The cookery writer. You know, she's always in *Vogue*. And she's written this super book about Mediterranean food. Why don't you come to lunch tomorrow? We can try one of the recipes."

Marina dropped me in Chepstow Road. After lunch, I went into the dining room. Charles kept cheque books and other documents relating to money on the top drawer of the bureau. I settled down and tried to work out how the money ebbed and flowed and ebbed again in our lives. I found the most recent bank statement among the pile of business letters which I had left on the hall table for Nigel. I wished he were here now.

At the date of the statement, our personal account had not been overdrawn, but it now was. In the week before his death Charles had made out a cheque for one hundred and eighty-nine pounds, nineteen shillings and eleven pence.

I leafed through the cancelled cheques enclosed with the statement. The cheque in question had been made out to H. R. Caterford Ltd and paid into a branch of Barclays Bank in Cardiff.

Feeling like a detective, I put on my hat and coat, walked to the telephone box on the corner of Victoria Road and consulted the telephone directory. H. R. Caterford Ltd was a jeweller's in the Royal Arcade. Suddenly the solution came to me: Charles must have bought me a present. The dear man knew I had been a little low since coming out of hospital in September. (Knowing one will never have children *is* a little depressing.) But in that case, where was the present? Christmas was two months away. He would hardly keep it until then.

On impulse I dialled the number in the directory. The phone was answered on the second ring, which was just as well as I was beginning to get cold feet about the whole business.

"Good afternoon," I said. "May I speak to Mr Caterford?"

"Speaking."

"This is Mrs Butter, from Lydmouth. Mrs Charles Butter. I believe my husband—"

"Mrs Butter. How pleasant to hear from you. You're well, I hope?"

"Yes, thank you. I was wondering—"

"Oddly enough, I was just thinking of you. Only yesterday afternoon the lady who sold us the brooch came in with the matching ring. Platinum and opal. Said she didn't want that either, because her daughter had told her that opals are unlucky unless you're born in October. Not that you need to worry about that, of course."

"Oh?"

"As you're one of the favoured few."

"Oh yes."

"It's rather a lovely ring. The opals are a perfect match for your eyes, if I may say so. Anyway, would you like to have a word with Mr Butter about it? Then perhaps he could telephone me. I'll hold it for a day or two. It's always a particular pleasure to oblige an old customer."

"Yes, thank you. Goodbye."

I put down the phone and walked home. A platinum and opal brooch. Charles knew I didn't like platinum. Then the opals: unlucky unless the wearer had been born in the month of October. My birthday was in March. And how could opals match my eyes? They are brown. Finally, Mr Caterford had spoken to me as if he knew me. But until this afternoon I had never heard of him.

The following morning, I found the rat. The rat-catcher had warned me this might happen. "That's the trouble with rats, look," he had said. "You can never tell where they're going to pop up."

The rat was lying on the path that led from the old stable to the road. It was dark, with a long tail. There had been a frost in the night and its fur was dusted with droplets of ice, like sugar. Actually, it looked rather sweet. Because of the frost, the ground would not be easy to dig, so I decided to bury it after lunch – my lunch with Marina Harper.

Marina lived in Raglan Court, a block of modern flats over-looking Jubilee Park. The place looked very nice, I'm sure – if you like hard, modern furniture and American gadgets. There was a lounge-cum-dining room with a huge picture window overlooking the park and a serving hatch to the kitchen. The place stank of garlic.

"I've just made dry martinis," Marina said. "You don't mind if I put the finishing touches to lunch, do you? We can talk through the hatch."

As she poured the drinks, light glinted on a silver brooch she was wearing. Rather a pretty brooch with opals set in it.

Not silver: platinum?

"That's a lovely brooch," I said.

"Yes, it is pretty, isn't it?"

"Aren't opals unlucky?"

Marina laughed, a gurgle of sound like water running out of a bath. "Not if you're born in October. Then they're lucky. Now why don't you sit here while I finish off in the kitchen?"

I watched her through the frame of the hatch – the flash of a knife, the glint of platinum – and all the time she talked.

"I thought we'd have *filet de porc en sanglier*. It's one of my Elizabeth David recipes. Pork that tastes like wild boar. The secret is the marinade. It has to be for eight days. And you can't skimp on the ingredients either – things like coriander seeds, juniper berries, basil. There's a little shop in Brewer Street where you can get them. I think it must be the only place in England."

Black market ingredients, I thought. *Pork and all. The bitch. The cow.*

While Marina talked, the rich, unhealthy odours of the meal wafted through the hatch into the living room. My hands were sweaty on the cold glass. In my nervousness, I finished the drink more quickly than I should have done.

"Can I get you a refill?" Marina called.

I stood up. "I wonder if I might – is it along here?"

"Second on the left."

In the hall, I opened my handbag and took out Charles's Yale key. Holding my breath, I opened the front door. I slipped the key into the lock and twisted. The key turned.

I drew it out of the lock, closed the door quietly and darted into the sanctuary of the bathroom. Marina was wearing the brooch. The jeweller in Cardiff had thought that Marina was me, had thought that she was Charles's wife. So they must have been in Cardiff together, and acting as if they were a married couple. The key in Charles's pocket fitted Marina's door. There could be only one explanation for all that.

It is strange how in a crisis one finds reserves of strength one did not suspect existed. Somehow I went back into the living room and accepted another dry martini. Somehow I made myself eat the ghastly, overflavoured pork which Marina served up with such a triumphant flourish that I wanted to throw the plate at her. I even complimented her on her cooking. She said that she would give me the recipe.

The meal dragged on. It was far too heavy and elaborate for lunch. Marina served it in the French way, with salad after the main course, and then cheese before the pudding. So pretentious. What was wrong with our way of doing things?

When at last it was time to go, Marina came into the hall and helped me on with my coat. Then she bent forward and kissed my cheek.

"I have enjoyed this," she said. "Let's do it again soon. I'm running up to town for a night or two but I'll be in touch as soon as I get back."

I walked home through the park and down Victoria Road. The rat was still lying on the path between the house and the stable. After I had taken off my hat and changed, I went outside and manoeuvred its stiff body into a bucket with the help of a spade. The ice had melted now, so the fur gleamed with moisture. I carried the bucket into the stable. I looked at the various places where the rat-catcher had left the poison. All of it had gone. I wondered if there were more rats. It was then that the idea came into my mind. I remembered the Kipling story.

Nigel and Charles thought Kipling was the greatest writer of the century. They were particularly fond of the Stalky stories, which are about schoolboys at a boarding school near the sea. I had read them in our early days, when I'd been friends with Charles and Nigel, just before Charles and I became engaged. A wife should try to like the things the husband likes. But I hadn't liked these stories.

In one of them, the boys kill a cat with an air gun. They push its dead body under the floorboards of a rival dormitory. The cat decomposes, and gradually its smell fills the dormitory, growing stronger and stronger, and more and more loathsome. If a cat could do it, so could a rat.

It was just a silly idea – childish, undignified and in any case impossible to carry out. I left the rat in the stable and went inside for a cup of tea. During the rest of the day, however, I could not help thinking about the rat. And about Marina.

Marina was going to London. I had a key to her flat, which she did not know I possessed. If I went there tomorrow evening, after darkness, there would be very little risk of my being seen as I went to or from the flat. There was a little gate from the park to the communal garden of the flats – I could go that way. People kept to themselves at Raglan Court so with luck I would not be noticed. In any case, I could take the precaution of wearing a rather bright headscarf, a pre-war present which I had never used, and an old mackintosh which had belonged to Charles.

As the evening slipped past, the idea seemed more and more attractive. Well, why not? It wouldn't harm Marina to have another smell in that evil-smelling flat. And it was a way of making a point about her beastly behaviour. There was no excuse for adultery. There was no excuse for stealing my husband. The following evening, I decided to act.

I put the rat, wrapped in brown paper, in my shopping bag, slipped a torch into my pocket, walked up to Raglan Court and let myself into the flat. I was not afraid. Indeed, I had the oddest sensation that it could not be me, Anne Butter, doing this. I felt as if I were watching rather than doing.

I went straight into the kitchen. This was where the nasty smells came from – so this was the place for the rat. I did not turn on the light, but used the torch sparingly. I unwrapped the rat and let it fall to the linoleum.

The gas cooker was raised on legs a few inches above the floor. I found a floor mop and used it to push the body under the cooker to the wall. The torch proved to be a blessing. With its help I was able to see that there was a gap between the wall and the back of the cupboard beside the cooker. With a little manoeuvring of the broom, I managed to push the rat into the gap. Even if Marina looked under the cooker she would not be able to see anything. I did not think it would be long before the rat began to smell: the flat was centrally heated, and the kitchen would be the warmest room.

I went home. Then it was simply a matter of waiting. Waiting for Nigel and waiting for the rat.

A few days after I had left the rat at her flat, Marina arrived on my doorstep with a small parcel in her hand.

"For you," she said, smiling. "Just a little something."

I asked her in for coffee. The parcel contained a copy of Elizabeth David's *A Book of Mediterranean Food*.

"The lovely thing about cooking is that when the pleasure's shared it's somehow doubled," Marina said. "You won't be able to get a lot of the ingredients in Lydmouth. Perhaps I can find what you need in London."

During the next two weeks, I saw Marina regularly. I even asked her to lunch. Many of Elizabeth David's recipes were really very simple. I found one – *tarte à l'oignon et aux oeufs* – which turned out to be very like the flans I used to cook Charles. Marina said my *tarte* was quite marvellous.

Why did she do all this? Why was she such a hypocrite? There were two possible explanations: either she felt guilty about stealing my husband, or she was doing it because she derived a malicious pleasure from pretending to be my friend. On the whole I thought the latter explanation was more likely.

On the second occasion I had lunch with her, I was sure I could smell something in the living room. It was a faint *blueness* in the air, an uneasy hint that lingered in the nostrils. After the meal, I helped Marina carry the plates into the kitchen.

I sniffed.

"Can you *smell* something?" Marina asked.

"Well..."

"I keep thinking I can. Something rather unpleasant. I really must turn out the cupboards soon. And the larder."

No more was said about it until a day or two later, when Marina drove me up to Cheltenham for a matinée at the Everyman. In the interval she brought up the subject again.

"Do you remember that smell in the kitchen? I think it might be the drains."

"Have there been complaints from the other flats?"

"Not as far as I know. I've got someone coming to have a look."

Two days later, she came to tea and gave me the next instalment. Unfortunately the plumber had turned out to be rather good at his job. He soon realized that the smell was not from the drains. He pulled out the cooker and found the decaying body of the rat squeezed between the cupboard and the wall.

"It was quite disgusting," Marina said. "It looked as it smelled, if you know what I mean. Anyway, the plumber was marvellous. He got the wretched thing out of the flat and now things are beginning to return to normal."

"Isn't it odd having a rat in a modern block of flats?"

"Unusual, I suppose. But apparently they are very agile creatures, and you never know where they are going to turn up. The plumber suggested that I get the rat-catcher." Marina shivered, rather theatrically. "Just in case there are any more."

"We had rats in the stable," I said. "The rat-catcher soon sorted them out. I've got his address if you'd like it."

Marina took out a little leather-bound diary and made a note of the details. As she jotted them down, the brooch gleamed on her cardigan. Platinum and unlucky opals.

The rat man came and left poison under the cooker and in the larder. Marina told me all about his reluctance to leave the poison in the kitchen, about the strictness of his instructions to her. This was just before she went up to London for the weekend. She was going to a party, she said, where she hoped Elizabeth David might be present.

"I know I've only met her once, but I feel I know her really well – as well as I know you – just through her writing." Marina patted my arm – she was always touching me, which was one of the things I disliked most. "I'll tell Mrs David I've been making converts in Lydmouth. I'm sure she'll be delighted. I'll be back on Monday, so I'll come and tell you all about it on Tuesday."

I was in a quandary for the whole weekend. Should I or shouldn't I? It was such a good opportunity, presented to me, as it were, on a plate. It would make up for the rather tame performance of the rat. I didn't want to hurt Marina, of course, not seriously. But there would be very little risk of that. The amount of poison that would kill a rat would surely give a human being nothing more than a mild bilious attack.

All weekend I toyed with the idea. *What if? What if?* On Sunday evening, when it was dark, I put on the headscarf and the raincoat and left the house. I had the torch and the key of Marina's flat in my pocket.

Everything went as smoothly as last time. In the refrigerator was a saucepan containing what I now knew was ratatouille. It looked and smelt quite disgusting. The rat poison was on saucers, one under the cooker and the other in larder. I took a little of the poison from each and rearranged what was left on the saucers so that they both looked untouched. I stirred it into the ratatouille. To my relief, it seemed to dissolve very quickly. I wondered if the poison would taste. Even if it did, I thought that the ratatouille was so strongly flavoured that it would mask any additions.

What if? What if?

I went home. That night I dreamed of Nigel. Funnily enough I had always dreamed more about Nigel than about Charles. On Monday morning, I woke with a light heart. Now I could put the past behind me and look to the future. In a sense, there was nothing personal in what I'd done at Raglan Court the previous evening. There was no reason to gloat. It had not been a question of being vindictive – merely of doing my duty. Someone had to teach the woman a lesson, and the someone had happened to be me.

I was washing up after breakfast when a man walked past the kitchen window and knocked on the back door. A plate slipped from my hand and broke when it hit the sink. I dried my hands and went to answer the door.

It was the rat-catcher, a grubby little man with a baggy tweed jacket and a collarless shirt.

"Morning, ma'am. Just come to see how the little fellows are getting on."

"I really don't know."

"No dead 'uns?"

"Who knows?"

"Shall I take a look? See if they need a second helping?"

"Yes, please."

The rat-catcher went down to the stable. I cleared up the broken plate and tidied the kitchen. A few minutes later, the man came back.

"They've eaten it all. I put down a bit more."

"Good." I opened my handbag and took out my purse. "Were there – were there any bodies?"

He chuckled. "Gone back to their nests. Give 'em a choice, they like to die in their own beds – just like us, eh?"

I paid the man. He wanted to stay and gossip – in my experience, men are far worse gossips than women – but luckily we were interrupted by the ring of the front doorbell.

It was a telegram. My heart lurched because telegrams usually mean bad news, apart from those connected with births and weddings; and I had nothing to do with either. I tore it open.

BOAT DOCKED LATE LAST NIGHT. COMING DOWN TODAY. IN CIRCUMSTANCES HAVE BOOKED ROOM AT BULL. SEE YOU ABOUT FIVE. NIGEL.

That was typical of my brother-in-law. Nigel could be very thoughtful. When Charles was alive, Nigel always stayed at the house. But now Charles was dead, the situation was different. Lydmouth wasn't London. If we were alone under the same roof, tongues might wag. People might even remember that before I became engaged to Charles, I had seen a good deal of Nigel.

By half-past four I was as ready as I could be – the lounge fire burning brightly, the brasses in the hall gleaming, the water near boiling point in the kettle, the tea tray laid. As I sat waiting, all sorts of foolish thoughts chased through my mind. *What if? What if?*

Nigel rang the doorbell at twenty-past five.

"Anne – wonderful to see you." He swept me into his arms. "I'm so sorry about Charles." He hugged me, then stood back. "Sorry I'm a bit late. Train was delayed. Nothing works properly in this country."

Nigel was taller than Charles had been, and age had been kinder to him. As a young man, he had been gawky and had had difficulty in talking to a girl without blushing. The war had changed all that. I brought the tea in and we chatted for a while – mainly about Charles.

"You must be wondering about the money side," Nigel said. "No need. As far as I am concerned, you can stay in the house for as long as you like. You own fifty per cent of it now, anyway. And Charles's share in the shop comes to you, so that should give you a decent income, even if we have to pay out a bit more in wages."

I asked him how long he was staying in Lydmouth.

"Only a couple of nights, I'm afraid. I'm popping over to Paris on Thursday." He grinned at me. "I'll see if I can find you some perfume."

"It's a shame you can't stay longer."

His eyes met mine. "I'll be back."

"I wonder – could I ask you to help me with Charles's things? There're all his clothes, for example. And I've not really been through the business papers in the bureau."

"Of course I will. When would suit you?"

"Come to lunch tomorrow – we can sort everything out afterwards." He hesitated.

"I'll see if I can do something interesting," I said brightly. "I've been experimenting lately. I love Elizabeth David. Her recipes are mouth-watering."

"Yes." He glanced at his watch. "Elizabeth David, eh? You've been acquiring cosmopolitan tastes in my absence."

"I try." I smiled at him. "Even with all the shortages, there's no excuse not to be adventurous in the kitchen."

Nigel stood up and tossed his cigarette end in the fire. He ran the tip of his index finger along the spines of the Kipling edition in the bookcase. I shivered. He turned to face me.

"Oh – by the way: I owe you some money."

"Really?"

"I asked Charles to pay a debt for me. He mentioned he'd done it in his last letter. A hundred and ninety-odd pounds."

A hundred and eighty-nine pounds, nineteen shillings and eleven pence?

"Oh – oh yes." I felt as if a horde of insects were crawling across my skin. "I'd noticed the cheque. To a jeweller's, wasn't it?" With immense effort I forced a smile. "Who was the lucky lady? If it *was* a lady."

Nigel's cheeks darkened. The young man I had known before the war was suddenly not so very far away. "I – I suppose I'd better tell you. The thing is, when I've come down to Lydmouth in the last year or so, I've had a sort of friendship with a woman. A special friendship."

"And Charles knew?"

He nodded, took out his cigarette case and fiddled with the catch. "And then I went to Paris on a business trip in the spring, and I met Ghislaine. One thing led to another – well, in fact we're going to get married."

He paused, looking at me, as if waiting for congratulations. I couldn't speak.

"But there was still this – this other lady. That had to end. But I wanted to give her something as a keepsake. Then I had to go to Tanganyika ... " He managed to open the case at last. He took out a cigarette and rolled it around in his fingers. Crumbs of tobacco dribbled down to the hearthrug.

"I asked Charles if he'd buy her a present. It was while you were in hospital. A piece of jewellery – something quite decent. So I gave him a rough idea of how much I wanted to spend and left him to get on with it. We were going to settle up when I got home. I do hope you don't think too badly of me."

He looked at me. In the end, I shook my head, which seemed to satisfy him. Men are easily satisfied.

"It wasn't serious," he said, as if that excused it. "Men tend to sow a few wild oats before they settle down. Women are different."

Were they? If all women were different, how could the men sow their wild oats?

He looked at his watch again. "Oh lord, I must go. I'll see you tomorrow. What time would suit you?"

"About twelve-thirty?"

"Splendid."

We went into the hall. He bent towards me and his lips brushed my cheek.

"You've always been a good pal. You're not shocked? Charles thought you would be."

"Don't be silly." I smiled up at him. "Boys will be boys."

We said goodnight and I closed the door behind him. I went back into the lounge. The room was empty and desolate. There was nothing left of Nigel except crumbs on a plate, a puddle of tea at the bottom of a cup and golden flecks of tobacco on the hearthrug. I went over to the bookcase and ran my finger along the spines of the Kiplings. I tried to think about Ghislaine but she was too abstract, too foreign for me to grasp. She wasn't flesh and blood like Marina. Marina, I thought idly, would be home by now.

One of the books was a little out of line. It was *Stalky and Co*, the schoolboy stories which had been Nigel and Charles's favourite. *Boys will be boys*. There was a slip of paper protruding from the pages, presumably a bookmark. I took it out, suddenly curious to re-read the story about the dead cat and the smell. The bookmark was buff coloured. I pulled it out and discovered it was a telegram. For a moment, I thought that Nigel's telegram to me had somehow found its way into *Stalky and Co*. But that was still propped up on the mantelpiece behind the clock. This one was addressed to Charles and dated in September, while I was in hospital.

YOU'RE WELCOME OLD BOY. WHILE THE CAT'S AWAY. HAVE FUN. NIGEL.

I sat down beside the bookcase in the chair that was still warm from Nigel's body. I read and re-read the telegram. It had come all the way from Suez. Nigel must have sent it on his way down to East Africa. Suddenly many things were clear. Nigel, Charles and Marina – they had all betrayed me in their different ways, even Nigel.

Nigel worst of all.

It was growing very cold. I stood up and put more coal on the fire. *A Book of Mediterranean Food* was on the sideboard. I riffled through the pages, looking for a suitable recipe for tomorrow. I knew I would find something. And I also knew that, whatever I cooked, Nigel would eat with apparent relish because he felt guilty.

A little later, I went outside. It was a cold night, with stars like diamonds. The moon gave a hard, clear light. Frost gleamed on the path to the stable. I opened the door. Moonlight streamed across the floor and showed me a saucer in the corner. I picked it up and left the stable.

As I was walking back to the house I heard the sound of an ambulance. The bell drew closer and closer. It was coming down Victoria Road from the direction of the park and Raglan Court. In the freezing night air, I stood still and listened to the sound of the ambulance as it slowed for the junction with the Chepstow Road, turned left and sped towards the hospital.

What if? What if?

HUNGRY EYES

Sheila Quigley

THE ARCHAEOLOGIST, A tall, very thin man with a heavy grey
moustache, smiled at his audience.

The hall was full of people eager to learn about the recent dig at
St Michael and All Angels church in Houghton le Spring. A new
floor was being laid, so the archaeologists had moved in.

His lecture was finished, and he summed up, "So what have we
learned? That this was once a prehistoric ritual site? Perhaps...A
Roman temple? Possibly; it was after all standard practice for
Romans to take over earlier religious sites. There is definite evidence
of Normans and Saxons, and during the last excavation in the
churchyard in the late nineties an erratic line of whinstone boulders,
probably from the Hadrian's Wall area, do suggest a prehistoric use
of the site. Several other such boulders have now been found inside
the church, so there is a suggestion – not proof, mind you – that
perhaps there was a stone circle on the site."

PC Steven Carter gasped in awe. He couldn't wait to get back to
the station and tell his boss, DI Lorraine Hunt. She was always so
interested in the history of Houghton le Spring, he thought,
applauding along with everyone else.

As Carter made his way outside, he was followed by three men. They
were locals from the Seahills estate in Houghton le Spring; Carter
hadn't noticed them because they had been sitting at the back.

"So what do yer reckon?" Danny Jorden asked his two friends.
Danny was a chancer, had been all his life, skirting the boundary
between legal and illegal, nothing big, nothing bad, just enough to
keep his kids in shoe leather and food on the table.

"Hmm, don't really know." His cousin Len Jorden scratched his chin, looking sideways at the other member of the trio. Like Danny, Len was dark-haired with green eyes. The resemblance ended there though; Danny was tall and thickset, and frequently wore a smile, while Len was as tall as the archaeologist but even thinner, and had the look of a professional pall-bearer.

"You're a bloody old woman, Len." Adam Glazier, at twenty-six the youngest by nine years, grinned at Len.

"And your jokes stink," Len retorted.

"Knock knock," Adam laughed.

"Piss off."

"Shut up, the pair of you. What we gonna do? I reckon there's a fortune in coins lying in this old church. We need to get to them before those archaeologist blokes do, and it has to be tonight. Tomorrow they start filling the floor in."

"It's a damn shame they couldn't go deeper – God knows what they might have found. I mean, all those old bones." Len shivered.

Danny shook his head. "That's the point, Len, they can't dig any further. But we can."

"I don't know, the church in the middle of the night…Kinda spooky if yer ask me."

"Old woman," Adam hissed.

"All right, for God's sake," Danny snapped, the pressure of new shoes for his oldest making him edgy. "Are youse in or not?"

Adam shrugged. "Yeah, fine by me."

"Len?" Danny looked at his cousin.

Len thought about it for a moment, sighed then answered, "I suppose so. But the first sign of a ghost…"

Adam burst out laughing. "Bloody ghosts, no such thing, yer soft shite…We gonna cut Jacko in?"

"Jacko." Danny thought for a minute. Jacko was a good mate and probably would have been here if he wasn't ill. "Depends what we find, I suppose."

They continued arguing all the way to Danny's van. When they got there Danny kissed his fingers and patted the wing mirror. Len tutted but Danny ignored him. The van, which he called Elizabeth after his dream woman Elizabeth Taylor, was his pride and joy. At the moment his girlfriend wasn't speaking to him because three nights ago he'd called out, "Oh more, Elizabeth, more," at totally the wrong moment, and not for the first time either.

As they drove away, another man came out of the church, tall and dark-skinned with a heavy beard. He was talking on his mobile phone in an East European accent, and he was angry. "You get to him and you get to him now. You have two hours, or it's your skin I'll be stretching over my lampshade." He snapped his phone shut and strode over to the waiting Mercedes.

DI Lorraine Hunt glared at her partner Detective Luke Daniels. "I swear I will kill him," she mouthed. "Any minute now."

Luke, tall, handsome and black, with a presence about him that turned heads, tried not to laugh out loud. Unaware that his boss was reaching meltdown, Carter was droning on and on about the history of St Michael and All Angels church.

Two minutes later Lorraine had had enough. She stood up. "Yeah, OK, Carter, that's all very interesting, but old bones and stones that may or may not be four thousand years old can't very well help us with today's problems, can they?"

Luke smiled. Carter actually got away with more than anyone in the station. Luke knew that Lorraine genuinely liked the young, naive officer, who had somehow got it into his head that Lorraine shared his love of the area's history. But at the moment Luke was as concerned as Lorraine about the news that had come over the wires less than an hour ago.

"So what's up?" Carter asked.

"Fill him in, Luke. I'm in need of some liquid refreshment; back in a mo." She left them, her long blonde ponytail swishing from side to side as she strode out of the office.

Five minutes later she was back, a can of Diet Coke in her hand. From the look of horror on Carter's face she guessed Luke had told him most of what there was to know about Kirill Tarasov.

"So." She sat down at her desk, eyebrows raised.

Carter swallowed hard, then felt sick. "A...a cannibal?"

"Yes. A cannibal who collects antiques."

"There's no accounting for tastes, is there?" Luke said, shaking his head.

Carter and Lorraine groaned in unison, and Lorraine went on, "He's been wanted all over the world for years, nearly caught twice. Believe me this guy makes Dracula look like a pussy cat. He skins his victims, eats them, then decorates his house with their skin."

"Oh, gross," Carter shivered. "But why haven't I heard about him before now?"

"Classified information. There's enough fear in the world today without adding to it. Besides, why give him glory? There's plenty of weirdos out there that would worship him...Actually Kirill, if that's even his real name, if he's even really Russian, is a variant of an old Greek word which means lord."

"Yeah, in his case lord of darkness," Luke put in. "No one's safe when this guy's around."

"Please don't tell me he's in Houghton, please." Carter was thinking of his mother, all alone until he got in from work, and it was getting dark out there already. The hairs stood out on the back of his neck when he thought of the gruesome things Luke had told him.

"Get a grip, Carter," Lorraine said. "He was followed from Germany to France, where they lost him for the second time this year. But then luck struck and he was recognized getting off a plane in Newcastle. He was followed, but the agent's car died on him. Tarasov was last seen heading for Durham."

As Carter opened his mouth to ask more questions the phone rang. Lorraine quickly snatched it up.

The two officers watched her face go from dismay to outright disbelief. She muttered a few words, put the phone down and stared at Luke and Carter.

"Well?" Luke urged.

Lorraine slowly shook her head, blew air out of her cheeks before saying, "There's been a prison break at Durham, one man dead, two escaped...Both escapees were doing life for murder...Vicious murder." She stood up. "Come on, guys, we're all out on patrol."

* * *

It was a dark night, no stars and hardly any moon. Danny, Len and Adam met up outside the church. They had each taken a different route up from the Seahills; some of the gossips on the estate hardly slept, and if the three of them were seen together after midnight, they'd have put two and two together and come out with an odd number.

"So where we gonna dig first?" Len whispered.

"I reckon up the front, near the altar," Danny replied.

Adam nodded. "Sounds good to me."

They made their way quietly to the door. Danny pulled out a crowbar and set to work on the heavy locks. "Once upon a time churches used to be open all the time," he grunted as he struggled with the lock.

"Aye, but that was before thieving bastards started to rob them," Adam said with conviction.

Len looked at him, "So what the hell are we, then?"

Adam shrugged. "That's different. We're not robbing the church. I reckon coins and ancient stuff belong to the people, it's our … our birthright." He nodded at Len then at Danny.

"Will the pair of yers shut the fuck up and give me a hand, for Christ's sake?"

"OK, OK, keep yer hair on." Adam lent his weight to Danny's and the lock snapped with a sudden crack like a gunshot.

"Shit." Len ducked and quickly looked around.

They all held their breath as Danny slowly pushed the door, expecting it to start creaking at any moment. But the hinges were well oiled and it opened silently. "Remember," he hissed, "keep the torches pointed at the ground; we don't want any lights showing through the windows."

They crept quietly along to the altar. They were three feet away from their target when Len squealed.

"What the …?" Danny glared at him.

"Yer nearly frightened the life outta me, yer great prat." Adam gave Len a push.

"Something ran over me foot," Len muttered.

"I'll run over yer fucking foot in a minute." Danny thrust a spade at Len. "Here, this is as good a place as any."

"It was probably a rat," Adam whispered. "Or maybes a ghost." He grinned.

Len glared at him, and started digging. Danny pulled a lantern and another spade out of the holdall. He handed the spade to Adam and lit the lantern. The light spread over a six-foot radius, enough for them to see what they were doing. All three of them started digging in a yard-wide square.

Twenty minutes later Len's spade hit something solid.

"Oh my God." He dropped to his knees, quickly followed by the others. Adam held the torches as Len and Danny began to scrape away at the soil. In moments they uncovered a large metal box.

"That doesn't look really old," Len observed, though he had to keep his feet solid on the ground to stop himself dancing with excitement. He gave a deep sigh; the others knew how he felt. Rich at last, was the one thought running through their heads.

"It's bloody heavy though." Danny lifted the box and carried it to the altar.

Practically slavering, Adam rubbed his hands together in excitement. "Bet it's full of gold coins. We should have had Jacko here."

"He's got the flu. He could hardly get out of bed this morning." Len stared at the box as Danny stepped back. "But we'll see he's all right, won't we, Danny?"

Kirill Tarasov watched as the two he'd been waiting for ran from behind the trees to the car. One of them was limping badly. He frowned; a weakling. When they had climbed into the back of the Mercedes he turned to face them.

"Everything went to plan, then?" He eyed them up and instantly dismissed the smaller man who had limped and was less than skin and bone. To register on Tarasov's radar you needed some meat on your bones.

"Yeah," Simon Dupri, alias the Slasher, a nickname he'd been given by the press, answered quickly. "He definitely buried the box in the church, in front of the altar. He swore to it as he begged for his life."

The smaller man sniggered. He was Vinnie Grey, doing life for murdering his whole family then starting on his neighbours one dark winter night. He was cut short by a look from Tarasov.

"OK." Tarasov pulled into the road, "We go to the church now, and you tell me all about how he died on the way."

And you, skinny man, he thought, will not be coming out of the church. Fatso, though, I will keep close, in case rations are hard to come by someday soon.

"Open it, open it," Adam practically shouted.

"Shh," Danny and Len hissed.

For a moment there was silence. Adam took a deep breath and controlled himself, then nodded at the other two. Danny slowly pried the lid off the box. A sound behind him made him gasp, and the three of them spun round.

There was nothing but the pitch darkness with a lighter patch right at the back where the stained-glass window reigned supreme. Len wiped the sweat off his brow, and Adam placed a shaking hand over his heart.

"Just the fucking rats again," Danny snapped.

The lid was off the box now, and all three peered inside, holding their breath in anticipation.

Tarasov, followed by Dupri and Grey, quietly made his way past the old gravestones to the church. When they reached the door, Tarasov held his hand up and stared in dismay at the broken lock.

He clenched his fists and gritted his teeth. He had searched for years for the box, and wasn't going to be outdone now. He put his finger to his lips to quell any outbursts from the others, and cocked his head like an inquisitive dog listening, stretching his senses.

At first he heard nothing. He stepped through the door and paused, listening again, concentrating hard, then looked towards the altar. As his eyes adjusted to the darkness he saw the light beneath the altar, beckoning like a beacon.

Bastards!

"Hurry up, hurry up." Adam was unable to control himself any longer. "What is it ... Is it gold coins? Fucking tell us, man."

Len squashed up to his cousin on the other side, every bit as excited. "Are we rich? I can't stand this any more – how much?"

Danny pulled a large piece of carefully folded canvas out of the box and held it up. The other two shone their torches on it. "For God's sake, it's just a bloody painting." Unable to hide his disappointment, he shook his head. "It's a painting of a woman, who believe me is no Elizabeth Taylor."

"Yer can say that again." Adam stared at the painting. "I've seen that ugly mug somewhere before though."

Len tutted. "Oh you bloody pair of idiots, for God's sake, it's the Mona Lisa."

Danny and Adam stared at Len. After a moment Danny said, "Do yer think it's the real I am?"

Len looked in awe at the signature. Slowly he nodded.

"Is it worth anything?" Adam beat Danny to the question.

The answer came from behind them. "Yes, gentlemen ... millions."

For a moment they froze, then slowly, as if trained by a choreographer, they turned together. Danny swallowed hard, feeling Adam and Len tremble beside him – and who could blame them, faced with a huge man holding a large knife in each hand?

Tarasov moved closer. "For years I have followed this painting, then seven years ago the trail went cold. The fools in the museum think they have the real one. Ha."

"What, er, what yer gonna do, like?" Danny didn't quite succeed in keeping the tremble out of his voice. Judging by the man's face, he could guess exactly what he was going to do.

He smiled at them, and Len trembled even more. Adam though found his voice. "Who are you like? Standing there like some crazy fuck out of a horror movie. Think we're frightened, like?"

"You should be, cocky twat." Grey stepped out from behind Tarasov.

"Oh God," Len moaned. "We're well and truly up shit creek without a paddle this time, guys." A second later he screamed as he was grabbed from behind.

The scream forced Adam into action. Without thinking he threw himself at Grey, leaving Danny to deal with Tarasov and his knives. Len bent over then quickly threw his head back, snapping his assailant's nose. More by luck than anything else, Adam kicked Grey in exactly the right spot on his injured leg; when he yelled in pain and reached down, Adam launched a left hook and knocked him out flat.

As Len peeled himself away from the dead weight still clinging to him, Adam quickly moved to Danny's side.

Tarasov laughed. "You think you can take me? Ha, I don't think so. Not even two or three of you." He jumped forward and the knife in his right hand slashed down, taking a piece of Adam's ear off and slicing the side of his neck. Blood spurted, and Adam collapsed to his knees in shock.

Advancing on Danny, Tarasov laughed again.

"Fuck off," Danny yelled, wondering if this would be a good time to run, but knowing he couldn't leave Adam at the mercy of this grinning freak.

Then he had a brainwave. He snatched the painting up and shook the canvas. Tarasov stopped, a look of pure horror on his face.

"No, no...Do not damage it." His eyes burned into Danny's. "I will give you anything."

"Do yer honestly think for one minute that I'd trust you, yer creepy bastard?" Danny shook the painting again, as Len, finally untangled from Dupri, bent down to help Adam.

Tarasov curled his lip, "Enough of this," he shouted, his arms held high. Each long blade caught the light as he prepared to leap forward again.

"Oh yes, well said, definitely enough of this." DI Lorraine Hunt hurried into the church with Luke Daniels and Carter close behind.

They had been cruising round the Seahills estate, visiting a couple of known criminals recently released from Durham prison when Lorraine had suddenly remembered something Carter had said about the church. On a hunch they had quickly sped up to Houghton.

"Kirill Tarasov, I am arresting you on...Well, just about any crime known to man."

"Fucking hell." Danny wiped sweat from his brow. "Talk about saved by the bell." He bent down to see to Adam, but Len stared at him and shook his head.

"NO!" Danny yelled.

Using the sudden distraction Tarasov ran at Lorraine, but she was ready for him. Using a karate sidestep, she swiftly moved to one side, and as Tarasov ran past her she kicked his leg from under him. He fell to the floor, and Carter and Luke were on top of him in seconds.

Luke cuffed him. Tarasov looked at Lorraine; mixed with the contempt was a smattering of admiration. "Brought down by a woman."

"Save it, creep." Lorraine moved to check on Adam. It took her a few moments to find a pulse, but find it she did: erratic, but still a pulse. She took Len's hand and pressed it over the wound in Adam's neck. "Keep it there ... " She looked over her shoulder. "Carter? Ambulance."

"On its way, boss."

Danny and Len breathed twin sighs of relief. Lorraine looked at them, shook her head and said, "Please tell me why I am not at all surprised to find you bloody lot here."

HOMEWORK

Phil Lovesey

English homework
Judy Harris – Year 10.

IN YOUR OPINION, is Hamlet merely faking his madness, or is he really insane?

This term we have been studying *Hamlet*, a play written ages ago by William Shakespeare. It's quite good, though the words are all strange for modern people to really understand. There's lots of stuff that is really, really old, that Sir needed to try and explain to us before it made any sense, not that most of the class seemed bothered, goofing around as usual.

Most of us thought that the film was better than the book, but that Mel Gibson bloke still used all the old words, so that when there wasn't much going on except him talking, I noticed quite a few of the class were either mucking about or texting. I even told Sir about this after one lesson, but all he did was sort of smile at me, then tell me that Shakespeare wasn't for everyone, and maybe it was better for me if the class didn't think I was telling tales, which seemed quite harsh, as I was only trying to help him.

The story of *Hamlet* sort of goes like this: There's this prince (Hamlet) who lives in another country a long time ago. His dad dies and his mum marries Hamlet's uncle, so Hamlet doesn't get to become the king. He gets real mad about this, and reckons his mum's a bit of a whore for marrying his uncle, especially when the ghost of his dad comes back and tells Hamlet that the pair of them were an item before he died, and that his brother even dripped poison into his ear and murdered him, just so he could get off with Hamlet's mum and become King.

This was quite a spooky bit in the film, the ghost thing, and most of the class were watching, except Cheryl Bassington, who was still texting her boyfriend under the desk. He's an apprentice plumber who lives down our road, and I often see him pick her up on his crappy little motorbike thing. She says they've done it lots of times, which I think is really lame at her age, as I reckon you should save yourself for someone who really loves you.

Hamlet has a woman who loves him. Her name's Ophelia, and she sort of hangs around the palace, pining for him. It's that Helena Bonham Carter in the film, and all the lads in the class were right crude about her in her nightie. Steve Norris made a sort of "joke" about boning-Bonham-Carter which even Sir sniggered at, but I just thought it was sick. I think Ophelia's really sad, because she really does love Hamlet, and when he starts acting a bit mental, she gets really upset. He even tells her that he never loved her, and that she should go away and become a nun. Even Polonius (her own dad) uses Ophelia to test if Hamlet really is mad, which seems, well, odd – but then Polonius gets stabbed behind a curtain anyway, which serves him right for being such a bad dad in the first place.

My dad wouldn't ever do such a thing to me, regardless of what the papers said about him at the time of the robbery.

It seems that in *Hamlet*, everyone's only after power, and that they're prepared to do anything to get it, even if it means killing their family, marrying incestuously, using their kids, or faking madness that really hurts people. I think that's very bad of all of them. Ophelia is so cut up about Hamlet being horrible to her that she goes and drowns herself, and even Hamlet doesn't seem that bothered. Neither did the boys in the class, who asked for that bit to be shown again, as they reckoned you could see Helena Bonham Carter's tits through the wet nightie. Thank goodness that someone tells Ophelia's brother what a schemer Hamlet is, so that he comes back really angry and tries to kill Hamlet in a duel.

We all thought that the ending was right crap, because nearly everyone dies, Hamlet, his uncle, his mum, Ophelia's brother; they all end up dead in this big hall, either poisoned or stabbed with poison-tipped swords. Dave Coles reckoned that the *Macbeth* we did for SATS in Year 9 was better because there were real nude women to perv over, and hangings and beheadings and stuff. When I told him I'd hated that film, loads of people laughed at me, and I felt right stupid, especially as Sir didn't tell them off for being so cruel.

Maybe that was when I decided to do what I've done to you, Sir. Maybe that was the moment that it all made a sort of sense. Like I've written, maybe some people simply want power, and don't care about other people's feelings. Like you, then. Just two terms in the school, obviously wanting to be the trendy young teacher, joining in with them, laughing at me, not stopping it like other teachers would have done. Perhaps it was just another tiny, all too quickly forgotten moment for you, but believe me, Sir, it went well deep with me. Well deep.

That night, I told my mum about what had happened in your class, how you'd let them laugh at me. She was cooking – well, I say cooking, putting a ready-meal in the microwave for Uncle Tony for his tea, more like. Because she has to have it on the table for him when he gets in, or there's trouble. He rings on his mobile from The Wellington Arms, tells her to have it ready in five minutes, then suddenly she's all action, heaves herself up from the sofa and sends me up to my room as she gets done.

Once, his meal wasn't ready. I heard the result. Lots of shouting, then a scream. Mum's scream. Then what sounded like moaning. I didn't come down until the door slammed half an hour later, and I saw Uncle Tony walking away from the house from my bedroom window. Mum wouldn't look at me, sort of flinched when I tried to put my arm round her. She was trying to stick a torn-up photograph of her and Dad back together, but her hands were shaking too much, and she was trying not to cry. I asked if I could help. It was a nice photo – her and Dad on honeymoon in Greece, both of them looking right young and happy on a beach in front of all these white hotels. She swore at me and told me to get back upstairs to my room.

Hamlet used to love his dad as well. Then he went away to some college somewhere, and when he came back his dad was dead, and his uncle had married his mum. The problem is that his dad is now a ghost, and tells him that he was murdered, so that makes Hamlet really angry. He also doesn't know if it's just his mind being tricky with him, so he decides to set a trap to see if his uncle is really guilty or not. Hamlet gets these actors to do a play which is sort of like his uncle killing his dad, and watches his uncle's reaction. He wants to "prick his conscience".

Dave Coles went "wheeey!" when Mel Gibson said the word "prick" – which everyone but me thought was real funny. I thought it was a good plan of Hamlet's. He wasn't saying "prick" like a penis; he was saying it like a needle, pricking his uncle's brain to see if he was guilty. I think I'm cleverer than most of them in the class because I read more and understand these things, know that words can have more than just the obvious meaning. I think it's because I'm not allowed to use the computer at home (Uncle Tony's on it most of the time he's in), so I don't have any MSN or anything. Or a mobile phone. Just books, really. A bit of telly sometimes, downstairs, when Mum's finished watching the soaps. But mostly I'm in my room, thinking and reading.

I write to Dad a lot. Tell him about school. Mum says I can't talk about some of the stuff that goes on in the house, as it would only upset him. She says that even though Uncle Tony isn't my real uncle, he's doing us a massive favour by staying with us when Dad's away. They used to be good mates, Dad and Uncle Tony, working at the warehouse together, going down to the pub, but when it all went wrong, and the police came for Dad, they sort of fell out.

What's really great is that Dad's letters are getting longer each time he writes back to me. Just a page in the beginning, now it's often three or four. His spelling's really coming on too, because of all the classes he's been taking. He's been well behaved, so they've allowed him more time to study. He says he's taking his GCSEs too! Strange, isn't it, Sir? There I am, in your class, studying *Hamlet* for my English GCSE Shakespeare coursework, and my dad's doing exactly the same thing. At thirty-eight, too. He reckons once he's done his English, Maths, and Science, he'll do loads more subjects after that. He says one bloke further down the wing he knows has got nineteen GCSEs! See, Sir? They tell you all this stuff about people in prison being right thick and scummy, but there's some of them really trying to improve themselves. Dad's got another two years left, so I reckon he'll have more qualifications than me when he gets out. How weird will that be?

In Dad's last letter, he talked about Uncle Tony, and said that even though they weren't best friends any more, it was good that he had agreed to lodge at our house, and help pay the rent and stuff. He said it was the least Uncle Tony could do, because really, he owed Dad big time. He also said that the years would fly by, and when he finally got released, he'd got a surprise that would keep me, Mum, and him happy for years. When I showed Mum the letter, she screwed it up and chucked it away, said my dad was talking nonsense, told me never to mention it again. I'm not sure, but I think it was to do with the robbery at the warehouse. Thing is, although the police had CCTV film of Dad loading stuff into a van when he shouldn't have been, the actual stuff was never found. The local newspaper said it was worth over a £100,000 – though you can't believe everything they say, *can you*, Sir?

Dad doesn't like me to visit, see him where he is, so every other Saturday, when Mum and Uncle Tony go to Norwich, I go to the reference library in town. It's nice there, warm. I don't use the Internet stuff. I prefer to look through the books and old newspapers they have on this stuff called microfilm. Honestly, Sir, it's amazing. Thousands and thousands of newspapers from all over the place going back years and years. All catalogued to make searches easier. People think that the Internet is the way to find out stuff, but I reckon searching through old newspapers in the reference library is better. There's loads of interesting stuff in those papers, articles people can't be bothered to upload on to the Web, because I guess it would simply take too long. Can be frustrating, though, and you have to have a little bit of luck and patience.

Yeah, luck. I guess that's how I managed to find you, Sir. Luck and patience, And, of course, a really good reason. And you made sure you gave me plenty of those, didn't you. Sir? Calling me a sneak, not helping me when the others laughed at me. I began to wonder why you did that. Why you wouldn't help me. And then I noticed, figured out why. Just one of those chance things that no one else saw, but I did.

It was a Wednesday, the last lesson before lunch, and we were all in your classroom as Mel Gibson was waffling on about whether or not to kill himself (*To be, or not to be*; remember, Sir, you made us watch the bloody thing ten times that lesson?), and true to form, I could see Cheryl Bassington texting away in the darkness on her mobile under the desk. Except it wasn't her plumber boyfriend she was texting, was it, Sir? Because when she pressed Send, the next thing that happened was you got your phone out from your jacket and read the screen as discreetly as possible. I saw you, Sir. Watched it happen. You, Sir. Someone who should be trusted to educate us; getting secret texts from a fifteen-year-old girl. Well, naturally, my conscience was "pricked", as Shakespeare might have said ...

I began wondering what Hamlet would do in my situation. You know, needing to find stuff out, but not wanting to be caught doing it. So I did what he did – pretended to be a loony for a bit. That lunchtime, I went and sat right next to Cheryl Bassington and started eating a bit weirdly, mixing my pudding into my pizza and making stupid noises and giggling. Very Hamlet, Sir, you'd have been proud. Anyway, I could see my plan was working, and that Cheryl and her mates couldn't wait to get up and leave. The next bit was so easy – just as they were going and calling me all sorts of names, I suddenly leant over and clung on to Cheryl, slipping a hand into her coat pocket and grabbing the mobile as she yelped and tried to hit me to get away. Mr Price came over and began shouting at us to behave, but Cheryl and her mates just swore at him and ran off. He asked me if I was all right, and I said I was fine. Next, I went straight to the toilet block, locked myself in, and went through the phone.

They're really quite easy to figure out, these mobile things. There's a kind of main menu with all sorts of helpful symbols to direct you to all the stuff stored on it. I found myself looking at Cheryl's pictures first, and let me tell you, Sir, there's some right rude stuff on there. Not just bits of the plumber, either, but stuff of you, as well. And not like shots taken in class when you weren't watching, but photos of you smiling right at the camera, in bed, with her... Well, you were there, you know the rest ...

I couldn't believe how bloody stupid you'd been, what a crazy risk you were taking. If Cheryl showed any of this stuff to the wrong person – you'd be out of a job, wouldn't you, Sir? They'd probably stick you in prison, too, wouldn't they? And my dad tells me what they do to people like you in prison, Sir. Really horrible things that even the wardens (he calls them "screws") turn a blind eye to. Really, really stupid of you, Sir.

Next, I went into the text menu, and found loads and loads. From you, to her; from her back to you. Some of them went back as far as six weeks, which, considering you've only been teaching here for just over two terms, kind of makes you a very fast worker, I guess. They have names for people like you, Sir.

Anyway, the most recent series of texts between the two of you were about meeting up on Saturday night. At the usual place, apparently, wherever that was. You suggested half-eight, and Cheryl had simply replied with one of those really lame smiley-face things. Sad. And sick.

But seeing as no one had complained, no rumours had started, I had to assume that no one else knew about you and her. Except me, of course. Which really made me think about things for a while.

Strange life you've led, Sir. Like I say, the reference library comes up with all sorts of stuff. One of the main reasons I went there was to find out more about what had happened to my dad. It even made one or two of the national papers, because I guess it was what those newspaper people refer to as a "slow news week". Seems one of the main things about it was the fact that the police reckoned Dad had to have had someone helping him that night. There were two CCTV cameras that covered the warehouse, but only one was trained where it was supposed to be, on the loading yard. The other one was pointing across the road at (and here I'm going to use a quotation, just like you told me to) "the entrance to a nearby youth club, where a group of underage girls could be seen to be drinking and cavorting with young lads".

See what I'm saying, Sir? If someone *had* been helping Dad (and he's never admitted as much, even to me) then the camera wasn't pointing the right way to catch them. It was watching young girls instead. Maybe it was looking for trouble from them, but then again, you know better than that, don't you, Sir? For guess what I found when I researched our town's CCTV company a little further? That's right, a picture of you, stood with the two other operators on the launch of the company five years ago. You – unmistakably. Your name on the caption thing, everything. A big photo of all three of you, smiling in front of loads of little television screens, the article telling people how you could remotely direct and move all these little cameras around the town to catch criminals and keep us safer. Sort of like you playing Big Brother, wasn't it, Sir? Only, not the crappy programme on the telly – the book by George Orwell. Like I say – I read a lot, I really do.

And once I found out about your "preferences" from Cheryl's mobile, things started to drop into place. I began piecing it together as I sat in those toilets on that Wednesday lunchtime. Just under a year, you've been teaching. Eighteen months my dad's been inside. According to the papers, at Dad's trial, the CCTV company admitted they'd received a resignation from one of their operators for "failing to comply with company policy whilst monitoring the immediate area around the warehouse". That was *you*, wasn't it, Sir?

I reckoned you left the job, took a quick teacher-training course somewhere, then got the job here. But, like I say, it was only a theory. I could have been wildly wrong. So I decided to do what Hamlet does, and devise a test (another conscience-pricker) to see if I was right. Here's what I did...

First, I texted you back on Cheryl's phone. You remember that one, Sir? The one where she asked to meet you that very night, at The Wellington Arms? That was me, not her. But less than a minute later, the phone buzzed in my hands with your reply, something about having to be really careful, it was quite a public place.

And I was giggling now, as I replied, insisting we must meet, that I was worried, had something to tell you that I might need to see a doctor about. I remember having to stop myself from laughing when I pressed Send.

Next, I deleted the messages and dropped the phone down the toilet. Now, even if Cheryl and her mates did find it, the thing wouldn't work. You wouldn't be able to secretly text her before the meeting in The Wellington. You were most likely going to show up, and she had no idea about it. Quite a scheme, eh? I think even Hamlet would have been proud of me, don't you, Sir?

It's a good play, *Hamlet*, and has often been interpreted in many different ways. It seems to me that the central question – does he fake his madness to get revenge on those who've betrayed him? – is almost impossible to answer. Perhaps Shakespeare was trying to say that all revenge is a form of madness, as it can consume our minds if we're not careful.

I think Dad's the sanest man I know. Yes, he did a stupid thing and got caught, and now he's being punished for it. But he's never talked of revenge – even though I reckon he'd probably want to get that CCTV operator who spent too long looking at young girls getting drunk, rather than catching Dad's accomplice on the night of the robbery. The police never found any fingerprints or anything, but the fact is that Dad *couldn't* have done it on his own. Someone else must have helped him, been inside the warehouse, handing him the boxes of stuff to load into the van, just out of shot of the properly sighted camera. But when the police went through the tapes, Dad was the only person on them. Doesn't seem very fair, does it, Sir? My dad in prison, and the other man going free because you didn't do your job properly?

Chances are, Sir, you never made the connection between me and Dad. Judy Harris, I mean, it's not as if it's a very uncommon surname, is it? Sort of invisible to you, aren't I? The swotty kid who complains about the others, tells tales on them; the easy one to ridicule. The plain one, the one that doesn't wear makeup, giggle at you as you pass by in the corridor. Just invisible old Judy Harris, gives in her work on time, does all the homework, tries her best. Strange how life can turn out, isn't it, Sir.

Back to my conscience-pricker. Having arranged for you to be in The Wellington, I decided that Mum and Uncle Tony needed a little more culture in their lives. I went to the shopping precinct on the way home, bought myself a copy of the *Hamlet* DVD, told them both that after tea, I thought it would be a really nice idea if we all

sat down and watched it together. Well, of course, Uncle Tony –
already a little drunk at this point – raised a few objections, said he
didn't mind watching Mel Gibson stuff, *Mad Max* and the like, but
he was buggered if he was going to sit down and watch a "load of
Shakespeare shit all night". (See, another quotation, that's two so
far; doing right well, aren't I, Sir?)

Anyway, I made a bit of a fuss, and eventually Mum decided to
smooth things over and asked Uncle Tony really nicely if he'd do
this one thing. I said it'd make us all feel more like a proper family,
and Uncle Tony sort of made a throaty noise, shrugged, and gave
way, saying he'd give it half an hour, and if it was bollocks, then
he'd leave it.

So, Sir, just after half-seven that night, I put *Hamlet* on our DVD
player. Imagine that – a bit of real culture in our grotty house.
Amazing, eh? And then I did what Hamlet does, watched my mother
and my uncle real close as the story unravelled…

It didn't take long, say twenty minutes at the most, and that's
even with all the old language to cope with. Mum and Uncle Tony
soon got the gist of it – the betrayal of Hamlet's father – and began
sort of shifting uncomfortably and giving these sideways looks at
each other. Honestly, Sir, it worked a treat.

Uncle Tony started coming out with all this stuff about Mel
Gibson going "poofy", and that he was much better in *Braveheart*
and the *Lethal Weapon* films. I just knew he was begging for an
excuse to leave what was becoming more and more embarrassing
for him. So at that point I decided to tell him about you, Sir. Not the
Cheryl Bassington stuff, or even the way you were so mean to me;
no, instead I told him about the other stuff.

Yeah, I know, I lied. But just a white one, really. And Hamlet
himself does that, doesn't he, when he tells poor Ophelia that he
doesn't really love her any more? I told Uncle Tony that when I was
in town buying the DVD a strange bloke had come up to me asking
me my name and where I lived, and when I told him, he asked me if
Tony Watts lived with us. When I said he did, the man told me he
wanted to speak to him about "the favour" he'd done my Uncle
Tony with the security cameras, and that as far as he was concerned

he thought that Tony Watts owed him, big-style, and that he'd be waiting in The Wellington at 8.30 to "sort it all out".

Well, my Uncle Tony being the sort of bloke he is, you don't have to try too hard to imagine his reaction. He was well angry, and began swearing and cursing, telling me I should have told him much earlier, asking for a description of you, then grabbing his coat and storming off, slamming the front door behind him so loudly that the walls shook. Mum looked right ashen, turned the DVD off, and told me to get straight upstairs to my room, that she thought I'd caused enough upset for one night. Uncle Tony didn't come home that night.

That was two weeks ago, and you've been off school ever since, haven't you, Sir? At Thursday morning's full-school assembly, the Head told us that you'd been attacked the previous night, and were staying away to recover. Two broken ribs and a fractured jaw, the local paper said, with a couple of witnesses saying you'd been beaten up by a Tony Watts (unemployed) in the car park of The Wellington Arms. Police, apparently, are still trying to find a motive, but I'm sure with a little "help" they'll have a clearer picture of why he did that cruel thing to you.

Uncle Tony's on remand, as we can't afford the bail, so he'll be inside till the court case, which should be really interesting. The police have already interviewed my mum about Uncle Tony, but they haven't got to me yet. I'm not sure whether to tell them what I know, or to keep quiet about it. I'll write to Dad and ask him what he thinks I should do.

Our substitute teacher isn't very good, but she's told us to finish these assignments and the school will send them to you to mark while you recover. I'm sure that when you read this, Sir, you'll realize why you were attacked that night, together with how much I know about you that you'd rather other people didn't.

In conclusion, I say that whether Hamlet was faking his madness is irrelevant. How sane are any of us, anyway? And isn't the very idea of faking madness a bit bad in the first place? Maybe you should know, Sir, the amount of faking you've done in the last few years.

I look forward to receiving my A for this essay. After all, I really did my homework on you.

NO THANKS, PLEASE

Declan Burke

HEADS TURNED, HALF-CURIOUS, then full-faced in horror. A man started towards her, one hand out as if reaching to catch a low driven ball, but she walked on, turning up off the river under the arch at Christchurch and on down Patrick Street.

A condom in the gutter with a used teabag inside. A Labrador puppy cocking a leg at its reflection in a puddle. Italian names on car tyres. Each new thing reminded her why she was looking in these places for the first time. Not to avoid the shame she would see mirrored in their eyes or the degradation she might glimpse in some angled shop window. It simply hurt too much to roll her right eye up against the bruising. So she kept her head down and her shoulders hunched, arms loosely folded to cradle her ribs.

Now her feet began to hurt. At first the pain was a sharp pinching where the stiff leather folded across the knuckles of her small toes but soon it became a chafing and melted down in a raw burn. She realized the blisters had burst but she did not stop. She thought that if she stopped walking she would fall down and die. This was who she was now: a woman who might die if she ever stopped walking.

She tried to remember her name.

He rattled the paper in folding it, then slammed the pen down. This was his quiet time, mid-afternoon, a time for the crossword, a smoke. He crossed the apartment in two strides and jammed a forefinger against the red button.

"Yes?"

But all he heard was the intercom hiss and a low, rasping breathing. "Look," he said. "If I have to go down there..." Then he heard the faint, choked-off sob.

"Janey?" His stomach churned. "Janey? Is that you?"

The sob broke.

He didn't open the door wide enough and slammed his shoulder on the frame on the way through.

He ministered to her cuts and bruises using paper tissues and Dettol. But it was awkward, leaning in from so far away. She would flinch back even before he touched her.

"I'm not going to hurt you, Janey. I just want to—"

"I know," she whispered.

She had bawled at first, raw and honking until the whiskeys seeped through. Then she had whimpered, shoulders shaking with rage and fear and the tremors of a pure adrenaline charge. Now she seemed blank and dry, like old cardboard. "I just," she said, "I…"

He waited for her to finish but she only winced and hunched forward, arms folded below her chest.

"Janey, I really think we should get you to ER. Those ribs should be—"

"It's too late now." She nodded at the empty glass. "It's the first thing they'll ask, was I drinking."

"But I gave you the whiskey, to calm you down. I'll be your—"

"Jay? James?"

"What?"

"Can you run me a bath? Can you do that for me? A warm bath?"

"But shouldn't you wait until after you get…?"

But she was rocking herself, features flinty and set against the world at an impossible angle. He put the paper tissues on the arm of the chair and left the room.

When she said, "I'll need you to help me get undressed," he could almost taste the loathing that coated her tongue.

"Of course," he said. "Whatever. Janey, just ask. Anything you want."

She nodded, staring at a fixed point between the coffee table and who she used to be.

"You can stay here, no worries," he went on. "He won't get in here." He ground his teeth. "He can fucking try, but he'll be leaving backwards, in three fucking body bags."

She made a sucking sound, ran her tongue between her teeth and her split upper lip. "Jay? Did you leave the bath running?"

"Fuck."

He mopped the floor with dirty towels, poured in a handful of fizzy salts. Called her from the bathroom door and watched her lurch down the hallway like an ageing monster. She turned her back to him and he eased her T-shirt up over her shoulders, unhooked her bra, slid her denims over her hips and down past her knees. He experienced the frisson he had been dreading but when it was past he was unable to say if it had been the expected sexual rush or a profound reaction to engaging with the most vulnerable intimacy he had ever known.

The abrasion on her back ran from one shoulder blade almost to her kidneys. It looked as if he had attacked her with a wire-wool scrub. He quivered, felt his jaws lock in place.

"I'll be right next door, Janey," he said, retreating. "If there's anything, just shout."

"It hurts when I talk."

He closed the door as gently as he knew how and backed away down the hall wondering what his next move should be. The grating of the key was a kick in the gut.

He slipped out to the small Spar on Patrick Street. A pizza, garlic bread, a bottle of vodka, a carton of orange juice, some Panadol. At the checkout a stout middle-aged woman leaned across the counter to the young bottle-blonde till-jockey. He edged closer until they could no longer ignore him. The older woman turned and drew herself up.

"Can we help you?" she asked. Dry pink powder grouted the corners of her mouth.

"My friend was beaten up," he said, nodding at the armful of groceries. "She's a woman," he explained. "Her husband beat her up."

Their eyes glazed over, tiny pools freezing fast.

"She's taking a bath," he added, as if that might help them thaw.

"You left her alone?" the bottle-blonde said.

"She locked the door."

"You shouldn't have left her alone," the stout woman said. "God love her." Her hand was a hummingbird as she blessed herself, bringing her forehead down to meet the fingers, the wicker carrier-bag heavy on her elbow. "How bad?" she said.

"I'm going to kill him."

The stout woman stood back to allow him to put the armful of groceries on the counter. "Now hush," she said. "That's no way to talk."

"How?" the bottle-blonde said, waving the pizza at the side of the till until she heard the beep of barcode recognition. He stared at her. "How are you going to kill him?" she said, picking up the orange juice.

"Now, Tricia," the stout woman said.

"I'm going to eat his fucking throat out," he said.

The bottle-blonde bagged his groceries and put out her hand. "Don't just say it," she said. She rang up the transaction, returned his change. "I don't believe you," she said.

She ate steadily, without interest or appetite, and he despised himself for having to look away from the loose gaping of the bathrobe. She took two more painkillers and sipped her vodka-orange and stared vacantly at the TV.

"Are you sure you don't want to ring the cops?" he said.

She nodded.

"And you definitely don't want to go to the hospital."

She nodded again, weary.

"Are you going to stay here tonight?"

"No." The word deader than stone.

"You're going back?"

She nodded.

"Jesus, Janey..." Her eyes flickered away from the screen and came to rest on his. "If he's done it once he'll do it again. Go back now and you're telling him it's OK. You're giving him the *right*, Janey."

"Don't you think that's a bit simplistic?"

"What's so complicated about being kicked in the head?"

She waited. "This is about me," she said quietly.

"It's you I'm trying to help."

Her eyes flickered back to the screen.

"At least let me ring Caroline," he said. "What's her number?"

"She's minding the girls," she said. She drained her vodka-orange and stood up slowly.

"At least they weren't around to see it," he said, and just like that, as if she had suddenly seen it through her daughters' eyes, a thin orangey vomit spewed.

"At least," he said, re-hooking her bra, "let me come in with you. Just so he knows you're not alone."

"So he knows there's someone like him, just ready to go."

"Fuck sakes, Janey…"

"You can come in," she said. "If you can admit that you need to come in for you, then you can come in."

"Okay," he said. "I'm only doing it for me. So my conscience is clear. Happy?"

"No," she said. She walked to the car barefoot.

He drove up past the canal, out through Donnybrook, taking the N11 all the way to Foxrock. He vaguely remembered the estate from the house-warming party. When they pulled in to the kerb she stared into the setting sun, face immobile below the sunglasses he'd given her.

"You don't have to do this," he said.

"See the icebergs?" she said.

"What?"

She nodded, and he turned to look. Light wisps of orange-tinged cirrus hung suspended above the sun. And it was true: three small, hard, glittering clouds had the appearance of icebergs floating in a patch of light blue sky. "How would that happen?" she said. "What are they?"

He shrugged. "I don't know."

She couldn't reach up far enough to open the front door and so she handed him the key. They walked through the downstairs, then checked upstairs, but he wasn't home. She didn't want him to wait.

"Not here," he said. "But I'm going to wait down the road. And when he comes home, I'm coming back in. Someone needs to tell him what's what."

"And what's that?" she said. They were standing in the hall, the front door ajar.

"This isn't about you," he said. "It's about him."

"It's about you," she said.

"He has to learn. I'm only going to warn him."

She bit her lip and looked down. "It wasn't Sean," she whispered.

He frowned. "Then who?"

"I don't know."

"You were jumped?"

"Jay," she pleaded, "trust me."

But he was adamant, insisting. She backed away into the corner behind the door and when he took a step towards her the words tumbled out as if they might fend him off. Job. Lost. Mortgage. Sean. Friend. Company.

"No fooling around, though," she said. She sounded dull, a sleepwalker. "That was the deal. Just company. For the races at Leopardstown. Just drinks and company."

And all he could think to say was, "You walked all the way in from fucking Leopardstown?"

"There was another girl," she said. "In the room. I think she was Thai." She reached up and removed the sunglasses, holding them out for him to take. Her right eye was closed behind a blackening bruise spreading from forehead to cheek. "They preferred her."

He swallowed dry. "Where is she now?"

"I don't know," she said.

"What room, though?"

"I don't fucking *know*," she whispered.

He didn't believe her.

He drove to the far side of the green in the middle of the estate and reversed the car so that he was looking directly at the house. He opened the boot, found the wheel-brace, sat in the car again and lit a cigarette, huddling back in the seat to watch the house over the rim of the steering wheel.

Sean arrived walking, maybe an hour or so later. Smaller than James remembered, stick-thin even beneath the overcoat. He trudged to the driveway and stood outside looking up at the house with his hands buried deep in the pockets. Then his shoulders seemed to fall forward and he trudged up the driveway. He reached with the key, reconsidered, and rang the doorbell instead. He rang three times before the door opened but when it did he stepped inside straight away.

Now Jay got out of the car and jogged across the green, sidling up the side of the driveway out of sight of the living room window. He gained the porch and stood with his back to the wall, half-crouched, the wheel-brace held rigid behind his thigh. Then he punched the doorbell with his forefinger and left it there, jammed down.

They didn't answer. Four times he pressed the doorbell, half-crouched against the wall, looking out at the quiet estate. Wondering if he could be seen from behind the lowered blinds that faced their house. He pounded on the door but no one came.

He looked out across the estate to where the sun was sinking behind the horizon. The icebergs were gone. The porch lights hummed, flickered, winked on. On the far side of the green his car seemed impossibly distant.

He wondered how long was reasonable to stay before walking away.

THE SAME AS SHE ALWAYS WAS

Keith McCarthy

I AM THE *same that I always was.*
 I am the same that I always was.

Acts do not change us. Acts spring from what we are, and what we believe, and perhaps most important of all, what we desire. I am still the Gilly I was on the first day I met Greg, as I was on the day that he left me, as I was on the day that the police came to call.

It was Greg that changed not me, Greg who altered the bargain, who changed the rules, who ripped up the contract. Greg who stole my life from me without even realizing it.

I still love Greg and I always will, until the day I die.

The rain comes suddenly but not unexpectedly. When Greg and Gilly set out on their walk from the pub in the Forest of Dean where they are staying for the weekend, the wind was blustering and clouds, fluffy and bright, moved briskly before it, casting huge, travelling shadows on the land around them. He said to her then that he thought it would rain and she said, "Maybe, but let's go anyway."

Gilly loves walking. When Greg first met her, eleven years ago, it was on a walk, one for a breast cancer charity, because her mother had died of the disease and because his mother had had a cancerous lump but was cured. She has vividly red hair and freckles and Greg has loved her from the first moment he saw her.

"We should take waterproofs."

"Why?" she asks. "If there's a shower, we'll find some shelter somewhere; wait for it to stop."

"If it does stop."

She laughs. "So what if it doesn't? We've nowhere else to go, nothing to be late for."

And so they set out, walking through the lush green valley, beside dry stonewalls, past pretty cottages and copses and fields of potatoes, corn and grass. They have not been here since their honeymoon and the smells, the sights, the tastes bring back that time, reminding them of just how much they need the relaxation and respite from the stresses of their oh-so-busy lives.

Especially now.

A marriage is a pact. Everyone knows that, don't they? And a pact involves sharing and pooling, giving and taking, so that something is created, something that exists that had no existence before. Gestalt. A third entity that is part man, part woman, but most important of all, part neither of them. A creation that is every bit as real as a work of art, or an invention...

Or a child.

They have come because they need to escape their troubles. They know that a week in the Forest of Dean will be only a temporary respite but they also hope that it will allow them to see each other anew, to regain something that they both know (without saying as much) they have lost and, more importantly, that their relationship has lost.

Recent times have been hard.

Greg's IT consultancy has been going through a difficult phase and he has had to lay off all but one of the eight people he once employed; he has hopes to gain a new contract from a national retail distribution company but fears that he is too close to the event horizon of financial breakdown, the point beyond which no business returns.

And Gilly...

Poor Gilly has just terminated a pregnancy. She is thirty-eight now and she fears that she has made the wrong decision.

Who can blame her?

Three miscarriages preceded this pregnancy, one of which was at eighteen weeks and therefore the worst; she had dared then to hope that she might gain her prize.

The only prize that she has ever really wanted.

When did I realize that a child was all I ever desired?

How odd it feels, to have longed for something for so long, yet not to have known it, not until recently. When I was young, I played with my dolls and teddies, yet I did not consciously appreciate that this was all that I wanted; when I was a teenager, I had boyfriends but not, I am sure, because I saw them as a means to motherhood. Yet now I know that that was precisely my reasoning.

It frightens me, this recognition that I am driven, that I always have been driven, that perhaps all my decisions in life were guided by an imperative over which I have had no control, that was wired into me, whether by fate, or blind chance.

Or God.

After forty-five minutes, when they have just stopped to admire two ponies in a field, he asks her, "Are you all right?"

She looks up at him and smiles. "Oh, yes."

This starts off fine but ends with a catch in her throat. She looks quickly away, back to the ponies.

"Hey," he says gently, tapping her on the shoulder.

A nod. Shoulders hunched and a nod that is tensely sprung. She does not look at him.

"Gilly."

He puts his arm around her shoulders, grasps the soft blue cashmere, squeezes them gently, lowers his face to be level with hers. Another quick nod but this time with a sniff; still no words.

The ponies are skittish, kicking and suddenly galloping in short spurts. Perhaps they sense the coming rain.

Greg says quietly, in her ear, "You did the right thing."

For a moment, she continues to stare fixedly at the ponies but the sniffs come more and more quickly until she suddenly begins to cry continuously. Another squeeze of her shoulders and she turns to him and buries her face in his thick, woollen jumper; she smells his eau de cologne, the one that she gave him for their first Christmas and that he still says that he likes.

"We couldn't have coped." He is so calm, so reassuring, so certain.

"But..."

"We both agreed, didn't we? Do you remember, Gilly? How we agreed?"

Face still buried in his sweater, still trying to burrow into him, to hide from her grief, she nods slowly and only after hesitation. He is holding her tightly but she likes this, draws comfort from it. He says, "You're not strong enough on your own. You would have needed me, and at this moment, with things so difficult, I couldn't have given you the support *and* got the business going again."

There is no nod this time. She withdraws slightly, looks up into his face where she has always found so much security. "I didn't realize that it would be so horrible."

He holds her face in his hands, smears tears with his thumbs. "I know, I know," he whispers although she wonders just *how* he can know. "In a few years, when we can more easily afford it, when we're more established."

"But I'm getting old. What if I can't have any more?"

A laugh, one that tells her she is being silly, that of course she will have more.

"You will," he says. There is something of a command about this but it is couched in the softest, most gentle of tones. "These days, no one is too old."

It is flippant, almost insulting. The easy response to the unimportant fears of a subordinate.

"I knew that it wouldn't be easy, but I didn't think it would be this hard..."

For a moment he does not speak, then, "You're too close to it, Gilly. It was only a month and a half ago. By the time Christmas comes, you'll be able to think logically. You'll see then that it was all for the best."

And this makes her realize that he does not understand at all, that he *had* thought it was easy, that he *still* thinks it is. A light anaesthetic, a short sleep and – hey presto! – no more problem.

Yet six weeks on, she still feels dirty, filled with sin, tainted by guilt.

She says, "I hope so." But she is thinking through his words, his tone, the thoughts that must lie behind them.

A smile and what he presumably believes is a warm laugh as he replies, "You'll get over it, Gilly. This will help. You'll see."

And then he kisses her and holds her again for a long, long time.

"Okay?" he asks.

She says that, yes, she is, because she can see that this is what he wants her to say.

They continue on their walk.

Greg rescued me.

That sounds like an overstatement – hyperbole, I believe they call it – but that is what I always believed.

My mother had died after a long illness and I thought that I was coping by being busy and by helping Dad come to terms with the situation, and by jumping into charity. Except that I wasn't. I was fading, day by day, good deed by good deed, and I was completely ignorant of it all.

Greg gave me back a skyline, something to aim for, a concept that there was an outside world as well as the place where I lived.

I just wish that I thought that he knew what he was doing.

I'm afraid, you see, that he did not perform any of his chivalrous acts consciously, that he had always been blithely unaware – if not uncaring – of what he did.

Which is fine, I thought at first.

After all, most good in this world is done unconsciously, as an unintended byproduct of acts performed for different, perhaps selfish, reasons.

Oh, dear.

I wish I hadn't said that.

They are staying in an old coaching inn. The bed is fairly comfortable although Greg complains that the mattress is too soft and giving him backache.

They have not made love for six months.

The meals are hearty, with far too much on the plate; the puddings are straight out of Gilly's childhood, gorgeous, fat-filled sweetnesses that steam and beckon the diner with siren sighs.

Gilly is not really hungry.

It is a friendly pub, with a husky, deep-voiced landlady and low beams and the scents of scenes still remembered.

Gilly suspects that Greg is having an affair.

The first drops come after two hours. They are large drops, cold but not startlingly so. Greg looks up into the sky, his prominent nose and Adam's apple silhouetted against the sky in which the clouds are now grey but still bright. He looks at Gilly. She has fully recovered, is back to a young, professional woman on a short break.

"I think it's going to be heavy," he says. There have been occasional, mild flurries of rain, but this is different; the wind has got up and there is a slight chilled dampness around them.

They are in the middle of a small hump-backed bridge that crosses a fast-running stream that cuts deeply into a gully. Greg is leading because Greg always leads and Gilly is happy with that. She loves him, after all.

She looks around, points. "There's an old cottage over there. Why don't we shelter there?" It is some distance away, through some overgrown woods; it looks deserted, almost a ruin, but the roof appears to be intact.

He nods, holds out his hand for her, then they run together over the bridge and to their right, off the single-track road and into the woods. The rain becomes harder, the noise of its attack louder. By the time they reach the cottage, it is surprisingly torrential and they are very, very wet.

How did I know that he no longer loved me?

This question torments me.

If I could answer it, I would be so much happier, so much more contented, but contentment is a rare commodity, worth killing for perhaps. I would be happy because then I would be certain in my mind, and uncertainty is killing me.

But it is not to be. Certainty is second only to contentment in scarcity.

Yet, without a doubt, I knew that he had a lover.

It was like something seen out of the corner of my eye, a dancing spectre that teased me by leaping away as I turned my head to catch it.

But that did not mean that it does not exist.

The knowledge was there in his smile, his kiss, his kindnesses.

All I lacked was proof.

But I still loved him. I will always love him. He had his faults but so do I. I thought to learn to live with it.

Because I love him.

The cottage had once been whitewashed, was now flaking. The faded blue front door is half off its hinges, the windows without glass. There are the remains of a garden with a path in front of it.

There is even a well.

Breathless from the exertion, Greg says, "The gingerbread's fallen off."

Gilly laughs. "I hope the witch has gone, too."

Greg looks around. There is no hallway and they are standing in the sitting room. There is no furniture and leaves are piled in the corners. The ceiling is low and beams cross it.

"It would have been a nice house, once."

"I guess."

He is taking every detail in, examining it, almost as an architect might, seeing possibilities in the decay. "We could live here," he says but he does not say it loudly, although she hears it.

"I couldn't."

He looks around and the thing that she sees is a good-humoured smile. "It's wonderful! What's wrong with it?"

"It's small and pokey and probably subsiding and almost certainly damp. And it's nowhere near anywhere."

He laughs. "But it's charming, too."

"I don't want to live in charming, Greg. I want to live in convenient, warm, spacious and cheap."

A shrug of the shoulders. "You can't have everything."

"And what about work, Greg? We're in the middle of nowhere here."

"You know that I can do most things remotely. If I arranged matters properly, I would only need to be in the office one day a week."

"Does that send the right message? I mean, does that tell your clients that you're completely committed?"

He becomes angry. "My clients understand that commitment is nothing at all to do with sitting in a box in a city."

Wondering why he is so defensive she backs away, changes the subject. "What about children? I'm not sure that this would be a particularly suitable place to raise a family."

At once he says, "Maybe not."

And she is puzzled. Such acquiescence is unusual for Greg. He likes to win arguments.

"I didn't know that you wanted to move."

"I was just thinking."

"If you're not happy where we are, we can start to look around."

"It doesn't matter."

"If you'd said something…"

"I said, it doesn't matter." His tone is abrupt, annoyed and she is forced into timid silence.

Gilly thinks that she has come to terms with Greg's infidelity. She believes that love will overcome everything and that whatever his reasons for the affair, love is not one of them. She fears that she has failed him in some way, that this is a message to her to improve. Her logic starts from the premise that he loves her; if he loves her, then he must need something more, or something different, from a relationship than he gets from her. All she needs to do is find what that thing is and supply it.

She has gone through in her mind everything that seems to her to be likely, but cannot think of anything. She is certain that he enjoys the sex, that her cooking and housekeeping are a reasonable standard. The only thing that she wonders about is the number of rows that they have had in recent months and she has made a conscious decision to be less confrontational. This is hard for her, for she is by nature combative, but she calculates that it is worth trying.

"I wonder why this is deserted," he says.

"It's probably unsafe," says Gilly.

Greg has begun to explore, examining recesses and alcoves; when he moves out of the sitting room into the darkness beyond she says, "Be careful, Greg."

"I will." He says this with marked irritation chiselled into the words and she bites down on her own annoyance at his retort because she thinks that perhaps she is being too maternal towards him.

She waits nervously, glancing around her and then back to the corridor down which he has disappeared.

"Greg?"

His voice comes back from the dimness, replete now with a hinted reverberation, "I'm fine." The reverberation does not disguise the tone.

She looks around again.

There is something pink on the dirty floorboards. It seems hard and out of place and she succumbs to her curiosity.

It is the leg of a doll.

A child.

My God! A child.

"Gilly! Gilly!"

At once, she is so scared that she drops it. Her breath is caught, her eyes are wide. She turns back to the darkness of the corridor down which Greg had walked.

Gilly does not know it, but she has had a nervous breakdown.

"Greg? Greg? What is it?" She walks forward but stops at the threshold to the darkness beyond. "Are you all right?" she calls into the heart of the house.

"Come and look at this. Out the back." His voice is some way off, a slight echo its handmaiden.

"Is it safe?"

"If you're careful."

How typical of a man, she thinks as she gingerly picks her way down the corridor.

The plaster has fallen in patches, exposing rotten wooden battens; the floorboards are a landscape of dirt, leaves, rubble and shapes that she cannot recognize but fears are rat droppings.

"Which way?" she calls tentatively.

"The hall turns right and leads into the kitchen. I'm out the back."

As she moves forward, she makes out light coming from the right and she can also hear a rushing sound. As she turns the corner, she sees the light is coming through a doorway from grimy windows.

The kitchen is as laden with melancholy and decay as the rest of the house. A range cooker stands resolutely to her left and a butler sink accompanies it. The only other occupant of this space is a single half-glazed cupboard, bowed by age and oblivion, staring blearily at its companions from the opposite wall.

Ahead of her are the windows, some of them broken, and a door to the outside. The rushing sound is louder now.

"Greg?"

But the rushing sound is too loud and she has to repeat herself.

"Outside."

She barely hears this word.

What is that noise?

When she moves outside, her question is answered.

The stream over which they had crossed now passed below her into a narrow, man-made gully. She steps out on to a rickety wooden balcony about fifteen feet above the crashing water and to her left is a huge waterwheel. Greg is on the balcony by the wheel; he is beckoning her excitedly. Rain falls steadily but the balcony is overhung by a sloping roof; bright sparkling drops of water hang and then fall from its edge.

"Isn't this fantastic?" he calls.

She certainly finds it exhilarating – the sound is loud, her position is high and the woodland around her is dense and green and beautiful – but she also finds it unsettling. The balcony on which she is standing seems to be dangerously fragile. Below her, the water moves from rain-specked flow to turbulent chaos as it passes through and under the wheel.

"Is it safe?" She has to raise her voice because of the white noise from below.

"I think so. Take it carefully, though."

"You are joking..."

"You'll be fine."

She moves forward gingerly, feels some give but is reassured that it seems to hold. Just to be safe she clings to the wooden railing that runs along the length of the walkway.

"It's incredible. Who'd have thought it?"

The wheel is about fifteen feet in diameter and reaches to about the level of their knees. It is in need of much repair and does not move despite the water rushing past it.

"I wonder what it's for," she says.

Greg leans over the balcony, scares Gilly. "The axle goes into the side of the house beneath us. There must be some milling equipment down in the basement."

"Be careful."

He straightens up, looks across at her and smiles. "It's perfectly safe," he says. To demonstrate this he wobbles the railing, making her gasp slightly, eyes widening. This is typical of him, playing the macho man, trying to scare her.

"Don't," she pleads, making him laugh.

Turning back to the wheel he says, "I can't work out why it isn't turning. It must be stuck. Probably silted up or something."

This is amazing!

Gilly is for the moment transported. The idea that she does not want to live here is suddenly absurd; this place is a paradise. Greg is right; of course, they must live here, deep in nowhere, surrounded by memories of things that perhaps never happened, enchanted and entranced.

Greg's phone rings. Although the noise is almost swamped by the water's rush, Gilly hears it.

She watches him reach into the breast pocket of his shirt, hardly look at the phone as he presses with his thumb, raise it to his ear.

She walks towards him, feeling the balcony giving slightly beneath her feet despite the fact that she is petite and light-footed.

Who's ringing?

Greg answers the call.
   "Hello?"
   A brief pause.
   "Oh, hi … "
   He glances up at her as he turns slightly away, takes a step back …
   But then there is a crack for he has not noticed that the wood where he stands has rotted because when the wheel worked the water splashed for decades against the underside of the balcony. He falls through with a scream of shock. His knee is struck as he falls and he is aware of a shaft of pain that skewers into his leg …
   His head strikes the side of the house.
   Gilly screams.
   Gilly's head has made perfection of her life, yet her life is far from perfect and the foundations of what she has made are already cracking. She watches Greg disappear through the wooden flooring, sees the phone flip upwards out of his grasp and fall in front of her.

Please, no. Please, God, don't do this to me.

She rushes forward, now even more aware of the fragility of the balcony on which she treads, made fearful by the knowledge of how precarious her own position might be.
   The phone is lying between two planks of the balcony, saved from falling into the water by an underlying strut but this is barely registered.
   "Greg? Greg?" She half asks this, half screams it as she approaches as close to the splintered hole as she dares, leaning forward to look down through it. What she sees makes her almost hysterical.
   He is half submerged in rushing water and she can clearly see that his legs are being pulled away by the strength of the current; but the upper half of his body is caught. He has fallen on to the wheel – fallen partly through it – and is now wedged, splintered beams

sticking into his abdomen just below his ribs, between the wheel and the house. The water falls and splashes around him and past him, only just missing his face.

"Greg?" she calls again.

She sees that he is dazed. He has hit his head and there is blood over the left of his face. When he looks up, she can see that he is having trouble focusing on her.

And then the wheel moves.

I remember a curious incident.

It was the good time, the time when I was pregnant and full of joy and expectation – and I mean, "full", as in replete, filled to bursting, completely consumed by them. This time things had gone without a hitch and we were just awaiting the result of the chromosome analysis...

I had lost my keys to the house and had looked everywhere. Greg's car was a last resort – I had driven it briefly the day before to pick him up from the station when my car was at the garage – and I came across a savings statement from a foreign bank, one I'd never heard of. It was in the glove box, under some travel sweets.

It said that Greg had saved twenty-six thousand pounds.

I asked him, of course. What wife (or husband) wouldn't?

He said that it was a tax avoidance scheme, a bolt-hole for money from the business. Not strictly legal, he said, but everyone did it.

He was perfectly natural, perfectly convincing.

I believed him.

"Gilly?" She hears the terror in his voice as he comes to full realization of where he is.

"Greg! Are you all right?"

It is a stupid question.

"It hurts, Gilly."

He is only two metres from her, but they are metres that stretch to infinity. His voice echoes and the noise of the water is loud and insistent and menacing. Above all this, she can still hear his panic, his pain, his terror.

Gilly can see that he has fallen on to the wheel, partly broken it and then come to rest in the narrow gap beside the sheer drop of the house wall. She sees also that his fall has loosened the wheel, that it is creaking faintly against the rush of the water, that it will soon start to turn and drag him under the water.

The creaking is getting louder.

Turning away from the wheel she looks around, searching for something to stop the wheel beginning to turn, without any ideas as to how she might achieve this. She sees a splintered plank, grabs it, but it is caught by nails at one end.

The wheel moves and she hears Greg scream.

Spurred by terror she finally wrenches it free, then thrusts it down into the hole that Greg has fallen through. It is just long enough – but only just – to reach down between the spokes of the wheel and stop it turning.

The day that they were given the results of the chromosome analysis has not faded into the past but lives with Gilly and always will. The events of the day – the emotions, the things seen and glimpses, the sounds heard and the places visited – revolve around a single discovery like dancers around a maypole, are tied to it for all of her eternity.

The obstetrician was very kind and very calm, the nurse with him even more so, but that counted as nothing when the implications of what he said burst into molten pain within her.

The baby had Down's Syndrome, probably severely so.

Greg had been with her, had held her hand, but all human contact was detached from her existence at that moment.

The clock on the wall behind the obstetrician's wiry grey hair had said that it was seventeen minutes past eleven; the calendar on his desk had said that it was the 6th of June.

"Gilly?"

The rain has begun again, adding to the noise. She peers down at him, now on her hands and knees.

"Help me, Gilly."

But the futility of this request is obvious. He is beyond her reach.
"I'll have to get help."

"It hurts when I breathe. And my leg ... I think it's broken."

"Don't worry ... I'll run and get someone."

But this only induces panic in him. "No! No! Don't leave me, Gilly."

"I've got to, Greg ... "

"What if the wheel turns again? It'll pull me under."

"But I can't do anything on my own ... "

It is then that the mobile phone rings. At once she thinks, "Of course! I'll phone for help." At the same time she wonders who is calling him, who called him not five minutes before.

She looks at the screen.

Nikki.

She does not know anyone called "Nikki": she does not know that Greg knows anyone called "Nikki".

It is a curiously intimate name, full of suggestion.

She knows then that it is the name of his lover.

She presses the red button, the one that cuts off the connection, sees a movement out of the corner of her eye, and looks around to see a small girl standing just behind her. She jumps in shock.

Greg sees Gilly's head disappear from his view above.

"Gilly?"

The child has Down's Syndrome – severely so. She does not speak, does not even react beyond a smile on her face that is part beatific, part eerie; the look in her eyes is unfocused, as if she does not see Gilly but far beyond her.

Gilly tries a smile; a friendly one, a gentle one. "Hello. What's your name?"

No reaction; neither response nor movement.

Greg's voice comes from below a second time, this time more urgent, more panicked and almost angry.

Gilly turns back to him and calls down, "It's all right, Greg. There's ... "

But as she turns back to the girl, she sees nothing there. There is no child, no sign that there ever was.

"What is it?" Greg is demanding, like a child himself.

Gilly has stood up, is looking all around her – through the windows of the mill, over on the other side of the fast-flowing stream. Nothing.

"Gilly, for God's sake…"

At last she turns back to him but she is still confused, wondering.

He calls, "Will you get me out of here?"

She remembers the phone, bends to pick it up, but this time her head is filled with thoughts beyond Greg's predicament.

Would my child have looked like that?
   I was going to call her Belle…
   She wasn't ugly, not ugly at all…
   I could have loved her…

Gilly has suppressed from her memory the fact that she was sexually assaulted as a seven-year-old girl by an uncle, a brother of her now dead mother. She has suppressed this but it lurks there, not dead, not even dormant, just stealthy.

It has poisoned her, turned her.

She believes that she is still essentially innocent.

But she is not.

Virginity, both sexual and moral, went long ago, stolen from her, and the only thing between Gilly and depravity is the construct she has made of her life, the one that she has built on a foundation of a lie.

Gilly does not carry a mobile phone, does not want the leash that it represents.

She called him.
   Now, this week of all weeks, she called him. Couldn't she let me have him to myself for just a week?

She looks at the phone. She is familiar enough with it to work her way through the menus.

She hears Greg call again. "Gilly? What's happening?"

Without looking down at him she replies, "I'm phoning, Greg."

She comes across the call log, is about to call back the last number received (although she does not know why), but then she hears, quite distinctly, a child's voice in her head; although she never heard the little girl speak, it carries with it certainty that it is hers. Nor does it come in words, only knowledge.

Gilly opts to look at the messages received.

The rain is falling hard now. The stream is rushing and there is a single but deeply menacing creak as the plank of wood that juts through the hole moves slightly.

"Gilly?"

Some are from her, some are from strangers, but most are from "Nikki".

The ones from Nikki are graphic, sexual, illuminating. As Gilly reads them, moving backwards in time through the past few days, then weeks, she comes to appreciate just how little she has known about Greg's life, about his thoughts, about his wishes for the future. She sees that Greg has gone elsewhere not just to complement something in his life that she is not supplying, that he has gone there for a completely different experience.

She is stunned.

The man with whom she has shared her pleasures and pains has been an actor. There is a facet to him that he has hidden from her, one that, now exposed, casts him as a liar, as contemptuous of her gullibility, as mocking of her sexual timidity.

This epiphany is a light in her head, but one that burns as bright as laser-light, one that destroys as it enlightens. It cracks the entire edifice of her life, the beliefs that she has been in the possession of "truth". It allows the evil that she went through as a child, that has adulterated her, to rise up and embrace her completely. It floods into the cracks in her mind and splinters it, making razor sharp shards with which to wound.

It spreads through her and throws shadows in places that once were lit, lights crevices and thereby allows her to see the monsters that lurk within.

She reassesses his actions and words of the past weeks and months, but there is worse to come...

"Where are you, Gilly?"

Gilly's head appears in the hole above him. "Here I am, dear."

"What's happening?"

She smiles. He is very, very cold; this helps the pain but dulls his thoughts. He can see that her attitude is somehow wrong, but he cannot bring his sluggish thoughts to wonder why. She says, "I'm sorting things out."

"Hurry up...please."

"It won't be long."

Another creak from the wheel.

He said, "We could live here."

He wasn't talking to me, but to himself.

Was he also talking to his girlfriend...?

And the money...

How far have your plans gone, Greg? How close are you to leaving me?

Gilly is starting to feel strange. Her head is filling with all sorts of ideas and possibilities that have sprung into febrile activity, that scurry from corner to corner, feeding on all that has been done to her. She makes a last effort to control them, to counter the dizzying revolution in her mind.

She glances back at the phone, sees for the first time a time and date.

It is from Nikki and it is full of anticipation, apparently agreeing to meet him that afternoon.

It is dated the 6th of June and it was sent at five minutes to two in the afternoon.

It would all have been different if we could have had children. Perhaps that is what the problem was, the reason for his infidelity; I have not been able to give him children, could only promise him a handicapped baby...

This attempt is futile; worse it is the fuel that causes the smouldering to erupt into conflagration.

No!

I'm being so stupid, so trusting, so blind.

He never wanted children. Not really. He was lukewarm about the idea, at best. He saw it as something to give to me, to shut me up. It probably would have suited him to give me a baby to look after; it would have been a distraction for me, while he bedded "Nikki", pleasured her as she desired...

No, no, no!

God, how could I be so stupid?

He doesn't want me to have children! They would only complicate matters for him, make leaving me more problematic...most expensive. His twenty-six thousand pounds wouldn't go too far then...

This serpent of thought is now alive and feeding hungrily. Within seconds it is all that there is in her soul.

He made me abort Belle. He said that it was for the best, but whose best?

He made me murder her.

She might have been beautiful, like that little girl. Sweet and passive and somehow luminous in her innocence.

All so that his life would be easier, so that he could screw around.

He will say that he is leaving me because he wants children and I haven't given him any.

Gilly looks down at the phone, decides that it is time to call for help.

There is yet another creak from the wheel.

Gilly looks down at Greg. He is only half conscious.

"Greg?" she calls.

He responds slowly, first of all looking around, only raising his eyes after a while. His face contains pain, his voice is husky as if he has phlegm in his throat.

"Yes?"

"I've rung for help."

"Thank God ... "

"She may take some time to get here."

He does not realize what she has said for a few seconds.

"She? Who do you mean?"

Gilly smiles.

"Nikki."

She enjoys the look on his face, savours it for a moment, then in a single movement grasps the plank of wood that is jamming the wheel.

"I hope she's in time," she says.

She pulls the plank free and the wheel at once begins to turn. Greg screams but it is a very short scream, ended abruptly as he is taken beneath the water and then wedged against the bed of the stream.

As Gilly walks out of the cottage she sees the little girl again. She is sitting on the wall of the bridge talking to a woman. The woman is laughing and joking with her, clearly her mother.

Gilly walks across to them to experience their shared pleasure.

I will have a child one day. I will be free of this curse.

I am the same as I always was.

I am the same as I always was.

OUT OF THE FLESH

Christopher Brookmyre

RESTORATIVE JUSTICE, THEY cry it. That's what happens when wee scrotes like you get sat doon wi' their victims, mano a mano, kinda like you and me are daein' the noo. It's a process of talking and understanding, as opposed tae a chance for the likes ay me tae batter your melt in for tryin' tae tan my hoose. The idea is that us victims can put a face tae the cheeky midden that wheeched wur stereos, and yous can see that the gear you're pochlin' actually belongs tae somebody. Cause you think it's a gemme, don't you? Just aboot no' gettin' caught, and anyway, the hooses are insured, so it's naebody's loss, right? So the aim is tae make you realize that it's folk you're stealin' fae, and that it does a lot mair damage than the price ay a glazier and a phone call tae Direct Line.

Aye. Restorative justice. Just a wee blether tae make us baith feel better, that's the theory. Except it normally happens efter the courts and the polis are through wi' their end, by mutual consent and under official supervision. Cannae really cry this mutual consent, no' wi' you tied tae that chair. But restorative justice is whit you're gaunny get.

Aye. You're shitin your breeks 'cause you think I'm gaunny leather you afore the polis get here, then make up whatever story I like. Tempting, I'll grant you, but ultimately futile. See, the point aboot restorative justice is that it helps the baith ay us. Me batterin' your melt in isnae gaunny make you think you're a mug for tannin' hooses, is it? It's just gaunny make ye careful the next time, when ye come back wi' three chinas and a big chib.

Believe me, you're lucky a batterin's aw you're afraid of, ya wee nyaff. Whit I'm gaunny tell you is worth mair than anythin' you were hopin' tae get away wi' fae here, an' if you're smart, you'll realize what a big favour I'm daein' ye.

Are you sittin' uncomfortably? Then I'll begin.

See, I used tae be just like you. Surprised are ye? Nearly as surprised as when you tried tae walk oot this living room and found yoursel wi' a rope roon ye. I've been around and about, son. I never came up the Clyde in a banana boat and I wasnae born sixty, either. Just like you, did I say? Naw. Much worse. By your age I'd done mair hooses than the census. This was in the days when they said you could leave your back door open, and tae be fair, you could, as long as you didnae mind me and ma brer Billy nippin' in and helpin' oursels tae whatever was on offer.

We werenae fae the village originally; we were fae the Soothside. Me and Billy hud tae move in wi' oor uncle when ma faither went inside. Two wee toerags, fifteen and fourteen, fae a tenement close tae rural gentility. It wasnae so much fish oot ay watter as piranhas in a paddlin' pool. Easy pickin's, ma boy, easy pickin's. Open doors, open windaes, open wallets. Course, the problem wi' bein' piranhas in a paddlin' pool is it's kinda obvious whodunnit. At the end of the feedin' frenzy, when the watter's aw red, naebody's pointin' any fingers at the nearest Koi carp, know what I'm sayin'? But you'll know yoursel', when you're that age, it's practically impossible for the polis or the courts tae get a binding result, between the letter ay the law and the fly moves ye can pull. Didnae mean ye were immune fae a good leatherin' aff the boys in blue, right enough, roon the back ay the station, but that's how I know applied retribution's nae use as a disincentive. Efter a good kickin', me and Billy were even mair determined tae get it up them; just meant we'd try harder no tae get caught.

But then wan night, aboot October time, the Sergeant fronts up while me and Billy are kickin' a baw aboot. Sergeant, no less. Royalty. Gold-plated boot in the baws comin' up, we think. But naw, instead he's aw nicey-nicey, handin' oot fags, but keepin' an eye over his shoulder, like he doesnae want seen.

And by God, he doesnae. Fly bastard's playin' an angle, bent as a nine-bob note.

"I ken the score, boys," he says. "What's bred in the bone, will not out of the flesh. Thievin's in your nature: I cannae change that, your uncle cannae change that, and when yous are auld enough, the jail willnae change that. So we baith might as well accept the situation and make the best ay it."

"Whit dae ye mean?" I asks.

"I've a wee job for yous. Or mair like a big job, something tae keep ye in sweeties for a wee while so's ye can leave folk's hooses alane. Eejits like you are liable tae spend forever daein' the same penny-ante shite, when there's bigger prizes on offer if you know where tae look."

Then he lays it aw doon, bold as brass. There's a big hoose, a mansion really, a couple ay miles ootside the village. Me and Billy never knew it was there; well, we'd seen the gates, but we hadnae thought aboot what was behind them, 'cause you couldnae see anythin' for aw the trees. The owner's away in London, he says, so the housekeeper and her husband are bidin' in tae keep an eye on the place. But the Sergeant's got the inside gen that the pair ay them are goin' tae some big Halloween party in the village. Hauf the toon's goin' in fact, includin' him, which is a handy wee alibi for while we're daein' his bidding.

There was ayeways a lot o' gatherings among the in-crowd in the village, ma uncle tell't us. Shady affairs, he said. Secretive, like. He reckoned they were up tae all sorts, ye know? Wife-swappin' or somethin'. Aw respectable on the ootside, but a different story behind closed doors. Course, he would say that, seein' as the crabbit auld bugger never got invited.

Anyway, the Sergeant basically tells us it's gaunny be carte blanche. This was the days before fancy burglar alarms an' aw that shite, remember, so we'd nothin' tae worry aboot regards security. But he did insist on somethin' a bit strange, which he said was for all of oor protection: we'd tae "make it look professional, but no' too professional". We understood what he meant by professional: don't wreck the joint or dae anythin' that makes it obvious whodunnit. But the "too professional" part was mair tricky, it bein' aboot disguisin' the fact it was a sortay inside job.

"Whit ye oan aboot?" I asked him. "Whit's too professional? Polishin' his flair and giein' the woodwork a dust afore we leave?"

"I'm talkin' aboot bein' canny whit you steal. The man's got things even an accomplished burglar wouldnae know were worth a rat's fart – things only valuable among collectors, so you couldnae fence them anyway. I don't want you eejits knockin' them by mistake, cause it'll point the finger back intae the village. If you take them, he'll know the thief had prior knowledge, as opposed tae just hittin' the place because it's a country mansion."

"So whit are these things?"

"The man's a magician – on the stage, like. That's what he's daein' doon in London. He's in variety in wan o' thae big West End theatres. But that's just showbusiness, how he makes his money. The word is, he's intae some queer, queer stuff, tae dae wi' the occult."

"Like black magic?"

"Aye. The man's got whit ye cry 'artefacts'. Noo I'm no' sayin' ye'd be naturally inclined tae lift them, and I'm no' sure you'll even come across them, 'cause I don't know where they're kept, but I'm just warnin' you tae ignore them if ye dae. Take cash, take gold, take jewels, just the usual stuff – and leave anythin' else well enough alone."

"Got ye."

"And wan last thing, boys: if you get caught, this conversation never took place. Naebody'd believe your word against mine anyway."

So there we are. The inside nod on a serious score and a guarantee fae the polis that it's no' gaunny be efficiently investigated. Sounded mair like Christmas than Halloween, but it pays tae stay a wee bit wary, especially wi' the filth involved – and bent filth at that, so we decided tae ca' canny.

Come the big night, we took the wise precaution of takin' a train oot the village, and mair importantly made sure we were *seen* takin' it by the station staff. The two piranha had tae be witnessed gettin' oot the paddlin' pool, for oor ain protection. We bought return tickets tae Glesca Central, but got aff at the first stop, by which time the inspector had got a good, alibi-corroboratin' look at us. We'd planked two stolen bikes behind a hedge aff the main road earlier in the day, and cycled our way back, lyin' oot flat at the side ay the road the odd time a motor passed us.

It took longer than we thought, mainly because it was awfy dark and you cannae cycle very fast when you cannae see where you're goin'. We liked the dark, me and Billy. It suited us, felt natural tae us, you know? But that night just seemed thon wee bit blacker than usual, maybe because we were oot in the countryside. It was thon wee bit quieter as well, mair still, which should have made us feel we were alone tae oor ain devices, but I couldnae say that was the case. Instead it made me feel kinda exposed, like I was a wee moose and some big owl was gaunny swoop doon wi' nae warnin' and huckle us away for its tea.

And that was *before* we got tae the hoose.

"Bigger prizes," we kept sayin' tae each other. "Easy money." But it didnae feel like easy anythin' efter we'd climbed over the gates and started walkin' up that path, believe me. If we thought it was dark on the road, that was nothin' compared tae in among thae tall trees. Then we saw the hoose. Creepy as, I'm tellin' you. Looked twice the size it would have in daylight, I'm sure, high and craggy, towerin' above like it was leanin' over tae check us oot. Dark stone, black glass reflectin' fuck-all, and on the top floor a light on in wan wee windae.

"There's somebody in, Rab," Billy says. "The game's a bogey. Let's go hame."

Which was a very tempting notion, I'll admit, but no' as tempting as playin' pick and mix in a mansion full o' goodies.

"Don't be a numpty," I says. "They've just left a light on by mistake. As if there wouldnae be lights on doonstairs if somebody was hame. C'mon."

"Aye, aw right," Billy says, and we press on.

We make oor way roon the back, lookin' for a likely wee windae. Force of habit, goin' roon the back, forgettin' there's naebody tae see us if we panned in wan o' the ten-footers at the front. I'm cuttin' aboot lookin' for a good-sized stane tae brek the glass, when Billy reverts tae the mair basic technique of just tryin' the back door, which swings open easy as you like. Efter that, it's through and

intae the kitchen, where we find some candles and matches. Billy's
aw for just stickin' the lights on as we go, but I'm still no' sure that
sneaky bastard Sergeant isnae gaunny come breengin' in wi' a dozen
polis any minute, so I'm playin' it smart.

Oot intae the hallway and I'm soon thinkin', knackers tae smart,
let there be light. The walls just disappear up intae blackness; I
mean, there had tae be a ceiling up there somewhere, but Christ
knows how high. Every footstep's echoin' roon the place, every
breath's bein' amplified like I'm walkin' aboot inside ma ain heid.
But maistly it was the shadows ... Aw, man, the shadows. I think fae
that night on, I'd rather be in the dark than in candle-light, that's
whit the shadows were daein' tae me. And aw the time, of course,
it's gaun through my mind, the Sergeant's words ... "queer, queer
stuff ... the occult". Black magic. Doesnae help that it's Halloween,
either, every bugger tellin' stories aboot ghosts and witches aw
week.

But I tell myself: screw the nut, got a job tae dae here. Get on, get
oot, and we'll be laughin' aboot this when we're sittin' on that last
train hame fae Central. So we get busy, start tannin' rooms. First
couple are nae use. I mean, quality gear, but nae use tae embdy
withoot a furniture lorry. Big paintin's and statues and the like. Then
third time lucky: intae this big room wi' aw these display cabinets. A
lot ay it's crystal and china – again, nae use, but we can see the
Sergeant wasnae haverin'. There's jewellery, ornaments: plenty of
gold and silver and nae shortage of gemstones embedded either.

"If it sparkles, bag it," I'm tellin' Billy, and we're laughin' away
until we baith hear somethin'. It's wan o' thae noises you cannae
quite place: cannae work oot exactly whit it sounded like or where it
was comin' fae, but you know you heard it: deep, rumbling and low.

"Whit was that?"

"You heard it an' aw?"

"Aye. Ach, probably just the wind," I says, no even kiddin' masel.

"Was it fuck the wind. It sounded like a whole load ay people
singin' or somethin'."

"Well I cannae hear it noo, so never bother."

"Whit aboot that light? Whit if somebody *is* up there?"

"It didnae sound like it came fae above. Maist likely the plumbing. The pipes in these big auld places can make some weird sounds."

Billy doesnae look sure, but he gets on wi' his job aw the same.

We go back tae the big hallway, but stop and look at each other at the foot of the stairs. We baith know what the other's thinkin': there's mair gear tae be had up there, but neither ay us is in a hurry to go lookin' for it. That said, there's still room in the bags, and I'm about to suggest we grasp the thistle when we hear the rumblin' sound again. *Could* be the pipes, I'm thinkin', but I know what Billy meant when he said lots ay folk singin'.

"We're no' finished doon here," I says, postponin' the issue a wee bit, and we go through another door aff the hall. It's a small room, compared to the others anyway, and the curtains are shut, so I reckon it's safe to stick the light on. The light seems dazzling at first, but that's just because we'd become accustomed tae the dark. It's actually quite low, cannae be mair than forty watt. The room's an office, like, a study. There's a big desk in the middle, a fireplace on wan wall and bookshelves aw the way tae the ceiling, apart fae where the windae is.

Billy pulls a book aff the shelf, big ancient-lookin' leather-bound effort.

"Have a swatch at this," he says, pointin' tae the open page. "Diddies! Look."

He's right. There's a picture ay a wummin in the scud lyin' doon oan a table; no' a photie, like, a drawin', an' aw this queer writin' underneath, in letters I don't recognize. Queer, queer stuff, I remember. Occult. Black magic.

Billy turns the page.

"Euuh!"

There's a picture ay the same wummin, but there's a boay in a long robe plungin' her wi' a blade.

"Put it doon," I says, and take the book aff him.

But it's no' just books that's on the shelves. There's aw sorts o' spooky-lookin' gear. Wee statues, carved oot ay wood. Wee women wi' big diddies, wee men wi' big boabbies. Normally we'd be pishin' oorsels at these, but there's somethin' giein' us the chills aboot this whole shebang. There's masks as well, some of wood, primitive efforts, but some others in porcelain or alabaster: perfect likenesses of faces, but solemn, grim even. I realize they're death masks, but don't say anythin' tae Billy.

"These must be thon arty thingmies the sergeant warned us aboot," Billy says.

"Artefacts. Aye. I'm happy tae gie them a bodyswerve. Let's check the desk and that'll dae us."

"Sure."

We try the drawers on one side. They're locked, and we've no' brought anythin' tae jemmy them open.

"Forget it," I say, hardly able tae take my eyes aff thae death masks, but Billy gies the rest ay the drawers a pull just for the sake ay it. The bottom yin rolls open, a big, deep, heavy thing.

"Aw, man," Billy says.

The drawer contains a glass case, and inside ay it is a skull, restin' on a bed ay velvet.

"Dae ye think it's real?" Billy asks.

"Oh Christ aye," I says. I've never seen a real skull, except in photies, so I wouldnae know, but I'd put money on it aw the same. I feel weird: it's giein' me the chills but I'm drawn tae it at the same time. I want tae touch it. I put my hands in and pull at the glass cover, which lifts aff nae bother.

"We cannae take it, Rab," Billy says. "Mind whit the Sergeant tell't us."

"I just want tae haud it," I tell him. I reach in and take haud ay it carefully with both hands, but it doesnae lift away. It's like it's connected tae somethin' underneath, but I can tell there's some give in it, so I try giein' it a wee twist. It turns aboot ninety degrees courtesy of a flick o' the wrist, at which point the pair ay us nearly hit the ceilin', 'cause there's a grindin' noise at oor backs and we turn roon tae see that the back ay the fireplace has rolled away.

"It's a secret passage," Billy says. "I read aboot these. Big auld hooses hud them fae back in the times when they might get invaded."

I look into the passage, expecting darkness, but see a flickerin' light, dancin' aboot like it must be comin' fae a fire. Me and Billy looks at each other. We baith know we're shitin' oorsels, but we baith know there's no way we're no' checkin' oot whatever's doon this passage.

We leave the candles because there's just aboot enough light, and we don't want tae gie oorsels away too soon if it turns oot there's somebody doon there. I go first. I duck doon tae get under the mantelpiece, but the passage is big enough for us tae staun upright once I'm on the other side. It only goes three or four yards and then there's a staircase, a tight spiral number. I haud on tae the walls as I go doon, so's my footsteps are light and quiet. I stop haufway doon and put a hand oot tae stop Billy an' aw, because we can hear a voice. It's a man talkin', except it's almost like he's singin', like a priest giein' it that high-and-mighty patter. Then we hear that sound again, and Billy was right: it is loads ay people aw at once, chantin' a reply tae whatever the man's said.

Queer, queer stuff, I'm thinkin'. Occult. Black magic.

Still, I find masel creepin' doon the rest ay the stairs. I move slow as death as I get to the bottom, and crouch in close tae the wall tae stay oot ay sight. Naebody sees us, 'cause they're aw facin' forwards away fae us in this long underground hall, kinda like a chapel but wi' nae windaes. It's lit wi' burnin' torches alang baith walls, a stone table – I suppose you'd cry it an altar – at the far end, wi' wan o' yon pentagrams painted on the wall behind it. There's aboot two dozen folk, aw wearin' these big black hooded robes, except for two ay them at the altar: the bloke that's giein' it the priest patter, who's in red, and a lassie, no' much aulder than us, in white, wi' a gag roon her mooth. She looks dazed, totally oot ay it. Billy crouches doon next tae us. We don't look at each other 'cause we cannae take oor eyes aff what's happenin' at the front.

The boy in the red robe, who must be the magician that owns the joint, gies a nod, and two of the congregation come forward and lift the lassie. It's only when they dae this that I can see her hands are tied behind her back and her feet are tied together at her ankles. They place her doon on the altar and then drape a big white sheet over her, coverin' her fae heid tae toe. Then the boy in red starts chantin' again, and pulls this huge dagger oot fae his robe. He hauds it above his heid, and everythin' goes totally still, totally quiet. Ye can hear the cracklin' ay the flames aw roon the hall. Then the congregation come oot wi' that rumblin' chant again, and he plunges the dagger doon intae the sheet.

There's mair silence, and I feel like time's staunin' still for a moment; like when it starts again this'll no' be true. Then I see the red startin' tae seep across the white sheet, and a second later it's drippin' aff the altar ontae the flair.

"Aw Jesus," I says. I hears masel sayin' it afore I know whit I'm daein', an' by that time it's too late.

Me and Billy turns and scrambles back up the stair as fast as, but when we get tae the top, it's just blackness we can see. The fireplace has closed over again. We see the orange flickerin' ay torches and hear footsteps comin' up the stairs, the two ay us slumped doon against a wall, haudin' on tae each other. Two men approach, then stop a few feet away, which is when wan ay them pulls his hood back.

"Evening boys. We've been expecting you," he says. The fuckin' Sergeant.

"I assume you took steps to make sure nobody knew where you were going tonight," he goes on. I remember the train, the guard, the bikes, the return ticket in my trooser pocket. The Sergeant smiles. "Knew you wouldn't let us down. What's bred in the bone, will not out of the flesh."

Four more blokes come up tae lend a hand. They tie oor hauns and feet, same as the lassie, and huckle us back doon the stair tae the hall.

"Two more sacrifices, Master," the Sergeant shouts oot tae the boy in red. "As promised."

"Are they virgins?" the Master says.

"Come on. Would anybody shag this pair?"

The master laughs and says: "Bring them forward."

We get carried, lyin' on oor backs, by two guys each, and it's as we pass down the centre of the hall that we see the faces peerin' in. It's aw folk fae the village. Folk we know, folk we've stolen from. I think aboot ma uncle and his blethers aboot secret gatherings. Auld bastard never knew the hauf ay it.

"This one first," the Master says, and they lie me doon on the altar, which is still damp wi' blood. I feel it soakin' intae ma troosers as the boy starts chantin' again and a fresh white sheet comes doon tae cover me.

I don't know whether there was ether on it, or chloroform, or maybe it was just fear, but that was the last thing I saw, 'cause I passed oot aboot two seconds later.

So.

Ye don't need many brains tae work oot what happened next, dae ye? Aye, a lesson was taught. A wise and skilled man, that magician, for he was the man in charge, the village in his thrall, willingly daein' what he told them.

Suffice it to say, that was two wee scrotes who never broke intae another hoose, and the same'll be true of you, pal.

I can see fae that look in your eye that you're sceptical aboot this. Maybe you don't believe you're no' gaunny reoffend. Nae changin' your nature, eh? What's bred in the bone, will not out of the flesh. Or maybe you don't believe my story?

Aye, that's a fair shout. I didnae tell the whole truth. The story's nae lie, but I changed the perspective a wee bit, for dramatic effect. You see, if you werenae so blissfully oblivious of whose hoose you happen tae be screwin' on any given night, you might have noticed fae the doorplate that my name's no Rab. I wasnae wan ay the burglars.

I was the Sergeant.

I'm retired noo, obviously, but I still perform certain services in the village. We're a close-knit community, ye could say. So I ought to let you know, when you heard me on the phone earlier, sayin' I'd caught a burglar and tae come roon soon as, it wasnae 999 I dialled. Mair like 666, if you catch my drift. 'Cause, let's face it, naebody knows you're here, dae they?

Are you a virgin, by the way?

Aye, right.

Doesnae matter really. Either way, you're well fucked noo.

*   *   *

Aye, good evening, officer, thanks for coming. He's through there. Sorry aboot the whiff. I think you could call that the smell of restorative justice.

Go easy on him. I've a strong feelin' he's aboot tae change his ways. A magical transformation, you could cry it.

How do I know? Personal experience, officer. Personal experience.

HARD ROCK

Gerard Brennan

THE SWEET SCENT of groupie sex hung in the air. I grabbed the tequila bottle by the neck and gulped down a mouthful. Another hotel room. They'd all merged into one. Especially since our manager had decided not to book us into five-star penthouses. He said the savings would buy us better equipment, but I was still battering out licks on the same old Les Paul I'd started out our first six-month tour with. We'd just played the last set. No more shows. No more hotel rooms. And no more groupies. Except this last one.

Buck-naked and handcuffed to the headboard, my last fuck of the tour smiled up at me. I stood at the foot of the bed, not wearing much more myself – just my silk boxer shorts and a smug smile. Her body was at my mercy. Five minutes she'd known me, but she trusted this much. I'd have passed it off as typical groupie dumb-bitch behaviour, but this one didn't strike me as the usual awestruck bimbo. She wasn't after a story to tell her friends. She wanted to give me a story to tell. I plonked my tequila bottle back down on the dressing table. She writhed a little on the crumpled sheets, just for show.

"You ready to go again, rockstar?"

"I need another minute." I smiled to myself. "Just lie there and wait for me." Like she'd a choice.

"Oh, you're so mean, Joey D. Leaving me all chained up like this. I need some attention."

"What are you, some kind of nympho? I already fucked you twice."

"They were intro-fucks. Now that we've got to know each other, we can really go wild."

I shook my head, but my dick twitched in my boxer shorts. She was something to look at, all right. Her golden brown skin and black shock of thick curly hair spoke of Latin blood, but her stunning green eyes had an Asian slant. Hawaiian, maybe? Certainly a world apart from the flame-haired cailíní I'd pursued in my youth. Forget those frigid Irish chicks. I'd moved on to better things. I ran my fingers through my mane, a match for hers in length, colour and volume. Rock and Roll, baby.

"Maybe a line or two of coke will get you going?" she said.

Seemed like a good idea. I scooped the baggie and my little pewter straw from the round table in the corner of the room. I held it out to her.

"Want some?"

"No, Joey. I want you." I poured some snow on the table. "Wait, Joey! Why would you want to snort off that old thing? Lay some of that powder on me, why don't you?"

"Party on, my lady."

She giggled. "My lady. What are you, a knight?"

I ignored the wisecrack. She'd told me her name earlier, but I didn't care about that shit. No need for names in this business. Something you learned pretty quickly on the road.

I powdered her from her tits to her trimmed pubes and got to work like a Dyson. She giggled as I disappeared the coke, working from the top down. I didn't get it all. Got distracted by that musky scent from between her muscled thighs. I tossed the straw over my shoulder and it pinged as it bounced off the wall. She raised her hips to meet my tongue, purring like a kitty cat.

When I'd had my fill, I crawled up her body, licking patches of the missed coke off her skin on the way. My senses hummed. As we kissed, she hooked her toes into the waistband of my shorts and slid them down to my ankles. I reached out to the bedside cabinet for a condom. I always kept them next to the Gideon Bible. I'm not sure whether or not I meant it as an insult. I bagged Little Joey and guided him towards her.

"Wait," she said.

"For what?"

"Let's have a little more fun."

"What do you have in mind?"

"I was wearing a silk scarf. It's on the floor by the door. Would you get it?"

"Why?" I tapped the headboard. "You're already tied up."

"I've something else in mind."

I wanted to fuck, but I humoured her. If she was into me wearing a white silk scarf it was no skin off my nose. So long as I got my hole. It's something that'll never change for me, but I can't help feeling ridiculous when walking naked with a hard-on. What's sexy about that? Worse still when it's wrapped in a luminous green rubber. So I wasted no time. Dashing to the door and back, embarrassed by the wobble and sway of my dick, I fetched the scarf. Back on the bed, I started to put it on. She giggled.

"It's not for you, Joey. It's for me." I shrugged, and wrapped it around her elegant neck. "Tighter," she said. I tugged on it a little. "Tighter." I pulled a little harder. "Tighter, Joey! Tighter!"

"What? You want me to fucking strangle you?"

"Yes!"

I froze. Was this chick for real? She stared me in the eye. "What? You never heard of erotic asphyxiation?"

"Girl, I can't even spell it."

"Oh, come on. You never dabbled in breath-control play? Baby, you haven't lived."

"Are you serious?"

"Hell, yeah. Joey, honey, you wouldn't believe it. It makes you cum so hard."

"It makes you die."

"No, no. It's breath-control. It reduces the oxygen flow to your brain to heighten the orgasm. But you release the pressure before going unconscious. You haven't heard about this before? I thought you were a man of the world."

"Hey, I've been around, but most of my lays are happy with the old bang-bang. None of them ever complained either."

She pouted. "I'm not most lays."

I nodded. "Okay, baby. Let's give this a go." When you're running on adrenaline, booze and cocaine, you'll try anything.

And I swear to God, as soon as I yanked on that scarf like I meant business, she became electric. I could almost feel static crackle between us as she bucked under me. I had to pull out after one short minute, not wanting to end the experience but knowing my limitations.

"Oh, honey, don't stop now."

Her voice was hoarse. Had I damaged her throat in such a short time? If so, she didn't seem to mind. She was hungry for more.

"You have to give me a minute. I'm ready to blow my load here."

"Put on another rubber. It might slow you down a little." So I did. And she was right. I went a little longer this time, choking and releasing at steady intervals as I drilled her. But I stopped when her eyes began to stream.

"Don't stop yet." This time, she barely managed a whisper.

"We're going too far," I said.

Again, that throat cancer whisper. "I'll be the judge of that."

And I wanted to go again. That feeling of power had me hooked. I hadn't felt in control since the start of the tour, ruled by time-tables, flight schedules and a fat-fuck manager. If she said she wasn't done, who was I to argue? But first I went back to my tequila bottle. I was still too close to filling my doubled-up condoms.

After four or five big shots of Mexican rocket fuel, I grabbed a handful of snow and pelted it at my handcuffed, kinky nympho. She smiled, and through puffy and reddened lids, her eyes glinted in the dull light.

I leapt on to her, raising a fine white cloud, and we went at it even harder than before. I'd decided the third time was the charm. No more pulling out. Finish the job, roll up the scarf and unlock the cuffs. We'd pushed our luck far enough.

And as I felt my own orgasm welling, I closed my eyes and continued to tighten and release the scarf every few seconds. The end came too soon. I sighed as I finally let go, then flopped on to my back beside her. I needed a cigarette.

"Holy fuck, baby," I said. "That blew my mind."

She didn't reply. I figured her throat was too sore. I rolled on to my side to look her in the face. Check out her post-coital glow.

"Hey, baby," I said, a hand sneaking out to squeeze her tit.

She didn't respond. I nudged her a little. Then I stoked the raw skin on her neck, tentatively checking her pulse. Her head lolled in response to my touch.

"Oh, no."

It was all I could think to say. She looked back at me with unseeing, blood-flecked eyes.

She wasn't glowing. She looked ... Dead. "Oh, no." Slowly, calmly, I got off the bed and went for my tequila. "Oh, no."

I took a slug. "Oh, no." And another. "Oh ... " Another. "No."

I'm not sure how long I stood there, drinking tequila and staring at a dead groupie handcuffed to my bed, but eventually I snapped out of my daze. Something had to be done, but I was fucked if I knew what. There was nothing for it. I had to tell Larry. I used the phone on the bedside cabinet to call my manager's room. As it rang, I looked at the Bible lying under a smattering of condoms. I swallowed hard and averted my gaze.

"Come on, Larry. Pick up the fucking phone."

"Fuck's this?"

"Larry! Man, I need to see you. Come up to my room, will you?"

"Fuck's this?"

"It's Joey D. Come on, man. I'm in room one-eighty-seven."

"Fuck you want?"

"I'll tell you when you get here. It's important, okay?"

"Fuck's sake. Be there in a minute."

He hung up. I dropped the handset back in its cradle and sat on the edge of the bed. Then I remembered the dead chick. I jumped up and crossed the room, back to the tequila. I raised the bottle to my lips then lowered it without taking a drink. Enough already. I had to stop before I passed out. I lit a cigarette instead, flicking the ash on to the carpet rather than returning to the bedside cabinet for the ashtray. Just as I was trying to figure out what to do with the butt, the doorknob rattled.

Larry's voice cut through the wood. "Let me in, Joey."

I moved to the door, pausing at the bathroom to flick my cigarette butt into the sink. Larry bustled past me, bleary-eyed and wearing a white dressing gown. His thick, ginger chest hair looked even thicker against the white towelling. He scratched his fat ass as he squinted at me.

"Jesus, kid. Put something on, will you?"

Fuck! I was still naked. Mumbling an apology, I retrieved my shorts from the foot of the bed and pulled them on. With my modesty covered, I turned to Larry. He blinked rapidly as he tried to focus on the groupie.

"Is she ...?" he trailed off.

"Yeah."

"What the fuck happened?"

"I strangled her."

"What for?"

"It was a sex thing, Larry."

Larry blinked at me now. "You sick fuck."

"It was her idea, man. I didn't mean to kill her."

Larry scratched his stubbly head. "Fuck."

"What are we going to do, Larry?"

"I don't know. Give me a smoke, will you?" I fetched him the pack and lighter. His hands didn't shake as he pulled out the cancer stick and lit it up. He slid the rest of the cigarettes into the pocket of his robe. I didn't complain.

"Fucking rockstars and their messes. I should have gone into hip-hop. At least real gangsters know how to get rid of the bodies."

It sounded like it wasn't the first time he'd encountered a disaster like this. But that wasn't something I wanted to pry into.

Larry glared at me. "Were you fucking her when she died?"

"No. I mean ... maybe. I'm not sure, man."

"How can you not be sure?"

"I, uh ... I had my eyes closed."

Larry snorted, puffing smoke from his nostrils. "You fucking pussy."

"How's this helping, Larry?"

"It just seems like the kind of thing you should know. Psychologically speaking. I mean, years from now, will you be able to put your hand on your heart and say that you've never humped a corpse?" He licked his chapped lips. "Though as far as they go, this is one fine-looking cadaver."

Sour spit flooded my mouth. I fought hard against the urge to puke. "Kid, you look like shit. Go freshen up while I think about this." He didn't need to tell me twice. I managed to keep down my tequila supper, but only just. My reflection squinted at me from the mirror over the sink, gaunt and sickly. I picked the cigarette butt out of the sink and filled the cool white porcelain with cold water. Then I took a deep breath and dunked my face in. My lungs burned in my chest before I pulled myself back out. I reached for a neatly folded towel and daubed at my face. Now I looked gaunt, sickly and wet.

I closed my eyes.

The sound of creaking springs from the bedroom froze me to the spot. What the fuck? Hoping to find a revived groupie sitting up on the bed, I forced myself out of paralysis and sprinted from the bathroom.

Larry kneeled between the dead girl's thighs. His gown hung open and he fumbled with a condom. I couldn't help but stare at his short, fat erection beneath the solid swell of his gut. "Want a picture, faggot?"

"What are you doing, Larry?" He laughed. The ugly, fucked-up sound of it raised gooseflesh on my arms and back. "Larry, what the fuck?"

"Dead or not, this bitch is smoking hot. No sense in wasting an opportunity."

"Stop it."

"Or what?" He stroked her inner thigh. "She won't mind." He rolled the condom on and I wondered why he'd picked a ribbed one. For her pleasure. What kind of a fucked-up thought was that?

"Seriously, Larry. I mean it, man."

"Fuck you. If you want my help, you'll give me and my new girl-friend some privacy."

But that wasn't going to fly. Bad enough I'd killed the poor girl. No way was I going to let fat Larry have his way with her dead body. I leapt and shoulder-barged him off the bed. We hit the floor with an almighty thud. A tangle of limbs. Me on top. I straddled his chest and tried to take the advantage. It felt so wrong to be struggling on the floor with a pink-skinned, almost naked, fat man wearing a ribbed condom. But life throws shit like that at you sometimes.

He grappled with my arms as I tried to land a punch. I couldn't get a clean hit. Then he was holding each of my wrists in an iron grip. We stared at each other. Stalemate. He smiled, as if he was embarrassed by the situation. Then the fat fuck caught me with a headbutt. He let go of my wrists and I fell back.

I cupped my nose with my hands. Blood ran down my face and filled my throat. I coughed and spluttered gobs of crimson into the air. It rained down on my chest. Larry was on his feet. He kicked my ribs and stomped on my head. I curled up into a ball. Helpless. But he'd figured the job was done. The mattress springs creaked again as he climbed back on to the bed.

"You fucking prick." Larry sounded amused. "I lost my erection. Talk about a fucking mood-kill."

I heard him roll off the bed and pad across the room. He snuffled and snorted. The bastard had his piggy snout in my coke.

"That's the business," he said. "I'll be back in the saddle in no time."

I got to my hands and knees then yakked on the carpet. Watery, bitter-tasting puke splattered my hands and forearms.

"Better out than in," Larry said. I groaned. "You should have left me alone, kid. I just wanted to clear my head. Now look at you." My stomach lurched again. I breathed deep to wrestle back control of my innards and inhaled the pungent scent of tequila puke. Larry said something else, but I lost it in a fit of coughing.

When my coughing stopped I pushed myself on to my knees. Larry stood before me, the tequila bottle in his pudgy hands. "Here, have a drink."

"Fuck you, Larry."

"Ah, don't be like that. We just had a little misunderstanding. No harm done."

I spluttered a choked, sarcastic laugh. I held up my blood-coated palms. "Yeah, Larry. Just a little misunderstanding."

"Come on, kid." His tone was kind. "Don't be a little bitch about it. Take a drink."

I took the bottle and drank deep, clearing the blood from the back of my throat. It felt good. Harsh. Cleansing. I wiped a forearm across my mouth and stood on Bambi legs. Larry smiled and nodded at me. Then he glanced at the dead chick.

"Okay, Joey. Give me ten minutes with her, while she's still fresh, and then we'll get to work. Okay? We can smuggle her out, and I know some people who'll take it from there. You listening?"

Still fresh.

I smiled back at him and he opened his arms as if to invite a hug. I hefted the almost drained tequila bottle. Grunting, I brought it down hard on top of Larry's head. His shaved scalp split neatly.

"Uhn!" he said, all surprised and wide-eyed.

"Okay, Larry." I smiled at him, then clunked the bottle off the side of his head. He wobbled. "Okay, Larry." I hit the other side of his head. Blood sprayed this time. "Okay, you fat fuck." His eyes rolled back in his skull and he toppled backwards. I looked down at the bottle in my hands. It surprised me that it was still intact. In the movies, they always shattered into a million pieces.

It looked like Larry was dead, but those same movies taught me never to wait for a fallen enemy to leap up for the final scare. I knelt by his side and pounded his face with the bottle. It was therapeutic. And when I realized that, I forced myself to stop. I didn't want to become some sort of psycho. I picked my leather jacket up off the floor and covered the pulpy mess that used to be Larry's face.

I stood up and looked around the room. Cocaine on the table. Dead girl cuffed to the bed. Dead fat man laid out on the floor. Blood-covered rockstar, stinking of puke and clutching the murder weapon, swaying on his feet.

It crossed my mind that jumping out my window might be my best option. But that was the coward's way. Besides, my room was on the first floor. I'd probably break a leg at worst. Better to face the music. The music. Fucking music.

Our album sales would go through the roof when this got out. When would I ever get a chance to enjoy that? Probably never. It would go to my family though, wouldn't it? See my parents right? I thought about calling my lawyer.

I picked up the phone and dialled down to the reception. "Hi. I'm going to need you to put me through to the police." Fuck.

ART IN THE BLOOD

Matthew J. Elliott

1

SOME MAY CALL it a tragedy, others a fantasy. My friend Sherlock Holmes will not have it that those terrible events surrounding the Tuttman Gallery are capable of anything other than a rational, albeit unorthodox explanation. While he admits that the violent death of Anwar Molinet is beyond our ability to explain at present, he is insistent that future scientific developments will one day show how such a thing might be possible. I confess, I do not share his confidence – should I call it hubris? – and to this day, he chides me for ever daring to suggest a supernatural solution to the mystery.

"Can it be, Watson," he says, "that you, a trained man of science, have fallen in with the spiritualists, soothsayers and other such frauds and self-delusionists?"

I make no reply, and never shall. But I set down here the full, unbiased account of our most mysterious adventure, and leave it to the reader to decide.

Sherlock Holmes did not, as a rule, encourage visitors at 221b, but he frequently made an exception for Inspector Lestrade. I confess, I have never understood his fondness for the company of the rodent-faced policeman over other officers for whose intelligence he expressed a higher regard, but I have rarely seen my friend happier than when sharing a bottle of the beaune with his old adversary. It was common on such occasions for Lestrade to voice his concerns regarding any recent problematic investigations. I expected today would be no different, but this afternoon the police official appeared agitated, glancing at the clock on the mantelpiece from time to time.

"Are we keeping you from your duties, Inspector?" asked Holmes, with more than a touch of mockery.

"Er, no, Mr Holmes. Not just at this moment. I was just thinking … it should be happening soon. Cawthorne's post-mortem, I mean."

It took very little effort on my friend's part to persuade him to elucidate.

"Anwar Molinet was the fellow's name," Lestrade explained. "Murdered in broad daylight, in the middle of a busy restaurant."

"Oh?"

He consulted his notebook. "Les Frères Heureux, it's called. Ever heard of it?"

"Your pronunciation could stand some improvement, Lestrade," I remarked. "But, yes, I believe we've dined there once or twice. An excellent cellar."

"Although the manager's cigars are quite as poisonous as I have ever experienced," Holmes added. "It's the curse of the modern age, I fear. I find it hard to believe that a detective of your undoubted abilities would experience even the mildest of difficulties running the culprit to ground. You seem to have an over-abundance of witnesses, and more than adequate supplies of the energy required for such a task."

Lestrade twitched visibly. "You might think so, Mr Holmes, but … Well, it's a peculiar thing … impossible, even."

"I make it a habit to eliminate the impossible before proceeding in an enquiry. Come, come! Surely this is a matter for which the old hound remains the best."

"I should have thought so, too. But you tell me what it means when a man is brutally murdered in front of some twenty-odd people and yet not one of them claims to have seen a thing … Almost as though the killer were *un*visible."

"Brutally?" I wondered aloud.

"You're a medical man, Dr Watson, and a soldier to boot but I doubt if even you have ever … " Lestrade's voice failed and I imagined for a moment that he was actually stifling a sob. "You'll never see anything like it this side of hell, I swear it".

Holmes rose to his feet and stuffed his pipe into the pocket of his dressing gown. I saw at once that his mood had altered from extreme languor to devouring energy.

"If we are content to sit here chatting about it, I too swear that we will never see it. You said that the post-mortem is due to begin at any moment. If we make a start now, we should be in time to interview the surgeon. Watson, Professor Cawthorne is a member of your club, yes? Then we should have no difficulty in breaching the inner sanctum of one of London's most respected police surgeons. No, no, Lestrade, you need not accompany us. I see from your haggard features that you have already had far too much of the unsavoury side of this investigation. By all means, finish your drink, and show yourself out when you are ready. But please take a moment to extinguish my pipe which, my nostrils inform me, is beginning to singe my dressing-gown."

I was struck, upon entering the mortuary, how long I had been away from the world of practical medicine. The smell of carbolic and decaying flesh could never be described as palatable, but our ability to become accustomed to even the most unattractive circum stance will invariably out. On this occasion, however, it took some effort on my part not to gag as the odour assailed my nostrils.

Cawthorne was soaping his hands as we entered, and gave no more than a brief backward glance. It was not his way, however, to be ungracious, even in the most morbid situation.

"Why, John, what a pleasant surprise. Though I shouldn't really be surprised at all, I suppose. And Mr Holmes." The two men exchanged no more than a nod of assent, for feelings were somewhat cool between them, ever since Holmes had called Cawthorne's competence into question during our investigation into the shooting of a vagrant on the grounds of Colonel James Moriarty's Chelmsford home. "You're here about the late Mr Molinet, I imagine?"

With his stick, Holmes indicated a corpse beneath a bloody shroud. "This is he?" he asked.

"It is. I've more or less finished with him, but you're welcome to take a look. I confess, there are still a good many questions concerning the nature of his death I'd like answering. You have George's permission to be here, of course?"

It took a moment before I realized that Cawthorne was referring to the Inspector, with whom, it seemed, he was on first-name terms. To Sherlock Holmes and myself, however, he was simply "Lestrade".

I explained, in the most diplomatic terms, that our mutual acquaintance had chosen to remain behind at Baker Street, rather than view the body once more.

"You won't judge him harshly, I hope. This is a shocking matter, even for an old war-horse like George. Indeed, your joint experience in examining dead bodies notwithstanding, you should perhaps prepare yourselves for something you may not have seen before."

He tugged back the sheet, and we found ourselves looking at what had once been a man but had now been transformed into a nightmare. I made no remark; no gasp of astonishment escaped my lips. I seemed, in fact, utterly incapable of speech at that moment.

"Well, well," Holmes breathed, "you do not exaggerate, Professor."

"Whoever did this to Mr Molinet aided my examination considerably. As you can see, I had no need to make a single incision."

In the moments that followed, I heard only the whistling of my own breath, as we three gazed in silence at the hideously mutilated corpse, his innards visible through the gaping hole in the stomach. I had witnessed something similar when examining the body of the unfortunate Catherine Eddowes, but on that occasion, identification of the weapon had been a simple matter.

"These tears are deep but also ragged," Holmes observed, without apparent emotion. "This was not done with a blade of any sort. Claws, perhaps... or teeth. Have you ever seen the results of an attack by a wolf, Professor?"

"Very few wolves in London, Mr Holmes," Cawthorne replied.

"Not the four-legged variety, in any case."

"In any event, there is an even greater mystery to be overcome, as you can see, since it would appear that this beast – whatever it may have been – clawed its way *out*, not in."

I heard someone say "There is devilry afoot," and it was a moment before I realized that the words were mine, the first I had uttered since the hideous corpse had been uncovered.

"I have, in the past, voiced the opinion that life is infinitely stranger than anything which the mind of man could invent," Holmes murmured, "but this is perhaps *too* strange even for life as we comprehend it." But I knew that he could not do anything other than proceed with his investigation, for he refused to associate himself with any matter which did not tend towards the unusual and even the fantastic. And I, who share his love of all that is bizarre and outside the conventions and humdrum routine of everyday life, could do nothing but follow in his wake.

2

For Holmes's sake I attempted, so far as seemed appropriate, to make light of the matter. "Well, Holmes, we have a rare little mystery on our hands," I commented, as we rattled along in the four-wheeler we had flagged down outside the mortuary.

"Your propensity for understatement never ceases to amaze me, Doctor. We seem to have been presented with someone's waking nightmare masquerading as a case. Molinet is slashed to pieces in a public place, apparently by a ferocious animal and in a manner that beggars belief … and yet no one seems to have seen anything."

"Witnesses to a particularly vicious crime are often unreliable," I noted. "I'm certain I don't need to remind you of the conflicting accounts we heard following the Pennington Flash Murder. Shock can play peculiar tricks on the mind."

"In one or two cases, I might agree, Watson, but surely shock cannot have affected ever single diner and member of staff in one of London's most fashionable restaurants."

"Perhaps we are approaching the matter from the wrong end," I suggested. "It may well be that knowing why Molinet was murdered will give us some indication of how it was done."

"Excellent, Watson! Really, you are coming along! How can I take you for granted when your clarity of mind comes to my rescue?"

Holmes had never said as much before, and I must admit that his words gave me keen pleasure, for I have often been piqued by his apparent indifference to my assistance.

Upon our return to Baker Street, we were advised by Mrs Hudson that Lestrade had only recently departed, and in a state of some merriment. Our long-suffering landlady was less than cheered, however, to learn that Holmes and I would not be staying for dinner, nor could we say when we were likely to return. Holmes searched through his ever-reliable index until he found the address of the late Anwar Molinet.

My earlier intuition, alas, proved of little use when we were confronted with a locked door. There were no servants at Molinet's Belgrave Square address, no one to answer our persistent knocking.

"Our first broken thread, Watson," Holmes noted, and though there was no malice in his tone, I could not help but redden with shame at the thought of a wasted journey taken at my suggestion.

"You'll find no one at home, I'm afraid," a strident female voice called to us. We looked about, and saw that the voice belonged to the occupant of the house next door. Though not born to the purple, she gave an excellent imitation, save for the fact that she had chosen to lean out of her window in order to address two perfect strangers.

"Anwar's nephew gave the servants notice as soon as he heard. The place has been locked up ever since. You're Sherlock Holmes and Dr Watson, aren't you? You're not unlike your pictures, if I might say so."

I raised my hat. "Madam, you were a friend of Mr Molinet?"

"An acquaintance would be the better term," she simpered. "Neighbour, really. The last time I saw him was at the auction. Oh, I'm terribly sorry, I haven't introduced myself. What on earth would my husband have said? Mrs Serracoult is my name. Actually, would you care to come inside? Susan was about to prepare tea."

I accepted cheerfully. Holmes, whose mistrust of the fair sex seemed to increase in direct proportion to their ebullience, murmured: "Watson, I leave this interview entirely in your hands."

In an experience of women which extends over many nations and across several continents, I have met none so flighty as Mrs Serracoult. She rushed about her sitting room as though in a constant panic, half-remembering some errand before forgetting it once again.

Holmes emitted several loud groans at this very feminine behaviour, but our host was far too preoccupied with at least half a dozen things simultaneously, and I am relieved to say she never noticed.

"Mrs Serracoult," I said eventually, having sat through several tedious anecdotes regarding her late husband's social connections, "you mentioned that the last time you saw Mr Molinet was at an auction?"

"At the Tuttman Gallery, that's right, Doctor. Which reminds me, I've been suffering from an unpleasant burning sensation recently, right here."

"I'd be happy to examine you, dear lady, but I regret I left my stethoscope at home." I turned my hat in my hand as I spoke, hoping to conceal the bulge made by the instrument. "Now, this auction...?"

"At the Tuttman Gallery, yes. Do you know the Tuttman Gallery?" I shook my head.

"They're very particular about their customers – perhaps I could put in a good word for you both, next time I'm there. Anyway, there was rather a fierce bidding war over a Redfern."

Holmes, who had the crudest notions regarding art, raised a quizzical eyebrow. "Redfern is a painter?" he asked.

"One of London's most exciting new talents, Mr Holmes." Without warning, she shot from her chair, rattling the tea things as she raced to a handsome landscape upon the wall. I knew that my companion could have no appreciation of its excellence, or of the artist's choice of subject, for the appreciation of nature found no place among his many gifts. "Rather marvellous, isn't it?" our host enthused. "And hideously expensive, of course. But that fact seems to make the very owning of it even more exciting. And I do so long for excitement. Curious, isn't it, Doctor, how one can be very, very bored and very, very busy at the same time?"

Despite never having experienced this condition, I expressed my sympathy. I was in the middle of lamenting the state of a society in which such a complaint could be allowed to arise, when Mrs Serracoult let out what I can only describe as a strangled shriek, and collapsed back into her chair. I did not even have the chance to enquire as to the cause of her distress, before she regained her composure and desire to speak.

"Goodness! It just occurred to me, Dr Watson – the last time I saw Oliver Monckton was also at the Tuttman."

I had no notion of who Oliver Monckton might be, or whether he had any bearing upon our current investigation, but I persisted nevertheless.

"Did you outbid Mr Monckton also?"

"Heavens, no! I hadn't even heard of Redfern then."

"So Monckton bought a Redfern also?" Holmes asked. Mrs Serracoult nodded, but before she had time to expand upon the fact, Holmes rose to his feet. "Well, thank you for the tea, Madam," – I noted that his cup was untouched – "but our duties require our presence elsewhere."

"The elusive Professor Moriarty, no doubt."

He gave a thin-lipped smile. "No doubt. Come along, Watson."

Our rooms were ankle-deep in newspapers, reference books and crime periodicals. From time to time, Holmes added to the general scene of chaos with another carelessly discarded document. I have made mention of this frustrating anomaly in my friend's character elsewhere, but under the circumstances, I had little cause for complaint; I had no keener pleasure than in following him on his professional investigations, and in admiring the rapid deductions with which he unravelled the conundrums submitted to him.

"What exactly are you looking for?" I asked in frustration as a crumpled-up copy of something called *Police News of the Past* flew past my face.

"This!" He announced, triumphantly, presenting me with a copy of the *Journal de Genéve*.

"Some of us have only the one language, Holmes."

"Please excuse me, old fellow. This article relates to the sudden death of Englishman Oliver Monckton while holidaying in Switzerland. I recall that the details were few, but I was struck by the journalist's claims that certain unsavoury details were suppressed by the coroner."

The word "unsavoury", which I recalled Holmes had used earlier, certainly suggested to my mind a connection between Monckton and Anwar Molinet, although I wondered whether any description could do justice to the horror I had witnessed in the mortuary.

"And Mrs Serracoult said that both men had purchased Redferns at the Tuttman Gallery, wherever that may be."

"It is in Knightsbridge, I believe – formerly the Gaylord Auction Rooms. The question is, if a connection exists, does it relate to the paintings, the artist, or the gallery? We are in unfamiliar territory, Watson; my own art collection consists solely of portraits of the last century's most notorious criminals."

"And my army pension would hardly stretch to spending afternoons at the Tuttman Gallery in the company of Mrs Serracoult," I added, ruefully.

"Then you must be thankful for small mercies, Doctor."

"Holmes ... I have been thinking."

"This is turning out to be a day of remarkable occurrences."

"Really, you're the most insufferable fellow alive."

"Quite possibly. Please, go on; I should be grateful to hear your theory."

I marshalled my thoughts with the aid of a stiff whisky. "Remember the affair of the Christmas Goose, or the busts of Napoleon? Might there not be something hidden away, perhaps within the frame itself?"

"A provocative notion, Doctor. And though it does no harm to theorize, we are at sea without—"

He got no further along his train of thought, however, for at that moment we were interrupted by a knocking on the door. I imagined it might be Mrs Hudson, and wondered what her reaction to the present state of the room might be, when the door swung open to reveal the familiar figure of Inspector Lestrade, his features more haggard than before, if such a thing can be imagined.

"Our good fortune, Doctor!" Holmes cried. "Inspector Lestrade, here to help us through the morass of officialdom. And with a gift of a somewhat unconventional nature, I see."

"Hardly that, Mr Holmes." I saw that he held in his right hand what had once been a lady's shoe. From its charred appearance, I supposed he must have extracted it from a bonfire.

"Where did you come by this singular souvenir, Lestrade?"

The police agent waited a moment before responding. "This shoe, Mr Holmes ... is all that remains of Mrs Bernice Serracoult."

3

My friend has so often astonished me in the course of our adventures that I am ashamed to admit a sense of fascination at witnessing his complete astonishment. A flush of colour sprang to his pale cheeks as he listened in silence to the Inspector's account of Mrs Serracoult's demise. Approximately half an hour after our departure, the maid, one Susan Foxley, had been alerted by the screams of her employer.

"She described being conscious of a peculiar odour for several minutes – an odour we now know to have been burning flesh. When she reached the sitting room, Mrs Serracoult was fully ablaze."

Holmes had been on the point of reaching for his pipe, but evidently thought better of it. "How much of the house was destroyed in the fire?" he asked.

"None, Mr Holmes."

"None?"

"Mrs Serracoult was burned to a crisp, but the chair she sat upon was not even singed."

"Impossible," I protested. "Such things might occur in Dickens novels, but never in real life."

"And yet it happened," Holmes noted, "suggesting that it is simply a badly observed phenomenon. I have said many times that life is infinitely stranger than anything the mind of man could invent, but we must stick to reason, or we are lost."

"Unlike Mr Holmes here, I don't believe in coincidences," interrupted the haggard policeman. "I can't explain it, but when the neighbour of a man who died a horrible death suddenly bursts into flames ... I don't know, gentlemen – it beats anything I've ever seen, and Lord knows, I'm no chicken."

Holmes hurried Lestrade from our rooms with an assurance that should any thoughts occur to him he would be in contact and a few moments later we were in a cab, on our way to the Tuttman Gallery.

I attempted to draw Holmes into conversation about our present investigation. When he would not be drawn, I sought to engage his power to throw his brain out of action and switch his thoughts to lighter things by changing the topic to Cremona violins, warships of the future and the obliquity of the ecliptic.

"It ... hurts my pride, Doctor," he said eventually. "It should have occurred to me that, as the owner of a third Redfern, she might be in as much danger as Molinet and Monckton. I'm a foolish old man. How long can it be before I must retire to that farm of my dreams?"

So accustomed was I to his invariable success that the very possibility of his failure had ceased to enter my head until that very moment. "But surely ... there's still a chance ... a chance to save anyone else who's become entangled in this sinister web. If any man can untangle it, that man is Sherlock Holmes."

Holmes gave a weak chuckle – he was always accessible upon the side of flattery. A moment later, he was the cold and practical thinker once again. "And faithful old Dr Watson, of course," he added.

I knew at heart that he would not give up so easily. It was when he was at his wits' end that his energy and versatility were most admirable. "May I ask what our present objective might be?"

"Firstly, to ascertain whether anyone at the Tuttman Gallery might have a reason to wish harm to these three persons; secondly, to discover the names of anyone else who might have purchased a painting by Redfern; lastly, to locate the artist himself. It may be at odds with my method of observation and deduction, but I have an intuition that he might be at the centre of this pattern of events."

And so it proved. Crabtree, the proprietor of the Tuttman Gallery, was a gentleman of amiable disposition, who was extremely distressed to hear of the deaths of three of his most frequent customers, and allowed us free rein to search his store, question his staff and examine his records. Given the outré nature of the deaths, I had no clear idea of what we might be looking for, but Holmes seemed satisfied that no one at the Gallery was acting with malicious intent. It appeared from Crabtree's register that he had sold only one other Redfern, to a Mr Phillimore. Holmes advised me that he had been consulted by Inspector Stanley Hopkins after Phillimore returned to his house one morning to fetch his umbrella and was never again seen in this world.

"I dislike ever having to hazard a guess," remarked Holmes, "but I think we have a fair idea of the reason for his disappearance, although I very much doubt whether even now we can count that case as one of my successes. Tell me, Mr Crabtree, have you had any dealings with Mr Redfern?"

"None personally, Mr Holmes," the proprietor replied in a nasal whine. "All his paintings come to us through Mr Milhause. You know him, I trust?"

"By reputation only. But it seems that we must make ourselves known to him. Mr Crabtree, might we rely upon you to provide us with an introduction?"

"As if you needed one, Mr Holmes," said a refined if somewhat affected voice behind us. We turned, and found ourselves facing a fellow I deduced to be Mr Bartholemew Milhause himself. If I could have pictured a more suitable brother for the rotund Mycroft Holmes than my colleague, then it would surely have been Milhause. He was only slightly smaller than the obese civil servant I had encountered during the affair of the Greek Interpreter and the business of the stolen submarine plans, but in all other respects – the thinning hair, the deep-set grey eyes – he might have been his twin. However, where I commonly associated Mycroft with the faint odour of expensive cigars, Milhause had apparently drenched himself in a perfume better suited to a vulgar music hall artiste than an alleged patron of the arts.

He shook Holmes by the hand with an enthusiasm I considered unseemly. "An honour, sir, an honour!" he cried. "And you must be the other one," he observed caustically, eyeing me with distaste. I pretended to ignore the obvious slight.

"Mr Milhause, you act for the artist Redfern, do you not?" Holmes enquired.

"A true talent, Mr Holmes – a young fellow of genuine ability. An oasis in the desert of mediocrity that passes for culture in modern London. I make an exception for the items to be found in the Tuttman Gallery, of course." Crabtree, to whom this remark was directed, responded in similarly fawning terms. I glanced at Holmes, but he did not return my grimace.

"It just so happens, Mr Milhause, that I am interested in sitting for a portrait."

"But surely Mr Paget—"

"That was some years ago, and I am no longer the man I once was. I thought that if any artist in London might be capable of capturing my – well, my spirit ... "

"That artist is Algernon Redfern!" Milhause declared, with a tiresome flourish. "Excellent, Mr Holmes, excellent! Portrait work is not really in his line, you understand, but I doubt that he could fail to pass up such a fascinating commission. Mr Sherlock Holmes himself – how very unique!"

"It is simply 'unique', Mr Milhause," I pointed out.

"But it is, my dear fellow – simply unique!"

Like every Londoner, I had, of course, heard of the artists' studios to be found off the long lean artery of the King's Road, but I had never seen them. Finding myself on that dark flagged alley, I must confess that I was not impressed by my surroundings. Indeed, the only hint of a bohemian air to the district was supplied by two disreputably dressed young gentlemen, no doubt on the way to their own studio. As they passed us, I heard the taller man say, "Honestly, Bunny, you really are the most frightful ass ... " in a cultured fashion greatly at odds with his attire.

We halted at an unlatched door, and Holmes raised his hand to knock.

"It's open, Mr Holmes, do come in!" called a male voice. My friend's expression betrayed none of the surprise I was sure he must have felt, and he pushed the door open.

I had imagined that the residence of a successful artist would be crammed to the rafters with sketches and paintings in various stages of preparation. But the lofty room in which we found ourselves betrayed little evidence of the tenant's occupation, save for an easel at the far side of the room and a small table in the centre. The painting upon that easel faced away from us, but had, in any case, been covered by a stained towel. A completed work, rolled up, rested against the easel.

As for Algernon Redfern himself, again my expectations were crushed. Given his flamboyant agent, and his apparent connection with a string of bizarre murders, I had begun to imagine him as a curious cross between Oscar Wilde and Edward Hyde; but such was not the case. Redfern was a man of approximately five-and-twenty, tall, loose-limbed, with black close-cropped hair and a pockmarked face.

"Forgive me for not shaking hands," he said, jovially, displaying his paint-smeared palms.

"How does it come about that you were expecting us?" I enquired.

He smiled, and I observed a row of uneven yellow teeth. "Perhaps as an artist, I have a keener instinct than most, Doctor. Or, a telegram might have reached me before your carriage. Then again, I might have that marvellously convenient invention, the telephone, installed somewhere on the premises. Pick any one you prefer. Cigarette?"

Under a copy of the *Pall Mall*, a plain cigarette box rested upon the small table. He brushed the newspaper to the floor and opened the box, revealing just one cigarette within.

"No thank you, Mr Redfern," Holmes replied.

"As you like," said the artist. In one swift movement, he placed the cigarette in his mouth and lit it. "This will probably be my last one, anyway. Plays hell with my chest. Is there any medical basis for swearing off them, Doctor?"

I must own that during my explanation – which took in findings made a century earlier regarding the connection between snuff-taking and certain nasal polyps, as well as my friend's frequent three-pipe sessions – I rambled more than a little, distracted as I was by Redfern's voice. That he was attempting to conceal his own nationality beneath a somewhat flawed English accent was clear.

"Well, Mr Holmes," he said, jovially, "to what do I owe the honour of this visit?"

"What does your keen artist's instinct tell you?" Holmes asked, dryly.

Redfern chuckled. "Most assuredly, *not* that you are interested in having your portrait painted. From what I know of you from Dr Watson's stories, I would not have said you were so vain."

"If you are an admirer of the Doctor's work, you have my condolences," said Holmes with, I felt, unnecessary relish. "But you are correct in stating that I have not come here today on my own account. I am more interested in your connection to James Phillimore, Anwar Molinet, Oliver Monckton and Mrs Bernice Serracoult."

Redfern expelled a long, luxurious cloud of smoke before responding: "Sorry to say, I've never heard of any of them. Who are they?"

"They each bought one of your paintings," I explained.

The artist shrugged, before stubbing out his cigarette on the lid of the box and picking up a pad and pencil. "I only paint them," he said. "The charming Mr Milhause handles the business side of things. You've met him, of course. Quite unbearable, isn't he?"

"They are also, as Dr Watson is too discreet to mention, all dead – Mrs Serracoult as recently as this afternoon."

Algernon Redfern appeared unperturbed by this news. "I should call that a rather extreme reaction to my work." He began to scribble absent-mindedly on the pad.

"Are you English by birth, Mr Redfern?" Holmes asked.

"How could you doubt it? I'm not native to London, however, but I've been here a while. And I'll remain until I've done what I came here to do."

"And that is?" I asked.

He looked up from his pad. "To sell my paintings, naturally. What else?"

I coughed to attract Holmes's attention.

"Your friend seems to have rather a nasty chest. Or is there something on your mind, Doctor?"

"You said...you said that Mr Milhause dealt with the sale of your works. And I would not have imagined that a true artistic soul would be interested in such vulgar matters."

"I don't play any part in the sales – I couldn't even tell you where they're sold. But as a professional writer, you must know that any artist who says they're not interested in public acceptance is a liar. That's what it's all about. And money, of course. Only the air is free, gentlemen, and I have some doubts as to its quality."

"Dr Watson likes to say that my pipe does little to add to the city's atmosphere."

"Another persuasive argument in favour of my giving up the cigarettes." Redfern dropped the pad at his feet, seeming not to notice. "I'm sorry I can't help you, Mr Holmes, but as I told you, I've never met or even heard of those people you mentioned. And I'm certain that as a professional detective, you must have all sorts of ways of telling whether I'm telling the truth or not." Again, he flashed a sickly yellow grin, and I had the certain feeling that we were being manipulated, as a cat toys with a wounded mouse.

Holmes scratched his long nose. "Well, it was a long shot at best. Thank you for your time, Mr Redfern."

We made to leave, but the young man bounded across the length of the room, the rolled-up painting in his hand. "Wait!" he cried. "Mr Holmes, as an … admirer of your work, I should very much like you to have this."

Holmes chuckled. "My services are charged at a fixed rate, Mr Redfern. I doubt that I could afford one of your paintings."

"I'm not selling it – I'm giving it to you. It's mine to do with as I wish, and I wish you to have it. Take it, please."

I was already on my guard, and should never under any circumstances have accepted a gift from a man so patently false as Algernon Redfern, so I was astonished by my friend's reaction, unrolling the picture with an almost childish enthusiasm of which I would never have imagined him capable. Holmes's eyes glittered as he examined the picture.

"Why, this is really very fine!" he exclaimed.

"If I have captured the colour of the mudstains, I take it you can identify the precise area of London depicted?"

"No need, Mr Redfern, I am quite familiar with Coptic Street; I had lodgings not far from there some years ago, and it has featured in one of our recent investigations. Watson, you recall the case of the Coptic Patriarchs?"

I attempted to convey my concerns to Holmes in a surreptitious manner by means of a loud cough, but he seemed completely oblivious.

"Well, goodbye, Mr Holmes," said the young man, his unhealthy grin now even wider. "It was nice to have known you, if only for a brief time. Goodbye, Dr Watson – paregoric is the stuff."

4

"I suppose it has occurred to you, Holmes," I remarked, tartly, "that thus far in this case, everyone who has owned a painting by Algernon Redfern has died the most horrible death...and you are the latest owner of a Redfern?"

Holmes's mood during our cab journey back to Baker Street had been irrepressibly cheerful, and he refused to allow my grim observation to spoil his mood. "You know my methods, Watson – I am well known to be indestructible. Besides, I trust that the two of us will be able to see danger coming in any direction."

"I wish us better luck than Anwar Molinet; we still have yet to determine the precise cause of his death, but I'd be prepared to wager a considerable sum that this fellow Redfern is behind it all somehow."

"Then perhaps it's wise that your chequebook is safely locked away in my drawer."

I ignored the sharpness of his retort. "I simply meant that I find it inexplicable that you choose to trust this fellow!"

"I did not say that I trusted him."

"But you said you were certain he was at the centre of this pattern of events, and now you're accepting gifts from the fellow."

"Well, evidently, I was wrong about his precise connection to the case. I simply view him now as another stop on our journey, rather than our destination point."

This pronouncement baffled me; so far as I could see, we had no lines of enquiry left to pursue. Holmes evidently noted the confusion on my features, for he continued: "It's interesting that, as an artist,

Mr Redfern prefers to write rather than doodle. You noticed, of course, his furious scribblings as we conversed?"

"I noticed," I admitted, "but I placed no importance in it."

Holmes tutted. "Just when I think I have made something of you, Doctor. As we spoke, he wrote the words 'Do they know about Ferregamo?'"

"How could you possibly have seen that from where you were positioned?"

Holmes winced, and I found myself reaching for my service revolver, imagining that my friend was in some danger. But he simply smiled weakly.

"I really must speak to Mrs Hudson about her cooking," he groaned. "I'm so sorry, old fellow, what were you saying?"

I repeated my question.

"No magic, Watson: one simply has to watch the end of the pencil in order to establish what is being written. It's a trick every detective should know. Now we have to establish who or what Ferregamo is—"

"That would be a Julius Ferregamo, of Bedford Square."

"Your average is rising, Watson. That's twice in a single day you've managed to render me speechless. I retract my earlier criticism. How do you come by this information?"

"No magic, Holmes. It just so happens that I met the fellow at a luncheon at the Langham Hotel. It was a good many years ago, but his reputation as London's premier art collector was unequalled even then. Many pretenders to the throne have come and gone in the interval, and Ferregamo retains his supremacy. Half-Italian, you know, but still quite a decent chap for all that."

"I'm sure he would appreciate your finding him so, Watson." Again, he winced, and clutched at his stomach.

"Holmes, you're unwell. We must get you back to Baker Street."

"If I am unwell, then I am extremely fortunate in having a physician at my side at all times." He rapped upon the roof of the carriage with his stick. "Driver, we've changed our minds! Take us to Bedford Square."

I shifted uneasily in my seat, as Redfern's painting brushed against my leg, and told myself that the chill I felt was entirely imaginary. I remembered Holmes's old maxim that the more bizarre a crime appears, the less mysterious it proves to be, and I wondered whether we might be witnessing the exception to that particular rule.

Julius Ferregamo was almost exactly as I recalled him from that luncheon so many years before. Where the years had taken their toll on my brow and waistline, he was as trim and dandified as ever, as he greeted us in the parlour of his lavish abode.

"Doctor, so good to see you again. Still producing your little yarns? How charming? And this must be Sherlock Holmes! You're very fortunate to catch me at home, you know. I've been in Amsterdam for some time, negotiating for a Hans Holbein. You're familiar with Holbein, I imagine?"

"Only with Anton Holbein, the Augsburg poisoner," Holmes answered. "The doctor will tell you that I have only the crudest notions about—" My poor friend's face had suddenly assumed the most dreadful expression. His eyes rolled upward, and his features writhed. For a fleeting moment, I feared he might be on the verge of collapse.

"Are you ill, Mr Holmes?" Ferregamo enquired,

"Merely beginning to regret my dining habits, sir." He laughed weakly.

"I always dine at Les Frères Heureux when I'm of a mind, but as I passed it today, it seemed to be closed. I'm so sorry, Mr Holmes, you were saying something about your crude notions?"

"Concerning art, Mr Ferregamo. In fact, I came here today to ask your opinion on a piece I recently acquired. That is, if you would deign to cast your expert eye…?" He passed the painting to the Italian, who accepted it cautiously. As Holmes released his grip on it, a curious change seemed to come over his face, as though the cause of his discomfort had suddenly evaporated.

"For a friend of the doctor, how could I refuse?" He unrolled the painting with care. "I must warn you, if you are hoping to make a fortune from it, you are likely to be disappointed."

"Mr Holmes is interested in art for its own sake," I explained. "But of late, I've learned a great deal about the importance of money in your world, Julius."

"Oh, indeed!" he beamed. "Why, that Hogarth etching behind you has probably appreciated in value about £100 since you entered my home. Why, this is very fine indeed."

Knowing that my own artistic impulses – though keener than Holmes's – were nowhere near as refined as Ferregamo's, I was cheered by the fact that our view of Algernon Redfern's abilities tallied.

"I should say that this would be the pride of your collection, Mr Holmes," he went on. Given that Holmes's entire collection was made up of illustrations from the crime news, I was forced to agree.

"I am gladdened to hear that you like it, Mr Ferregamo," Holmes said with uncharacteristic glee. "You must have it."

I was startled by this sudden act of generosity. What was Holmes thinking? Had he not accepted the same painting as a gift from Algernon Redfern an hour earlier?

"How much are you asking for it? As I said, it is not valuable, I merely appreciate it as a work of art."

"If you value it so highly, I am happy to present it to you as a gift. The doctor will tell you that I do not ordinarily act on impulse, but I feel very strongly that this painting should be yours."

A crease of doubt appeared on Ferregamo's high domed forehead. "Really? You know, I don't recognize the style, but there's something oddly... familiar. I pride myself that I can identify an artist's brushstrokes just as you, Mr Holmes, could spot the typeface of any newspaper."

"Not quite *any* newspaper. When I was very young, I mistook the *Leeds Mercury* for the *Western Morning News*. But the artist in question is Algernon Redfern. Doubtless you're familiar with him?"

"As I say, I've been out of the country – I'm a little out of touch with recent developments. This Redfern... young fellow, is he?"

"In his early twenties, I should say," I answered. "Strange chap – claimed to be English, but he had an accent I couldn't place."

Without warning, Julius Ferregamo grabbed me by the lapels. "His teeth! His skin! Describe them!"

"Then you *do* know him!"

As quickly as he had accosted me, the frightened man released me, before staggering as though wounded. "My God!" he breathed. "Ruber! He's found me out! My God!" His face had reddened, and heavy beads of sweat ran down his face. I feared his heart might be under some tremendous strain.

"Julius!" I cried. "Julius, what's happening to you?"

In describing what occurred next, I realize that I risk straining my readers' credulity. Even the famously eccentric Professor Challenger, the one man in London I imagined would be sympathetic to my tale, dismissed it as some form of narcotic delusion when I related this event to him. Nevertheless, I insist that I speak the absolute truth.

Ferregamo was acting like a madman, first scratching at the painting, then flailing about wildly. I attempted to restrain him, but without success. Holmes, meanwhile, was paralysed by the strange scene, his expression pale but exultant, his lips parted in amazement. At last, our host collapsed to the floor, heaving. But the worst was not over. It seemed from the unnatural movement in his gullet, that something was attempting to force its way out of his body … something alive.

When I viewed the remains of Anwar Molinet – was it really only that morning? – I thought I had witnessed the most hideous sight man could ever see. But now, crouching on all fours, Julius Ferregamo proceeded to disgorge a stream of bile … and live scorpions, more than could ever have been contained within a man's system, should he have chosen to swallow them whole in the first place. Freed from their unnatural prison, the creatures then proceeded to scuttle about the room, some of them heading towards Holmes and myself.

"Run!" Holmes cried, suddenly himself once more. Needing no further encouragement, I followed him out into the hallway, slamming the door firmly shut behind us.

"Holmes … " I gasped. "What just happened … " It was neither a question nor a statement, but Holmes nodded vigorously.

"It happened, Watson. But I'm at a complete loss as to explain why or how."

5

"When you start a chase, Mr Holmes, you really do it!" With the passing of the day, Lestrade had become quite his old self. Holmes and I, however, were both exhausted and less than willing to accept the Scotland Yarder's customary twitting. "And you say this fellow's death is connected to the Molinet business?"

Holmes nodded, dumbly.

"And ... you saw live scorpions coming out of his mouth? I don't mean to question your skill for observation, but really ... "

"I am as dumbfounded as you, Inspector – not a sensation I much enjoy. But if you open that door, you will find that what we say is true. But please draw your pistol before doing so; you will have need of it."

With some hesitancy, Lestrade pushed lightly against the door to the parlour. Then, with a sly grin, he shoved it wide open.

"Having a laugh at the expense of the slow-witted policemen, eh? Well, no scorpions in here. Also no tarantula spiders and no venomous swamp adders."

Disbelieving, I pushed my way past Lestrade. Julius Ferregamo lay where we had left him, quite dead. But of the ghastly creatures, there was no trace.

"Impossible!" I breathed.

"Merely improbable, I should say." Sherlock Holmes brushed by and knelt to examine the body. "If there were no scorpions, then there remains the question of how Ferregamo was stung to death."

"Sounds as though I should have a word with the keepers at London Zoo," Lestrade suggested, unhelpfully.

I joined Holmes as he lifted Ferregamo's right hand gingerly. Under the fingernails were traces of paint. "He did begin scratching at the Redfern just before ... the end," I observed.

"Perhaps he wanted to see this other painting underneath," said Lestrade. We both turned to see the police official examining the picture.

"Underneath?" I repeated. Looking closely, I could see that he was correct; there was a second picture, but it was impossible to tell what it might be.

"No doubt Mr Holmes has some chemicals in his laboratory that could help reveal it."

"No need for that," Holmes responded, "I already know what it is. Lestrade, Watson and I have an appointment elsewhere. I can trust you to take care of the body before you begin waking up the zookeepers?"

Sherlock Holmes was transformed when he was hot upon such a scent as this. As the gleam of the street-lamps flashed upon his austere features, I saw that his brows were drawn in deep thought and his thin lips compressed. His face was bent downwards, his shoulder bowed, and the veins stood out like whipcord in his long, sinewy neck. His eyes shone out from beneath his brows with a steely glitter. Men who have only known the quiet thinker and logician of Baker Street would have failed to recognize him. But I recognized the battle-signs; the time of crisis had arrived.

It was close to midnight when we returned to Algernon Redfern's studio off the King's Road. Holmes did not wait, but simply pushed the door open and entered. I followed closely, my heart thumping so loudly in my chest, I was certain that I could be found in an instant by whoever or whatever awaited us.

I lack my friend's cultivated eyesight, but I doubted that even he could make out any details in the darkness. The lamps were unlit, the blinds drawn and were it not for the fact that I knew Redfern possessed virtually no furniture, I would have feared to take a step in any direction.

"You didn't knock, Mr Holmes," said a familiar voice from the other end of the room. "I sensed at heart you were a poor sport. The artist in me ... knows these things."

"Any pretence at sportsmanship vanished when you attempted to kill me, Mr Ruber," Holmes replied, stridently.

I strained my eyes, but I could not make out the shape of Algernon Redfern. He chuckled. "Ferregamo told you my real name. Oh, please tell me he said it with his dying breath. It would mean so much to me. Or don't you propose to give me the satisfaction?" The last traces of his forced English accent were gone for good, I realized.

Holmes remained silent, a fixed point.

"Oh, very well," sighed the man I had known as Redfern. "If it helps – and I doubt it will – I'm sorry. Not about Ferregamo, of course, but about any discomfort you may have experienced."

I could remain silent no longer. "You seem to have forgotten, Redfern – I mean, Ruber – that four other people are dead, and I take it you are responsible."

"Haven't you told him, Mr Holmes?"

"If I have kept the good doctor in the dark … so as to speak … it is only because I find it difficult to credit that such a thing could occur in the world as I understand it. Very well, perhaps explanations are in order. All these terrible crimes were committed with just one target in mind: the late Mr Julius Ferregamo. I realized that very late in the day – both figuratively and literally – when I passed on the painting that had been a gift from Ruber here, and all my digestive problems vanished."

"And were inherited by Ferregamo?" I asked, hardly daring to believe the implications.

"Had he not taken it, I daresay *I* should have suffered the same ghastly fate, a notion that should give fuel to my nightmares for some years to come."

From the tone of his voice, I knew that Ruber was mightily pleased with himself. "I was worried you might not have picked up on the little clue I left you – I never even saw you examine the paper I was writing on – but when word reached me about Ferregamo's death, well … I knew you'd done exactly what I'd wanted you to do."

"It was not as though I had any choice in the experience. Once you led me to him, I found I could do nothing but give him your painting. With the assistance of Watson here, I swore off the evils of cocaine because I disliked the sensation of not being in control of my thoughts and senses. All the works you created under the alias of Algernon Redfern – they were meant for Ferregamo, were they not?"

I had some vague notion of what Holmes was driving at, but it seemed simply too fantastic to credit. "What do you mean, Holmes?" I asked. "What are you saying?"

"I am saying that Ruber here … "

"*Felix* Ruber, in case you were wondering," the man in the darkness interrupted.

"Very well," Holmes continued, "*Felix* Ruber, you see, has … an ability. I cannot classify it scientifically, but it seems that his paintings are somehow able to affect their owner – adversely, I need hardly add. Hence, Mrs Serracoult's fiery demise, the mysterious disappearance of James Phillimore, the invisible creature that clawed its way out of Molinet's stomach, and so on. You have a very vivid imagination, sir, if more than somewhat disturbed." Holmes touched my sleeve. Whether he could see my response or not, I nodded my understanding. "Given that you have achieved your goal," he asked, "would you at least satisfy my curiosity and tell me your story?"

"If you're hoping that my story will contain an explanation of my gift, I'm afraid you're destined to be disappointed, Mr Holmes. But why not?" As Ruber spoke, I began to take short, silent steps, tracking the voice to its source. "I was living on the streets of Vienna, when I first met Julius Ferregamo. I was little more than a child, trying to make money any way I could. You might think you've seen some terrible things today, gentlemen, but believe me, nothing can compare to the horrors I experienced growing up. Ferregamo was there to see what artwork he could snatch up for the so-called civilized world. The man was no better than a vulture. He'd heard some talk about my work...my abilities. You'd think that would have made me blessed. But once the word spread, life became impossible...I was the miracle-worker, the modern-day messiah. Believe it or not, I simply just wanted to paint. It is what I do, what I *am*. Ferregamo promised me a new life, away from that hell. I believed him. But he just wanted to use me like all the others. To be richer than he already was, to see his enemies crushed. It was my job to see that those things came to pass."

I remembered that Ferregamo had somehow retained his position as the premier art collector in London, perhaps even in Europe, but his competitors had all come and gone. Now I had some inkling of *how* they had gone. "So...you simply paint something and it happens?" I asked, and instantly regretted doing so. Had I given away my position?

"Not quite, Doctor. You have to possess the painting to feel its power. People must have thought Ferregamo was a very generous man – he was always giving them gifts."

"And those gifts were your paintings," Holmes responded. "Then you were his accomplice."

"I was his prisoner! Locked in a cell in his home, with a guard watching over me at all times. But finally, during my one mealtime a day, I was able to scratch a drawing into a metal plate with my fork

– it was a drawing of a heart exploding. The guard took my plate and…I was free." In his rage, he did not seem to have noticed my approach. I continued, step by careful step, as he expounded.

"I disappeared, studied, changed my style. Then returned to destroy Julius Ferregamo. But that wasn't easy if he had to possess my work. That was why, in addition to reinventing myself, I hid my revenge paintings under those rather more conventional landscapes. I found that using Brickfall and Amberley's lead-based paint seemed to block the effects for a time. Don't ask me to explain it; I don't really understand it myself. But, of course, I couldn't just send him one of my pictures, he would have known instantly. The only way was for him to buy one at auction. I had no idea he was out of the country until I saw it in the newspaper."

"And tell me, Mr Ruber, does that make you any less of a murderer?" asked Holmes. In the gloom, I could see only the easel on which Ruber's last painting still rested. Where *was* the devil?

"I won't ask for your forgiveness. And I can't ask for it over… over all those other people you just mentioned whose names I'm ashamed to tell you I've already forgotten." I still could not see my quarry, but I was certain that I had traced the voice to its source, somewhere close to the easel.

"Of late, I've given a great deal of thought to questions of captivity and freedom…it strikes me that I have been a captive for my entire life – even these last few months, living in self-imposed imprisonment, unwilling to go out in public for fear that Ferregamo might recognize me. I have been my own jailer, Mr Holmes; perhaps, in a way, that is true of us all. And I think that, for once, I should like to taste *real* freedom. The whole of Europe is open to me."

"I'm afraid that may not be possible. You must be called to account for the deaths you have caused."

Another chuckle. I knew that I was close. "I would not have categorized you as a wishful thinker, Holmes. It seems you still possess the ability to surprise me, after all. But you recall I said earlier today that I would stay in London until my work was completed. Well, Ferregamo has been dead some time now…and I departed the moment I knew."

I pounced. There was a crash – and then I experienced the sudden, overpowering numbness that comes seconds before the onset of great pain. My ribs burned, as I lay on the floor, and I could only hope that I had somehow succeeded in waylaying Felix Ruber as I fell. But I knew in my heart that I had not. Not only had he vanished without trace, but a search of the studio revealed no other entrance or exit. The windows had clearly not been opened in many a year, and we left some hours later, infinitely sadder but no wiser for our experience. Surely, I told myself, the voice could not have emanated from the self-portrait of Felix Ruber, which I had succeeded in knocking from the easel to the dusty floor?

Holmes and I did not discuss the incident upon our return to Baker Street, and we have talked little of the case since. If his own words are to be believed, Ruber is at large somewhere in Europe as I write, and though my friend could easily use his influence with the high officials of several international police forces to arrange a wide-scale search, he has not done so.

"Having given the matter further thought, it strikes me that it would be nearly impossible to bring the fellow to trial in a satisfactory manner," he explained, some months later. "The average British jury is not composed of massive intellects, and a prosecutor might just as well accuse hobgoblins and fairies of the crime. I fear that the finer scientific points would be lost on the great, unobservant British public."

For a man who has turned the docketing of fresh and accurate information into an art-form, it seems odd that he should be able to deny that these events occurred as they did, and as – so far as I am aware – the only other surviving witness, I fear that no one will place any stock in this account. So I lay it aside for now, in the hope that perhaps my friend is at least partially correct, and by the time it is published, long after my death, we will at last have come to comprehend the nature of Felix Ruber's remarkable abilities.

I should add that I hear rumours, from time to time, of queer noises emanating from the vaults of Cox and Co, where the portrait of Felix Ruber is stored, but I have not felt a pressing need to investigate further.

UNHAPPY ENDINGS

Colin Bateman

I SAY YES to a lot of things I shouldn't really say yes to, like the writing of this short story. It's worth about a grand, but out of that there's an agent to pay and a few pounds whittled away on research. It'll appear under a pseudonym, nobody will ever connect me to it; it's quite liberating, actually, I don't have to worry about what critics think or my literary reputation and I can just indulge in flights of fancy or get away with murder or generally just please myself. The problem is that there's always an unhappy ending, and that depresses me. Not at the time, you understand, but later. I just have a thing about writing unhappy endings.

My research isn't much more than sitting in the pub having a few pints watching and listening, because I'm not really one for learning the intricate details of anything. If there's brain surgery in my story, I don't feel the need to talk to a brain surgeon. I look it up on the net, give it a cursory read and then wing it. If you crash landed on a desert island and the pilot had a fractured skull and you had to operate to save his life so that he could, after a substantial period of recovery and perhaps physiotherapy and rehabilitation, together with the frequent consumption of the milk of coconuts, somehow repair the plane and fly you out of there, you wouldn't want to use my story as a guide to how to drill into his head to relieve the pressure or take out the blood clot, because you'd really mess him up. He'd be slobbering in a wheelchair for the rest of his life, pointing the finger of blame at me, though of course he wouldn't be able to literally point the finger of blame at me because well, you would have drilled into the area of the brain that controls the finger of blame. On my advice you would also have used the corkscrew you rescued from the premier seats at the front to do the drilling, pausing only to comment sardonically that planes don't reverse into crashes and they should have the rich seats at the back. Actually using the corkscrew would be pretty damn sore unless you improvised chloroform using a mixture of vodka, egg whites and broccoli. You can't really improvise chloroform using vodka, egg whites and broccoli. Don't try it at home, because it's really difficult to get the right kind of broccoli. You need Spanish broccoli, grown in the foothills of the Andes. You see, when information is presented in fiction you have a tendency to accept it as fact just because it's there on the page before you; you presume we've done the research. Think about it. The Andes aren't in Spain, but you just blithely accepted that they were.

This story features a woman who works in a bank. She could work *anywhere* because it's not really relevant, but having her work in a bank adds a certain *je ne sais quoi* given what later develops with the banknotes. I can toss in *je ne sais quoi* because it's French everyone understands. I don't speak French. If I made her a French banker I'd really be screwed because even though the story would be in English, you'd expect her to come out with a couple of French words just to make her character seem kosher. A French Jew, in fact. She's from Montmartrelle, I might say, which shows that I can look up a map of Paris, and then corrupt not only the specific area but the entire *arrondissement* just enough to make it appear like it's really based on Montmartre and I've changed it subtly because what I'm writing is too damn close to the truth to allow me to use its real name. What I'm writing must be closer to *roman à clef* than fiction, which also adds a certain *frisson* which will be further advanced by the pointless and distracting use of *italics*. All of which will be entirely irrelevant, because she's not a French Jewess from Montmartrelle, but a banker from Derby.

The hotel bar is modern with a pale wooden floor. You would think it would stain, but it can be wiped clean with a damp sponge. The ambience is provided by Sky Sports News with the sound high enough to be distracting but low enough not to impart any information, and the screen is just far enough away from where I'm sitting to prevent me from accurately reading the tickertape information at the bottom or the league tables and fixtures at the side. Sky Sports News is thus failing to inform me of anything on several different levels. The situation could be rectified if I simply moved closer, but I've become captivated by the Derby woman having a heart to heart with her boyfriend. I never actually see her boyfriend's face because they're both hidden by a pillar, and I don't hear anything he says because he's quietly spoken, but I hear everything she says because she's louder, and I'm drawn to her because I was once engaged to a woman who said she came from Derby. I killed that woman because she tried to break it off. When the Jehovah's Witnesses came to the door shortly afterwards, I still had blood and soil on my hands. They asked to speak to the woman from Derby, with whom they clearly had already established some kind of relationship, or she must have at least hinted at some stage that she might be willing to let them in, which is a dangerous thing to do with Jehovah's Witnesses, or Mormons, or insurance salesmen, because they're like multiple dogs with multiple bones, but I told them that I had just murdered her and buried her under the patio. People will accept anything if you present it in the right way. They laughed politely and left, no doubt discussing my unusual sense of humour, and I was able to make a clean getaway, that time, even though I would have been quite intrigued to discover if Jehovah's Witnesses actually made for good witnesses.

It takes a lot of work to dig up a patio.

It's useful to have a power point nearby.

I catch a glimpse of the guy leaving. When I peer around the pillar and ask her if she's okay, because she's sobbing, she says there was no need for him to storm off like that. For the purposes of this story, she is good looking. If she was some big thunder-thighed porpoise, what follows would feel rather sordid, and you would probably allow it to colour your perceptions of me as a person. It is a universal truth that people prefer to read about attractive people making love, because you can understand the animal passions they might arouse in each other. If she had thick ankles and sagging arms and skin like a peppered mackerel, then it would just read as if I was taking advantage of her despair. So for the purposes of this story she is attractive. We are both, in fact, attractive. In fact, I'm gorgeous.

Also, it would probably work better if it was set in Montmartrelle, with the bells of the Eiffel Tower peeling softly in the background, but for the purposes of this story the location will remain firmly here, in this dull city. But don't worry, she is not another one who ends up under the patio. That would be ridiculous. Her room is on the nineteenth floor of this hotel, up where there are no patios.

In retrospect, I will remove the bells from the Eiffel Tower. I could only justify them by creating an alternative history for France in general and the Tower in particular, one in which Napoleon wasn't defeated at Waterloo etc., etc. and I would have to continue you right up to the modern era and actually make her a French banker, but this is a short story and they're paying by the word, and it's really not worth the effort.

I get into her room by telling her the story about the man who won the lottery. It always works. He was an ugly man who very occasionally had ugly girlfriends, which is another universal truth. But when he won the lottery he decided that now he was entitled to enjoy the company of the most beautiful woman in the world. He found her in a hotel just like this one, I say. He watched her all night, and she too had had a row with her boyfriend, and he too had stormed off leaving her without any money of her own, which was ironic, because she worked in a bank.

It wasn't really ironic, but I was playing my game.

"I work in a bank too!" my lady cries.

"Really? What a coincidence. Anyway, the woman in my ugly lottery man story wanted to stay out and have a good time, but now she was going to have to go back to her room all by her lonely self and cry. Except, this ugly lottery guy sidles up to her and says, you don't normally talk to guys like me, and you'll probably slap me in the face, but today I became richer than I ever thought I could be, and I want to do something really special, I want to make love to you. He told her she was the most beautiful woman he had ever seen and that he knew that under normal circumstances she would never look even once at him, but he had seen her being abandoned by her man, and observed her checking her purse for money she did not have, and now he wanted to make her an offer. He told her he had thirty thousand pounds in cash in his jacket and that he would give her all of it in exchange for one hour in bed with her.

Her first instinct, naturally, was to call security, but she hesitated, and she started to think about how awful her boyfriend was to leave her like that, even though she still loved him, and how much thirty thousand was, and how nobody would ever have to know what she'd done for it; she could say that she had won the lottery, and in some ways she had.

And I pause there and take a sip of my drink.

"Well, did she do it, did she?"

The Derby woman is well and truly sucked in.

I nod.

"Oh, the little ... and did she ... did she enjoy it? You know what they say about ugly men. Did she fall in love and ...?"

"She hated it. He did all sorts of despicable things to her, but she didn't think she could protest. She kept thinking of the money."

"And I'll bet he ran off without paying her!"

"No. He paid her. Thirty thousand. And an extra five for her tears. But before he handed it over, and when he was still lying on top of her, he said, just one more thing. Kiss me and this time use your tongue."

She hadn't used it at all. She was keeping it for her boyfriend. Using her tongue somehow seemed more intimate than any of the unspeakable acts she had so recently partaken of.

I ask the Derby woman if she understands why the woman in my story was so reluctant to use her tongue.

The woman from Derby nods. "But did she, in the end? Did she give in and use her tongue?"

"She did. She did. And he gave her the money, and he left and she never spoke of what had happened, never told a living soul."

"Gosh," the woman from Derby says.

It is not a word you hear very often these days.

Gosh.

"What kind of despicable things?" is her next question.

Despicable is another word you don't hear very often.

The chances of somebody coming up to you in a courtroom, after the verdict has been handed down, and saying, "Gosh, you are despicable," must be extremely remote indeed.

I tell her about his despicable acts in considerable detail, and she pretends to be shocked, but it brings colour to her cheeks and there's a coy look to her as she murmurs, "Still, thirty-five thousand pounds."

I smile, and pat my jacket pocket, and her brow furrows, and I raise an eyebrow, and there's a sudden sparkle in her eyes and for a long, long moment she believes that I have thirty-five thousand pounds for her.

She whispers, "You're not ugly at all," and she's right, because as we have already established, for the purposes of this story, I am gorgeous. But then I laugh and tell her that I'm a writer and the story of the lottery winner with the cash for sex offer is from one of my short stories. She looks disappointed. I say, forget the money, I'm still capable of despicable acts. And that gets her laughing, where really, it shouldn't. She asks me if that's really how the story ends and I tell her no, that after the lottery winner left the woman went back down to the bar and ordered a bottle of champagne, being thirty-five thousand pounds better off, but when she tried to pay for it the bar man held her twenty up to the light and said it was counterfeit, and upon further examination, they all were. She took the thirty-five thousand pounds out of her bag and threw them on the ground and stamped and tore at them, and just at that point her boyfriend returned, all ready to apologize, but such was her rage that she blurted out what had happened, and he stormed out again, this time for good.

My woman goes, "Oh!" and "Oh!" and that's just a *horrible* story.

She's quite drunk now, and she is relatively easily persuaded to her room. She finds it exciting, at first, the tearing off of the clothes and the fumbling and tumbling, because her boyfriend might return at any moment, but when we make love she seems disappointed that I do not perform despicable deeds upon her, and she urges me to hurry up and finish, which is difficult now that I can sense her regret.

As I lay upon her, I say there was an alternative ending to that story about the lottery winner and the woman of easy but expensive virtue.

And she says, "What?" as in what are you talking about the short story for while you're supposed to be finishing off.

And I say, she didn't really go down to the bar and find out she'd been fobbed off with dodgy banknotes. Didn't you pick up on the fact that if she worked in a bank, she would probably have recognized straight away that the twenties were fake?

She sighs and says: "Well, *what* then?"

My lips move to her ear and I whisper, "The reason she never spoke about it again was that she couldn't. When she put her tongue in his mouth, he bit it off. She bled to death there beneath him, and he stared at her the whole time she was dying, and she couldn't move because of the weight of him upon her, and the fact that he was still inside her."

I think it is unlikely that she will have an orgasm now.

"What kind of a writer are you anyway?" she hisses as she tries to get out from under me. "Who would come up with a nasty, disgusting sort of a story like that?"

And I tell her that when I was learning how to become a writer, the best piece of advice my tutor ever gave me was to write about what you know.

He was a good creative writing teacher.

He came to our prison every week.

But he always had a problem with my unhappy endings.

RUN, RABBIT, RUN

Ray Banks

TERRY DAVIES STARTED on the beers around kick-off, and continued through final whistle until his knees felt loose. Now he held on to a table, a fresh pint in his free hand, nodding as Marto gave him the lad's name.

Billy Lewis.

Didn't ring any bells; could've been anyone. But the way Marto told it, nobody called the lad Billy, anyway: to him and the blokes Marto had been talking to on Terry's behalf, the lad's name was Rabbit, and Rabbit was a smackhead on licence with priors coming out his arse. It was juvenile odds and sods that put him in the big boys' nick, and Marto wanted to make it clear that this wasn't Keyser fucking Soze they were dealing with here.

"Lad's done some shite – breaking and entering you know about. Handling stolen goods. Got done for possession with intent, and that's the most serious, like. But I don't want you to think he's owt worth getting scared about."

"I'm not scared."

"Nah, I know you're not scared," shouted Marto against the noise of the pub. "I didn't mean it like that. All I'm saying, you want to do something—"

Terry waved his hand, looked behind Marto at the people lining the far wall, but didn't really see any of them. "I haven't made a decision yet."

"You were the one wanted us to keep an ear out."

"I know. I appreciate it."

"Not like I give a fuck what you do, like. I'm not putting any pressure on or nowt."

"I know you're not, man." Terry smiled, but it didn't seem to stay on his face. "I'm just saying that I want to have a think about it."

Marto held up one hand. "Nae bother, son. You do that, take all the time you need." He leaned in, trying to keep his voice down, but the gist was clear: "But he's not fuckin' hard, if that's what's worrying you. Streak of piss, stiff breeze'd knock him on his arse."

"He's a runner," said Terry.

"How'd you know that?"

"Rabbit."

"Wey aye, that's why. I never thought."

Terry tapped a temple. "Fuckin' brains, me."

"So y'are." Marto gulped back some of his beer, showed his teeth and bucked his head as he belched. "How, tell you, see if it was me? And he'd done to me what he did to you?" He pulled a sick face. "I'd chin the cunt into the middle of next week."

"I know you would."

"But that's me."

"Aye, that's you."

"I'm fuckin' emotional." One last drink to punctuate, then: "All I'm saying is, you want to find him, the lad's easy fuckin' found."

"That right?"

"Has to go to the Addictions to give a sample, else he's back in the nick. Big car park outside the place, you could wait there, nobody'd bat a fuckin' eye."

Terry rolled his tongue around the inside of his mouth. He was warm, felt sweaty. "What does he look like?"

"Like a smackhead streak of piss," said Marto. "Shaved head, got this tattoo of a Jew star on the side of his neck."

Terry grimaced. "His neck?"

"That don't make him hard. He's soft as clarts, everyone says."

"Everyone?"

Marto grinned, held up his empty pint glass. "How, you want all the gen, you're gonna have to get another round in."

***

They stepped out of the pub and leaned against the wall to focus. Their breath misted in front of their faces.

"You need any help ... on it," said Marto.

"Nah."

"You'll think?"

"Aye."

"Wey, then. Take care."

Terry clapped him on the shoulder, and Marto lumbered off down the road. Terry watched him go, the street lights throwing a sick orange glow over everything. Marto walked with his legs going in opposite directions, and Terry knew he'd be the same once he pushed away from the wall.

Promised he'd think about it, but there wasn't a lot to think about. What Marto told him, if Terry didn't do it, someone else would. This lad Rabbit owed cash all over the fucking shop, pissed off the kind of villains who wouldn't think twice about battering fuck out of a junkie, even if it was just for giggles and small change.

He launched himself off the wall and dug both hands in his jacket pockets, striding forward as straight as he could. He wanted a tab, but didn't think he'd be able to smoke and walk at the same time, so he kept concentrating on the pavement, watching his feet, until he got home. There he fished around for his keys, scratched at the front door for a good minute before he realized they'd had to change the locks.

His missus came to the door, one fist keeping her dressing gown closed, her other hand trembling with something other than the cold. She opened up on the chain first and regarded him with blank eyes. Then she unlocked the door, left it ajar and went back to the lounge.

She hadn't been sleeping, which meant Terry hadn't been sleeping, either. Wide awake and stiff as a board at the slightest noise, convinced that it was happening again, and she wouldn't take anything for it, wouldn't relax. When he suggested medication, it was as if he'd suggested she take cyanide instead of Nytol. So he stopped suggesting it, and tried to find other options.

"You're late." She was perched on the edge of the settee, watching the telly, some cheap drama about cops and killers. "You stink an' all."

"I know." He sat on the settee next to her, watched a couple of cops banter on for a bit. "I saw Marto."

"What'd he say?"

"He got us a name."

She nodded, a sharp little movement. "That all?"

"No."

"Okay."

He glanced across at her. In the flickering light of telly, she looked older than she was, her eyes hollow and short wrinkles slashing at the edges of her perpetually pinched mouth. She looked at her hands, knotted together in her lap, and swallowed.

"So what you going to do?"

He looked back at the telly. The cops were at a crime scene, a body face down in the middle of the floor, and they were talking about the pretty patterns the blood had made when it sprayed up the wall. Terry put one hand over hers and squeezed.

"I'm going to sort it," he said.

* * *

On Monday morning, nice and early, he phoned in sick. Said he had a bug, he'd been up all night with the sickness and diarrhoea, didn't think he'd be in for a couple of days at least. There weren't many questions after that. People he worked for, they didn't want to know the gory details, and with Terry's clean sick record, he reckoned they probably owed it to him anyway. He drove to Freehold Street, where he parked a good way back from the entrance to the Addictions place and got settled in for the day.

By nine o'clock, the Addictions place was open. He watched them come and go, got to know the clients by the way they looked. A couple with a bairn in a pushchair, the girl with a fat arse and telling the stocky bloke that she'd seen these lush tops in Primark, and as soon as she got her dole, that'd be her. An old man with a face like a burst balloon who looked more like an alkie than a smackhead, shambling pigeon-toed and tired, and who trailed a lingering smell that could strip paint. Two lads on bikes, swinging around the car park, waiting on a third, older lad, who came out of the Addictions smiling yellow and black, announcing that his piss test was done.

The afternoon came, and Terry put on the radio, confident that nobody had seen him. Classical music filled the car. Sort of thing he listened to when he had the Cavalier to himself, none of your avant-garde stuff, just the standards. Relaxation music.

Terry took a drink of water. Just a sip to wet his mouth. Last thing he needed was to be bursting for a piss when Rabbit showed his face. He put the cap on the bottle, and the bottle on the dash, and he swallowed against a quickly drying throat. Got to thinking about what he had to do, like if he was the kind of bloke to go out and bray a lad, even if he had a fucking good reason. He hadn't been in a fight since he was a kid, and even then it'd been mostly just him defending himself against bigger lads. Marto – oh aye, Marto – now he was the kind of bloke who could be the full-on radge merchant, no sweat, but Terry wasn't sure about himself. Wasn't that he didn't have the bottle – he had plenty of that; enough to spare, even – but it wasn't something he'd done before, and there was a loud part of him that was worried he'd freeze.

He looked at the rounders bat. He'd taken it from the garage, where it had sat in the summer box with the swingball. Kids wouldn't miss it, and he'd replace it before the holidays. Couldn't have his bairns playing rounders with a bloodstained bat. Just like he couldn't have his missus staying up all night every night, going steadily mental to ITV Nightscreen. It wasn't right. Terry looked up, blinked against the sunshine. The radio was playing Wagner, that tune that reminded him of the old Bugs Bunny cartoon where Elmer Fudd ran around in a horned helmet.

Kill da wabbit and all that.

He smiled, moving away from the light. Shielded his eyes and saw a figure heading towards the Addictions. He was a long lad, a wide walk on him, and a thin layer of stubble covered his head. Terry shifted in his seat, tried to get a better look.

Rabbit. Maybe. Could've been. He couldn't really tell at this distance. Terry reached for the bat.

The lad turned a little, and then Terry saw it, the tattoo, the one of what Marto had called a Jew star. It was large and spindly and blue, and it covered the left side of Rabbit's neck from shoulder to just under the ear. Couldn't miss it.

And then he was gone, ducked inside the Addictions place.

Terry took another swig of water, a large one. No longer worried about needing a piss. This would be over soon enough. He felt the weight of the rounders bat and breathed through his nose. His heart threw itself against the inside of his ribcage, and he noticed a tremor in his arms. He didn't know how long Rabbit was going to be in there, but he needed to get himself sorted for when the lad came out. He wouldn't get many chances like this, not if the lad was a runner.

So he focused on the entrance to the Addictions. Pictured the lad going up the stairs to reception, taking a seat. If he was on licence, he was probably doing a piss test, and it didn't take very long to drop off a sample. Terry watched a couple of blokes, same loose limbs as the rest of the smackheads who'd been in there this morning, and his gut lurched. He hadn't thought about witnesses, had it all planned different.

The two blokes stopped by the entrance, their backs to the door. One of them, a gadgie with long black hair, lit a tab and passed the pack to his mate, who had the strong but fattish build of a doorman.

Fuck it, it didn't matter if there were people around or not.

Three minutes by the clock in the dash, and Rabbit stepped out of the Addictions. Terry pushed out of the car in one movement, picking up the bat as he went. Kept his head down, thinking it was now or never, thinking about the missus, thinking about the kids, thinking about the broken conservatory window and the stolen jewellery, PS3 and DVDs. Thinking about that junkie fuckin' scum, deserves everything he gets, and getting his blood up so Terry could do this, go back to his missus and tell her everything was okay, everything was sorted, that she could sleep tonight safe in the knowledge that the man who'd violated their home was twitching in the gutter outside the Substance Abuse Team office—

He heard a scream, and a car alarm went off.

"Howeh, the fuckin' money, Rabbit, eh? You fuckin' holding or what?"

Terry looked up. Saw the doorman with Rabbit thrown up on to the bonnet of an old-style Merc, and Rabbit was trying to yell for help through the blood in his mouth. The bloke with the long black hair had something in his hand, something wicked sharp that caught the light and flashed it across the tarmac, while the doorman went to work on Rabbit's gut.

Terry ran towards them. Couldn't help himself. He yelled at them, the words scrambling out of his mouth before he had a chance to stop and think. "Fuck off, the pair of youse, he's *mine*."

The doorman turned his head, the other bloke stepping back. Both glanced at the bat in Terry's hand, then at the look in his eyes. Terry kept walking, couldn't stop now. The doorman laughed and let Rabbit slide off the bonnet, then the pair of them started backing off.

"Fuckin' hell, Rabbit, you're popular the day, aren't you?" The bloke with the hair grinned at Terry. "You're welcome to sloppy seconds, mate."

Terry raised the bat, and the two men moved a little quicker. The car alarm still shrieked, made his head hurt. Rabbit lay in a pile on the tarmac. Blood all over his face. Already beaten. There was a gash in his side, and his T-shirt was soaked red, but he was still breathing. Terry looked up at the Addictions building; people in the windows, looking back at him and Rabbit.

His arms buzzed with adrenaline, and he was aware he was breathing through his teeth.

Rabbit looked up. "Thanks, man."

Terry felt the energy drain from him, and he lowered the bat. His brain screamed at him to use it, but his body had other ideas. He looked around him, and he felt like crying. He gripped the bat in both hands like handlebars, then threw it on to the tarmac. It clattered and rolled towards the Merc. Rabbit watched it, then looked back up at Terry. "I know you?"

Terry heard sirens through the wail of the car alarm. Probably an ambulance, probably for Rabbit, and probably called by the Addictions staff who were watching him right now.

"Nah," he said. "You don't know me, kidda."

And he turned back to the car where he slept like a baby for the first time in weeks.

SLOW BURN

Simon Brett

MURDER RATES ALWAYS rise during the Christmas holiday period, and Greg Lincoln was determined to add to them. Just by one. The additional statistic would be his wife Shelley.

It's not on Christmas Day itself that the bulk of the murders happen. Most relationships can survive the enforced bonhomie for sixteen waking hours (particularly when some are spent comatose in front of bland television). It's in the days afterwards, the inert sag between Christmas and New Year, that's when people turn homicidal.

The Lincolns had married because Greg had been attracted to Shelley's money, and Shelley had been attracted to … Actually, Greg never knew exactly what it was in his character that had attracted her. He had reasonably good looks and suave manners, but even he recognized that he had no moral qualities whatsoever. Still, Shelley, a good Catholic girl, had agreed to marry him. Maybe he was the only man who had ever asked her. The fact had to be faced, she wasn't that pretty. But she was beautifully rich.

She was also rather mousey, which suited Greg very well. He'd never wanted a wife who would be too assertive, or who might question the lifestyle choices he had made. In this sense Shelley was perfect. She never suggested – as some wives might have done – that perhaps he ought to do some work and thereby make a contribution to their mutual finances. Nor did she show unhealthy curiosity as to how he spent his time away from home. She accepted his mumbled excuses about "going off to play a round of golf", without ever wondering why the golf bag in the boot of his BMW still looked as fresh as when it came out of the shop. Shelley's lack of curiosity was convenient, as it was years since Greg had stepped inside a golf club. And the only "playing around" he did was in the bedrooms of bored Sussex housewives.

Perhaps, he sometimes idly wondered, Shelley was unsuspicious simply because she was so preoccupied with her two obsessions. The first of these was her Catholic faith. To Greg, who had never believed in anything except for his own superiority, this was no more than a puzzling eccentricity. Shelley's second obsession he found equally inexplicable. *Gardening*. Greg Lincoln's lips could not shape the word without an expression of contempt. To him one plant looked much like another, and none of them was very interesting. But to Shelley her inheritance from her parents, not Lovelock Manor itself but the garden surrounding it, was her *raison d'être*. She was never happier than when spending long hours with her gardener Dan in his shed, discussing their plans for the forthcoming season.

Though unable to understand his wife's horticultural obsession, Greg concluded with a mental shrug that it didn't do any harm. And, so long as the garden kept her from taking too much interest in his activities, it was all fine by him.

So that was the Lincolns' marriage, no better and probably no worse than many another. Greg had announced early on that he didn't want to have children, a decision that Shelley, though it challenged her Catholic principles, had greeted with characteristic meekness. They still had occasional sexual encounters, on days when Greg hadn't managed to find a convenient bored housewife, but with decreasing frequency. Whether Shelley enjoyed these interludes, or regretted their dwindling away, Greg had no idea.

And so their marriage rubbed along. And might have rubbed along for a good many years, but for one thing.

Greg Lincoln fell in love.

It was unwished for, it was inconvenient, but it was a fact. Greg, who had never regarded women as more than means of gratification, had fallen head-over-heels in love.

Inevitably, the woman he fell for was as tough and cynical as he was. Vicki Talbot. They'd met at a pre-Christmas drinks party. She had had in tow a husband called Alan, in whom she clearly took as little interest as Greg did in Shelley. A few drinks and a quiet chat in a kitchen sticky with mulled wine led to an agreement to meet the following afternoon for what both knew would be a sexual

encounter. Like Greg, Vicki showed no coyness. She had no illu-
sions that there might be anything romantic involved, while Greg
looked forward to carving another notch on his metaphorical
bedpost, before moving on to his next conquest.

And yet, from the moment he had made love to Vicki Talbot, he
could not eradicate her image from his mind. At the age of forty-six,
Greg Lincoln, hard-bitten, self-serving Greg Lincoln had fallen
calamitously in love. Not the kind of warm love that might make
him feel good about himself, but an obsessive, jealous love, over
which he had no control. Thoughts of what Vicki might be doing
when he was not with her burned like hot wires through his brain.
The idea of anyone else just being in her company, let alone touching
her … He tried to force his mind away from the images that tortured
him, but to no avail. Greg Lincoln was hooked.

The agony had been increased by the fact that, after a series of
torrid, snatched encounters running up to the holidays, he'd actually
had to meet Vicki socially on Boxing Day. A drinks party given by
mutual friends, an occasion of jaded bonhomie, no one really yet
ready for another celebration after the excesses of Christmas Day
itself. It was the kind of occasion at which Greg could normally
excel, drinking too much, patronizing Shelley, getting cheap laughs
from his less quick-witted friends.

But at this drinks party he was like a coiled spring, his mental
radar aware only of where Vicki was standing, who she was talking
to, who placed a casual hand on her arm. He thought he would
explode if he couldn't get just a moment alone with her. The
prospect of their reaching the end of the party, of Vicki being
whisked away by the odious Alan with nothing more than a
communal wave and wishes for "A Happy New Year", was more
than Greg could bear.

There were moments at the party when he thought Vicki was
feeling the same pressure. At times he thought he could read an
undercurrent of anguish in her jokey social manner, but he couldn't
be sure. Though it had never bothered him much before, he was
brought up hard against the impossibility of knowing what went on
inside a woman's mind.

They did get their snatched moment, ironically in the kitchen, mirroring their first fatal encounter.

"I need you," Greg hissed in desperation. "I have to be with you all the time."

"Nice idea," said Vicki, in a manner that sounded sincere, "but there is a problem."

"What? There's no problem we can't get round."

"Shelley. You can't be with me all the time if Shelley's on the scene."

"It's the same with you and Alan."

"No," she said contemptuously. "I only stay with Alan because I have expensive tastes, and he can afford to cater for them. With you and Shelley it's different."

"What do you mean?"

Her greyish-blue eyes found his. "I mean that you and I can't be together unless Shelley is out of the equation."

Further intimate conversation was prevented by the entrance of a very drunk Alan. "You two having a secret snog, are you?" he asked with a guffaw that cut through Greg like a serrated blade.

For the next twenty-four hours, he kept trying to analyse the four words Vicki had spoken. "Out of the equation." What did they mean? That he should leave Shelley? He could do that readily enough. That he should divorce her? Shelley's Catholicism might make that more difficult, but it was not insoluble.

Greg Lincoln, however, knew Vicki had meant more than that. Coming so close to the reference to her expensive tastes, there was only one conclusion that could be reached. Greg had no money of his own. Divorce from Shelley would leave him virtually penniless. But were Shelley to die, he would inherit all of her estate. At the start of their marriage they had made wills, each naming the other as sole beneficiary. All at once the meaning of the phrase "out of the equation" became blindingly clear.

Once he had decided to murder his wife, Greg Lincoln felt a lot calmer. And he started to think in a very logical way.

The most important consideration was that Shelley's death should look like an accident. And ideally should happen while her husband was absent from Lovelock Manor. His plans would be ruined by any suspicion attaching to himself. Shelley would have to die, Greg would have to play the grieving widower for a suitable length of time (or at least till probate on the estate was sorted out), and then he could be with Vicki Talbot for ever.

He spent most of Boxing Day evening striding restlessly around Lovelock Manor, assessing various forms of domestic accident. Rewired electrical boobytraps, loosened carpets on the stairs, combustible gas leaks in the kitchen...he contemplated them all, but none promised the guarantee of success. And many would put him too near for safety to the scene of the crime.

Through the night too he lay sleepless, his mind churning over other ways of eliminating the woman who lay softly sleeping beside him. And it was only as the gleamings of a truculent winter dawn could be seen through a crack in the bedroom curtains that Greg Lincoln's great idea came to him.

Rather than in the house, it would be much easier to engineer his wife's death in the garden.

At lunch the following day, Shelley was surprised when, for the first time in their relationship, Greg showed some interest in her hobby. "Will you be doing gardening stuff over the next few days?" he asked casually.

"Yes, I'll hope to," his wife replied. "Dan'll be back at work tomorrow, and there's a lot we need to do."

"I'm sure there is," he replied with an uncharacteristically generous smile. "Planting seeds and things...?"

"More planning this time of year."

"You and Dan in a huddle in the shed?"

"Yes, a bit cold to be outside too much."

"I'm sure. I was just interested, Shelley..."

"Yes, Greg?" There was a pathetic hopefulness in her look. Was her husband finally getting interested in gardening?

"...because I've got a golf thing on tomorrow, so I won't be here."

"Ah." She looked crestfallen.

"But you're here today, are you, Shelley?" She nodded. Greg smiled and took an envelope out of his pocket. "Unless, of course, you decide to go off and spend these...?"

A hundred pounds-worth of gardening tokens, which he had been out to buy that morning. There was a childlike gleam of excitement in her eye as she took the present. For Shelley the tokens represented the possibility that her husband might finally be showing some interest in her life. For Greg they were a means of getting his wife away from Lovelock Manor while he devised a way of ending that life.

Predictably, she went straight off to a garden centre. Greg Lincoln made sure that her car was out of sight, before moving to explore what was new territory for him, the garden of Lovelock Manor. As he pottered around, his mind catalogued potential murder methods. Poisoning, yes... there must be plenty of poisons in gardens. Commercially available mixtures to kill off weeds and insects. But how much would be needed to kill a healthy woman in her forties? And, more importantly, how could she be persuaded to swallow the stuff...? In a manner that would appear to be accidental...?

Then again, there was hazardous garden equipment. Greg had hazy recollections from his schooldays of reading books in which horny-handed sons of the soil suffered terrible injuries from sickles and scythes. Then, of course, farmers kept getting trapped under tractors. And didn't people die in grain silos?

He realized his fantasies were getting a little out of hand, and decided to curb them until he had actually assessed the possibilities offered by the garden shed.

So far as he could recollect, Greg Lincoln had never been inside the place. Lovelock Manor had come as part of the package with Shelley, and he'd had no curiosity as to what happened outside the house itself. So walking down the path to the shed was a new experience. There had been rain on Boxing Day, the red bricks underfoot were slippery and Greg winced at the idea of getting slime on his tasselled loafers. He passed an almost dead bonfire from which frail tendrils of smoke fought their way up through the mist. Amazing how long some things burned for. Dan the gardener, who must have lit the fire, hadn't been to work since the day before Christmas Eve.

Greg was surprised to find how spacious the interior of the shed was. Also how neat and well maintained. He had never taken much interest in Dan. A muscle-bound young man probably around thirty, the gardener seemed to be a man of few words. (That was to say that Greg had never heard many words from him; then again he'd never addressed many to the young man either.) But the neatly aligned hanging spades, forks, hoes, rakes and other garden implements suggested a tidy mind, which was confirmed by the carefully labelled pots, boxes and jars on the benches that ran below the small windows. The minimal light these gave was further diminished by creepers growing outside, and Greg was not surprised to see that Dan had a large fat candle in a holder. Nor that there was a lighter lying on the bench beside it.

There was no electricity running to the shed, but the space was surprisingly snug. Two dilapidated armchairs gathered round a butane gas heater, and a sofa-bed slumped against one wall. A small butane gas stove suggested Dan could keep himself supplied with hot drinks and snacks. There was a small cabinet containing instant coffee, UHT milk, sugar, a biscuit tin.

Greg Lincoln only vaguely took in these details. What his mind focused on was the predominant smell inside the shed. Petrol.

The odour emanated from a large fuel can, and from the mower, chainsaw and strimmer which had been filled from it. Greg smiled at his own good fortune, as all the elements of the plot that had been eluding him fell neatly into place.

The next day Dan would be back at work. The next day Shelley would inevitably join him in the shed to discuss their future planting strategy.

The next day there would be an unfortunate accidental conflagration in the shed. An explosion caused by leaking petrol coming into contact with a naked flame.

Of course, the plan probably meant that Dan would die as well as Shelley. But, Greg Lincoln reflected with a self-satisfied grin, you can't make an omelette without breaking eggs.

Having decided where and how to arrange his wife's murder, Greg Lincoln began to concentrate on the details of his plan.

It was absolutely certain that she would spend some time the following day in the shed with Dan. Shelley, for whom – inexplicably to her husband – a day without gardening was a day without meaning, had been restless over the holiday period, and the presents of gardening books she'd received had clearly been a poor substitute for actually getting her hands dirty. And yet she seemed unable to do anything in the garden on her own initiative; she needed Dan there as a guide and sounding board. Shelley really did have a very weak personality. Once the shock of her death had passed, Greg felt sure he would have real difficulty in remembering anything about his former wife.

Anyway, by then he would be permanently with Vicki Talbot. The tantalizing image of her body strengthened his resolve – which didn't really need any strengthening – to dispose of Shelley as quickly as possible.

So…a conflagration in the garden shed. The windows would be too small for Shelley and Dan to escape through, but the door would need to be locked somehow. Locked in a way that would not be a giveaway to post-conflagration forensic examination…?

Greg Lincoln enjoyed the challenge this problem presented to him. He was feeling even more confident than usual. The energy given to him by his passion for Vicki would be channelled into devising Shelley's death.

He studied the outside of the shed door. A broken old-fashioned wooden latch had been superseded by a more robust system with an eye screwed into the frame and a clasp to the door. An open padlock hung from the eye. It could be removed to fit the clasp over the ring, then replaced and closed to secure the building. But a locked padlock in the embers of Shelley Lincoln's funeral pyre would be far too much of a giveaway.

Greg concentrated on the older fixture instead. It was a traditional Sussex design – a wooden bar pivoted by a screw into the door and fitting when closed into a wooden slot on the door frame. A rectangular hole cut into the door would once have held a handle attached to the bar, which someone inside could lift to let themselves out. But the crosspiece was missing, and the bar hung downwards.

He tested the bar, which he found still rotated on its screw fitting. Hardly daring to believe his luck, he moved it round like the hand of a clock until it stood upright above its pivot. He then gently banged the door closed. Shaken off balance, the bar very satisfyingly moved through an arc to settle into its welcoming groove in the door frame. The shed was locked from the outside.

Greg Lincoln felt a surge of glee. The Sussex craftsman who had made the latch had made it good and robust. Greg used a screwdriver to tighten the screw and, after a few adjustments, found that every time he closed the door, the bar would infallibly fall into the locked position. With no inside handle to reopen it.

Deliberately leaving the latch bar hanging in its downward position, he moved into the shed. Petrol next ... petrol to fuel the conflagration. The smell inside was already so strong that he didn't reckon Shelley or Dan would notice however much more of the stuff he sprinkled around. But he was careful. Glossy pools on the floor would raise suspicions. So he poured his petrol trail out of sight beneath the benches and armchairs. He shifted the sofa-bed and generously soaked its back, which would be out of sight against the wall.

Greg Lincoln moved deftly, glorying in his own cleverness. While he prepared his fire-trap, his mind coolly assessed possible methods for igniting it. Had to be something remote, something that would activate while he was safely off the scene. He'd decided that the following day he actually might do what he had claimed to be doing so many times before, and go to the golf club. There'd be plenty of old bores there, escaping the cloying bonds of a family Christmas, able to give him an alibi for the time of his wife's murder.

The ignition method couldn't involve anything electronic. That too might leave traces. No, he needed something that would disappear in the general conflagration, offering no clues to outside intervention.

A fuse, it had to be some kind of fuse.

He looked around the shed for inspiration. He still felt confidently calm. He was in a zone where he knew that the right solution would come to him. Greg Lincoln could not fail.

But nothing he saw inside rang the right bells. Pensively, he moved out into the garden, and found himself drawn to the bonfire he had observed earlier. The bonfire that was still burning three days after Dan had lit it.

The centre of the fire was dead white ash, but from the circle around the edges little spirals of smoke rose. Greg's tasselled loafer

probed tentatively into the smoulderings, and instantly found what
he was looking for.

Amidst the embers were some strands of brown garden twine.
One or two were glowing, alight but burning very slowly.

He found a big ball of twine in the shed. Unwilling to risk accidents inside the incendiary bomb that he had created, he conducted
his experiments in the garden.

First he tried soaking a length of the twine in petrol, but it burnt
too quickly. Besides, that might leave some forensic trace. Then he
just lit the twine as it was and found, to his intense gratification, that
it worked perfectly. If he held his fuse up and lit the end, it flamed
only for a few seconds, but continued to burn. A red glow moved
slowly along, and the twine was consumed at a satisfyingly steady
rate. The smouldering burn was resilient, too; however much he
shook the fuse or waved it about, the twine continued inexorably to
burn. It must have been treated with some flammable preservative.

He tested his fuse's effect on a pool of petrol on the red-brick
path. When the tiny red glow reached the fluid, a very rewarding
flare-up ensued.

Consciously slowing down his pulse rate, Greg Lincoln experi-
mented until he had a fuse that would burn for almost exactly
twenty minutes. Perfect. The following morning he would wait until
Shelley and Dan had gone into the shed, then come down the garden,
check his locking device had worked, and bang on the door to say
he was off. By the moment of combustion he would be safely in the
golf club, surrounded by witnesses.

He laid the fuse to run through a knothole into the shed and to
end up in a pool of petrol behind the impregnated sofa-bed. He set
the latch bar in the upright position. Then he returned to Lovelock
Manor to reward himself with a large Scotch. He resisted the temptation to ring Vicki Talbot. Much better to contact her with the *fait
accompli*, the news that his wife was dead, and that he was free to
spend the rest of his life with his lover.

That evening he was particularly solicitous to Shelley, showing
uncharacteristic interest in the booty she had brought back from the
garden centre. He didn't dislike his wife. Her personality was too

pallid to inspire dislike. And he felt a mild regret about the fate that
awaited her the next morning. But not enough regret to make him
change his plan.

He slept surprisingly well, but woke early, round six, to the sound
of heavy rain. His first reaction was delight. Rain would ensure that,
once Shelley and Dan got into the shed, they wouldn't leave it in a
hurry. They would work out their horticultural strategy in the dry,
rather than venturing out into the garden.

But no sooner had he had this heart-warming thought than he
was struck by another, less pleasing, consequence of the heavy rain.
His twine fuse would get soaking wet!

Greg managed to get out of bed and collect his clothes without
rousing Shelley. His wife continued to breathe evenly, little knowing
that what she would wake to would be the last morning of her life.

Greg's carefully cut twenty minutes of twine was indeed very wet.
Not wishing to re-enter the booby-trapped shed, he had brought a
lighter with him from the kitchen. When he fed a flame to the frayed
end, the twine did catch alight and flare briefly, but then sputtered and
soon no glow showed. He threw it down on the ground in frustration,
and tried to think of some other way of detonating his time-bomb.

For a tiny moment he felt doubt. The possibility crept into his
mind that he might fail. But he quickly extinguished the unworthy
thought. Of course he would succeed. He was Greg Lincoln.

It didn't take long for the solution to come to him. Simple, really.
Better than the twine fuse. The only surprise was that he hadn't
thought of it earlier.

He opened the shed door, and carefully left it open. To lock
himself in would not be very clever, he thought with a chuckle. And
as soon as he walked inside, he realized just how perfect his new
plan was. The overcast sky made the interior darker than ever.
Which meant that when Shelley and Dan came in, the first thing
they would do would be to light the candle.

Cylindrical and large, probably three inches in diameter – ideal
for his purposes. A half-inch of blackened wick showed at the top.

Taking advantage of the tools he found in the shed, Greg worked
with confident efficiency. First he used a Stanley knife to take a

quarter-inch slice off the top of the candle. Careful not to cut through the wick, he eased off the disc of wax and put it to one side. Then, again digging around the wick, he excavated a hole about two inches across and three down into the centre of the candle.

He cut the wick, so that it was three inches long, and poked the blackened end through the hole in the disc. Lighting the wick briefly ensured that the surrounding wax melted and cemented it into position.

The next bit was easy. He simply poured petrol into the little wax reservoir that he had created and replaced the lid he had cut off, so that its trailing white wick was immersed in the fluid. He then used the warmth of his fingers to seal the wax and hide the mark of his cut. He would rather have used a flame, but prudence warned him against the unnecessary risk. Anyway, Dan wasn't going to look at the candle closely. The first thing he'd do when he and Shelley entered the gloom would be to find his lighter and put it to the candle wick.

And then – boom. Conflagration. Greg Lincoln almost hugged himself at his own cleverness.

He was about to leave the shed when he was stopped by the sound of approaching voices.

"Where's Greg?" asked Dan's voice, deep and throaty.

"He's gone. He said he had some golf thing."

"At this time in the morning?"

"I don't know. I never ask what he's doing."

"No, you let him ride roughshod over you."

"Dan … " There was a note of pained pleading in Shelley's voice.

"Well, the way he treats you … it makes me mad."

"He's my husband, Dan."

"Useless kind of husband. He doesn't care about you at all. The only person he thinks about is himself."

"That's not true. Yesterday he bought me a hundred pounds-worth of gardening tokens, and he really sounded interested in the garden."

Greg was touched by his wife's tribute to his solicitude. But he remained aware that he was in rather an awkward situation – geographically, at least.

"Oh, yes?" asked Dan cynically. "He doesn't care about you. I'm the only one who cares about you. I'm the only one who loves you, Shelley."

Hm, thought Greg, there's a turn-up for the book. And he waited with interest to hear what would come next.

"I know you do, Dan. But—"

"And you love me too. Go on, you've told me you do."

"I may have said things like that in the past, Dan ... " Shelley wasn't finding what she was saying easy. "But the fact is that Greg is my husband. I'm a Catholic, and I believe that marriage is for life."

"Even a rotten marriage that makes you unhappy?"

"Maybe it's only a rotten marriage because I haven't worked hard enough to make it a better one. And the fact is that Greg is my husband and we have both sworn to stay together until death do us part."

Oh, thought Greg, what a splendidly loyal little woman I married. Pity I've got to murder her.

"And if death did you part?"

"What do you mean, Dan?"

"If Greg died, then would you marry me?"

There was a long silence, then Shelley's voice said quietly, "Yes, Dan. I can give you that satisfaction at least. If Greg were to die, I would marry you."

Oh well, there's a nice warm thought for them to end their lives with, thought Greg.

"Thank you for saying that," murmured Dan, his voice thick with emotion. Then Greg heard him approaching the shed, even putting his hand on its open door. "So I can't tempt you in?" asked the gardener. "Just for a quick cuddle?"

"No," said Shelley firmly. "It wouldn't be fair to Greg."

Her husband was divided between respect for his wife's loyalty and annoyance at the realization that, if she wouldn't go into the shed, he was going to have to find another way of murdering her.

"All right. If that's what you feel ... " And, as a petulant punctuation to his words, Dan slammed the shed door shut.

Things happened very quickly then. Just at the moment Greg heard the clunk of the wooden door latch finding its slot and locking him in, he was aware of a sudden roar of combustion behind him. He turned back to the inferno that had once been a sofa-bed, and saw flames licking along the floor towards him from every direction.

Greg Lincoln had been a very good planner, after all. His twenty-minute twine fuse hadn't really gone out. Burning more slowly because of the damp, its spark had still crept inexorably towards the knothole and the pool of petrol inside the shed.

Realizing that that's what must have happened was the last thought of Greg Lincoln's unlamented life.

And his last sight, through the flames and the cracking windows of the garden shed, was his wife Shelley, held in the protective arms of the gardener Dan. Which was where she would stay for the remainder of her very happy life.

FINDERS, WEEPERS

Adrian Magson

THE RUNNER STANDS blinking into the sunlight like a small, pudgy rodent. He's wearing a neat Paisley-print silk dressing gown and leather slippers, and looks like one of the Wise Men from a nativity play.

I don't need to check the photograph to see we've got the right man. Plumper than when the snap was taken, and wearing a tan he didn't have a year ago, but it's him: Gerald Martin Bream, once of south London – until he decided to go runabout with a bagful of his employer's money.

Problem is, he's got one hand behind his back and I can't see what he's holding.

Even small, paunchy rodents have teeth.

I look at the large brown envelope in my hand. "Uh... Mrs Tangmere? I've got a package."

Bream's gaze slips instinctively to the envelope, which holds a couple of old magazines, but he shakes his head.

"This is Mandeville Cottage, though, right?"

"Yes. But there's no Mrs anybody here. I'm renting."

"Oh. Must be a computer glitch. Sorry."

I leave the Paisley-print dressing gown and go back to the car where my partner, Reece, is waiting. We'll come back later and pick him up.

Reece and I are people finders. We get called in when all other methods have been exhausted. Understandably, not all of the people who disappear want to be found – it's why they did a runner in the first place. Among their reasons for going are debt, guilt, anger, confusion, loss and fear. Fear is the biggie; it makes people go deeper than most. Fear of death, fear of retribution – sometimes fear of fear itself.

Bream, though, doesn't quite fit this category; he'd just got greedy without thinking it through; an accountant with dreams of freedom. After a lot of pointless dithering – mostly to do with professional reputation – the company had called in Reece and me.

By then, Bream had probably already spent a lot of the stolen money trying to hide his tracks. But he'd been dumb enough to hang on to his mobile phone. One call to the number, pretending to be a call centre offering a big cash prize, and he'd given away where he was hiding.

All we have to do now is go back and pick him up when he's dropped his guard, and we'll collect our fee. We don't always get asked to take the runners back, but Bream is what we call a "take-away" – the client wants him on a plate.

Back down the lane, Reece is in the Range Rover, scowling over the *Telegraph* crossword. He's stuck on twenty-six down.

"It's our boy," I confirm, sliding in alongside him. "Dinner or coffee?"

"Too many letters." He hurls the *Telegraph* into the back, a sign the crossword isn't going too well. "I need sustenance." Another sign.

We find a decent restaurant, eat dinner, then go back for Bream. We park down the lane again and walk up to the house and through the front door.

But someone has got there before us.

Bream's Paisley-print gown is no longer neat, due to two bullet holes in the front.

Unfortunately, Bream is still inside it.

* * *

"Stone me," says Reece. We split and do a rapid tour of the place to make sure no one is waiting to pounce on us. It's soon obvious that nothing has been touched. Even if we've never been inside a place before, we can tell if a place is naturally tidy or if it's been cleaned up after a search. This one looks normal.

I feel uncomfortable and peer out of the window. The street lights are just coming on, and if anyone is waiting for us to come out again they'll have a clear shot.

"This is some weird shit," mutters Reece, staring around the room. "If they were after the money, why didn't they toss the place?"

"Maybe that wasn't the point." I peer closely at Bream's body. Just visible in the skin of his upper chest are two vivid impressions, like knuckle marks, only deeper.

He'd been punched before being shot. One of his slippers is across the other side of the room, confirmation of a struggle, as if he'd been forced back in off the doorstep.

We hoof it back to the car. Death doesn't happen often in our business – at least, not by our hand. We've tracked down people who died before we got to them, and we once found a man who had a heart attack the day after he returned home.

But nothing like this.

I ring Jennings. He's a sort of Mr Fixit who makes his living in various ways, mostly security related. Rumour says he used to be a high-level government spook. He approached us not long ago when one of his regular stringers was off sick, and we'd picked up several tracing jobs since then. Some were on the run after doing something illicit; others were unfortunate souls who went walkabout with no rational explanation. Either way, someone wanted them back and was willing to pay.

Jennings doesn't react well to the news.

"What the hell were you wasting time on Bream for?" he explodes, as if we've been laying waste to the home counties with a flame-thrower. "Melinda Blake is your current assignment."

Melinda Blake, late of Her Majesty's armed forces, is a private investigator whom nobody has seen for over a month, which is apparently out of character. Jennings sent us the brief a week ago, with a key to her flat so we could do an audit of her belongings. It wasn't going well, but along the way, we'd tripped over Bream's trail. Sometimes multi-tasking does that; one door closes, another opens.

"Change of plan," I explain. "We got a lead to Bream's whereabouts. It paid off. Well, almost. Blake's next on the list. What's the problem?"

"Leave it," he says after a lengthy pause. "I'll deal with the Bream thing. Get on Blake – and ring me when you find her." He clicks off before I can use the phrase I keep for people who upset me.

*   *   *

The Corpos Fitness Centre is a modern, single-storey building near Battersea Park, catering to those who like their exercise in air-conditioned comfort. Forget pounding the streets in the wind and rain; that's for freaks, army types and London Marathon wannabes.

Melinda Blake, according to a membership card we'd found in her flat, is a member, so it seems a good place to start our search.

Finding where runners might have gone can be a laborious process. Nine times out of ten, there's a link, a clue, no matter how tenuous. Usually it's to a place from their past life – maybe their childhood – even somewhere they've fantasized about but never been. Reece and I work on the basis that tucked away in the fabric they leave behind, there's always something, often overlooked by friends and family.

We call this process the audit. It involves going through any rubbish we can find, from theatre tickets to the fluff in their pockets. We once found a runner from a dumped photo album. After drawing a blank everywhere else, we'd noticed snaps of a tiny village near St Tropez, southern France. It was a long shot, but that's where we found him one afternoon, drinking a cold Stella at a bistro in the local square, enjoying his new life.

So he'd thought.

Five thirty in the afternoon is evidently a quiet time in the world of sweatbands and leotards, and from our vantage point in a café across the road, we count three people entering the gym. All are young-ish, good looking and self-aware in the latest sportswear, which draws from Reece a sour comment about some people having no jobs to go to. He's still having trouble with the crossword.

"What's the story here?" he says with a sigh.

"Slim," I tell him, like the information we'd been given by Jennings. "Ex-army, a private investigator. Her brother is worried about her and reckons she might have been threatened by somebody – possibly from a past job. A couple of her regular clients say she hasn't reported in, which isn't like her."

We give the last fitness freak two minutes, then leave the café and push through a set of glass doors. The foyer shows photos of muscular men and women doing unnatural things with complicated equipment, and the décor is a mixture of Greek tiles, thick carpets and tinkling fountains. A vague smell of air-freshener and soap hangs in the air, with that faint gamey element wherever bodies gather together in exercise.

Behind the desk is a friendly looking young woman with an orange tan and big hair. She takes one look at Reece and thrusts out her chest. I don't even rate a glance.

"Mandy," Reece says smoothly, eyeing the badge on her chest. "I wonder if you can help me?" His tone makes it perfectly clear that she can and, even if she can't, it might be fun anyway. Mandy swells with anticipation and I look away.

Much more of this and I'll get a bucket of cold water.

Two minutes later, Mandy is sashaying down the corridor on her high heels. If she'd had eyelashes painted on her rear, we'd have both been winked to death.

The moment she disappears, I slip behind the desk and run Melinda Blake's membership card through a swipe machine.

"You didn't promise her anything, did you?" I say, while the machine clicks and whirs.

"I asked for details of the company's lawyers," he replies. "Said I'd slipped and fallen in the showers a couple of weeks ago, and need details of her people so my people can contact their people." He smiles proudly at his inventiveness.

I look at him. We'd discussed tactics on the way here, such as which ruse to employ to gain access to their customer records. Somehow, his plan seems almost half-hearted, like Indiana Jones waving a silk handkerchief instead of a bullwhip.

"That's it? You slipped? I thought you'd come up with something like…"

"Like what?"

"I don't know. Something interesting…daring." The computer stops clicking and reveals an address – a new one.

In the background I hear a familiar clattering of heels in the corridor.

We're up and out of there in seconds, before Reece can be called to task by the pneumatic Mandy.

* * *

The new address turns out to be a small flat above a letting agency. Access is by a flight of metal stairs from a service yard at the rear. We hang back, watching the place, and I call Jennings as instructed.

"Okay, leave it for now," he says, which surprises me. He usually likes to get these things done and dusted. "I've got something urgent for you."

Ours is not to reason why, so we go to check on this other job. It keeps us busy for a couple of hours, by which time the traffic in the area has died down.

We park the car and Reece leads the way up the metal stairs. The door at the top is fitted with a simple Yale lock. At least, it had been. Someone has kicked the door in.

Reece and I exchange a look. Shades of the late Mr Bream. This doesn't look good.

We step over splinters of wood into a short, carpeted hallway. The atmosphere has a dead, musty sadness about it, as if the soul has fled the scene. No memories, no presence, no trace of past warmth and not much future.

The bathroom is empty save for some washing on a line and a faint smell of soap and perfume. A pair of tights lies coiled in the bottom of the bath like a wet snakeskin, and one of the taps is dripping into a brown stain on the enamel with a plunk-plunk sound.

Across the hall is a small kitchen. It smells of fried food and spices and needs a clean.

"Alec." Reece is standing just inside a bedroom along the hallway, looking down at the floor. I join him.

A woman is curled on the carpet, clutching her stomach. She's face down, as if trying to bury herself in the worn pile. A pair of spectacles are a yard away and her shoes are lying nearby. One heel is broken off, the nails shining like a rat's teeth.

I check her pulse. She's gone.

Closer inspection reveals a soggy area of tissue just below her ear, and by the way the fingers of her right hand are twisted into her clothing, she'd been hit in the stomach first, doubling her over. The killer blow had come from above. No matter what the chop-socky experts claim, it's a blow which requires considerable force.

"Still warm." Whoever did this isn't long gone. We might even have passed him in the street.

I survey the scene, trying to read what happened. I check out the living room, and find a briefcase sitting on top of a folded blanket on the settee. It's empty save for a crumpled sandwich wrapper, a three-day-old *Standard* and a Starbucks napkin. A travel bag on the floor holds some casual clothes, the sort you'd take if you were going on a trip and weren't fussy about creases. Apart from that, the room is depressingly clueless.

We check the rest of the flat. Nothing stands out; no paperwork, no receipts, none of the detritus of an established life. On top of the wardrobe in the bedroom, in a recess behind a moulded surround, is a Jiffy bag containing a photograph in a plain black frame. It's the sort issued by official photographers, where necessity and cost triumph over style. A group of men and a woman in army camouflage are smiling self-consciously at the camera. The woman looks like the one on the floor, but as we haven't actually seen her face full on, it's difficult to tell. She looks confident and tough and her head is cocked to one side as if she'd been caught off-guard. Not for the first time, I consider sadly.

"Provost," says Reece, pointing to a spot on Blake's uniform. "Army cop."

That figures. As a military policewoman, she'd have been drawn naturally to working as a private investigator.

In the kitchen, a pair of faded Marigolds are hanging over the edge of the sink. While Reece watches the street I do a thorough search of the place, starting with the back of the wardrobe, then a chest of drawers. They yield layers of dust and cobwebs but little else.

The bed and bedside cabinet yield nothing, so I move on to the kitchen and bathroom, checking cupboards, boxes and air vents. There aren't many places to look because there's so little furniture.

Ten minutes later it's clear that whoever killed Blake has cleaned out anything which might have helped fill in her background. No correspondence, no letters, no invoices. No character.

"Nobody's life is this empty," I mutter. Even after a few days you pick up some rubbish. I check the bin in the bedroom. Not even a liner. Unnatural.

"A pro," says Reece. It would take a pro to be this efficient. Or someone living a very ascetic life. Then he says, "Hello."

There's something in his tone, and he's looking at the door. I turn and stare down the barrel of an automatic pistol, held unwaveringly at shoulder height. Behind it stands a youngish woman, slim, fit-looking, with short-cropped, dyed-blonde hair and eyes that tell me I'm in trouble if I try even to breathe loudly.

"Who are you?" she says. Her voice is shaky, but steadier than mine would be in similar circumstances.

"I'm Alec," I reply. "He's Reece. By the way, we didn't do this." I'm not sure I'd believe me if I was her, but there's no harm in trying.

She moves sideways and says, "Sit. Both of you." We sit on the bed, while she looks down at the body. Her air of calm is surprising, and I wonder if I can get out of the way if she starts shooting.

"Unusual piece," says Reece, nodding at the gun. "Baikal, isn't it?"

It's hardly relevant, but that's Reece all over. If this woman is feeling hormonal, we're dead meat.

"Why are you here?" she asks. She moves to the chest of drawers and rests her gun on it, still pointing at us. Never believe it when you see people in films standing around holding a gun like a plate of cucumber sandwiches; they're heavy as hell and play havoc with the wrists and arm muscles.

I explain what we do, and how we just discovered Melinda Blake's body on the floor. She blinks when I mention the information from Blake's brother.

"Blake doesn't have a brother," she says.

Then Reece says, "That's not Blake."

He's still holding the photo frame. He's got his finger on the face in the photo. The one we thought was Blake.

It's the woman with the gun.

"Her name was Cath Barbour," Melinda Blake explains. "We were in the same unit. She was staying with me for a couple of days."

"What kind of trouble are you in?" asks Reece.

"Who says I'm in trouble?"

"You must be – for this." I indicate her dead friend. And the gun.

She sighs, then surprises us by dumping the gun on the chest of drawers and kneeling down by the body. If she thinks we're a threat, she doesn't care any more.

"Can we move?" I ask. I don't, though, in case she has a miniature Uzi tucked in her bra.

"Are you two ex-army?" she murmurs, ignoring my question and running her fingers across the dead woman's face.

"No. Didn't like the haircuts." The closest we ever got was as Ministry of Defence investigators. It took us to Iraq for a while, working undercover, but it's not something we like to talk about.

"Then this won't be something you're used to." Her voice is soft, almost regretful, as if we're not what she was hoping for.

"Death, you mean?" I give a shrug when she looks at me. "Actually, we're more accustomed than you might think." I explain about Bream, and how two deaths inside twelve hours is a little unusual.

She takes it all in, then nods and gets up, scooping up the gun on the way. "We need to find a photo printer," she says. "Bring the frame." Then she walks out.

We get in the car and she directs us to a shopping centre where there's a medium-size chemist with a photo printer in one corner.

Melinda makes sure nobody is too close, then asks Reece to tear off the back of the photo. There's a small plastic object taped to the inside. It's about the size of a postage stamp, with one corner cut off.

"It's a smart card," Melinda explains, and points to a slot in the photo printer. "Put it in there."

Reece does that, too, and when the screen asks us what we want to do, Melinda leans across and taps the screen until it dissolves into a grid of thumbnail snaps of what is on the card.

"Don't let anyone see these," says Melinda, and moves out of the way while Reece and I take a look.

Good thing she warned us. We're looking at a series of still shots. A young woman is lying on a single bed, with two men standing over her. It's clear what the scenario is, but the scene is given a sharp twist in the final four frames. One of the men is hitting the woman. Only this isn't some aggrieved punter taking his guilt out on a luckless street girl; he's twice her size and he's wielding a set of knuckle-dusters.

Knuckle-dusters? The indents on Bream's chest.

The final shot shows the woman lying back, lower face destroyed, eyes open and staring. The expression reminds me of Melinda's friend.

"Jesus," whispers Reece, who doesn't shock easily. "He killed her."

I don't say anything; I'm not sure I can trust my voice. Instead, I concentrate on the photos and point at two of the frames. "Can we print these?"

Melinda taps the screen. Seconds later, we're studying the enlarged prints.

"They're army," I say.

"Officers." Reece sounds disgusted.

Just visible in the two shots is a uniform jacket, resplendent with ribbons and braid, hanging on the back of a chair. Beneath the chair is part of a hat brim.

"The hitter's name is Collinson," Melinda Blake informs us as we leave the shop. "He's a major attached to an Intelligence unit. The other is a Major Pullman. They go everywhere together.

"I received a complaint one day from a female private," she continues as we walk back to the car. "She said Collinson and Pullman had picked her up in a bar and taken her to a hotel. They ordered her to strip off, threatening to end her career if she disobeyed or told anyone. Then they raped her." She shrugs. "I filed a report, but the following day the complainant backed out. Said she'd made it up."

"Why would she do that?" I ask.

"That's what I wondered, so I did some digging. There's a lot of history on these two, mostly anecdotal. They run a small group called the Hellfire Club. It's an exclusive gathering for people of similar rank and inclinations, although I think they limit the kind of

excesses you just saw to themselves." She shudders, the first real sign
of emotion. "They're sick, and whoever they touch is left ruined."

"So how come nobody's stopped them?" says Reece.

The look she gives him should have withered him to a crisp.
"They're experts, that's why, good at covering their tracks. It's
what they do." The way she says it makes my neck tingle.

"What do you mean?"

"They've been trained in a branch of the Intelligence Corps
dealing with Psychological Operations. They know how to influence
people ... to find their weaknesses and draw them in. Exploiting
circumstances is what they do for a living. It's how they find the
other Hellfire members." She looks drawn. "After I submitted the
report on the rape complaint, things started going wrong. It was like
I'd picked up a disease. Weird stuff began to happen ... stupid,
mostly, but in the army it was enough to get me noticed. Then
rumours started to circulate."

"What rumours?"

"About me ... and another female private. And an officer. Neither
was true, but that didn't matter. When somebody reported missing
funds and stolen weapons, even my own CO began to doubt me. I
was frozen out and threatened with a transfer to some God-forsaken
depot in Germany. The only alternative was to leave. I didn't need
the hassle."

"But you got hold of this memory card," says Reece. "How come?"

"The private who'd alleged the rape sent it to me later. She'd
found their camera bag in the hotel bathroom. Thinking they'd taken
photos of her, she took the card. She didn't look at it until recently.
When she did, she brought it to me. They must have found out."

"What happened to this private?"

Melinda nods bleakly at the body on the floor. "You found her."

***

Reece and I exchange a look, probably thinking the same thoughts.
The death of Melinda's friend is a warning of what's in store for
her, too, if the officers catch up with her.

But it's not great news for us, either.

"We've been used," Reece mutters quietly, getting there a moment before me. "They set us up like gun dogs."

He's right. We find Melinda Blake and, hey-presto, they find her, too. I think back to see if I can recall any tail on us over the last couple of days. But when you're not expecting to be followed, why check the rear-view mirror?

I remember Jennings's response when we told him we'd called on Bream. He'd been frosty. Okay, he's not the most sociable type we've ever worked for, but even for him it was more than cool.

Because he'd been expecting us to find Blake first, not Bream.

"Jennings," I say, and Reece nods in agreement. It was Jennings who'd supplied us with the story on Blake's "brother". If whoever was following us had been expecting us to lead them to Melinda Blake's hideout, simply because that was our current assignment, they would have gone in hard. It must have been a shock finding a short fat man in a fancy dressing gown instead of a former female army provost with a dye job.

It was too late to back out, so they shot him.

And now this. If the killers knew where Melinda was hiding, it could only have come from the information we'd given to Jennings.

And he'd expressly delayed us coming in here. Now we knew why.

"They'll be looking for us now," concludes Reece.

* * *

We settle Melinda in a small hotel with plenty of exits and head for Jennings's place in west London. It's in a Georgian terrace near the BBC, with state of the art security cameras everywhere, and we park the Range Rover right outside. Just so he gets the message.

I should feel like one of the Magnificent Seven walking across the pavement, but remembering what happened to most of them, I feel vulnerable instead.

Reece kicks on the heavy front door and it opens with a sigh.

A bad sign.

We step inside and find one of Jennings's assistants, a chinless wonder with more muscle than brain, waiting for us. He advances

like a runaway train, but Reece simply side-steps and clips him in
the throat with the edge of his hand. He collapses and flops about
on the carpet like a beached haddock.

We head on into the inner sanctum where Jennings has his office.

Or rather, had his office.

He's sitting in his chair behind his desk, and whatever he had in mind
for his final action, improving the decor clearly wasn't uppermost.

"An officer and gentleman to the core," mutters Reece sourly, looking
at the automatic in Jennings's dead fist. "He hasn't paid us yet."

I open a desk drawer and find a wad of notes in an envelope. I
liberate the assets for our greater good, then go back to the outer
office, where the assistant is just about sitting upright. He sees us
coming and tries to crawl away across the carpet, but Reece steps on
his ankle, pinning him to the floor.

"Where are they?" I say, bending down so he can see me. By the
look in his eyes, it's clear he knows what happened, and wants to
get away before he becomes suspect number one. He also knows
who I'm talking about: Majors Collinson and Pullman, pride of the
Intelligence Corps.

"They … they've gone," he gasps, struggling to stay out of Reece's
reach. "I don't know where. I saw them leaving … and found him
like that."

"Makes your heart proud, doesn't it?" I say. The cream of the
army, and they turn out to be sadists and women-killers. Thank God
we didn't need them for something serious. Like fighting a war.

I reach for the assistant's tie and give it a nasty twist on the way
past. I know – not gentlemanly.

But I'm no officer.

* * *

Reece and I return to the hotel, during which time we agree a plan
of action. It's clear we can't let things go, because Collinson and
Pullman now know who we are.

We collect Melinda and take her to another, larger hotel,
surrounded by busy streets, bus routes and underground stations.

I hand her a key-card and a holdall. "Go to room two-one-one. Here's a change of clothes and some cash. Take off everything you own – jewellery included. Get dressed in the new stuff and leave the hotel through the rear cark park."

She takes the key. "What then?"

"Just keep walking," says Reece. "Don't look back. Your trail needs to be clean."

"Why?"

"Because if they get to us, they'll surely get to you."

It's cold and brutal, but she needs to see the facts.

"You need to make a fresh start," I explain. "Temporarily, anyway. Go to the beach, get a new job, invent a new name and background. It sounds drastic, but with those two still out there, it's the only way. It won't be for ever."

She still looks doubtful. "What are you going to do?"

"Go after them." We don't really have a choice. It's no good going to the police, and while Collinson and Pullman are out there, they'll always be a threat – to us as well as Melinda. They'll never let up.

For them, it's become part of the game.

The only thing they haven't reckoned on is that we know how to find people, too. However good they are, or where they go.

And like I said, we don't always take them back.

Melinda blinks and tries a smile. It's shaky, but comes out right in the end. "Okay. But when it's finished, how do I find you?"

"You won't have to. We'll come find you." I give her my best cheesy smile. "It's what we do, remember?"

THE HARD SELL

Jay Stringer

THEY'D BEEN BROUGHT together by Ed Baker, the only real long-con player in the Midlands. People said he never got involved in anything that had fewer than ten moves.

There were five of them at the meeting:

Jake Nichol, former pro wrestler. He'd got as far as the big two in America before dropping out. He never quite made it, but he did get pinned by Hulk Hogan.

Returning to England, Jake got put away for holding up a petrol station without a gun. The cops eventually found him with a mashed-up banana in his pocket. He went in a failure but came out a minor legend.

Tom McInnes. Young and green, he was making a name at short con. Nobody liked him because he had the charm of a dead rat, but he was willing to learn. He had some nervous disorder and was always moving or twitching.

Jamie Prescott. He talked a lot. He did it well. Put him in a suit, he was the smoothest lawyer you'd never seen. Put him in overalls, he could convince you he could turn your car into a spaceship.

The strangest member of the group, the one everyone's eyes kept drifting to, was Claire Gaines. She was the youngest daughter of Ransford Gaines. Everybody in the room was scared of Ransford Gaines and they all decided to be scared of his daughter, too.

They sat around a pool table in the back room of Ed's favourite pub and waited until he arrived. Jake leaned back and swigged from his bottled beer.

"You know the problem with modern wrestling?"

"No, go on," Tom took the bait.

"It's the endings. Everybody knows how it's going to happen, like."

"Yeah, well, it's all fake, innit?"

"Of course it is, but that's like saying a movie is fake. You get someone good in that ring and it's like a great film, or a great song, it's telling you a story. It's making you feel something, or that's what it should do. It doesn't, not any more."

Jake's speech was interrupted when Ed finally arrived. He was wearing a suit and carried a laptop. He looked like he was about to do a presentation at a board meeting. He set the laptop on the pool table.

"Have you all heard of the safety deposit con?"

Two heads nodded, one shook.

Claire didn't seem interested.

"Okay. It's been around forever. Until a couple of years ago, I thought it was a myth."

"What changed your mind?"

"I tried it, up in Glasgow."

"Wow," said Jake, impressed.

"So, you get two guys dressed as security guards. You take your two guys to a bank, on a busy street, and you cover up the deposit box with a metal sheet. Hold it in place with whatever cheap glue you can find, but it needs to look real."

"You did it with a metal sheet?"

"No, actually, I did it with hazard tape. Covered the deposit box and crossed over it with the tape, like a big X. But I think metal looks better."

"Okay."

"So, you've got your two security guards, you've got the safety deposit box sealed, and you've got a sign put up saying the deposit box is out of order."

"You never mentioned the sign," said Claire.

"I'm mentioning it now. The trick is, you see, that you'll get all sorts of people coming to deposit their money. It depends on the timing, but if you do it on a Friday, just before five o'clock, you'd get a lot of impatient shop workers. They want to drop their cash and be done with their day. If you do it at the right bank, you can do it on a weekend, and get people who are in a hurry to be done with their week."

"And they just give it to you?"

"That's the job, you have to make them believe you're a security firm acting on behalf of the bank. They put their cash into whatever you're using – a metal briefcase, maybe, or a security van – and you give them an official-looking receipt. They go on their way, and so do you."

"It's one of the first scams I ever heard of," said Jamie, "No way does this work."

"I swear, I thought the same thing. But I tried it."

"And you made good?"

"Five grand."

"I need another drink," said Claire.

After another round of drinks, Ed tapped the laptop again.

"You want us all to work the security con?" said Jake.

Jamie didn't like the idea. "Where's the money in it? I mean, five grand is good, and would pay for that nice shiny laptop of yours and maybe a Chelsea season ticket, but it won't pay for five of us to be involved."

"You talk as if five grand is nothing," said Jake. "You're young."

Ed raised his hand and nodded at both Jake and Jamie in turn.

"Okay. Jake, Jamie, you're both right. But what if I told you I have an idea to make a hundred grand out of it?"

He had everyone's attention at this point.

"Jamie is right, basically. It's a short con, and there's no fortune in it. I wanted to find a better angle. Do you know the trick to the long game? It's finding the human interest. In this case, everyone always looks at the trick itself. I bet, even as I told you about it, you were thinking about the job. About which bank to hit, who to put in uniform, and how much money you'd get in your case when you walked away."

Jake nodded.

Jamie shrugged.

Tom twitched.

Claire drank.

"You know what I thought the first time I heard of it? I wanted to know what happened to all those people."

"The people you stole from?" Claire said in between her drink and a raised eyebrow.

"Exactly. What happens to them? All these people putting their hard-earned cash into my briefcase. It's their money and I got to keep it. So what happened to them?"

"Banks cover it, don't they?" said Jamie, "I mean, like if a bank vault is robbed, or if someone uses your identity to scam money, the bank's insurance covers it, right?"

"They do. That's why I did the job, to watch and see. And in every case they paid up. To the exact penny. Banks can't afford any bad publicity right now."

"Good for them. I don't see the profit in it though. I mean, we steal a bit of money, the bank pays back a bit of money, and everyone goes home happy. But we're still only up by five grand."

"But what if we were the ones being stolen from?" said Claire.

Nobody spoke for a moment.

"Exactly," said Ed. "We combine the short and the long con. We go through with it as normal. We also provide some victims. Some expensive and trusted clients. Say, for instance, the daughter of Ransford Gaines. The bank will cover whatever amount she was to have written on her receipt."

Everyone set their drinks down and didn't pick them up again.

"Brilliant," said Jake.

"Fucking brilliant," said Jamie.

"I don't get it," said Tom.

"If that's the end of your presentation," said Claire, "what was the laptop for?"

Ed picked it up and dropped it; it made a hollow plastic thud.

"Case in point. It's all about making people believe in what you're doing."

Everyone nodded. Everyone drank several more drinks. The last two to leave, Ed and Claire, sat on the pool table talking through the plan.

"You'll need to find out which bank your father has most of his money in and, if you haven't already, open an account with them."

Claire looked at Ed over her final drink.

"You're scared of me, aren't you?"

"I think we all are."

She had very dark eyes.

"You can kiss me, if you want to."

* * *

On the 1st of April, Ed Baker walked into the bank in Solihull and opened an account.

He opened it with a deposit of three thousand pounds and over the following month he paid in another two. Five thousand pounds in a month was enough for the bank manager to earmark him as an important customer.

Claire Gaines already had an account. She'd been having large sums of money paid in on a regular basis from her father's account, and similar sums going out.

Living is expensive.

On the 1st of May, at four in the afternoon, an unmarked van pulled into the alley beside the bank.

Josh and Tom, dressed as security guards, took a thin metal sheet from the back of the van. Using cow gum glue they fixed it into place over the deposit box. Ed had given them a sign with the bank's insignia printed at the top, stating that the deposit box was out of service. Ed had even put the bank's phone number on.

Jake didn't like that last touch because it made him nervous.

"Everybody's got a mobile," he said. "It won't take them nothing to ring and check before depositing the cash."

"Relax. It's just like the laptop, it's all for show. They'll see the number and they'll assume everything's okay. I promise you they won't call."

"And if they do?"

"Run like hell."

"We get to carry guns?"

"Nah. You ever see a guard carry a gun? Not over here. Nobody will give you money if you carry a gun. Unless you're pointing it at them."

At quarter past four, they got their first drop. A local shop owner making his weekly drop. He put seven thousand pounds in the case.

Jake wrote him out a receipt on official bank slips.

At twenty past the hour, Ed Baker walked up. He was wearing his best suit and he made a point of walking past a couple of cameras near the bank. He stopped to chat with a traffic warden. Outside the bank, he let the security guards explain the situation to him. They pointed to the sign. Ed opened his briefcase and handed the bigger of the two guards, the one who was writing the receipts, four bundles of plain paper. The paper was cut to look like bank notes. The fake money was locked in the case and Ed walked away with his receipt.

Between twenty past and half past, they received two more drops totalling thirteen thousand.

Claire was late.

It had been arranged that she would turn up at half past, and be the last customer. At thirty-one minutes past, maybe thirty-two, the guards were due to get into their unmarked van and drive away.

By thirty-four minutes past, Claire still hadn't turned up. Ed had never heard of this job going longer than thirty-five minutes, which is why he'd planned it the way he did.

There was some scientific study he'd heard of once, where scientists proved that neutral observers will watch crimes like this for twenty minutes before calling the police. Violence or murder, or crimes committed against themselves, they'll call straight away. But if they are watching something like this, they will wait twenty minutes before it annoys them enough to call the police.

At thirty-six minutes past the hour, with Claire still not turned up and Ed starting to sweat, a police car cruised past. It stopped at the traffic lights, ten feet away from the bank, and sat there while the light stayed at red.

Tom's nervous tic kicked in, and Josh began deep breathing.

When he'd wrestled in front of crowds, he'd learned that the only way he could get by was to block out the crowd. Think through the script, think a few moves in advance, and you're not thinking of what's going on outside the ring.

He blocked the police car out.

He thought about Claire turning up, they'd talk for a minute. She'd deposit her fake money. Tom would put the case in the back of the van, Jake would pull down the metal plate, and they'd drive away.

That's what he thought about.

The lights took forever to change. The police looked right at the bank, one of them made eye contact with Jake. He nodded a stranger's greeting, uniform to uniform.

The lights changed and the car drove on.

Ed was no longer keeping track of the time when Claire turned up a few minutes later. Even from the safety of a coffee shop across the road, he was preparing to run. Claire strolled up, carrying half a dozen shopping bags.

"There was a sale on."

She deposited her fake money, and collected her genuine receipt.

She was barely ten feet away when Jake and Tom pulled away in the van.

* * *

Police were called. By the time they got there, all they could do was canvass for witnesses and speak to the bank management.

The bank's security cameras picked up the whole thing, but it was impossible to make out the features of the security guards. They did pick out the faces of the people depositing their money, and the cash as it was handed over.

Everyone held their breath and waited.

They didn't have to wait long. Three working days later, the first of the shopkeepers noticed that the money hadn't appeared in their account, and they came in to complain. Not long after that, another victim came in; bringing a copy of the local newspaper that ran the story of the crime.

It was a full week after the crime that Ed Baker came in with a receipt for ten thousand pounds and demanded the bank cover his loss. The bank was still reeling from that blow when, the following week, Claire Gaines visited the manager. She brought with her a young ambitious lawyer by the name of Jamie Prescott. She produced a receipt showing that she had, in fact, paid two hundred thousand pounds into the bank that day.

Her lawyer not only pointed out the bank's liability, but also how much he would enjoy making his name out of suing them if they refused to cover the loss.

* * *

"And they paid?"

"They paid."

Claire, Jamie and Jake were sharing a drink in one of Ransford Gaines's restaurants. It was after hours, they could talk about whatever they wanted.

"It took some major bluffing," said Jamie. "For a while I thought they were going to call us on it."

"I just had to mention my daddy's name a few times, the manager shit himself."

"Hey, don't talk down my contribution. That was my best suit that I wore, and my best legal bullshit."

Jake called a taxi and left while Claire fetched drinks. She sat down close to Jamie, toying with her glass.

"Does your dad mind you doing things like this?"

"Oh no. He's always offering me work. But, you know, it's impossible to make your own name when your dad is one of the most feared men in town. I can't get a normal job, and I don't want to work for him. I mean, he'd let me run any of his places, like my sister does, but I'd hate it, and the staff would hate me."

"Must be tough."

"It is. I keep trying to find something that's all my own, you know? Even this, the whole thing revolves around cashing in on my daddy's name."

"Sorry."

"You're scared of me, aren't you?"

"A little bit."

"You can kiss me, if you want to."

* * *

Once Ed gave the all clear, they met in the old church hall.

Four guys, one woman, several beers and a pile of money.

Tom and Jake had been first, bringing in the twenty thousand pounds they'd collected on the day. They emptied the money out on the table, piling the bundles as high as they could for the best effect. Ed was next, bringing a crate of beer and a briefcase holding twenty-five thousand pounds.

They sat and drank for an hour, talking about football and films. They tried not to show how worried they were that Claire was, again, late.

It was just over an hour later when Claire and Jamie walked in. They were carrying a suitcase each. Two hundred thousand pounds; they set it on the table.

Everyone who wasn't already drunk caught up.

Jake drank the most but didn't really show it.

"You guys know the problem with modern wrestling?"

"Yeah, you said it was because it was fake." Tom thumped the table.

"No, I said it was the endings. Everyone knows how a match is going to end. The finishing moves are all that anybody bothers with."

"But isn't that what they pay for?"

"No. They pay for the drama, we sell them a story, the hard way. The little guy, the monster, people giving in or people going the distance. It's about guys who have no right to win, but do. It's—"

"It's about selling tickets. It's about money."

Everyone turned to see who the new voice belonged to. It was Ransford Gaines, flanked by an armed escort.

"Dad," said Claire. "What kept you?"

Everyone now turned to stare at Claire. Everyone except Jake, who kept his eyes fixed on Gaines.

"I was busy," said Gaines. "I had a few other things to do. Is this all the cash?"

"Yes."

"Come on, kids, get it together."

Claire and Tom stood and shovelled the cash into the bags while nobody else moved.

"Think of it as a lesson," Gaines said. "Next time you decide to use a man's name, make sure you've asked first. And you really want to take a man's money? Point a gun at him."

His escort smiled and waggled his gun.

Gaines reached into one of the bags and tossed a bundle of notes on to the table.

"Get drunk and learn your lesson," he said to all of them. He turned to Jake, who was still staring at him, "What you staring at?"

Jake just shrugged and leaned back in his chair.

Gaines smiled, "You're the guy who held up a store with a banana, right? Give me a call, you've got balls."

He nodded and left, followed by his escort and, holding hands as they carried the cash, Claire and Tom.

The room stayed silent for a long moment.

Jake reached for a fresh beer and took a long swig.

"Now that there? Exactly the kind of ending I'm talking about."

PARSON PENNYWICK
TAKES THE WATERS

Amy Myers

"SOMETHING IS AMISS on the Walks, Caleb."
Looking most agitated, Parson Jacob Dale came into his parlour, where I was taking my breakfast. My old friend and host had just returned from conducting the daily service in the church. He is an elderly man, of even greater years than mine own, and not in good health. "It requires your assistance," he continued ominously.

"Of what nature?" I asked cautiously. My stay in his parsonage on Mount Pleasant in the delightful spa of Tunbridge Wells was a yearly delight, and I would help where I could, although the coffee and toast before me had greater appeal.

"I cannot say." Jacob looked at me helplessly. "It centred on the bookseller's store, so Lady Mopford informed me. A threat of death, she cried. Send for Parson Pennywick."

I have some small local reputation for successful intervention in such situations, and unsought though that honour is, I find my services called upon from time to time. Lady Mopford, whom I knew from previous visits, was a better source of accurate information than the *London Gazette*.

"Threat to whom?" I asked.

"I do not know."

Poor Jacob finds matters outside the daily norm distressing. He is more at ease with his learned books than with the problems of his flock, dearly though he would like to help.

"You could take the waters, Parson Pennywick," Jacob's delightful daughter Dorothea teased me, attracted by the unusual hullabaloo.

"Thank you, but I put my faith in rhubarb powder."

Dorothea laughed, and I could not blame her. She is young and therefore all that is old and tried and true is of no value to her – yet. It is hard for me to change my ways, and I cannot believe that a glass of spring water taken in the Walks, popularly known as the Pantiles, would prove a tonic more beneficial than the fresh air of Mount Pleasant. For no one but Jacob and Dorothea would I go to the Walks during the fashionable hours. It was late in June and the high season was upon us. Earlier this century the Wells would have been host to every person of fashion in London, but by this year of 1783 the delights of Brighton offer an alternative that it cannot match, particularly for the younger visitors. Nevertheless the spa is still crowded with its admirers.

With a wistful glance at Jacob settling down to my coffee and toast, I hastened to remove my cap and to seek wig, hat and cane. I too must look my best, as Dorothea insisted on accompanying me.

"Make haste, Caleb," Jacob urged me from the comforts of his own table.

"The spring will not run dry," I assured him somewhat crossly, "and doubtless the threats of death will by now have cooled." I was only reconciled to my fate by the thought of the wheatear pie, a Kentish delicacy that I had been promised for dinner that afternoon.

On the Upper Walk of the Pantiles a threat of death seemed as out of place as a Preventive Officer in a parsonage. I suspected Dorothea was less concerned about the fate of some unknown person than about missing the excitement of the day – which would doubtless be long over when we arrived. To enter the Upper Walk was like stepping on to the stage of Mr Sheridan's Drury Lane straight from the rainy muddy streets of London town. Gone are the dull cares of everyday and around one is a whirligig of colour, chatter, riches and culture. Here one may take coffee, read newspapers and books, write letters, dance, play cards, buy Tunbridge Ware – and above all converse. Death does not usually dare speak its name. And yet today, according to Lady Mopford, it had.

How could death be contaminating such a paradise, I wondered? This was a paradise with strict social rules. By now, at well past ten o'clock, the Upper Walk should be all but deserted as society would have returned to hotels and lodgings to "dress" for the day. Before then the ladies appear here in déshabillé with loose gowns and caps and the gentlemen are unshaven, as they greet the day by taking the waters. After their departure they would not return until noon, by which time they are boned and strutting peacocks in silks and satins of every hue – a delightful spectacle for one whose calling demands more sober colours.

Today, however, I saw to my unease that a great many were still here. Something must indeed be amiss.

"There," cried Dorothea. Her arm tensed in mine, but I did not need her guidance, for I could see the crowd outside Mr Thomas's book store and circulating library for myself. He caters for visitors who, having paid a subscription, may have such books as they choose delivered to their lodgings. Mr Thomas's shop is always well attended, but today it seemed all Tunbridge Wells wished to advance its knowledge of literature and science. As we pushed our way forward through the throng, Dorothea caught the vital words.

"The Book of Poets," she exclaimed.

Even I had heard of this tradition – and indeed read the Book in the past with much amusement. For well over a hundred years, this weighty tome containing copies of lyrics from would-be poets had been displayed in the book store. At first these verses had been of a saucy nature circulated amongst gentlemen in the coffee shop but then they had been requested by a wider public. Ladies now read the love poems in the Book of Poets, each imagining herself the fair damsel addressed – fortunately in more tasteful terms than in earlier times. Nevertheless the quality scarcely rivalled Dryden, nor their content John Milton.

Seeing Dorothea, who looked most attractive in her printed cotton morning gown, Mr Edwin Thomas – a fine-looking man of perhaps thirty years – immediately hurried to her side.

"I'm honoured, Miss Dorothea."

His wife did not look quite so honoured, but was too preoccupied in appeasing the sensibilities of the elderly ladies clustered eagerly around the Book, which lay open on a table of its own. Dorothea was equally eager to view it, and so, with Jacob's mission in mind, was I, as this could be the source of the threat.

Mr Thomas cleared our path to the Book, after I had explained my presence. "Let me show you yesterday's verse first, Parson Pennywick," he said gravely.

A sheet was laid between two pages, and I read:

Fairest nymph, fair — of the Wells
Whose magic spells
Are cast upon thy humble slave
Who but the merest glance doth crave…

These most unmemorable lines were writ in a cultured hand, but lacked talent, however heartfelt the sentiment that lay behind them. It was the custom that the lady's name should be anonymous, but not that of the author. Thus a bold *Foppington*, followed by a flourish of which only an English aristocrat would be capable, adorned the end of the poem.

Even I had heard of this fop, whose name was so well bestowed. Lord Foppington was the grandson of the Duke of Westshire, and prided himself on his reputation as the most fashionable macaroni in London society, clad in exquisite silks and satins.

"And now," Mr Thomas said even more gravely, "see today's verse, in the same hand but hardly of the same nature or intent." He turned the page, where I read on the next sheet:

Alas, I am spurned by fairest —, my love divine
But no other shall with her form entwine
No other hand shall win her favour
From death's cold grasp no man can save her.

"It is not the thing, sir; indeed it is not," Mr Thomas moaned.

"It is a jest," Mrs Thomas quavered. A slender woman of far less height than her husband, she was clearly indignant that the world had singled out her beloved spouse for such tribulation.

As indeed tribulation it was. I did not like this affair. I perceived that no name was attached to this verse, but it looked to be the same hand as its predecessor. "How did it come?" I asked. "Did the poet bring it?"

"It was by our door this morning," Mr Thomas told me. "Many of our poets spend their evenings in the Rooms, either dancing or playing cards according to the evening, and they pen their tributes during the midnight hours, leaving them by our door to find in the morning."

By the cold light of day, I thought, many must rue their hot-headed declarations. No wonder the fashion for anonymity of the damsels so highly praised by the poets. Did the author of this last verse rue his violent declaration, or was it merely a lovers' quarrel which time had solved? Somehow I did not think so. "Have you spoken to his lordship today?" I asked.

"Lord Foppington has not appeared this morning, and no wonder," Mr Thomas said in a tone of disgust. "Nor, fortunately, has the fair Miss Olivia Cherrington, whom all know to be the nymph he threatens."

"He is coming," squealed Mrs Thomas, running to the window. "Husband, pray *do* something. Miss Cherrington accompanies him."

There was a hush outside as all turned to the approaching couple, who seemed to take such attention as their rightful due. Her maid walked dutifully behind her. Both Lord Foppington and Miss Cherrington were in full dress, despite the early hour, he in berib-boned breeches and elegant frock coat, she a delightful shepherdess with ornate polonaise drapery, white stockings peeping below the calf-length skirt, and her hair piled high on her head. They looked as though they indeed graced a stage.

"Mr Thomas, Miss Cherrington is impatient to read my latest poem," Lord Foppington drawled, seemingly unaware of the twit-tering disapproval around him.

"I would," lisped Miss Cherrington. She looked a sweet child for all her affectation, although more a dainty automaton than a young lady with a mind of her own.

"Pray do not," Mr Thomas said anxiously.

"Why?" she asked indignantly, turning the fateful page to read it. I made no attempt to dissuade her. If this was a true threat against her life, she should know about it.

"Oh!" A gasp, then Miss Cherrington grew very white and swooned into Mr Thomas's arms. Mrs Thomas hastened to bring salts, which, firmly removing the young lady from her husband's arms, she applied to the victim's nostrils with no immediate effect.

"This is your doing, my lord," Mr Thomas said angrily.

Lord Foppington smiled. "She swoons for my love."

I stepped forward. "She fears, my lord. You must assure her it is a jest."

"Fears? A jest? Who are you, sir?" Lord Foppington eyed me querulously.

"Parson Pennywick of Cuckoo Leas. Miss Cherrington fears you wish to kill her."

"*Kill* her?" Lord Foppington looked blank.

"Your poem threatens it, sir."

He cast a look at the verse and looking up, frowning. "This is not my poem. I wrote of love, I wrote of her beauty – not this."

Miss Cherrington quickly opened her eyes. "It is your hand, my lord," she snapped, and swooned again.

His lordship looked alarmed. "Fairest nymph, let me recite my poem for today. Hark – When fairest — takes the waters, Withdraw, all ye other daughters, So far in beauty—"

Mr Thomas had heard enough. "Do you deny you wrote this?" He pointed to the disputed verse.

"Certainly I do."

Miss Cherrington, now fully awake, burst into tears. "You are a villain, my lord."

Lord Foppington dropped instantly upon one knee. "Fair lady, it is not my hand," he pleaded. "Depend upon it, this is Percy's doing."

"Lord Foppington's rival for her hand," Dorothea whispered to me in excitement. "Mr Percy Trott, younger son of the Earl of Laninton."

"Of what am I guilty, pray?" The languid voice belonged to a full-bodied gentleman dressed à la mode, who was surveying the assembled company through an eyeglass without enthusiasm – until he spied Miss Cherrington.

A dozen voices enlightened him.

"You insult me, you mushroom," Mr Trott accused his lordship indignantly, then turning to Miss Cherrington: "Madam, pay no attention to this clunch, this clown." And back to Lord Foppington: "At dawn tomorrow, my lord, we shall meet. My seconds shall call upon you."

Miss Cherrington's recovery was now remarkable, and she beamed at the prospect of a duel. "I shall forgive you both," she announced. "Whether alive or dead," she added generously.

The three left their stage together, apparently all restored to good humour. Play-acting? Perhaps. But plays only succeed if based on true emotions – and what those might be here, I could not guess. The crowd began to disperse, no doubt reminded that it was long past the hour when they should be seen in déshabillé.

As for myself, Dorothea reminded me that I had apparently clamoured to take the waters, and docilely I agreed. Overhearing this exchange, Mr Thomas immediately said he would accompany us to the spring, although Mrs Thomas' displeasure at having to remain in the store was obvious. The spring was at the end of the Upper Walk and it was the custom for visitors to the Wells to pay a subscription on leaving to one or other of the dippers for service during the course of their stay. This hardly applied to poor parsons but it pleased Dorothea when I produced a halfpenny.

Most of the dippers were of mature years, with a practised eye for the richest visitors, but Miss Annie Bright was a merry-eyed girl. Annie, so Dorothea explained to me, was the niece of Jacob's housekeeper, Mrs Atkins, and so I acquired her services in filling the metal cup for me.

The pretty little hand closed around my halfpenny and its new owner gave me a merry smile – at which Mr Thomas too decided to take the waters. Annie spun me a tale of the wondrous properties of the spring and insisted I drank not one but *three* cups. An even number of cups would bring ill fortune she told me gravely, but an odd number would give speed to my legs, make my liver rejoice and my spirits rise. I felt neither of the first two effects, only the flat metallic taste of a chalybeate spring, but as for the third, my spirits did indeed rise, as she smiled at me.

But then I saw Lord Foppington chatting amiably to both Miss Cherrington and Mr Trott, the threat of the poem forgotten. Except by Caleb Pennywick.

***

That evening I was late to my bed, having been persuaded by Dorothea that I wanted nothing more than to attend Mrs Sarah Baker's theatre on Mount Sion to see a performance of Mr Sheridan's *The Rivals*. A most amusing piece. Early the next morning I was awoken by Dorcas. She is my housekeeper, and at home my dearest companion by day and often by night. It is she not I who keeps the difference between us for she maintains she has no wish to play the part of parson's wife. She chose to come with me on my visit to Jacob, but remains in the housekeeper's rooms, as she is eager, she claims, to learn new receipts for our pantry at Cuckoo Leas. Every morning therefore she visits the market on the Walks, and today had been no exception.

"Caleb, wake up, lovey." She was gently shaking me.

I sat bolt upright in my bed. "Are there no more wheatear pies?" I cried, having dined and dreamed happily of them.

"There's been a murder done."

"Miss Cherrington?" I was fully awake now.

"No, Caleb. Young Annie Bright, one of the water dippers."

The lass who had so eagerly received my halfpenny yesterday. My heart bled for the loss of innocence and joy in this world.

"Found by the sweeper at the spring this morning," Dorcas continued. "A paper knife was stuck in her. In a rare taking is Mrs Atkins. I told her you'd find out who did it."

My Dorcas looked at me with such trust and confidence that I quailed. As I sat in my nightshirt in a parsonage not my own, it seemed a most unlikely prospect that I could track down this murderer. "We are strangers here, Dorcas," I pleaded. "In Cuckoo Leas I know my flock."

"You can do it, Caleb." She assured me. "You brought your brain with you, didn't you? It's not left behind in that old cocked hat of yours?"

I was forced to smile. That beloved hat was now so old it was forbidden to travel with me.

"Has a runner been requested?" If the local magistrate deemed this case beyond the powers of the Wells' parish constable, he had the power to summon a Bow Street runner.

"Not yet, Caleb. Annie was a dipper, not a duchess." There was no bitterness in Dorcas's voice. We both knew the ways of this world.

The constable would be unpaid and unskilled, and even a country clergyman might do as well. And I could refuse Dorcas nothing.

***

I was quickly out that morning. I could not wait for breakfast at ten but would take a coffee in the Coffee House. Dear Jacob, who heard the news with perturbation, offered to accompany me to the Sussex Tavern, where he had been told the coroner was to hold an inquest at two o'clock that afternoon and where the constable might now be found. I refused Jacob's offer, to his relief. I would be better on my own, as I could more easily assume the role of well-intentioned meddling old parson rather than that of an aspiring Bow Street runner.

"Oh, I solved it already, Parson," young Constable Wilson said with some pride, when I found him in a rear room of the tavern, the grounds of which abut the Lower Walk.

It was my turn to be relieved. "Who committed this terrible crime?"

"Jem Smith, Annie's sweetheart. Twas a lovers' quarrel. Killed her late last night and the body was found early this morning."

"A lovers' quarrel?" I said, forgetting my planned role. "And he happened to be carrying a paper knife with him while he was wooing her?"

The constable gave me a strange look. "Must have been," he pointed out kindly. "That's what killed her, see? That's the evidence, that is. Proof for the magistrate. Jem will be up in front of Sir John Nicholls after this inquest and then be in the lock-up until the assizes."

So much for justice. The lad was already condemned, it seemed. I resolved to return here at two o'clock, but in the meantime I would stroll in the Lower Walk. I have not yet explained that the Lower Walk plays just as important a role as the Upper. By unspoken assent the gentry and aristocracy gather alone on the Upper Walk, and at times dictated by the strict timetables that have been in place for many decades. In the Lower Walk however the tradesmen and citizens of Tunbridge Wells flock through for the whole of the day, and it is here on the steps at the far end that the market is held from seven to ten o'clock each day.

Here, if Jem were innocent, I might learn the truth. I was uneasy about that paper knife; it spoke of planning and preparation not of a lovers' quarrel, and I was even more uneasy about the coincidence of a death on the Walks so soon after the threat to Miss Cherrington – although of course the verse had been anonymous.

I stopped so suddenly at this thought that I received a sharp blow in my back followed by a curse. A pedlar had been following in my wake and my apology did nothing to assuage the glare I received from this individual. It was to be hoped that his demeanour would change before customers or he would do little trade. It was the tray carried before him that had jolted my back.

"My apologies, sir," I said once more. "My thoughts were with the poor girl who died last night."

Malevolent eyes greeted me. "Aye. The girl-flirt." His Kentish vowels were so drawn out it was hard to be sure of what he said.

"That is a harsh word," I answered him.

"I've worse." He peered at me and so strong a sense of evil seemed to come from him that I almost stepped backwards. "The devil's filly she was."

"The constable has taken up Jem Smith for her murder," I remarked.

He stared at me. "There's plenty had cause."

Including himself, I wondered? "Was Lord Foppington one of her suitors?" I thought of that anonymous poem.

A grimy finger touched the side of his nose in a meaningful way. "Could be. And that gentleman friend of his – the one with his nose in the air and his stomach before him." I identified this as the Honourable Percy Trott. "Then there's Black Micah," the pedlar added maliciously. "Saw him here last night. Him who sweeps the Walks."

"And he found the body this morning, I understand." This was usually an interesting starting point to consider. When Widow Hart was found dead in Cuckoo Leas, her neighbour had found the body – and it was he had done the frightful deed. "Did you see Annie Bright here last night?"

I saw sudden fear on the pedlar's face and in answer he pushed rudely past me. I glanced at his tray with the usual ribbons and pins, but pens and knives also. Did he sometimes carry paper knives, I wondered? I could see none, but perhaps because one had found a tragic home last night.

I could see the crossing sweeper, seated on the shallow steps that led to the trees lining the Upper Walk. Black Micah was a solitary figure, bent in gloom, though many people went up to him and spoke a few words. I went to greet him, introducing myself as a parson – much is forgiven of such a calling which in others would be impertinence.

"A great shock, sir, finding Miss Bright's body."

He looked up at me; tears were clearing a path through the grime of his face. "My Annie," was all he could say.

"Our Lord will judge her from her heart, but I heard she was free with her favours," I said. "But that is mere tittle tattle no doubt."

"Lies," Micah roared. His ancient three-cornered hat and beard gave him the look of the Bible prophet after whom he was named. "Their tongue is deceitful in their mouth," he quoted. "She was my friend, she was, and I saw her there dead, with such a look of such surprise on her dear sweet face."

"Was Lord Foppington a friend also?" I needed to establish this.

Another roar. "Rich men are full of violence, so the prophet tells us. Always there he was, he and that Mr Percy Trott. Promised her a pound when the season was over. She just laughed at them, knowing they didn't mean it."

Had Annie laughed once too often? Had she and not Miss Cherrington been his lordship's fairest nymph?

"You swept the Walks last evening. Did you not see her then? Did you see anyone with her?"

He stared at me, then said, "I will bear the indignation of the Lord, for I have sinned against him." He would say no more but rocked to and fro in his grief.

I sighed. Was Micah's idea of sin that he loved Annie more than he should, or that he had not protected her – or that he himself had killed her?

The market was nearly over now, but the day's bustle continued, as groups gathered and spoke urgently amongst themselves. There was an edge to the atmosphere today. The voices were low and none invited me to join him. I was a visitor, and, worse, an enemy when one of their own had died.

On the Upper Walk society was reluctantly vanishing to prepare itself for the next stage of their day. But as with yesterday many still lingered. The crowd at the well of ladies in their negligées spoke less of enthusiasm for the cure than of worldly prurience. The dippers were making the most of their companion's tragic death and who could blame them? Coins were changing hands with great speed for accounts of what an angel Annie had been – or, as I listened to another, what a devil she had been. My heart was full as I thought of Annie's dead body lying here alone last night. I was paying dearly for the cups of water I had taken from her hands, and vowed I would first be sure that Jem Smith had not been her murderer, but if in doubt would seek the truth.

I could endure no more, and walked quickly to the book store where another crowd had assembled outside. A distraught Mr Thomas guarded the door and caught sight of me with relief.

"Come quickly, Parson. There's another verse from Lord Foppington."

I could scarcely believe it. If his verse referred to Annie's death, not Miss Cherrington's, then surely he would not write another. I hastened inside where Mr Thomas led me to the table where the Book of Poets lay, with Mrs Thomas grimly guarding it. The verse was brief and to the point:

Fairest nymph, thy end was just indeed
Thy beauty too great for this world's need.

I blenched. If I had needed proof that the fairest nymph of yesterday's poem had been Annie, this was it. And yet to what purpose had the foul deed been advertised? A fearful thought came to me.

"Miss Olivia Cherrington?" I cried. "She is safe?" Could there have been another death besides Annie's?

"Thanks be to God, she is," Mr Thomas said fervently. "I sent to her lodgings for word."

"It seems it was the water-dipper on whom Lord Foppington's true fancy fell," Mrs Thomas said sadly. "His lordship has a roving eye, I fear, and no doubt the girl was all too willing – at first."

"Hush, wife," her husband said angrily. "Annie is dead, and must be mourned. She was a bright star in this most unnatural world. And we must recall that Lord Foppington denied writing yesterday's poem."

Mrs Thomas looked chagrined and I hastened to ask, "Did this verse arrive this morning?"

"It awaited me at the door again. The poet, whether Lord Foppington or Mr Trott, would hardly have brought it in person, any more than he cared to sign his name."

"But why display the poem at all? If he killed the girl, would he blazen the fact abroad?"

"Because he might kill again?" Mrs Thomas ventured.

"I think not," I assured her gently. "But why should her murderer wish to announce her forthcoming death here, where Annie would not see it? Only the *ton* would do so. Poor Annie could doubtless not even read, let alone appreciate verses, even of the dire quality displayed here."

"Lord Foppington is a loose fish," Mr Thomas observed, "who professes weariness with everyday life. He and Mr Trott were members of the Hell Fire Club, where such monstrous folk fed on the death of others for their pleasure."

This was a new thought to me, and must be considered. Held in the caverns of Wycombe, terrible practices were said to have taken place at these orgies — practices to which the Miss Cherringtons of this world would be strangers, but which were part of the risks of living for the Annie Brights. Had she fallen prey to either or both these fops? Were the poems merely part of their sinister game?

"How could Lord Foppington have met Annie last evening?" I enquired. "Surely he would be escorting Miss Cherrington?"

"After yesterday," Mr Thomas suggested, "it is possible that Miss Cherrington decided to avoid the Walks."

"And so he wreaked his revenge on Annie?"

"Having laid a false trail deliberately with these poems," Mrs Thomas contributed.

I frowned. "But were Lord Foppington or Mr Trott seen here last evening?"

The evenings were as strictly regulated as the days. On Tuesdays and Fridays dancing took place at the Upper and Lower Rooms respectively. Yesterday being a Wednesday, they would have been playing cards or conversing at the Lower Rooms.

"Both were," Mr Thomas informed me. "Mrs Thomas was unwell, but I met friends for a game of cards, and saw them both. And," he added authoritatively, "I saw Lord Foppington talking to Annie Bright."

"Did he go to take the waters?" This seemed strange when wine and cognac would be flowing.

"There was no such need. Annie Bright was a serving maid at the Rooms on some evenings, and Jem worked there too."

"You saw her leave with him?" I asked.

"I did. I tarried for one last game – forgive me, my love – and when at last I left Annie and Jem had long gone. All seemed quiet in the Walks."

It looked bleak for Jem Smith, and were it not for those verses, I would believe in his guilt myself. Whom would the coroner and magistrate believe? Jem Smith – or Lord Foppington and Mr Trott? It was time I met Jem. Alas, breakfast in Jacob's cosy parlour had not seen me, but if the inquest were brief I could be present for dinner at four o'clock. Meanwhile a coffee must suffice, and I made my way to the Upper Walk.

Here I could see the waters of society begin to close over the tragic story of Annie Bright. It was twelve o'clock and the musicians in the gallery opposite overlooking the Upper Walk had begun to play, just as the peacocks began to return to the parade. To my surprise and admiration I saw Miss Cherrington arrive on the arm of an elderly gentleman, whom I presumed to be her father, as she made her entrance on to the Walk. Clad in blue silk, she made a lovely sight and was a braver lady than I had given her credit for. She had heard the news and yet decided to make her appearance despite it. Behind her companion, followed Lord Foppington and Mr Trott, apparently on the best of terms, despite their duel. Neither bore any marks that I could see. They too were in their fine feathers, but what did those feathers guard? The party entered the Coffee House where I sat, and my attention was reluctantly diverted from the charming music of Wolfgang Amadeus Mozart.

Then word came that Jem Smith had been taken to the Sussex Tavern, guarded by Constable Wilson, and his hands firmly tied. I could not miss this opportunity and hurried to join them there, on the pretext that Jem might need a parson.

When I arrived, Constable Wilson was still full of his importance as the representative of the law, his rattle at the ready as though even now Jem might make a bid for freedom. The prisoner looked to be a fine upstanding young man, who in twenty years' time, if proven innocent, would be a solid member of society. Today, he was in a miserable quake.

"I not be condemned yet," he yelled when he heard I was a parson. The poor fellow thought I had come to escort him to the gallows, and I hastened to make my role clear.

"I would hear your story, Jem," I told him. "God must judge you as well as the coroner's jury and Sir John, and I stand here as His messenger."

He took a careful look at my face and burst into tears. "Annie and me had words," he managed to say.

"See, he admits the crime," Constable Wilson broke in triumphantly.

"No, sir," Jem gasped. "We fell out as she left the Rooms. She was wanting to be wed, but I was waiting until I had a home to take her to. She thought I did not love her. If you don't want me, there's others that do, she said, and she went running off across the Walk. I went back inside and Mr Dale, he's the owner, told me to leave her be and come back inside. I never saw her again."

"You didn't walk past the spring on your way home?"

"No, sir. It's dark in that corner. Why would I look there? She'd gone to her home – or so I thought." The tears flowed as he must have realized that he had walked right past Annie's dead body.

"Did you see Lord Foppington last night, or Mr Percy Trott?"

His face darkened. "Both of them. Always hanging around her. Annie couldn't see they had nothing good in mind for her. She told me they

offered her a position in London. I thought she might go and leave me."
It was ingenuous of Jem to tell us this, as it provided another reason for
his guilt, and yet it was because of that I felt sure he was innocent.

"You heard about Lord Foppington's poems?"

"Yes, parson." He looked suddenly hopeful. "You think *he* might
have killed my Annie? Or Mr Trott? They were gambling in the
Rooms that evening." His face fell. "But gentlemen like that don't
soil their hands with murder."

"What about Black Micah or the pedlar?" I asked. Constable
Wilson was looking most annoyed at my persistence.

"Annie liked old Micah, but that pedlar – he's a wrong 'un. Oh
sir, you'll save me?"

I longed to say yes, that God could do that, perhaps through my
hands, if he were innocent, but I could not raise his hopes. There was
little more than an hour remaining before the inquest would begin.

At first I told myself that it was a good sign that Jem accused no
one else, but I was forced to change my mind. Jem's guilt might lie so
heavy upon him that he wished to face the penalty. Promising I would
return for the inquest, I made my way back to the Upper Walk, where
the peacocks were strutting in their finery. It would have made a
pretty sight, if I could have expunged the thought of Annie Bright's
body lying by the side of the spring. Soon the peacocks would mostly
depart for the afternoon to walk upon the Common or take an
excursion to Rusthall or High Rocks. And all the while Jem's fate
would be determined. I began to despair, seeing no way forward.

And then I saw Miss Cherrington again, walking with her
companion down the Upper Walk, a dainty parasol guarding her
from the sun – although the sun did not require much to banish it
today. I went to greet her and she recognized me immediately.

"Parson Pennywick, that poor girl," she cried. "I thought it would
be me."

"I too, Miss Cherrington," I said bluntly, taking more kindly to
her. "But you are safe now. I do not believe the verses were meant
for you," I assured her.

To my surprise, Miss Cherrington looked annoyed, not relieved.
"But *I* am the fairest nymph," she complained.

"Dearest lady, there is no doubt of that." Like bees to the fragrant flower, Mr Trott had joined us, with Lord Foppington at his side.

Miss Cherrington looked at them both severely. "I am going to the book store. I am told you have written another verse today, Lord Foppington."

"No," he bleated indignantly. "Fairest lady—"

Mr Trott interrupted him. "We must see the Book for ourselves. There is some mistake as neither his lordship nor I has written a poem for today. Permit us to escort you, Miss Cherrington."

Did they want this poor lady to suffer unnecessarily? Fortunately from the look in Miss Cherrington's eye, as she regarded her two suitors, her suffering was not too great at present, despite the tragedy of Annie Bright.

Mr Trott offered Miss Cherrington his arm, as he led her into the bookshop. Lord Foppington and I followed in their wake. Mr Thomas immediately helped her most solicitously to a chair. The Book of Poets was brought to her, and she read the two lines most carefully.

"But I am *not* dead," she pointed out, puzzled. "And you yourself, Mr Trott, said I was the fairest nymph."

"You are the fairest," squealed Lord Foppington, but Miss Cherrington took no notice.

"Do you still deny you wrote these verses, Lord Foppington?" I enquired, as he and Mr Trott read the new addition to the Book of Poets for themselves.

"I do," he said. He cast his rival a look of displeasure. "And Percy has a gift for copying work."

Mr Trott drew himself up. "My seconds shall call *again* on you, my lord."

"And I shall ask my husband to take these verses from the Book," Mrs Thomas declared. She drew me to one side, as Miss Cherrington's swains departed to discuss their next duel. Her husband was occupied in escorting Miss Cherrington and her companion to the door. "They are the work of one, if not both of those gentlemen," she continued.

"And Annie Bright's murder too?" I asked gently.

But Mrs Thomas was intent on the verses. "I do not believe that those verses have anything to do with the murder, parson."

I still could not believe that. Had Lord Foppington written them in the hope that with Annie dead, Miss Cherrington would be off her guard? Or had Mr Percy Trott hoped to ruin his rival's suit? No. There had to be another solution.

Vexed, my stomach began to object to the absence of a soothing breakfast, and even lacked enthusiasm for the dinner ahead. I could not contemplate taking the waters today, with the memories of Annie so vivid. My mind was in a whirl, a dizziness that came of too much imagination, and too little sustenance. If I was convinced the verses had to do with Annie's death, I must first reason out why. Could I discount the pedlar and Black Micah from my thoughts on that basis? Possibly. Lord Foppington again assumed monstrous proportions in my mind, with Mr Trott leering over his shoulder.

This is balderdash, Caleb, I told myself firmly, merely the results of an upset digestion. And to think I had brought no rhubarb powder with me! I took prompt action. I asked Mrs Thomas for directions to an apothecary.

I had not far to go, and there I had the delight of meeting not only with rhubarb powder but with my dear Dorcas.

"Parson Pennywick," she said in delight. Caleb was used only on informal occasions. "Fancy that. I was here to buy you some rhubarb powder."

"And I was on the same mission." We looked at each other, highly pleased. "Shall we attend the inquest together?" I asked.

Dorcas was doubtful about the propriety of this, but I persuaded her, and having taken my rhubarb powder with water, we made our way back to the Lower Walk and along to the Sussex Tavern. I could still hear the strains of music and that, together with my faithful remedy, did much to calm me.

"For what reason," I asked her, "would Lord Foppington write those verses himself? Did he announce his plan to murder Annie Bright only because of his vanity as a poet?"

"No, parson," Dorcas declared sensibly. Her comfortable figure at my side, clad in the familiar caraco jacket, gave me strength. "These society folk know well how to look after themselves, when their skins are at stake."

"You are right. It would be too dangerous for him or for Mr Trott to do so."

We were already at the Sussex Tavern garden and we would shortly reach the room at the rear of the inn where the inquest would be held. And my mind was still in a jumble. And then Dorcas said: "I'll take a cup of those waters tomorrow, in memory of Miss Bright."

I remembered pressing the coin into Annie's hand. I remembered who had been at my side. Who had sought the excuse to come with me. Whose trade would give him ample opportunity to seize a paper-cutting knife. Whose wife was so devoted, he found it hard to get away. Yet he had got away. He said he had been playing cards that evening; he doubtless had the skills to copy Lord Foppington's hand, and the opportunity to place the poems in the Book, thus to take the attention away from himself. Mr Edwin Thomas, beloved of the ladies. Had he expected Annie Bright to love him too, and when she refused his favours killed her?

I was jubilant. I had the story. I was sure of it. Now I must speak to the coroner and to Sir John himself.

"We will soon have this wheatear pie cooked," I told Dorcas, thinking to please her by a reference to the dish she is so eager to try at Cuckoo Leas.

"No. You will only eat it, Caleb," she jested. "'Tis the kitchen where the pie is put together."

I stared at her. The kitchen? My mind clarified like liquid passed through a jellybag.

Not Mr Thomas, but *Mrs* Thomas. So possessive of her husband that she would be rid of the woman she falsely believed to be his light o'love. She did not wish her husband to be incriminated and so wrote those verses to deflect attention from him. Under pretence of being ill, she took a paper knife from their store and stabbed her supposed rival. It was she who had cooked this pie, and thought to enjoy the results.

We were at the door of the inquest room now. Before we entered, I took Dorcas's hand and pressed it to my lips. Jem Smith would owe his life to her – and, of course, to rhubarb.

SUCKER PUNCH

Nick Quantrill

I TRIED NOT to flinch in my chair as the punches landed. One after another. Relentless. The taller boxer was on top. A left hook connected with his opponent's nose, which exploded on impact. Those nearest the ring were on their feet, encouraging the fighters to continue. Another left hook landed, quickly followed by a sharp right. The combination rocked the smaller fighter and forced him backwards, and on to the defensive. And then it happened. The smaller man sprung forward, and with one vicious swipe of his right hand sent the taller man sprawling on to the canvas. The crowd went silent for a brief moment. Even the winning boxer looked surprised.

A click of the remote and the television screen faded to black. A drink was placed in front of me. I didn't want alcohol at this time of the day.

"What do you think?"

I turned to Burrows, not sure what I was expected to say. "Looks like it was a good fight."

Burrows laughed. "Not from where I was sitting. It cost me a lot of time and money to organize that fight."

I swallowed the alcohol, forcing it down, not sure why he'd called me to his office. I didn't want the job. I didn't have a choice.

"The tall lad is called Jordan. He's fought for me a few times. Not a bad fighter as it goes, but as you can see, he lacks ring craft. He's got a punch, but he's not really going anywhere. Too many flaws. You were a rugby player, weren't you?"

I nodded.

"You'll understand there are certain things you can't coach into people, then. They've either got it or they haven't. It's about natural talent. The point is, Joe, I can't do any more for Jordan, so we came to an arrangement."

He left it hanging there, forcing me to ask what the arrangement was.

"I'm a man who cares, so when I have to part company with someone, I make sure they're well looked after."

Burrows reeked of insincerity. I knew of him by reputation but this was the first time I'd met him. One of his men had collected me from my office. I was hired. End of discussion.

"There's a problem, though." He flicked the fight back on and searched for the final punch. We watched it again in silence. "I'm told you're good, Joe. Probably the best in this city." He forced me to meet his stare. "Jordan took a dive and cost me a lot of money. And as the bookmaker, I think I'm entitled to a few answers. Now I can't find him."

I'd left Burrows's office with a list of Jordan's known haunts and a couple of hundred pounds in my pocket. I'd get the same again if I found my man. The nearest place on the list was a boxing club on the edge of the city centre. I decided to walk there, feeling like I needed the fresh air. The club was situated in the loft of an old warehouse. Downstairs was a fitness gym. I assumed the club had little spare money. The room was dominated by a tired-looking ring. Two teenagers were sparring and feeling each other out in front of a watchful coach and small crowd of other boxers.

"Help you?"

I turned around. He was in his early sixties, but he was still in good shape and I had no wish to mess with him.

I passed him a business card and introduced myself. "I hope so. I'm looking for someone."

"Yeah?"

"I need to speak to Jordan."

"He doesn't have anything to do with us any more. He left a while back."

"I was told he did."

"I'm telling you he doesn't."

"Fair enough." I looked around the club. "Nice place you've got here."

"And it'll be staying that way." He introduced himself as Bill Armstrong. "I opened this place over thirty years ago to give teenagers somewhere to go, something positive to do. I got nothing given to me, so I built it up over the years by myself. I've even produced some good boxers over the years. Some have gone on to bigger and better things. It's a shame Jordan's gone down this road. I thought he was really going to kick on, but the lad he was fighting the other night, Shane, he was something else. He could really have pulled up some trees." He stared at me. "I assume Burrows sent you?"

I nodded. "I need a quick word with Jordan, get last week's fight straightened out."

The man laughed. "It's unlicensed boxing. Things happen. You take your chances in that kind of game. I understand the attraction of it for people like Jordan, but it's not something I approve of or encourage my fighters to get involved in. It's a dangerous game." He paused and stared at me. "For everyone."

It didn't take me long to find Jordan. I sat in the pub opposite his flat with a newspaper and waited it out. He had to go home at some point. It seemed the most likely option on the list of potential places. He wouldn't be looking out for me. He sat down in the corner, watching Sky Sports News, well away from the front door. I'd done my job, but I held off making the call to Burrows. I walked across to Jordan and sat down.

"All right?" I said.

He looked like he was going to run, but I'd angled my chair to block his only escape route.

"Who are you?" he asked me.

"I need to talk to you."

"Touch me and I'll go to the police."

"I'm not going to touch you." His face was a mess from the fight. He looked younger in the flesh. On the fight footage I couldn't see the acne or the wispy facial hair. Still a teenager.

"I know who sent you," he said.

"He needs to speak to you."

"About the fight?"

I nodded.

"I can't talk to him."

I said nothing. I wanted to walk away, but I knew Burrows would hold me responsible. I'd been warned at the boxing club. Unlicensed boxing was a dangerous game and I didn't want to be involved. "He won't go away," I said. "It needs to be dealt with."

"I know."

I saw a tear in his eye.

"I'm scared."

"I know you are."

"I hate those fights. Everyone's stood right up close to you, shouting at you. You can't hear yourself think and it gets so hot. Part of me wishes I was back in Billy's gym, doing it the right way, but it's gone too far for that now. If I fight, it's for people like Burrows. I hate it. I hate what I've become." He paused. "You need to speak to Shane."

Jordan called Shane on his mobile and he joined us five minutes later.

"That was quick," I said. Shane's face was in a similar state to Jordan's.

"I'm staying in Jordan's flat until this blows over," he said.

"Until what blows over?"

Shane shrugged. "Burrows was going mental after the fight, so we got out of the place. I got a text message from a mate at the gym telling me he was looking for me."

"Looking for you?"

"That's right."

"I didn't realize you two are friends."

They both nodded.

"It was just a fight," Shane said. "Nothing personal."

I gave Jordan a note from the bundle I had and told him to buy us all some drinks. I waited for him to leave. "Unlicensed boxing?" I said to Shane. "And Burrows?"

He shrugged. "I need the money."

"I spoke to Bill at the club. He said you were a good boxer. You don't need to be doing this."

"I don't have a choice."

"Of course you do." Any sport requires dedication if you're going to do it at a high level, but it's the price of the ticket. "Why don't you go back to the club?"

"There's no point."

"Why not? You can start again, work your way back up?"

"I can't. I'm diabetic."

Jordan put the drinks on the table.

"I was good, wasn't I?" Shane said to Jordan. "A couple of years ago, I could really fight."

Jordan nodded.

"It was going well. I was clearing up at junior level and I had a chance of making it as a pro. Bill was going to put me in touch with some people who could sort me out."

"Burrows?"

He shook his head. "Proper boxing people. A proper manager."

"But the diabetes stopped that?"

He nodded. "It's not easy to fight professionally with it. It's a big hassle and nobody would touch me now I've got it. I'm damaged goods."

I sympathized with him. My rugby career had been ended by injury when I was barely out of my teens. "So you turned to un-licensed boxing?"

"It's not illegal."

"I know it's not."

"I've got debts to pay. I need to earn some money and all I know is how to fight. There's no jobs about, anyway."

Fair point. "How did you end up fighting for Burrows?"

"He runs all the unlicensed stuff in the area. Billy wasn't able to help me any more, so I went to see Burrows, told him what my position was like. Said I needed the work."

"And he signed you up?"

"He's always looking for new fighters."

I didn't know much about unlicensed boxing but it was obviously going to be more dangerous. I knew I'd be wasting my breath. He needed to fight.

We drank up in silence. I suggested we go back to their flat.

*　*　*

"How did you end up fighting each other?" I asked. I'd moved the newspapers and cans until there was space to sit on the settee.

"Burrows told us we had to," Jordan said.

Shane nodded. "Since we were kids. We practically live together like a married couple nowadays."

I mulled it over and got down to business. "Why did you throw the fight, Jordan?"

Jordan looked terrified. "I didn't throw no fight."

"Burrows says you did."

He looked at Shane. "I wouldn't throw a fight, would I?"

"Course not. We're proper fighters."

"Why would Burrows tell me you'd thrown it?"

Jordan slumped back further into chair. "He's mentioned it to me before. He said it was the only way I'd make some money because he was thinking of getting rid of me."

"Why would he get rid of you?"

He shrugged. "Don't know. It's his business." He leant towards me. "You've got to tell him I didn't throw the fight. I wouldn't do that."

I doubted Burrows would listen. I looked up as Billy walked into the flat. He unzipped his jacket and sat down with us. "I take it you've all got yourselves into a spot of bother?"

Billy sat there silently as I explained what had happened. And the overriding problem of Burrows.

"Throwing unlicensed fights?" Billy looked appalled, but I suspected not too surprised. "Is that what it's come to? If you needed money, Jordan, you only had to ask. I would have found you something. I always need people at the gym. Anything so you didn't have to mix it with the likes of Burrows."

Both Shane and Jordan were shaking their heads. "We wouldn't do that to you, Billy," Shane said.

"I didn't throw the fight," Jordan repeated.

"Neither did I," said Shane.

I looked at both of the fighters. "I believe you. Both of you."

"What do you mean?" said Billy.

"Jordan didn't throw the fight," I said.

"Why is Burrows looking for him, then?" asked Billy.

"Because he knew Shane wouldn't be far away. He's the one Burrows really wants."

We all turned to Shane. "I didn't throw the fight." He looked away from us. "I didn't get the chance. I was supposed to go down in the third. It wasn't meant to happen. I didn't mean to put Jordan down."

It would have been an unpleasant surprise for Burrows. An expensive one, seeing as he was the bookmaker and organizer. Shane was the one with the talent, the youth champion. I assumed most of the punters would have been betting on him winning. Maybe he wasn't able to help himself. Maybe he got lucky. Either way, one punch was enough to bring the fight to an end. It could happen. I looked at Billy. "Can you sort this?"

He nodded. "I run a gym full of the city's finest boxers. I can sort it." He paused. "I could use some new equipment for the gym, though."

I smiled and took the money I'd got from Burrows out of my pocket. Passed it to him. "Will that cover it?"

He counted it before putting it in his pocket. "Perfect. I guess sucker punches can come in many forms, Mr Geraghty."

TOP HARD

Stephen Booth

THE LORRY I'D been watching was a brand new Iveco with French registration plates. All tarted up with flags and air horns and rows of headlights, it was like the space shuttle had just landed in a layby on the A1.

I'd got myself a position no more than thirty yards away, slumped in the driver's seat of a clapped-out four-year-old Escort that had last been driven by a clapped-out brewery rep. Or that was the way it looked, anyway. It was one o'clock on an ordinary Monday afternoon. And all I had to do was wait.

The trouble was, the lorry hadn't been doing very much. So all I had to look at was a red and white sticker on the Escort's dashboard thanking me for not smoking, and a little dangling plastic ball that told me what direction I was going in. I might have been facing the soft south, but at least I was nicotine free.

I already knew a few things about this French truck by now, of course. I'd counted its sixteen wheels and admired the size of its tail pipes. I'd seen the sleeping compartment behind the cab, which contained a little ten-inch colour telly, a fridge and even a microwave oven for warming up the driver's morning croissant. I knew that its forty-foot trailer was packed full of leather jackets, jeans and denim shirts – all good stuff that's really easy to shift. And I also knew that somebody was going to be really pissed off about that trailer very soon.

Well, it definitely looked like a solid job so far – good information, and a plan that might actually come together for once. And that's saying something in this part of the world. So all I had to do was sit tight and wait for the action. Yeah, right. It's funny how things can start out really good and solid in the morning, and then turn totally brown and runny by tea time. It's one of my own little theories. I call it the Stones McClure Vindaloo Lunch Rule. It's as if the bloke with the beard up there likes a bit of a joke now and then. And this was going to be one of his joke days. Well, I might just die laughing.

Meanwhile, sitting in a tatty motor was in danger of ruining my image – the Escort just wasn't worth looking at. Well, that's the point of it, I suppose. There were an incredible 85,000 miles on the clock of this thing, which proved it hadn't been handled by a used car dealer recently. The floor seemed to be covered in empty sweet wrappers, the mouldy debris of a cheese sandwich, and dozens of screwed-up bits of pink and white tissue. The inside panels looked as though they'd been trampled by a gang of miners in pit boots. The cover had fallen off the fuse box, and a tangle of wires and coloured plastic hung out of it, for all the world as if I'd just botched a hot-wire job. The car smelled of stale beer, too. Maybe a pack of free samples had split open some time. Or maybe a brewery rep just goes around smelling like that. You can take low-profile a bit too far sometimes.

In a word, it just wasn't the sort of motor that folk round here are used to seeing Stones McClure in. My style is more poke than parcel shelf, if you know what I mean. More turbo charge than towbar. Not to mention a spot of F and F across the fake fur seat covers.

For the last few minutes, I'd been dozing a bit, clutching my plastic bottle of Buxton Spring Water in one hand and a half-eaten Snickers bar in the other. Don't believe that means I had no idea what was going on. I've got this trick of keeping one eye half open at all times, like an old tom cat. It's saved me a lot of grief on jobs like this.

One fifteen. I sat up to take a quick look round. Along the road a bit there was a roundabout where the traffic was grinding its way on to the A614 towards Nottingham or heading west on the A57 into Lincolnshire. Apart from a roadside café, there was nothing around me in the layby – just empty fields on one side, and a bit of Sherwood Forest on the other. I mean there was nothing apart from four lanes of traffic thundering by on the A1, obviously. But the drivers weren't taking notice of much. They were busy fiddling with their Black-berries and Bluetooth, or counting the miles ticking off as they hurtled towards their next meeting or their latest delivery of widgets. This is what vehicle thieves rely on. Nobody sees anything going on around them when they're on the road.

Well, people never learn, do they? That's my second rule. And thank God for it, because this is what keeps blokes like me in beer and Meatloaf CDs for life.

I glanced at my watch. Shouldn't be long now. Earlier on, I'd watched the driver who brought the lorry disappear into the café, shrugging his shoulders at the smell of hot fat drifting from the window of Sally's Snap Box. He was a short, thickset bloke wearing blue overalls and a five o'clock shadow. You could practically hear him singing the Marseillaise. This bloke's load might be headed for Leeds or Glasgow. But it wouldn't make it to its destination. Not today.

It was the load that was important, you see. Thieves don't target brand-new trucks for their own sake. If you're planning to cut a vehicle up for spares, you go for an old Bedford or something. There's a big export market for old lorry spares. But if you're nicking the load, it's a different matter. That's where the really big business is – at least £1.6 billion worth a year, they say. And people will do anything to tap into dosh like that.

For the sake of authenticity, I was tuned in to a local radio station on the Escort's battered old Motorola. But the presenter had just stumbled off into one of those endless phone-in segments they seem to like so much. Grannies from all over the county were passing on tips for getting cocoa stains out of acrylic armchair covers, or swapping back copies of *People's Friend* for a second-hand budgie cage. It was dire enough to kill off my remaining brain cells – I mean, the few that last night's booze had left intact.

And then – bingo! An unmarked white Transit van slowed in the inside lane of the A1 and pulled slowly into the layby in front of the French truck. Action at last.

I have a really good memory for registration numbers, but the plate on the Transit was a new one to me. That was no surprise, though. It would have been nicked from a car park in Worksop or Mansfield some time during the past hour, and that was someone else's worry.

From my position, I could just see a bloke jump down from the passenger side of the van. He had the collar of a red ski-jacket turned right up and a woollen hat pulled low over his face, making it impossible to get an ID on him. As soon as he'd slammed the door shut, the Transit pulled out into the traffic again and disappeared south.

I stayed low in my seat. I ate a bit of my Snickers bar. The chocolate was starting to melt on to my hand and my fingers were getting sticky. I wiped them with a windscreen wipe out of a little packet that I found in the door well. I would have stuffed the used wipe into the fold-out ashtray, but it was already jammed full with more crumpled bits of tissue, all yellow and crusty. Anonymity is fine, but I draw the line at catching some disgusting disease for the sake of camouflage.

The bloke in the cap was fiddling with something I couldn't see, right up close to the near side of the Iveco's cab. No one took any notice of him, except me. Then he looked round once, took a step upwards, and was gone from sight.

I speed-dialled a number on my mobile, then waited a minute or two more until I heard the rumble of a diesel engine and the release of air brakes. As I started the Escort's motor, I glanced in my rearview mirror and saw a large figure emerge from the café. It was a bloke so big that he had to duck and walk out of the door sideways to avoid bringing the side of the caravan with him. He lumbered up to the side of the car, hefting something like a lump of breeze block in his left hand. And suddenly it was as if the sun had gone in. Oh yeah, meet my sidekick, Doncaster Dave. He's my personal back-up, my one-man riot squad. A good bloke to have watching your arse.

Dave had been stuffing himself with sandwiches and cakes in Sally's at my expense. Well, it's better than having him sit in the car with me. He gets twitchy when there's food nearby, and he'd probably enjoy the phone-in programme and laugh at the DJ's jokes. And then I'd have to kill him.

"Come on, come on."

Dave was starting to go into the monkey squat necessary for him to manoeuvre his way into the passenger seat, when the door of the café flew open again and a second figure came out. This one was dressed in blue overalls, and it was gesticulating and shouting. The sight of the lorry pulling on to the A1 seemed to infuriate him and he ran a few yards down the layby, yelling. Then he turned and ran back again, still yelling. This was far too much noise for my liking. And definitely too much arm waving. Even on the A1, he might get attention.

I could see Dave speaking to him, and nodding towards the Escort. The bloke came eagerly towards me, and I sighed as I wound down the window.

"Mon camion," he said. "My truck. It is being stolen."

"Let him in, Donc, why not?" I said. So Dave opened the back door of the Escort without a word. The Frenchman climbed in, and Dave squeezed into the front. The breeze block in his hand turned out to be the biggest sausage and egg butty you've ever seen, dripping with tomato sauce. The car filled with a greasy aroma that would linger for days. It didn't go too well with the stale beer either.

The Iveco was already a couple of hundred yards away by now, and the Frenchman began bouncing angrily.

"What's up, monsieur?" I said, as I indicated carefully before pulling out. I was waiting until I spotted some slow-moving caravans to sneak in front of. Getting on to the A1 from a layby is a bit dicey sometimes – you can easily end up with a snap-on tools salesman right up your backside, doing ninety miles an hour in his company Mondeo.

"We must follow the thieves. They steal my truck."

"Dear, oh dear. It happens all the time, you know. You can't leave anything unattended round here."

"Hurry, hurry! You are too slow."

I shook my head sadly. Well, there you go. You give somebody a lift, do them a favour, and the first thing out of their mouths is criticism of your driving. The world is so unfair.

"It's always been like this, you know," I said helpfully. "This bit of the A1 was the Great North Road. You know, where Dick Turpin used to hang out? You've heard of Dick Turpin, have you, monsieur?"

"*Comment?* What?"

"Highwayman, you know. Thief."

This is straight up, too. Well, the original Great North Road is a bit to the east, but it's been well and truly bypassed now. Some of it has deteriorated to a track, fit only for horses and trail bikes. But make no mistake. This whole area is still bandit country.

"Then there was Robin Hood," I said. "Robbing from the rich to give to the poor. Oh, and we had Mrs Thatcher, of course, who got it the wrong way round."

The Frenchman wasn't listening to my tour guide bit. He was gesturing down past the gear lever towards the bottom of the fascia, where there was my mobile phone, a pile of music CDs, and the world's worst in-car stereo system.

"Yeah, you're right, it's crap, this local radio. Le crap, eh? I don't know why I listen to it. What do you fancy then, mate? Some Sacha Distel maybe?"

I poked among the CDs as if I was actually looking for *Raindrops Keep Falling On My Head*. It wasn't likely to be there. Not unless there was a cover version by Enya or UB40. Whoever normally drove this Escort had different tastes from mine. No doubt about it.

"How about this? This is French." I held up Chris Rea's *Auberge*. "Auberge. That's French, right?"

I slipped the cassette into the deck, and Rea began to sing about there being only one place to go. It's really funny how you can always find Chris Rea tapes in sales reps' cars. I reckon they have them so they can play "The Road to Hell" and feel all ironic.

"No, no. You must call for help," the trucker shouted in my ear over the music. "Roadblock. Stop the truck."

And then he reached forward, trying to grab the phone. Dave barely moved. He gave the Frenchman a little flip and the bloke hit the back of his seat like he'd bounced off a brick wall.

"Sorry, mate, but the signal's terrible round here," I said. "It's all the trees. Sherwood Forest, this is."

The lorry driver called me a *cochon*. I failed French O-level, but even I know that isn't polite.

"Look, I'm really sorry it's not Sacha Distel, but I'm doing my best, right?"

As we approached the big roundabout at Markham Moor, the Iveco was already halfway up the long hill heading southwards, growling its way past the McDonald's drive-thru and the Shell petrol station. I could catch up with the lorry easily. No need for lights and sirens – which was lucky, because we didn't have any.

But the sight of the red and yellow arched signs across the carriageway put me in mind of something.

"Hey, it's a bit like a scene in that film, what's it called? You know, with John Travolta and the black bloke in a frizzy wig. What do they call a Big Mac with cheese in France?"

Dave's ears pricked up at the Big Mac, but he didn't know the answer.

The Escort's steering juddered and the suspension groaned underneath me as I twisted the wheel to the right and we swerved into the roundabout, across the A1 and towards a little B-road that leads past the Markham Moor truck stop. As we passed, I couldn't resist a glance into the truck stop for professional reasons. On the tarmac stood two orange and white Tesco lorries, a flatbed from Hanson Bricks and a Euromax Mercedes diesel, all backed up against a couple of Cho Yang container trucks. There was a load of NorCor corrugated boarding, and even a Scania full of Weetabix. To be honest, though, I couldn't see anyone shifting fifty tons of breakfast cereal too easily. Not in these parts.

The Frenchman started gibbering again and pointing to the main road, where the back of his lorry had just vanished over the hill.

"Non, non. Turn round. That way. The thieves go that way."

"It's a short cut, mate. What do they call a Big Mac with cheese in France?"

"*Merde!*"

Then he began to poke his finger at Dave's shoulder. Well, that was a mistake. Dave stared at him, amazed, like a Rottweiler that finds a cat pulling its whiskers. His immense jaws opened and his teeth came down on the round, stubby thing in front of his face. It disappeared into his mouth with a little spurt of red, and he began to chew. The Frenchman pulled back his finger fast, in case it went the same way as that sausage.

We passed through a couple of little villages before I turned on to a road that was more mud than tarmac. A track led us over the

River Maun, past some derelict buildings, through some woods, over another river and into more woods. The trees closed all around us now, dark conifers that wiped out any hope of a view.

But in the middle of the trees a space suddenly opened up on a vast expanse of wasteland – acres and acres of black slurry and weed-covered concrete. There were old wheel tracks down there in that slurry, and some of them were two-feet deep. This was one of our dead coal mines, whose rotting bodies lie all over Nottinghamshire these days – a memory of the time when thousands of blokes and their families lived for the seam of coal they called Top Hard.

Finally we ran out of road and pulled up by a series of slurry lagoons. These lagoons are pretty deep too, and I wouldn't like to say what the stuff is that swirls about down there.

"Okay, Monsieur Merde. Out."

The Frenchman looked from me to Dave, who helpfully leaned back to unfasten his seat-belt. The trucker flinched a bit, but looked relieved when the belt clicked open. He got out and looked at the devastation around him, baffled.

Well, this little bit of Nottinghamshire is no picnic site, that's for sure. We were on the remains of an old pit road, where British Coal lorries once trundled backwards and forwards all day and all night. In some places there are old wagons dragged off the underground trains, filled with concrete and upended to stop gypsies setting up camp in the woods. But there are always ways in, if you know how. Up ahead was a bridge where you could look down on the railway line that had carried nothing but coal trains. The lines are rusted now, but the coal is still there, way below the ground. Top Hard, the best coking and steam coal in the country. Top Hard made a lot of the old mine owners rich.

Yes, this was once the site of the area's proudest superpit. A few years back, when it was still open, a report came out with the idea of making it a Coal Theme Park, preserving the glory days of the 1960s. There would have been visits to the coal face, a ride underground on a paddy train, and maybe a trip to the canteen for a mug of tea. They had a dry ski-slope planned for the spoil heap.

You'd need a heck of an imagination to picture this theme park now. The buildings have been demolished, and the fences are a futile gesture. There's just the black slag everywhere and a few churned-up roadways where they came to cart away the debris of a way of life.

The Frenchman stared at the lagoons, then turned round and looked across the vast black wasteland of wet slurry behind him. It would be suicide to try to walk through that lot. He shrugged his shoulders and waited, his eyebrows lifted like a supercilious customs man at Calais. Suddenly, his complacency annoyed me.

"Take a look at this then, mate. What do you think? Pretty, isn't it? This is what's left of our mining industry. Coal mining, yeah? It may not mean much to you. You grow grapes and make cheese in France, right? But coal was our livelihood here in Nottinghamshire, once. Blokes went down into a bloody great black hole every day and got their lungs full of coal dust just so that we could buy food after the war. You remember the war, do you? When we kicked the krauts out of your country?"

Of course he didn't remember the war. He wasn't old enough. Nor am I, but I've read a history book or two. I know we bankrupted ourselves fighting the Germans, and it was the miners like my granddad who worked their bollocks off to get this country out of the mess afterwards. And since then their sons and grandsons carried on going down those bloody great holes day after day to dig out the coal. Decades and decades of it, with blokes getting crushed in roof falls and burnt to death in fires, and coughing their guts out with lung disease for the rest of their lives.

And this is what thanks they got, places like this and a score of other derelict sites around Nottinghamshire, Derbyshire, Yorkshire. Maggie Thatcher betrayed us, the whole country let us down. Even our own workmates stabbed us in the back. It was 1984. Write it on my gravestone.

Somewhere north of Newark, the French truck would be picking up speed on the flat. In a few minutes it would hit the bypass and turn off westwards on the A46. Within the hour it would be in a warehouse on an industrial estate outside town, and it would be nothing to do with me at all. All thanks to Slow Kid Thompson.

Oh, I forget to mention Slow Kid, didn't I? Slow Kid Thompson is one of my best boys. He's got a lot of talents, but his number one skill is driving. If Slow can't drive it, it hasn't got wheels. Today, he'd just delivered our first big load, a job worth quite a few grand to us all. After years of doing small-scale business, shifting dodgy goods and re-plating nicked motors, we were finally moving into the big time. That Iveco represented the start of a new life.

"You're lucky, monsieur. I'm feeling in a good mood."

By now the Frenchman had gone as quiet as Doncaster Dave. I guess it had finally dawned on him that we weren't going to help him catch his stolen lorry after all. Maybe he'd realized that there'd be no nice British bobbies rushing up to arrest the villains who'd ruined his day. No high-speed pursuit, no road blocks, no one to pull him out of the brown stuff.

Oh yeah, that's another thing I forgot to mention – you just can't rely on anyone these days. I call it the Stones McClure Top Hard Rule.

COP AND ROBBER

Paul Johnston

THE COP CAUGHT the robber and sent him to jail.

When he finishes his sentence, the cop's waiting for him outside the prison gate.

"Need a lift?"

"Seems you're the only person offering."

They head back to town.

"What is it you want from me?" the robber asks, after he's smoked one of the cop's cigarettes.

"It's not like that."

"Sure it isn't."

"All right, I've got something I want you to do."

The robber looks out at the suburbs – grey buildings, people with their heads bent against the scouring wind, trees with bare, bony branches. "I've got a choice?"

"Not really. If you do this for me, I'll keep off your back."

"How long's it going to take?"

"Just tonight."

"Any money involved?"

"Sure. Whatever you find in the place."

The robber's gut overdoses on acid. The last time that happened was in the shower block. He's always been able to tell when he's about to be shafted.

"You want me to break the law?"

The cop laughs. "That's what you do, isn't it? Look, it's simple enough. I'll give you the address of a residential property. You go there after dark and use your talents to get inside. Then you locate a certain something."

The acid is half-way up the robber's oesophagus now. "What about the people who live there?"

"They'll be out."

"You sure about that?"

The cop gives him a hard-man look. "Trust me."

The robber doesn't do that with anyone, never mind cops.

It's one-thirty in the morning. There are no lights showing inside the medium-sized detached house, and the only one outside is above the front door. Checking the street for movement, the robber goes up the garden path and round the back of the building. He sees no sign of an alarm system, but takes the necessary precautions. He's inside in under three minutes, using a torch with a narrow beam and the tools he retrieved from a friend earlier.

The robber stands stock-still in the kitchen, the only sounds those coming from kitchen appliances. He goes into the hall, casts his light around the sitting and dining rooms, and then moves slowly up the wooden staircase. He tests each step before putting his weight on it.

The doors to two of the three bedrooms are open, as is that of the bathroom. The rooms are furnished, but unoccupied. Only the main bedroom is left. That's where he's been told the envelope will be. The robber puts his ear to the closed door and listens. Silence. The heating units are cold. That just makes him more suspicious. Taking a deep breath, he turns the handle and pushes the door inwards. The curtains are open and the light of the waxing moon floods over a large bed. On it, a naked male is lying on his back, arms wide and legs apart. There is a dark stain on his chest and the smell of fresh blood is strong. The shaft of a knife is standing vertically in the middle of the blood slick. As the robber has suspected from the start, it's a set up. He has to get out before law enforcement arrives, but he can't stop himself moving towards the body. He looks down at the dead man's face, which is twisted in agony. He still recognizes him. It's the cop. So what happened? Did he kill himself or did someone else oblige?

As the seconds pass and no sirens approach, the robber wonders if he's been framed after all. Then he sees an envelope under the cop's head. It looks like the one he was told to look for, brown and size A4. Pulling it out with latex-sheathed fingers, he sees his name scrawled on it.

He kneels down, holding the torch between his teeth, and slides his fingers under the flap. He takes out a photograph and a sheet of paper. The photo shows his wife. He hasn't seen her in the flesh for nearly three years, when she made her single, sorry prison visit. She is naked from the waist up, an inviting smile on her lips and a male hand on her right breast.

The robber reads the hand-written words on the sheet of paper.

"We were together when you were inside. She said it was you or me when you came out. I've had enough of her and the job. She'll be back from her shift at the bar around two-thirty. Think about it, you've got options."

The robber rocks back on his heels and does what he's told, a large wad of banknotes falling unnoticed between his knees.

Not long before two-thirty, a key sounds in the front door. Footsteps move up the stairs and along the hallway. A slim form comes through the open door. He clamps his hand over his wife's mouth before she can scream.

"You've been screwing the man who put me inside."

She feels the point of the knife that was in the cop's chest against her abdomen. "I…I…"

"I'll gut you if you cry out." The robber slowly removes his hand from her face.

His wife stares at the bed and then turns towards him, eyes wide. "You killed him!"

"If that's what you want to think."

"I suppose…I suppose you're going to do the same to me."

"And soil myself with your blood? No, I've got other plans."

She stares at him uncomprehendingly. "What…"

He thrusts the knife into her hand, pushes her on to the bloody body on the bed, and makes a rapid exit. He hears a couple of screams before his wife realizes that calling attention to herself is a bad idea. To make sure, he calls the cops from a pay-phone. By the time the first patrol car arrives, he is out of sight.

The robber isn't sure if framing the woman had been one of the options his benefactor had hinted at. He puts a hand in his pocket. For once in his life he's loaded with cash that he hasn't stolen. On the other hand, the cop stole his wife. He remembers the statue on the court building. Justice is blind, but her heart's obviously in the right place.

OFF DUTY

Zoë Sharp

The guy who'd just tried to kill me didn't look like much. From the fleeting glimpse I'd caught of him behind the wheel of his brand new soft-top Cadillac, he was short, with less hair than he'd like on his head and more than anyone could possibly want on his chest and forearms.

That was as much as I could tell before I was throwing myself sideways. The front wheel of the Buell skittered on the loose gravel shoulder of the road, sending a vicious shimmy up through the headstock into my arms. I nearly dropped the damn bike there and then, and that was what pissed me off the most.

The Buell was less than a month old at that point, a Firebolt still with the shiny feel to it, and I'd been hoping it would take longer to acquire its first battle scar. The first cut is always the one you remember.

Although I was wearing full leathers, officially I was still signed off sick from the Kerse job and undergoing the tortures of regular physiotherapy. Adding motorcycle accident injuries, however minor, was not going to look good to anyone, least of all me.

But the bike didn't tuck under and spit me into the weeds, as I half expected. Instead it righted itself, almost stately, and allowed me to slither to a messy stop maybe seventy metres further on. I put my feet down and tipped up my visor, aware of my heart punching behind my ribs, the adrenaline shake in my hands, the burst of anger that follows on closely after having had the shit scared out of you.

I turned, to find the guy in the Cadillac had completed his half-arsed manoeuvre, pulling out of a side road and turning left across my path. He'd slowed, though, twisting round to stare back at me with his neck extended like a meerkat. Even at this distance I could see the petulant scowl. Hell, perhaps I'd made him drop the cell phone he'd been yabbering into instead of paying attention to his driving ...

Just for a second our eyes met, and I considered making an issue out of it. The guy must have sensed that. He plunked back down in his seat and rammed the car into drive, gunning it away with enough gusto to chirrup the tires on the bone-dry surface.

I rolled my shoulders, thought that was the last I'd ever see of him.

I was wrong.

Spending a few days away in the Catskill Mountains was a spur-of-the-moment decision, taken in a mood of self-pity.

Sean was in LA, heading up a high-profile protection detail for some East Coast actress who'd hit it big and was getting windy about her latest stalker. He'd just come back from the Middle East, tired, but focused, buzzing, loving every minute of it and doing his best not to rub it in.

After he'd left for California, the apartment seemed too quiet without him. Feeling the sudden urge to escape New York, and my enforced sabbatical, I'd looked at the maps and headed for the hills, ending up at a small resort and health spa, just north of the prettily named Sundown in Ulster county. The last time I'd been in Ulster the local accent had been Northern Irish, and it had not ended well.

The hotel was set back in thick trees, the accommodation provided in a series of chalets overlooking a small lake. My physio had recommended the range of massage services they offered, and I'd booked a whole raft of treatments. By the time I brought the bike to a halt, nose-in outside my designated chalet, I was about ready for my daily pummelling.

It was with no more than mild annoyance, therefore, that I recognized the soft-top Cadillac two spaces down. For a moment my hand stilled, then I shrugged, hit the engine kill-switch, and went stiffly inside to change out of my leathers.

Fifteen minutes later, fresh from the shower, I was sitting alone in the waiting area of the spa, listening to the self-consciously soothing music. The resort was quiet, not yet in season. Another reason why I'd chosen it.

"Tanya will be with you directly," the woman on the desk told me, gracious in white, depositing a jug of iced water by my elbow before melting away again.

The only other person in the waiting area was a big blond guy who worked maintenance. He was making too much out of replacing a faulty door catch, but unless you have the practice it's hard to loiter unobtrusively. From habit, I watched his hands, his eyes, wondered idly what he was about.

The sound of raised voices from one of the treatment rooms produced a sudden, jarring note. From my current position I could see along the line of doors, watched one burst open and the masseuse, Tanya, come storming out. Her face was scarlet with anger and embarrassment. She whirled.

"You slimy little bastard!"

I wasn't overly surprised to see Cadillac man hurry out after her, shrugging into his robe. I'd been right about the extent of that body hair.

"Aw, come on, honey!" he protested. "I thought it was all, y'know, *part of the service.*"

The blond maintenance man dropped his tools and lunged for the corridor, meaty hands outstretched. The woman behind the reception desk jumped to her feet, rapped out, "Dwayne!" in a thunderous voice that made him falter in conditioned response.

I swung my legs off my lounger but didn't rise. The woman on the desk looked like she could handle it, and she did, sending Dwayne skulking off, placating Tanya, giving Cadillac man an excruciatingly polite dressing down that flayed the skin off him nevertheless. He left a tip that must have doubled the cost of the massage he'd so nearly had.

"Ms Fox?" Tanya said a few moments later, flustered but trying for calm. "I'm real sorry about that. Would you follow me, please?"

"Are you OK, or do you need a minute?" I asked, wary of letting someone dig in with ill-tempered fingers, however skilled.

"I'm good, thanks." She led me into the dimly lit treatment room, flashed a quick smile over her shoulder as she laid out fresh hot towels.

"Matey-boy tried it on, did he?"

She shook her head, rueful, slicked her hands with warmed oil. "Some guys hear the word *masseuse* but by the time it's gotten down to their brain, it's turned into *hooker*," she said, her back to me while I slipped out of my robe and levered myself, face-down, flat on to the table. Easier than it had been, not as easy as it used to be.

"So, what's Dwayne's story?" I asked, feeling the first long glide of her palms up either side of my spine, the slight reactive tremor when I mentioned his name.

"He and I stepped out for a while," she said, casual yet prim. "It wasn't working, so we broke it off."

I thought of his pretended busyness, his lingering gaze, his rage.

No, I thought. *You broke it off.*

Later that evening, unwilling to suit up again to ride into the nearest town, I ate in the hotel restaurant at a table laid for one. Other diners were scarce. Cadillac man was alone on the far side of the dining room, just visible round the edges of the silent grand piano. I could almost see the miasma of his aftershave.

He called the waitress "honey", too, stared blatantly down her cleavage when she brought his food. Anticipating the summer crowds, the management packed the tables in close, so she had to lean across to refill his coffee cup. I heard her surprised, hurt squeak as he took advantage, and waited to see if she'd "accidentally" tip the contents of the pot into his lap, just to dampen his ardour. To my disappointment, she did not.

He chuckled as she scurried away, caught me watching and mistook my glance for admiration. He raised his cup in my direction with a meaningful little wiggle of his eyebrows. I stared him out for a moment, then looked away.

Just another oxygen thief.

As soon as I'd finished eating I took my own coffee through to the bar. The flatscreen TV above the mirrored back wall was tuned to one of the sports channels, showing highlights of the latest AMA Superbikes Championship. The only other occupant was the blond maintenance man, Dwayne, sitting hunched at the far end, pouring himself into his beer.

I took a stool where I had a good view, not just of the screen but the rest of the room as well, and shook my head when the barman asked what he could get me.

"I'll stick to coffee," I said, indicating my cup. The painkillers I was taking made my approach to alcohol still cautious.

In the mirror, I saw Cadillac man saunter in and take up station further along the bar. As he passed, he glanced at my back a couple of times as if sizing me up, with all the finesse of a hard-bitten hill farmer checking out a promising young ewe. I kept my attention firmly on the motorcycle racing.

After a minute or so of waiting for me to look over so he could launch into seductive dialogue, he signalled the barman. I ignored their muttered conversation until a snifter of brandy was put down in front of me with a solemn flourish.

I did look over then, received a smug salute from Cadillac man's own glass. I smiled – at the barman. "I'm sorry," I said to him. "But I'm teetotal at the moment."

"Yes, ma'am," the barman said with a twinkle, and whisked the offending glass away again.

"Hey, that's my kind of girl," Cadillac man called over, when the barman relayed the message. Surprise made me glance at him and he took that as invitation to slide three stools closer, so only one separated us. His hot little piggy eyes fingered their way over my body. "Beautiful *and* cheap to keep, huh?"

"Good coffee's thirty bucks a pound," I said, voice as neutral as I could manage.

His gaze cast about for another subject. "You not bored with this?" he asked, jerking his head at the TV. "I could get him to switch channels."

I allowed a tight smile that didn't reach my eyes. "Neil Hodgson's just lapped Daytona in under one-minute thirty-eight," I said. "How could I be bored?"

Out of the corner of my eye, I saw Dwayne's head lift and turn as the sound of Cadillac man's voice finally penetrated. It was like watching a slow-waking bear.

"So, honey, if I can't buy you a drink," Cadillac man said with his most sophisticated leer, "can I buy you breakfast?"

I flicked my eyes towards the barman in the universal distress signal. By the promptness of his arrival, he'd been expecting my call.

"Is this guy bothering you?" he asked, flexing his muscles.

"Yes," I said cheerfully. "He is."

"Sir, I'm afraid I'm gonna have to ask you to leave."

Cadillac man gaped between us for a moment, then flounced out, muttering what sounded like "frigid bitch" under his breath.

After very little delay, Dwayne staggered to his feet and went determinedly after him.

Without haste, I finished my coffee. The racing reached an ad break. I checked my watch, left a tip, and headed back out into the mild evening air towards my chalet. My left leg ached equally from the day's activity and the evening's rest.

I heard the raised voices before I saw them in the gathering gloom, caught the familiar echoing smack of bone on muscle.

Dwayne had run his quarry to ground in the space between the soft-top Cadillac and my Buell, and was venting his alcohol-fuelled anger in traditional style, with his fists. Judging by the state of him, Cadillac man was only lethal behind the wheel of a car.

On his knees, one eye already closing, he caught sight of me and yelled, "Help, for Chrissake!"

I unlocked the door to my chalet, crossed to the phone by the bed.

"Your maintenance man is beating seven bells out of one of your guests down here," I said sedately, when front desk answered. "You might want to send someone."

Outside again, Cadillac man was going down for the third time, nose streaming blood. I noted with alarm that he'd dropped seriously close to my sparkling new Buell.

I started forwards, just as Dwayne loosed a mighty roundhouse that glanced off Cadillac man's cheekbone and deflected into the Buell's left-hand mirror. The bike swayed perilously on its stand and I heard the musical note of splintered glass dropping.

"Hey!" I shouted.

Dwayne glanced up and instantly dismissed me as a threat, moved in for the kill.

OK. Now I'm pissed off.

Heedless of my bad leg, I reached them in three fast strides and stamped down on to the outside of Dwayne's right knee, hearing the cartilage and the anterior cruciate ligament pop as the joint dislocated. Regardless of how much muscle you're carrying, the knee is always vulnerable.

Dwayne crashed, bellowing, but was too drunk or too stupid to know it was all over. He swung for me. I reached under my jacket and took the SIG 9mm off my hip and pointed it at him, so the muzzle loomed large near the bridge of his nose.

"Don't," I murmured.

And that was how, a few moments later, we were found by Tanya, and the woman from reception, and the barman.

"You a cop?" Cadillac man asked, voice thick because of the stuffed nose.

"No," I said. "I work in close protection. I'm a bodyguard."

He absorbed that in puzzled silence. We were back in the bar until the police arrived. Out in the lobby I could hear Dwayne still shouting at the pain, and Tanya shouting at what she thought of his stupid jealous temper. He was having a thoroughly bad night.

"A bodyguard," Cadillac man mumbled blankly. "So why the fuck did you let him beat the crap out of me back there?"

"Because you deserved it," I said, rubbing my leg and wishing I'd gone for my Vicodin before I'd broken up the fight. "I thought it would be a valuable life lesson – thou shalt not be a total dickhead."

"Jesus, honey! And all the time, you had a gun? I can't believe you just let him—"

I sighed. "What do you do?"

"Do?"

"Yeah. For a living."

He shrugged gingerly, as much as the cracked ribs would let him. "I sell Cadillacs," he said. "The finest motorcar money can buy."

"Spare me," I said. "So, if you saw a guy broken down by the side of the road, you'd just stop and give him a car, would you?"

"Well," Cadillac man said, frowning, "I guess, if he was a pal—"

"What if he was a complete stranger who'd behaved like a prat from the moment you set eyes on him?" I queried. He didn't answer.

I stood, flipped my jacket to make sure it covered the gun. "I don't expect you to work for free. Don't expect me to, either."

His glance was sickly cynical. "Some bodyguard, huh?"

"Yeah, well," I tossed back, thinking of the Buell with its smashed mirror and wondering who was in for seven years of bad luck. "I'm off duty."

GUNS OF BRIXTON

Paul D. Brazill

1

"WHITE AND RED, Richard!" said Caroline Sanderson as she lay on her massive four-poster bed massaging her temples. She did this at the start of each day, saying that it helped her focus, as if White House level decisions awaited her. She propped herself up on her elbows and exhaled deeply.

"But, whatever you do, don't buy bloody Chardonnay. Everybody hates Chardonnay now, you know? It's so unfashionable," she continued. "Remember, okay?"

Richard resisted the temptation to ask her how, pray tell, a human's taste buds could be affected by the fickle whims of what was considered fashionable but he knew from experience that he'd be pissing in the wind.

Caroline was in a planet far, far away from him these days. And all the better for it. Her voice was starting to sound like a squeaking gate or a leaky tap dripping throughout a sleepless night.

Richard was bursting to get out of the house. His hangover was surprisingly mild; fighting the tedium of the night before's New Year's Eve party at the Oxo Tower, he'd got sloshed and satisfied himself with a few sneaky tokes of wacky backy in the toilets with one of the glamorous Eastern European waitresses. Anyway, it wasn't the drink that gave him headaches these days.

Richard walked into the migraine-bright bathroom. The face in the bathroom mirror wasn't exactly what you'd call handsome but neither was it particularly ugly. A lived-in face, perhaps. With more lines than the London Underground, though.

Well, he was a kick in the arse off fifty and teetering on the precipice of a mid life crisis. What did he expect?

He was lucky, though, in that, unlike most of his mates, he hadn't developed a beer belly. The fake, black Hugo Boss suit fit him as well as it had fifteen years ago when he'd bought it in Bangkok, in fact. The fact that he still wore it pissed Caroline off no end, which was an added bonus, of course.

Richard straightened his tie in the bedroom mirror, picked up his stainless-steel briefcase and headed downstairs, barely noticing his long-neglected guitar that was propped up in the corner.

"Oh, and Richard. Could you pop into Muji and get some of that string stuff?" shouted Caroline as he reached the bottom stair.

"Eh?" said Richard.

"You know, it was in Australian *Elle*? To make the plant pots look more rustic."

Richard grunted an affirmative but he was already on his way out of the door; the more he listened to Caroline, the more he felt as if he was drowning in a well of disappointment. He supposed he should have asked her a little more about who was going to be at the dinner party but the weight of numb indifference overwhelmed him. Probably the usual hodgepodge of fourth-tier media tossers and middle-management wankers, he guessed.

Richard got into his Mercedes, threw his briefcase on to the back seat and opened up the glove compartment. He took out a fist-sized hip flask. Drinking in the morning – especially when he had a drive south of the river to Vinopolis – probably wasn't the best idea in the world but it would help him keep his life at arm's length. He thought of the W.C. Fields line: "She drove me to drink, it's the one thing I'm indebted to her for."

Richard pushed the hip flask into his jacket pocket and opened a packet of L&M cigarettes. He took a big hit and gazed up at his six-bedroom West London home. There was only him and Caroline living there but it still felt claustrophobic, suffocating.

One of his old mates had referred to it as Xanadu – like the cavernous house in *Citizen Kane*; stuffed with "the loot of all the world" but containing nothing Kane's wife "really cared about".

Roxy Music's "In Every Dream Home a Heartache" corkscrewed through Richard's mind every night as he walked up the garden path after another uneventful day at work.

Richard buckled up and started the engine. He switched on the radio and Dexy's Midnight Runners were singing "Burn It Down" as he pulled out of the driveway into Sycamore Road. Not a bad idea, he thought. Not bad at all.

He turned into Bath Road and headed south. It was a cold, granite-coloured morning. He stared out of the car window, barely focusing on the rows of detached houses being smudged by the January rain. For a while he drove aimlessly, listening to the music.

Ten years of this he thought. You'd get less for murder.

2

"Learned it from Andy McNab books, didn't I, Ken?" said Big Jim, cleaning the blood from the dagger. He threw the stainless-steel briefcase on to the back seat of his red Jag.

"You stab 'em under the ribcage, see? So the blade isn't deflected by bone and then you puncture the heart and twist," he continued.

Kenny Rogan wheezed as he lifted Half-Pint Harry's body from the ground. Shit, I'm out of condition, he thought. Once a semi-professional footballer now a full-time barfly. He'd even given up the Blue Anchor's Sunday league and he got a hot flush when he bent down to fasten his shoe laces.

Big Jim nodded as he took the legs. Jim was as much use as a condom in a convent most of the time, thought Kenny, but when it came to the heavy lifting he was the man for the job; built like a brick shithouse and bearing more than a passing resemblance to one too. His face was so lived-in, even squatters wouldn't stay there.

"Looks a mess, eh, Kenny?" said Big Jim.

"Was no oil painting when he were alive, mind you. Would make a good Jackson Pollock, though, eh?" said Kenny. "Picasso, even…"

"Jackson Bollocks, more like it." said Jim, with a 5,000-watt grin.

"Very droll, James. Very sharp. You'll be cutting yourself if you're not too careful," said Kenny.

They stuffed the body in the boot of the Jaguar and slammed it shut. The car was Jim's pride and joy. He'd had it since it was new and he considered it a classic car from back in the good old days.

Jim was a man who didn't like change. An ageing Teddy boy, his car even had an old eight-track cartridge that exclusively played the two Eddies – Eddie Cochran and Duane Eddy.

"Right annoying fucker, though, eh? Non stop motormouth. Geordie twat," said Jim.

Jim took the hosepipe and sprayed it around the lock up.

"Wasn't a Geordie," said Kenny.

"Eh?" said Jim.

Kenny grinned.

"Half-Pint Harry. He wasn't from Newcastle. He was from Sunderland, James. Was a mackam," he said.

"What's a fackin' mackam when it's at home?" said Jim.

"A mackam's … like a decaffeinated Geordie," said Kenny, chuckling to himself.

"The north's all the same to me," said Big Jim.

"I wholeheartedly agree," said Kenny. "Mushy peas, black pudding, pease pudding, fishy-wishy-fuckin'-dishy. I usually start to hear the duelling banjos from *Deliverance* as soon as I get north of Finchley."

Jim wasn't listening, though. He was rubbing a pair of black tights between the fingers of one hand and scrutinizing a pair of black patent leather high heels like they were a magic-eye painting.

"Not too keen on Plan B, then?" said Kenny with a grin as he dropped his trousers.

"Do we have to?" said Jim.

"Not much choice now that Half-Pint Harry's worm meat. This clobber is our best front door key," said Kenny.

He clumsily stripped to his snowman boxer shorts and struggled to pull a gold sequined dress over his shaven head.

3

"You go the Lord Albert last night?" said Lynne, before using the Clarkeson's Jewellers complimentary pen to snort a hill of cocaine. Eight o'clock on New Year's Day wasn't the best time for her to start work and she knew she'd need a little lift.

She passed the pen to George. It was mass-produced shit and the Brixton address had been misspelled but then Clarkeson's were cheap bastards. They'd made money hand over fist over the last few years but still cut costs wherever they could.

Lynne had been manager there for four years now and had only had one pay rise. It was a trap but there she was in her mid forties, single and under-qualified. She didn't exactly have a bucket-load of choices.

"Oh, I did," said George, "but it was completely dead. As much fun as Morrissey's stag night." He took a big snort.

Lynne checked her make-up in the mirror and pushed up her breasts, her best asset, she thought.

"Somewhere to park your bike," said George looking at her cleavage.

Lynne tossed her dyed red hair back dramatically.

"Sure you don't want me to turn you straight, Georgy Porgy?" she said, almost rubbing her breasts in George's face.

She was only half joking. George was a good-looking lad. Tall, blond and half her age. And he was always immaculately dressed. He was a cut above the rough and tumble types she met in the Brixton Hill Arms. However, he was as camp as Christmas, unfortunately.

"Mmmm," said George. "Well, maybe if I can flip you over and play your B-side!" he guffawed, loud and vulgar, as Lynne battered him with a feather duster.

4

Kenny and Big Jim sang "Summertime Blues" at the top of their voices.

Kenny held the steering wheel in his left hand and checked his make-up in the mirror. It was a good job he'd shaved that morning, he thought. The stubble still showed, though. He adjusted his curly blond wig as he pulled up at a pelican crossing and waited for a staggering smackhead to wobble across the road.

Kenny usually loved driving in London on a Bank Holiday; there was almost no traffic, leaving the city to the real Londoners. But today was New Year's Day and it was like a zombie scene from *Dawn of the Dead* with the overspill from the night before's parties wandering the streets.

As he raced down Walworth Road he swerved around the Elephant and Castle roundabout, narrowly missing a group of rat-boys being chased by a red-faced Santa Claus; he started to feel nostalgic.

"Remember the sixties, Jim?"

"Just about," said Jim, opening up a can of Stella and handing one to Kenny who held the steering wheel with one hand as he opened it.

"August Bank Holiday Monday. Brighton Beach. Mods versus Rockers. Kicking ten bags of shit out of those little twats on hairdryers."

"Happy days," said Jim.

Kenny sipped his can of Stella, gazed at the fading bat-wing tattoos on his hands and remembered a drunken night at a Brighton tattoo parlour that then segued into the time he first met his wife, Deborah. Ex-wife now, of course.

Twenty-five years ago now. There'd been a lot of booze under the bridge since then, he thought.

"Grab a bunch of them," said Kenny. He threw a well-stuffed wallet to Big Jim. Jim opened it up and pulled out a wad of cash. "More leaves than you'd see in a cabbage patch, eh?" said Kenny. "Help yourself. Half-Pint Harry doesn't need them."

"Won't Uncle Frank want this?" said Jim, an edge in his voice.

"It's a little bonus from Frank, James. He don't give a toss as long as he gets that back," said Kenny. He gestured over his shoulder towards the shining metallic briefcase.

"After we get rid of Half-Pint Harry and do this next little job we can head off down the Blue for a gargle, eh?"

Jim fiddled with his bra strap and adjusted his long blond wig.

"Great minds drink alike, Kenny," he said.

5

Lynne wiped her nose and looked up as a black Jaguar pulled up outside the shop.

"No way! Customers at this time of the morning?" said Lynne, putting on an extra layer of make-up. "It's New Year's Day. We're supposed to be shut."

"Now, you know that Mrs Clarkeson says that we have a no closing policy. Tight twat, that she is," said George.

"They'll have to wait until we've finished the stock-taking," said Lynne, indignantly.

The car door slammed and two tall, glittery blondes got out, wearing more gold than you'd find in Fort Knox or on Jimmy Savile.

"No! Russian Princess alert," said George, perking up.

Russians usually spent a fortune and he worked on commission. The men – bullet heads with no necks – terrified him but the women usually seemed to take a shine to him.

"We've got to let them in, I'm off to Barcelona next weekend."

Lynne just shrugged and finished off the cocaine.

"Time for some serious rimming," said George.

Lynne grimaced.

"Metaphorically speaking, of course," said George. He wiped the white powder from his nose, pressed the button to open the security door and painted on a smile as wide as the Grand Canyon.

"Morning, ladies," he beamed. Then he saw the Glock and his jaw dropped so much you could have scraped carpet fluff from his bottom lip.

Lynne screamed as glass from the shattered cabinet showered her and pebble-dashed her face.

"Shut the fuck up," said Kenny, pressing the gun against George's left eye as Jim stuffed a big black bag with jewels.

6

"I'm as happy as a pig in shit," said Kenny, swigging on his can of Stella and swerving the car around the corner into Druid Lane. He pulled off the wig and threw it on to the back seat.

"Let's have a butcher's at this," said Jim, wiping the make-up from his face. He leaned into the back of the car and pulled the bag of jewels towards him. He opened the bag and took a swig of Stella.

"Oh, for fuck's sake," said Jim. The beer he'd spilt over his crotch was cold. He started rubbing at the wet patch.

"Looks like you're enjoying that," said Kenny.

"Sure you're not shaking hands with the one-eyed milkman?" They both howled with laughter and then Kenny froze.

"Bollocks!" said Kenny, as a white Mercedes hurtled towards them.

* * *

Richard was feeling pretty smug. It had been an effort but he'd managed to find as many bottles of Chardonnay as his credit card would allow. He deliberated over stopping off for a swifty in one of the striptease pubs that were bound to be open, even on New Year's Day. He felt bloody good.

He felt the urge for another nip from the hip flask. Resisting the temptation, he fumbled in the back of the Mercedes' glove compartment for a CD.

"Shit," said Richard. As he looked up, *The Best of The Undertones* in his hand, he saw a black Jaguar career toward him.

"It's a one way … " Richard floored the pedal and swerved the car away. He bounced the Mercedes on to the pavement.

* * *

Kenny swerved and slammed into a wall between a kebab shop and a pound shop. The airbag deployed, punching him in the stomach.

Fuck, he was trapped. Taking a deep breath, he struggled in his trouser pocket for his Swiss army knife and punctured the airbag which deflated with a wheeze.

He struggled out of his seat, the radiator hissing like a snake as the steam escaped. The car alarm was wailing and Big Jim didn't look too good at all.

* * *

Richard staggered out of his car and saw the Jag: a face was sliding down the passenger-door window like a snail leaving a trail of blood.

"Christ…" he said.

"Hey, you."

He looked up and saw a bald transvestite stumble out of the mashed Jag carrying a big black bag, spilling necklaces and jewels, in one hand and a silver briefcase in the other.

Richard fumbled in his pocket for his phone and felt cold steel against his forehead.

"I'm taking your car," said Kenny, who looked as dazed and confused as Robert Plant. "And you're driving."

Shit, Richard thought, as he heard the approaching sirens in the distance. Why not? Can't be any worse than Caroline's dinner party.

THE DEADLIEST
TALE OF ALL

Peter Lovesey

H<small>E WROTE</small> "A Troubled Sleep", stared at it for a time, sighed and struck it out.

"The Unsafe Sleep" didn't last long either.

"In the Death Bed" was stronger, he decided. He left it to be considered later. A good title could make or break a story. He'd tried and rejected scores of them for this, the most ambitious of all his tales. "Night Horrors"? Possibly not.

Then an inspiration: "It Comes By Night". This, he thought, could be right. He barely had time to write it down when there was a knock at the door.

He groaned.

The man from the *Tribune* was creating a bad impression. His manner verged on the offensive. "Have a care what you say to me. My readers are not to be deceived. I will insist upon the truth."

The inference was not lost on Edgar Allan Poe.

"Do you take me for a deceiver, then?" he said, scarcely containing his annoyance. He had consented to this interview on the assumption that it would prop up his shaky reputation.

"You will not deny that you are a teller of tall tales, a purveyor of the fantastic."

"That is my art, sir, not my character, and you had better make the distinction if you wish to detain me any longer. What did you say your name is?"

"Nolz. Rainer Nolz."

"Ha – it sounds Prussian."

"Is that objectionable to you?"

"It is if you are unable to temper your questions with courtesy."

"My family have lived in Virginia for two generations," Nolz said, as if that absolved him of Prussian tendencies. He seemed bent on establishing superiority. Overweight – fat, to put it bluntly – and dressed in a loud check suit stained with food, he was probably twenty years Poe's senior – too old to be a hack, notebook in hand, interviewing a writer. A competent journalist his age should surely have occupied an editor's chair by now.

He threw in another barbed remark. "Since you raised the matter of names, yours is an odd one. Poe – what's the origin of that?"

"Irish. The Poes arrived in America about 1750."

"And the Allans?"

"The family who took me in when I was orphaned. Do you really need to know this?"

"It's not a question of what I need to know, but what my readers will expect to be informed about."

"My writing," Poe said, raising his generally quiet voice to fortissimo.

"On the contrary. They can pick up one of your books. Anything from me about your writing would be superfluous. The readers – my readers – are interested in your life. That's my brief, Mr Poe. I've come prepared. I have an adequate knowledge of your *curriculum vitae* – or as much of it as you have put in the public domain. You aren't honest about your age, subtracting years as if you were one of the fair sex."

"Is that important?"

"To posterity it will be. You were born in 1809, not 1811."

Poe smiled. "Now I understand. You've been talking to the unctuous Griswold."

"And you've been lying to him."

Rufus Griswold, self-appointed arbiter of national literary merit, had first come into Poe's life probing for personal information for an anthology he was compiling ambitiously entitled *The Poets and Poetry of America*. At twenty-six, the man had been confident, plausible and sycophantic – a veritable toady. Poe had recognized as much, but failed to see the danger he presented. Writers with a genius for portraying malice do not always recognize it in real life. Griswold was a third-rate writer who fancied himself one of the literati, a parasite by now embedded in Poe's life and repeatedly damaging him. Ultimately the odious creature would take possession of the writing itself. At the time of their first meeting there had seemed no conceivable harm in embellishing the truth.

Nolz was a horse of a different colour, making no pretension to charm. "But you'll oblige me by answering my questions honestly."

"Before I do," Poe said, liking him less by the minute, "I'm curious to know how much of my work you have read."

"Not much."

"The poems?"

"A few."

"The tales?"

"Fewer. I don't care for the fantastic and horrific. I prefer something of intellectual appeal."

"You think my work is not for the intellect?"

"Too sensational. At my age, Mr Poe, one has a care for one's health."

"Are you unwell?"

"My doctor tells me I have a heart murmur. Too much excitement aggravates the condition. But I am here to talk about you, not myself. You are fond of claiming that you could have emulated Byron and swum the Hellespont because as a youth in Richmond you once won a wager by swimming a stretch of the James River."

Poe was pleased to confirm it. "Correct. At the mere age of fifteen I swam from Ludlam's Wharf to Warwick against one of the strongest tides ever known."

Nolz was shaking his head. "Unfortunately for you, I know Richmond. I have lived there. To have achieved such a feat you must have swum at least six miles."

"As I did," Poe answered on an angry rising note. "I assure you I did. In those conditions there is no question that my swim was the equal of Byron's."

"And I say it is impossible."

"Mr Nolz, it happened, and others were there as witnesses. I was an athletic youth. Were I fifteen again and fit, I would not hesitate to duplicate the deed. Sadly, in recent months my health, like yours apparently, has suffered a decline. But I have achieved other things. Shall I tell you about *The Raven*?"

"I would rather you didn't."

The sauce of this fellow! "Your readers will expect to be told how it came to be written."

"I know all that," Nolz said and smiled in a way that was not friendly. "I have a copy of your essay, 'The Philosophy of Composition', which purports to explain the genesis of the poem."

"*Purports*?"

"The piece is self-congratulation, a paean to Mr Poe. You omit to mention how much you borrowed from other writers."

"Name one."

"Miss Elizabeth Barrett."

"I am on the best of terms with Miss Barrett."

"You are on the best of terms with any number of ladies. And I am sure you are on the best of terms with a poem of Miss Barrett's entitled *Lady Geraldine's Courtship* because in *The Raven* you aped the rhythm and rhyme and offered not a word of your debt to her in the essay."

"She has not complained to me."

"As a critic you are quick to accuse others of imitation and lifting ideas, but you seem blind to the same tendency in yourself. You are also indebted to Mr Charles Dickens. Allow me to remind you that you were planning to write a poem about a parrot until you read of the raven in *Barnaby Rudge*."

Poe was silent. The man was right, damn him.

"I suggest to you" – Nolz gave the knife a twist – "that a parrot saying 'Nevermore' would not have impressed the public. It might well have made you a laughing stock."

Poe said in his defence, "Whether or not the raven in the Dickens novel put the idea in my head is immaterial. I might as easily have seen one perched on a churchyard wall. The artist cannot choose the source of his inspiration."

"But he ought to acknowledge it when he claims to be expounding his *modus operandi*. I recall the scene in the novel where Barnaby is imprisoned with Grip the raven for company and the sun through the bars casts the bird's shadow upon the floor while its eyes gleam in the light of the fires set by the rioters outside. Somewhat reminiscent of your unforgettable final stanza, is it not? '*And his eyes have all the seeming of a demon's that is dreaming, And the lamp-light o'er him streaming throws his shadow on the floor.*'"

"Would you tax me with plagiarism?"

"No, sir. Forgetfulness."

"How charitable! Is there anything else you hold against me?"

Nolz gave a nod, as if tempted to go on. Then he hesitated before saying, "Mr Poe, you may not appreciate this, but I am your best hope."

"Best hope! God save us! Best hope of what?"

"Of a lasting reputation."

"Sir, my written work will ensure my reputation."

"Without wishing to be offensive, it has not achieved much for you thus far."

Poe sighed. "I grant you that. *The Raven* is the most popular poem ever written and I remain in penury."

Nolz spread his palms. "You were a fool to yourself, publishing in a newspaper without the protection of copyright. Any cheapjack publisher was free to reprint without redress."

"And has, a thousand times over." Poe put his hand to his mouth and yawned. "Put me out of my suspense. How will you improve my prospects?"

"Materially, not at all," Nolz said. "I am a journalist, not a businessman. I spoke just now of your reputation."

"It doesn't have need of you," Poe said on the impulse. "It's second to none." Yet both knew the statement was untrue. He'd acceded all too eagerly to the request for an interview. He needed shoring up if it wasn't too late already.

Nolz was looking at him with pity. The man had the power to unnerve, as if he knew things yet to be revealed. The world might be – ought to be – aware that the writer of "The Gold-Bug" and *The*

Raven was a genius, but this dislikeable old hack seated across the table was behaving as if he was the recording angel.

"Who are you?" Poe cried out. "Why should I submit to your churlish questions?"

"I told you who I am," Nolz said. "And as to the questions, most of them have come from you."

"There you go, maligning me, twisting my words. Why should I trust you?"

"Because I have a care for the truth above everything. You have enemies masquerading as friends, Mr Poe. They seek to destroy your reputation. They may succeed."

Much of what the man was saying was true.

"You keep speaking of this reputation of mine as if it matters. My work is all that matters and it will endure. Poor Edgar Poe the man is a lost cause, a soul beyond hope of redemption."

"With a well-known flair for self-abasement. Coming from you, this is of no consequence. But when others damn you to kingdom come, as they will, you are going to have need of me."

"As my protector? You are not a young man, Rainer Nolz."

"Ray." He extended his fat hand across the table. "Address me as Ray. My fellow writers do."

Poe reached for the hand and felt revulsion at the flabby contact. "So, Ray ... "

"Yes?"

"Are there any other failings of mine you wish to address?"

Nolz raised a shaggy eyebrow. "Are there any, Edgar, that you care to confess?"

"Plenty, I should think! When I drink, I drink to oblivion. One or two glasses are usually enough. I am a fool with women, writing love letters to one whilst pursuing another. I am hopeless with money. Are you writing this down?"

"It's too well known. Let's address some of the misinformation you have unleashed on the world."

"Must we?"

Nolz gave a penetrating look with his brown, unsparing eyes. "If I am to be of service, yes."

The examination that followed was uncomfortable, depressing, shaming, a ledger of Poe's falsehoods and exaggerations. Why did he endure it? Because Nolz, like the Ancient Mariner, was possessed of a mysterious power to detain. He dissected more of the myths blithely confided to Griswold and given substance in *The Poets and Poetry of America*. The myth that as a young man Poe had run away from home to fight for the liberty of the Greeks in their War of Independence against the Turks. The myth of a trip to St Petersburg where he got into difficulties and was supposedly rescued by Henry Middleton, the American Consul. All this in an attempt to gloss over two years in the ranks, of which Poe was not proud.

Nolz had said he knew the *curriculum vitae*, and so he did, in mortifying detail. He must have gone to infinite trouble to find out so much.

Finally he said, "Was that good for your soul?"

"Against all expectation, yes," Poe admitted. "I am tempted, almost, to ask you to absolve me of my sins."

Nolz laughed. "That would be exceeding my duties."

"I feel shriven, nonetheless, and I thank you for that."

"No need, Edgar. Instead of absolution I will offer a piece of advice. Beware of Rufus Griswold. He is not your friend."

"Ha! I don't need telling," Poe said. "After all his blandishments how many of my poems appeared in his book? Three. One Charles Fenno Hoffman had forty-five. I counted them. Forty-five. A man whose name means little to me or the public."

"I saw."

Poe was warming to his theme. "And who was offered and accepted my job after I was dismissed as editor at *Graham's*? Griswold."

"And the magazine suffered as a result," Nolz said, beginning to show some sympathy.

"He even shoulders me aside when I show affection for a lady. There is a certain poetess—"

"Fanny Osgood?"

"You know everything. The first I heard of it was that she had dedicated her collection of poems to him – 'a souvenir of admiration for his genius'."

"Why then, Edgar, do you continue to have any truck with a man who treats you with contempt?"

Poe rolled his eyes and eased his finger around his stock. All this was making him sweat. How could he explain without damning himself? "Griswold has influence. That wretched book of his must have gone through ten editions. Oh, I've tried cutting free of him more than once, but he'll remind me that I have need of him. Since you know so much, you must be aware that he put together another anthology, *The Prose Writers of America*."

"And invited you to contribute. To which you responded that he was an honourable friend you had lost through your own folly – *your own folly*."

Now Poe flushed with embarrassment. "Swallowing my pride. He included several of my tales."

"He continues to tell his own tales about you to all that will listen, shocking scurrilous stories."

"I know."

"Griswold will bring you nothing but discredit."

He nodded. He knew it, of course. He was destined for the sewers. But surely the work would keep its dignity, whatever was said of its creator?

"And you, Ray? What may I expect from you after this interrogation? Should I be nervous of what you will write in your newspaper?"

"The truth."

"Exposing the lies?"

"Oh, no. We disposed of them this evening. I needed to make certain. I am now confident that what I write has the force of verified fact. It will not be to your detriment."

"And when may I look forward to reading it?"

"Never."

Poe frowned, and played the word over in his brain. "I don't understand."

"You will never read it because you will be dead."

The statement was like a physical blow. His brain reeled. Deep inside himself, he'd feared this from the moment he admitted the stranger to his room. Nolz was not of this world, but an agent of destruction.

"You've turned pale," Nolz said. "I must apologize. It was wrong of me to speak of this."

"Tell me," Poe whispered, eyes wide. "Tell me all you know."

"Edgar, I know only what I have confirmed with you this evening."

"You spoke of my imminent death."

"No. I said you will never read what I write because you will be dead. I am a writer of obituaries."

A shocked silence ensued.

"You are my obituary writer?"

"It's my occupation. I was commissioned to prepare yours."

"By whom?"

"The editor of the *New York Daily Tribune*. You, as a journalist, will know that obituaries of eminent men are prepared in advance, sometimes years in advance. One cannot write an adequate account of a life on the morning a death is announced."

"My obituary! I am forty years old!"

"*Ars longa, vita brevis.*"

"I don't want this," Poe said, panicking. "I wish I had never spoken to you. How can you compose my death notice when I am still of this earth? It's ghoulish. You've put the mark of death on me."

Nolz looked shamefaced. "I have committed an unprofessional act. I should never have told you."

"I'm still creative. God knows, I still have the talent."

The journalist cleared his throat. "With due respect, Edgar, you have not produced much of significance this year."

"I have not suffered a day to pass without writing."

"What manner of writing?"

"I revise my earlier work."

"Previously published work. All this tinkering with things that appeared in print ten years ago is the symptom of an exhausted talent."

"And poems. I wrote a new poem longer than *The Raven*."

Nolz lifted his eyebrows, leaving the last four words to resonate. "I doubt if anything you have written in the last six months is worthy of mention in the obituary."

"Cruel!"

"But true. I told you I must be honest." Nolz closed his notebook and pushed his chair back from the table. "I shall take my leave of you now. Take heart, Edgar. Your place in the Pantheon is assured. In your short life you have written more masterpieces than Longfellow, Hawthorne and Emerson between them."

Poe's next words were uttered in a forlorn cry of despair. "I am not finished."

"I think my hat is hanging in the passage."

"Damn you to kingdom come, I am not finished!"

Nolz crossed the room.

Poe got up and followed him, grabbing at his sleeve. "Wait. There is something you haven't seen, a work of monumental significance. I've been working on it for five years, the best thing I have ever done."

Nolz paused and turned halfway, his face creased in disbelief. "Unpublished?"

"You must read it," Poe said, nodding. "It's a work of genius."

"A poem?"

"A tale. It will stand with 'The Tell-Tale Heart' and 'The Pit and the Pendulum'."

"One of your tales of horror? I told you how I feel about them."

"Not merely one of my tales of horror, Ray, but the ultimate tale. If you neglect to read it, you will undervalue my reputation, whatever you write in that obituary."

"What is the title?"

He had to think. "It Comes By Night". He rushed to his desk in the corner of the room and started riffling through the sheets of paper spread across it, scattering anything unwanted to the floor. "Here!" He snatched up a pen and inscribed the title on the top sheet. "If I die tomorrow, this is my legacy. I beg you, Ray. If you have a shred of pity for a desperate man, give it your attention." He thrust the manuscript into Nolz's hands. "Take it with you. I swear it is the best I have ever done, or will do."

Shaking his head, Nolz pocketed the handwritten sheets, retrieved his hat and left.

Two days later, the script of "It Comes By Night" was returned to Poe by special messenger. With it was a note:

Dear Sir,

I understand that you are the author and owner of these pages discovered in the rooms of Mr Raymond Nolz, deceased. I regret to inform you that he was found dead in bed yesterday morning. The physician who attended was of the opinion that Mr Nolz suffered some spasm of panic in the night which induced a fatal heart attack. He was known to have an irregular heart rhythm. In these sad circumstances it may be of some consolation to you that your story was the last thing he ever read, for it was found on his deathbed. I return it herewith.

Sincerely,

J. C. Sneddon, Coroner

Poe threw the script into the fire and wept.

Edgar Allan Poe himself died the next month in Washington College Hospital, Baltimore. The mystery surrounding his last days has baffled generations of biographers. He had been found in a drunken stupor in a gutter. Dr John Moran, who attended him in hospital, reported that even when he regained consciousness the writer was confused and incoherent. "*When I returned I found him in a violent delirium, resisting the efforts of two nurses to keep him in bed. This state continued until Saturday evening (he was admitted on Wednesday) when he commenced calling for one 'Reynolds' which he did through the night up to three on Sunday morning. At this time a very decided change began to affect him. Having become enfeebled from exertion he became quiet and seemed to rest for a short time, then gently moving his head he said, 'Lord help my poor Soul' and expired.*"

The identity of "Reynolds" has never been satisfactorily explained. Poe had no known friend of that name. In *The Tell-Tale Heart, the Life and Works of Edgar Allan Poe*, his biographer, the poet, critic and mystery writer, Julian Symons, wrote: " ... this last cry, like so much else in his life, remains a riddle unsolved".

Just as the sudden death of Ray Nolz was never explained.

On the day of Poe's funeral, the *New York Daily Tribune* published an obituary announcing the death and stating *"few will be grieved by it"* because *"he had no friends"*. Poe had been worthless as a critic, always biased, and *"little better than a carping grammarian"*. This savage piece was balanced with praise of the stories and the poetry, but the impression of the man was devastating. He was likened to a character in a Bulwer-Lytton novel: *"Irascible, envious, but not the worst, for these salient angles were all varnished over with a cold repellent cynicism while his passions vented themselves in sneers ... He had, to a morbid excess, that desire to rise which is vulgarly called ambition, but no wish for the esteem or the love of his species."*

The obituary had been prepared by Rufus Griswold.

And the damage didn't end there. The appalling Griswold approached Poe's mother-in-law, Maria Clemm, and by some undisclosed arrangement obtained a power of attorney to collect and edit the writings. The first two volumes were in print within three months of Poe's death, with a preface announcing that they were published as an act of charity to benefit Mrs Clemm. She received no money, just six sets of the books. Griswold's *Memoir of the Author*, published in 1850, became for many years the accepted biography. It contained all the old distortions and lies and added more.

AUTHOR'S NOTE: Rainer Nolz and "It Comes By Night" are inventions. Everything about Rufus Griswold has been checked for the truth.

THE BEST
SMALL COUNTRY
IN THE WORLD

Louise Welsh

Henryk couldn't understand what the old man was trying to say to him.

"Are you all right, son?"

The man's lips were pulled back into what might have been a grin, but his harsh tone matched the flint greyness of the world beneath the railway bridge.

"It's just that you look a wee bit out of sorts, if you don't mind me saying so."

Henryk wanted to walk away. He hadn't eaten since the night before and he was cold. Of course it was colder at home, but the Glasgow chill had a damp quality that had seeped through his trainers, stiffened his feet and crept into his bones.

He couldn't go. If he left the spot now he might miss Tomasz, and there was still an outside chance that it had all been a misunderstanding and Jerzy might yet come back.

"You've been standing here for three hours now. It was the wife that spotted you and sent me down."

Maybe the old man was asking for money. A dishevelled youth had approached Henryk an hour or so ago nursing a meagre hoard of coppers in a battered polystyrene cup. Henryk had scowled and the thin boy had shambled on. But now that he looked more closely this old man was too well dressed to be a beggar. Cleaner too, his white hair cut short under his tweed cap, a checked scarf tucked neatly into the neck of his padded jacket.

"You want to watch yoursel' round here, son. There's some would have the hide off you if you stop still for long."

Henryk moved the old man's hand from his arm and said the few words of English that he knew.

"No…no, thank you."

Tomasz had been angry, more than angry – furious – but Henryk knew in his heart that he'd be back. All he had to do was wait and eventually he would see his friend striding his way through the pedestrians, still angry – Tomasz was often angry and this time the Virgin herself knew he had a right to be – but resigned to facing trouble together.

"You've no' got a clue what I'm rabbiting on about, do you? DO…YOU…SPEAK…ENGLISH?"

Henryk shook his head and moved down the wall a little, but his persecutor's attention had already shifted to an elderly lady in a red coat who was caught midway between the moving traffic. A black cab, like the ones Henryk had seen in movies, stopped to let her cross and she gave a cheery wave to the driver who shook his head resignedly then rolled on.

"Just you wait here a wee minute. That's the wife coming. Now she's seen you're not a suicide bomber she's keen to get her neb in."

Jerzy's face had invited trust. It was the kind of face used to advertise fresh mint chewing gum of the sort that didn't interfere with your teeth, but whose sugar-freeness didn't mean it wasn't sweet. Henryk had warmed to Jerzy as soon as he had caught sight of him holding up the paper neatly printed with their names at the arrivals gate of Prestwick Airport.

"Look, Tomasz," he'd said. "Our chauffeur awaits."

But Tomasz had merely grunted and given Jerzy the sideways stare he reserved for strangers. It was this look, a look which seemed to hold all their recent difficulties in its reproach, that had sent Henryk's hand into his pocket for the envelope they had both agreed to hold on to until the last possible moment. He had handed it to

Jerzy without a single question and so six months of scrimping and self-denial had slipped effortlessly into a stranger's pocket. And with it went some of the glint in the toothpaste-slick smile.

"Okay," Jerzy had said. "Come with me".

And they'd had no choice but to follow.

"I don't think he speaks any English, Jeanette."

"Is that right?" The old lady looked at Henryk's bag. The tag that had been attached at the airport in Wroclaw was still there. "Are you lost, son? Look, Tam, he's just off some flight. Are you waiting on a pal?"

"Ach, maybe we shouldn't be bothering him."

"Of course we should be bothering him. Look at him, he's almost greeting. How would you like it if it was Robert or Kirsty lost somewhere they didn't speak the lingo? I am Scottish." The old lady pointed at herself. "Where are you from?" She repeated the action. "Me Jeanette, me Scottish. You?"

And suddenly he understood what she wanted.

"Henryk. Polski."

"Henryk, Polski." She gave him a smile, then turned back to her husband. "He's from Poland."

"How d'you know?"

"You heard him. *Polski.*"

"That might be his second name. Plenty of folk are called after places. Clare English, Joan Sutherland, Ian Paisley."

"Aye, and Miss Scotland. No, he's Polish right enough. He has a look of that boy that works in Raj's. You know the one? Cheery wee fella."

"Aye, mibbe, except this one's not looking very cheery."

"No, he is not."

Henryk had tried to keep his spirits up as Jerzy had driven them along stretches of motorway that had slowed almost to a standstill as they neared the city.

"It's always this way," Jerzy had said. "The first twenty miles fast, the last two slow."

"The same at home." Henryk had glanced at Tomasz, hoping he would join the conversation, but his friend's eyes were closed, his head resting against the van window.

Of course it was harder for Tomasz. Henryk was leaving behind his home, his friends and his language, but he was unmarried, his mother still in good health. For him the trip held promises of adventure, the freedom to be himself. Tomasz was leaving behind a good job and years of training. Whatever the tensions at home, the move was always going to hit him harder.

The van drove up a slip road and suddenly the old city was all around them. Tomasz looked up. "Where are the hills and the heather?"

Jerzy laughed. "Not so far away. Maybe we'll go to them at the weekend."

Henryk had noticed Jerzy's expression then and wondered what life here was really like. He had got an impression of cafés and restaurants, a blood-red tattoo parlour, the shining glass front of a theatre. Everything was different from home and yet, he comforted himself, the substance was the same.

"Okay." Their driver pulled into a parking space. "Flat first. You can get washed, have a shave, something to eat and then we'll go to the supermarket where you'll be working."

They'd unloaded their luggage and Jerzy had led the way. Henryk's bag was heavy, and he was glad when Jerzy finally stopped outside one of the sandstone tenements that lined the street.

"Okay, here we are."

Tomasz had glanced at the rows of names next to the entry buzzers.

"A lot of people live here."

Jerzy was fumbling in his jacket pocket.

"It's a workers' district."

"But no Poles?"

"Two Poles from today." He took out a set of keys and swore softly. "Unbelievable. I took the wrong keys from the van. This is for a flat I'm taking people to this afternoon. I'll have to go back and collect yours. Wait here, I won't be long."

He gave them the clean, even, grin, and then jogged off in the direction of the van. It had been as quick and as casual as that.

Henryk wasn't sure how long they'd stood there before the truth dawned, but he guessed that Tomasz had also clutched the knowledge of their betrayal wordlessly in his chest, still hoping that Jerzy would return, keys in hand, his smile shining.

"Hello, Jeanette, Tam." An elderly woman laden with shopping bags greeted the couple.

"Oh, no, here we go." The old man looked at Henryk. "You'll soon be wishing we'd left you to your misery."

"Is this your grandson? He's a fine-looking fella, isn't he?"

"Hello, Bella." The first woman looked important. "No, this isn't my grandson. Mind you met Robert? They're the same height right enough, but Henryk doesn't look anything like him, Robert's much darker."

"Oh, aye. So who's this then?"

"We don't know. He's been standing here for almost three hours now. I noticed him when I went out to the shop. That was at eleven, and he was still here when I came back. Then we had a bite to eat and watched a bit of telly. When I went to do the washing up I could see him from the kitchen window. I said to Tam there's something not quite right there and he came down to check on him."

"And what does he say?"

"Nothing, not a peep, but you can see the way he is."

The newcomer stared intently into Henryk's face.

"He's awfy glum-looking." She reached into one of her bags, brought out a packet of biscuits, opened them and thrust them at Henryk. "Here, a Jaffa Cake can be very sustaining in a crisis."

"Oh, for goodness sake." The old man took a mobile phone out of his pocket and started to dial. "I should have done this at the off."

Eventually Tomasz had pressed the door's buzzers. His English was good and though he found the Scottish accents crackling down the entryphone hard to understand, it was clear no one was expecting them, and no one was about to welcome them in with an offer of a bed for the night.

The worst had happened. After all the exchanges of emails and promises, there were no jobs, no lodgings waiting for them in

Glasgow. Jerzy had gone, taking their cash and their hopes with him, leaving the two men stranded.

Tomasz had given Henryk a look that was close to a curse.

"Why did I listen to you?"

He turned his back and walked quickly away.

Henryk followed. Men smoking outside pubs tailed them with their eyes and the stream of shoppers parted, giving the couple a wide berth.

"I'm sorry. I shouldn't have given him our money."

"Supermarket jobs and minimum wage! All just lies. I'm a teacher. What did you expect me to do here? Stack shelves? Collect trolleys?"

They had reached the railway bridge now. Henryk grabbed his friend by the shoulder. Some youths in football strips *ooohed* at them as they passed.

"Kiss and make up!" one of them shouted and his friends laughed.

Henryk ignored the taunts.

"They weren't going to let you teach any more."

Tomasz pushed him away.

"And whose fault was that?"

He turned and ran, leaving Henryk standing beneath the bridge.

The old people were talking amongst themselves. The woman with the biscuits said, "Are you sure he's no' up to something? He could be casing a joint."

Her friend laughed. "Away with you, he's just a wee, lost boy."

"A wee, lost Polish boy come to take our jobs." The woman popped a biscuit into her mouth. "My Davie says there's too many of them. Sounds like Gdansk round here some days."

"Your Davie says more than his prayers. They're hard workers, the Poles. My mother said the Polish airmen were always the smartest dressed during the War. All the lassies wanted to dance with them. Them or the Yanks."

Old Tam harrumphed.

"Aye, your father came back from North Africa to find your house bombed out and your ma with a whole new set of dance moves. Mind, they had a terrible time of it during the War, the Poles ... "

Their voices drifted into the grumble of passing traffic. Henryk forgot them. Tomasz was coming towards him, flanked by two policeman. The old man looked up. "That was quick. I only called youse a minute ago. We're a wee bit concerned about this lad here."

One of the policeman took out his notebook and asked Tomasz, "Is this the man who robbed you?"

"No." Tomasz managed a smile. "We came here together. We are together." He squeezed Henryk's shoulder and said in their own language, "I'm sorry."

Henryk clasped Tomasz in a brief hug. However hard things were, they would be all right now.

The policeman looked from one to the other, his eyes wary. He nodded, then turned away and said to his partner in a low voice, "Just a couple of poofs having a domestic."

Henryk saw Tomasz flinch. He wondered what the policeman had said and how long it would take him, Henryk, to learn English properly. How long before he understood everything.

MR BO

Liza Cody

M Y SON NATHAN doesn't believe in God, Allah, Buddha, Kali, the Great Spider Mother or the Baby Jesus. But, he believes passionately in Superman, Spider-Man, Batman, Wolverine and, come December, Santa Claus. How he works this out – bearing in mind that they all have super powers – I don't know. Maybe he thinks the second lot wears hotter costumes. Or drives cooler vehicles, or brings better presents. Can I second guess my nine-year-old? Not a snowball's hope in Hades.

Nathan is as much a mystery to me as his father was, and as my father was before that. And who knows where they both are now? But if there's one thing I can congratulate myself on, it's that I didn't saddle my son with a stepfather. No strange man's going to teach my boy to "dance for daddy". Not while there's a warm breath left in my body.

I was eleven and my sister Skye was nine when Mum brought Bobby Barnes home for the first time. He didn't look like a lame-headed loser so we turned the telly down and said hello.

"Call me Bo," he said, flashing a snowy smile. "All my friends do."

So my dumb little sister said, "Hi, Mr Bo," and blushed because he was tall and brown eyed just like the hero in her comic book.

Mum laughed high and girly, and I went to bed with a nosebleed – which is usually what happened when Mum laughed like that and smeared her lipstick.

Mr Bo moved in and Mum was happy because we were "a family". How can you be family with a total stranger? I always wanted to ask her but I didn't dare. She had a vicious right hand if she thought you were cheeking her.

Maybe we would be a family even now if it wasn't for him. Maybe Nathan would have a grandma and an aunt if Mr Bo hadn't got his feet under the table and his bonce on the pillow.

I think about it now and then. After all, some times of year are special for families, and Nathan *should* have grandparents, an aunt and a father.

This year I was thinking about it because sorting out the tree lights is traditionally a father's job; as is finding the fuse box when the whole house is tripped out by a kink in the wire.

I was doing exactly that, by candlelight because Nathan had broken the torch, when the doorbell rang.

Standing in the doorway was a beautiful woman in a stylish winter coat with fur trimmings. I didn't have time for more than a quick glance at her face because she came inside and said, "What's up? Can't pay the electricity bill? Just like Mum."

"I am not like my mother." I was furious.

"Okay, okay," she said. "It was always way too easy to press your buttons." And I realized that the strange woman with the American accent was Skye.

"What are you doing here?" I said, stunned.

"Hi, and it's great to see you too," she said. "Who's the rabbit?"

I turned. Nathan was behind me, shadowy, with the broken torch in his hand.

"He's not a rabbit," I said, offended. Rabbit was Mr Bo's name for a mark. We were all rabbits to him one way or another.

"Who's she?" Nathan said. I'd taught him not to tell his name, address or phone number to strangers.

"I'm Skye."

"A Scottish Island?" He sounded interested. "Or the place where clouds sit?"

"Smart *and* cute."

"I'm not cute," he said, sniffing loudly. "I'm a boy."

"She's your aunt," I told him, "my sister."

"I don't want an aunt," he said, staring at her flickering, candlelit face. "But an uncle might be nice." Did I mention that all his heroes are male? Even when it's a woman who solves all his problems, from homework to football training to simple plumbing and now, the electricity. I used to think it was because he missed a father, but it's because you can't interest a boy in girls until his feet get tangled in the weeds of sex.

I fixed the electricity and all the lights came on except, of course, for the tree ones which lay in a nest on the floor with the bulbs no more responsive than duck eggs. Nathan looked at me as though I'd betrayed his very life.

"Tomorrow," I said. "I promise."

"You promised tonight."

"Let's have a little drink," Skye said, "to celebrate the return of the prodigal sister."

"We don't drink," Nathan said priggishly. He's wrong. I just don't drink in front of him. My own childhood was diseased and deceived by Mum's drinking and the decisions she made when drunk.

"There's a bottle of white in the fridge," I said, because Skye was staring at my second-hand furniture and looking depressed. At least it's mine, and no repo man's going to burst in and take it away. She probably found me plain and worn too, but I can't help that.

She had a couple of drinks. I watched very carefully, but she showed no signs of becoming loose and giggly. So I said, "It's late. Stay the night." She was my sister, after all, even though I didn't know her. But she took one look at the spare bed in the box room and said, "Thanks, I'll call a cab."

When the cab came, Nathan followed us to the front door and said goodbye of his own free will. Skye was always the charming one. She didn't attempt to kiss him because if there was one thing she'd learnt well it was what guys like and what they don't like. She said, "I'll come back tomorrow and bring you a gift. What do you want?"

Now that's a question Nathan isn't used to in this house, but he hardly stopped to think. He said, "Football boots. The red and white Nike ones, with a special spanner thing you can use to adjust your own studs."

"Nathan," I warned. The subject of football boots was not new. I could never quite afford the ones he wanted.

But Skye grinned and said, "See you tomorrow, kid," and she was gone in a whirl of fur trimmings.

Mr Bo used to buy our shoes. Well, not buy exactly. This is how he did it: we'd go to a shoe shop and I'd ask for shoes a size and a half too small. Mr Bo would flirt with the assistant. When the shoes arrived I'd try to stuff my feet in and Mr Bo would say, "Who do you think you are? One of the Ugly Sisters?" This would make the assistant laugh as she went off to find the proper size. While she was gone, Skye put on the shoes that were too small for me and slipped out of the shop. Then I'd make a fuss – the shoes rubbed my heels, my friends had prettier ones, and Mr Bo would have to apologize charmingly and take me away, leaving a litter of boxes and shoes on the floor. It worked the other way round when I needed shoes, except that he never made the Ugly Sister crack about Skye. I hated him for that because although he said it was a joke I knew what he really thought.

The only time he paid hard cash was when he bought tap-shoes for Skye. He'd begun to teach us dance steps in the kitchen. "Shuffle," he'd yell above the music, "kick, ball-change, turn ... come on, girls, dance for Daddy."

The next day Nathan didn't want to go out. His friend came to the door wanting a kick-around but ended up playing on the computer instead. I didn't say anything but I knew he was waiting for Skye.

At the end of the day there was nothing I could do but make his favourite, shepherd's pie, and read Harry Potter to him in bed. I could see his heart wasn't in it.

I wasn't surprised – Skye had been taught unreliability by experts – but I was angry. She'd had a chance to show him that a woman could be as good as Batman and she'd blown it. All he had left was me and I was not the stuff of heroes. What had I done in the past nine years except to keep him warm, fed, healthy and honest? Also, I made him do his homework, which I think he found unforgivable. I thought I was giving him solid gold, because in the end, doing my homework and passing exams were the tools I used to dig myself out of a very deep hole. But how can that compare to the magic conferred upon a boy by ownership of coveted football boots? At his age he thought the right boots would transform his life and give him talents beyond belief. Magic boots for Nathan; dancing shoes for Skye.

Mr Bo tried to teach us both to do the splits. Maybe, at eleven or twelve, I was already too stiff. Or maybe, deep down inside, I felt there was something creepy about doing the splits in the snow-white knickers and little short skirts that he insisted we wear to dance for him. Either way, I never managed to learn. But Skye did. She stretched like a spring and bounced like a ball. She wore ribbons in her crazy hair. Of course she got the dancing shoes.

One evening he took us to the bar where Mum worked, put some money in the juke box and Skye showed off what she'd learnt. Mum was so impressed she put out a jam-jar for tips and it was soon full to overflowing.

Now that I have a child of my own I can't help wandering what on earth she was thinking. Maybe she looked at the tip jar and saw a wide-screen TV or a weekend away at a posh hotel with handsome Bo Barnes. Or was she just high on the free drinks? Once, she said to me, "Wanna know somethin', kid? If you're a girl, all you ever got to sell is your youth. Make sure you get a better price for it than I did. Wish someone tol' me that before I gave it all away." Of course she wasn't sober when she said that, but I don't think sobriety had much to do with it; it was her best advice. No wonder I did my homework.

Skye showed up when Nathan had stopped waiting for her. "C'mon, kid," she said, "we're going shopping."

"You're smoking." He was shocked.

"So shoot me," she said. "You have dirty hair."

"So shoot me." He grinned his big crooked smile.

"Needs an orthodontist," she said. "I should take him back to LA."

"Over my dead body," I said. "Nathan, get in the shower. Skye, coffee in the kitchen. Now."

She wrinkled her still pretty nose at my coffee. I said, "What're you up to? What's the scam?"

"Can't an auntie take her nephew shopping?" She widened her innocent eyes at me. "'Tis the season and all that malarkey."

"We haven't seen each other in over fifteen years."

"So I missed you."

"No you didn't. How did you find me?"

"Were you hiding?" she asked. "How do you know what I missed? You're my big sister, or have you forgotten?"

"I wasn't the one who swanned off to the States."

"No, you were the one who was jealous."

"I tried to protect you."

"From what? Attention, pretty clothes, guys with nice cars?"

I said nothing because I didn't know where to begin.

She stuck her elbows on the table and leant forward with her chin jutting. "It all began with Bobby Barnes, didn't it? You couldn't stand me being his little star."

"He was thirty. You were nine."

"A girl doesn't stay nine forever."

"He ended up in prison and we were sent to a home. He robbed us of our childhood, Skye."

"Some childhood." She snorted. "Stuck in that squalid little apartment – with no TV or anything."

"And how did Mr Bo change that? Did he stop Mum drinking? Did he go out to work so that she could look after us? Okay, he brought us a flat-screen telly, but it got repossessed like everything else."

"He gave us pretty clothes and shoes … "

"He *stole* them. He taught us how to steal … "

"But it was fun," Skye cried. "He taught us how to dance too. You're forgetting the good stuff."

"He taught *you* to dance. He taught me how to be a look-out for a pickpocket and a thief. You weren't a dancer, Skye; you were there to distract the rabbits."

"Why're you two quarrelling?" Nathan said from the doorway.

"We're sisters," Skye said. "If you're good I'll tell you how a pirate came to rescue us from an evil wizard's castle and how your mom didn't want to go and nearly blew it for me."

"No you won't," I said.

"Is it true?" He was as trusting as a puppy.

"Do you really believe in wicked wizards and good pirates?" I asked.

"Next you'll be telling him there's no Santa Claus or Tooth Fairy."

"I know there's no tooth fairy," he said. "I caught Mum *putting* a pound under my pillow and she pretended she'd just found it there, but she's a rubbish liar."

"She is, isn't she? Bet you took the cash anyway. Now let's go shopping."

"I'm coming too," I said, because I didn't know my own sister and I was afraid she might have inherited Mr Bo's definition of buying shoes.

"You'll spoil it," my loyal son complained. "The only thing she ever takes me shopping for is school uniform."

"What a bitch … sorry, witch." Skye dragged us both out of the house with no conscience at all.

A big black car, just a couple of feet short of being a limo, was waiting outside – plus a driver with a leather coat and no discernible neck.

Oddly, Mr Bo was not sent down for anything serious like contributing to the delinquency of minors or his sick relationship with one of them. No, when he was caught it was for stealing booze from the back of the bar where Mum worked. Of course she was done for theft too, thus ensuring that we had no irresponsible adults in our lives, and forcing us to be taken into Care.

By the time I was fifteen and Skye was thirteen we'd been living in Care for two and a half years. Foster parents weren't keen on me because I didn't want to split up from Skye, and foster mothers didn't like Skye at all because she was precocious in so many ways.

Crockerdown House, known for obvious reasons as Crack House by the locals, was a girls' care home, and judging by the number of non-visits from social workers, doctors or advisors, and the frequency of real visits by the cops, it should've been called a No Care Home. No one checked to see if we went to school or if we came back. Self-harm and eating disorders went unnoticed. Drugs were commonplace. There was a 60 per cent pregnancy rate.

I was scared rigid and spent as much time as I could at school. Teachers thought I was keen – most unusual in that part of town – and they cherished me. After a while I *became* keen.

Skye was the opposite.

It was only when a strange man turned up at the school gates in a car with Skye sitting smug as you please on the back seat that I realized she'd stayed in touch with Mr Bo while he was inside.

I knew that she and some other, older, girls regularly went to the West End to boost gear from shops and I lived with my heart in my mouth, fearing she'd be caught. She was never caught and she always had plenty of money. What I hadn't been told was that she supplied an old friend of Mr Bo's with stolen goods which he sold in the market. This friend kept Mr Bo in tobacco and all the other consumables that could be passed between friends on visiting day.

"He's coming out today," she told me excitedly. "We're going to meet him."

I looked at her in her tight jeans and the trashy silk top which would've cost a fortune if she'd actually bought it. I burst into tears.

"We're not going back to Crack House," she said. "It's over."

"What about school?" I wept. "What about my exams?" I was taking nine subjects and my teachers said I had a good chance in all of them.

"We never have to go to bogging school again. We're free. He's taking us abroad."

"What about Mum?" Mum was still inside. She wasn't just a thief; she was a thief who drank, and she was a bad mother who drank and thieved. Three strikes against her. Only one against Mr Bo. Classic!

"Oh, she'll join us later," Skye said vaguely, breathing mist on to the car window and drawing a heart.

"Is this your car?" Nathan asked the driver, impressed.

"Huh?"

"It's mine," Skye said, "for now."

"Will you have to give it back?" Nathan was sadly familiar with the concept of giving a favoured book or computer game back to the library.

"Where are we going?" The last time she and I were in a car together was a disaster.

"Crystal City. I heard it was the newest."

"It's the best," Nathan breathed. "We don't go there."

"Why not?"

I said, "It's too expensive and too far away."

"I know, I know," Skye said, "and you got a mortgage to pay and your tuition fees at the Open University. Studying to be a psychotherapist, aren't you? And both your lives gonna stay on hold till you qualify and hang out your shingle. When's that gonna be – 2050?"

"How the hell do you know that?"

"*You said hell.*"

"You'd be surprised what I know. Some of us use technology for more than looking up difficult words."

"You've been *spying* on us."

"Cool," Nathan said. "I want to be a spy when I grow up."

"You can be a spy now," Skye said. "Don't look back, just use this mirror and if you see a car following us, tell Wayne. Okay?" She handed him what looked like a solid gold compact.

"What sort of car?"

"Black Jeep," no-neck, leather-clad Wayne said. "Licence plate begins Sierra, Charlie, Delta."

"That's SCD to you, kid."

"Clever," I said. "Have you got kids of your own?"

"Do I *look* like a mother?"

"No need to sound insulted. It's not all bad."

"Coulda fooled me. Do you do *all* your shopping from Salvation Army counters?"

"Bollocks," I muttered, but not quietly enough.

"*You said b—*"

"Okay, Nathan," I said. "Haven't you got an important job to do?"

"Of *course* I looked you up," Skye said. "How the hell else would I find you? You're my big sister – why wouldn't I want to? I didn't know about the kid when I started. And I must say I'm surprised you felt ready to start breeding, given the mom we had. But I guess you were always kinda idealistic – always trying to right wrongs."

"No one's ready," I said.

"Hah! Got caught, did ya?"

That was an incident in my life that I didn't want to share with Skye while Nathan's ears were out on stalks.

Crystal City is five enormous interlocking domes. It's a triumph of consumer architecture and weather-proofing. You could spend your entire life – and savings – in there without drawing one breath of fresh air.

Wayne dropped us at the main entrance and Nathan, who can smell sports shoes from a distance of three and a half miles, led the way.

Walking with Skye through a shopping centre was strange and familiar. We both looked around in the same way as we used to. Searching for good opportunities, I suppose – only nowadays all I was looking for were half-price sales.

Skye bought football boots, flashy beyond Nathan's wildest dreams. They had ten differently coloured inserts for designer stripes, extra studs and a tool kit. She threw in an England strip for nine-year-olds and paid for everything with a credit card in the name of Skye Rosetti. She caught me looking and said, "I had to marry a Rosetti for the Green Card. But I liked the name so I kept it."

I called on all my nerve and asked, "What happened to Mr Bo?"

"Oh look, *shoes*," she cried and flung herself through the door of the fanciest, most minimal shoe shop I'd ever seen.

"Do we have to?" Nathan whined. He wanted to change into his England strip.

"Ungrateful little toad," Skye said cheerfully. "Here, kid, take your mom shopping." She handed him a roll of twenty-pound notes.

"Wow!" he said.

"No," I said. "Absolutely, no."

"Fuck off," she said. "Have a good time. Meet me at the Food Court on the ground floor in an hour. Don't be late. And kid? I want to see at least one strictly-for-fun gift for your mom. Don't try to scoop it all – I know you guys."

"*She said fu—*"

"Nathan," I warned as we walked away, "grown ups say stuff. And don't think we're going to spend all that money. You don't want your aunt to think you're greedy, do you?"

"I wouldn't mind."

All kids are wanty – they can't help it. But I love the way he's shocked by swearing. I melt at his piety. He wouldn't believe it if I told him what I was like at his age. And I was the goody-goody one who crawled away from a smashed-up childhood via the schoolyard.

An hour later he had the hoodie jacket he'd wanted for months. He also bought a notebook and the complete range of metallic coloured gel pens. I chose *The Best of Blondie* CD for myself because for some reason I can't listen to Blondie without wanting to dance. There was still a thick wedge of money to give back to Skye.

She was ten minutes late, and when she turned up she was followed by Wayne who was carrying enough bags to fill my spare room from floor to ceiling.

We sat in the octagon-shaped food court which had a carp pool and a fountain at its centre. Wayne took most of the bags back to the car.

Skye said, "C'mon over here, kid, I got something else for you."

"Skye." I held my hand up. "Stop. We have to talk about this. You're putting me in a very awkward position."

"I *knew* you'd spoil it." Nathan's mutinous lower lip began to shake.

Skye said, "Look at it this way, sis – how many birthdays have I missed? How many …?"

"Nine," Nathan interrupted, "and nine plus nine Christmases make, um, eighteen."

"See how smart he is? He's a good kid who goes to school and learns his times tables, and I got a lot of auntying to catch up with. Right, kid?"

"Right."

"But I understand your mom's point of view. She doesn't want me to spoil you. Your mom likes to do things the hard way, see. And I don't want to spoil you either 'cos I think you're perfect the way you are. So here's what we'll do. Do you have a cell phone?"

"We call them mobiles over here," Nathan said bossily. "Mum's got one but it's old and she says we can't afford two."

"I can't afford two sets of bills," I said. "Skye, you would not be doing me a favour if you're thinking of giving him one." I put the roll of twenties we hadn't spent into her hand. "You've been very kind, but rich relations can be too expensive."

She stared at the money in astonishment. Then she closed her hand over it and tucked it safely into her handbag. "Okay, okay. But I've got two phones and they have lots of cool applications. Want to play a game, kid?"

I watched them poring intently over the phones, two curly heads close enough to touch. Nathan's love of technology has been obvious since he first tried to feed his cheese sandwich into the VCR slot, so he didn't take long to master Skye's phone. I kept my mouth shut, but I was proud of him.

Suddenly I was content. I was drinking good coffee and eating a fresh Danish with my clever son and my unfamiliar sister. I was not counting pennies and rationing time. Worry went on holiday.

"Can I go, Mum?" Nathan was tugging my sleeve, his eyes alive with fun.

"What? Where?"

"Just down the end there." Skye pointed to the far end of the mall. "He'll have my phone and be in touch at all times. You don't need to worry."

"I'm Nathan Bond, secret agent."

"I don't know," I began, but exactly then Skye turned her face away from Nathan, towards me and I saw with dismay that she'd begun to cry. So I let him go.

"Gimme a minute." She blotted her eyes on her fur-trimmed cuff. "That's a terrific kid you got there. I guess you musta done something right."

"What happened to you, Skye?"

"Mr Bo died a year ago. He was shot by some county cops in a convenience store raid. Stupid bastard. I wasn't with him – hadn't been for years – but we kept in touch. That's when I started to look for you. I thought if he was dead, you could forgive me."

"Oh, Skye." I took her hand. Just then I heard my son's voice say, "Nathan to HQ – I'm in position. Can you hear me?"

She picked up her phone. "Loud and clear. Commence transmission. You remember how to do that?" She held the phone away from her ear and even in the crowded food court I heard the end of Nathan's indignant squawk. She gave me a watery smile but her voice was steady.

He must have started sending pictures because she forgot about me and stared intently at her little screen. Then she said, "HQ to Nathan – see that tall man in black? He's got a black and red scarf on. Yes. That's the evil Doctor Proctor."

"Skye?" I put my hand on her arm but she shook me off, got up and moved a couple of steps away.

I got up too and heard her say, " ...to the men's room. Wayne will be there. He'll give you the goods. Can you handle that?"

"No he can't handle that," I shouted, grabbing for the phone. "What're you doing, Skye?"

She twisted out of my grasp. "Let go, stupid, or you'll wreck everything. You'll put your kid in trouble."

I took off, sprinting down the mall, dodging families, crowds, balloons and Santas, cracking my shins on push chairs, bikes and brand-new tricycles.

I arrived, out of breath and nearly sobbing with anxiety, at one of the exits. There was no Nathan, no tall man in black, no Wayne. I saw a security uniform and rushed at him. "Have you seen my son? He's wearing the England strip, red and white boots and a black hoodie. He's nine. His name's Nathan." I was jumping up and down. "I think he might've gone into the Gents with a tall man in black and a black and red scarf." Terror gripped the centre of my being. "I don't know where the Gents is."

"Kids do wander off this time of year," the security man said. "Me, I think it's the excitement and the greed. I shouldn't worry. I'll go look for him in the toilets, shall I? You stay here in case he comes back."

But I couldn't wait.

He said tiredly, "Do you know how many kids there are in England strips this season? Wait here; you aren't allowed in the men's facility."

I couldn't wait there either. I pushed in behind him, calling my son's name. There were several boys of various ages – several men too – but no Nathan, no Wayne and no man in black.

"Don't worry," the security man said, although he was himself beginning to look concerned. "I'll call this in. Natty..."

"*Nathan.*"

"We'll find your boy in no time. Wait here and..."

But I was off and running back to the food court to find Skye. She had the other phone. She knew where Nathan was.

Except, of course, there was no sign of her.

I found our table. No one had cleared it. Under my seat was the carrier bag containing Nathan's old shoes, his ordinary clothes, his gel pens and my CD. I lifted his sweater to my nose as if I were a bloodhound who could track him by scent alone.

My heart was thudding like heavy metal in my throat. I couldn't swallow. Sweat dripped off my frozen face.

The most fundamental rule in all the world is to keep your child safe – to protect him from predators. I'd failed. My family history of abuse and neglect was showing itself in my nature too. Whatever made me think I could make a better job of family life than my mother? Neglect was bred into me like brown eyes and mad hair. There could be no salvation for Nathan or me.

I was fifteen when I lost Skye.

"We'll start again in the Land of Opportunity," said ex-jailbird, Mr Bo. "But we'll go via the Caribbean where I know a guy who can delete a prison record." Skye sat on his lap, cuddled, with her head tucked under his chin.

"But my exams," I said. "Skye, I'm going to pass in nine subjects. Then I can get a good job and look after us."

"You do that." She barely glanced at me. "I'll stay with Mr Bo."

"Looks like it's just you and me, kid," he said to her, without even a show of regret.

I was forced to borrow money from Skye for the bus fare back to Crack House. I had a nosebleed on the way and I thought, she'll come back – she won't go without me. But I never saw her again.

I sat in a stuffy little office amongst that morning's lost property and shivered. They brought me sweet tea in a paper cup.

Skye lent Nathan her sexy phone and I'd watched him excitedly walk away with it. It looked so innocent.

She was my sister but I knew nothing about her except that childhood had so damaged her that she experienced the control and abuse of an older man as an adventure, a love story. Why would she see sending my lovely boy into a public lavatory with a strange man as anything other than expedient? She'd been trained to think that using a child for gain was not only normal but smart.

I was no heroine – I couldn't find him or save him. I was just a desperate mother who could only sit in a stuffy room, drinking tea and beating herself up. My nose started to bleed.

"Hi, Mum – did someone hit you?" Nathan stood in the doorway staring at me curiously.

"Car park C, level five," the security man said triumphantly. "I told you we'd find him. Although what he was doing in the bowels of the earth I'll never know."

"Get *off*," Nathan said crossly. "You're dripping blood on my England strip."

"Nathan – what happened? Where have you been?"

"Don't *screech*," he said. "Remember the black Jeep – Sierra, Charlie, Delta? Well, I found it."

"Safe and sound," the security man said, "no harm done, eh? Sign here."

Numbly I signed for Nathan as if he was a missing parcel and we went out into the cold windy weather to find a bus to take us home. There would be no limo this time, but Nathan didn't seem to expect it.

On the bus, in the privacy of the back seat, Nathan said, "That was awesome, Mum. It was like being inside of Xbox. I was, like, the operative except I didn't have a gun but we made him pay for his crime anyway."

"Who? What crime?"

"Doctor Proctor – he hurts boys and gives them bad injections that make them his slaves."

"Do you believe that?" I asked, terrified all over again.

"I thought you knew," he said, ignorant of terror. "Skye said you hated men who hurt children."

"I do," I began carefully. "But I didn't know she was going to put you in danger."

"There hardly wasn't any," said the nine-year-old superhero. "All I had to do was identify the bad doctor and then go up to him and say, 'I've got what you want. Follow me.' It was easy."

I looked out of the window and used my bed-time voice so that he wouldn't guess how close I was to hysteria. "Then what happened?"

"Then I gave him the hard-drive and he gave me the money."

"The what? Hard..."

"The important bit from the inside of computers where all your secrets go. Didn't you know either? You've got to destroy it. It was the one big mistake the bad doctor made. He thought he'd erased all his secrets by deleting them. Then he sold his computer on eBay but he forgot that deleting secrets isn't good enough if you've got enemies like me and Skye. She's a genius with hard drives."

"I'll remember to destroy mine," I said. "What happened next?"

"*You* haven't got any secrets, Mum," Nathan Bond said. "After that I gave the money to Skye and hid in the bookshop till she and Wayne went away. Then I followed them."

"What bookshop?" When I ran after Nathan to the end of the mall there had been shops for clothes, cosmetics, shoes and computer games. There had not been a bookshop. I explained this to him. He was thrilled.

"You didn't see me. Nobody saw me," he crowed. "I did what spies do – I went off in the wrong direction and then doubled back to make sure no one was following. You went to the wrong end of the mall."

"Is that what Skye told you to do?"

"No," he said, although his eyes said yes. He turned sulky so I shut up. I was ready to explode but I wanted to hear the full story first.

When the silence was too much for him he said enticingly, "I know about Sierra, Charlie, Delta."

"What about it?" I sounded carefully bored.

"You know I was supposed to look for it but I never saw it? That must've been a test. You know how I know?"

"How do you know?"

"Cos Skye knew where it was all along. She and Wayne went down to level five in the lift, and I ran down the stairs just like they do on telly. You know, Mum, they get it right on telly. It works."

"Sometimes," I said. "Only sometimes."

"Well anyway, there they were – her and Wayne – and they got into the Jeep and the other driver drove them away. I looked everywhere for the limo, but I couldn't find it. I thought maybe it was part of the game – if I found it we could keep it. I wish we had a car."

"We couldn't keep someone else's car." I put my arm round him but he shrugged me off. He was becoming irritable and I could see he was tired. All the same I said, "Describe the man who drove the Jeep."

I was shocked and horrified when he described Mr Bo. But I wasn't surprised.

Later that night, when Nathan had been deeply asleep for an hour, I crept into his room and laid his bulging scarlet fur-trimmed stocking at the end of the bed. Then I ran my hand gently under his mattress until I found the shiny new phone. Poor Nathan – he was unpractised in the art of deception, and when he talked about wanting to keep the limo, I saw, flickering at the back of his eyes, the notion that he'd better shut up about the limo or I might guess about the phone. I hoped it wasn't stolen the way the limo and Jeep almost certainly were.

I rang the number Skye gave him. I didn't really expect her to answer, but she did.

"Hi, kid," she said. Her voice sounded affectionate.

"It's not Nathan. Skye, how could you put him at risk? You're his only living relative apart from me."

"Did he have a good time? Did his little eyes sparkle? Yes or no?"

"If you wanted him to have fun, Skye, you could've taken him to the fun-fair. Don't tell me this was about anything other than skinning a rabbit."

"Well, as usual, you've missed the point. It was about making a stone bastard pay for what he'd done. Nathan was the perfect lure. He looked just like what the doctor ordered. And he's smart."

"If I see you anywhere near him again I'll call the cops on you – you *and* Mr Bo. You're right, Nathan *is* smart. He followed you too." That shut her up – for a few seconds.

Then she said, "Tell me, sis, what present did you buy yourself with my money?"

She'd probably looked in the bag when I went running after Nathan so there was no point in lying. I said, "A CD – *The Best of Blondie*. What's so funny?"

She stopped laughing and said, "That was Mr Bo's favourite band. He taught us to dance to Blondie numbers."

I was struck dumb. How could I have forgotten?

"Don't worry about it, sis," Skye said cheerfully. "On evidence like that, if you never qualify, and you never get to hang out your shingle, you can comfort yourself by knowing you'd have made a lousy psychotherapist. Oh, and Happy Holidays." She hung up.

Eventually I dried my eyes and went to the kitchen for a glass of wine. I sipped it slowly while I opened my books and turned on the computer. I will be a great psychotherapist – I can learn from the past.

Lastly I put my new CD on the hi-fi. It still made me want to dance. Mr Bo can't spoil everything I love.

FOXED

Peter Turnbull

Monday

THE MAN WAS about thirty years old, the woman, thought George Hennessey, was approximately the same age, perhaps a little younger. Both were slender, both athletic looking and they lay fully clothed side by side in the meadow, among the buttercups. Hennessey pondered their clothing, both wore good quality designer wear: she has a blouse and skirt and crocodile-skin shoes; he wore a safari jacket over a blue T-shirt and white trousers. Both had expensive wrist watches. She wore a wedding ring and an engagement ring; he wore a wedding ring only. And they both looked like each other, both in their feminine and masculine way, they looked similar, same balanced face, and Hennessey could see the basis for mutual attraction: if they looked at each other they'd see the opposite sex version of themselves. He took off his straw hat and brushed a troublesome fly from his face. He glanced around him, meadows, woods and fields in every direction and above a vast near cloudless sky, scarred it seemed to him by the condensation trail of a high flying airliner, KLM or Lufthansa probably, flying westwards from continental Europe to North America. Then, nearer at hand the blue and white police tape suspended from four metal posts which had been driven into the rock hard soil, for this was mid June and the Vale of York baked under a relentless sun.

Dr Louise D'Acre stood and glanced at Hennessey. "Well, all I can do is confirm Dr Mann's finding. Life is extinct. There is no obvious cause of death, not that I can see. They look as though they are sleeping, no putrefaction, just the hint of rigor, but they are definitely sleeping their final sleep. If you have done here, they can be removed to the York City Hospital for the post-mortem." Dr D'Acre was a slim woman in her forties, close-cropped hair, a trace of lipstick, but very, very feminine. She held a brief momentary eye contact with George Hennessey and then turned away.

"Yellich." Hennessey turned to his sergeant. "Have we finished here? Photographs, fingerprints?"

"Yes, all done and dusted. Still to sweep the field though."

"Of course." Hennessey turned to Louise D'Acre. "All done."

"Good. I'll have the bodies removed then." She placed a rectal thermometer inside her black bag. "Just as soon as they've been identified, then I'll see what I find."

"Identification won't be a problem."

"You think so?"

"Two people, young, wealthy, both married, probably to each other … they'll be socially integrated and easily missed. It's the down and outs estranged from any kin that take a while to be identified."

"I can imagine."

"Nothing so useful as a handbag or a wallet to point us in the right direction. Strange really, if they had been robbed, their watches would have gone."

"There's definitely the hand of another here though," Louise D'Acre spoke quietly. "What I can tell you is that they died at the same time, at the same instant, possibly within a few seconds of each other, as if in a suicide pact, but with such a pact, we would expect to see some evidence of suicide, a bottle of pills, a firearm. Death came from without, most definitely, by which I mean they didn't die of natural causes; two people, especially in the prime of life, do not die from natural causes at the same time in the same immediate, side by side proximity of each other. They just don't. But I'll get there." She smiled and nodded and walked away across the meadow, of green grass, ankle-high buttercups, and of the occasional fluttering blue butterfly, to the road where her distinctive motorcar was parked beside a black, windowless mortuary van.

* * *

Wealth. It was the one word which spoke loudly to Hennessey. He'd used it in talking to Dr D'Acre earlier that morning and now examining the clothes he used it again. "There's money here, Yellich. Real wealth."

"There is isn't there?" Yellich examined the clothing; all seemed new, very little worn, even the hidden-from-view underclothing had a newness about them. His offhand comment about there being nothing useful like a name stitched to the collars earned him a disapproving glance from the Chief Inspector. "Well I don't know about the female garments," Yellich struggled to regain credibility, "but you know, sir, there's only one shop in the Vale of York that would sell gents clothing at this quality and price and that's 'Phillips and Tapely's' near the Minster."

"Ah...I'm a Marks and Spencer man myself."

"So am I, sir, police officer's salary being what it is, but you can't help the old envious eye glancing into their window as you walk past. Only the seriously wealthy folk go there, only the 'Yorkshire Life' set. So I believe."

"Be out of my pocket as well then. Right, Yellich, you've talked yourself into a job. You'll have to take photographs of the clothing, especially the designer label, and take the photographs to the shop..."

"Phillips and Tapely's?"

"Yes...the actual clothing will have to go to the Forensic Science lab at Wetherby to be put under the microscope."

"Of course."

"Every contact leaves a trace, and often said trace is microscopic. I'll ask the advice of the female officers about the female garments, they might suggest a likely outlet."

* * *

Yellich being a native of York knew the value of walking the medieval walls when in the city centre, quicker and more convenient than the twentieth-century pavements below. That day the walls were crowded with tourists, but it didn't stop his enjoyment of the walk, the railway station, the ancient roofs, the newer buildings blending sensitively and the Minster there, solid, dependable, a truly magnificent building in his view. Without it there just wouldn't be a city. He stepped off

the wall, as he had to at Lendal Bridge, walked up Museum Street
and on into Drummond Place, and right at the Minster where stood
the half-timbered medieval building that was the premises of Phillips
and Tapely's, Gentlemen's Outfitters since 1810. Yellich pulled open
the door, a bell jangled, and he stepped into the cool, dark silence
and, he found, somewhat sleepy atmosphere of the shop; with dull-
coloured rather than light-coloured clothing on display, of wooden
counters and drawers constructed with painstaking carpentry. A
young man, sharply dressed, near snapped to attention as Yellich
entered the shop. "Yes, sir, how can I help you?"

"Police." Yellich showed his ID, and was amused by the crestfallen
look on the assistant's face as he realized he wasn't going to sell anything,
that this caller was not a customer. "I wonder if you can help me?"

"If I can, sir."

"I have some photographs here … " Yellich took the recently
produced black-and-white and colour prints from a brown envelope,
and placed them on the counter, " … of clothing, as you see … "

"Yes … we do sell clothing like this. I presume that's what you'd
like to know?" said with a smile, and Yellich began to warm to the
young man. "The jacket particularly, and the shoes … the label
'Giovanni', an Italian manufacturer, very stylish, favoured by the
younger gentleman … We are the only outlet for the 'Giovanni'
range in the north of England."

"Good, progress … " Yellich handed the shop assistant a photo
graph of the male deceased who appeared as though he was in a
restful, trouble-free sleep. "Do you recognize this gentleman?"

"As a customer? No I don't but we don't have many such young
customers … Mr Wednesday will help you if anyone can. Top of the
stairs, turn left. Mr Wednesday is the under manager. I'd escort you,
sir, but this is what we call the 'door' counter, always has to be
staffed. I welcome and say 'good day' to customers as they enter and
leave, as well as sell, of course."

"Of course."

"Just keep walking when you turn left, his office is the door just
beyond 'evening wear'."

"Just after evening wear," Yellich echoed.

"I'll let him know you're on the way up, sir." The assistant reached below the counter and lifted a telephone.

James Wednesday, for that was the name on the door of his office, was a short and portly man, rather severely dressed, to Yellich's taste, in his black suit. He had the appearance of an undertaker, and Yellich found him to have the sombre, serious manner of an undertaker. His office window looked out on to Minster Yard and the Minster itself. He invited Yellich to sit in the upholstered leather chair which stood in front of his desk. The chair creaked as Yellich sat.

"This photograph, Mr Wednesday," Yellich handed the photograph of the deceased male to the under manager. "Do you recognize him? One of your customers perhaps?"

"Yes. I can. It's Dominic Westwood, yes, that's Mr Westwood the younger all right. He has an account with us. Pays it sometimes as well, unlike most of our customers, who seem to think that a man really shouldn't pay his tailor."

"How do you stay in business?" Yellich couldn't resist the question.

"Often by refusing credit when debt has reached a certain level, by charging interest on overdue accounts and occasionally our lawyers have to make a claim on the estate of a customer if they have departed this life with outstanding debt to the shop. We stay afloat, Mr Yellich, and have done so for two hundred years. So, the police, a photograph of one of our customers who appears to be sleeping – has this particular customer departed his life perchance?"

"Perchance he has."

"Oh dear, it's so tedious making a claim on the estate of the departed, but I don't do it, personally ... " He tapped the head of the compact computer on his desk and Yellich was amused that a very conservative gentlemen's outfitters can still embrace modern technology. "So ... " James Wednesday spoke with a matter-of-fact, no trace of emotion manner. "Dominic Westwood, son of Charles Westwood, grandson of Alfred Westwood, gentlemen of this shire. All three have outstanding accounts. Dominic owes us £5,000, not a large sum, his credit limit is £20,000, last paid us two years ago, he owed over £10,000. Both his father and grandfather were customers, I dare say that's why the manager allowed him a £20,000 credit limit."

"Address?"

"His, Westwood the younger? It's the Oast House, Allingham."

"Allingham?"

"A small village to the north and east of York."

"We'll find it. Is he, was he, married?"

"Oh yes, he married Davinia Scott-Harrison a year or two ago. It was the wedding of the year in the Vale. We sold or hired much of the costumes."

"We'll go and visit the house." Yellich retrieved the photograph. "Thank you, you've been very helpful."

***

"They're not man and wife." George Hennessey spoke softly.

Yellich gasped. "I assumed the female…"

"It's always dangerous to assume, Sergeant. Very dangerous. The female deceased is believed to be one Wendy Richardson, aged about twenty-nine years. Wife of Herbert Richardson, gentleman farmer."

"How did you find her name, sir?"

"Exactly the same way as you found his, sergeant. I showed the clothes to a group of female officers; they told me that the only outlet for clothing of that cost in York is an outlet called Tomkinson's. I asked D.C. Kent to visit the shop which is in St Leonard's Place, very small frontage she tells me, but a deep floor area, and four storeys. But the staff recognized 'madam' in the photograph and the manager gave her address. 'Penny Farm' in the village of… can you guess?"

"Allingham."

"Got it in one. Not man and wife, but lived in the same village, were of the same social class, and in death were neatly laid out side by side, as if peacefully sleeping."

***

Hennessey watched the man from out of the corner of his eye. The curtain was pulled back by a solemn nurse who tugged a sash cord, and revealed Wendy Richardson with a clean face, wrapped tightly in bandages so that only her forehead to her chin was exposed; even the side of her head was swathed in starched white linen. She lay on a trolley tightly tucked into the blankets and was viewed through a large pane of glass, in a darkened room, so that by some trick of light and shade, she appeared to be floating peacefully in space.

"Yes," the man nodded, "that is my wife," then breathed deeply, and hard, and then lunged at the glass and cried, "Wendy! Wendy!" It was all the overacting George Hennessey wanted to see. He knew then, as only an old copper would, that he was standing next to a guilty man.

Hennessey smiled and nodded to the nurse who closed the curtain.

"Do you know how she died?" Herbert Richardson turned to Hennessey. He was a big man, huge, a farmer's hands, paw-like. His eyes were cold and had anger in them, despite a soft voice.

"We don't." Hennessey and he walked away from the room down a corridor in the York City Hospital. "We don't suspect natural causes, but there's no clear cause of death."

They walked on in silence, out of the hospital building into the sunlit expanse of the car park which Hennessey scanned for sight of Louise D'Acre's distinctive car, and seeing the red and white and chrome Riley circa 1947, her father's first and only car, a cherished possession, lovingly kept, allowed his eyes to settle on it for a second or two. Then he turned his thoughts to the matter in hand. "When did you last see your wife, Mr Richardson?"

"What!? Oh … don't know … sorry, can't think."

"Well, today's Monday … "

"Yes … well, yesterday morning. She went out at lunch time, just before really, about eleven-thirty, to meet her sister she said. Phoned me to say she'd be staying at her sister's house overnight, so I wasn't to worry if she didn't return. She often said that. She and her sister were very close."

They stopped at Richardson's gleaming Range Rover.

"You're a farmer, I believe, Mr Richardson?"

"Yes, I don't do much of the actual work, I have a manager to attend to that. I'm more of a pen-pusher than a bale-heaver, if you see what I mean."

"I think I do." He patted the Range Rover. "It clearly pays."

"Don't be too taken in by the image. It's run out of the business, still being paid for as well."

"Even so ... Mr Richardson, I can tell you that your wife was found out of doors; she and a deceased male were lying next to each other."

"She was what!?" Richardson turned to face Hennessey.

"She was lying next to the life extinct body of a man we believe to be called Dominic Westwood."

"Westwood?"

"Do you know the name?"

"Westwood ... there's a family with that name in the village but we do not mix socially."

"I think he will be of that family. Allingham is not a large village, there cannot be many Westwoods."

"I know only the one family in the village of that name."

"I see. Were you and your wife happily married?"

"Very. We hadn't been married long and we were enthusiastic about our union, wanted children. Yes, yes, we were happy."

"You know of no one who'd want to harm your wife?"

"No one at all. She was well liked, much respected." Richardson opened the door of his Range Rover.

"Where will you be if we need to contact you, Mr Richardson?"

"At the farm. Penny Farm, Allingham. Large white Georgian house, easily seen from the village cross."

* * *

"Yes, that is my husband," Marina Westwood said, and she said it without a trace of emotion. Then she put her long hair to her nose and sniffed. "Chlorine." She turned to Hennessey. "The constable said I could dry but not shower. I was in the pool you see, when the constable came, told me I was needed to identify someone. I wanted to shower the chlorine out of my hair but that takes an hour. So he said I couldn't. Smells of chlorine. Shower when I get back."

Detached, utterly completely detached. Hennessey was astounded, frightened even. This smartly dressed woman with long, yellow hair, high heels to compensate for her small stature, was looking through a pane of glass at the body of her husband and all she was concerned about was the chlorine in her hair. "Yes," she said, "that's Dominic. He looks like he's sleeping, sort of floating. I thought you were going to pull him out of a drawer."

And the nurse, used to many and varied emotions at the viewing of the deceased for purposes of identification, could only gasp at Marina Westwood's lack of emotion.

Hennessey nodded his thanks to the nurse who shut the curtains and seemed to hurry from the room – to escape Marina Westwood? To tell her colleagues what she witnessed? Hennessey thought probably both.

"Your husband died in mysterious circumstances, Mrs Westwood." Hennessey and she remained in the viewing room for a few moments.

"Oh?"

"He was found deceased in the company of a woman identified as Wendy Richardson, of Penny Farm, Allingham."

"Oh."

"Do you know her?"

"Yes…no…know of her, not speak to."

"Do you know of anyone who'd want to harm your husband, Mrs Westwood?"

"I don't. Dominic had no enemies. Rivals perhaps, but no enemies."

"He was a businessman?"

"He had a computer company. Software."

Whatever that is, thought Hennessey, who was proud to be the last surviving member of the human race who didn't possess or know how to use a computer.

"A farm worker found the bodies," Hennessey confirmed. "He thought they were two lovers, though it was a bit early in the morning for that sort of thing. Also thought they were a bit long in the tooth for it as well, but left them at it. When he returned, retracing his steps an hour later, saw they hadn't moved, he took a closer look. And we are here."

"I was getting a bit curious." She sniffed at her hair. "I wondered where he'd got to when he didn't turn up last night. I thought he had had too much beer again, and stayed somewhere rather than drive home. He's done that before. He's sensible like that."

"Who would benefit from his death, do you know?"

"Me, I suppose, I'm his wife. I'll get everything. Everything that's paid for anyway. Debt didn't seem to bother Dominic."

"Were you happily married?"

She shrugged her shoulders.

***

Yellich drove home to his modest new-build house in Huntingdon, to his wife and son. His wife explained that Jeremy had been "impossible" all day and she needed "space", so she put on a hat and went for a walk. Yellich went into the living room. Jeremy, cross legged and sitting far too close to the television set, turned and beamed at his father. Yellich smiled back. Jeremy was twelve years old, he could tell the time and point to every vowel sound letter in the alphabet, including the letter "y".

***

Hennessey too drove home, to his detached house in Easingwold, to a warm welcome from "Oscar", his brown mongrel. Later in the evening, he stood in the landscaped rear garden which had been planned by his wife shortly before she died, suddenly, inexplicably, as if she fainted, but it was life, not consciousness, which had left her. "Sudden Death Syndrome" was entered on her certificate, "aged twenty-three years". And in the thirty years since her death, her garden, where her ashes were scattered, had matured to become a place of tranquillity. Each day, winter and summer, rain or shine, Hennessey would stand in the garden telling Jennifer of his day. "Just lying there," he said to the grass, to the shrubs, to the apple trees, to the "going forth" at the bottom of the garden, where lived the frogs in a pond, "the farm worker thought they were lovers at first. Don't like the widow of the deceased male, haven't made up my mind about the widower, but the widow, she's an odd fish and no mistake."

Tuesday

Hennessey held the phone to his ear. "They drowned?"

"That's what I said." Louise D'Acre trapped her phone between her ear and her shoulder, using both hands to read through her notes. "In fresh water, or they had had a heart attack."

"I'm sorry, Dr D'Acre, I don't follow." Hennessey moved the phone from one ear to the other as he "heard" Dr D'Acre smile down the phone.

"I'm the one who should be sorry, I'm not making a great deal of sense, am I? I was puzzled because the cause of death was apparent upon investigation, both corpses show evidence of vagal inhibition of the heart, which brought on a fatal heart attack. Death from such causes is often associated with shock, especially in the frail elderly, but as I pointed out, both died at exactly the same time. So what caused two young and healthy people to die of shock at the same time? That had me foxed. And if their deaths hadn't been linked, if their bodies had been found miles apart for example and at different times, I probably wouldn't have looked for a link, and so put death down to heart failure, cause by vagal inhibition. But they were clearly linked, so I had a closer look and found the answer in the marrow of the long bones."

Thus far Hennessey had written "heart attack" on his notepad but continued to listen patiently.

"I found diatoms in the long bones."

"Diatoms?"

"Wee beasties, as a Scotsman might say. Micro-organisms that live in the water, they get into the marrow of the long bones of a drowning victim. They differ from salt water to fresh water, these are fresh-water diatoms. The victims blood has expanded in the veins caused by the fresh water joining the blood stream, salt water doesn't do that, so they drowned in fresh water. And I would guess a struggle for life induced vagal inhibition, which brought on a heart attack. No signs of violence though, except for small areas of light bruising round the ankles of both victims. Both of her ankles, and one of his ankles."

"The ankles?"

"They were held face down in a large body of water by someone holding their ankles. The water was clean, not polluted, and heavily chlorinated. A swimming pool, for example."

"Funny you should say that."

"Why, is that significant?"

"Very."

"Well, diatoms differ from one body of water to another; if you could obtain a sample of water from the pool in question, I could tell you if our two friends here drowned in that pool."

* * *

"What are you looking for, boss?" Yellich drove out to Oast House, Allingham.

"A swimming pool." Hennessey sat in the front passenger seat and went on to tell Yellich about Marina Westwood's hair smelling of chlorine; he also told him about diatoms and vagal inhibition.

The Westwood house in Allingham was a sprawling bungalow set in expansive grounds. A large car and a small car stood in front of the building, saying clearly "his and hers".

Marina Westwood opened the door almost immediately upon Hennessey ringing the door bell. She looked surprised to see Hennessey. Hennessey remarked upon the fact.

"No...no..." she stammered. She was dressed fetchingly in faded jeans, leather belt and a blue T-shirt. "Well I suppose I am...I thought that yesterday was it, just identify him. What do you want?"

"Your husband died in suspicious circumstances. We'd like to look at your house."

"Do you have a warrant? On television..."

"Do we need one?" asked Hennessey.

"Are you hiding something?" asked Yellich.

"No," she shrugged offhandedly, and stepped aside, allowing the police officers to step over the threshold.

It was a large, spacious house inside, very light, very airy, with interior walls of unfaced brick.

"Where is the swimming pool?" Hennessey asked suddenly.

"Down there." Then Marina Westwood's face paled.

Hennessey saw her pale and he knew a chord had been struck, and he knew this inquiry was drawing to an early close. It was so often the case, he thought, before you look at the outlaws look at the in-laws. "If you'd lead the way?"

Marina Westwood led them down a narrow corridor to the indoor swimming pool. Thirty-feet long, twenty wide, brick walls on three sides, the fourth wall was given over to tall windows which looked out over the rear lawn. Hennessey took a test tube from his pocket and knelt and dipped it into the pool and sealed the contents. "You haven't changed the water in this pool since they drowned in it, have you?"

"No."

A pause, a look of horror flashed across her face. Marina Westwood screamed and ran from the poolside into the body of the house. Yellich lunged at her as she ran past him, missed and started to run after her.

"Don't." Hennessey placed the test tube in his jacket pocket. "She's not running from us, she's running from herself, either that or she's engaging with life for the first time. Either way, we'll find her sobbing on the sofa somewhere."

In the event they found her on the rear patio looking out over the garden, sobbing quietly. Hennessey stood beside her.

"You know," she said, "this was all going to be mine."

"Was."

"Can't profit from a crime, can you?"

"No."

"His brother will inherit it all now."

"But it wasn't your idea to murder them?"

"No, it was his."

"Richardson?"

"Yes," she nodded as she watched a pair of swans, keeping perfect stations with each other like aircraft in formation, swept low over the house. "Won't see that goal will I?"

"No. No, you won't. Wasn't even your idea, was it?"

"No. It was his. My marriage wasn't good. My husband was carrying on with Wendy Richardson. I found out about it. Went to see Herbert Richardson. He went cold with anger. He said we should do something. I told him that every Sunday afternoon they swim at our house, I'm out then, but I know they do it. I gave him a key. Came back Sunday evening and he was in the house, by the pool, soaked to the skin. My husband and her lying on the poolside. He'd just jumped into the pool, grabbed them, held them by their ankles face down until they drowned. He's a big man, strong enough to do that."

"Then?"

"Well, then we dressed them. It's not easy dressing a dead body."

"I can imagine."

"But we managed it. Took them out and laid them side by side in a field. Herbert Richardson said, 'That'll fox 'em.'"

"Which it did," Hennessey thought… "and there lay your undoing."

"Where will we find Richardson now?"

"At home. He said to carry on as though nothing had happened. So he'll be at Penny Farm. There's nothing between us, me and him. We have nothing in common."

And Hennessey thought, but did not say, "Except double murder. You've got that in common."

* * *

That evening, with both Herbert Richardson and Marina Westwood in the cells having been charged with the murders of Dominic Westwood and Wendy Richardson, Hennessey drove out to Skelton, taking an overnight bag with him. He walked up to a half-timbered house and tapped on the door. The door was opened, by a woman who smiled warmly at him.

"Evening, madam." Hennessey stepped over the threshold and kissed the woman.

"The children are in bed," said Louise D'Acre. "We can go straight up."

MURDER

Nicholas Royle

W ITH THE OCEAN in front of you and waves crashing only a few feet below, close enough for you to taste the salty spray on the air, Canglass Point feels like one of the ends of the Earth. Great black-backed gulls hang steady in the buffeting wind, the bold curly bracket of their wingspan tipping this way and that, while further out gannets cut through the white space like dashes, before one turns into a W as it dives, then a Y and finally, as it drops into the sea, an almost perfect I.

If you were to climb the rock ledges behind you, they would eventually yield to a plateau of close-cropped grassland 120 feet above the waves that in turn leads to a gentle climb to the top of Slievagh more than 600 feet high. If you're likely to spot the blood-dipped beak of the glossy black chough anywhere on the mainland, you're likely to spot it here, somewhere between hilltop and cliff.

In the middle of the plateau is a hole 150 feet by 100. The only way to approach the edge – on your belly. A sheer drop, the odd grassy ledge from which there's no route back up and only one way down. Narrow bands of black rock forced by unimaginable pressures into a series of looping curves. A jagged archway at the western end leading to the ocean, the deep water clear enough to reveal rocks at the bottom.

If you walked over the edge one night, no one would ever know. If you ran down the hill on a foggy day, they would never find you. The waves would drag you out into the ocean to become food for fish. Picked clean, your skeleton would disintegrate and sink to the sea bed to be found, maybe, a few pieces anyway, a bone at a time in trawl nets over decades to come.

* * *

My friends Alice and John stay in a farmhouse in the west of Ireland every year with their friends Virginia and Donald. The four of them are academics with elevated positions in English departments at various universities – in the north of England in Alice and John's case, while Virginia and Donald live and work in the US.

Academia is meant to be an incestuous world, but if you avoid conferences and turn down ridiculously low-paid offers to work as an external examiner, it can be fairly isolating. I have heard of Humanities departments where nobody knew that a colleague had left, and another where a senior lecturer was challenged on entry to the building since it was believed she had retired. My wife, Diana, is Professor of English and head of department – twin roles that exact a steep price in terms of simple happiness. Nothing pleases me more than hearing her unselfconsciously girlish laughter, whether prompted by TV comedy or dinner party or (still occasionally) something I have said. But laughter is rare; I'm more likely to hear "I could kill that woman" or "I despair, I just despair". My professional life, as a fractional lecturer in creative writing, is less stressful.

I first met Alice at a conference on motivation in crime fiction held at the University of Verona, which marked one of my few forays from southern England, since when we have enjoyed a regular and stimulating correspondence. At first we would write to each other about books and birds, two shared passions. We maintained a week-long exchange of emails in which we talked about collective nouns for different types of birds. We would also discuss Virginia and Donald. I would lightly tease Alice about what I perceived as her tendency always to defer to them. I knew, for instance, that it was always Virginia and Donald who made the farmhouse booking, after which they would invite Alice and John to join them. Virginia and Donald would accept payment of half the rent, but they would handle all dealings with the owners, and either they gave the impression – or allowed Alice and John to form the understanding – that they were somehow vaguely in control.

Last year, in the early spring, Alice emailed me to ask if Diana and I wished to join them for a week's holiday in the west of Ireland.

"In the farmhouse? Is there room for six?"

Alice explained that she and John, having heard nothing from Virginia and Donald, had taken the initiative and emailed them to say they were thinking of going to the farmhouse again and wanted to check to see what Virginia and Donald's plans were before asking anyone else to join them instead.

"We got a noncommittal answer," Alice wrote. "I inferred that they didn't really want to go this year, but didn't want to give offence by saying so straight out."

After which, Alice had let a few weeks go by before asking Diana and me if we wanted to join them.

"You'd love it," she wrote to me. "Oystercatchers, rock pipits, even reed buntings. And there's always a murder of crows in the field behind the farmhouse."

"How many crows make a murder?" I asked.

We decided on three; two would be pushing it.

I said I would talk to Diana and we would look at our diaries.

A week later, Alice telephoned. Virginia and Donald had been in touch to propose the same arrangement as usual.

"Oh," I said.

"Oh no, you were going to say you would join us, weren't you?"

"Well, I know I hadn't got back to you, but you know how it is," I said.

"Oh damn! I would much rather we could go with you and Diana."

"We'll go another year," I said. "Don't worry about it."

I didn't hear from Alice for a while and assumed she was busy, which I certainly was, having agreed to be an external for a neighbouring institution. Plus I was trying to complete a couple of papers for academic journals to bolster my department's RAE submission.

These two papers finally off my desk and with days of unending rain denting any hopes of a decent summer, I emailed Alice to ask how the week in Ireland had gone. She replied with a brief report on bird species spotted. The reed buntings had materialized, also gannets, great black-backed gulls and lots and lots of crows.

"A murder?" I asked.

"Oh yes."

It continued to rain and although Diana and I ticked the days of August off the calendar, we never really felt that summer had arrived before the leaves started to change colour and the return to university unequivocally announced the arrival of autumn. The new term and the next were busier than ever and when Alice emailed in the spring to ask if we would like to join them for a week in the farmhouse, I didn't even have time to enter into banter about their needing to check first with Virginia and Donald.

The farmhouse is situated on a peninsula. You have to drive through the town – a single street lined with shops and pubs with hand-painted wooden signs – then turn left on to the stone bridge. Once over the river, you head left again. There are fewer houses and the hedgerows are alight with a fiery combination of purple and red fuchsias and bright orange crocosmia lucifer.

As you approach the end of the peninsula, the road turns a sharp left in front of a shallow bay and after a hundred yards you have to stop to open a gate. Now on private land, you may take pleasure in leaving your safety-belt unfastened. The way is rutted; grass grows in a line down the middle of the path. Cows amble in the fields alongside. Like clockwork soldiers, jackdaws march.

In the farmyard, hens will scatter. A marmalade cat may be lying on a bale of silage enjoying the low sunlight. Gravel will crunch beneath your tyres and your handbrake will sound a little like the ratcheting cry of a magpie in the otherwise still air of the late afternoon.

They appeared on the doorstep, Alice implausibly attractive for an academic with her long golden hair, hazel eyes and plump red lips, while John's wide-eyed grin hovered somewhere between boyish enthusiasm and the honest astonishment of a man who still can't quite believe his luck.

We got out of the car, joints creaking after the long drive from Dún Laoghaire. I stretched theatrically, but necessarily; Diana approached the open arms of Alice and fell into her embrace. I shook hands with John, who was as hearty as ever.

A third person had appeared between Alice and John. Blonde, sun-blushed from working outdoors, she was introduced by Alice as Marie, the owner.

"Ah, it's grand to meet you, so," Marie said, surprising and unsettling us with sudden warmth and hugs.

We all moved back inside where Alice resumed food preparation. She was in the middle of peeling vegetables. John put the kettle on for a cup of tea. Personally I would have killed for a glass of Guinness, but four mugs had been lined up on the work surface. Granted they looked as if they were china, but still.

As he removed the spent tea bags from the pot, John turned to Marie.

"So you put these on the flowerbeds?" he said to her.

"Around the hydrangeas, yes. They work a treat."

I helped Alice, gathering the potato peelings.

"What about these, Marie?" I asked. "You must have a compost heap somewhere?"

"Just put them in the back field," she said. "The cat'll like them."

I looked at her and she beamed at me. I turned to Diana, frowning, then looked back at Marie.

"Really?" I said.

"Oh yes, the cat'll like them."

Neither Diana nor I had ever owned a cat, but I was pretty sure cats didn't eat potato peelings.

Marie eventually left and we opened a bottle of wine. The food was good, the company excellent. Night fell softly around the farmhouse almost without our noticing.

I awoke to the cawing of crows in the back field. Diana was sleeping quietly. I eased my body out of the unfamiliar bed, grabbed my jeans and a T-shirt and walked softly out of the room.

As I brushed my teeth, I wondered if Alice and John, who now had the much better bedroom upstairs, had previously been obliged to use the one in which Diana and I had slept. It was a strangely inhospitable room, chilly despite the season. The tiled floor was cold underfoot. The convex mattress precluded a decent night's sleep.

Finding the kitchen empty, I wandered outside. The potato peelings still lay in a little pile in the back field where I had thrown them the night before. Obviously the cat was not hungry.

Three or four crows picked at the topsoil in the middle of the field, among them a solitary rook. At this distance, I couldn't see the rook's white snout and identified it by its shaggy silhouette and awkward-looking gait in relation to its sleeker cousins. The birds were behaving against type since it is the rook that is sociable, while the territoriality of crows normally keeps their numbers down.

In the distance, the summit of Knocknadobar was still wreathed in low grey cloud. I imagined huge ravens tumbling acrobatically out of sight, their playful nature belied by their grim demeanour.

Alice was making tea. There was no sign of either Diana or John.

"I love this house," she said, running her hand along the grain of the worktop.

"I know," I said.

"No, I *really* love it," she said, looking out of the window.

I asked about the bedrooms and she confirmed they had used our room on all previous visits apart from the last one, when Virginia and Donald had sought to make amends for the confusion by offering Alice and John the upstairs suite.

Diana appeared dressed in loose flowing clothes and wearing a little make-up that helped to make her eyes shine. Her thick reddish-brown hair had gone wavy, as it always seemed to do when we went away anywhere; she hated it, but I loved it. I got up to give her a kiss and felt her body relax against mine. She needed this holiday. Over her shoulder I watched the crows moving about in a random pattern in the back field.

We went to a harbour on the north side of the peninsula where John and Alice swam and Diana read a book (as a reaction against creative writing students' ever lengthening portfolios she had brought a number of very short novels and was currently rereading Márquez's *Chronicle of a Death Foretold*) while I fished from the rocks, casting out a silver lure and retrieving it, a repeated action that seemed as if it might never end unless I actually caught a fish. This finally happened as Alice and John joined us on the rocks, Alice towelling the ends of her damp hair.

At first I assumed the lure had merely become snagged in weed, which had happened once every five or six casts. But on this occasion the weed pulled back. The rod tip bent and I felt that unique and familiar conflict – the desire to let the fish have its head and take line from the spool, thus extending the fight, balanced against the need to land the fish before it swam into weed. I managed a few turns on the reel and glimpsed the glimmer of a golden flank turning in the deep water just beyond the rocks. It was a decent size, but beaten. I used the lowest ledge of the rocks to land it and knelt to unhook the lure. I turned to display my catch to the others, who applauded.

"What is it?" Diana asked.

"It's our dinner," I said. "A pollack. Couple more like this and we'll eat well."

"Really?" Diana's eyes were wide. Perhaps she had thought I might put the fish back.

Alice stepped forward.

"May I?" she said and took the fish from me. She grasped its tail in her right hand and turned it over. In one swift movement, she cracked the top of its head against the nearest rock. I heard Diana gasp and John spoke his wife's name as if in reproach. Alice shrugged and dropped the dead pollack on the rocks. "Catch some more," she said, making it sound like a challenge.

Grilled and served with lemon and steamed green beans, pollack proves a more than adequate substitute for cod or haddock. A New Zealand sauvignon blanc or a pinot grigio will be the perfect accompaniment. At some point as the sky darkens, the house martins and swallows swooping over the back field will be replaced by bats, but you will be unable to identify the moment when this happens, or even if it actually has. The one thing you can be sure of is that the black dots in the background, the murder of crows, will not go away. They may change their configuration, flapping in and out of vision, altering their numbers, but two or three will always remain.

Scented candles will burn, keeping midges and mosquitoes at bay and causing shadows to flicker over faces. Intellectual arguments will ripple back and forth as the precise meanings of words will be debated, assumptions about the nature of existence questioned. Doubts, fears, uncertainties at the back of your mind will fade and retreat, but not quite disappear.

Conversation will turn, as usual, to books, to art, to films. Someone will talk about a black and white Czech film they have recently seen, made in 1968 but set in the 1930s. They will say it deserves to be better known. Someone else will confess to not liking subtitles. Another person will say that *The Third Man* is their favourite film of all time and you will remember the scene in the Ferris wheel, Harry Lime talking to Holly Martins, describing the people below as dots and asking him if he would really feel any pity if one of them stopped moving for ever.

The four of us in one car, we drove past the harbour where I had caught the pollack and on uphill towards the forest. We passed a rustle of reed buntings dispersing from their perch on a barbed-wire fence. Cows chewed on the long grass, their huge jaws grinding and crushing and it suddenly hit me. Cows. Cattle. *The cattle like them.*

"What are you smiling at?" Diana asked.

I grinned at her. "I'll tell you later."

When the road petered out in a pine wood, we left the car and threaded our way between the trees, startling a jay, which clattered away with a telltale flash of white rump.

Diana's question seemed to come out of nowhere.

"Don't you miss being here with your other friends?" she said. "Only, because you normally come with them."

I noticed John look at Alice, who merely grunted and made a dismissive gesture with her hand.

Leaving the wood, we tramped through bracken to the unmarked summit of Slievagh. Soon after we began our descent on the seaward side, I noticed a strange black disc on the surface of the promontory ahead of us. It reminded me of the black rubber mat a bowls player will drop on the green before starting to play. Because of the changing angle of slope and the lack of other topographical features, it was difficult to tell the size. I was walking with Diana; Alice and John had pulled ahead. We exchanged shrugs, puzzled looks.

It soon became obvious it was a hole, but how deep? Was it merely the result of peat cutting? Or a landslip? It was too big for a pot hole. Once we reached the plateau, the narrow angle meant the hole resembled a sheet of water sitting on the grass. Alice and John had reached the edge and were looking down. It took Diana and me a minute or so to join them and finally get a look over the edge.

"It's a long way down," Diana said.

Alice and John smiled.

"There's an easier way down to the sea over there," John joked, pointing to where the cliff edge and a series of huge boulders appeared to offer a reasonably easy climb down to the lower rocky ledges on to which the waves could be heard perpetually pounding. Diana left the edge of the hole and walked towards the boulders. John went with her.

I looked at Alice. We were both standing a few feet from the edge and several yards apart. Taking great care I knelt down, then eased myself on to my front so that I could see right over the edge. Alice followed suit. As I looked down at the waves sloshing against the rocks more than a hundred feet below, I could feel my heart beating against the cropped turf. I looked at the sheer rock face on the far side of the hole dotted with patches of grass that clung to the most negligible of ledges, running on a diagonal towards the bottom. Half-way up, my eye was drawn to the down-turned bright-red beak of a blue-black bird bigger than a jackdaw but smaller than a crow that was perched on one of the ledges. I caught my breath and looked up at Alice to see if she had seen it. She was looking at me and her scarlet lips formed a curve, but you couldn't really call it a smile.

DRIVEN

Ian Rankin

I'M THE ONE you all hate, the one you've been hearing and reading about. I was a hero for a short time, but now I'm the villain. Well, not *the* villain. Do you want to hear my side of the story? I have this need to tell someone what happened and why it happened. Here's the truth of it: I was brought up to believe in the sanctity of life, and this has been my downfall.

I am a son of the manse. A curious phrase; it seems to be used by the media as shorthand of some kind. But it happens also to be true. My father was a Church of Scotland minister in a career spanning nearly forty years. He'd known my mother since primary school. I was their only child. In my late teens, I calculated that impregnation (a word my father would probably have used) probably took place on their Isle of Mull honeymoon. Early July they were married (by my grandfather, also a kirk minister), and I entered the world on April 1st the following year. A hard birth, according to family legend, which may explain the lack of brothers and sisters. My mother told me once that she feared I'd been stillborn, so quiet was I. Even when the doctor slapped my backside, I merely frowned and gave a pout (family legend again).

"I knew right then, you'd grow up quiet," my mother would say. Well, she was right. I studied hard at school, did as little sport as possible, and preferred the library to the playground. At home, my father's den became my refuge. He'd collected thousands upon thousands of books, and started me with parables and other "wisdom stories", including the Fables of Aesop. I grew up, quite literally unable to hurt a fly. I would open windows to release them. I would lift worms from the baking summer paths and make a burrow for them with a finger-poke of the nearest soil, covering them over to shield them from the sun. I turned down my parents' offer of pets, aware that everything had to die and that I would miss them terribly when the time came. Nobody ever called me "odd"; not until very recently. But then you know all about that, don't you?

What you can't know is that I thought my upbringing normal and untroubling, and still do. After school, there was university, and after university a lengthy period of speculation as to what should come next. Lecturing appealed, but I was torn between Comparative Religion and Philosophy. I could train for "the cloth", but felt two generations of church service was perhaps enough. It wasn't that I didn't believe in God (though I had doubts, as many young people do); it was more a feeling that I would be better suited elsewhere. My father had taken to his bed, in thrall to the cancer which had slumbered inside him for years. My mother was strong, and then not so strong. I helped as best I could – shopping, cleaning and cooking. Between chores, I would retire to the den – it had become mine by default – and continue my studies. I learned at long last to drive, so as to be able to visit the supermarket, loading the car with porage oats, smoked fish and loose-leaf tea, tonic water, washing-powder and soap. Once a week I wrote out the shopping-list. Other days, I stayed home. Sometimes we would manoeuvre my father into the walled garden, a rug tucked around him, the transistor radio close to his ear. My mother would pretend to weed, so he couldn't see she wasn't able.

Then the day came when he asked me to kill him.

The bed had been moved downstairs, into the sitting room. There was a commode in one corner. Some furniture had been removed from the room, meaning the hallway was more cluttered than before. A few of his old congregation still visited, though my father was loath to let them witness his deterioration.

"Still, some people find it necessary," he told me. "It strengthens them to see others weaken."

"But it's kindness, too, surely," I answered. He merely smiled. It was a few days after this that, having just accepted another small beaker of the green opiate mixture, he said he was more than ready to die. I was seated on the edge of the bed, and reached out to take his hand. The skin was like rice-paper.

"That stuff you keep giving me – don't think I don't know what it is. Liquid morphine. A couple of glassfuls would probably do the job."

"You know I can't do that."

"If you love me, you will."

"I can't."

"You want to see me get worse?"

"There's always hope."

He gave a dry chuckle at that. Then, after a period of silence: "Best not say anything to Mother." I know now what I should have said to him: it's *your* fault I'm like this. *You* made me this way.

It took him another six weeks to die. Three months after his funeral, my mother followed him. They left me the manse, having bought it from the Church fifteen years before. The parish had moved the new minister and his young family into a new-build bungalow. After a time, I was forgotten about. My parents' old friends and parishioners stopped visiting. I think I made them feel awkward. They looked around the rooms and hallway, as if on the lookout for expected changes of décor or ornament. The bed, freshly made, was still downstairs. The commode was dusted weekly. The lawn grew wild, the beds went unweeded. But curtains were changed and washed seasonally. The kitchen gleamed. I ate sometimes at my father's old desk, a book propped open in front of me.

The years passed.

I became a keener driver – maps plotting my course into the countryside around the city, then further afield – west to Ullapool, north to the Black Isle. One daring long weekend, I travelled by ferry from Rosyth to the continent. I ate mussels and rich chocolate, but preferred home. Books travelled with me. I became adept at finding cheap editions in Edinburgh's various secondhand shops. Every now and then I would see a job advertised in the newspaper, and would send off for the application form. I never got round to returning them. My life was busy enough and fulfilling. I was reading Aristophanes and Pliny, Stendhal and Chekhov. I listened to my parents' records and tapes – Bach, Gesualdo, Vivaldi, Sidney Bechet. In the attic, I discovered a reel-to-reel deck with a box of tapes my father had recorded from the radio – concerts and comedy shows. I preferred the former, but concentrated fiercely on the latter. Laughter could be disconcerting.

Oh, God.

I say "Oh, God" because it's now time to talk about *him*. No getting around it; pointless to tell you any more about my shopping trips, tastes in music and books… All of it, pointless. My life has been condensed. For all of you, it begins with the moment I met *him*. Everything that I was up to that point you've reduced to words like "bachelor" and "loner", and phrases like "son of the manse". I hope I've shown these to be reductive. I'm not excusing myself; I feel my actions merit no apology. It was a country road, that's all. Not too far out of town, just beyond the bypass. A winding lane, edged with hedgerows. The sun was low in the sky, but off to one side. Then a bend in the road. Dvorak on Radio Three. A fence, with trees beyond it. Smoke, but not very much of it. A car, concertinaed against one of the largest trunks. Tyre-marks showing where it had torn through the fence.

I pulled to a stop, but only once I was safely past the bend. Flashers on, and then I ran back. A blue car, leaking petrol, its engine exposed. Windscreen intact, but frosted with cracks. Just the one figure inside. A man in the driving seat. He was conscious and moaning, head rolling. The airbag had worked. I managed to yank open his door. It made an ugly grating sound. He was not wearing the seatbelt.

"Are you all right?"

It was an effort to pull him from the wreck. He kept saying the word "No" over and over.

"You'll be okay," I assured him.

As I hauled him to safety, hugging him to me, his face was close to mine. He half-turned his head. I could feel his breath on my cheek. There was warm blood running from a wound in his scalp.

"Don't," he said. And then: "I'll do it again."

I realized almost immediately what he meant. No accident, but an attempt at suicide. Seatbelt unfastened, picking up speed as the bend came into view…

"No, you won't," I told him.

"Just leave me."

"No."

"Why not?"

"I believe in the sanctity of life."

I had laid him on the ground, a bed of leaves beneath. At first I took his spasm for a seizure of some kind, but he was laughing. Laughing.

"That's a good one," he was able to say at last, blood bubbling from the corners of his mouth. Another car had stopped. I walked towards it, hoping the driver would own a mobile phone. There was an explosion of hot air from behind me. The crashed car was on fire. The heat was bearable. The injured man, I realized, had craned his neck so he could watch me rather than the explosion. His shoulders were still shaking. A young couple had emerged from their open-topped sports car. I felt sure they would own phones; indeed, led lives which felt them necessary.

"You all right, pal?" the male said. He was wearing an earring. I nodded. His girlfriend was wide-eyed.

"Another minute, he'd've been toast," she commented. Then, fixing her eyes on me: "You're a hero."

A hero?

The description would send me to the den that night, to consult any books I could find. I didn't feel like I'd committed an act of bravery. I didn't feel "heroic". Heroes were for wartime, or belonged to the realm of mythology. I wished my father were still alive. We could have discussed the notion and its implications.

A police car had arrived first at the crash site, followed a few minutes later by the paramedics. The driver was sitting up by this time, arms wrapped around his chest. He was in his thirties, around the same age as me. His hair was thick, dark, and wavy, with just a few glints of grey. It had been a couple of days since he'd shaved. "Swarthy" was the description that came to mind. His eyes had dark rings around them. Tufts of chest-hair welled up from beneath his open-necked shirt. His arms were hairy, too. Even when I wasn't looking at him, I sensed he was keeping a careful eye on me. He had been holding a white handkerchief – my handkerchief – to his scalp-wound.

"He was trying to kill himself," I told one of the policemen. "That's a crime, isn't it?"

He nodded. "And we only prosecute the failures." I think he meant this light-heartedly, but I spent part of the evening mulling his words over, reading meaning into them.

"Did he say as much?" he asked me. I nodded. But later that night a different policeman came to my door with what he termed "a few follow-up questions". I learned that the man whose life I had saved was called Donald Thorpe, and that he was denying being suicidal. It was "just an accident", caused by his lack of acquaintance with the route and some mulchy leaves on the road surface.

"But he told me," I insisted. "He said he would do it again."

The officer stared at me. His hands were in his pockets. Previously, he'd seemed interested only in his surroundings, but now he asked me if I lived alone. When I nodded, he asked if the house had been in my family a long time.

"It has," I agreed.

"It's almost like a museum," he commented, looking around him again. "You could open it to the public." I decided to ignore this. "Gashes and bruises, maybe some pelvic damage and a rib that'll cause him gyp." He turned his attention back to me. "He was dazed when you reached him; might explain what you heard him say."

I made no reply.

"Papers'll be after you for a picture."

"Why?"

"They like the occasional feel-good story. You're a hero, Mr Jamieson."

"I'm not," I was quick to correct him. "I only did what anyone would do."

"Well, *you* were there. And that's all that matters."

Less than an hour after he left, the first reporter arrived. I started to let him into the house, but then thought better of it – which is why the word "recluse" appeared in his third or fourth version of the story.

"Just tell the readers what happened," he explained. "In your own words."

"Who else's would I use?"

He laughed as though I'd made a joke. He was holding a tiny recording device, holding it quite close to my mouth. But he was looking past me at the hall's "cramped furniture and outdated floral wallpaper" (as he himself put it later). I told him the story anyway, deciding to leave out the suicide bit.

"The other couple who stopped," he said, "they saw you drag the victim clear as the car burst into flames..."

"That's not quite how it happened."

But it was how he wrote the story up. It didn't matter that I'd told his recorder differently. I became the CRASH INFERNO HERO. When his photographer arrived on my doorstep, he asked me if I had any burns to my hands or arms, any blood-stained or charred clothing. I had already showered and changed into fresh clothes, so I shook my head. The bloodied handkerchief, discarded when the medics had arrived on the scene, was steeping in the sink.

"Any chance we can get a shot of you at the site?" he then asked. But he had second thoughts. "Car's probably already been towed..." He rubbed at the line of his jaw. "The hospital," he decided. "Bedside, how would that be?"

"I don't think so."

"Why not?"

How could I tell him? Meeting Thorpe, the first question I would need to ask would be: why did you lie? Why keep the suicide attempt a secret? And then: *will* you do it again? (Of course, I *would* meet Thorpe again, at his hospital bed. But that was for later.)

After further negotiation, the photographer settled for me on my doorstep, then standing beside my car, arms folded.

"Don't you feel a bit of pride?" he asked. "You're a bloody life-saver. What about a smile to go with it?"

I lost count of the number of pictures he took – well over twenty. And as he was finishing, another photographer arrived, five minutes ahead of *his* reporter. And so it went for much of the rest of the night. Even the neighbours became curious and emerged from their homes, to be collared and interviewed by the press.

Very quiet... private income... looked after both parents up to their death... no girlfriend... goes out in his car sometimes...

The Reluctant Hero.
Quick-Thinking Quiet Man.
Brave and Bashful.
Local Hero.

This last they used most often over the next few days. Faces I hadn't seen for a while came calling – members of my father's congregation, the ones who'd visited him during his illness. A neighbour over the back called to me one day and passed a home-baked cake across the fence. There were more requests from the media for bedside photos. Just a quick handshake. I appeared on two radio shows, and there was even talk of a civic reception, some sort of bravery award or medal. And then, just when it seemed to be quieting down, a call from the police.

"He'd like to see you. I said we'd pass on the message."

Meaning Robert Thorpe; Robert Thorpe wanted to see me.

"But why?"

"To say thanks, I suppose."

"I don't need him to say thanks." But then again, maybe I did. Maybe in saving his life I'd convinced him that life itself was worth living. And wouldn't it be heartening to hear him say as much?

So I went.

And I wonder now – was that my fatal mistake?

There were only a couple of photographers this time. They were waiting in the corridor outside Thorpe's ward. They had found a young nurse to stand next to the bed. She was to pretend to be changing a drip. I'd be shaking hands with the man I'd rescued. This was all being explained as we walked into the ward. Thorpe was sitting up. Part of his hair had been shaved, and the black stitches in his scalp looked fierce.

"Are you Mr Jamieson?" he asked, holding out a hand. I could only nod that I was. He gripped my hand and the cameras clicked. "As I keep telling them, I don't remember too much."

"But you're all right?"

"So the scan says."

"Just one more, please, gentlemen," one photographer was saying.

"How about a smile, Mr Jamieson?" asked the other.

"And if our glamorous assistant could lean a little further in towards the patient..." (He meant the nurse, of course.)

Then the other photographer took a call on his phone and handed it to me. "Newsroom want a word."

More questions, all about how I felt and what had been said to me. Then it was Thorpe's turn to speak.

"Saved my life, so I'm told...eternally grateful to him...don't know how I'll repay...It's all a bit of a blur..."

I realized I was drifting towards the swing-doors, keen to be leaving. But Thorpe waved for me to stay. When he handed the photographer's phone back, he asked if he and I could be left alone for a minute. One of the photographers was asking the nurse for her name and a contact number as they left. There was a chair next to the bed, so I sat down.

"I'm sorry," I said, "I didn't bring you anything." There was nothing on the bedside cabinet except a plastic jug of water and a beaker. No cards from family, no flowers or anything. Thorpe just shrugged.

"They're letting me out tomorrow."

"You'll be glad to get home."

He gave a low chuckle, reminding me of the crash scene. His eyes were boring into mine.

"'...the sanctity of human life'."

"You remember that much then?"

"I remember everything, Mr Jamieson."

I was silent for a moment. I wanted some of the water in the jug, but couldn't bring myself to ask.

"Go on," he said with a smile. "You're dying to ask."

"You were trying to kill yourself." It was a statement rather than a question.

"Is that what you think?"

"You didn't want to be saved. You said you'd do it again."

"Do what, Mr Jamieson?"

"Kill yourself."

"Is that what you told the police?"

I swallowed and licked my lips. I could feel sweat on my forehead. The ward was stifling. Thorpe gave a shrug.

"Doesn't matter anyway."

"*Are* you going to do it again?"

"I'm not going to kill myself, if that's what's bothering you."

"So it sunk in then?"

"What?"

"What I said to you about the sanctity of life."

"Is that what you want?"

I nodded again. Thorpe closed his eyes slowly.

"Go home, Jamieson. Enjoy it while you can."

"Enjoy what exactly?"

The eyes opened a little. "Everything," he whispered. To my ears, it seemed louder than any explosion.

You know what happened next.

Thorpe walked out of the hospital and disappeared. It was a couple of days before neighbours began to complain of a smell in the tenement stairwell. Police broke down the door on the second floor and found two bloodstained corpses. Ten days they'd been there. Both men were unemployed. They shared with a third, and he was missing. His name was Robert Thorpe. The car he'd crashed had belonged to one of the two. There were signs in the living room that a card game had been underway. Poker, according to reports. Cigarette-butts littered the carpet. They had been emptied from one of the murder weapons – a solid glass ashtray. It had been reduced to fragments by the force of impact against the first victim's skull. Three empty bottles of vodka, traces of cannabis, the remains of a dozen cans of super-strength lager…The second victim had attempted escape but made it only as far as the hallway. He had been punched, kicked and bludgeoned in what the media kept referring to as a "sustained and horrific assault", quoting one of the police officers.

Questions were asked. Why had police not checked on the flat in the aftermath of the crash? Why had none of the neighbours come forward earlier? What did it say about the state of our society that no one had intervened?

And why had Richard Jamieson felt it necessary to save the killer's life?

THE MONSTER WHO LIVED – that was the headline I'll always remember. Thorpe was pictured in his hospital bed, shaking my hand. It seemed to me that the pretty nurse should have been in the shot, but she wasn't. I was aware that software existed which could alter photographs. I wished they'd used it on me instead of her, but of course I was the subject of their follow-up stories. The journalists were back at my door. They wanted to know if I felt anger, embarrassment, even shame.

"Aren't you ashamed, Mr Jamieson?"

"Shouldn't he have been left to die?"

"Don't you regret …?"

"Didn't he say anything …?"

I stopped answering the door. I left the house only in the middle of the night, shopping at the 24-hour supermarket on Chesser Avenue. I kept the curtains closed in the den. I ate from tins and drank from cans. I even let the bin go uncollected, so they couldn't accost me as I walked up the path with it to the pavement.

Did I feel angry? No, not really. But I better understood the situation a few days later when he killed again. A shopkeeper this time, the event caught on the security camera which had been installed to deter shoplifters. It had failed to deter Thorpe. His haul consisted of cigarettes, alcohol and cash from the till. The victim left behind a wife and five children. My doorbell rang and rang. The voices called questions through the letter-box. One of them pretended to be a postman with a delivery. I opened the door.

"He's killed again, Mr Jamieson. Do you have anything to say to the grieving widow? She wouldn't be a widow if you'd … "

I slammed the door shut, but could still hear his voice.

Your father was a man of the church … your grandfather, too … how would they feel, Mr Jamieson?

Did I feel regret?

Did I feel shame?

Yes, yes, yes. Most definitely yes. And anger, too, eventually, as the meaning of his words sunk in. He hadn't wanted to be saved because he'd known he would do it again – as in kill again. *Don't... I'll do it again...* And I had allowed this to happen. I had allowed the monster to live.

The TV and radio kept me up to date with the manhunt. Police questioned me several times. Could I shed any light? I explained it to them as best I could. One of the officers was the same man who'd come to my house that night with the follow-up questions, the one who had doubted Thorpe's attempted suicide. He kept shifting in his chair, as if he could not get comfortable. His face was pale. I knew from the media that the police were under a good deal of pressure. They had let Thorpe go. They hadn't checked his flat. They hadn't noticed that the blood on his clothes belonged to more than one person. They shared a certain culpability with me in the minds of the press.

"If only you'd left him to die," the officer said as he paused on my doorstep.

"I thought I was doing the right thing."

"Turns out you were wrong, Mr Jamieson."

Wrong? But when I rescued him, he was still an innocent man, his crimes a secret. He was victim rather than monster, and I was the hero of the hour, wasn't I?

Wasn't I?

Well, wasn't I?

I turned to my father's library again in search of answers, but found too little comfort. There were books about the nature of evil and the more complex nature of good. Why do we do good deeds? Is it in our nature, or does communality dictate that what is best for others is also likely to be of benefit to us? Do people become bad, or are they born that way? Robert Thorpe's life was picked over in the days that followed. His father had been a domineering drunk, his mother addicted to painkillers. There was no evidence that he had been abused as a child, but he had grown up an outsider. His spells of employment were short and various. Girlfriends came and went. One opened her heart to a doubtless generous tabloid. He watched violent films. He liked loud rock music. He was "a bit of an anarchist". Photos were printed, showing the trajectory of the killer's life. A blurry child, clutching a funfair ice-cream. A teenager in sunglasses, no longer smiling for the camera. A man at a party, cigarette drooping from his mouth, sprawled across a sofa with a woman in his arms (her face softwared out, to preserve anonymity).

Lucky her.

The manhunt continued, but the media interest began to wane. There were rumours that Thorpe could have disguised himself and headed to Northern Ireland – no need of a passport. From there, it would have been straightforward to cross to Ireland proper. The Western Isles was another possibility. Or far to the south, melting into Manchester, Birmingham, or London. His photo was on show at every mainline station, and in shop windows and at bus stops. He had taken around three hundred pounds from the shopkeeper. It was only a matter of time before he struck again.

I started to emerge from my house, as a butterfly from its chrysalis. The neighbours showed little interest. There were no reporters waiting kerbside. But everywhere I went, Thorpe's eyes stared back at me from all those wanted posters. I felt I would never be free of him. I dreamed often of crashed cars, mangled corpses, stained carpets, shattered ashtrays. I reached into my parents' drinks cabinet for bottles of whisky and sherry, but found both foul beyond words. One night, I decided to go for a drive. I hadn't been out of the city since the evening of the crash. I found myself steering the same route, slowing at that curve in the road, headlights picking out the remaining scraps of police tape. From a distance, there was no other sign that anything had happened here. I drove on, stopping at the all-night supermarket on my way back into the city.

Of course he was waiting for me, but I couldn't know that. I parked the car in the driveway. I lifted out the bag of shopping. I unlocked the door of the house. I closed it after me, placing the bunch of keys on the table in the hall, the same way my father and mother would have done. There was a draught, meaning an open window. But I still wasn't thinking as I carried the shopping into the kitchen. Glass crunched underfoot. There was glass in the sink, too, and spread across the worktop. The window frame was gaping. I put down the shopping and checked the den. Someone had raided the drinks cabinet. I switched on the light in the living room. He was lying on my father's bed. The whisky bottle was on the floor next to him, emptied. He had his hands behind his head. He had twisted his body to face the doorway.

"Hello again," he said.

"What do you think you're doing here?"

He had removed the stitches from his scalp. The wound hadn't quite healed. There was a baseball-cap resting on his chest. He placed it to one side as he began to swing his legs over the side of the bed.

"I missed you," he said. "This where you sleep?"

"I sleep upstairs."

"That's what I reckoned. Took a look around, hope you don't mind."

"The window's broken."

"Windows can be fixed, Richard."

"How did you find me?"

"Your old man's still listed in the phone book – Reverend Jamieson." Thorpe wagged a finger. "Time you did something about that."

"You've been killing people."

"Yes, I have."

"Why?"

There was that smile again, as if he knew some joke no one else in the world did. "I couldn't believe it," he said, "when they took me to hospital, cleaned me up and had me checked. And the cops, asking me questions but never quite the *right* questions. Every time those doors swung open, I reckoned I was done for. But they patched me up and then they let me walk right out of there." He was pointing towards the doorway. He was still sitting on the edge of the bed, and it seemed to me that he was offering me the chance to escape, indicating the direction I should take. But I was too busy listening to his story.

"It struck me then," he went on, "that I could do it again."

"Kill, you mean?"

He nodded, eyes fixed on mine. "Again and again and again. So tell me, Mr Richard Jamieson, how does that square with your 'sanctity of life'? What does the Bible tell you about that, eh?"

When I didn't say anything, he raised himself from the bed and walked towards me.

"Is this where your old man died?" he asked.

I nodded.

He was very close to me now. He had forgotten his baseball cap. He squeezed past me without making eye contact. I followed him into the hall. He turned left into the den.

"This where he spent all his time?"

I nodded again, but he had his back to me, so I cleared my throat. "Yes," I said.

"And now it's all yours. We're not so different, you and me, Richard."

"So biology would have us believe."

"The old human DNA ... go back far enough, we'd even be related, am I right?"

"I suppose so."

"Darwin says the apes, the Bible says Adam and Eve. Do you think Adam and Eve were apes, Richard?"

"I don't know." He had turned to face me. "What are you doing here?" I asked him again. "The police are looking for you."

"But they're not very clever – we both know that."

"How clever do they need to be?"

He answered with a twitch of the mouth. "I've been thinking about you, Richard. Papers have been giving you a hard time. They reckon you should have let me top myself. How do you feel about that?" He was resting the base of his spine against my father's desk, one foot crossed over the other, arms folded. When I didn't answer, he repeated the question.

"Why do you need to know?" I asked him instead.

"Does there always have to be a reason? I'd have thought you'd have learned that much, despite all these bloody books." He nodded towards the shelves. "I'll tell you why I wanted to see you again – to thank you properly." He gave a bow from the waist, still with arms folded. Then he eased himself upright. "Now, if you'll excuse me ... "

"What are you going to do?"

"You know what I'm going to do, Richard."

"You're going to kill again?"

"And again and again and again." His voice was almost musical. "And all thanks to you and your sanctity of life. Learned from your father, I'm guessing, years before you watched him wither and die. Were there any words of comfort, Richard? Did he meet his maker with a happy and a fulsome heart? Or had he twigged by then that it's all a joke?" He waved his arm towards the books. "All of it."

He waited for my answer, then gave up, brushing past me again as he stepped into the hall.

"I can't let you go," I told him.

"Good for you."

"You know I can't."

I had lifted the bottle of sherry from the cabinet. There was less than an inch of liquid left inside. I was holding it by the neck. He stood there in the hall, waiting with his back to me, head angled a little as if consulting some hidden force beyond the ceiling.

"I know you can't," was all he said. It was as if he'd become the passenger and I the driver.

I lay down on my father's bed that night, a baseball-cap resting on my chest. Was I hero or villain? I'm hoping you'll tell me. I'm hoping one of you will tell me. I need to know. I really need to be told.

Again and again and again.

ACKNOWLEDGEMENTS

THE VERY LAST DROP by Ian Rankin © 2009. First appeared on the Royal Blind website, www.royalblind.org. Reprinted by permission of the author and his agent, Robinson Literary Agency Ltd.

DOLPHIN JUNCTION by Mick Herron © 2009. First appeared in *Ellery Queen Mystery Magazine*. Reprinted by permission of the author.

CHRIS TAKES THE BUS by Denise Mina © 2009. First appeared in *Crimespotting: An Edinburgh Crime Collection*, Polygon. Reprinted by permission of the author.

THE MADWOMAN OF USK by Edward Marston © 2009. First appeared in *Ellery Queen Mystery Magazine*. Reprinted by permission of the author.

DEAD AND BREAKFAST by Marilyn Todd © 2009. First appeared in *Ellery Queen Mystery Magazine*. Reprinted by permission of the author.

AFFAIRS OF THE HEART by Kate Atkinson © 2009. First appeared in *Crimespotting: An Edinburgh Crime Collection*, Polygon. Reprinted by permission of the author and her agent, Rogers, Coleridge & White.

THE BALLAD OF MANKY MILNE by Stuart MacBride © 2009. First appeared in *Uncage Me*, edited by Jen Jordan, Bleak House Books. Reprinted by permission of the author.

THE CIRCLE by David Hewson © 2009. First appeared in *Thriller 2*, edited by Clive Cussler, Mira Books. Reprinted by permission of the author.

A GOOSE FOR CHRISTMAS by Alexander McCall Smith © 2009. First appeared in *The Strand Magazine*. Reprinted by permission of the author and his agent David Higham Associates Ltd.

AN ARM AND A LEG by Nigel Bird © 2009. First appeared in *Crimespree Magazine*. Reprinted by permission of the author.

THE LOVER AND LEVER SOCIETY by Robert Barnard © 2009. First appeared in *Ellery Queen Mystery Magazine*. Reprinted by permission of the author's agent, Gregory & Co.

DEAD CLOSE by Lin Anderson © 2009. First appeared in *Crimespotting: An Edinburgh Crime Collection*, Polygon. Reprinted by permission of the author.

THE TURNIP FARM by Allan Guthrie © 2009. First appeared in *Uncage Me*, edited by Jen Jordan, Bleak House Books. Reprinted by permission of the author.

AS GOD MADE US by A. L. Kennedy © 2009. First appeared in *Crimespotting: An Edinburgh Crime Collection*, Polygon, and the author's collection *What Becomes*, Vintage. Reprinted by permission of the author's agent, Antony Harwood Ltd.

ROBERT HAYER'S DEAD by Simon Kernick © 2009. First appeared in *Uncage Me*, edited by Jen Jordan, Bleak House Books. Reprinted by permission of the author.

ANOTHER LIFE by Roz Southey © 2009. First appeared in *Radgepacket*, Byker Books. Reprinted by permission of the author.

THE WOMAN WHO LOVED ELIZABETH DAVID by Andrew Taylor © 2009. First appeared in *The Strand Magazine*. Reprinted by permission of the author and his agent, Sheil Land Associates.

HUNGRY EYES by Sheila Quigley © 2009. First appeared in *Criminal Tendencies*, Creme de la Crime Ltd. Reprinted by permission of the author.

HOMEWORK by Phil Lovesey © 2009. First appeared in *Ellery Queen Mystery Magazine*. Reprinted by permission of the author.

NO THANKS, PLEASE by Declan Burke © 2009. First appeared in *Uncage Me*, edited by Jen Jordan, Bleak House Books. Reprinted by permission of the author.

THE SAME AS SHE ALWAYS WAS by Keith McCarthy © 2009. First appeared in *Ellery Queen Mystery Magazine*. Reprinted by permission of the author.

OUT OF THE FLESH by Christopher Brookmyre © 2009. First appeared in *Shattered: Every Crime has a Victim*, Polygon. Reprinted by permission of the author and his agent, United Agents.

HARD ROCK by Gerard Brennan © 2009. First appeared in *Thuglit*, www.thuglit.com. Reprinted by permission of the author.

ART IN THE BLOOD by Matthew J. Elliott © 2009. First appeared in *Gaslight Grimoire: Fantastic Tales of Sherlock Holmes*, edited by J. R. Campbell and Charles Prepolec, Edge. Reprinted by permission of the author.

UNHAPPY ENDINGS by Colin Bateman © 2009. First appeared in *The Red Bulletin*. Reprinted by permission of the author.

RUN, RABBIT, RUN by Ray Banks © 2009. First appeared in *Shattered: Every Crime has a Victim*, Polygon. Reprinted by permission of the author.

SLOW BURN by Simon Brett © 2009. First appeared in *Ellery Queen Mystery Magazine*. Reprinted by permission of the author and his agent, Michael Motley.

FINDERS, WEEPERS by Adrian Magson © 2009. First appeared in *Thuglit*, www.thuglit.com. Reprinted by permission of the author.

THE HARD SELL by Jay Stringer © 2009. First appeared in *Beat to a Pulp*, www.beattoapulp.com. Reprinted by permission of the author.

PARSON PENNYWICK TAKES THE WATERS by Amy Myers © 2009. First appeared in *Ellery Queen Mystery Magazine*. Reprinted by permission of the author and her agent, Dorian Literary Agency.

SUCKER PUNCH by Nick Quantrill © 2009. First appeared in *Radgepacket Online*, www.bykerbooks.co.uk. Reprinted by permission of the author.

TOP HARD by Stephen Booth © 2009. First appeared in *Criminal Tendencies*, Creme de la Crime Ltd. Reprinted by permission of the author.

COP AND ROBBER by Paul Johnston © 2010. Reprinted by permission of the author and his agent, Broo Doherty.

OFF DUTY by Zoë Sharp © 2009. First appeared in *Criminal Tendencies*, Creme de la Crime Ltd. Reprinted by permission of the author and her agent, Gregory & Co.

GUNS OF BRIXTON by Paul D. Brazill © 2009. First appeared in *Crime Factory*, www.crimefactoryzine.com. Reprinted by permission of the author.

THE DEADLIEST TALE OF ALL by Peter Lovesey © 2009. First appeared in *On a Raven's Wing: New Tales in Honor of Edgar Allan Poe*, edited by Stuart M. Kaminsky, Harper Paperbacks. Reprinted by permission of the author.

THE BEST SMALL COUNTRY IN THE WORLD by Louise Welsh © 2009. First appeared in *Shattered: Every Crime has a Victim*, Polygon. Reprinted by permission of the author and her agent, Rogers, Coleridge & White.

MR BO by Liza Cody © 2009. First appeared as a chapbook published by Crippen & Landru. Reprinted by permission of the author.

FOXED by Peter Turnbull © 2009. First appeared in *Ellery Queen Mystery Magazine*. Reprinted by permission of the author.

MURDER by Nicholas Royle © 2009. First appeared as an art print. Reprinted by permission of the author.

DRIVEN by Ian Rankin © 2009. First appeared in *Crimespotting: An Edinburgh Crime Collection*, Polygon. Reprinted by permission of the author and his agent, Robinson Literary Agency Ltd.